A Game of Proof

A GAME OF PROOF

Megan Stark

CARROLL & GRAF PUBLISHERS
New York

Carroll & Graf Publishers
An imprint of Avalon Publishing Group, Inc.
245 W. 17th Street
NY 10011
www.carrollandgraf.com

First published in the UK by Constable,
an imprint of Constable & Robinson Ltd 2004

First Carroll & Graf edition 2004

ISBN 0-7867-1341-0

Printed and bound in the EU

1

'My lord, I call Sharon Gilbert.'

A gust of small movements disturbed the still air of the courtroom as people coughed, shuffled papers, and leant forward to get the best view of the witness box. The court usher, a woman in a pink blouse and black robe, opened the door in the panelled wall at the back of the court. 'Sharon Gilbert, please.'

At the barristers' table in the well of the court, Sarah Newby leant forward, her fingers laced under her chin. This was the first time she would see the victim, the woman the prosecution said her client had raped. The woman whose evidence she would have to demolish, to keep Gary Harker out of prison. The woman whose reputation she would have to destroy, to continue the steady rise of her own. Sarah had been a qualified barrister for three years and this was her first rape case. A great opportunity, if she did well. The first step on the ladder to becoming a Queen's Counsel, like the Crown Prosecution barrister, Julian Lloyd-Davies QC, who stood next to her facing the jury.

Lloyd-Davies placed his notes on the portable lectern which he had brought with him and tapped a silver pencil on it nonchalantly as he waited for his witness to appear. Where Sarah was intent and nervous he appeared calm, relaxed and confident. The lectern, silver pencil, silk gown and expensive tailored suit were all signs of a status that Sarah both coveted and feared. Beside him sat his junior, James Morris, pen poised to take notes. I belong here, all these things said, this is my stage to command. Sarah felt like a novice beside him. Even in her best Marks and Spencer black suit, tight starched wing collar and bands, she was painfully conscious of how the black cotton of her gown marked her out as a junior barrister like James Morris, someone who would normally assist a QC in a case like this rather than lead it herself.

In front of the barristers sat the judge, His Lordship Stuart Gray, raised high on his dais under the prancing lion and unicorn of the royal coat of arms. His long cadaverous face surveyed her from under his wig with drooping bloodhound eyes. He had once practised as a QC too, Sarah reflected gloomily, and before that no doubt attended one of England's best public schools – perhaps the same one as Julian Lloyd-Davies.

Certainly he had not left school at fifteen and spent his teenage years, as Sarah had, bringing up a baby on one of the worst council estates in Leeds.

Sarah drew in a slow, deep breath and let it out again, tensing the muscles of her stomach as the butterflies danced within. I've earned the right to do this and here I am, she thought. *They* didn't have to fight to get here, but I did. And if I win this time, it will be the best ever.

A woman came through the door in the back of the court and looked about her uncertainly. She was a tall, slim woman in her late twenties, smartly dressed in a green suit with three-quarter length sleeves. The waves in her long, bleached shoulder-length hair suggested hours of careful attention in front of the mirror. She entered the witness box and took the testament and card from the usher.

'Take the book in your right hand and read the words on the card.'

'I swear by Almighty God that the evidence I shall give shall be the truth, the whole truth, and nothing but the truth.'

The words were clearly, almost defiantly spoken. Sarah watched as Sharon Gilbert handed the book and card back and looked around. Like many witnesses, she seemed struck with a sense of shock and wonder that she could actually be here, beneath the great domed roof and stucco pillars of York's magnificent eighteenth-century courtroom. Or perhaps she was shocked by the audience of students and idlers in the public galleries, as well as the row of pressmen, all here to listen to the intimate evidence she would have to give.

Sarah watched carefully, trying to assess her character. Many witnesses were terrified by this court, and mumbled their way miserably through their evidence as though in a public library; others seemed to revel in the theatrical opportunities the public stage gave them. It looked as though Sharon Gilbert might be one of the latter. She could hardly fail, after all, to have read the pre-trial press publicity; she knew how important she was.

As Julian Lloyd-Davies began his introductory questions, designed to establish a few basic facts and put the witness at ease, Sarah Newby sat quite still at the table beside him, listening intently. What sort of person was she, this victim of a brutal, humiliating rape? Well-dressed, attractive, certainly – she had taken great care with her appearance today. The accent was local, however, uneducated; the way Sarah herself had spoken until she had learned to moderate her vowels at the Middle Temple. Probably most of the jury spoke as Sharon did.

More important was the sense of character that came through Sharon Gilbert's voice. It was strong, clear, brash – the voice of a woman who knew her own mind, or thought she did, but was also afraid of contradiction and expecting it. One of life's victims, perhaps, but not a submissive one; not someone who would break down in tears on the stand and have to be coaxed through her evidence as many rape victims did, Sarah thought.

She was glad of that, at least. From the moment she had been given this case, she had been concerned about what she might have to do in cross-examination. She was not worried that she might not be incisive or brutal enough; she believed she was good at that and hoped she was getting better all the time. In her three years of practice she had already taken several notable scalps. One defendant had left the box blustering vainly, entangled in his own deceit; a second had stood silent, unable to answer her final, devastating question; two more had wept. A surge of mixed pride and pity had flooded through her in those moments: pity, at the public humiliation she had inflicted; but far greater pride, that her own skill had won the case, and she could rejoice in her success in the vicious game played out in court.

But so far she had been lucky, for her victims had deserved it – burglars, a mugger, a fraudster, a brutal policeman.

A rape victim would very different. Sarah was enough of a feminist to have felt some initial reluctance about defending a man – particularly a violent petty criminal like Gary Harker – accused of rape; but as Lucy Sampson, her solicitor, had said, 'If *you* don't do it, a man will, and how will that help the victim?' After all, everyone deserved a good defence, she told herself; if she was to be a proper barrister she must take what came; there could be no no-go areas. But that had all been in the abstract; now she was here, watching a woman prepare to tell the story of her brutal rape by the man it was Sarah's job to defend.

To do that she would have to divert some of the jury's sympathy away from the victim to her client. And to herself. The witness might feel she was on stage; but the barristers controlled the drama. If the woman were shy or nervous it would be child's play to humiliate her by dwelling on the physical details of the crime or her previous sexual morality – techniques practised by male lawyers over many years. But Sarah wanted to avoid this, if she could. A tearful victim, bullied by the defence lawyer, would only turn the jury's sympathies even more against her client, who was an unpleasant enough thug in the first place.

But nonetheless, he denied rape; so it was Sarah's job to test the truth of Sharon's story with all the skill at her command. She was hugely relieved that her first impression was of a tough, forthright woman who would stand up to questioning.

'Do you have children, Ms Gilbert?' Lloyd-Davies enquired politely.

'Yes, two. Wayne is seven and Katie's four.'

'I see. So they were both born some time before you met Gary Harker.'

'Yes, he's not their dad, thank God. He'd be rubbish as anyone's dad.'

She didn't say who their father was, Sarah noted, and Lloyd-Davies didn't ask. But Sharon tossed her head and risked a swift glance at the jury, as though defying them to infer anything from the fact that the children's father – or fathers – were no longer around. It had nothing to do with the case, after all. She was a mother, and she had been raped; that was all the jury needed to understand.

But there was more to it than that, as Sarah knew only too well. How could she not know, she who had been pregnant at fifteen? She knew why two young men in the jury gazed at Sharon with open admiration, while others looked away, avoiding her gaze. She even knew how that *felt*. She was certain that Sharon was promiscuous, and it was more than likely that she was, or had been, a prostitute – a game as old as the law. Once Sarah had flirted with that idea herself. Far less training, instant fees. I could have ended up like this, Sarah thought; proud of managing as a single mother, daring anyone to challenge me, defiant. And lonely as hell underneath.

So far, Sharon had looked everywhere in the court except at Sarah's client, the man accused of raping her. It was as though he were a stucco pillar or a chair; her eyes slid past him without interest. But now Julian Lloyd-Davies mentioned him for the first time.

'Could you tell the court where you first met the defendant, Gary Harker?'

'Yes. It was at a club. The Gallery, in Castle Street. About two years ago.'

'And did a relationship then develop?'

'Yes. He moved in with me.'

'I see.' Lloyd-Davies peered at her thoughtfully over his half-moon glasses. 'By that you mean he lived together with you in your home, as though you were man and wife?'

'He lived with me, yes. For about a year – something like that.'

'I follow. And – to make things quite clear for the jury – during that year you slept in the same bed together, did you? And had regular sexual intercourse?'

'Well, he wasn't just there for decoration, was he?' Sharon seemed gratified by the ripple of amusement which greeted her answer. It was part of the age-old comedy of the court: the contrast between the fussy precision of the barristers' language and the earthy facts the witnesses described. Part of the language barrier reflected a genuine need for precision in court; but another part was to do with the social gulf which separated the lives and experiences of people like Sharon and Gary from those of Julian Lloyd-Davies and His Lordship Stuart Gray. A chauffeur had delivered the judge to court; Lloyd-Davies, Sarah recalled wryly, had driven a black Jaguar with the number plate LAW 2. She had been tempted to scratch it with her engagement ring as she walked past. That was the least that would have happened to a car like that in Seacroft; it would have lost its wheels and been standing on bricks by morning, if it was there at all.

'And when did this relationship come to an end?' Julian Lloyd-Davies continued.

'Last April. He didn't come home for three nights and I found out he'd

8

been sleeping with another woman. So I slung his stuff out on the street. Cheating bugger.'

'I see. And what happened when Gary came home and found it there?'

'We had a fight. He broke my finger. But I changed the lock and he didn't come back.'

'Was this the first time he had been violent to you?'

Sharon shook her head. 'You're joking. He used to slap me round all the time. Specially when he was drunk. He's a violent man, been in prison several times for it.'

Quickly, Sarah stood up, her eyes on the judge. 'With the greatest respect, my lord . . .'

'Yes, yes, of course, Mrs Newby.' Judge Gray knew as well as she did how vital it was for the defence to keep Gary's criminal record from the jury. 'Ms Gilbert, you must only answer the questions that are put to you. You mustn't talk about anything else unless Mr Lloyd-Davies asks you. Do you understand?'

'Yes, all right. But he asked me if he's been violent and he has. And it's true what I say, he has been in prison.' For the first time, Sharon looked directly at Gary Harker in the dock. It was a look of recognition – a defiant challenge. *I've got you now, you pig: see how you like this*, it seemed to say. She held the gaze for a long second, then turned contemptuously away.

But her words were potentially devastating. Gary Harker's criminal record ran into three pages, with several convictions for violence, some against women, for which he'd been sent to prison. According to the rules of evidence these facts, which might prejudice the jury against him, could not be mentioned in court. Now they had been. Sarah remained on her feet. It was within her power, she thought, to stop the trial now. But the judge's long, bloodhound face concealed a quick mind. Instead of addressing Sarah he turned to the witness.

'Ms Gilbert, answer this question yes or no, will you please. Has Gary Harker ever been sent to prison for any act of violence against *you*? Yes or no, remember – nothing else.'

'Well, no, but he has –'

'*No*, that's your answer then,' Judge Gray interrupted her smoothly. 'Now one more question, yes or no. Has he ever been convicted of any act of violence against you?'

'Well, no, not against me, but –'

'Thank you, Ms Gilbert, that's all. You see, Gary Harker is not on trial for anything else he may have done in his life, he is simply on trial because he is accused of raping you. So you must only tell the jury about things that he has done to you personally, or to your children. That's all this jury can consider, nothing else. Now Mr Lloyd-Davies asked if he'd been violent towards you and you answered that he used to slap you

9

around when he was drunk. But it's also true to say that he has never been convicted of any offence of violence against you. Isn't that right?'

'Yes,' admitted Sharon sullenly. 'Not yet, anyway.'

'Very well then.' The judge looked at Sarah, who was still standing, and raised one lugubrious hairy eyebrow. 'Does that satisfy you, Mrs Newby?'

'I . . .' Sarah hesitated, then capitulated. 'For the moment, my lord. I am most grateful.' She sat down submissively, but she was boiling inside. Sharon had effectively told the jury that her client had convictions for violence. Should she have protested more, or asked for the trial to begin again with a fresh jury? Her hands shook as she wondered. The hesitation, and perhaps the capitulation too, were signs of her inexperience. She could still do it, she supposed; but even at this early stage it would cost time and money, which Judge Gray clearly wanted to avoid.

She had already lost one battle with the judge before the trial started, when she had tried to get the case dismissed because of the exceptional pre-trial publicity. A national tabloid had described Gary Harker as 'the man arrested by police hunting York's serial rapist', and Sarah had argued that this article made it impossible for any jury in the York area to give Gary a fair trial. The judge had listened courteously but ruled against her, specifying only that jurors who admitted reading the offending newspaper article could be excluded.

Now he had allowed the jurors to hear of her client's criminal past. What should she do? Dare she – a very junior barrister – challenge a high court judge twice in one morning? She might turn him against her for the rest of the trial. Would that help her or destroy her case?

She turned it over furiously in her mind. If the judge had ruled unfairly there would be grounds for appeal. On the other hand, she might gain a possible benefit. If the judge allowed the prosecution to attack Gary's character by mentioning his criminal past in court, then perhaps she could attack Sharon's character too; and she was no angel either. Sarah sat very still, thinking hard. What would a more experienced barrister do? Was that a hint of smugness on the judge's face? Two up to him for the moment – pompous sod.

Lloyd-Davies resumed. 'So on 23rd April last year Gary Harker left your home because of this quarrel, and so far as you were concerned he didn't live there any more. Is that correct?'

'Yes.' Sharon tossed her hair defiantly. 'I told him I never wanted to see him again.'

'And did you see him again?'

'No. Well, not for months. I met him at a party at the Royal Station Hotel in October. I wasn't expecting him, he was just there.'

'I see. What day was this exactly?'

'Saturday the 14th. The same day I was attacked in my house.'

'I see. Would you tell us in your own words, please, exactly what happened that night.'

So here we go, Sarah thought. She sat quite still, quite focused – a slim dark figure with her elbows on the leather-covered table and her fingers folded delicately under her chin, staring intently at the witness. She has noticed me now, Sarah thought coolly; twice she's met my eyes, looked away, and back again. She knows I'm here; listening; waiting.

'Well, it was a big party, and there was a lot of people in the hotel, drinking and singing and carrying on. I was having a good time, and then suddenly there was Gary in front of me.'

'What happened then?'

'Well, at first it was OK; I even had a dance with him. But then he got nasty. He said I'd kept his watch when he left, and he wanted it back. When I said I hadn't got it, he called me a thieving slag and said he'd get it back himself. So I told him to piss off and he did.'

'All right. Did you see him again that night?'

'No. Not until he came to my house and raped me.'

There was a stir of interest in the public gallery above Sarah's head. This was what they came for, she thought. Ghouls. She glanced at the jury – eight women, four men; Lloyd-Davies had been lucky there – and saw a look of pity on the face of a motherly woman in the front row.

'All right, Ms Gilbert. Take your time, and in your own words tell the court exactly what happened when you got home that night.'

At first Sharon did not speak. She glanced down and fiddled with a bracelet as though uncertain, now the moment had come, what to say. But then she lifted her head, stared straight at Lloyd-Davies, and began the story she had, no doubt, rehearsed many times before.

'Right. Well, I got a taxi home at eleven – I couldn't be any later, because I had a sitter in for the kids, my friend Mary. When I got home they were tucked up on the sofa in front of the telly. My youngest, Katie, had an ear infection so Mary'd brought both of 'em downstairs. After Mary left I made the kids a hot drink and settled them down in bed. It took a while because Katie was still grizzling so I had to give her a cuddle and play one of her tapes.'

'What tape was that?' Lloyd-Davies prompted.

'Postman Pat, I think. I've bought all those stories for her – she loves 'em.'

Oh wonderful, Sarah thought. She raised an eyebrow in cynical admiration of the point of Lloyd-Davies' question. Hot drinks, Postman Pat – the perfect loving home.

'So how long was it before you managed to get Katie off to sleep?'

'About half an hour, probably – perhaps a bit more. I don't know exactly – I was dropping off myself in the chair by the bed. Then I heard this noise downstairs.'

'What sort of noise?'

'A crash – like a window breaking. I wasn't sure if I'd imagined it at first, so I just sat quiet, listening to see if there was anything else. Then after a couple of minutes I heard someone moving around downstairs, so

11

I thought, Oh my God, and went out on to the landing and then I saw him, coming up the stairs . . .'

Sharon paused, and Sarah watched intently. This was the crucial part of the story – was there any possibility that she was making it up, or was it all true? Sarah's gloom deepened. It seemed to her that a genuine memory was flooding back to Sharon as she spoke, as if the events she was describing were clearer in her mind than the courtroom she stood in.

'Who did you see?' Lloyd-Davies asked softly.

'A man in a hood coming up the stairs. One of them balaclava hoods that terrorists wear.'

'So what did you do?'

'Nothing. Screamed, I think. But then he grabbed me, put his hand over my mouth and shoved me back into Katie's room. I tried to stop him but he was too strong. And he had a knife.'

'Did you see this knife?'

'No. I just felt it. He stuck it into my throat, here.' She touched the left side of her neck. 'Just a little, so I'd know it was there. I felt it go into my skin.'

'Did he say anything?'

'Not then, no. He just laughed, and started pulling at my clothes. I was terrified. He pulled my skirt and knickers down and then he . . .' Sharon took a deep breath and plunged on, determined to get it over with. '. . . he turned me round and pushed me face down over the side of the armchair and then he . . . he shoved my legs apart and raped me from behind.'

She stopped and looked at Lloyd-Davies, knowing probably what was to come, but unable to phrase it for herself. The precise, necessary legal language.

'When you say he raped you, you felt his erect penis enter your vagina?'

'Yes. Oh yes, he got it in all right. It hurt, too, it hurt a lot. The doctor saw that after.'

'Yes. And while all this was happening, where was your four-year-old daughter Katie?'

'In her bed, of course, by the armchair. That was the worst part of it. She thought he was killing me, poor kid. I can see her now, in that bed with her mouth wide open screaming her head off. It was like all her nightmares come true – she still dreams about it now, almost every night she wakes up and wets the bed, screaming. Then little Wayne came in and started hitting him to get him off me.'

Lloyd-Davies held up a hand for her to pause. Then he repeated her point slowly and clearly, to make quite sure the jury had taken it in.

'You're saying that your seven-year-old son, Wayne, came into the room and started hitting the rapist in order to rescue his mother. Is that right?'

'That's right.' For the first time Sharon had tears in her eyes. 'I told him to get out and run but he's a little hero, that son of mine. Sticks up for his mother no matter what.'

'So how did the man respond to this attack by a seven-year-old boy?'

'Well, he shoved him off, didn't he? But Wayne wouldn't stop, so he said, "Get off me, Wayne, you little bugger," something like that. That was when I guessed who he was.'

Lloyd-Davies held up his hand again, to emphasize the point. 'He said "Get off me, *Wayne*," did he? He used your son's name?'

'Yes, he did, definitely. I remember that.'

'And was it that, the use of Wayne's name, that made you realize who this man was?'

'Well, yes – that and his voice. I recognized that too. It was him – Gary bloody Harker.' Again she glared at Gary in the dock, and Sarah wished she could see his reaction.

'So what happened then?'

'Well, Gary pulled out of me and stuck the knife in my throat. He said he'd kill me if Wayne didn't piss off. Then he grabbed my hair and dragged me into another room. My own bedroom.'

'What was your response to all this?'

'Well . . . I was screaming, at both of them. I was screaming at Gary to let Wayne alone and at Wayne to stay away. I thought he'd kill him. I didn't care about myself, I just didn't want my kids hurt.'

'And were you asking him to leave *you* alone as well?'

Sharon stared at him pityingly. 'What do you think? Of course I was.'

'And how did he respond?'

'Like the animal he is. He smacked me round the face and told me to shut up and do what he said or he'd kill me and the kids too.'

'And you recognized his voice when he said that, too, did you?'

'Oh yeah, it was him all right. Filthy pig.'

'All right. So when he got you into your bedroom, what happened then?'

'Well, he hit me in the face and I fell down and lay there on the floor. Then he grabbed me by the hair and I thought, it's all going to start again. But it didn't, not the rape anyway. Instead he grabbed the cord of my dressing gown and tied my hands behind my back with it, and then tied the long end round my throat so it started to choke me if I didn't hold my hands high, up my back. Then he put the knife to my throat again and . . . I thought I was going to die.'

'Did he say anything?' Lloyd-Davies asked softly.

'No, not this time.' Sharon shook her head, lost in the horror of her memory. 'But there was a noise. I didn't know what it was at first, then I realized – it was him laughing. I could see it in his eyes too. He just stared at me through that black hood, and . . . laughed. I could hardly

13

breathe and he had his knife to my throat and I thought, He's going to kill me now and then he'll murder the kids as well.'

Her eyes flooded with tears and Sarah thought, it's too much even for her. Too much for any woman to have to say in open court in front of bewigged lawyers and twelve members of a jury and the furiously scribbling newspaper reporters and the serried ranks of German language students in the public galleries above, simultaneously appalled and delighted by the example of British justice they had stumbled upon. To say nothing of the accused, Gary Harker, watching her coldly from the dock. And me, whose job it is to cast doubt on all this.

Sarah felt ill as she contemplated the magnitude of her task. But it was Sharon's comfort the judge was concerned with.

'Would you like a break, Ms Gilbert?' he asked courteously, when the pause had gone on for nearly a minute. But Sharon shook her head determinedly. She wasn't crying; she had just needed a pause to regain her courage. And she had nearly reached the end of her story.

'What happened next?' Lloyd-Davies asked.

'He shoved me down on the bed, went to my chest of drawers and pulled out the bottom drawer. And that proved who he was, too.'

'Could you explain that, please?'

'Yes, well, he went straight to the bottom drawer, where I keep my jewellery in case anyone breaks in. There are six drawers but he went to the bottom one straight away. And the first thing he pulled out was his watch, the one he'd asked about in the hotel. After that he took some rings as well. Then he left, I suppose. Thank God he didn't hurt the kids.'

'What happened after he left?'

'Little Wayne came in and untied me, bless him. I was nearly choking, I could hardly breathe. Soon as I recovered I called my friend Mary and the police.'

Sharon looked at Lloyd-Davies with relief. She had done it; the first part of her torment was over.

Almost over.

'Just a couple more questions, Ms Gilbert, then I've finished. You say that you recognized Gary by his voice and the fact that he knew your son's name, and then you felt even more certain when he went straight to the jewel box in your bottom drawer. Is that because Gary knew you kept it there?'

'Yes. He saw it when he lived with me. And he said in the hotel, I bet I know where that watch is.'

'I see. And did anything else about your assailant make you sure it was Gary?'

'Yes, everything. He was the same size, same build. The kids recognized him. Even his prick was the same, if you really want to know.'

Sarah Newby raised her eyebrows slightly. Not the wisest point to

14

make to a respectable jury, Sharon, she thought. Did Lloyd-Davies expect her to say that? Surely not.

But Sharon hadn't finished. 'Anyway, he's done it to other women, hasn't he? I saw that in the papers.'

Swiftly Sarah was on her feet, but once again Judge Gray forestalled her. 'Ms Gilbert, you are here to give evidence about what happened to *you*, and nothing else, do you understand me?' He looked directly at the jury. 'Members of the jury, I must ask you specifically to disregard that last remark. I can tell you categorically that Gary Harker has never been convicted of rape in his life before, and no evidence will be presented in this court about any other charge than the one before you; and if it is you are duty bound to disregard it.'

'I am grateful, my lord.' Slowly, Sarah sat down. But she had been outmanoeuvred for the second time today, and she wondered bitterly if Sharon's outburst had been spontaneous, or whether Lloyd-Davies had put her up to it. Was this how you got a silk gown and black Jaguar with a personalized number plate? Am I just going to sit back and take this? *No.*

Julian Lloyd-Davies glanced at the clock on the wall. 'Would my lord like Ms Gilbert to remain for questions from my learned colleague?'

The judge smiled protectively at Sharon, as Lloyd-Davies had expected he would. 'No, no, I think in view of the time and the distressing nature of the evidence, we might adjourn for today. But you must be here tomorrow to answer questions from Mrs Newby, Ms Gilbert. Do you understand?'

He rose to his feet, the usher bawled, 'All stand!' and court was over for the day. Julian Lloyd-Davies tied his notes in red tape with a casual, practised hand, and smiled urbanely at Sarah. 'And the best of British luck, I have to say.'

Sarah met his gaze coolly. 'I'm going to need it, if this kind of thing goes on,' she said. 'I'm requesting a meeting in chambers straight away. I want this stopped right now.'

2

The meeting in the judge's chambers was brief and tense. Judge Gray had divested himself of his wig and red gown, and sat comfortably at his desk in a white shirt with blue braces. Through the window behind him Sarah could see trees in the park by the River Ouse. She, Julian Lloyd-Davies and his junior James Morris had also taken off their wigs but still wore their stiff collars and black robes. They sat in upright chairs before the judge's antique leather-topped desk.

'Well, Mrs Newby?' Judge Gray sat back with a curt nod which indicated that he knew exactly what she wanted to say and was irritated with her for troubling him with it. Sarah took a deep breath and began.

'My lord, on two occasions this afternoon the witness made extremely prejudicial references, one to my client's record and the other to newspaper allegations. Despite your lordship's ruling this morning, I must insist that these two references taken together will inevitably blacken my client's character in the minds of the jury, even if they have not read the press publicity against him. In my respectful submission this jury are now irredeemably prejudiced and I can see no way in which they can be expected to give him a fair trial.'

She stopped, conscious that it had all come out in a rush and that she was blushing slightly. But she had decided to say it and had said it clearly. The fact was that over the past year in York two women, in addition to Sharon Gilbert, had been attacked. One, Maria Clayton, had been raped and murdered; the second, Karen Whitaker, had had a lucky escape. The local press, convinced that the attacks were the work of a single man, had written a story entitled 'The Hooded Knifeman', which – to the embarrassment of the police – had been picked up and elaborated by the nationals, some of whom were in court today. Despite extensive police investigation the only man so far brought to trial was Gary Harker. As all the lawyers in the room knew, the police had tried very hard to link him with the other attacks – one of which had involved a hood and both a knife – but had so far failed.

Gary was charged with the rape of Sharon Gilbert, and no one else. But after Sharon's remark, Sarah's contention was that the jury must suspect that he was guilty of those crimes too, even though there was one key piece of evidence – a hair found on a tape used to bind Karen Whitaker – whose DNA did *not* match Gary's and seemed to prove his innocence. But since he was not charged with attacking Karen Whitaker, Sarah could not mention this in court.

Wearily, Judge Gray raised a bushy eyebrow. 'Do I take it that you were not satisfied with my specific instructions to the witness and jury in both instances?'

Sarah frowned. 'I am most grateful to your lordship, of course, but . . .'

'But you feel I could have done better?'

'Not exactly, my lord, no.' Sarah was determined not to be patronized. 'I make no criticism of your lordship's interventions but my submission is that the damage has been done and cannot be undone.'

'And so?'

'For my client to receive a fair hearing there should be a new trial and a new jury, my lord. Preferably not in York where there's been so much publicity about this "Hooded Knifeman".'

So there, she thought. I've said it. Now what?

The judge inclined his head to the man in the silk gown beside her. 'Julian?'

Lloyd-Davies smiled – that conspiratorial, collegiate smile that Sarah knew and loathed so well. *Julian* indeed!

'It seems to me that both incidents were dealt with admirably by your lordship.' He favoured Sarah with an avuncular glance. 'I have the greatest respect for my learned friend's zeal to defend her client, but I believe there have been several directives from the Lord Chancellor's Office about the cost to public funds of such retrials, have there not? The CPS would strongly oppose such a ruling on the grounds of cost alone.'

'I am aware of the importance of cost, my lord,' Sarah replied determinedly. 'But public funds exist to provide justice, and I repeat that my client cannot now receive a fair trial from a jury whose minds have been unfairly prejudiced by this witness. Twice in one afternoon!' she added, almost as a personal accusation.

Judge Gray raised a hand wearily to stop her. 'Yes, yes, I understand your point fully, Mrs Newby, and it does you credit. I am also fully aware of the purpose of public funds.' He paused for a moment, rubbing his thumb along his jaw and staring intently at an area just below her chin. Did her collar have a stain on it, she wondered anxiously? But no, of course not – it was merely another technique for humiliating people, putting them in their place. The judge cleared his throat and resumed.

'I have already directed the jury to ignore both remarks and will repeat those instructions in my summing up. In my opinion that will suffice to ensure your client the fair trial which he undoubtedly deserves.'

The words appeared impeccable but the sarcastic final phrase was a deliberate reference to the fact that everyone in court – except, she hoped, the jury – regarded Gary Harker as an unpleasant thug who was almost certainly guilty and belonged in prison. Not that the judge had actually *said* that, of course, but . . .

'In that case, my lord, I hope that any uncharitable references to Ms Gilbert's character which may come out in court will be treated with equal leniency.'

It was waspish, petulant and unwise. The judge's face grew cold. 'You mistake me, Mrs Newby. There was no *lenience* in my directions this afternoon, and there will no *leniency* either for you or your client. This is a most unpleasant rape case and will be tried with proper respect shown to the victim. I would have thought that you, as a young woman, would appreciate that.'

Young woman, Sarah thought. Odd how a phrase that might be a compliment in one context could be an insult in another. Foolishly, she floundered on. 'Of course, my lord, but she does have a very chequered

17

history and if my client's record is to be brought before the jury then in all fairness –'

'You fail to grasp the point, Mrs Newby. Your client's record has *not* been brought before the jury and it will not be unless you choose to tell them about it yourself. Therefore it would be quite improper for you to make irrelevant accusations about Ms Gilbert's sexual past. Do I make myself clear?'

'Yes.' Sarah bit her lip, counted to ten under her breath, and said, 'I am grateful to your lordship.' Then she got to her feet and moved to the door.

The men, either out of reflex politeness or as a further subtle insult, rose to their feet when she did, but did not immediately follow her to the door. When she opened it and turned to bow she saw an ironic smile on the judge's heavy jowl.

'After all, Mrs Newby, we're all feminists here, you know.'

She strode down the softly carpeted corridor, seething with anger and humiliation. Half-way along she paused, wondering if she heard laughter from the judge's chambers, from which *Julian* and his junior had still not emerged. Then she burst into the robing room and tore at the stud in her stiff collar with her fingers.

I've made a complete mess of it, she thought. My biggest case so far and on the very first day I antagonize the judge to no purpose whatsoever. I sound off about justice with as much emotional control as a teenager on her first date, and now they're going to be needling me about it for the rest of the week.

She glanced into the mirror and saw with relief that her face was only slightly flushed, not nearly as hot as it felt. It was an attractive face, with neat shoulder-length dark hair and hazel eyes around which a network of tiny wrinkles had begun to appear. Perhaps they had always been there but she had only noticed them since she had begun to wear contact lenses eighteen months ago. There's the problem. Your vision improves and you see faults in yourself, she thought wryly.

As Sarah unbuckled her collar another barrister came into the room – Savendra Bhose, a young Indian from her own chambers. Although he was seven years younger than her they had qualified at the same time, and apart from Lucy he was the person she felt closest to at work. He smiled. 'Hi! The big rape defender! How'd it go?'

'Dreadful!' Sarah dropped her wig into her briefcase. 'The victim's as hard as nails, shoots her mouth off about my client's record, and when I complain the judge tells me he's a feminist!'

'What?' Savendra laughed. 'You don't mean old Baskerville Gray?'

'Yes, the old bloodhound himself. He must be sixty-five if he's a day, and eighteen stone into the bargain, and he's in there now with his buddy

Julian choking over his port because he told me to respect the rights of women!'

Savendra grinned delightedly. 'Well, so you should, you know! The man has a point. The world's changing – even women and blacks can vote nowadays.'

'Really? I hadn't heard. No one tells me anything.' Sarah smiled ruefully. 'I just blew it, that's all. Rushed in like a rookie and asked for a retrial and *of course* he told me the grounds weren't strong enough and it would be a waste of public funds, et cetera, et cetera . . . but what am I to do, Savvy, eh? Sit there and smile meekly while they pull a fast one on me?'

'That hardly sounds like you –' Savendra began, but got no further before Julian Lloyd-Davies swept in. He nodded at Sarah.

'No hard feelings, I hope?'

She picked up her briefcase and made for the door. 'Of course not. It was a long shot anyway.'

He smiled genially. 'Like the whole case, I should think.'

'Yours, do you mean? I'll tell my client that – he'll be delighted!'

She winked at Savendra and left. Pleased with her smart remark, she ran down the wide eighteenth-century staircase to the entrance hall, where Lucy Sampson sat amid a cluster of security guards, witnesses and departing students. Lucy, a large, motherly solicitor in a baggy black suit, rose to her feet expectantly.

'Any luck?'

'No, sorry, I just set them all against me. Come on, let's go and see Valentino.'

The two women made for the staircase to the police cells, where Gary Harker would be held until the Group 4 van took him back to Hull prison for the night. As they went through the door they left the imposing pomp of the courtroom with its ancient oak panelling, stucco pillars and exotic domed ceiling, and entered a grey, comfortless world of bare stone corridors and clanging cell doors. At the foot of the stairs they met a detective on his way out.

'Aha, the devil's advocate! Hello, Sarah. And Lucy Sampson, isn't it?'

'That's right. My solicitor.' Sarah smiled coolly at DI Terry Bateson, one of the few CID men she actually liked. Bateson, as usual, was managing to make his double-breasted suit hang crumpled around him like a tracksuit. Perhaps it was something to do with the tie, strung several inches below the top button; or the loose-limbed, broad-shouldered frame that supported the clothes, but every time Sarah saw the man he looked more like an athletic teenager than the senior criminal detective that he actually was. And despite her cool smile, conversations with Terry seldom failed to fluster her. He was a widower, too, which made him all the more attractive.

It was Terry who had charged Gary with rape; and as the officer investigating the murder of Maria Clayton and the attempted rape of Karen Whitaker, he suspected that Gary was guilty of these crimes too. Maria Clayton, an upmarket prostitute, had been found strangled on Strensall Common last summer. Her hands had been bound behind her with the belt of her own raincoat, and the belt looped through its buckle round her neck, so that the harder she struggled the tighter the noose became, just as Sharon had described this afternoon. It seemed she had been half strangled like this and then throttled with her attacker's hands. She had been sexually assaulted and there was a small cut in her neck. Her dog, a Yorkshire terrier, was found with its throat cut in a ditch.

Karen Whitaker, a university student, had been posing nude in the woods for her boyfriend to photograph when the couple were attacked by a hooded assailant with a knife, who snatched their camera, hand-cuffed the boy to the steering wheel of his car, bound Karen's hands with tape, and was attempting to rape her when the boyfriend managed to set off the car alarm and attract some walkers, who chased the attacker away.

This attack, which happened less than three weeks after the Clayton murder, led to the Hooded Knifeman articles in the *Evening Press*; and when Sharon Gilbert was raped a month after that, the pressure on the police to make an arrest was enormous. But although Gary was Terry's prime suspect for all three attacks, the evidence he had to link him to the first two was very thin. Gary had been one of a small team of builders who had built an extension to Maria Clayton's kitchen two months before her death, and had boasted of having sex with her once. He had also been one of a gang of builders repairing Karen Whitaker's hall of residence, and had seen the naked pictures in her rooms. But scores of men had visited Maria Clayton's house, and dozens of students and building workers had known about Karen Whitaker's exhibitionist hobby. A smudged footprint from a size 10 Nike trainer had been found near the scene of both crimes, and a battered pair of size 10 Nike trainers had been found in Gary's flat; but this, as Lucy had pointed out scornfully when the police presented it, would put about two million other men in the dock alongside Gary. Although she had been sexually assaulted, no semen or body hairs were found on Maria Clayton's body, but Terry's team had been triumphant when they had found a male hair stuck to the tape used to bind Karen Whitaker's hands. But their triumph turned to ashes when DNA analysis of the hair turned out not to match Gary, effectively acquitting him of the Whitaker assault. Despite the similarities between the cases and Terry's continued suspicions, the evidence was simply not there to prosecute Gary for anything except the rape of Sharon Gilbert.

'I hope you haven't been harassing my client, Terry,' Sarah said, half seriously.

'I never touched him, Sarah,' Terry protested, drily. 'Personally, I think someone should cut off the man's dick and float it away on a weather balloon, though I'll deny it if you ask me in court. But tell me – how can you ladies bring yourselves to defend a bastard like that? He's a menace to every woman in Yorkshire. You do realize that, don't you? Next time it could be someone like you. He's killed already, you know.'

'If you're still trying to link him to the Clayton murder, Terry, he's not charged with that here today,' Sarah said firmly. 'As you well know.'

'Well, he damn well should be!' Terry snapped. 'So the jury could see the similarities. Same cut in the neck, same method of bondage . . .'

'Different women, different places, Terry. And no evidence that my client was even there.'

'A client with a record three pages long, including four assaults on women –'

'None particularly serious –'

'Oh, sure? Until it's your face on the end of his fist!' Terry stopped, aware that he was losing his temper. *Again.* It was happening too often these days. This was not the impression he wanted to convey, of some emotional, out-of-control bully. Not to this woman of all people. But he did care, strongly, about convicting Gary Harker. He took a deep breath and began again.

'Look, I hear you tried to get the case thrown out this morning. How can you, as a woman, square a trick like that with the search for justice? Tell me that.'

Sarah touched his arm softly. 'I'm not a woman, Terry, I'm a barrister. My job's to play the game in defence of my client. The game of proof. And when I play, I play to win.'

Terry shivered. Perhaps it was her hand, the delicate fingers gently touching his arm; but it was also the cynical, lightly spoken words, the opposite of all he believed the law should be about, that frightened him. The three attacks on women had been his main investigation over the past six months, and the single positive result so far was Gary's appearance in court today.

Now Sarah Newby, of all people, was defending him.

He scowled. 'Well, I wish you the worst of luck. The sooner the vile pillock's banged up for life the better. You can tell him that from me.'

'I wouldn't dream of it,' Sarah smiled, and took her hand from his arm. 'I might hurt his feelings. And that would never do, would it?'

Terry Bateson watched her go. It annoyed him intensely to see Sarah defending this case. He hated defence lawyers; he regarded them as a sort of parasite growing fat on the wounds of society. They worked in the courts of law but the one thing that seemed to concern them least was justice. If they could get a man released on a technicality they would, with no concern for the hard, sometimes dangerous detective work that had led to the arrest in the first place, or for the effect on the public of a smirking villain released to rape, rob or burgle once again. How would those two women feel, he wondered, if Harker broke into *their* homes and did to them what he had done to Sharon Gilbert?

Serve them bloody well right. But even as he thought it the idea made him ill. Not Sarah Newby, please God not her.

He had first met her when she had prosecuted two of his cases a year ago. The case against the first man had been thin, and the defendant and his expensive London barrister had come into court laughing, convinced he would get off. Terry's heart had sunk, certain he was about to see months of police work trashed. His first sight of the pretty, dark-haired prosecution barrister had discouraged him further. In her mid-thirties, and only recently qualified, he'd heard. Nice legs, but probably no brain. But in fact it was the expensive London brief – only an ageing junior rather than a silk, for all his Savile Row suit and Jermyn Street shirt – who had failed to do his homework, not Sarah. The trial had ended with the defendant sweating in the witness box, snared like a fat fly in the web of his own lies. At one point a juror had actually laughed aloud. And her performance in the next case had been even better. Terry had become a fan. And, he thought, a friend.

But now she was on the other side, defending Gary Harker of all people. Her cynical words echoed in his mind. *My job's to play the game in defence of my client. The game of proof. And when I play, I play to win.*

He respected her too well to think it was bluff – she really thought she could get the bastard off. All those virtues which he had so admired in her as a prosecutor were to be deployed in defence of a violent rapist. She didn't care that Gary was probably the biggest danger to local women for many years. It was her own performance she was interested in. She was just like all the other lawyers after all; a hired advocate, a hooker who would prostitute the truth for a fee slipped into the pocket in the back of her gown.

Let her cope with Gary Harker then. She chose him.

Gary was sitting on the blue plastic mattress in his cell. It was the same colour as the graffiti-scarred walls, and matched the tattoos of the grim reaper on his right bicep and the snake that writhed around his solid neck and appeared about to savage his left ear. He scowled at his lawyers morosely as they came in.

'Well, what did I tell you? Lying bitch, ain't she?'

Sarah folded her arms in her gown and leaned against the door. Lucy stood by her side. The only other choice was to sit on the bed beside Gary, and neither woman fancied that.

'I tried to persuade the judge to dismiss the jury because she referred to your record, but I'm afraid he didn't agree.'

'No, well, he wouldn't, would he?' Gary looked unsurprised by the news. 'What did you think of Sharon?'

Sarah shrugged. 'She made a good impression. Any woman would, with a story like that.'

'Aye. Well, she's a lying bitch who made the whole fucking thing up!'

Silence. Neither woman could think of any response. At last, in a tone of weary disgust, Lucy said, 'It's no part of our case to say she wasn't raped, Gary. It's a fact that she was.'

'Yeah, well, maybe. But it weren't me. If she's telling the truth then there's some shite out there who needs his throat ripped out! And I'll do just that if I ever find him, the little pisshead!'

'Yes.' Sarah contemplated her client with distaste, considering what would happen if she put him on the stand. What would impress the jury most – the sincerity of feeling with which he denied the charge, or the foul language he would use to do it? She imagined Julian Lloyd-Davies needling him with his deliberately languid, pointed questions. The man might run amok, bursting out of the witness box like a tethered bear snapping its chain.

She wasn't obliged, of course, to put him on the stand at all. She could simply tell the court that he denied the charges and rely on her ability to cast doubt on the prosecution case. But she was unlikely to win like that, since the law now specifically allowed the judge to comment adversely to the jury about a witness's refusal to give evidence on his own behalf.

But if he did give evidence, Lloyd-Davies would shred him into small slices, like salami.

'Look, Gary,' she began. 'I need to know I've got everything right. Tell me again exactly what happened at the hotel, first of all.'

For a while she checked details. She doubted Gary's innocence, but it *was* possible, after all. He certainly denied all guilt. It was the jury's job to decide whether they believed him or not.

Anyway, tomorrow she had Sharon to deal with.

On the way out of the court Sarah nodded at a couple of the barristers from Court 2. They would know she was defending a difficult rape case on her own, which was a step up. If she did well, her status would rise. And she didn't intend to lose; not without a fight, anyway. From her point of view, the prejudice and weight of evidence against Gary were a bonus. If she lost, few people would blame her, but if she won, more serious cases would follow.

She walked out into the afternoon sunshine. The eighteenth-century architect had not designed the elegant court building so that people could look out of it, so it was easy to forget, in the windowless dome of the courtroom and the claustrophobic cells beneath, that there was a quite different world immediately outside. In front of Sarah tourists queued up to visit the Castle Museum and the Norman castle, Clifford's Tower. Tourists and children carrying balloons and ice cream glanced up idly at the statue of Justice above the court. For a moment Sarah stood on the court steps, breathing in the soft breeze and luxuriating in the warmth like a cat.

But the machinery of justice ignored the weather. Below Sarah the prison van waited, its tiny cells with square blackened windows designed to ensure that neither Gary nor any of the other prisoners had even the smallest sensation of freedom between York and their remand cells in Hull.

Sarah watched it go. Then she and Lucy walked briskly down the steps and turned left to Tower Street, their offices, and work.

3

While Sarah went back to her office, Terry Bateson collected his colleague, DC Harry Easby, and drove south of York to investigate an incident that had been reported the day before. Easby stopped the car on a bridge over the A64, and the two policemen gazed at the muddy desolation of a building site half a mile ahead. Grimy yellow JCBs toiled like great insects in the mud, while a crane with a wrecking ball casually demolished an abandoned hospital.

'Looks like progress, sir,' Harry offered, breaking the oppressive silence between them.

'Progress?' Terry grimaced. 'More like the battle of the Somme, you mean.'

'That's how uniform see it,' Easby nodded. 'But they pushed the buggers out of their trenches last week, any road. Just look at the hairy sods.'

He nodded towards a wood behind the JCBs. The building site was protected from the wood by an elaborate boundary of high wire fences, security men and dogs . The fence was festooned with flowers and scraps of paper, and a long whitish banner floated between two tall trees. SAVE OUR TREES, SHOP IN TOWN, it read. The leafy treetops also supported a network of aerial walkways and tree houses, where the eco-warriors lived.

The park-like woodlands that had surrounded the old maternity hospital were being redeveloped for an out-of-town designer shopping centre. Trees planted by Victorians had reached their full, beautiful maturity just in time to become a hindrance to a twenty-first century plan for floodlights, car parks and upmarket designer units. The shops would market a style of beauty which would be packaged, bought, worn and replaced every year with something newer, fresher and more up-to-date. Against this the useless, magnificent trees stood no chance. After all, they made no money and offered nothing but the same, endless, wearisome repetition of natural style – every autumn, every spring the same.

News of the project, however, had spread to the hairy unwashed army of eco-warriors, who had a profound and perverse lack of interest in style, markets and fashion. They came from every hedge, cave, bender and battered caravan in the country. They moved swiftly, with energy, secrecy and determination. The developers' chainsaws were confronted by an army of bloody-minded economic rejects whose main aim, it seemed, was to be seriously injured by the lackeys of global capitalism, and thus become martyrs to the movement. And so the police had become involved, in order to remove the protesters peacefully before one had his arm trimmed off accidentally on purpose.

'Daft buggers!' said Easby contemptuously. 'Thousands of jobs, this place'll bring.' He drove on, past the village of Portakabins where the contractors' workmen and security guards lived, fenced in with their guard dogs. Terry observed it with distaste.

'I don't see why they couldn't build it in town,' he mused. 'You wait, son – in six months this'll be one vast car park, and another dozen shops in the city centre'll go out of business. Soon the whole city'll be boarded up or vandalized.'

'All the more work for us, then,' said Harry philosophically, looking ahead for the farm entrance. 'You sound like one of these tree people, sir.'

'And you sound like a taxi driver,' Bateson snapped. 'Just drive, constable, will you.'

'Sir.'

Terry regretted the words, but made no effort to call them back. This was happening more and more, he knew – he was becoming impatient, crusty, like all the worst officers he'd known. It was as though his personality was changing. It was attracting wry comments among his colleagues. When he tried to make amends, it just made matters worse. They seemed to fall over themselves offering sympathy. 'So sorry to hear about your, wife, sir . . . is there anything I can do? . . . come out for a drink . . . terrible thing about your wife . . .'

Two years ago it had been so different. Terry had seemed able to square the magic circle – hardworking, successful, ambitious, but also popular with his fellow officers. His aim to get the DCI's job when Jim Carter retired was supported, he believed, by most of his colleagues.

And then in one night it was all destroyed. Two fifteen-year-old boys had hot wired a Jaguar, blasted it up to eighty miles an hour, and smashed it head-on into his wife's Clio. It had taken four hours to cut Mary's lifeless body from the wreckage. It would take Terry the rest of his life to cut the image from his mind.

For two weeks he had been in despair. His sister had come to care for him and his two daughters. The Police Federation counsellor advised him that grief was natural, and that it was no sin for a man to cry. But

Terry had cried already and it didn't seem to help, it just felt painful and frightened him. So he drank most of a bottle of whisky in one night, and the rest the day after. What happened in between he couldn't remember, but it made his sister tighten her mouth and his children look afraid. That, more than anything, purged him. After the funeral, where he was ashamed by his pounding headache, he sat down with his two little girls and talked to them quietly about the future.

They wanted to know who would look after them. He said *he* would, of course. He would leave the police. But to his surprise, this idea seemed to scare them; perhaps because it scared him, too. He knew nothing else, had never wanted to. And so his sister and the counsellor advised him about childcare, and Trude, a young nanny from Norway, entered their home.

She was cheerful and active, eager to help and to please. His girls took to her at once. After a halting expression of sympathy in broken English she didn't speak much about their mother, but entered enthusiastically into what, to her, were the fascinating foreign details of their everyday English lives. She was a messy but surprisingly good cook, making things like waffles and meatballs and rice porridge which they had never tasted before. She seemed content to be with them, undemanding. Above all she was genuinely interested in children and had no reason to feel sad. When she had been there two days the children went back to school, and the week after that Terry went back to work. Life, of a sort, began again.

But his ambition, his ability to concentrate were gone. He kept a photo of Mary on his desk and found himself staring at it, silently, for half an hour at a time. So he put it in a drawer and only took it out occasionally, when he was alone. But she was always there, at the front of his mind, while the work seemed an irrelevance, a side issue to be sorted and swiftly forgotten.

He took up running again. He had once been a promising 800 metre runner, not quite fast enough to get into the big time. Now he found that the exercise calmed his body and his mind at the same time. In the evenings he cuddled his little girls and told them bedtime stories as he had done when they were babies. At night they seemed to need him most. They talked about their mother and remembered the good things they had done when she was alive. Sometimes they prayed for her, all three together. But during the days, life had to go on.

Gradually his concentration returned. But he lost all thoughts of promotion. He tried to arrange his hours to be at home after school and at weekends like a normal parent. It was not ideal for a detective but it was the best practical help his colleagues could give him. He was discreetly withdrawn from the front line, to office work and routine enquiries. DCI Carter retired and instead of Terry a sharp, clever southerner, Will Churchill, got the Detective Chief Inspector's post. At the time, Terry had been so numb, he scarcely cared.

But time passed and the little girls began to forget, as young healthy creatures do. When Terry first saw them laugh and play like other children he resented it. How could they be happy when Mary was dead? But they *were* happy and they were only little children after all. He watched them gratefully, drawing healing from them. They resumed contact with their friends, and sometimes he came home to find a chaotic houseful of children with the nanny in the middle. The sight cheered him, gave him confidence to take on serious enquiries again.

And so two years had passed. Life went on, but he was not the same detective he had been before. He cut corners and turned down overtime to be at home with his children. He made mistakes, he forgot things. And worst of all he snapped at people for no reason, as he had done with young Harry Easby just now. He had to get a grip on this.

If only he could stop thinking about Mary, seeing her face suddenly when he was looking at something else, remembering the feel of her beside him in bed, the small of her back lithe under the palm of his hand when they danced . . .

'Here we are, sir,' said Harry Easby, turning on to a farm track. 'Bank House Farm.'

Sarah didn't leave her office for another three hours, and when she did, very little about tomorrow's cross-examination was left to chance. She had prepared her questions and tried to anticipate how Sharon Gilbert might respond. Much of this was logic, based on the written evidence in the prosecution file and Gary's story; but the rest was intuition, based on her impression of Sharon's character this afternoon.

She had an advantage here, for she had lived among women like Sharon. She was used to their brash, slightly resentful manner. She understood how they felt patronized by teachers and doctors, cheated by boyfriends and husbands, short-changed by employers and the DSS. She felt sure that Sharon's assertiveness in court today masked a fear that somehow the police and lawyers were going to betray her again, as the authorities had always done in the past.

A fear that Sarah was determined to bring true.

The softer part of Sarah felt sorry for Sharon. Not just because of the rape – of course she deserved sympathy for that – but because of what she was. Sarah could so easily have ended up like that herself. But she had chosen not to. And for that very reason, a much stronger part of Sarah despised Sharon. The part of Sarah that had made that choice didn't believe in luck or genes or social excuses. She believed that if you worked, you could succeed. As she had done.

One by one the other barristers, the clerk and the secretaries called out their goodbyes and left the office. By seven thirty, Sarah looked up and saw that only Savendra had his light on across the corridor. His door was open; she could see him in his shirtsleeves and red braces, making detailed notes at his desk. She yawned, and stretched her arms over her head with her fingers linked, easing the joints in her stiff neck and spine. Savendra looked up and smiled.

'Finished already?'

'Yup.' She crossed the corridor, leaning on his door frame curiously. 'What's your brief?'

'Mass poisoning.'

'What, you? Advocate for the Borgias?'

'Hardly. My client's a farmer who let his slurry pit overflow into a village borehole. Diarrhoea and vomiting all round.'

'Charming. Still, you know what they say, don't you?'

'What?'

'Where there's muck there's brass. A case like that should make you stinking rich.' She ducked as he flung a paper clip at her. 'I'm off home.'

She crossed the corridor to her own room, leaving her door slightly ajar, just to tease Savvy who knew what happened next. She kicked off her court shoes and took off her jacket, hanging it neatly on a hanger behind the door. Then she stepped out of her skirt. Savendra whistled softly. Sarah strolled across her room, took a black leather jacket from a hook on the wall, pirouetted as she put it on, and blew him a kiss. Then she sat on the edge of her desk and pulled on some black leather trousers, smiling as they creaked around her. Finally she pulled on heavy black boots, locked her door, and waved to Savvy as she went downstairs.

Her office was on the fourth floor of an old Victorian building in Tower Street, a stone's throw from the courts. The barristers had chambers on the top floors; the solicitors, where Lucy worked, were downstairs. The building had lots of disadvantages – the narrow stairs, the small rooms, the fire risk – but one good part of it from Sarah's point of view was the servants' passage leading to a small back yard, where the Victorians had once had a loo and a coal shed. Now the lawyers had transformed it. There was an array of potted plants, some expensive wrought iron garden furniture; and in the coal shed were two gleaming motorcycles.

One – the larger – belonged to Savendra; the other, a jet black Kawasaki 500, was Sarah's. She regarded it with a mixture of amusement and excessive, secret pride. She had bought it first as a solution to the problems of traffic and parking, but it meant far more to her than that now.

It was a joy she only shared with Savendra, when they compared, with sparkling eyes, the beauty of the machines and their accessories. She had grown to love everything about the Kawasaki – the shining black paintwork and gleaming chrome; the smooth responsive purr of the engine and the bike's sensitivity to the slightest shift of her weight in the saddle; the sensuous creak of leather; the glorious freedom of weaving through traffic and accelerating to speeds that, though perfectly legal, seemed to her risky in the extreme. She loved the style of it too – black helmet, black leather clothes, black bike – and the way it marked her out, made her at once anonymous and different, her own person, not like the rest.

Not like a wife or a mother. Like a free spirit, like no one at all.

It was something, perhaps, to do with her desire to become a barrister in the first place. A free spirit who was faster than others, who played to win. A similar instinct, no doubt, had led Julian Lloyd-Davies QC to drive a black Jaguar with LAW 2 on the number plate. Sarah couldn't afford that – in fact her bike was cheaper than a small car – but it marked her out as someone to be taken notice of, someone not to mess with. And that was how she wanted to be. Not a victim ever again, but a person who made things happen.

Whose life belonged to herself.

The car bounced along the track towards a solid, brick-built farmhouse. Cows watched them from a field on their right, and a black and white collie streaked towards them. As the two policemen got out, the collie danced around them, barking hysterically. Terry put out his hand to it, to no effect. It danced away and growled ferociously at Harry Easby.

'Come on, boy. Where's your missus?'

'I'm over here!' They looked up and saw a sturdy woman in gumboots and a torn, muddy coat coming towards them.

Terry showed his badge. 'Mrs Steersby? I'm Detective Inspector Bateson and this is DC Easby.'

''Bout time too.' The woman held out her hand and Terry shook it. Her grip was strong, the hand redolent of cow dung. 'D'you want to see Helen, then?'

'If she's home from school, yes.' Terry took an incident report out of his pocket. 'Your daughter was frightened by a man two nights ago, Mrs Steersby. Is that right?'

''Course it's right.' The woman turned her back, cupped her hands round her mouth, and in a voice loud enough to be heard in Lancashire yelled: 'Helen! Come here now!'

Terry saw a girl riding a pony on the far side of a field. She popped the pony over a line of jumps and cantered towards them, pulling up in a flurry of mud.

'What d'you want, Mum?'

'It's the police to see you!'

'Again?' The girl looked bemused. 'But they came yesterday.'

'These are different. Inspector Bateson – top brass Sherlock Holmes feller – so you'd best answer his questions. That pony's done enough for today, anyhow.'

'OK. But I've got to cool him down first.'

'Right. Ten minutes then. I'll put kettle on.'

Terry watched as the girl walked the pony quietly around the field, and pondered what he knew of her story so far. Someone had tried to attack her while she was riding alone in the woods. A man in a black tracksuit and woolly hat, similar to his image of the man who had murdered Maria Clayton, and assaulted Karen Whitaker. That was why he was here now.

It disturbed him. It couldn't be Gary Harker this time, unless Group 4 had taken to letting their rapists out for a run in the woods on the way back to Hull. So what was it? Coincidence? Copycat? Or false alarm?

Terry watched as she unsaddled her pony. She was a pretty girl in a grubby blouse and jodhpurs. How old was she? Fourteen, the report had said.

So if there had been an attack, what sort of pervert were they dealing with? A child abductor, a paedophile – or just a common lecher who fancied young girls in tight trousers? Or a monster the girl had made up? That was why he had come, to hear it in her own words.

In the farm living room, the four of them sat in faded brown armchairs grouped round an open fireplace. Terry smiled at Helen. 'You told Constable Watson that you were riding in the woods at about half-past seven when a man came up to you. Can you remember what he was wearing, Helen?'

'A black sort of tracksuit thingy, trainers, and a black woolly hat.'

Not a hood, then. 'So you could see his face, could you?'

'Yes.' She nodded, looking thoughtful, a little apprehensive perhaps.

'And you have no idea who he was?'

'No. I've never seen him before. And I do meet people quite often in those woods. I ride there most days.'

'How old was he?'

'I don't know. Thirty, perhaps.'

'I see. So what exactly happened when you met him?'

'Well, I was just walking down the track on Toby at the time, and I saw him jogging towards me. Then he put his hand on my bridle and said something, like . . .'

She hesitated and looked down, and Terry saw tears in her eyes. Not such a big girl after all then. She *had* been frightened.

'He said, "That's a nice pony, darling," something like that, and asked me how old Toby was. So I told him, and he said was he nice to ride, and I said he was brilliant but a bit lazy sometimes, and then he said could *he* have a ride. So I said no and he said, "Oh come on," something like that, and put his arm round my waist trying to pull me off, so then . . .'

Helen looked up at her mum, who nodded for her to go on.

'. . . I screamed and hit him hard with my riding whip. He didn't let go at first so I tried to kick him too and then Toby reared and we got away. Then I galloped home and told Mum.'

Terry nodded. 'You must have been very frightened.'

'I was, yes. 'Course I was.'

'Did you see what the man did when you got away?'

'No. I looked back once and saw him running into the woods. Then he was gone. I didn't want to see him.'

'No, of course not.' Terry watched her for a moment in silence. He was fairly convinced she was telling the truth; there seemed no reason not to. 'How did he speak? Like someone from round here?'

'No. It was a funny accent – not local.'

'And you're sure he tried to pull you off the horse? You couldn't have made a mistake – he wasn't just trying to be friendly?'

'No! What do you mean, mistake? I can feel him doing it, now!'

'All right, I'm sorry.' He had really upset her now, he saw. She was crying, and her mother reached out to hug her. This *was* serious, he thought angrily. It could have been very serious indeed. But the great thing was, she had seen his face. And heard his voice.

He waited for a moment while the tears subsided, then, as gently as he could, said: 'Listen to me, Helen. It's important to catch this man, isn't it? So I want you to do one more thing for me – in a while, when you're feeling better. I want you to help us make a photofit picture. We've got a lady officer who's very good at that. Will you come and see her, please?'

She nodded, still with tears in her eyes but determined, too. Encouraged, Terry made the arrangements with her mother and left.

He sighed as Harry drove down the track, the collie streaking alongside. After Gary Harker's arrest, this sort of thing should be over. Of course there were other men like Gary, but statistically, Terry knew, this sort of behaviour was odd. Most rapists were known to their victims; more rapes were committed by relatives in the home than by strangers in the woods.

He thought how angry he would feel if such a thing happened to his own girls. It would be insupportable. I'd kill the bastard, he thought, his hands tightening on his knees. Kill him and ask questions after.

4

As Sarah wheeled the Kawasaki into the street something tugged at her memory. She glanced at her watch and swore. Seven forty. Her daughter Emily had a school concert that night and she had promised to go. When did it begin – eight? Eight thirty? Pray God it was the latter. Quickly she fastened her helmet, settled herself in the saddle, and turned the key. The engine purred smoothly. I must be quick, she thought. Not so much freedom after all.

But as the bike wove its way swiftly down the street the old thrill returned. It was so powerful and free, compared to a car. Why shouldn't she enjoy it, this daily adventure on the roads? It was her reward for long hours of work, for all the disasters of her childhood.

If Emily was late for the concert and threw a tantrum, so what? Secretly Sarah regarded her daughter as spoilt. What did Emily know of trouble or poverty? Nothing, compared to her mother.

Sarah had been fifteen when she met Kevin Mills, and he had been seventeen. She had been an ordinary conscientious working-class girl at her local grammar school, not particularly clever or pretty, five foot six with short dark hair. The first risk she had ever taken was to drink two halves of lager and lift her miniskirt for Kevin in the back of his parents' yellow Ford Capri; and that risk had ruined her life. She still remembered, almost every day, the lonely dread for weeks afterwards waiting for a period that never came. And then the morning sickness, and telling her mother.

And Kevin.

Kevin was of course a devil, a satyr to have seduced an underage schoolgirl, but he had great pride. He was shorter than other boys, but wiry and strong, able to command respect with a look or sharp word. Nobody put him down; he was too dangerous for that. He was also capable of great charm. She knew he'd had other girls but he'd chosen her. She had felt proud and excited to be with him. Not afraid, not then.

Not even when she told him she was carrying his baby.

At that moment, he had been brilliant. Or so she had thought at the time. She could remember how the angry pimple on his forehead flared red as the rest of his face went white with shock. But then, when the truth had sunk in, he had puffed out his chest like a little fighting cock – he had been *proud*! She was pregnant with *his* baby – he had done it before most other boys on the estate! So two days later he had stood in her front room with her hand in his and told her parents he was going to marry her. Not asked them, *told* them. At seventeen years old he said he loved her and wanted her children and they were going to get married.

Such fools they both were.

They were married when she was sixteen, and Social Services found them a council house on the Seacroft estate in Leeds. It was a dreadful estate; their house had damp running down the walls so freely that they saw snails crawling above the cot. The wallpaper was peeling off, the window frames were rotting and the weeds were two feet high in the garden.

But at first it didn't matter. It was their own house and they were young and determined and it almost seemed like a game. They furnished it with second-hand carpets and a plastic three-piece suite, a brand-new cot from Social Services for the baby and a mattress on the bedroom floor for themselves. In the kitchen they had a Baby Belling cooker with two electric rings only one of which worked when the oven was on. Her mother gave her a cookbook called *Healthy Eating for Less Than a Pound a Day*, and Sarah came to know all its recipes by heart. Often things were burnt or underdone but in those first few weeks it didn't matter because afterwards, so long as the baby was asleep, they could go up to their own bedroom in their own house and make love as long and adventurously as they liked.

And they did like. When Sarah's father had described Kevin as a randy little sod he had been telling the exact truth and Sarah, aged sixteen, responded with delight and enthusiasm. That grubby bedroom, with a mattress and a rug on the floor, a stained mirror and an old chest of drawers with paint peeling off it, became for that brief period their version of the Arabian Nights. In those first few weeks of marriage Sarah's sexuality blossomed as suddenly and completely as a flower in an Arctic spring.

But then it faded, never to be the same again. The demands of real life piled up outside the bedroom door. Unwashed dishes, crying baby, dirty nappies, shopping, social worker, doctor, colds, cystitis, measles, vaccinations, electricity bills, pegging out the washing, rent demands, broken windows, cleaning, cooking, milkman's bills. Sarah wanted to go home, but she couldn't – this *was* home.

And Kevin was away so much. He was a plumber's apprentice, off to work at eight in the morning and then not back again for eight, ten, even twelve hours. Then he wanted food, sex and sleep, in that order. He would play with the baby for a few minutes but wanted it to go to sleep afterwards. When it didn't, he became jealous. When it woke in the night, he was annoyed. When she cooked badly, he became irritable. When she was too tired or ill for sex, he became angry.

The first time he hit her was when she tried to discuss an electricity bill as they were undressing for bed. She had read about this technique for extracting money from your husband in a magazine in the doctor's waiting room, whose agony aunt had clearly met no one like Kevin. Kevin just slapped her and continued with his lovemaking as though nothing had happened. The electricity was cut off a week later. She covered the bruise on her face with powder.

After that he began to stay out longer and longer. She prepared meals for him that dried up in the cooker. What do you want me home for? he asked, cruelly. You've got cystitis, you can't do it. Anyway we need the money. It's only me that earns it. They screamed at each other over the baby's head. When she stood in the doorway to stop him going out he smacked her head against the door post so that it bled. He didn't come back until one in the morning.

A week later he told her it was all over. He had met someone else, he said, an older woman called Sheila. He'd got to know her when he'd been fixing her pipes. Sheila and he had the same interests, and he was moving in with her. *Now*, today. There would be a divorce. She could keep baby Simon but he might want to see him sometimes at weekends

33

when he was older. Teach him to play football. That was what people did, wasn't it?

And then he was gone. The bubble burst, just like that. A week before their first anniversary the fairy tale was over. The coldness, the lack of emotional interest, stunned her so much that for the first, and only, time in her life she completely lost the power of action. When the social worker visited two days later Sarah had done nothing – no housework, no washing up, not even fed little Simon, who was howling upstairs. She just sat blankly on the green plastic sofa, staring at the wall.

The social worker put Simon in a foster home under a place of safety order. Sarah went back to her parents, there was nowhere else to go. The doctor gave her Valium and for a month she walked around like a zombie. Then her mother forced her to sign up for evening classes and take up studying again.

Which was the best thing my mother ever did for me, Sarah thought now. The one really good thing she did, the old cow. The thing that changed my life.

Just as refusing to have little Simon in her house was the very worst. The thing that ruined him, perhaps. Unless it was Kevin's genes.

Her mother's plan was for her to make a complete break with the past. Have Simon adopted, never see Kevin again, go back to school.

The last part of it worked perfectly. Sarah signed up for evening classes to complete her GCSEs and found, suddenly, a voracious hunger for learning. The more she learned the more she wanted to know; the harder she worked the more she wanted to work. It was an escape, a recreation of herself. It was something that gave her control again. It became as necessary to her as breathing. It lasted the rest of her life.

But the pain, the guilt about her baby didn't leave her. She didn't want him to be adopted. As the work replaced the Valium she railed at her hard-faced mother for refusing to have him back in the house. No, her mother said. Have him adopted. It'll hurt now but you'll thank me one day. It'll turn out best for you both in the end.

One night at the evening class she read the papers explaining adoption and then screwed them up. They're screwing my mind, she thought. That was when the teacher, Bob, found her crying at her desk half an hour after the class had ended. He took her out for a coffee and three months later they were married.

Bob was everything that Kevin was not – intelligent, well educated, thoughtful, witty and kind. Where Kevin had been short, cocky and macho, Bob was tall, with a neat beard and glasses, physically weak, gauche and unassertive. Where Kevin had been a ravenous, demanding, insatiable lover Bob was gentle, sensitive, almost shy. He was also idealistic. He was fascinated not by Sarah's body, as Kevin had been, but by her story. It seemed to him she had lived a whole novel by the age of eighteen. Her hard work and determination to succeed reflected something in himself; her disastrous circumstances challenged him to help her.

If she married him, he would adopt Simon too. It was the right thing to do.

And so it might have been, too, if they hadn't had Emily.

Not that Emily was a mistake, of course not, Sarah told herself, as she turned her bike on to the quiet country road that led to home. The mistake had been having her so soon after they married. While Bob's relationship with Simon, his project to demonstrate the benefits of having a teacher for a stepfather, had only just begun. Of course Bob tried to be fair and kind to Simon but his enormous delight at Emily's birth had been obvious to everyone. Especially to the troubled little boy, who had just come back to live with the mother who had abandoned him, and now had a new baby. And this strange, bearded man who wanted to teach him things.

Perhaps if we'd waited a year, Sarah wondered sadly. Would that have made the difference? Or were the difficulties in his genes? Simon was Kevin's son, that had become clearer the older he got. But he was hers too – if only he'd wanted to *learn* from her and Bob, instead of defying them as he always had. But now he was nineteen and had left home. He had his own life to lead, his own mistakes to make. There was no more she could do.

Whereas Emily and Bob *were* at home, waiting for her impatiently. Sarah pushed her guilt about Simon into a drawer at the back of her mind, and closed it. For the moment, Emily and Bob were more important. And things were not going particularly well with them, either.

As she approached home Sarah saw Bob's Volvo parked in the drive. When Sarah had first seen this house three years ago she had thought it entrancing. It was a detached modern house, in half an acre of its own grounds. It had a lawn and a golden Robinia tree in front. But it was the back that was its real glory. The spacious rooms had large picture windows which opened on to a fifty yard lawn which sloped away towards a meadow with grazing cows the far side of a little gate. Beyond the meadow was a footpath and willow trees on the banks of the river, and beyond that again, more meadows and the church of a distant village whose bells they could hear on Sunday mornings. Socially it was as far from Seacroft as you could get.

With Sarah earning fees for the first time and Bob just having become a head teacher they took a deep breath, an enormous loan, and joined the middle classes.

Or at least, Sarah, Bob and Emily did.

Simon hated it from the start. He had been sixteen then, beginning his last year at school. The new house meant long bus journeys, and hassle when he wanted to meet his friends. To him it was the final proof that he meant less to his mother than her own lust for success. Two years later he moved into a small terraced house in town, the deposit paid by Sarah and Bob.

The loss of Simon twitched in Sarah's mind daily, like the nerves from a missing limb. He was the family ghost, the casualty of her conflict with Kevin.

She parked her bike in the garage, and walked into the dining room. Bob was in his shirtsleeves, eating baked beans and reading the paper. Emily was nowhere to be seen.

'Hi!' she said. 'Anything for me?'

'Beans in the warmer,' Bob answered, frowning. 'You've got ten minutes.'

'Why ten minutes?'

'Emily's concert. She's got to be there by eight fifteen. Or have you forgotten?'

'Oh Christ!' She went into the hall and began to peel off her boots and leather trousers. The trousers snagged in her tights, pulling them half down too, and as she struggled, bent over, Emily came down the stairs.

'Mum! For God's sake!'

'Hello, Em. I'm sorry I'm –'

'We've got to go! I'm late! And nobody wants to see your bum!'

The tone of mingled exasperation and pure disgust in Emily's voice made it quite clear to Sarah that the girl saw nothing attractive or funny about her mother's nether regions. Emily herself had clearly taken pains with her appearance – hair neatly brushed, eye-liner, blusher and lipstick generously applied. The only drawback was the anxious, petulant frown on her face.

Sarah extracted her leg from the trousers, hoisted up her tights, and smiled encouragingly. 'You look really nice, Em . . .'

'Well, make sure *you* do. We've got to go *now*, Mum!'

'Five minutes.' Sarah hurried upstairs, changed, brushed her hair quickly, and gulped four mouthfuls of dried baked beans before Bob and Emily hustled her into the Volvo.

'You forgot, didn't you?' said Bob, reversing the car. 'Again!'

Sarah sighed. 'It's an important case and I'm cross-examining tomorrow. Anyway –'

'Stop!' Emily screamed from the back. 'Dad, go back – I've forgotten my music!'

'For heaven's sake . . .'

'Why on earth they have a concert the week before their GCSEs I cannot understand,' Bob said, as Emily dashed back into the house. 'The poor child's in a bad enough state as it is.'

'She's a clever girl. She'll manage.'

'How would you know?' Bob snapped. 'You never see her. She was in a dreadful state when I got home – tears, books and papers all over the place!'

'She did well enough in the mocks.'

'Yes, well.' Bob fell silent as Emily ran down the drive, got in, slammed the door, and shouted, *'Drive!'* in a voice whose nerves contrasted severely with the cool appearance she had presented on the stairs.

Sarah said nothing. Clearly they were both too wound up to accept comfort from her anyway. Despite what Bob said, Emily was a conscientious student who had got mostly As and Bs in her mock GCSEs a few months ago. If her work ethic lacked the intensity and rigid self-discipline of her mother's, that was because her life was so much easier. Emily had a comfortable home, loving parents, no babies to look after . . .

Sarah remembered how phenomenally organized she'd had to be in those early years of her marriage to Bob. He'd had a full teaching job and she, with a toddler and a baby to care for, had begun studying two A levels. But it had always been worth it. As she began studying at a higher level, she felt as if wires in her head that had fused together with rust were being cleaned and pulled apart and tuned. It became a pleasure that she couldn't do without.

When she got an A in both subjects her addiction was confirmed. Simon was six by then and Emily three. She began an Open University degree, getting up at five each morning to study. She even protected her desk from the prying hands of children by fencing herself in with a playpen. The sight of their mother in there with her books became such a common family sight that the first time little Emily saw a monkey in a cage at the zoo she proudly informed everyone that it was 'studying'.

But to Sarah her studies opened up such vistas of freedom that it was those outside who were in prison. She learned to inhabit two worlds – one in which she cooked, cleaned and cared for the children, and the other in which she studied and passed exams – always with the highest grades so that she could move on to the next stage. After the OU degree she read law at the University of Leeds, and then spent a year at the Inns of Court School in London, coming home only at weekends on the train. By then Simon had been fourteen, Emily ten, and her constant study was a fact of family life. And finally it had paid off. She got a pupillage and then a place in chambers as a barrister.

And so she had climbed to the top of her ladder, only to find another stretching away above – the ladder to becoming a QC and eventually, perhaps, a judge. And the case of Gary Harker was one of the first squalid, slippery rungs.

She began thinking about the case in the car and resumed, guiltily, during the school concert. She had no ear for music and although she was proud that Emily had passed so many flute exams she couldn't concentrate on it for long. Tomorrow's questions began to replay themselves in her mind, and she imagined the responses Sharon would make. There were a couple of awkward points, she realized, which she would have to work on when she got home.

Emily stood up to play the flute solo she had been practising, and her mother smiled encouragingly. But Emily wondered, not for the first time, whether the mind behind her mother's smile was really concentrating on her at all.

5

At breakfast that morning Terry's younger daughter Esther let her pet hamster out of its cage, and by the time Terry had retrieved it from behind the sofa the rush hour traffic was gridlocked across the city, so that he was late for the team meeting which he was due to lead. When he arrived at the incident room his new boss, DCI Will Churchill, was striding back and forth at the head of his new troops, some of whom were looking distinctly resentful.

'And when it comes to police work, what I'm looking for is *commitment*,' he barked in his sharp Essex accent. 'That's what will finally nail the killer of Maria Clayton and the rapist who attacked Karen Whitaker.' He waved at the photographs, maps and articles about the Hooded Rapist displayed around the incident room walls. 'I may be new here, but that has is own advantages. An outsider can often see more clearly.'

And annoy people more deeply, Terry thought bitterly. Before Mary died, I was in line for this job. And it would have been enough for me, I didn't want to rise higher. But Churchill, a man ten years younger and six inches shorter than himself, had been fast-tracked within the service from the moment he joined. He would be with them for a few years, no more, trampling on everyone in this room as he scrambled to the next rung of the ladder. Seeing Terry sliding into a back seat, he broke off his tirade.

'Ah, DI Bateson, I presume. Good of you to join us. Forgive me, I have used the general's absence from his post for a little pep talk. One serious crime solved, two more to go. Or three, if your visit to the farm girl proved anything yesterday.'

Terry signed, registering the implied criticism, and rose from his back seat.

'Shall I brief the team about it now, sir?'

'Of course, old son, you carry on.'

Churchill parked himself in a front seat to judge the performance of his second-in-command, and began picking his teeth with a match.

Terry looked around the room, feeling grateful for the moral support he detected in several faces. Unlike Churchill he knew these people, he had worked with them for years. Briefly, he outlined what he learned at the Steersby farm yesterday. All of them knew the details of the Clayton and Whitaker cases; most still believed, with Terry, that Gary Harker was the likeliest suspect for both. But clearly, he could have had nothing to do with this Steersby girl.

'Most likely, then, it's a copycat,' he concluded. 'But no hood this time, so at least we'll get a photofit. In the meantime,' he said, staring straight at Churchill as he spoke, 'I know the amount of dedicated police work that has gone into the these investigations, and today we have our chief suspect up in court, thanks to the efforts of this team. But he's only facing one charge. If Gary Harker is convicted today – as we all hope and expect he will be – we need to go over the Clayton evidence especially with a fine-tooth comb. He's still not ruled out of that. And if someone else attacked Whitaker then we need to find that person too. It's our job to ensure that the women of York can sleep easy in their beds once again. Thank you. That's all.'

As the meeting broke up Churchill approached Terry. 'You're still set on Harker for the Hooded Rapist, then, Terence?'

Terry winced. Terence was his Christian name but he hated anyone to use it. To him it sounded like some cheap gangster, not himself at all. Terry was uncertain if Churchill knew, or cared, much about the tragedy that had shattered his personal life; but he certainly did know which version of his name he preferred to be called by, because Terry had told him, several times.

'I've known Gary a long time, sir. He's moved from petty theft to assault, GBH and rape over a period of ten years. He has exactly the profile we're looking for.'

'Yes, but the DNA in the Whitaker case wasn't his, was it, old son? So until we have positive evidence to the contrary, I suggest you assume that Harker didn't murder Clayton or attack this schoolgirl either, and get out there looking for the man who did.' He paused. 'Any reason why Harker won't be convicted?'

'I don't think so, no, sir. I'm giving evidence against him tomorrow, of course.'

'Yes, well make sure you don't cock that up, at least. He's your one good catch so far. But there are more sharks than him – this Steersby case proves it. You've caught one, Terence – but we need two!'

With an odd supercilious smile on his face, Churchill held up two fingers to illustrate his point. Two fingers that looked, to Terry's eyes, uncannily like the first V-sign from his new boss.

For her second day on the witness stand, Sharon Gilbert appeared in a navy blue skirt and jacket over a white blouse. It conveyed exactly the right impression – sober, respectable, the sort of thing a business secretary might wear. She flicked back a curl of hair as Sarah began.

'Ms Gilbert, I believe Gary Harker lived with you for a year, didn't he?'

'About a year, yes.'

'And during that time you slept in the same bed together, had regular sexual intercourse, and generally behaved as man and wife. Is that right?'

'Yes. That's right.' Sharon nodded suspiciously, unable to disagree so far.

'You must have been very fond of him, then?'

'Well . . . yes, I were at first . . .'

'Were you in love with him?'

Sharon smiled contemptuously. ''Course not, no!'

'Really? Not in love?' Sarah glanced at the jury. 'But you let him move into your house, slept with him every night. How *did* you feel about him, exactly?'

Sharon looked confused. 'Well, I mean, I quite fancied him, like – he was a good lay, we had some laughs together.'

'I see. He was good for sex and a laugh, but you didn't love him.'

'Love him? No.'

'All right. But during that year you had the house to look after, and two children to bring up. Did Gary help you with that – contribute to the housekeeping, perhaps?'

'Well, yes, 'cause I made him. We wouldn't have had money to eat, else.'

'So he gave you money. Did he ever play with the children, take them places?'

'Well, yeah, he did sometimes, what do you think?'

'But they weren't *his* children, were they? How did Gary get on with their father?'

'With their fathers? Well, I dunno if he met them. I suppose he met Wayne's dad once or twice, 'cause he took him to football. But not Katie's dad – he's gone. I never see him.'

So far, so good, Sarah thought. She was treading a thin line, as the judge had warned in chambers. It was no longer an acceptable defence to cross-examine a rape victim about her sex life, in order to suggest that the woman was so immoral that she somehow asked for it; but it was quite legitimate to ask about her relationship with the accused. And if Sharon chose to reveal that her children had two different fathers, and that she shacked up with Gary for sex rather than love, then so much the better. At least it began to alter the impression of a perfect mother that Julian Lloyd-Davies had tried to create yesterday.

'All right, Ms Gilbert, I want to ask you a little more about your relationship. You say that Gary contributed to the housekeeping and sometimes played with the children, and that you liked him because he was a laugh and – a good lay, I think you said. When you made love with him, it was a good experience, was it?'

Sharon smiled, embarrassed. She seemed almost more embarrassed by this easy question than by the horrific details she had given yesterday about the rape; but then she had been prepared for those, psyched herself up to tell them. Now she hesitated. 'Well . . . yeah, it was OK.'

'He was a good lover to you?'

'Sometimes, yes. When he weren't drunk.'

'All right. And during that year, did he ever force you to do anything – any sexual act, I mean – that you didn't want to do?'

This was a risky question. The wrong answer would make things worse for her client. But there were benefits, too, if it went the way she hoped.

Sharon hesitated. 'Well . . . he could be a bit rough, like . . .'

Wrong answer. Quickly, Sarah minimized the damage. 'What I mean is, did he ever treat you the way the intruder treated you on the night of the rape? Did he ever do anything like that?'

'Oh, nothing like that. God, no.'

Right answer. The risk had paid off. 'Did he ever tie you up in the way you described yesterday?'

'No. No, he never done that.'

'All right. So during that year, he regularly made love to you in a perfectly acceptable way, a way that you enjoyed, that gave you pleasure?'

'Yeah . . . I suppose.' As Sharon hesitated, Sarah moved on quickly.

'Very well. Now, I want to ask about the events of the night of the rape, Ms Gilbert.'

Sarah paused, remembering the surprise change of direction she had planned. With luck, the jury would understand before Sharon did.

'When you first saw this hooded man on the stairs, you were frightened, weren't you?'

'What? Yeah, of course. I were terrified.'

'But you didn't think it was Gary at that point, did you?'

'No . . . not then. I just saw the hood and screamed.'

'I understand. You were frightened because you suddenly saw a hooded man, a complete stranger, coming up your stairs. That's what you're saying, isn't it?'

'Yeah.' Sharon nodded her head sarcastically, and stared at Sarah as though she were a simpleton. 'That's what I'm saying, yeah. You deaf or something?'

Sarah ignored this, and continued smoothly. 'If you had thought the man on the stairs was Gary, would you have been less frightened?'

'What?'

Sarah repeated the question. Sharon thought about it. 'Well, yes, I suppose a bit . . .'

'You would have been less frightened because Gary had never seriously hurt you or raped you before. Isn't that right?'

Sharon looked confused. 'Well, yeah, but I didn't know it was Gary then, did I? I mean, he had a hood on!'

'Yes, exactly. You were afraid because you had no idea who the hooded man was.' Sarah paused again, to let the point sink in. 'So when you began to think this man was Gary, you were less afraid, were you?'

'What? Well, yeah . . . I dunno.'

'Were you more or less afraid when you began to think the man was Gary?'

'What's it matter?' Sharon was confused now. 'I was scared because this man had bust into my house and was raping me! It didn't matter if it were Gary or not – I was bloody terrified!'

'You were afraid of rape, of course, I appreciate that. But did you think the man might kill you as well, or hurt your children? Were you frightened of that?'

'Yes, I bloody well was! He had a knife, you know – he stuck it in me throat. I thought I were going to die, and he'd murder my kids an' all!'

'Yes, I understand. So what I'm trying to get at, Ms Gilbert, is that while all these terrible things were happening, your mind was quite naturally full of all sorts of fears and terrors because you had no idea what the man was going to do next or who he was or whether you and your children were going to be alive at the end of it all; is that right? You were completely terrified because all these dreadful thoughts were rushing through your mind.'

'Of course I was terrified. Wouldn't you be?'

'I'm sure I would be, Ms Gilbert. So would any woman. If a masked man with a knife broke into my house, I'd be in a complete panic. Is that how you were?'

'Yes, right. You got it at last.' Sharon looked at Sarah pityingly.

'So if you were in a complete panic, with your mind full of all these natural terrors for yourself and your children, you weren't in a very good condition to identify a man whose face was covered by a mask, were you?'

Sharon hesitated. Sarah hoped the jury had understood the question quicker than Sharon had, and were wondering why she didn't answer.

'Ms Gilbert?'

'I know it were him,' she insisted finally. 'I told you – I recognized his laugh, and . . .'

'And his penis, I believe you said, Ms Gilbert,' Sarah broke in smoothly. 'We'll come to that in a minute.'

'He said, "Wayne" too!' Sharon almost shouted. 'He said, "Get off me, *Wayne*"!'

'So you say, Ms Gilbert. But before that . . .' Sarah pretended to consult her notes, though she knew the phrase by heart. '. . . you said yesterday, "I told him to get out and run but he's a little hero, that son of mine." Do you remember saying that?'

'Yes, 'course I do! He is a hero, too, my Wayne is!'

Sarah smiled. 'I agree with you, Ms Gilbert. You must be proud to have a son like that. But what were your exact words to him? Do you remember? Something like "Get out, Wayne, call the police!", perhaps? "Keep away, Wayne – you'll get hurt!" Something like that?'

'Something like that, yes.'

'So you did say "Wayne"?'

'Maybe. I can't remember.'

'Well, it would be natural to use the child's name, wouldn't it? And if you did, it's likely the man heard you use it, isn't it?'

'I dunno. He might have. So what?'

'Well, if he did hear you use Wayne's name, that may be why he used it himself, you see, Ms Gilbert.' Sarah smiled sweetly. 'That's common sense. It hardly proves that the man was Gary, does it?'

'Well, I think it does!' Sharon glared angrily. 'Anyhow, Wayne recognized him too!'

'After you had talked to him, Ms Gilbert, yes.'

'What?'

'You did talk to Wayne afterwards, didn't you? Before the police came?'

''Course I did. Poor little sod, he was shitting himself.'

'Yes, I understand. He's a very brave little boy. How old is he – seven? He saw his mother attacked and tried to defend her. He's a little hero; any mother would be proud of him. So naturally you picked him up to comfort him, and told him it was Gary, and the police were going to arrest him, didn't you?'

'Yeah, well – what of it?'

Sarah heard the slight sigh from Julian Lloyd-Davies beside her, and stifled the urge to grin. She was beginning to make progress. The key thing now was to make her point crystal clear to the jury, without looking too triumphant about it. 'It's a perfectly natural way for a mother to behave, Ms Gilbert. I'm sure everybody understands that and sympathizes. But it does mean, you see, that Wayne almost certainly got his idea about the man being Gary from you. He didn't think of it for himself. He's only a child – he thought it was Gary because you told him it was.'

'That's not true. He recognized him!'

Sarah shook her head. The jury had got the point; she didn't need to labour it.

'So we are left with Gary's voice, aren't we? Tell me, Ms Gilbert, this hood the man was wearing – did it cover all of his face?'

'Yes. All but his eyes.'

'It covered his nose and mouth too, did it?'

'Yeah. I think it did.'

A little imp in Sarah's mind began to laugh. That was more than she had hoped for. 'So his voice must have sounded rather muffled, mustn't it? If he spoke through a woollen mask?'

'Yes, I suppose so.'

'Tell me, Ms Gilbert, how often have you heard Gary talk through a thick layer of wool?'

'What? That's not the point. *I knew it was him*, I tell you!'

'You knew it was him because you think you recognized his voice through a thick woollen hood, when you've already admitted you were in a complete panic which made you so terrified you hardly knew what was happening? That's not possible, Ms Gilbert. I don't think anyone could make a proper identification in a situation like that.'

'It was him, I tell you. *I recognized his voice!*'

'That's for the jury to decide.' A vital skill, Sarah had learned from a QC in her first year, was how to wrong-foot a witness by stepping out of an argument just at the right moment. Never be drawn into a slanging match, he said. Always keep the initiative, and remember the impression you're making on the jury. She glanced at the clock, and saw there were about ten minutes to go before lunch. But Sharon hadn't finished.

'Look, I recognized the bastard, and that's it! Why would I say it were him if it weren't, eh? You tell me that!'

Sarah nodded calmly: 'Well, in fact that is exactly the point I intend to come on to next, Ms Gilbert. But . . .' She glanced at the clock, and then at the judge. '. . . I anticipate it may take some time, and as it is now twelve thirty, I wonder if your lordship might think . . .'

Judge Gray nodded, and pushed back his heavy chair. 'Yes, very well, Mrs Newby. We will adjourn until half-past one.'

As the usher called out, 'All stand,' and the judge withdrew through the panelled door behind his throne, Sarah studied the jury, wondering how her morning's performance had gone down with them. They certainly looked lively, and several eager discussions had already begun. So far so good, then – the more they began to question the evidence, the better. Then her gaze travelled up to the public gallery, where students, relatives, and idlers were beginning to climb back over the wooden benches to the door at the top.

But to her surprise, one young man was not moving. He leant over the rail at the front of the gallery, watching the unravelling scene below. His eyes fixed on hers as soon as she saw him, and she recognized her son, Simon.

6

She met him in the entrance hall, amid the throng of witnesses, security men and the general public. Sarah ran up to Simon quickly, her papers still under her arm.

'Simon! Whatever brings you here?'

Simon shrugged. 'Day off. Thought I'd see what you actually do.'

'Well! What a wonderful surprise!'

Sarah looked up at her son in delight. He was six inches taller than her, with a handsome, broad-nosed face and a shadow of stubble on his chin. His reddish-gold hair was cut brutally short and he had the ring in his left ear that she hated. But he looked fit and relaxed, in jeans and a sleeveless shirt that showed off the muscles of his upper arms. He had always been a natural athlete, much fitter than Bob had ever been.

Simon touched her wig. 'You look daft in that.'

'I'll take it off then. Wait there – have you got time for lunch?'

'Maybe.' He looked around apprehensively. 'Don't you eat here?'

'No. We'll buy a sandwich – sit by the river.'

'OK then.'

She ran up the wide staircase to leave her gown, wig and papers in the robing room. She glanced hurriedly at the questions she planned to ask later, but there was nothing she needed to change. Anyway Simon was here, that was what mattered – her son whom she hadn't seen for weeks!

As she came down she was surprised to see Simon talking to a witness, Graham Dewar. As she approached they moved apart. She took Simon's arm and went out into the sunshine.

'Do you know that man?'

'Yeah, a bit. Met him on a building site.'

'He's a friend of Gary's, you know. Witness for the defence.'

'Yeah?' Simon's uninterested response forced Sarah to suppress a slight jolt of irritation. It was a mannerism which had provoked many quarrels between them over the years. But she had no intention of nagging him today.

'What do you fancy? Sandwich? Pizza? Burger?'

'A sandwich'll do fine. I thought all you barristers ate posh. You know – fine linen, champagne, pass the port?'

'Not my style. Anyway, you know what wine does to me, Simon – do you want to see me weaving into court all tipsy with my notes upside down?'

'That'll be the day. They'll not catch you with your buttons undone, no way.'

'I should hope not.'

They bought sandwiches, fruit and mineral water in Marks and Spencer's. All the benches in the park by the river were occupied by tourists or shoppers, so they sat with their feet dangling over the quay, watching the river buses and rowing boats pass on the water.

'So how come you've got a day off?' she asked.

'I just took it. Most o't labourin's finished, any road. It's nowt but tidyin' up today, so I mitched it.'

Sarah sighed. Everything about the answer depressed her. It was bad enough to have a son whose ambitions extended no further than labouring on building sites, but it seemed Simon couldn't even manage that without skiving. And then he had to use this exaggerated broad accent, to emphasize how he was moving in exactly the opposite social direction from her.

But I won't nag, she told herself. It does no good – that's how we lost him before.

'How's Jasmine?'

Jasmine was Simon's girlfriend, a startlingly beautiful young woman with whom he had lived for the past ten months. Sarah had hated her at first, partly because she seemed to have no more ambition than Simon, but also in the way that all mothers find it hard to relate to the girl their son has chosen to replace them. But as time passed and she seemed to make him happy, Sarah had begun to resign herself to the situation and search for good qualities in the girl that she hadn't noticed before. So his answer distressed her further.

'She's gone.'

'What?'

'Left me – weeks ago. Ran off with a bloody male nurse from the hospital. Namby-pamby little wuss who loves trees.'

'Oh Simon, no!' She touched his arm but he shrugged her off.

'Oh Simon, yes. You're too messy, Simon, your home's a tip. I'm off to get meself a life.'

'She said that?'

'Summat like it, yeah.' He slung the crust of his sandwich to a seagull on the water. ''Course there was mess, I'd been painting. And putting up shelves.'

'*You*, Simon, decorating?' The squalor of Simon's house was legendary in their family.

'Yeah. I thought that's what she wanted. What all women want, in't it – a nice home?' He looked at her sideways, as though this might be the answer he had come for. *What is it women want, Mum? How can I get Jasmine back?* Of course he would never ask these questions so explicitly but that was what he wanted, she felt sure.

Sarah felt touched, flattered and afraid. Touched and flattered that he should come to her, afraid that she had no idea of the answers. How could *she* know, who paid so little attention to her own home and marriage, these days? It was, she knew, somehow unsatisfactory despite all the efforts she and Bob had made over the years. Years in which Bob had put up shelves and units and wallpaper in every house they had had. And now Simon had for once tried to copy his stepfather, and Jasmine – his one spectacular achievement – had walked out on him. I could weep, she thought.

'When did she go?'

'Six weeks ago. I know where he lives. He takes her to them bloody protesters at fashion centre. Clowns – diggin' holes and climbin' trees.'

Like everyone, Sarah knew of the environmental protest at the designer centre. Emily might have supported it, but Simon hated things like that.

'So Jasmine's involved with the protest too?'

'Probably. I saw her there once.'

'Oh Simon.' She touched his hand gently. 'Is there no chance she'll come back?'

'Only when she fancies a bit of . . . you know. Then she comes back for an afternoon. But it's not the same, is it?' He flung the mineral water bottle viciously into the river, missing a duck by inches. She kept her hand on his but he wouldn't look at her.

'You still see her then?' Sarah could easily believe it. She had always suspected Jasmine of using her son for her own purposes, as an amusing sexual accessory. 'Well, couldn't you . . . I don't know, discuss it with her when you meet? I thought you got on so well!'

The answer, when it came, was surprisingly loud and strong, a gale of sound that turned heads nearby. 'Don't you think I've tried that, Mum? She just laughs at me. I've even followed her back to his house, to tell that little bastard to leave her alone. But it's no good, is it? She wants it all her own way, the bitch!'

The strength of his emotion frightened her. If he showed this much anger towards Jasmine, she thought, the girl might be afraid to come back.

'I . . . I don't think that's quite the way, Simon,' she began hesitantly. 'I mean . . .'

'Oh, forget it,' he said suddenly. 'There's nowt you can do, I never thought there were!'

But he had, she thought. He'd hoped. 'Perhaps if you tell me about it, the things you quarrelled about . . .'

'No, there's no point.' He recovered himself, patted her hand. 'We didn't really quarrel, Mum, we just . . . fell out, you know. It's happened before and it'll happen again. I'll just have to live with it.'

Only I can't, his body language said. He clenched his fists on his thighs, and slowly pressed them together until his arms tensed with the strain. It looked like an unconscious expression of all the violence and tension in his emotions. Then, suddenly, he relaxed.

'Anyhow, what about you? You're not going to get this sod Harker off, are you?'

'I'm doing my best, Simon. You know me.'

'Yeah. Leave no stone unturned. But what d'you reckon to him, eh? Hardly your sort.'

Sarah smiled ironically. 'Criminals aren't my sort, Simon, you know that. My job's to defend them, not admire them.'

'He's a criminal all right. Nasty violent thug.'

'He . . . how do you know that?' An unpleasant sensation of shock squirmed in her stomach. Just those two sentences of Sharon in court yesterday about Gary's criminal record, and here was her son parroting them back to her. It must be from last night's *Evening Press*, which she hadn't bothered to read.

'Everyone knows who's met him,' said Simon. 'I've seen him on building sites.'

'You've met Gary Harker?'

'Yeah. Ugly bastard, isn't he? Thinks he's hard but he's scum really.'

And they probably say the same about you, she thought bitterly. You, my son, working with Gary Harker. She shook her head, trying to take it all in. 'So you didn't come just to see me? You came to see him!'

'Both of you,' Simon said. 'I saw it in't paper and thought, I've got a family interest here. I'll go along and see what's what.'

'I see.' Sarah sighed. 'So what do you think, now you've seen it?'

'I think you're giving that woman a hard time. Does she deserve it, really?'

'I have to, Simon, it's part of the game. She says Gary raped her, he says he wasn't there. I have to test the evidence – you know that.'

'Yes, Mum, but what do you really think? Did he do it, or not?'

'I don't know, Simon. It's not my job to know.' It was an old argument, but the rest of her family had never really accepted it. Like that detective, Terry Bateson, yesterday.

'Oh, come on, Mum – you must have an opinion! Hasn't he told you?'

'Yes. He's told me he didn't do it and I have to respect that. Isn't that what you'd want, if I was defending you?'

'Yeah, but I mean, Gary Harker! He's a right hard case. And all that stuff with the knife and the mask and the little kid – if he did all that he should have his balls cut off!'

'If he did it, Simon, yes,' said Sarah sarcastically. 'And if he didn't? What then?'

'He's still a pillock. I've met him – remember?'

'So have I. I'll remember your views when I have to defend you. In the meantime . . .' She stood up, looking for a litter bin for the sandwich wrappers. '. . . even pillocks need defending, so I'd better get back. Coming?'

'Maybe, for a bit. Nowt else to do.'

Once again his answer irritated and pleased her at the same time. As they walked back, two young female backpackers, sunbathing in bra and shorts and heavy boots, glanced at Simon appreciatively, and for a moment Sarah saw him through their eyes and thought how attractive he was, this tall muscular young man who was her son. If only she could be more proud of him; but there was always this awkwardness between them. Impulsively, as they approached the court, they turned to each other and both began to speak at once.

'Simon, would you like me to come round to your house after . . .'

'How's Emily?'

48

Recovering, Sarah spoke first. 'Emily's fine. Worried about her GCSEs though. I went to a concert of hers last night.' She paused. 'Would you . . .?'

'My place is a bit of a tip at the moment . . .'

'I don't mind. I could help you to clear it up.'

'Not your scene really is it, Mum? You've got books to read, pillocks to defend. I'll see you around.'

She sighed. 'All right then. Any time, Simon, really. Just drop round.'

'Yes.' Living near each other in the same city, separated by emotion rather than distance, they had never really solved the issue of whether to kiss or embrace at parting. Other people seemed to manage it well but they were not a family who touched much. So now she just gave him her hand. 'See you then.'

'I'm coming to watch, remember?' Trying to make amends, he drew her to him briefly and kissed the top of her head as though she were a child. Then, going up the steps past Julian Lloyd-Davies who stood watching with his junior, Simon said loudly: 'I'll be in't gallery then, Mum. Ready to gob on't pillock's head if he misbehaves!'

7

When Sarah entered court everyone else apart from the judge was already in their places. Hurriedly, she poured herself a glass of water, and scanned the questions on her pad.

'All stand!' the clerk called, and everyone rose. Judge Gray entered, bowed and sat down. Everyone except Sarah resumed their seats. Despite her hurried entry she felt quite calm, clear in her mind about what she had to do.

'Now, Ms Gilbert, you say you met Mr Harker at a party at the Royal Station Hotel on Saturday 14th October. What time did you arrive?'

'About eight, eight thirty, I suppose.'

'And you left just before midnight, you said?'

'Yes. I had to get home because of the kids.'

'Yes. Your little girl was ill, I think you said. So you stayed at this party for what? Three hours? Four?' Sarah glanced at the jury, hoping they would take the point about Sharon's standard of child care.

'About that, yeah.'

'I see. And while you were there, what did you drink?'

'Vodka and lime. That's what I usually have.'

'That's the only thing you drink, is it?'

'Usually, yes. Sometimes a glass of wine or a gin.'

'All right. So you went to this party to enjoy yourself, and you were there for three or four hours. Think back, Ms Gilbert. So how many vodka and limes did you have in the course of the evening? One? Three? Five? Ten?'

Up to this point Sarah had met Sharon's eyes as she questioned her, but now she looked away, at a point on the wall about a yard to Sharon's right and above her head. It was a technique she had learned from other barristers – at crucial points look away, break eye contact. It keeps your mind clear to focus on the most precise, awkward questions while at the same time leaving the witness floundering, unable to enlist your sympathy with body language. It's a sort of calculated insult, too – it shows the jury you're in charge, that you're listening to the answers but don't necessarily trust the person who is giving them.

'About . . . four, five perhaps.'

'All right. Four or five vodkas with lime. What about gin? You drink that sometimes.'

'Yeah, Gary bought me one. Trying to make up to me, I guess.'

'All right. So you had four or five vodkas, and a gin. A double gin, was it?'

'Yes.'

'All right. So it was a good party and you had quite a lot to drink.' Sarah looked pointedly at the jury. 'Nothing wrong with that, but it all adds up to . . . what? Maybe eight units of alcohol altogether. And for the sake of comparison, an average woman exceeds the drink drive limit after three or four units, so you were well over that. Were you drunk, Ms Gilbert?'

'Drunk? No. A bit merry, perhaps.' Sharon was looking flushed now, annoyed. 'I'm never drunk. I can't be, can I, with the kids?'

'Never drunk. So you feel you were in a perfectly fit state to look after your children, one of whom was ill. Is that right?'

'Yes, of course I was! All I had to do was give them a bit of a cuddle and put 'em to bed! Anyway, so what? I'm not here because of my kids, I'm here because that man raped me!'

'Well, that's exactly the point I'm coming to, Ms Gilbert. You see, we've already established that it would be very difficult for you to positively identify a man who broke into your house with a hood over his face, when you were naturally very frightened – terrified – and the man only spoke a few words through his hood. Now when I asked you about that this morning, I imagine the jury assumed you were sober; but you weren't, were you? You were not only terrified out of your wits – as you had every right to be – you were drunk!'

'No I bloody well wasn't! I just had a few drinks at a party. What's wrong with that?'

Sarah faced the jury, hoping to appeal to their common sense. She studied them carefully – a frowning middle-class woman in her fifties, a young man in a suit, a vacant young woman in a fluffy pink cardigan, a heavy-set man in a leather jacket, resting his chin in his hand.

'You had consumed eight units of alcohol, Ms Gilbert. Do you know why people are prohibited from driving with that amount in their blood? It's because their ability to react correctly, and perceive accurately what is going on around them, is seriously impaired. But you had drunk twice the permitted driving level, Ms Gilbert! Twice as much! It's a simple medical fact – everything was a blur to you that night, wasn't it?'

'No!'

'Yes, Ms Gilbert.' To her delight Sarah saw the man in the leather jacket and the middle-aged woman nod in agreement. 'Let me put it simply. It's hard enough for anyone to identify a man with a hood over his face when they're sober, but you weren't sober, you were drunk. So you were in no state whatsoever to identify a man whose face you never even saw!'

'Yes I bloody well was! It was him – Gary Harker! He broke in and raped me, damn you – how would you like it!'

I wouldn't like it at all, Sarah thought. I'd be scared witless and it might ruin my life for ever. She noticed accusing frowns from two jury women who were probably thinking the same. Be careful, she thought. This is a battle for the jury's sympathy as well as to establish the facts. She kept her voice calm and reasonable.

'Please understand me, Ms Gilbert. I'm not suggesting for a second that you weren't raped. What I *am* suggesting is that you were far too drunk to be sure that the man who raped you was Gary Harker. It could have been somebody else, you see, not Gary at all!'

'No. It was Gary,' Sharon insisted stubbornly.

'All right then.' Sarah sighed, and began a new tack. 'Let's go back to the party at the hotel where you met Gary earlier. What sort of things did you talk about?'

'This and that. Where he was living, jobs he'd had. *Whether he'd been in jail again.*' Sharon brought this last remark out with vindictive spite, no doubt remembering the effect her reference to Gary's record had had yesterday.

It was a good hit, but Sarah moved quickly on. 'He asked about his watch, didn't he?'

'Yeah. He said he knew where I kept it, it was in my bottom drawer with all my rings and things, and if I didn't give it back he was going to get it himself.'

'All right, Ms Gilbert. Now I want you to think carefully.' Sarah thought carefully herself. The next point had to be built up step by step if it was to work. For the next few questions Sarah carefully established that the hotel had been crowded, and yes, Sharon and Gary had argued quite loudly enough about the watch for other people to overhear them talking about it and where it was kept. And after all, she had had this watch for six months, a man's watch, not one she would wear herself.

51

Had she shown it to a few friends, perhaps, men who might be interested in buying it? Sharon shrugged, not seeing the relevance.

'I may have shown it to a few people, perhaps. So what?'

Sarah smiled inwardly. 'The point I am putting to you, Ms Gilbert, is that plenty of people other than Gary must have known that you kept that watch in your bottom drawer. So even if the rapist did go straight to your bottom drawer, that doesn't prove it was Gary, does it?'

'Yes it bloody well does!' Sharon saw the point now, and was angry. 'He knew it was there and he took it, and anyway I recognized him by his voice, and the fact that he knew Wayne's name, and . . .'

'. . . and his penis, Ms Gilbert. Yes, we covered all that this morning. And we have also just established that you were terrified out of your wits and drunk at the time. Are you quite sure that you're telling the truth about this watch? It *was* there in your bottom drawer, wasn't it? And the rapist definitely took it?'

'Yes. I told you. How many times?'

'All right. So how do you account for the fact that when the police arrested Gary next morning, they didn't find the watch? He hadn't got it. Surely if he was so fond of this watch he would have put it on his wrist, wouldn't he?'

'He must have hidden it. Like the rings and the hood that might incriminate him.'

'Yes, the balaclava hood.' Sarah shook her head slowly. 'The police didn't find that in Gary's flat either, did they? Well, you may be right, Ms Gilbert, he may have planned things carefully and hidden the watch and the hood and the rings before going home. But isn't it equally possible – much more likely, in fact – that the reason the police didn't find these things in Gary's flat is because *he didn't rape you*? You made a mistake, and identified Gary when *it was someone else!*'

'No! It was him. I told you!'

'Was it?' Sarah paused, and as she did so she was suddenly aware of herself from outside, as though she were looking down from the gallery on this woman in a wig and gown, the focus of attention of everyone in the courtroom. It was a weird sensation, lasting only a second, but she delighted in it. This was exactly where she had wanted to get to in her cross-examination and she had done so without mishap. She felt like an actress on centre stage who is about to launch into her main soliloquy. Her voice was clear, resonant, persuasive.

'You see, Ms Gilbert, you had two big shocks that night, didn't you? The second one was the rape, which was a terrifying, awful thing; but the first one came earlier, when you met Gary Harker in the hotel. Gary, the man who'd betrayed you. It wasn't a particularly nice surprise meeting him again, was it? You felt bitter towards him because of the way you'd broken up. Then you had an argument about this watch. You were angry with him, weren't you?'

'Angry? I was sick of him. Still am!'

'Yes.' The more shrill and angry Sharon's voice became, the more Sarah tried to keep her own calm, reasonable, understanding. 'So there you are, going out for a nice evening, when Gary turns up. You have a quarrel and it spoils your evening. You're angry – sick of him, as you say. And you've had a lot to drink, too, we've established that. So on the way home, these feelings of anger towards Gary are still there in your mind; you can't get rid of them. He's nothing but trouble, you think – the last thing you want is to see him again. He spoils everything. It's perfectly natural to think that, of course – nothing wrong with it. But then, in the middle of this, a masked man, a stranger, breaks into your house and rapes you. You're confused, drunk and terrified. So when he's gone and the police start asking you questions you put the two things together in your mind and think, That man must have been Gary.'

'It *was* Gary! I recognized him!'

'What I'm putting to you, Ms Gilbert, is that in your drunken, terrified state you *imagined* it was him, when in fact you didn't recognize him at all, did you?'

'I did! I told you! It was Gary – I know it was!'

'But you have no real proof, Ms Gilbert, do you? You're just imagining these things about recognizing his voice and his penis because you're angry with Gary and you want to get your own back on him, but the truth is that you don't really know who raped you, do you? That's the terrible truth. You were raped by a man who you simply didn't recognize at all!'

'No . . . no . . . I don't know. I've told you it was Gary. It had to be.'

'*You don't know.* Exactly; you say it yourself. It's much more terrifying to be raped by a complete stranger but that's the real truth of the matter, isn't it? *You don't know.* You really don't know who the man was, do you?'

Sarah had expected another instant denial but to her surprise there was a pause. Sharon looked down, fiddling distractedly with a ring. Every second the pause went on Sarah felt a rising thrill, a rush of adrenalin along her bloodstream as she thought, *I've done it! I've got her!* In reality the pause only lasted perhaps fifteen seconds but it seemed to go on for ever. Everyone in court watched Sharon intently, fascinated, waiting.

When Sharon finally raised her head there were tears in her eyes but she made no attempt to wipe them away. She looked directly past Sarah at the man in the dock, and when she spoke her voice was hoarse, quieter than before, almost a whisper.

'It was Gary Harker who raped me.'

And so she had not broken. Sarah stood for a moment, irresolute, wondering what to do next. Part of her wanted to go on, to worry the woman like a bitch who has wounded her prey but not killed it, but she doubted now if Sharon would ever surrender. Anyway she had no new questions and if she simply repeated the old ones the judge would stop her for bullying the witness. She remembered a point from her training –

if you can't break your witness, stop when the doubt is uppermost in the jury's mind. She had reached that moment now.

'That's all I have to ask.' She folded her gown about her and sat down.

'Thank you, Ms Gilbert,' the judge said courteously. 'You may stand down now.'

As the usher guided Sharon out Sarah watched the jury, trying to gauge their reaction. The middle-aged lady looked disapproving, the girl in the pink fluffy pullover vacant, the man in the leather jacket sympathetic, as though he would like to get up and wrap Sharon in his arms. No joy there, then. But a grey-haired man in tweeds, whom Sarah had not noticed before, shook his head sadly as Sharon went out, and a younger man was scribbling intently on his note pad.

That must have put some doubt in their minds, Sarah thought, her hands trembling with suppressed excitement. I did the best I could; I couldn't have done better.

She looked over her shoulder at Lucy, who smiled encouragement. Then she looked up, to see what Simon had made of her performance. At least he must see she wasn't a complete dud at this job she had spent so long training for. Perhaps they could talk about it afterwards.

But to her surprise and intense disappointment, Simon was no longer there.

8

Sarah awoke at six as usual, and lay for a while thinking. In these first moments after waking her mind was always clear, and she could often solve problems that had been obscure the day before. Bob, still dozing beside her, was the exact opposite. He wouldn't surface for half an hour, and then only with groans and sighs. She had often tried to discuss things with him at this time, but it was hopeless – he was scarcely human until she was showered, dressed and ready for work. It was a daily irritation in their marriage.

But family matters were not uppermost in her mind this morning; they seldom were. Today she might have to cross-examine Sharon Gilbert's little boy by video link. It would not be easy. Then there were the forensic scientist and DI Terry Bateson, both tough nuts too. She replayed the questions she had planned in her mind as the dawn light filled the room.

She sat at her dressing table by the window, looking out. This was the time of day she liked the house best. There were dew-covered spiders' webs on the long grass in the meadow. She saw a heron float on its wide, creaky wings down to the river bank, where it folded its wings and stood, silent and intent, among the reeds on the further shore. There had been nothing like this in Leeds – it belonged in a nature film on the telly, not in real life where you could actually walk about in it if you wanted. Occasionally Sarah did that – put on a coat and wellington boots and trudged along the river bank; but she felt out of place in it then. It was too cold or damp or muddy; there were insects that bit her; it was eerily quiet and hostile.

It was better looking at it through the window. After all, the fact of having a detached house with a view like this proved she and Bob had made it; they were a success at last. So she sat for a while longer, as other people did t'ai chi or meditation, and told herself she enjoyed it. Then she crossed the room to have a shower, tickling Bob's toes wickedly under the end of the duvet just before the alarm went off.

She was putting on her face before the mirror when Bob came back with a cup of tea, his hair still tousled from sleep. He slumped down on the bed and, to her astonishment, spoke.

'Can you talk to Emily before you go?'

She turned to stare at him. 'What about?'

'Her exams. I was up with her for an hour last night. She thinks she's going to fail.'

'Of course she's not going to fail.' Sarah turned back to the mirror to finish her eye-shadow. 'She's a clever girl, she's done the work. She'll be fine.'

'*She* doesn't think so. The poor kid's in a dreadful state.'

'So what do you want me to do?'

'Talk to her, that's all. Show some sympathy. You've passed enough exams, you know what it's like.'

'All right.' Sarah glanced at her watch. 'But I've got to go in twenty minutes. Is she up?'

'Probably not.' Bob sighed, and took a life-saving draught of tea. 'You don't have to be first person in every day, surely? Have a heart, Sarah.'

'It's a brain she needs, not a heart.' Sarah walked quickly across to her daughter's bedroom. 'Emily, are you up? I want a word.'

'What? Oh, Mum, no.' Emily was still in bed. She opened one eye, saw who it was, and buried her face in the pillow.

Sarah softened a little. She sat on the edge of the bed and touched Emily's shoulder. The shoulder shrank away. 'Emily, wake up. I just want to talk to you for a bit. Dad says you're worried about your exams.'

A mumble that might have been 'So I am' came from deep in the pillow.

'Don't you want to talk about it?'

'No, not now – I'm asleep.'

Sarah sighed. 'You've got to get up anyway to go to school.'

'No, I haven't. Not going today.'

'Don't be silly, of course you're going. You're not ill, are you?'

'No. I'm revising at home.'

'But you can't just skip school when you feel like it.'

''Course I can. Everyone's doing it. The lessons are finished now – all we do at school is revise or sit around and talk. I can work better here.'

Emily hunched up to a half-sitting position facing her mother. Her face was puffy from sleep, but there were no signs of tears. Sarah felt her forehead. 'You're not feverish, are you?'

'*No*, Mother! For God's sake, I'm just staying home to revise! It's only a week to German, you know!'

'All right.' Sarah looked around the room. There were books and papers spread on the desk, clothes scattered all over the floor. 'Have you got all your books here?'

'Yes.'

'Well, you can at least pick up these clothes if you're going to be here all day.' She regretted the words as soon as she'd said them; predictably, they brought tears to Emily's eyes.

'I haven't got time for that – don't you understand? I've got all this work and almost no time left to do it and you go on about stupid things like clothes! I don't know any German and I'm going to fail, I know I am!'

She was crying, and turned her face towards the wall. Sarah groaned inwardly, and surreptitiously checked her watch. She really would have to go soon, to get ready for court. Clumsily, she tried to embrace her daughter, but Emily shoved her away.

'Don't! Leave me alone!'

Frustrated, Sarah tried to speak sensibly. 'Look, you did all right in the German mock, didn't you? You got an A . . .'

'A B! And I only just got that!'

'All right, a B then. But that's not too bad –'

'*You* never got Bs, did you? You never got a B in anything!'

'Well, maybe I didn't, but . . . I *thought* I was going to get Bs lots of times, so I did a bit more work and got an A. That's what you should do, darling. If you sit here and work hard –'

'It's not just German, you know! There's nine other subjects!'

'I know. But they don't all happen on the same day, do they? What you should do is set out a plan, a revision timetable, and then –'

'What do you think I'm doing?' Furiously, Emily leapt out of bed, scrabbled in the mess of papers on her desk, and waved a coloured chart under Sarah's nose. 'See – look at that! That's what I'm doing! Supposed to be doing, anyway. That's what my life is now!'

'Good, well, stick to it then. I *do* know, Emily, I have done a few exams myself. Do the work, and you'll be OK.'

'Yes, but you're different,' said Emily, shaking her tousled hair and glaring at her mother bitterly. 'You're just Superwoman, you can do anything, no one else is like you. I don't even *want* to be like you, why should I? I'll fail and be like Simon – he's happy!'

A cold panic flooded through Sarah. Simon wasn't happy, she didn't believe it. The worst pain of her adult life had been when Simon dropped out of school to become a labourer. It had been a rejection of everything she and Bob had wanted for him. At least Emily had always been diligent, conscientious, found schoolwork easy. And now, at the first big hurdle, to talk of dropping out . . .

'Don't be stupid, Emily! Of course you'll pass. Just stick at it for another few days, and you'll do well. I promise!'

'I can't, Mum! I don't want to anyway!'

Sarah didn't know how to deal with this. Nor did she have time. If she carried on talking now it was just going to blossom into a big discussion which would lead nowhere and make her late. She got up from the bed. 'Of course you can, Emily, and of course you want to. Do your German revision this morning, and I'll give you a ring at lunchtime, OK?'

'If you must.' Emily slumped dejectedly back on her bed as if she might go to sleep.

'I will.' Sarah smiled brightly, opened the door, and went out.

The conversation irritated her, filling her mind as she rode into town. Probably she should have been more sympathetic, but . . . it was *irritation* rather than sympathy that inflamed her mind. Why did the girl make so much *fuss*! After all, at her age, Sarah told herself, I had a baby, I had been slung out of school, I was a social pariah in a cold smelly house with damp walls and rotten plastic furniture but I didn't cry, did I? Not until Kevin left, anyway – I just got on with it.

So why can't Emily do that? All that panic and emotion – it just gets in the way. Bob's too soft with her; she's got to stand on her own two feet. I'll ring at lunchtime like I said but I'll keep the talk light; she'll manage best if no one takes the fuss too seriously.

And with that, she closed the file in her mind on Emily, and opened the ones on Gary Harker and Sharon Gilbert.

These weren't just mental files, but real piles of paper wrapped in red tape which she carried into court a little later. The day began well, with a significant victory for Sarah. Before the jury entered, there was a brief conference between the barristers and the judge, at which Julian Lloyd-Davies conceded that there was no longer any point in presenting the evidence of Sharon's little boy, Wayne. He had intended to do this via a video link, with the little boy in a separate room chaperoned by a trained police psychologist, but in view of Sharon's admission yesterday that she had probably called Wayne by name during the assault, and certainly talked to him about Gary afterwards, there was no longer any point.

So the first witness was the forensic scientist from the Rape Crisis Centre. She confirmed that Sharon had suffered extensive bruising to the vaginal area, entirely consistent with her story of forced, unlubricated penetration. There were marks on her wrists and throat consistent with having been bound; bruising to her cheek and nose, entirely consistent with the right-handed blows to the face which she had described. Julian Lloyd-Davies extracted these facts with careful, polite questions, dwelling on every detail of the injuries to emphasize to the jury the brutality that must have caused them.

But the most important point, for Sarah, was what the scientist did *not* say. When Lloyd-Davies had finished she stood up confidently.

'Dr Marson, I would like to take you back to your examination of Ms Gilbert's vagina. You testified to bruising, did you not? But I heard no mention of semen. Did you not find any?'

The scientist, an intense young woman with short-cropped hair and steel-framed glasses, shook her head. 'No, I'm afraid we didn't.'

Sarah affected to look puzzled. 'But you did look, I take it? I mean, evidence from semen is very important in cases of rape, is it not?'

'Yes, indeed it is. In this case I took a number of swabs from the vaginal area, but I could detect no semen on any of them.'

'And what conclusion do you draw from that?'

The young woman shrugged. 'That the rapist withdrew from the victim's vagina before an ejaculation took place. Either that or she had cleaned herself with a douche, but there was no evidence of that.'

'Very well. But from your point of view as a forensic scientist this is a pity, isn't it, because if there *had* been any semen you would have been able to send it for DNA analysis, which could have established the accused's guilt or innocence beyond doubt. So no doubt you searched very diligently to find such a sample?'

'I did my best, yes.'

'So to summarize your evidence, Dr Marson, your findings confirm the victim's story that she was forcibly raped, beaten and bound. Am I right?'

The young woman nodded earnestly. 'I would say so. Yes.'

'But nothing in your findings can help us establish the identity of the man who did these terrible things. Is that also right?'

'Well, no . . . that's true, yes.'

The answer was hardly as clear as Sarah wanted. She tried again.

'Just to make that crystal clear, Dr Marson, what you are saying is that you know that Sharon Gilbert was raped, but that you have no idea at all whether it was Gary Harker who did it, or my learned colleague Julian Lloyd-Davies here beside me, or his lordship up there on the bench, or any man walking around York today. It could have been any one of those people, couldn't it, as far as you know? All you can tell us for certain is that it was – a man!'

The young scientist flushed. 'Well . . . I'm afraid – yes.'

That had woken them up. Sarah smiled, noticing the raised, bushy eyebrows of the judge, the broad grin of a young newspaper reporter, and the wide, astonished eyes of several jurors.

'Thank you very much, Dr Marson.' Pleased with her *coup de théâtre*, she sat down.

9

'Hello, this is the Newby house. There's no one home at present, but if you'd like to leave a message after the tone . . .'

Damn, Sarah thought. The tone beeped. 'Come on, Emily, pick up the phone if you're there. I'm just ringing to see how you're getting on. Emily? Are you there . . .?'

No answer. She snapped the phone shut, instantly regretting the action. It was hardly an ideal place to show her irritation. She was outside the court on the main steps, where a policeman, a car thief and his solicitor were deeply enjoying the sight of the bewigged lady having a tantrum with her mobile. But Emily had left no message on it this morning.

Where *was* the girl? All that fuss about staying at home to work and now no answer.

She dialled Bob's number and persuaded the officious school secretary to trek to the school dining hall to fetch him. After a three-minute wait she heard his voice, breathless from running. 'Sarah? Yes – what now?'

'Have you heard from Emily this morning?'

'No. Why should I?'

'I just rang and the answerphone's on. Her mobile's switched off.'

'So leave a message. She's probably gone out to buy a Mars bar – refresh the brain cells.'

'She was supposed to be revising, Bob, you can't do that in a sweet shop. What was she like when you left this morning?'

'Oh, so-so, I suppose. I told her not to worry about the exams – I wish you'd do the same.'

'What do you mean, you wish . . . *Bob*? You *asked* me to talk to her this morning and I did. I told her to stick to her revision and she'd be all right.'

'She said you put the wind up her. You always do, somehow. Poor kid, she's terrified she won't do as well as her mother. You don't have to remind her of that, you know.'

'Bob, I didn't do that! I wouldn't, surely you know that!'

'You remind her just by being there, a living example of over-achievement. You . . .'

59

'Well, thanks a lot, Bob Newby.' Sarah held the phone at arm's length while Bob's voice chattered away tinnily to itself. Why had he started doing this to her recently? She didn't know but she hated it. Everything they'd shared for so many years – her academic success, their daughter – had suddenly become a cold wet cloth which he slapped in her face. What was going wrong?

Whatever it was, this was no place to sort it out. 'Look, Bob, I can't talk now and I'll be in court all afternoon. Give her a ring from your office sometime and check she's OK, will you? Bye.'

As she turned back to go in again she collided with a man coming out. 'Oh, excuse me.'

'Sarah! The devil's advocate – I was looking for you!' Terry Bateson grasped her arm. 'Fancy a spot of lunch?'

'It's not . . . the best moment, Terry.'

'Nonsense. Not a word about the case, I promise. Just a pie in the Blue Lion.'

She sighed. That hadn't been what she'd meant but that was why he was here, of course – to give evidence this afternoon. But if they didn't discuss the case, there was no reason why not. And the alternative, a moody meal on her own, suddenly seemed vastly unattractive.

She had no idea what made this detective so cheerful, particularly given the flaws in the evidence he was here to give. Maybe he wasn't aware of them, yet. Anyway, she might as well profit by it. He might not be the brightest detective in the world, but he *was* handsome.

'All right. Just wait while I disrobe.'

'Who could resist?'

Whether she heard those words or not Terry didn't know, but six minutes later he found himself squeezed into a seat opposite Sarah in a corner of the pub. On the small round table in front of them he set down two halves of lager and a numbered white ticket entitling them to chef's special pasties with gravy. The cramped space forced their knees companionably together. He smiled, and tried to wave away the money she fished out of her purse.

'My treat.'

'Oh no. I'm not having my meal subsidized by a prosecution witness. Besides, you'll want your money back when I've finished with you this afternoon.'

'Sounds ominous.' He raised his glass.'Here's to a long painful sentence for Mr Harker.'

'*Terry!* One more word and I'm out of here. No shop, remember?'

'I remember.' The waitress brought the pasties with white napkins, gleaming knives and forks and gravy in a jug. Terry poured for them both, smiling. 'This place is one of our few rewards for bringing villains to court. Every time we fail I have to eat in the police canteen.'

'Shame.' Sarah tucked in her napkin carefully. 'You should learn to cook for yourself.'

'Our nanny does that.'

'Oh yes.' Sarah knew a little of Terry's personal circumstances, but not much. 'Norwegian open sandwiches, isn't it?'

'Sometimes. You should try them.'

'Ask me and I will.' She smiled. He thought, it's just an offhand remark, *but I wish* . . .

'How's your daughter – Emily, isn't it?'

Sarah sipped her lager, frowned. 'Don't ask. She's a teenager, she's got GCSEs next week, she hates her mother . . . what else? You wait, Terry, you've got it all to come.'

But Terry was feeling like a teenager himself, on a date. That frown, he thought wryly, the way it crinkles her forehead, the little feminine gestures she makes as she sips her beer and pats her lips with the napkin – they're such tiny, normal things yet I could watch them all day. This is how it was with Mary, all those years ago – so beautiful that it hurt.

Don't be daft, he scolded himself, you're forty years old. Still, any man can dream . . .

'What's the joke?' Sarah asked, her napkin patting the puzzled half-smile on her lips.

'What? Oh – nothing. Just you.'

'Me? What did I say?'

Careful, Terry. This is a married woman, a barrister, a dangerous lady who's about to cross-examine you in court. Not a fantasy in your dreams.

'Just – a look on your face. It took me back, that's all. To a girl I once knew.'

'Your wife, you mean?' A look of careful sympathy crossed Sarah's face.

'No, no. Before that. Long ago. When I was a student.' That's it. Clever move, old son. Get her interested in your exotic past.

'Where were you a student?'

'Here in York.'

And for a while he told her about his running career, and his reminiscences of student life. His ambitions then had been to bed all the pretty girls on campus and win the Olympics, neither of which he had quite achieved. He knew very little of her background, but realized as they talked that she did not seem to have the same sort of carefree student memories. She had studied in Leeds, he gathered, as a mature student. There seemed to be some mystery about what had happened before, but before he could solve it she glanced at her watch.

'Court resumes in ten minutes, Detective Inspector. I hope you're ready for a roasting. I mean it.' The sharp, ironic, smile irritated him somehow.

'What for? Putting a serial rapist in the dock? As a woman you should be grateful.'

61

'For providing such a brief with so many flaws in it? Oh, I am, Detective Inspector, I am!'

This time the cynicism definitely got beneath his skin. She might be pretty and clever with words, he thought, but if she'd seen the things I've seen . . . Sharon Gilbert shaken and bruised in front of her little kids . . . Karen Whitaker sobbing in the woods . . . Maria Clayton's dead body . . .

'No, not that. For making the streets safer by getting scum like Harker locked up. Play your games in court if you like, Sarah, but his place is behind bars, because he's guilty as hell. You know that as well as I do.'

Sarah flushed. She had enjoyed the banter over lunch, but she was in no mood to be lectured. She seldom was. 'You may *think* you know that, Terry, but can you prove it? The courtroom game, as you call it, means that you must prove his guilt to the jury. And my job is to defend him, in case you get it wrong. Which you have done, I'm sorry to say.'

'Have I? How?'

'You'll see. In court this afternoon.'

'I hope not.' Terry's anger made him clumsy. 'I've worked hard on this case, you know.'

'So have I.' She shrugged and walked to the door. 'We'd better not go back together, it wouldn't look good. Anyway it's a different world in court. We meet as strangers.'

Just how right she was, he was about to find out.

As she came back into court, Sarah checked her mobile. But there were no messages, from Emily or anyone else. Probably she was still in a sulk, or revising hard. And Bob would ring sometime in the afternoon, if he remembered. Maybe her father's voice on the answerphone would induce her to pick up the receiver.

The judge entered, and Julian Lloyd-Davies began to take Terry Bateson through his evidence. Terry explained how he had gone to Sharon's house when she had called the police, at 1.22 a.m. Sharon's friend Mary had been there with her. A female officer had stayed with Mary and the children while Sharon was taken to the rape suite and examined by a female doctor.

Both during and after the medical examination Sharon had stated clearly that she had recognized the rapist as Gary Harker. Terry had arrested Gary in his flat at five that morning.

Lloyd-Davies then played parts of the tape of Terry's interview with Gary. He had asked the judge to allow this, because he believed that the tone of what was said was as important as the substance. The real reason, Sarah guessed, was to ensure that even if Sarah kept Gary off the stand, the jury would still hear him speak in his own coarse, brutal fashion. Sarah had resisted, but not as strongly as she could have done. When he had won his point Lloyd-Davies had smiled smugly at his junior; and Sarah had been inwardly delighted, realizing he had made his biggest mistake so far.

On the tape Gary was surly, aggressive and uncooperative. After he left the Station Hotel, he said, he had been to another pub with a friend called Sean. There they met two prostitutes, and screwed them up against a wall for a tenner each. He could remember neither of their names. The older jurors looked appalled and disgusted, just as Lloyd-Davies had hoped.

On the tape Terry insisted that Gary had gone to Sharon's house, broken in, and raped her in front of her kids. Gary denied it. *'She's a lying bitch if she says that.'*

'But that's exactly what she says, Gary. She recognized the man who did it. It was you.'

'Well, she's lying then. She couldn't have recognized me, the cow!'

'Why couldn't she recognize you, Gary?'

'Because I wasn't bloody there, that's why!' The retort was followed by a long silence, broken at last by a nervous Gary. *'Do you hear what I said, copper? She couldn't have recognized me because I wasn't there.'* Silence. *'Can you prove I was there, eh? Go on then, tell me how.'*

And then came the statement which Sarah had noticed.

'We know you were there because she recognized you, Gary. She saw your face!'

There was a silence which seemed, to Sarah watching the jury's pained faces, to be longer than all the others. Gary's voice on the tape was having the effect Lloyd-Davies had anticipated: it was loud, aggressive, mocking. *'Silly bitch, that's all crap, she's lying! Recognize my arse!'*

As the court clerk switched off the tape, Lloyd-Davies turned to Terry Bateson in the witness box. 'Now, officer, I have a few questions about that interview.'

'Very well.' Terry glanced at Sarah, who sat watching him intently. There was nothing flirtatious or friendly about her eyes. They were as cold as those of a lizard watching a fly.

'Did you look for this man Sean – Murphy, or Mulligan, or Moriarty?' Lloyd-Davies was practised in the use of sarcasm and it oozed from him now. 'The one Mr Harker claims to have spent the evening with?'

'Yes, sir, we did. Without result.'

'No. Well, were you able to find these two prostitutes that he claims to have met?'

'No, sir. We had no name or address, no real description . . .'

'So what is your opinion of Gary Harker's *alibi*, as I suppose we must call it?'

'I think it's a pack of lies, sir.'

'Thank you. Now, in the interview you repeatedly told the accused that he had been recognized by Ms Gilbert. How did he appear to react to that?'

'Well, I think you can hear it on the tape, sir. He was really surprised and upset. But he wasn't upset when I told him she'd been raped, or even that it had happened in front of her kids. That didn't seem to worry him much. What really got to him was that she claimed to have *recognized* him. He went white when I said that. He couldn't speak.'

Lloyd-Davies stood silent for a while after Terry had finished speaking, pretending to think, while Terry's last words echoed in the jury's minds. The silence continued until Judge Gray raised a quizzical eyebrow and Lloyd-Davies reluctantly sat down.

'Thank you, Inspector, wait there, please.'

Sarah stood up. She looked across the court at Terry Bateson. No flicker of recognition passed between them. The easy conversation of a hour ago was forgotten. They were strangers. As she asked her first question, the hair rose along the back of his neck.

'Detective Inspector, you lied to Mr Harker, didn't you?'

For a long telling moment Terry didn't answer. 'I . . . don't understand you.'

'Let me help you then. Do you recall these words: "We know you were there because she recognized you. She saw your face." You said that, didn't you?'

'Yes.'

'Was it true?'

'Ms Gilbert recognized Gary Harker, yes. That's why we arrested him.'

'Was it true that she saw his face?'

'No.'

'So you lied to Mr Harker, didn't you?'

Terry recovered himself slightly, and addressed his reply to the judge as the police were trained to do. It was a subtle way of insulting defence counsel, making them seem unimportant in the eyes of the jury. 'She didn't actually say she saw his face, my lord, that's true, but she stated very clearly that she recognized her assailant as Gary Harker, and the reason I –'

'I didn't ask you *why* you lied, Detective Inspector, I asked you *if* you lied. And the answer is yes, isn't it?'

The judge leaned forward protectively. 'Nevertheless, I think it might help the jury if the Detective Inspector were allowed to give his reasons, Mrs Newby. Inspector?'

Thank God for judges, Terry thought. 'The reason was simple, my lord. I wanted to see what his reaction would be if he thought he'd been recognized. And his reaction was quite clear. He was silent, as you could hear on the tape, and he went very white. That convinced me that he was guilty.'

Sarah glanced at the judge. It seemed he had finished, for the present at least. Once again she had the electrifying feeling that all eyes were on her. Mostly hating her, at this moment.

'I see. What would you say, Detective Inspector, if I told this court that at lunchtime you put your hand up my skirt and indecently assaulted me?'

A collective gasp sucked the air out of the court. Someone in the public gallery began to giggle helplessly. Terry opened his mouth to speak but no sound came out.

Before he could recover Sarah went on, smoothly: 'I think the jury can see exactly what you would say. Your face has gone white and you are lost for words. Well, let me reassure the jury straight away that that was a hypothetical question. The Detective Inspector did not assault me, members of the jury. But even though he knows the suggestion is untrue he is shocked and lost for words, as you see.'

A young jury woman laughed and her neighbour grinned. The other expressions ranged from delight through dismay to disgust. She had their undivided attention, at least.

But it was not a line of attack she had planned – where did she go from here? When you've made your point, move on. In a quiet, reasonable voice she asked: 'Detective Inspector, did you find a balaclava hood in Gary Harker's flat?'

'No, my lord, we didn't.' Terry's voice was wooden, stolid, but underneath he was seething. What a bitch the woman was! Was she planning this in the pub? Her questions continued, swift and relentless.

'Did you find the watch that Sharon Gilbert described?'

'No, my lord.'

'No hood, no watch. You *did* search the flat, I suppose?'

'Yes, we did.'

'But you found no hood and no watch. Did you find any evidence at all in the flat, to suggest that Gary Harker had raped Sharon Gilbert?'

'No, my lord. But –'

'So your only justification for arresting Mr Harker at five o'clock that morning was Sharon Gilbert's identification of a man whose face she had *not* seen. Is that correct?'

'It . . . was the main reason for arresting him, yes.'

'Was there any other reason?'

'No.'

'So it wasn't just your *main* reason, it was your *only* reason, wasn't it? Tell me, Detective Inspector, when you interviewed Ms Gilbert that night, was she sober?'

'I . . . understood she had been drinking, my lord, but she didn't seem particularly drunk. She was quite clear about what she was saying.'

'Not particularly drunk, you say. Ms Gilbert has told this court that she drank five vodkas and a double gin at the party, plus a vodka just before you arrived. But she was not particularly drunk, in your view. Detective Inspector, how many units of alcohol can a woman drink without exceeding the drink drive limit?'

Terry hesitated. 'Er . . . one or two, I believe. Maybe three, if it's consumed with food.'

'You *believe*? You're a police inspector. Aren't you sure?'

'It varies with circumstances and body weight. Anyway I'm not a traffic policeman.'

'Let me tell you then. An average woman is unfit to drive if she has consumed more than three units of alcohol in three hours. Sharon Gilbert had consumed at least eight units of alcohol. She was nearly three times over the driving limit. And yet you say she wasn't drunk.'

'I didn't say she was fit to drive. I said she could identify the man who raped her.'

'Even though that man was wearing a balaclava hood?'

'Yes. He was a man she knew very well.'

'Well, look, Detective Inspector, it seems to me that you're asking this jury to believe one of two impossible things. Either you believe that a woman who has drunk six vodkas and a double gin is perfectly sober, or, if you accept that she wasn't sober, you are saying that a woman who was hopelessly drunk can positively identify a man with a hood over his face. Which is it?'

There was smothered laughter from the jury box. It sounded like applause to Sarah, mockery to Terry, who sighed.

'Neither of those. As I said, she wasn't completely sober but she was clear enough in her mind to identify the man she believed had raped her. And she repeated those allegations the next day when she *was* perfectly sober. She has always been perfectly clear about that.'

'I see. Well, is it also true, Detective Inspector, that Mr Harker denied the allegation of rape when you first arrested him, and has clearly and consistently repeated those denials every time you've asked him?'

'That is true, my lord, yes.'

'Very well. And you found no other evidence whatsoever in his house or on his clothing to substantiate this charge. That's correct too, isn't it?'

'That's true, my lord.'

'Very well. That's all I have to ask.'

She folded her gown about her and sat down. And as he made his way to the back of the court she watched him with a slight enigmatic smile on her face. A smile signifying what, Terry wondered. Irony? Mockery? Self-satisfaction?

Bitch.

10

The final prosecution witness was a man called Keith Somers. His testimony was straightforward and damning. He knew Gary Harker, and he had seen him in Albert Street just after 1 a.m. on the night of the rape. Gary had been wearing black jeans and a black shirt, and had even acknowledged him with a wave.

The significance of this was that Albert Street ran parallel to Thorpe Street, where Sharon Gilbert lived. The houses had small back gardens with low fences which backed on to each other. The rapist could easily have left Sharon's house, climbed the fence and come out in Albert Street.

From Sharon's phone bill, Lloyd-Davies demonstrated that she had phoned her friend Mary at 1.08 a.m., and the police at 1.22 a.m. Somers had seen Gary at about 1.05. This, Lloyd-Davies insisted, put Gary in exactly the right place, at exactly the right time.

As Sarah stood up to cross-examine she felt her pager tremble in her pocket. Looking down she saw her husband's work number. What did he want – more problems with Emily? Nothing she could do now, anyway.

Somers was a good, credible witness. She tried to cast doubt on the time he had seen Gary, but he would have none of it. He had been at a friend's house watching a film which ended at 12.50 a.m. He'd left immediately: no lingering conversations, no cups of coffee. He'd had a few beers but he wasn't drunk. He'd seen Gary's face clearly under a streetlight. Sarah tried to turn this, at least, to her advantage.

'You could see all of his head, could you?'

'Yes. He was bare-headed.'

'So he wasn't wearing a balaclava hood?'

'No.'

'Did you see any sign of a hood – something in his hand, a bulge in his pocket, perhaps?'

'No. No, I can't say I did.'

'I see. Well, thank you very much.' She sat down. It was the best she could do – Gary admitted being in the area that night, after all. Sarah remembered the pager again. What did Bob want? She felt suddenly tired, unaccountably low after the adrenalin rush of the early afternoon.

Julian Lloyd-Davies said: 'That completes the case for the prosecution, my lord.'

'Very well.' The judge looked enquiringly at Sarah, who stood up.

'My lord, I would like to address the court on a point of law.'

'I see. In that case, members of the jury, I must ask you to retire for a short time.'

As the jury filed out of court the barristers digested the phrase *a short time*. Lloyd-Davies knew very well what Sarah was about to say, and no doubt regarded it as a forlorn hope. But she was determined to give it a try.

'Before I present the case for the defence, I would like to invite your lordship to dismiss the case as being unsafe to put before a jury. As your lordship will have seen, the prosecution have completely failed to produce any evidence which puts my client at the scene of the crime. They have no forensic evidence at all. My client has consistently pro-tested his innocence, and the only evidence against him is that of identification. The evidence of the victim's child has been discounted, and that of the victim herself is highly suspect and tainted by her own extreme animosity towards my client, whose face she never saw. In view of all these points it seems to me that the only proper course for your lordship is to dismiss the case now rather than running the risk of an unsafe conviction before a jury.'

Julian Lloyd-Davies stood to reply but the judge waved him away.

'No, Mr Lloyd-Davies, it won't be necessary. I hear what you say, Mrs Newby, and I agree with you that there are a number of difficulties with the identification evidence, and the child's evidence has been excluded. But the fact remains that Ms Gilbert was very well acquainted with the defendant, and can be presumed able to recognize his voice, even from behind a mask. The last witness puts your client in the area at precisely the time the rape was committed. Even if the Crown have not been able to produce the watch, its existence does give your client a motive, in addition to the intention to rape, for entering the house, and its theft suggests that the intruder knew the layout of the bedroom. So in view of all these points I am satisfied that the Crown have produced a case to answer.'

Sarah bowed. 'As your lordship wishes.' It was no more than she had expected. But any appeal court would know that she had tried three times to get this case thrown out. The judge's decision would have to be proven right in all three instances; no one could say she had not tried.

'So, Mrs Newby. The jury are chafing at the bit. Shall we begin?'

Sarah sighed. 'Very well, my lord.' The jurors filed morosely back into their seats, looking far less eager than the judge had suggested, and she called Graham Dewar.

Dewar was a bricklayer who had worked with Gary for a company called MacFarlane's. When Lucy had first discovered him Sarah had been delighted. Whatever else, he would embarrass the police. He was a respectable, red-faced man, uncomfortable in his shiny blue suit.

'Mr Dewar, when you worked with Gary Harker, did you know a man called Sean?'

'I did, yes.'

'Did you know his surname?'

'Never did, no. Always called him Sean, that's all.'

'Was he friendly with Gary?'

'Quite friendly, yes, I suppose. I think they met in prison, like.'

That's just what I didn't need, Sarah thought. Quickly, she moved on.

'What sort of man was he?'

Dewar considered. 'Well, sort of fitness fanatic, I suppose. Did a lot of training. Not very chatty. I didn't know him right well, like. He were there for two or three weeks and then gone.'

'Is that unusual?'

'No. We get lots like him. Work for a bit then go back on t'dole. Happens all't time.'

'When did he leave?'

'Well, I can't say for definite – but it were about same time as Gary got arrested. Middle of October, maybe. Around then.'

'I see.' Sarah glanced at the jury. 'One last question, then, Mr Dewar. Did the police ever come to your building site, to ask you or your mates if this man existed?'

Dewar shook his head. 'No. Definitely not. If they'd come I'd have told them like, but nobody ever asked before your solicitor did.' He indicated Lucy, sitting behind Sarah.

'Thank you, Mr Dewar. Stay there, please.' Sarah glanced at Terry in the well of the court, and sat down. Lloyd-Davies, perhaps as a sign of contempt, had asked his junior, James Morris, to cross-examine. The young man stood up eagerly, and began in a well-educated southern voice. 'That's all a pack of lies, Mr Dewar, isn't it?'

Dewar took his time answering, examining the young lawyer curiously, as though he had never seen anything quite like him before and was curious how he was put together. 'No, young man, it isn't bloody lies. It's the truth, like I swore to tell on yon book.'

James Morris flushed. 'Well, we'll see what the jury think, shall we? You're a close friend of Gary Harker, aren't you?'

'No, not particularly.'

Sarah glanced at Lloyd-Davies, to see how he was taking his protégé's performance.

'Well, you came here to testify on his behalf.'

'Don't make me his friend, does it? As a matter of fact I don't like the feller much.'

'But . . . if you don't like him, why have you come?'

'To tell't truth, young man. For justice' sake. In't that what you do 'ere?'

Morris was sunk. He floundered on for some time but only dug himself deeper into a hole. Sarah blew Lucy a silent kiss. Despite the unfortunate comment about prison, Dewar was a gem. She had hit the bull's-eye this time. The only trouble was, he was the only shot in her locker.

James Morris sat down at four o'clock. The judge peered at Sarah over his spectacles.

'Will your client be taking the stand, Mrs Newby?'

'That remains to be decided, my lord. I need to take instructions from my client.'

'Very well. We will resume in the morning.' The judge levered himself to his feet, the clerk cried out, 'All stand!' and court was over for the day.

Lucy came out of court with her. 'Will you put him on the stand?'

'I would advise not.'

'Why? We're doing well, and he's consistently denied it.'

'You know how he talks. Lloyd-Davies will prick him and goad him until he explodes. The jury will loathe him.'

'But if we don't, they'll think he's got something to hide.'

'He has. His voice, his temper, the lies about his alibi. He's got everything to hide. But if he doesn't speak they won't hear it from his own mouth. They'll just hear me.'

In his cell Gary grinned at them. 'We're doing well, lasses, eh?'

'*I'm* doing well,' said Sarah coolly. '*You're* probably going to jail.'

'Eh? What d'yer mean, you stuck-up bitch? It's your job to keep me out of jail, in't it?'

'Yes, but unless you prove your alibi, the jury are going to draw the obvious conclusion.'

'What d'you mean? You've just heard about Sean, haven't you?'

'We've heard he exists but that doesn't mean he was with you that night, does it? And their last witness saw you in Albert Street, for heaven's sake! What were you doing there?'

'I've told yer. I was on me way home after shagging this bird I met.'

'A bird whose name we don't know, with a friend called Sean who's conveniently vanished. The prosecution will crucify you about that, Gary. It would have been better to say nothing than tell the police a tale about girls whose names you can't even remember.'

'Have you never had a feller whose name you forgot next day? It happens all't time.'

'To you, maybe, but not to me,' Sarah said primly, thinking bleakly of Kevin and how similar he was in some ways to this thug before her. 'And my girlfriends didn't do a bunk the next day, either. You do realize, if we

70

could find this shagging companion of yours – Sean – and he confirmed your story, you'd be a free man tomorrow.'

Gary grinned, amused by her unexpectedly coarse language. 'I know, but he's scarpered, ain't he? He always were a devious bugger.'

'Not much of a friend, then, after all?' Sarah said sarcastically. 'If he was ever there.'

'You calling me a liar, woman?' He rose suddenly to his feet, six foot three of tattooed brawn and beer belly towering above them. Lucy flinched, but Sarah stood her ground. She was not surprised; she had intended to provoke him.

'That's what Lloyd-Davies will say tomorrow. He'll say you're lying about this man Sean and the two prostitutes. Sean's scarpered and they never existed.'

His fists opened and closed like claws. Sarah imagined them closing around her throat. But he looked more sly than angry. 'Aye, well. It's not a crime is it, to have the coppers on?'

'It's not exactly a brilliant idea to lie to the police when they're accusing you of rape. Is that what you're going to say in court tomorrow, that this alibi was just a fantasy of yours?'

'What if I do? It don't prove I raped the cow, does it? You said so yourself!'

'I didn't call her a cow, Gary.'

'No. But she is for all that. You don't know her.'

'All right, Gary.' Sarah became brisk, preparing to leave. 'We've done quite well, like you say, and tomorrow is the final speeches. As a defendant you have the right to give evidence on your own behalf if you choose, but as your advocate I strongly suggest you say nothing. If you go in the witness box Julian Lloyd-Davies will do his best to make the jury dislike you, and to be frank I think he'll succeed. If you say nothing then I can emphasize the weaknesses in the prosecution case, which will give us a better chance. But it's for you to decide. Do you agree?'

He frowned at her, thinking. 'You want me to keep me trap shut and tell no more lies?'

'Exactly. If you'd done that in the beginning you'd be better off now.'

'I'll think on. I'll tell you in't morning.'

'All right. But think hard, Gary. Juries don't like liars. Nobody does.'

With that she left. In the corridor outside she looked at Lucy. 'Did you hear that?'

'Tell *no more* lies,' Lucy sighed.

Sarah went back to her chambers to write her speech for tomorrow. There were plenty of questions she could raise about the evidence; her real problem was how to appeal to the jury, to get them to feel good about acquitting a man who not only looked like a horrendous thug but probably was one. Particularly when the acquittal would be so devastating for Sharon. And for her children too.

Well, that's what I'm paid to do. Not the easy things, but the difficult ones. That's the whole point of the challenge.

For an hour she tried out phrase after phrase, rejecting one after another. All the time Gary's words haunted her: *Keep me trap shut and tell no more lies.* It was as close as she was likely to get to an admission of guilt. Gary was an old enough lag to know the game; a client must never admit guilt to his barrister. If the client did admit it, it was the barrister's duty to advise a guilty plea, even at this late stage. If that advice was rejected the barrister could, as some did, withdraw from the case there and then, or more likely, offer only a token defence, questioning the evidence with a lack of conviction that clearly signalled to everyone in court – except the jury, who were new to the game – how little you believed in your task. Sarah had seen that done but always hated it. She wanted to do the job properly, go all out for victory.

After all Gary, repulsive as he was, had consistently professed his innocence.

Until now.

Keep me trap shut and tell no more lies. You sod, Gary – why didn't you keep it shut with me! But of course he hadn't admitted his guilt – she and Lucy had just inferred it from a couple of words. There was no ethical reason why she shouldn't continue to defend him, and every practical reason – including a substantial fee from the legal aid fund – why she should. It was a good case, a step up in her career. If only it didn't feel so tacky and sordid, suddenly.

The phone rang and she picked it up.

'Sarah?'

'Bob. Hi.' She'd meant to ring him earlier but got absorbed in her work. 'How's Emily?'

'That's just it. I don't know.'

'Don't know? What do you mean? Where are you ringing from – school?'

'No, I'm at home. But she's not here.'

'What time is it?' She glanced at her watch. Half-past six. 'Did she leave a note?'

'No, nothing. I got home at five and she wasn't here. No plates or sign of lunch. I've rung her friends – Michelle and Sandra anyway – and they haven't seen her either.' There was a hint of anxiety in Bob's voice – unusual for him.

'Didn't you ring this afternoon like I asked?'

'Look, I've had two teachers sick and a football match to referee, for God's sake! Anyway the answerphone was still on when I got here.'

'Have you tried her mobile?'

'It's here in her bedroom. She told me this morning the card has run out.'

'Well . . .' Sarah was nonplussed. 'Have you tried Joanne? She sometimes goes there.'

'I haven't got the number.'

'Well, go round by car. You know where she lives.'

'All right. But someone should be here in case she comes home. It's not like her, Sarah – you know what a state she was in this morning.'

'I'll be back in an hour or so. I've got this speech to write –'

'The hell with your speech! Bring it home, Sarah, do it later – you should be here!'

Sarah's face tightened. She didn't need this, not now. 'Stop panicking, Bob. She'll be OK. She's probably gone for a walk to get her head together. There's nothing we can do until she comes back anyway. If I get my speech out of the way I can talk to her later.'

Silence came from the phone. Don't play silly games with me, Bob Newby, not now. In a light voice intended to reassure, she said: 'In about an hour. OK?' And put the phone down.

Now – how to appeal to the jury's emotions. The deadline would concentrate her mind, as it always did. She bent forward over her desk, and her mind closed down all thoughts of Bob and Emily.

It would open again in an hour.

She got home at eight to find Bob alone. He had tried Emily's friend Joanne and two more without success, he said. The schoolgirls had phoned their network of friends – none of them had seen or heard from Emily today.

Bob looked distraught. When Sarah came in he rushed downstairs, hoping it was Emily. One of the mothers had suggested he search her bedroom to find out what clothes she had been wearing, but he had no memory for girls' clothes at the best of times. The idea, the fear in the mind of the woman who had put him up to it, made Sarah shiver as she unzipped her black leather jacket.

'Why do you want to know what she's wearing?'

'I don't know . . . well, in case, the police . . .'

'Bob . . .' She put a hand on his arm. 'She'll be all right.'

'So you say. You haven't been here – you've been writing your wretched speech to defend some rapist! Sarah, *it's eight o'clock in the evening* and none of her friends have seen her all day. It'll be dark in an hour.'

'Well, maybe she's gone for a walk.'

'Where?'

'Well, you know – where does she go? By the river.'

Oh God no! The same thought struck them both at once. 'I didn't know she went by the river,' Bob said.

'She has done once or twice recently. She told me about it. She saw a heron . . .'

'We'd better go and look.' He grabbed a coat and went to the back door. She followed. Outside in the garden he turned. 'No, one of us ought to stay here, in case she comes back . . .'

'But if we both go, one can go upstream and one down. As you say, it'll be dark soon.'

'But what if she comes back?' Bob's panic was infectious. They stood there, indecisive, staring at each other on the carefully mown lawn, beside the weeping willow and the rose trees they had worked so hard to afford. This is absurd, Sarah thought. Nothing is going to happen.

'We'll leave a note,' she said firmly. 'Surely you left a note when you went out before?'

'No. I didn't think.'

Christ! And you a head teacher! 'All right, I'll write one.' She turned back to the house. 'You go on. Which way will you go?'

'Upstream.'

'I'll go down then. See you soon.'

She wrote two large notes – GONE FOR A WALK BY THE RIVER, BACK SOON, MUM AND DAD – and left one on the fridge door and one on the stairs. If Emily came in she would either look for food or go to her room, surely. Then she put on her wellington boots and went out through the garden gate, across the field to the river bank. She set off downstream.

She could hear birds singing in the trees, and a blackbird called out in alarm as she approached. A lawnmower hummed in the distance. But other than that the silence was eerie, empty as she often found it. The sound of her boots on the grass, the creak of her leather jacket, became large as they never were in the city. The sudden croak of a moorhen startled her, and without warning two ducks skimmed round the bend and crash-landed on the river in front of her.

I'm supposed to like this place, she thought. It's luxury. Emily likes it anyway, that's why she may be out here. But why so late? She noticed a tangle of green weed close under the bank and shuddered. *God what am I looking for?* She braced her shoulders resolutely and strode on. For Christ's sake the child can swim well enough and anyway why would anyone be so crazy as to try swimming here when there are perfectly good swimming pools in town?

But she might have slipped and fallen in. Then she would climb out and come home. The girl's not an idiot.

So where is she?

A woman, a matronly figure in stout boots, tartan skirt and woolly hat, came along the path walking two labradors. 'Hello,' she said politely. 'Lovely evening, isn't it?'

'Yes,' Sarah said. 'Er . . . you haven't seen – a girl, have you?' *A corpse, a drowned body floating up from under the water, her long hair drifting around her like water weed?*

'Girl? No, I don't think so. Do you mean a small child?'

'No – no, not a child, a teenager. She's got long dark hair, looks a bit like me, fifteen years old . . .'

'What was she wearing?'

'I don't know, I'm afraid. She's my daughter, and she went out before I came back from work. I'm a bit worried – but you haven't seen anyone?'

'No one like that, dear, no, I'm sorry. They're a worry, aren't they, children? Specially at that age. I remember –'

'Yes – well, thanks anyway.' Sarah moved on swiftly to avoid getting entangled in the woman's reminiscences. But after fifty yards she thought, There's no point, if that woman's already been along here. I should have asked her how far she went. She looked back and saw the woman and the dogs in the distance. If I go back I'll get involved in conversation and that's pointless too. I'll go half a mile further on and then back. Emily wouldn't have gone further than that, she's no great walker *but she's been gone all day* and Bob's right, it's getting dark. Christ, this is bloody absurd, she can't have been abducted. She's probably gone into town and run out of bus fare.

Did I leave the answerphone on? I didn't check it when I came in – surely Bob did that? What happens if she hasn't got any money and she rings the operator for a reverse charge call and gets the answerphone?

Nothing, probably. No message at all.

Sarah walked another hundred yards, stared despairingly at the empty towpath winding through vacant fields beside the river in the gathering twilight, and turned back. I'm no good here, I'd be better in the house. I can organize things there.

When she got back the house was empty and there were no messages on the answerphone. She dialled 1471. A flat mechanical voice said: 'Telephone number 0 - 1 - 9 - 0 - 4 - 3 - 3 - 6 - 8 - 9 - 4 called today at 12.47 p.m. If you wish to return the call press 3.'

Sarah pressed 3. The phone rang five, ten, fifteen, twenty, twenty-five times. She put it down, dialled 1471 again and wrote the number down. That's something, she thought. She looked at the number but didn't recognize it. That's where she must be. I can ring it again and if it doesn't answer the police can find out where it is.

The police. It isn't going to come to that, is it?

The back door opened. She turned with hope singing in her heart but it was Bob. He stood there in boots and anorak, breathing heavily as though he had been running.

'Have you found her?'

'No. You?'

'No. There's a number on the phone.' She showed him. 'I rang it but it didn't answer.'

'I don't recognize it, do you?'

'No. I thought . . .'

'What?'

75

'The police could find out who it was if . . .' Sarah hesitated, not wanting to draw the conclusion. It seemed so ridiculous. Things like this didn't happen to them. '. . . if she doesn't come home soon,' she finished more firmly.

'*Soon*? She's been gone over twelve hours! I'm going to ring them now. Give me that.' Bob took the receiver out of her hand. For a moment she thought of resisting but then she looked out of the window and saw it was nearly dark. He was right. It was already far too long.

11

'So when they sing, they're calling their families over hundreds of miles,' Jessica explained earnestly. 'They haven't got ears, but they feel the sounds in their heads . . . they've got, like . . .'

'Supersonic earsight,' ventured Terry helpfully, spooning up his cornflakes.

'We saw a whale in a museum once, didn't we, Dad?' Seven-year-old Esther was determined not to be left out. 'It was as big as a bus.'

'Two buses, actually. We measured it, remember?' Jessica, two years older, was used to competition for her father's affections. Diplomatically, Terry wiped the spilt milk from around his younger daughter's plate while smiling encouragement at the elder one.

'Who's ready for waffles? Esther?' Trude came in bearing two hot waffles on a plate and wearing a T-shirt cut to display her exquisite belly-button to perfection. She flopped a steaming waffle on to Esther's plate. 'Strawberry jam or blackcurrant?'

'Treacle.'

'Oh no. Not before school,' said Terry firmly. 'Remember yesterday.'

'But I like treacle!'

'No one in Norway has treacle for breakfast,' said Trude supportively. 'It's a law.'

Esther gaped at her, then gave in and reached for the blackcurrant jam. Even without treacle, waffles for breakfast were an incredible luxury, one of Trude's best introductions. The young nanny had been amazed to find herself in a family with no waffle-iron. Every Norwegian family had one, she said. She immediately sent for one and now it was in constant use, delighting Terry and his daughters equally.

The mobile in Terry's pocket rang. Irritated, he answered it. 'Yes?'

It was Sergeant Rossiter at the station. 'Sorry to trouble you at home, sir, but there's been a flap overnight about a missing person out your way and I thought you might want to go straight there before you come in.'

'A misper? Aren't uniform dealing with it?'

'Well, yes, sir, they are, but like I say it's out your way and one of the parents is someone you know, as it happens. A Mrs Sarah Newby.'

Terry groaned. 'All right. But I'm having breakfast with my kids first. OK?'

'Sir.' It was not a thing CID officers usually said. 'I'll tell them you're on your way.'

At the Newby house no one had slept.

Bob had called the police at 8.30 p.m. but at first it had been hard to get them to take him seriously. A fifteen-year-old girl, still early in the evening – it didn't seem urgent. Nonetheless they would send a car round.

When the two PCs arrived Sarah and Bob were bemused by the uniforms and crackling radios in their own living room. They gave the details anxiously, submissively almost. No, Emily had no problems except her exams; no, there had been no family quarrel; yes, she was nearly sixteen; yes, she had been out at night before but always with friends; yes, she had a mobile but it was at home. Sarah gave them the number she had got from ringing 1471 and a constable wrote it down without comment. They checked Emily's room, took a photograph that Sarah gave them, wrote down Sarah's guess at the clothes her daughter had been wearing, and then – left.

'They're not bloody interested!' she fumed after they had gone. 'They think it's just a family quarrel. They're not going to do anything at all!'

Bob frowned. 'We did say she might turn up at any time, after all.'

'If she does I'll kill her, the spoilt brat.'

'Maybe that's why she went.'

'Oh, it's my fault now, is it?'

'You didn't show her much sympathy over her exams this morning, did you?'

'I talked to her, didn't I? You were still semi-conscious, as you are every morning. I said I'd phone her at lunchtime and I did, too. I can't help a person who isn't there!'

'Maybe she thinks *you're* never there when she wants you.'

'Oh shut up, Bob, this is no time for pop psychology. The fact is the wretched girl *has* vanished and you're quite right, it *is* out of character and it *is* late and the useless plods aren't interested.'

'They did take her photo.'

'Yes.' That was the thing that had shaken Sarah. It was a school portrait in a frame, of a slightly younger Emily smiling engagingly at the camera. The sort of photo of someone posed and pretty and full of bubbling happiness which the newspapers splash on their front pages when a girl has been stripped, raped, mutilated and murdered. Look at me, the photos always seem to say. I'm a star at last!

But unlike newspaper readers, the police and lawyers get to see the real photos, of the naked strangled corpse with the wounds and swollen eyes and the purple tongue hanging out.

That's not going to happen to Emily, Sarah thought. It can't. It won't. This is all a bad dream.

At 11.05 p.m. the police rang to say the phone number was from a public call box in Blossom Street, and had Sarah and Bob been in touch with Emily's grandparents? Might she have gone there?

They hadn't. Sarah and Bob each rang their parents, spreading the ripples of anxiety further. No, of course Emily wasn't with them. Bob rang the police and asked testily what they were doing now? At 1 a.m. a second police car with a uniformed sergeant arrived to ask many of the same questions, and probe further. Which were her closest friends? When had Bob spoken to them? Had Emily ever been out longer than expected, or with someone they didn't know? Where exactly did she like to go for walks?

The man was serious, concerned, avuncular. They would make some enquiries of her friends, he said, and if she still hadn't turned up by morning a proper search would be considered.

'Considered?' Bob asked. 'Meaning what, exactly?'

'Well, sir, we need to know where to look, really. I mean if you said she had gone out to a particular place we could start from there, but it's not as simple in this case, is it? But we'll do our best. Her description's already been circulated.'

Then he, too, left. Neither Bob nor Sarah smoked so they were reduced to pacing up and down, arguing, drinking coffee. Then at two o'clock Sarah remembered Simon! That was it, of course – it had to be! Emily and Simon weren't particularly close but surely Emily had said something about him that morning. What was it now? *I'll be like Simon – he's happy, at least!*

'Why didn't you mention that before?' Bob asked, aghast.

'I don't know, I just . . . didn't,' she faltered.

'Didn't think, more like,' said Bob angrily. 'OK, I'll give him a ring.'

'No, Bob, I'll do it. He's my son!'

'And she's my daughter! You've done enough damage today already!' He walked out to the phone in the hall. 'If she is there I'll give that boy a piece of my mind. This is the very last time he's going to screw up our lives, I promise you that!'

Sarah sat down and thought, How could we be so stupid? Of course it must be Simon – why was I blocking it out? Is he so very distant from me as well as Bob now, that we don't think of him at all in a situation like this?

She slumped on the sofa, listening for Bob's voice in the hall. Why does he blame *me* for all this – it's not just my fault, surely? If this is what they call a bad patch in your marriage I hope it doesn't get any worse. Then she heard Bob talking.

'You're quite sure . . . you're telling me the truth now, Simon . . . if I come round there and find she's been with you I'll . . . no, I don't think you need to do that . . .'

He stood in the doorway with a wild expression on his face and said: 'She's not there.'

'What? You've got to be joking.'

'No, I'm not. Unless he's lying, but I don't think he is. He swears he hasn't seen her, in fact he seemed quite upset when he got over the shock. He wanted to come over here but I said not to bother.'

'Why ever not? He might help.'

'I don't see how. Anyway she's not with him, Sarah – he hasn't seen her.'

'Oh God, no.' She moaned as the full realization hit her.

And so the nightmare continued. When Terry Bateson arrived just before 9 a.m. Sergeant Hendry was already there. He had sent two officers along the river bank behind the house, and four more were making enquiries round the village. Bob had just come in from the river bank wearing an anorak and rubber boots. He was pale and unshaven. He gazed bitterly at Terry.

'And who the hell might you be?'

Terry showed his card. 'We've met before, actually, Mr Newby. At the judge's ball.'

'Have we? Well, that doesn't matter now. What I need is someone to find my daughter.'

'Yes, of course.' Terry followed him into the living room where Sarah sat, her hands clasped round a cup of coffee. To his surprise she was wearing black motorcyclist's trousers, jacket and boots. Her face was pale, with dark bruises of sleeplessness round her eyes. She didn't appear to notice him.

'Hello, Sarah. I'm sorry to hear about all this.'

She looked up, startled. 'Oh, it's you. Hello, Terry.'

He glanced at Bob. 'Your wife and I work together sometimes at the courts, Mr Newby.' Where she shows the world how useless I am. Well, the boot's on the other foot now.

'Yes, no doubt. Well, what are you going to do?'

'I've only just come on duty, sir, I'm afraid. I need to know all the facts.'

'For God's sake! She's been missing nearly twenty-four hours and they send a complete newcomer on the case!'

Sergeant Hendry intervened. 'DI Bateson is the most senior officer to be involved so far, sir. If we set up a full-scale search he'll be the man to co-ordinate it.'

'Yes, all right. Let's get on with it then. For all we know every minute counts.' As Hendry explained the details Terry scrutinized Bob and decided that a display of anger and nervous energy was the only way he had of coping with the situation. A cocktail of fear and despair drove him to constantly interrupt the sergeant, creating more confusion rather than less. Sarah, on the other hand, sipped her coffee in silence, apparently withdrawn into herself.

The basic rule in child disappearances was: first look for the child, then look for the problem. If the child hasn't simply had an accident or got lost then there must be a reason for its running away, and very often the reason had something to do with family conflicts.

Was there a conflict here? The father pacing up and down manically, the wife silent. Neither offering the other any comfort, hardly looking at each other. Probably. After all, he knew from personal experience what a bitch the wife could be.

'You're quite sure, Mr Newby, there's nothing else your daughter might have said or done to indicate where she might be now?'

'I've told you that – no! Not that I can think of.'

'And there was no unusual quarrel or family row yesterday?'

'Not with *me*, anyway. Emily was worried about her exams, and I asked Sarah to talk to her before she went to work. She was supposed to comfort her but I don't know what she said.'

'I told her to stick to her revision plan and she'd be all right. I promised to ring her at lunchtime, which I did.' In comparison to her husband's voice Sarah's was perfectly calm and controlled. But that was the danger of it, Terry thought, wryly. It was the same controlled, deadly voice she had deployed against him in the witness box yesterday, when his friendly lunch companion had transformed herself into a razor-tongued witch. If that was how she behaved as a mother, God knows how many emotional wounds her daughter had.

Terry shut his notebook. 'All right. I think I've got the picture. It seems Sergeant Hendry has done all the correct things so far. When your men come back from the river, Tom, we'll put them on house-to-house enquiries with the others – it's not a big village, someone must have seen her if she was about yesterday. Get on to the bus company too, see which drivers came here yesterday and show them her photo. Then I want to check that phone box where the call came from –'

'How on earth will that help?' Bob interrupted irritably. 'If it's a public phone anyone could have used it.'

'Yes, sir, of course. But it's our only real clue so far, and unless it's at the station or in the city centre it probably has its own group of regular users. Most public phones do. So I'll check that, and then I'll need to talk to that son of yours, Sa . . . Mrs Newby.'

It didn't seem right to use her first name, in front of her husband. But the surname felt awkward too.

She picked up her motorcycle helmet with a faint, strained smile. 'All right. I go near his house on my way to work. If you follow me I can take you right to his door.'

Bob exploded. 'What the hell are you talking about, Sarah? You can't go to work! For Christ's sake – Emily's missing!'

Sarah's voice remained quiet and dry; exhausted but determined. 'I know that, Bob. I've already been out on the bike to look for her but it does no good. I don't know where she is and neither do you. And now we've got the police to search for us. I've got a job to do.'

'Defending a bloody rapist – when your own daughter might be lying dead somewhere! You're out of your mind!'

'It's *you* that's out of your mind, Bob. You've been shouting non-stop for four hours, and I can't take any more. I think Emily will come back when she's good and ready. In the meantime I've got one speech to make in court and that's it. I'll ring when I can. Do you want to follow me, Terry?'

Terry, like Bob, was aghast. 'I . . . don't need to do that, Sarah. Just give me your son's address and I'll find it.'

'Oh, all right. Bob knows it.' She turned for the door. Terry had the impression she was sleep-walking. Her husband tried to block her path.

'For God's sake, Sarah – I need you here! Just ring the court and explain – the judge'll adjourn the trial!'

To Terry's amazement, she walked right past him, out of the door. 'Don't stop me, Bob. I have to do this. Nothing I do here will make any difference this morning, anyway.'

And then she was gone. The three men heard the motorbike engine start up, cough to a crescendo as she roared out of the short drive, and gradually fade into the distance. Terry had a sense that something was wrong here, something surreal. That woman had just put the defence of a brutal rapist before the search for her own daughter.

12

It was, ironically, a sunny day. The sky was a brilliant blue as Sarah rode into York, and sunlight slanted diagonally across her desk to light up the brief, tied with faded red tape. Beside it were the handwritten notes for her speech, prepared last night before going home.

Last night. So long ago it seemed.

She tried to recall what the speech was about. That was why she was here, why she had come in. Wasn't that what she had learned over the years? Never be distracted by the accidents of daily life; identify your main goal, focus all your efforts on achieving it. The other things will sort themselves out on their own.

Emily will come back. Of course she will.

So how was she going to present this case? Sarah bent over her notes, and tried to concentrate.

Anyway, Bob's at home and the police are the professionals, not us.

Concentrate. The main thing is to destroy the identification evidence. Without that there's no case. Accept the jury's sympathy for Sharon as a victim but insist it wasn't Gary who did it. Get them to accept the possibility that the brutal rapist is still out there, wandering free. Looking for another victim.

A teenage girl perhaps.

Shut up. Focus. Concentrate. The police found no hood, no watch, no witnesses apart from Keith Somers. He's damaging, but his evidence is circumstantial – how exactly did I plan to deal with him . . .?

Emily, dragged by the hair into some grotty bedroom, forced to her knees, punched in the face, her legs dragged apart . . .

'Hi there, sunshine!'

'What?' She looked up, took her hands away from her eyes.

'Are you OK?' It was Savendra, his cheerful face suddenly registering concern.

'Not really, Savvy. No.'

'What is it? Family row?'

'Worse than that. Family's vanished. Emily's gone walkabout.'

'What *are* you talking about?' He sat down in front of the desk. Sarah explained, briefly, trying to make light of it. 'Of course she'll come back, it's just a mega teenage tantrum aimed at causing us all maximum embarrassment, that's all . . .'

'The police are searching, and you're still here?'

'Of course I'm here. I've got a case to defend, haven't I? Last day, speeches, summing up, verdict. You remember verdicts?'

'Yes, but . . . you could get it adjourned. These are exceptional circumstances beyond your control, surely. The judge – who is it, Gray – he'll understand.'

'Will he? Perhaps – but *what* will he understand? That I can't be a mother and a barrister at the same time? That the courts have to make special allowances for women? That everything gets slowed up because of my daughter's stupid tantrum? No, Savvy.'

'He won't see it like that –'

'He will, Savvy, he will, because he's an unreconstructed chauvinist who thinks women should be at home doing the dishes and not in court at all. And even if *he* doesn't think it others will. It'll go the rounds, you know it will. "That Sarah Newby, she knows her stuff but she's not reliable. Family problems, likely to take a day off to look after the kids. Better off with a man." That's what they'll say.'

Savendra shook his head. 'There's world of difference between looking *after* the kids and looking *for* them, Sarah. The courts aren't completely full of sharks and jackals, you know.'

'Aren't they? Which courts do you work in?' A wry, bitter smile dispelled the tears that had been threatening.

'Well . . .' Savendra saw the point. All barristers needed good cases to build up their reputation. Of all those who took law degrees less than ten per cent took bar exams; of those called to the bar only fifty per cent found a place in chambers; of those who found a place in chambers only a tiny fraction made a living in their first years. If a colleague dropped a case for whatever reason, there was a feeding frenzy of others to snap it up.

'Anyway, Bob's there. They don't sack headmasters for taking a day off.'

'Well.' He reached across to pat her gently on the arm. 'Where do you think she is?'

'If I knew that, don't you think I'd be there now?' Sarah's eyes would have shrivelled him to a burnt crisp on the seat of his chair, if they hadn't been suddenly softened by tears. 'Anyway, Emily's just trying to get at me, Savvy. To criticize my success. I won't let her.'

The contrasting sentiments were so harsh and shocking Savendra could find no response. He decided to step back from this emotional quicksand on to safer ground.

'So do you think you'll get the rapist off?'

'Rapist?' *Emily dragged into the back of a van, driven hundreds of miles to the south of England, sealed in a cellar to die of abuse and starvation . . .* 'Oh, you mean Harker?'

'Of course. Who else?'

'Do my best.' She indicated the notes on her desk. 'He claims he's innocent, Savvy.'

'So you have to defend him.'

The two barristers smiled at each other, knowing how seldom it was that they really believed in the innocence of the clients they defended. Savendra got to his feet. 'I wish you luck, then. But if you want me to take over . . .'

'No chance.'

He shut the door softly behind him, leaving her alone with her notes.

After Sarah's dramatic departure Terry looked at Bob Newby with concern. The man seemed unable to keep still. He paced up and down the room anxiously . . .

'What now, Mr – Inspector Bates, isn't it?'

'Bateson, sir. Well, I think you should stay here, sir, in case your daughter rings or simply turns up . . .'

'You think she'll turn up, just like that?'

'Quite often that's exactly what happens, sir. And it's important that someone's here to meet her or she might just go off again.'

'I'm sure you're right. But I'd feel better out there doing something, not just sitting still. That's why Sarah should be here.'

'Yes, sir.' Terry agreed, but it was not his place to do anything about it.

'*Bitch.*'

The word was spoken softly, so Terry pretended not to hear. He turned to Sergeant Hendry. 'Tom, have you got a constable to stay with Mr Newby? In case . . .'

'I'm not a child, you know!' Bob snapped. 'You get your men out searching – I may be upset but I do see the sense in what you're saying.'

'All right, sir, thanks. But Tom'll call in regularly, keep you in the picture. Here's my mobile number, if you need it. Now, er, can I have the address of that son of yours?'

Bob took a deep breath, trying to regain self-control. As he wrote the address he muttered: 'He's my stepson, really. Sarah had him before we met. He's a brickie – works here there and everywhere.'

'All right, sir, I'll find out. And we'll check that phone box too.'

As Terry turned to go, Bob clutched his arm. 'You've run this sort of search before, haven't you? What are the chances?'

Terry saw fear in the man's eyes, a barely suppressed panic that could quickly break through. 'Well, in two cases out of three the child just turns up of its own accord. So the chances are good, if you look at it that way. But we'll do our best to find her even if she doesn't.'

Outside he said: 'Keep an eye on him, Tom. He's likely to crack any time.'

In the cramped cell below the court, Gary Harker scowled at his lawyers.

'I've thought about it and I'm going in the box.'

'Why?' Sarah stood by the door, wig in hand, Lucy beside her.

'Well, if I don't, the judge is going to slag me off, in't he? You said so yourself. I'm not going down just because of some crap advice my brief gave me.'

'*As* your brief,' Sarah said firmly, 'I'm giving you the best advice possible. If you don't give evidence the judge is entitled to draw the jury's attention to your silence, Mr Harker; but if you go into the box, with your temper, the prosecution are going to hang you out to dry.'

'What's that bloody mean when it's at home?'

'Julian Lloyd-Davies is going to needle you about all the lies you've told, until you swear and curse and the jury despise you. He's an expert – he'll run rings round you.'

'I have given evidence before, you know! You think I'm fucking stupid or what?'

'I think you have a violent temper which you find hard to control.'

'Well, that's a load of crap, that is, thanks a lot! Me own bloody brief trying to bollock me before the trial!'

Sarah drew a deep breath. 'I'm trying to present your case in the best light possible, Mr Harker. If you want to dismiss me and defend yourself you're quite at liberty to do so.'

Gary considered it. 'No, that's not what I want, you know that.'

'Right then. Well, my advice is that if you go into that box and start swearing at people like you are now, you'll destroy yourself more effectively than the judge ever could. So I suggest you exercise your right to keep silent, and let the judge say what he likes.'

'And what if the jury listens to him, eh? What am I looking at?'

'For a violent rape like this? Fifteen years, maybe. Minimum of eight.'

'Fifteen fucking years! But it only lasted ten minutes, for fuck's sake!'

Gary stood, his huge hands clenching and unclenching by his side. Sarah said nothing. This is what I came to work for, she thought. Bob's right. I should be at home looking for Emily. Leave this tosser to rot. She saw the great vein swelling in his thick neck six inches from her face, as he shouted. 'Fifteen years, and you don't want me to speak? It's *me* that's going down, not you, you know, Mrs Pretty Barrister! For a ten-minute shag.'

'Are you admitting your guilt, Mr Harker? If you do that I can no longer represent you.' And you can rot in hell, she thought. Where you belong. She turned to go, but the man grabbed her shoulder.

'No, I am not admitting no fucking guilt. But I'm not staying silent, neither. I'm going in that box to tell the truth, so you'd best sharpen up your fancy brain too, because if you don't, I'll be looking for you after those fifteen years and it won't be no ten minutes' revenge I have in mind, neither.'

She put her hand on his to push it away, but realized she could no more move it than pull a brick from the wall. As her fingers scrabbled on his she met his eyes and to her horror he smiled. Then he let go.

I'm losing control of this, she thought. Get out now. But she had to preserve some dignity. 'Very well,' she said shakily. 'If you insist on giving evidence, that's your right. I'll see you in court.'

I'm not going to try very hard, Sarah thought. There's no point. Even if he hasn't actually admitted it the bastard's guilty and deserves to go down. Anyway I'm too tired. She stood up.

'My lord, I call Gary Harker.'

Gary took the oath in a strong, loud voice, stumbling slightly over the words as he read them.

'Mr Harker, you have heard all the evidence brought by the prosecution. Did you rape Sharon Gilbert?'

'No.'

'Did you go to her house on the night of Saturday 14th October last year?'

'No.'

'Very well. Let me take you through the events of that night. Did you meet Ms Gilbert earlier that evening, at a party at the Station Hotel?'

'I did, yes.'

'Why did you go to that party?'

'Why not? I knew some lads there.'

'Did you expect to meet Ms Gilbert?'

'No. I hadn't seen her for . . . six months, mebbe.'

'What were your feelings when you met her?'

'Well, I weren't bothered really. I mean, I bought her a drink, asked her to dance, like. That were it, really.' To Sarah's surprise Gary seemed quite calm, almost respectable in the way he spoke. The jury were listening intently, no sign of disgust on their faces as yet.

'Did she seem pleased to see you?'

'Not really. She's a stroppy cow at times.'

Here we go, Sarah thought. Sink yourself if you want to. I don't care.

'Did you have an argument?'

'I asked her for me watch back. She said she hadn't got it.'

'And how did you react to that?'

'I said she were, er . . .' Gary paused, glanced at the jury, seemed to take a grip on himself. 'I said it weren't true. I reckon she'd sold it and she owed me t'brass.'

'Were your voices raised when you had this argument?'

'A bit. You had to speak up to be heard.'

'All right. Did you threaten her in this argument, say you might come to her house and take the watch back, perhaps?'

'No.'

'Did you go to her house to get the watch back?'

'No.'

'So when did you last see this watch?'

'When she slung me out of her home, last year.'

The bastard's really trying, she thought. So far so good. For him, anyway. But now the silly lies start. The fake alibi.

'Tell the jury in your own words, what happened when you left the Station Hotel that night.'

'Well, I met a lad called Sean and we went to the Dog and Whistle. Cruising.'

'Cruising?'

'Yeah. Looking for lasses, like. Girls.'

'Did you find any?'

'Yeah. Two.'

'What happened then?'

'Well, they were tarts, like. Prostitutes. So we shagged 'em.'

'What happened then?'

'I went home to bed.'

'Did Sean go with you?'

'No. We split up when we met t'lasses. I didn't see him again.'

'What about the girl? Did she come home with you?'

'No.'

'What was her name?'

'Can't remember, sorry.'

'You've never seen her before or since?'

'No, I haven't.'

'Now, you've heard Keith Somers say he saw you in Albert Street just after 1 a.m. that night. Were you in Albert Street at that time?'

'Yeah. Probably. I could have been.'

'Is it on your way home from where you met the girls?'

'It's one way home, yes.'

'Keith Somers says you waved to him. Is that right?'

'Could be. Can't remember.'

'Very well. Albert Street runs parallel to Thorpe Street, which is where Sharon Gilbert lives. So I ask you again, did you go to Sharon Gilbert's house at any time that night?'

'No.'

'Did you rape her?'

'No.'

'So you say you are totally innocent of this crime that you are charged with?'

'Innocent? Yeah, that's right. I am.'

'Very well, then. Wait there.'

There had been a smile on Julian Lloyd-Davies' face ever since he'd learned that Sarah was calling Gary Harker to give evidence. Now he rose with what appeared to be a weary sigh, some sheets of notes in his hand. He peered at the notes intently for a few seconds, then tossed them aside in disgust.

'Mr Harker, this is all a pack of lies, isn't it?'

'What? No.'

'You don't have a friend called Sean, do you?'

''Course I do. I thought I did any road.'

'Where does he live then?'

'I don't know. He's left York. Must have done.'

'You were just wasting police time, weren't you?'

'I bloody weren't. They were wasting my time, more like!'

Here we go, Sarah thought. Score one to Lloyd-Davies. Or two, if we count the way he threw his notes away. The jury loved that.

'Oh, I see. You think it's a waste of police time to investigate a brutal rape, do you?'

'I never said that.'

'Oh? Forgive me, I thought you did.' Lloyd-Davies peered at Gary contemptuously over his reading glasses, deliberately affecting a superior, educated tone, and Sarah thought: That's it. He's got beneath his skin. Wait for the explosion.

To her surprise it didn't come. Gary gripped the edge of the dock in those huge, cruel hands, flushed, and said – nothing.

Lloyd-Davies began again. 'Do you have an unusually bad memory, Mr Harker?'

'No. I don't think so.'

'Well, tell me then. What's your friend Sean's second name?'

'I'm not right sure. I always called him Sean.'

'Do you remember where he works, perhaps?'

'He worked wi' me. At MacFarlane's. In Acomb.'

'At MacFarlane's, in Acomb.' Lloyd-Davies sighed elaborately. 'You see, that's all lies too, Mr Harker. The police have checked. There was no one called Sean working for MacFarlane's at that time.'

This time Gary shouted back. 'It's not bloody lies. He were there and he worked wi' me. You heard Graham Dewar!'

'Do you take this jury for complete fools, Mr Harker? To believe that you have a friend who simply doesn't exist?'

'I'm not a bloody fool! You may be!'

It was going as Sarah had predicted now. A contented smile played around Lloyd-Davies' smooth, rather prominent lips. He phrased his next question with deliberate enjoyment.

'Well, tell the jury this, then. Do you often "shag" girls, as you put it, without even learning their names?'

'Sometimes, yes. It happens. Mebbe not to you.'

There was a stir of muffled laughter in court, and Sarah saw to her surprise that two of the younger male jurors were grinning broadly. Irritation crept into Lloyd-Davies' voice as he sensed the exchange had not gone his way.

'Well, it's not a very good story, is it, because none of the people you say were with you that night actually exist, do they? It's all a tissue of lies, isn't it?'

'No, it bloody isn't.'

'Oh yes it is, Mr Harker. The truth is, that when you met Ms Gilbert that night you were angry with her, and you wanted to get your revenge. So after you left the hotel you waited in Thorpe Street until she was home, and then you broke into her house with a hood over your face, and brutally raped her in front of her children. That's what really happened, isn't it?'

'No.'

'Oh yes it is, Mr Harker. We know it's true because she recognized you.'

'No she didn't! She couldn't bloody recognize me because . . .'

Just for a second Gary hesitated, staring straight ahead of him, apparently at nothing. Sarah thought, This is it. The silly berk is actually going to admit it. Good thing too – for justice if not for me.

'Yes, Mr Harker? Why couldn't she recognize you?' Lloyd-Davies goaded him, gloating. His voice snapped Gary out of his trance.

'Because I wasn't bloody there, that's why! Because the feller who raped her wasn't bloody me! And if the police weren't wasting time with all this load of crap here, they'd be out trying to catch the beggar who did do it, wouldn't they?'

And so it went on, inconclusively, for a few more minutes, Lloyd-Davies needling sarcastically, Gary bludgeoning his attacks away. Neither complete triumph nor utter disaster, Sarah thought, when he sat down at last.

Lucy, however, was more upbeat. Dressed in a particularly vast and unflattering blue peasant smock, she confronted Julian Lloyd-Davies during the fifteen minute recess the judge granted before speeches.

'Do you play cricket, by any chance, Mr Lloyd-Davies?' she asked.

'Why yes, as a matter of fact I do.' Lloyd-Davies smiled, acknowledging her existence for the first time in the entire trial. 'Most weekends, actually.'

'I could tell from your style of cross-examination. Like England held to a draw by the Soweto second XI, I thought.'

'Lucy, that was wicked,' Sarah said, as the great man stalked away. 'Do you always talk to opposition barristers like that?'

'Only when they really get up my nose, like he does.'

'But how did you know he played cricket? An inspired guess?'

'Oh no. He boasts about it in *Who's Who*. Played for Eton and Oxford. Got a blue.'

A faint smile, brief as winter sunshine, lit Sarah's face and was gone.

'I doubt Gary's ever played cricket. Unless he could kill someone with the bat.'

13

Julian Lloyd-Davies stood to face the jury. One hand clutched the edge of his gown, the other was behind his back somewhere. The pose looked odd and pompous to Sarah. She hoped the jury felt the same.

It was his duty, he said, to prove Gary's guilt beyond all reasonable doubt. Confidently, he set about doing so. 'Let us remind ourselves exactly what Gary Harker has done. We say that on the night of 14th October last year, he deliberately entered the house of Sharon Gilbert . . .'

Seamlessly, he progressed into a precise, detailed description of the horrors of the assault. For nearly an hour he painstakingly constructed Gary's guilt from the evidence. He tore up Sarah's arguments and cast them aside like rubbish. How was it possible for any woman to be mistaken about the identity of a rapist, hooded or not, when she had lived with him for over a year? Lloyd-Davies invited the jury to consider their own partners – would they fail to recognize them, just because of a balaclava hood? Surely not.

Do QCs wear hoods in their wives' bedrooms, Sarah wondered flippantly? We should be told. *But then ordinary barristers' daughters can go missing, can't they?* her mind screamed back. *Lost alone in some pervert's bedroom.* Oh shut up, please. Concentrate.

Sharon, Lloyd-Davies reminded the jury, had heard the rapist's voice. She had seen his body, he had even used her son's name. How could she be mistaken? And Gary had two clear motives – to gain revenge after their quarrel that evening, and to recover his watch. He knew exactly where she lived, alone and defenceless with her children. He knew where she kept the watch; she had seen him take it. The police couldn't find it because he had hidden it, that was all.

And what about his so-called alibi? Well, it relied on three people who could not be proved to exist at all. But a witness who *did* exist had seen him in the adjacent street just a few minutes after the rape took place.

Finally there was the question of character. Someone was lying in this case, clearly. Well, the jury had seen Sharon Gilbert in the witness box; and they had seen the police inspector. Both those people believed Gary was guilty. Then the jury had seen Gary himself. So who did they believe? Sharon and the police? Or Gary Harker?

Quite, Sarah thought. A man with a criminal record three pages long, including violence against women. My charming client.

'We know who is telling the truth, don't we, members of the jury?' Lloyd-Davies concluded. 'We know who broke into Sharon Gilbert's house and raped her in front of her two small children. It was that man there. Gary Harker.'

So far Lloyd-Davies had been dry, calm, understated, allowing the horror of the facts to make his points for him. Now, he raised his right arm, and pointed at Gary. Then he sat down.

The judge eyed the clock. Eleven thirty. Too early to adjourn for lunch. 'Mrs Newby?'

The phone box was in Blossom Street – near the Odeon cinema, a bus stop, a Kentucky Fried Chicken outlet, and a few streets of Victorian tenements.

'All right,' Terry said, to Harry and two young uniformed constables. 'We've got the girl's photo. Let's see if anyone's seen her. Or knows who rang from here at 12.47 yesterday.'

It was the only clue he had, so far. His visit to Sarah's son Simon had yielded nothing. The door of the terraced house in Bramham Street had been opened by a truculent, muscular young man in a T-shirt and shorts. He had short reddish-gold hair, a round face with a broad nose, and a ring in one ear. He had led Terry into a cramped, untidy front room and answered his questions while putting on a pair of old socks and ancient, mud-stained trainers. Yes, his stepfather had rung at 2 a.m. last night; no, he had no idea where Emily had gone. He had last seen her a month ago in Tesco with their mother. He and his sister weren't particularly close but he could readily understand that the pressure from their highly academic parents had become too much for her. Probably she would come back in a day or two. Terry was welcome to search his house if he wanted but if not, he was going for a run.

Terry had considered a search but decided against it. Everything in the boy's demeanour suggested innocence. What disturbed Terry was how little the lad seemed to care. What sort of family is this, he wondered as he drove away? Son a half-employed brickie, husband a gibbering wreck, daughter run away from home. What does that woman do to people?

Terry and Harry took alternate houses down the street. Some had offices downstairs, others were entirely given over to bedsits. At quarter to twelve they crossed the road to confer with the uniformed branch. Or youth wing, as Harry called it.

'There are two possibles, sir,' reported PC Kerr eagerly. 'A woman who saw a man using the box yesterday morning – he was on for ages so she had to wait; and another bloke who said his neighbour always used the phone at the same time. Said he was obsessive, like.'

'Could your woman describe this man at all?'

Kerr consulted his notebook. 'About forty, balding, grey suit, camel coat.'

'Hm. And the obsessive neighbour? What did he look like?'

PC Kerr flushed. 'I didn't think to ask, sir. But he lives in flat 3a, number 7. He's out now but he usually watches telly in the afternoons, I was told.'

'All right, we'll check him out later today,' Terry said. 'Now I'd best get back and see the anxious parents. Anxious dad, at least.'

Sarah tried to listen to Lloyd-Davies, but her ability to concentrate was gone. She'd had no sleep last night and in the warm courtroom she found her eyes closing. Behind her eyelids she saw Emily running away. Someone was holding her hand, but who? She'd been about to find out when she awoke with a jolt and looked round wondering if anyone had noticed. Pray God the jury weren't laughing at her.

She stood up mechanically, her notes in her hand. 'Members of the jury, Mr Harker is, as you know, accused of a quite horrendous crime.' Which he almost certainly committed, she thought miserably. What now?

She stopped, transfixed by the extraordinary sensation that the jury were in a glass tank where she couldn't touch them.

Wake up, for God's sake. Concentrate.

I can't. I'm too tired.

Somehow, despite the turmoil in her tired mind, her voice continued without her. 'It is no part of Mr Harker's case to minimize the terrible suffering Sharon Gilbert has endured, or the harm done to her children. No decent man or woman could fail to sympathize with it.'

Not even me. As Emily's mother I sympathize with it, too. *Shut up.*

'What Mr Harker says is quite simple. It wasn't me, he says. You've got the wrong man. These terrible things happened but I didn't do them.'

Which is just what a child says when there's milk spilt on the carpet, a voice nagged in her mind. I didn't do it, the milk jumped straight out of the cup. Come on, you can do better than that.

Several jurors were shuffling or fiddling with their hands. A young woman gazed up at the decorated roof. *Come on. You're losing them.*

'Mr Lloyd-Davies says that the evidence proves Gary Harker's guilt. But that's not true, members of the jury, is it? The evidence in this case is really very thin indeed. The prosecution can't even prove that Gary was in the house, never mind that he committed this horrible rape. He wasn't there, members of the jury. It's the prosecution's job to prove he was there and they have totally failed to do so. Let's take a closer look at the evidence.'

Mercifully, the words were trickling out, but they were not flowing. The glass screen between Sarah and the jury remained. But the logic of the case was clearly laid out in her notes. She consulted them desperately.

'The only evidence that really counts is Sharon's belief that she could identify Gary. Well, do you remember how many drinks Sharon had that night? She was drunk, members of the jury – hopelessly drunk and terrified. How could she possibly identify anyone in that state? Could you? A man wearing a hood, wielding a knife, who spoke two or three words at most before forcing you to do terrible acts? I doubt it. I doubt if anyone could think clearly in that situation.'

Better. The adrenalin was beginning to flow. If only that juror would stop playing with his watch. This is important, damn you!

'Of course Ms Gilbert was angry and upset. Something terrible had happened to her and she wanted to blame someone for it. So she blamed the first man who came into her mind – the man she'd had an argument with that night. But she didn't *know* it was him, she couldn't possibly know. Nor could her little son. He was brave, wasn't he? Heroically brave. But he was only a child, he believed what his mother told him.'

So what about the rest of the evidence, she asked. The prosecution claimed Gary had gone there to steal a watch – well, where was the watch then? Why wasn't it in Gary's house? Where was the hood? That wasn't there either. There was no semen, no fingerprints, no forensic evidence to show he had ever been in Sharon's house. True, he'd been seen in a street not far away, but he had an explanation for that. The police claimed his friend Sean didn't exist – well, a witness had come to court who'd met him, after all. Gary's alibi didn't show him as a very pleasant character, but that wasn't the point. They didn't have to like him to believe him. And if they believed him, he was not guilty. Simple as that.

'The prosecution have failed to prove their case beyond reasonable doubt, members of the jury. There are many doubts in this case, very reasonable doubts indeed. Their case is as full of holes as a colander. They can't prove that Gary entered Ms Gilbert's house; they have failed to prove that he raped her. And so the only verdict you can possibly reach is not guilty.'

She sat down. It sounded lame to her, not the sharp, incisive perform-ance she had planned. But she had done her job. It was as much as – more than – a lying thug like Gary was entitled to. Now she could think of Emily.

The judge adjourned the court for lunch and Sarah went immediately to a phone.

'Hello?' Bob's voice sounded hopeful, desperate.

'Bob? It's me. Any news?'

'No.' The hope in his voice faded to a flat, bitter resentment as he recognized hers. 'Did you get your rapist off?'

'Don't know yet. Have the police been in touch?'

'Yes. They're all over the village, they've seen Simon, they're trying to trace this phone call but it won't be any good, how can it be? She's just gone, Sarah – vanished!'

'Have you been by the phone all morning?'

'What the hell do you think I've been doing? You should be here, so I could go out and look!'

'As soon as we have a verdict I will be. But there's not much we *can* do, is there? If she's gone of her own accord she'll come back when she wants to.'

'And if she hasn't gone of her own accord?'

'Don't say that, Bob, please. Of course she has.'

'What're all these policemen doing here then?'

'Bob, don't let's quarrel, please. I'll be home as soon as I can and you can page me any time if something happens. I'll talk to her when she comes back. That's when I can really help. When she's actually there.'

'And *you're* actually here too. That's the point, isn't it?'

'All right, yes, when we're both there. And you. All three of us.'

'Right,' Bob said quietly. And put the phone down.

There was a bicycle in the hallway, and Terry caught his foot twice in the stair carpet. As he knocked he could hear the sound of the TV inside. No one answered. He knocked again, louder this time, and the door jerked suddenly open.

'Not now, for Chrissake! It's two thirty-five!'

The door slammed shut and the volume of the TV inside reached a crescendo. An angry voice yelled something. Then the door opened.

'Well, what is it?'

'Police.' Terry showed his warrant card. 'Can we come in?'

'Christ, it never rains but it pours! I ain't done nothing.'

'We're investigating a missing girl . . .'

Inside there was an armchair, and a bed with *The Racing Post* on it. The man, about forty, balding, in a shiny grey suit, glared at them defensively. Terry explained why he had come.

'Yeah, all right, so I did phone from there yesterday morning. It don't make me a child snatcher, does it?'

'No, sir, of course not, but we have to investigate, that's all. Would you mind telling us who you were telephoning?'

'Who I always phone, o' course.' The man jerked his thumb at the TV. The sound was off but Terry could see a racehorse loping nonchalantly into the winners' enclosure, surrounded by an ecstatic crowd of owners, trainer, jockey and stable lad, all delighted at their good luck.

'Blasted 33–1 nag gets up to the favourite on the line. I had twenty quid on at 4–1. Sounds pathetic, don't it, but that's a big bet for me nowadays.'

'You were ringing your bookie, you mean?'

'Got it in one, my son. I used to make money at it. And will again, I promise you. OK?'

A dejected Terry was already leaving when Harry Easby asked: 'You didn't happen to notice anyone in the phone box before you, did you, sir?'

The man frowned. 'Dunno. Yeah, wait a mo, I think there was, matter of fact. Student, probably – lots of 'em round here. Music on all bloody night, sometimes.'

'You couldn't describe him, could you?'

'Long hair, ponytail, ring in one ear. I *think* I've seen him before, in that house over there.' He pointed out of the window. 'I could be wrong, though.'

Outside, Terry looked at the list from this morning's search. The house the man had indicated contained eight bedsits. There had been no one at home in three of them that morning.

Sarah tried, but failed, to find anything unfair in the judge's summing up. He gave reasonable weight to all aspects of the evidence, asking the jury to focus their minds particularly on the question of identification, and the impressions they had formed of the truthfulness of the two key witnesses, Sharon Gilbert and Gary Harker.

Which if they have any sense will send Gary down, Sarah thought.

He repeated that they should ignore anything they had read in the press, and disregard the remarks Sharon had made about Gary having attacked other women.

'He is charged with one crime only before this court, and that is the only matter you are to consider, members of the jury. And in view of what Ms Gilbert alleged, I must emphasize that the defendant is charged with no other crimes against women at all, apart from this one. It is fair that you should know that.'

It is indeed, Sarah thought, surprised. He must be very confident of a conviction to say that. It probably dishes my chance of an appeal, too. My presentation must have been awful.

But she cared less than she once had. As soon as the jury were out she took out her mobile.

'Bob? Any news?'

'They rang to ask if she knows any students living off Blossom Street. Does she?'

'Not that I know of.'

'That's what I said too. Where would she meet students? She's only a kid.'

'Clubs. Parties. She's been to a few, you know.'

'She's not old enough, Sarah!'

'She's fifteen. I was her age when I met Kevin.'

'Christ! Don't remind me!'

But you weren't there, Bob, Sarah thought. You don't know what it was like. When I first met Kevin it was magic, for a while. As though the world had been black and white and then someone switched the colour on. Maybe it's like that for Emily now.

'When are you coming home?' Bob asked.

'After the verdict. I've got to stay for that.'

'Oh yes, of course. Mustn't let your rapist down, must you?'

I don't think I've ever really hated Bob before now, Sarah thought as she put the phone down. Why does he keep slipping the knife under my nails? To make me feel guilty for going to work? Or because he knows there's a part of me that doesn't think Emily's in danger at all, but is having the time of her life with some boy just as I did with Kevin? And he can't stand that because he's not half the lover Kevin was. Never could be.

Even though Kev was a brutal selfish arrogant cocky little git, and not intelligent or hardworking or sensitive as we always wanted our daughter to be. Of course Bob's right, this is a disaster but . . . oh Emily, what sort of a man have you chosen to run away with?

If you had any choice at all.

It was always a tense moment, but today, for once in her career, Sarah couldn't feel it. She walked into court isolated, anaesthetized inside her own bubble of indifference.

'Members of the jury, have you chosen a foreman to speak for you?'

'We have, yes.' A young man, in a smart suit and tie, stood up.

'Mr Foreman, answer these questions yes or no. On count one of the indictment, the unlawful rape of Sharon Gilbert, have you reached a verdict on which you are all agreed?'

'We have, yes.'

'And on that charge, do you find the defendant Gary Harker guilty or not guilty?'

'Not guilty.'

'*Yeessss!*' The shout came from behind her. Sarah turned, as everyone did, to see Gary standing in the dock, a triumphant grin on his face. The judge contemplated him coldly.

'In that case, Mr Harker, you are free to go.'

As Gary left the dock, Sarah rose to her feet to demand costs from public funds. Then she gathered up her papers as the judge turned to thank the jury.

'Congratulations. A feather in your cap, no doubt.' With stiff politeness, Julian Lloyd-Davies essayed the smile of the gallant loser.

'Thanks.' Sarah thought how in other circumstances she would have been proud – cock-a-hoop with bubbling delight at having achieved such a triumph in the teeth of fierce pre-trial publicity, a prosecution headed by a QC, and firm control of the trial itself by a judge who clearly believed in Gary's guilt. But with Emily missing, it was ashes in her mouth.

In the foyer, she saw Sharon Gilbert sobbing, supported by her friend. Gary saw Sharon too. He laughed, and jerked his forearm upwards in the traditional footballer's gesture of triumph – shafted!

14

'So what do they say?'

'Who? The police? Nothing much.' Bob's eyes met hers – dark accusing eyes in a face pale with exhaustion. 'Do you really care?'

'Oh come on, Bob, of course I care. *What did they say?*'

He took a deep breath. 'The only one who's said anything of any consequence is that Inspector – Bateson I think his name is, the one who was here this morning. According to him someone saw a young man use that phone box around 12.47 yesterday. But it could have been one of three possible young men who live in Blossom Street. The snag is, none of them are at home. So, as far as I can make out, they're just sitting outside watching.'

'Watching?'

'Waiting for these lads to come back. Ridiculous, isn't it! Emily might be in one those flats right now. Why don't you just smash the door down, I said, go in and have a look! This is my daughter you're talking about, a fifteen-year-old child! But oh no, they can't do that, they say. They need a search warrant, they haven't got enough evidence, they can't say if these lads have anything to do with it at all. I ask you! I ought to go down there myself!'

'It wouldn't help, Bob. They have to act within the law. They're bound to make reasonable attempts to contact the occupants first, before breaking in. That's how it works.'

'Law, law, law!' he yelled. 'That's all there is with you, isn't it? And meanwhile Emily's been missing for over a day and nobody cares a toss!'

'Don't be silly, Bob – I care!'

'Like hell you do! Off all day in your bloody court. No wonder the kid ran away, when she's got a mother with ice in her veins!'

'Bob, please! We don't know why she went.'

'Don't we? No, but I can guess.' He went to the sideboard and poured himself a whisky. 'What happened in your wretched trial, anyway?'

'Not guilty.' Bob's face mirrored the expressions she had seen on the face of Judge Gray when the verdict was announced – surprise, followed by consternation and disgust. In the judge's case the visible signs of these emotions were swiftly smothered by long practice, but in Bob's they were sustained, open and bitter.

'So you got him off, did you? Set a rapist free. I suppose you're proud of that?'

'Not proud, no, not exactly, Bob, but . . .'

'But you won the fight. Trouble is you thought he was guilty, didn't you?'

They had discussed the case on a couple of occasions. Calmer occasions, normal evenings. He knew her too well for her to deceive him.

'He never actually admitted it, Bob. I'm not the jury, I'm his defence.'

'So now . . .' Bob swirled the whisky around his gums, as though he were trying to anaesthetize some toothache. '. . . now your rapist is out there walking free, God knows where, just like our daughter Emily. Makes you feel great, I suppose?'

'No, of course not . . .'

'It makes me sick!' He finished the drink, strode to the door, and put on his coat.

'Bob? Where are you going?'

'Out. To walk along the river bank, look for Emily, anywhere. You stay by the phone, see how you like it!'

'Bob!' But he was gone, and didn't come back for two hours. When he did, the evening and night passed in similar style, with recrimination, sullen silences and occasional unsuccessful attempts at a truce. Towards dawn Bob fell asleep, exhausted. Then at eight he showered, dressed and came downstairs.

'Where are you going?' Sarah asked, from the armchair where she slumped, gazing at the garden listlessly.

'To work, like you yesterday. I've got some reports to sign, they can't go off without me. Then . . . I don't know. I can't just sit. You'll stay here, won't you?' It was more of a plea this time, less of an insult.

'If that's what you want. I'll give you a ring if anything happens.'

'Of course.'

But in the event, that was precisely what she was unable to do.

Terry's phone rang as he was entering the school playground. Jessica had skipped away with a bright wave and a kiss; but Esther was miserable that morning. It was something about some boys who had torn her book; he had promised to speak to her teacher about it, and her seven-year-old hand gripped his forefinger tightly as they made their way through the screaming, jostling crowd of tiny figures.

Then his mobile rang.

Terry cursed silently. He had told them time and again not to do this unless it was an emergency. He fumbled the phone from his inside pocket. 'Bateson.'

'Sir, there's been a development in that missing child case of yours. They've found a body.'

'*Oh no.*' Terry stopped in the middle of the playground. 'Where?'

'In some bushes near the river, sir. Not far from where they're building the new designer outlet. A man walking his dog found it this morning.'

'What makes you think it's connected with the Newby case?'

'Clothing, sir. There's a car there now. Says it's a teenage girl with a blue and red jacket like the one in the description you've circulated. She's had her throat cut.'

'Mr Bateson, good morning! Hello, Esther, how are you today?' A friendly, motherly woman in a cream blouse and tartan skirt – Esther's class teacher – approached them, and noticing the anxious look in Esther's eyes, squatted down to smile at her. 'Have you come to see me?'

'OK, I'll go straight there.' Terry clicked the phone off and nodded vaguely at the woman. 'Er, yes, we were, but there's been a bit of an emergency . . .'

'*Dad!*' Esther's grip tightened round his finger and her other hand clutched his wrist. 'You promised!'

'Yeah . . . yeah, OK, love.' He looked down, saw his daughter was near to tears, and scooped her up on to his hip. 'Can we go inside for a moment?'

'Of course, follow me.'

In the light, airy classroom Terry found it hard to concentrate on Esther's problem of the torn book, and the petty dispute which had led the boys to tear it. But thank goodness the teacher, Mrs Thomson, seemed to have a clear grasp not only of the crime but also, more importantly, of a solution to make everything better. Five minutes later Terry left Esther comfortably ensconced on Mrs Thomson's knee, and waded out through a cloakroom full of small chattering bodies hanging up their coats and bags.

What a thing it must be to have a job that can make things better, he thought, crossing the playground to his car. What will I tell Sarah Newby, later today? I'm sorry, love, but that child you brought up for fifteen years – she's lying by the river with her throat cut.

The body, like all bodies, looked pathetic. It was only the second corpse Terry had seen since Mary was killed and he coped with it by concentrating on the way it was no longer a real living person but something essentially, fundamentally different. Something not just dumped here by the murderer but also discarded by the original occupant; a wrapping, no longer required on the journey. There has to be some sort of afterlife, he thought. Otherwise – this is it.

The body lay twisted, half on its back and half on its side, the limbs asprawl, the face wrenched sideways, half buried in brambles and nettles. The uppermost side of the face, the left side, was discoloured by mud and a bruise on the cheekbone just under the eye. The other side, which he gingerly lifted with a latex-gloved finger before letting it fall, was imprinted with twigs and mud and leaves, among which ants and worms crawled industriously. But it was not the face or the white, stiffening limbs which caught the eye the most. It was the red gash in the throat, wide enough for a man's hand and so deep he thought he could see bone and cut sinew inside it, from which the blood had gushed out and dried all over the girl's blouse and arms and on to the trampled grass around.

Terry stepped carefully, where the Scenes of Crime Officer, Jack Middleton, showed him. The body was in a group of bushes a few yards from the river path down which, presumably, a man had come walking his dog early this morning to meet this unwelcome surprise.

'Looks like your misper, doesn't it, Terry?' Jack Middleton said. He wore white overalls, and in one latex-gloved hand he held the print of a proud, smiling Emily Newby that Terry had copied from the school photo on Sarah's mantelpiece. Underneath was a brief description of the clothes she was believed to be wearing.

'Probably,' Terry agreed gloomily. 'Can't be sure from the face, but the hair colour and jacket are the same. Poor kid. When was she found?'

'About seven thirty, I think. But she's been dead for hours before that. Arms and legs are pretty much rigid.'

'When's the doc coming?'

'Any minute now.' As they spoke a slim young man in a suit came up the track, carrying a doctor's bag. Terry went to meet him.

'Dr Jones?'

'Yep. Where's the patient?'

'Over there. This officer will show you where to walk. We don't want to spoil any footprints.'

'Don't worry. I'll keep out of the mud as much as I can. I only bought these shoes last week. Hand-sewn.'

Terry had worked with Andrew Jones before and knew he was precise, thorough and very acute. The down sides were his vanity, and the defensive callousness he affected towards human corpses, approaching them with as much emotional involvement as a master chef contemplating a prime side of beef.

His initial examination did not last long. Death was obvious, and the cause equally apparent. While the SOCO took photographs Terry asked: 'When did it happen, roughly?'

'Ten to twelve hours ago, I should say, judging by the stiffness of the limbs.'

'Late last night then, an hour or so before midnight, you'd say?'

'Yep. Can't really be more precise than that.'

'Anything else you can be precise about before you get her in the lab?'

'Clearly she died from the throat wound – carotid artery severed, arterial blood everywhere. Presumably a knife, probably inflicted from behind. A right-handed assailant – probably held her head up by the hair, baring the throat, and then slashed from left to right. Hell of a big sharp knife too – machete maybe – he's cut right through to the vertebrae. I'll be able to tell you more after a closer examination.'

'Any other obvious injuries? There's a bruise on the face, isn't there?'

'Mm, yes – not sure when that was inflicted. She's also been raped.'

'What?' Dear God, how much worse can it get, Terry thought? Dr Jones flashed him a mocking, clinical smile.

'Didn't you lift her skirt? No doubt about it, I'm afraid. No knickers, bloodstains on her thighs and vaginal bruising. That's good news, at least.'

'Good news? How do you make that out?'

'We'll almost certainly find semen. Then if your budget can stretch to it we'll do a DNA profile and snap! You've got him. Open and shut, no argument.'

'We've got to find him, first, doc. And her knickers, it seems. Are they lying about somewhere?' He glanced at Jack Middleton, who shook his head.

Dr Jones shrugged. 'Probably took them home, as a souvenir. His version of a teddy, to keep on the pillow at night.' The disgust on Terry's face stopped him from going further. 'Sorry. It's a filthy murder, I know. When that photographer's finished we'll get the body down to the lab. I'll start the PM as soon as she's identified. Have you any idea who she is?'

Terry sighed. It was the task he was dreading. 'Oh yes. That's one thing we *can* be sure of, I think.'

'Is your husband at home?'

'He went to school. It's my turn by the phone today. Punishment for yesterday.' Sarah attempted a wry smile, conscious she must look a mess to Terry. Only a couple of hours' sleep for the second night running, on a diet of coffee and arguments – hardly the best beauty regime. As Terry frowned she thought, He's furious with me about the Harker case. No doubt he was, but his face showed a far deeper worry, a more profound concern which she didn't want to acknowledge. She shivered. 'Can I offer you coffee?'

'No, thank you. Mrs Newby –'

'*Sarah*, please. We are still colleagues, aren't we? In a sense, anyway – or haven't you forgiven me for . . .' Keep chattering and he won't say it.

'We've found a body.'

'What? *Oh.*' She sat down quite suddenly on a chair, as though the strings in her legs had been cut. 'Oh my God.' Her hand over her mouth.

Terry sat opposite her, waiting for the shock to sink in. It's like wounding a person, he thought. I might as well walk in here with a gun and shoot her. If a gun could stun and not kill, that is. The reaction is the same. The shock, often numbness before the pain.

She drew a deep shuddering breath, and looked up at him. There was a mute appeal in her eyes but she didn't ask.

'I'm very sorry. We think it's Emily but we can't be sure. It's a girl of her age and appearance wearing the jacket you described to us. Blue and red leather.'

'Dead?' A tiny hope, a plea.

'Yes.'

'Oh. *Oh God!*' The tears came suddenly, in a rush, and she would have collapsed altogether on the floor if Terry hadn't caught and held her. For a while they stayed like that, he kneeling awkwardly in front of her armchair, she sobbing with her arms around his neck. He held her, patted her back. 'I'm so sorry, love. So very very sorry.'

After a few minutes, an age, she scrambled awkwardly to her feet. Terry found a pack of tissues in his pocket – he had come prepared. But they were the devil to unwrap.

'Thanks.' She wiped her eyes, mascara all smudged, blew her nose. 'Terry, it *is* her, is it?'

'We think so but we can't be absolutely sure. We need you – or your husband – to identify her, I'm afraid.'

'Oh God, no. *Emily!* Is she badly – injured?'

'I'm afraid so, yes. But you'll only have to see her face.'

'Tell me.' The hazel eyes stared straight into his, like a wildcat defending her kitten.

Terry didn't want to go into this. 'Her throat was cut. But you do need to identify the body, Sarah, I'm sorry. Or your husband can do it if you prefer.'

'I'll ring Bob.'

She fumbled her way to the phone. The school secretary answered. 'I'm sorry, Mrs Newby, he's gone out. He didn't say when he'd be back. Can I take a message?'

Tell him his daughter's had her throat cut. 'No. Ask him to ring home, will you? It's important.' She turned to Terry. 'He's not there.'

'Would you like to wait until he comes home?'

Sarah drew a deep breath. 'No.' She sobbed, put her hand over her mouth, swayed, stood up straight. 'No. I want to see her, Terry. I want to see her *now.*'

Visiting his school had brought Bob little relief. His secretary, a motherly, talkative woman, had told everyone why he had been away yesterday, so he had to accept sympathy from each colleague he met. For a while he hid in his office, signing the school reports, but by mid-morning the restlessness, so strong that it was akin to panic, caught up with him.

'I'm going out, Mrs Daggett. Anything you can't deal with ask Mrs Yeo.'

'Yes, of course. Don't you worry about us. I'm so sorry . . .'

In the car his suspicions about Simon returned. The boy had sounded shifty the other night, he thought. Why hadn't he been in touch yet to ask if they'd found her? After all, she was his half-sister, even if they didn't get on so well. And it would be just like Simon to delight in turning Emily against him if he had the chance.

He drove straight to Simon's house, parking in the street outside. But although he knocked several times, and peered through the window, there was no answer. He called through the letterbox. 'Simon? Simon, are you there? . . . Emily? It's me, Dad!'

'Reckon he's bogged off, mate. Good riddance, too, I say.'

'What?' Bob whirled round and stood up from his cramped, embarrassing position with his mouth to the letterbox. A wizened old man in a flat cap, ancient cardigan and carpet slippers stood on the pavement behind him. 'Who are you?'

'Archibald Mullen, number 17, 'cross the road.' The man jerked his thumb. 'You from't landlord, are you?'

'No. I'm . . . Simon's stepfather.'

'Oh. Well, you won't want to hear what I say then.' The old man shuffled away.

'No, wait!' Bob grabbed his arm. 'What do you want to say?'

The man stood in the gutter in his carpet slippers, considering. Then he pulled an ancient, smelly pipe out of his cardigan pocket, turned the bowl upside down, and began to scrape ash out of it with a nicotine-stained little finger. 'Well, about all't rows, that's all.'

'What rows? Tell me. Please – it might be important!'

The old man inspected him quizzically. 'Don't know as I should, you being his stepdad.' He sucked his pipe experimentally.

'Look, I really need to know. My daughter's missing and I'm trying to find her. Was there a girl here last night? Do you know?'

'Girl? Aye, there might have been. What's your daughter look like then?'

Bob began to describe her, while the old man found a tobacco pouch in his pocket and began filling the bowl of the pipe. He looked down, absorbed in the task, and Bob suppressed a rising tide of rage as he was forced to describe the most precious thing in his life to the top of the old bastard's greasy flat cap. But when he mentioned Emily's red and blue leather coat the narrow, wizened face looked up sharply.

'Aye, that's it. That's what she was wearing.'

Hope flashed through him, like a knife. 'What *who* was wearing? Tell me – what did you see?'

'Well...' He had the wretched pipe full now, and proceeded to put it in his mouth, strike a match, cup his wrinkled hands around the bowl, and draw slow measured puffs of smoke for what seemed like an age. 'It was last night about half ten, summat like that. I were off to bed when late News came on, I don't watch that, seen it all earlier like, and I were in me nightshirt just coming out o't bathroom after doing me teeth – that's my bedroom over there, just over't yellow door, so I've got a clear view...' The pipe, it appeared, was going out. A second match was struck, held between cupped hands over the bowl, the flame ducked downwards.

'Yes. What did you see?'

'Well, there's this row, see. Slamming doors and screaming – a lass and a feller, like. So I looked – I mean, I'm not right nosy like some folk, but it's human nature like, in't it?'

'*What* did you see?' Bob was not a violent man, but the desire to snatch the pipe from the man's mouth and crush it underfoot was becoming so overpowering that he had to clasp his hands behind his back.

'Well, the young lass, the one in the blue and red coat, she were in't middle o't road with him, yelling at each other fit to bust. Right old ding-dong it were!'

'By *he*, you mean the young man who lives here, do you? Simon Newby?'

'Is that his name? Aye. I recognized him well enough. I'd seen't lassie before, a few times, like. Anyhow, he's trying to drag her back inside, but she won't come, so he smacks her in't chops. A fair clout, it were. Knocks her into't side o' yon car.' The old man took the pipe from his mouth to indicate a battered hatchback across the street, and grinned evilly. 'Like proper Wild West it were! Anyhow she storms off up street, and he goes back inside. For a bit.'

'For a bit? You mean he came out again?'

'Aye. After about ten, twenty minutes. Got in that old Escort of his and drove off.'

'Did he come back later?'

'Might have done, after I were asleep, like. But his car's not here now, is it?'

Simon's car was certainly missing. Anger flooded through Bob – Simon had hit Emily, so hard that she'd fallen against the side of a car! He wrote down the old man's name and address, then got back in his car to drive home.

I knew I'd find something if I tried, he thought. I've really got something, at last! I'll go home and phone the police and then come out again and look for that bastard Simon.

But why would Simon hit Emily?

*   *   *

104

'We're ready for you now, Sarah.' Terry came back into the dreary functional waiting room. Sarah sat hunched up next to a woman constable, and seemed to have shrunk, somehow. 'Are you sure you can manage this?'

'No, I'm not sure.' Was it the reflected light from the vile green plastic sofa that made her face look so seasick, or was she really ill, he wondered?

'We can wait a while if you like.'

'No.' She took a deep breath, and stood up. 'Let's get it over with.' The WPC held open the door and Sarah walked through it alone. Terry and the WPC followed.

The body was just across the corridor, laid out on a trolley in the morgue. It was covered with a sheet, and everything in the room had been carefully tidied up – no open chest wounds in sight, no skulls sawn in half, no pickled internal organs. Just the instruments, washed and clean in their places and the body fridges all along one wall, the doors carefully closed like long narrow lockers in a changing room. It was the smell that struck Sarah first. Disinfectant like in a hospital, but something quite unlike a hospital too. Formaldehyde? You don't preserve dead things in hospitals, you try to keep them alive.

And then the silence. The forensic pathologist, Dr Jones, stood by the head of the trolley, his hair covered by a white cap, his young face in the round glasses composed in respectful solemnity. He might be arrogant but he knew how to behave before grieving relatives, Terry thought. Sarah's shoes squeaked on the vinyl floor as she walked towards the trolley. Terry was close behind her on one side, the WPC on the other, both ready to catch her if she fainted.

'I'm the forensic pathologist, Mrs Newby,' Andrew Jones said. 'We'd just like you to look at her face, that's all, and tell us if you recognize the body. Let me know when you're ready.'

Sarah met his eyes, and nodded. Very gently, as though taking infinite care not to hurt the body any more, he pulled back the sheet as far as the chin. The great gaping wound in the throat, tactfully covered with a second sheet, remained hidden. But nothing could hide the bruise on the left cheek, or the marks of leaves and sticks in the rigid waxy pallor of the lifeless skin. Sarah shuddered, and almost fell. Terry and the WPC caught her elbows. Under his hands Terry could feel her trembling, trembling . . .

'Well,' he said very softly. 'Sarah, is it her?'

The trembling was worse now. Sarah leaned forward and gripped the side of the trolley with both hands, shaking her head vigorously.

'No,' she said at last. 'No, it isn't Emily. No, no, no, it's not!' She turned to look up into Terry's stunned eyes. Tears were flooding down her cheeks. 'It isn't her, Terry, it's not Emily, oh *thank God!*'

He put his arms round her and held her, and thought, Thank God too, the poor woman, but *who is it?* Over Sarah's shoulder he caught Dr

105

Jones's raised eyebrows and after another age of sobbing she drew back from him and he asked what he had to ask, for formality's sake only.

'So if it's not your daughter, Sarah, do you have any idea who this person is?'

The difference between a smile of relief and the rictus of agony is not so very great, particularly when smudged by a storm of tears. 'I'm sorry, it's wicked of me to be so happy but it's only because it's not Emily. Not because of this poor girl here. Yes, I do know who she is.'

Bob was on the phone to the police when the doorbell rang. The duty sergeant at the other end was being oddly obtuse, as though he couldn't fully take in what Bob was saying.

'Look, it's important, I want you to tell Inspector Bateson as soon as he gets in. The sooner he gets on to it, the sooner we'll get my daughter home. And she may be hurt.'

'Just one moment, sir. I'll put you through to someone who's dealing with this.' There was the sound of another phone ringing at the end of the line. Bob was about to go and see who was at the door when a voice said: 'Mr Newby? Detective Chief Inspector Churchill here. I understand DI Bateson hasn't made contact with you yet?'

'No. But I've found out something that may be very important. I went to my stepson's house this morning you see, and . . .'

Before Bob could describe his discovery further the doorbell rang again and then, a few seconds later, he thought he heard the front door open and voices talking, as though they were actually coming in. He hesitated, wondering what to do, and DCI Churchill took advantage of the break in conversation to say: 'Well, I'm very sorry to tell you this over the phone, Mr Newby, but there's been a rather unfortunate development. Inspector Bateson found the body of a young girl in a wood near the river this morning and I believe he's taken your wife in to identify . . .'

There were definitely voices in the hall. Then the kitchen door opened and Bob dropped the phone on the floor, where it continued prattling busily to itself.

'Mr Newby? Are you there, sir? I'm really very sorry indeed to have to tell you this but there is a strong likelihood that the body may be that of your daughter . . . Mr Newby? . . . Mr Newby, sir, are you all right . . .?'

Churchill could hear screams and cries which sounded like hysterics at the other end of the line, and he thought, I shouldn't have done it like this, I should have taken time to go round there and break it to him myself, but a man like a headmaster, I would have expected more self-control, what the hell's going on down there?

'A girl's body, is that what you said, Chief Inspector?' Bob broke in on his thoughts, his voice sounding oddly inappropriate, much nearer laughter than tears.

'Yes, sir. I'm really very sorry I have to break it to you like this –'

'Oh, that's all right, don't worry, no offence. You see it isn't my daughter anyway, so it doesn't matter.'

'Can you really be sure of that, sir?'

'Yes. Oh yes. You see she's standing right here in front of me. With the young man who took her away, I take it.'

'He didn't take me away, Dad,' said Emily earnestly. 'I decided to go myself, and we both came back together. You see I haven't run away or anything, and if you'd only listen we can explain it all.'

Bob put the phone down and gave his daughter a second hug, to comfort himself as much as her. Then he looked, somewhat less fondly, at the young man with the ponytail and scrubby beard who stood beside her, calmly holding her hand.

'Yes. I think you'd better do that. You've got a lot of explaining to do, young lady.'

'So who is it, then?' Terry asked.

'It's my son's girlfriend, Jasmine. Well, ex-girlfriend really. Oh God, I don't mean it like that, I mean I don't think he's seen her for some time.'

'But you're quite certain? Positive?'

'Yes. Oh yes. Oh God, now I suppose her poor parents will have to go through all this.'

'I'm afraid they will. You don't happen to have their address, do you?'

'I'm not sure, I suppose I must have got it somewhere. Do you mind if we get out of this awful place now? I think I want to sit down.'

'Of course.'

On the grimy green sofa across the corridor Sarah began to recover her poise. The WPC brought her a cup of hot sweet tea while she fumbled in her diary and found an address for Jasmine's mother. She took a deep draught of the tea, grimaced, and said: 'The worst of it is I didn't really like the girl. I never wanted this to happen, of course.'

'But she was your son's girlfriend for some time.'

'Yes. For nearly a year, I suppose. We never got on. I was probably her idea of a mother-in-law from hell.'

'Perhaps you can tell me all you know about her. I shall have to interview your son, of course.'

'Oh. Of course.' The shock must have made Sarah's brain slow because this was the first time this idea had occurred to her. She saw the seriousness in Terry's face, and underneath that, pity. Oh no, not Simon, she thought. 'You don't think he had anything to do with . . . . that?'

'I've no idea at present,' Terry said carefully. 'But I'm going to have to ask him a few questions, at least.'

15

'So perhaps you'd better take it from the beginning. Where exactly have you been?' Bob's voice wavered between relief and harshness as he confronted the pair on the sofa, Emily clutching her bearded young man's hand as though joined to it from birth. They were both, he noticed, as grubby as a street couple but there was a radiant glow in his daughter's face that made his heart sink.

'Well, we've been at the protest, you see – we spent two nights there, on a platform. It was fabulous, Dad, you could feel the tree creaking around you, and see all the birds and squirrels that depend on it too! The whole wood is like that and they're cutting it down just for a tacky shopping centre –'

'No, hold on a moment.' Bob raised both hands. 'Who's this young man, anyway?'

'I'm Larry,' the wispy beard and ponytail said. 'You're Bob, I guess.'

'Yes,' Bob admitted reluctantly, offended by the boy's use of his first name. 'Emily's father, as I'm sure you know.'

'Yeah, well, it's because of me that it happened, you see. I mean about Emily coming.'

'Coming where?'

'To the protest, Dad!' Emily burst in. 'You're not listening. You see, Larry phoned me, three days ago was it? – when I was pissed off with all this shit about the GCSEs . . .'

Bob registered the new foul language with shock. She had rarely used such words at home before, and never with such brutal fluency. It was all of a piece with the dirt and the fleece-lined denim jacket which, he thought vaguely, was different, too. But then this glowing self-assured Emily was not someone he'd seen before, either.

'. . . so he said why not come down to the protest and so I did, Dad, and it's brilliant. I mean it's so much more *real* than anything else – there are people who've actually got the guts to stand up and do something to stop the fucking meathead bastards tearing the place to shreds. I mean do you know what they do? Some of those trees are more than a hundred and fifty years old and they just go in there with bloody great chainsaws and cranes and tear them down in a few minutes. And nobody gives a toss! It opens your eyes, Dad, it really does!'

'So you spent two nights there?' Bob managed, as she paused for breath.

'Yes, and I'm sorry I didn't phone, Dad, I really am, only I didn't have my mobile and you can see I'm OK now, can't you . . .?'

'Have you *any idea* . . .' Bob began, but then the front door opened and Sarah walked in with the detective, Terry Bateson.

When she saw Emily she stood quite still, trembling. To Bob's surprise Bateson put an arm round her shoulder. Emily stood up, smiling nervously. 'Hi, Mum.'

What's happened, Bob wondered? Sarah's struck dumb. This is having an impact on her, at last. *Why doesn't she move?*

Emily stepped forward, nervously, but Sarah stayed frozen and Bob thought, Oh no, it's not relief or joy she's feeling but anger. The cruel vindictive bitch – she's going to punish the child for coming home! Then Sarah reached out and smothered the girl in an embrace that became a storm of tears. First no emotion and then too much, Bob thought. There were tears in Emily's eyes, too, but her feelings seemed more like embarrassment and guilt.

After almost two minutes of weeping Sarah stepped back, shaking her head slowly.

'Where in hell have you been?'

'At the tree protest, Mum. With Larry. This is Larry.'

Sarah ignored the young man as though he were a log which Emily had dragged home and dumped on the sofa.

'You have *no idea*, have you . . .? We thought you were dead!'

'Oh Mum, don't exaggerate. I mean, I know I didn't phone but –'

'Why do you think I'm here with a policeman? I've just been to the mortuary, Emily. There was a body there. They thought it was you.'

In the stunned silence a flush of increasing embarrassment mottled Emily's face. 'But that's just stupid, Mum! How could it be me? I'm just fine –'

'It's not stupid, Emily. The body was wearing your coat.'

'My coat? Oh . . . Oh no.' Watching, Terry thought he'd never seen anyone's face go from red to white so quickly. She swayed, and he stepped forward to catch the girl under her arms and lower her to the sofa as Sarah continued, looking at Bob for the first time.

'It was Jasmine. Jasmine Hurst. She's had her throat cut.'

When Emily recovered Terry found out what he needed to know, for now. Numbly, with her new boyfriend's arm around her shoulder, Emily explained how she had met Jasmine that first night, at the protest camp. They knew each other, of course, but according to Emily not particularly well; Jasmine had been Simon's girlfriend, that was all. Emily didn't see her brother often, didn't get on with him that well. She shuddered and looked away.

'Emily?' Terry prompted gently. 'Is there something else?'

The words were too quiet at first, so he asked her to repeat them. 'Neither did Jasmine,' she murmured defiantly. '*She* didn't get on with Simon either. They quarrelled. She told me.'

'Emily, for heaven's sake!' Sarah whispered.

'When was that, Emily?' Terry asked.

'A while ago, I think. That's why she left him. She isn't . . . wasn't his girlfriend any more. She had another bloke, one of the protesters. Dave, I think?' She looked to Larry for confirmation.

'Dave . . . Brodie, his name is,' Larry agreed. 'He's a nurse.'

'Address?'

'No, sorry.' The young man scratched his wispy beard, then shook his head. Bob found himself having to suppress a deep, irrational hatred for this boy, as though all this were somehow his fault, and could be put right if he would leave now, and never come back.

'Don't worry, we'll find it.' Terry turned back to Emily. 'So why did she have your jacket?'

'We swapped. This is hers.' Emily looked at the grubby fleece-lined denim jacket she was wearing with sudden horror, and almost took it off before hugging it tightly round herself instead. 'She said she wasn't going to sleep out and if I was this'd be warmer, and anyway I never really liked that red and blue jacket. Sorry, Mum, I know you gave it me but . . .'

'It doesn't matter,' said Sarah quietly.

'When did you change the jackets, Emily?' Terry persisted.

'That same night. Wednesday, was it? Yes, Wednesday.'

'And where was Jasmine going?'

'Back to her boyfriend's, I suppose. I can't remember.'

'Did you see her again?'

'No.' Emily began to cry and Terry got up. 'That's all for now,' he said to Sarah and Bob. 'I'll need proper statements later, for the inquest, but that can wait. At least your daughter's back. I'll let myself out.'

'So what have we got, doc?'

To Terry's irritation, Will Churchill was cleaning his teeth with a match. His very presence at the initial post-mortem report was an implied criticism, without that.

'As you see, the cause of death is obvious. Massive haemorrhage due to the fact that someone's had a go at cutting her head clean off. Severed the neck right back to the vertebrae.'

'Anything you can tell us about the weapon?'

Dr Jones shrugged. 'Big, sharp. Possibly serrated.'

'Serrated? You can tell that?' Terry asked.

'Can't be certain yet, but it's a possibility. Look at these marks on the bone, here. I'll know more when I've had them under a microscope.

Maybe a bayonet, hunting knife, something like that. A long blade anyway, six inches at least.'

'So he went prepared,' Will Churchill said.

'Unless he needed a six-inch knife for self-defence, by the river,' Dr Jones said wryly. 'Have you found a weapon yet?'

Terry shook his head.

'Well, if you do find one pop it in here. I'll see if it matches the wounds. There'll be bloodstains too unless it's been thoroughly washed. On his clothes too almost certainly.'

'What about the bruise on the face?' Terry asked. 'Did he beat her up beforehand?'

Dr Jones frowned. 'Some time before, if he did. That bruise is a few hours old. Didn't happen at the time of death. This did, though – or just before.'

He whisked away a sheet from the lower half of the girl's body, and Terry looked at her hips and genital area, the focus of so much attraction in life, so waxen and meatlike in death. Once a lithe young woman, now a carcass on a butcher's slab, defaced by their cuts and probes, prying into her most private place of all, sliced open now for ease of inspection.

'Bruising to the external labia, here and here. Internal bruising too. These bruises aren't very developed though. Must have been done within half an hour of death, I'd say.'

'Any semen?'

Dr Jones actually smiled, and produced a microscope slide with a triumphant flourish. 'Taraaa! Just a trace, but quite conclusive nonetheless – you find the wicked laddie, gentlemen, and I'll send him down. No room for doubt.'

Churchill smiled. 'That'll make a nice change, at least. Now all we need is a suspect.'

When Terry left, the four of them sat silent for a while, staring at nothing, like survivors of a bomb blast. Bob was still taking in the fact of Jasmine's death, and the horror of what he alone knew. Simon hadn't been quarrelling with *Emily* outside the old man's house – it had been *Jasmine*, it must have been! And that was hugely, horribly important. Why hadn't he told Terry Bateson just now?

And what would Sarah say if he had? She had always been protective of Simon. She was protecting him now. 'You shouldn't have said that, about Simon quarrelling with Jasmine,'she was saying to Emily.

'But it's true, Mum. She told me.'

'Yes, but don't you see? They'll think he killed her!' Sarah started walking nervously up and down. 'That's how the police work – any little hint like that sends them rushing off in the wrong direction – towards Simon, for God's sake!'

'Don't be silly, Mum – of course he couldn't *kill* her.'

111

'Of course not, no – but you see how important it is what you say.' Suddenly her attention was distracted by the sight of Emily's young man. What's *he* doing here, she thought? We don't need him. She attempted a polite, hostess-type smile. 'I think you'd better go.'

'Er, yeah, OK.' The young man began to get up. 'It's a bad time.'

But Emily dragged him down again beside her. 'No! I want him to stay. I've just come home and you're thinking about Simon again, aren't you, Mum? At least Larry cares about *me*.'

'And we don't, I suppose? We've been looking for you for two days, Emily! And Jasmine's dead!'

'I do know that, Mum. It's awful.'

'You don't know it, not really. I've just seen her body, wearing your jacket. Emily, I thought it was going to be *you*!'

'So it's all *my* fault now, is it?' Emily shook her head furiously, tears in her eyes – of self-pity, Sarah thought coldly. Teenagers. As if *she's* the one suffering here.

The young man put one arm round Emily's shoulder while he stroked her hair with the other. 'It must have been terrible, seeing that body, Mrs Newby,' he ventured, to Sarah's surprise.

'Yes, it was.' This mediation from a complete stranger who had caused such trouble confused Sarah deeply. She struggled to remain polite. 'Look, I'm sorry, I don't remember your name.'

'Larry. Larry Dyson.'

'Well, Larry, since you're here, do you mind explaining exactly why you asked Emily to go away with you to this . . . tree protest of yours for two nights? You can see the monumental amount of trouble it's caused.'

Sarah's sharp tone infuriated Emily further. 'He didn't *ask* me, I chose to go!'

Larry nodded. 'Yeah, well, that's right. You may not realize it, Mrs Newby, but Emmy really was very unhappy. She told me how she was feeling and when I said where I was going she asked to come with me. No one knew anything was going to happen to Jasmine. And direct action is important. Just as important as getting a few bits of paper from school.'

Emmy, Sarah thought. This ridiculous boy even wants to change her name. But before she could respond Bob took over, in headmaster mode.

'GCSEs aren't just bits of paper, young man – they can affect your whole life. You'd know that if you were a student.'

'I *am* a student, thank you very much. At St John's.'

'Well, that's something, at least. Doing what?'

'Earth sciences. I do *know* what I'm talking about. I study the environment, as it happens, as well as actually trying to do something about it.'

'You could have phoned, Emily,' Sarah said. 'Didn't anyone have a mobile?'

'Yes, but I thought if I phoned you'd just chew my head off – like you're both doing now! Come on, Larry, we'd better leave.' She stood abruptly, but Bob blocked her way to the door.

'Oh no. You're not going anywhere. Not again.'

'Dad! Please – let me go!'

'No.' It seemed to Sarah that Bob was about to resort to physical restraint, which would be ridiculous, because he was the most clumsy of men. But of course he was right, Emily couldn't possibly just walk out again. Not now, after all this. Sarah stood beside Bob for support. If he had no arguments, she had.

'Look, we've all had a terrible shock, and walking out now won't make it any better. Anyway, Emily, you're not sixteen yet, so if Larry has had any kind of sexual relationship with you he's committing an offence. You do realize that, don't you?'

'Yes, well, it's a bit late for that now!'

Silence. Mother and daughter stared at each other. 'You mean, you *have* . . .'

Emily smiled. 'There's no need to look shocked, Mum, everyone does it! *You* did!'

'That's different,' Sarah responded, weakly. 'You know it is . . .'

'No it isn't. How old were you when Simon was born? Sixteen?'

'You're not pregnant?' Bob burst in.

'Oh come on, Dad! I do have some sense. More than Mum had, anyway. I brought Larry here for you to meet him. It's important, Mum.'

And so it comes full circle, Sarah thought. Did my parents feel like this too, all those years ago? She tried and failed to make a pattern out of the kaleidoscope of emotions swirling through her mind – anger, regret, a piercing sense of loss, a sense of her own and Bob's growing irrelevance in Emily's eyes. But after the horror of Jasmine's death it was hard to focus on this too. She was going to have to tell Simon about Jasmine soon, poor boy. But first there was this.

Sarah looked at the young couple standing defiantly in front of her and thought, That's how I was, that's exactly how Kevin and I must have looked. She began to feel a strange joy, too, as well as enormous anxiety, and a growing curiosity about this intense skinny grubby young man who had sneaked into their house like a gypsy thief and stolen their daughter away. Succeeding all these was a desire not to get this wrong as her own parents had done; as she and Bob had done with Simon. We mustn't fail with Emily too.

Bob was floundering too. 'Look, Emily love, we're not Neanderthals. If you want to have a boyfriend that's fine. But you don't have to move out, of course not. You're far too young for that. This is your home, for goodness' sake.'

Emily hesitated. 'Yes, Dad, that's why we came here. But if you won't accept Larry . . .'

Sarah found her voice. 'We've only just met him, Emily. And we've been through the most terrible two days. But maybe it's a blessing that you've found this young man, after all. We *would* like to get to know him, really. Please, don't go.'

It was, Emily reflected later, very possibly the first time in her life that her mother had actually *asked* her to do something. She hesitated, not having learnt the appropriate response. Larry tugged her hand gently, pulling her back towards the sofa, making up her mind for her.

'I'll get some coffee,' said Bob. 'I think we all need some.'

'I'm taking over this case, Bateson,' Will Churchill observed casually on the steps outside the mortuary. 'You've enough unsolved mysteries on your plate as it is.'

Terry was stunned. There was no way this decision was based on concern for his personal welfare. 'May I ask why, sir?'

Churchill strolled towards his car. 'Simple. This is a high profile case that's likely to receive a lot of media exposure, so it deserves the best quality attention from our side.'

'And you think I can't provide that, sir?' The insult had to be deliberate. Churchill put a patronizing arm on his shoulder but withdrew it hurriedly at the look on Terry's face.

'What I think, Terence old son, is that your mind's on other things. Even this morning, you were late at the crime scene . . .'

'I was at my kid's school when I was called, sir. It only took a few minutes but it was important for her!'

'Well, exactly, there's an example. We all understand your family problems but it doesn't help your work. Look at this Harker case – the bugger gets off and why? Because his fancy knickers barrister catches you telling lies during interrogation! It was in the *Evening Press* – "York detective lies to rape suspect". How's that help public confidence in the police, eh? You tell me!'

'It was a trick with words, sir. All lawyers do it.'

'Only if we give them the chance. Plus she found an alibi witness you should have known about. So there we are, a public laughing stock. What's tonight's headline, do you think? "Serial rapist strikes again"?'

'More than likely, yes, sir.' Terry nodded, remembering the string of such articles since the Clayton and Whitaker cases. 'But this time we may have got him. After all, this girl Jasmine Hurst was killed in the same way as Maria Clayton – throat cut with a knife, out of doors in a lonely area – only this time he's left some semen. So maybe her killer killed Clayton as well.'

'Back to your serial rapist theory, eh, Terence?' Churchill laughed.

'Didn't you come to me, time and time again, claiming Gary Harker did all these crimes? Or did I dream that, perhaps? Tell me I dreamt it.'

'No, sir, that's what I said.'

'Yet here he is walking the streets again with three crimes unsolved. Or four, if you include this one. And even you can hardly tell me that Harker killed that girl in there!' His eyes widened in disbelief at the look on Terry's face. 'Oh come on, you can't believe that!'

'It is a very remote possibility, sir. As it happens he was free six or eight hours before she was killed. But there's no motive, no other connection.'

'No?' Churchill looked at him pityingly. 'Then I suggest you concentrate on the facts. Do you have any leads?'

'There is one, sir, yes. I was intending to talk to him later today.'

'Who's that then?'

'A lad called Simon Newby. Jasmine Hurst's ex-boyfriend. They quarrelled, apparently, and she left him.'

'Newby . . . Newby . . .' Churchill pondered. 'Don't I know that name?'

'His mother, sir,' Terry admitted reluctantly. 'She happens to be the barrister who defended Gary Harker.'

Churchill's mouth widened in a slow, incredulous grin. 'You're kidding.'

'No, sir, I'm not.'

'Well, there you are then!' Churchill laughed aloud. 'What's his address?'

Terry told him, and Churchill got swiftly into his car and drove away, still laughing. Terry sighed, thinking of Sarah trembling beside Jasmine's body, and the words of Dr Jones, the forensic pathologist, in front of Churchill later. *Evidence conclusive – you find the wicked laddie, gentlemen, and I'll send him down. No room for doubt.*

This was just the sort of case an ambitious Detective Chief Inspector would want, he thought, to make his mark in the media.

16

It was late afternoon when Terry located Jasmine Hurst's mother. According to Sarah the father had left and gone to Australia; Jasmine had one younger sister who lived with her mother in a small lodging house near the racecourse. Terry met a tall handsome woman of about fifty, cooking in a large kitchen where a pretty dark-haired twelve-year-old was doing her homework with her feet resting on an ancient Alsatian under the table.

The woman welcomed him with a friendly smile. I'm about to destroy your life, Terry thought. 'Mrs Miranda Hurst?'

'Yes.'

He showed his card. 'Are you the mother of Jasmine Hurst?'

'Yes.' The atmosphere of domestic happiness was jarring now. As though someone were screeching his fingernails down a blackboard slowly. 'Is she in some sort of trouble?'

'I'm afraid I have some bad news, Mrs Hurst. Perhaps you'd better sit down.'

In Terry's mind, the screech grew louder.

Bob didn't discuss it with Sarah. He knew it would create an impossible scene. She would want to prevent him and know that she shouldn't; the conflict would tear her to shreds. The responsibility must be his alone; with luck she'd know nothing about it.

Nonetheless his fingers shook as he pressed the buttons on the phone.

'Police. Can I help?'

'Er – hello. I want to talk to . . .' What was the name? . . . 'the detective investigating the death of Jasmine Hurst, please.'

'Hold the line.'

At least the police, thank God, did not play Vivaldi interspersed with recorded protestations about how all their detectives were busy right now. Just silence and the sound of his own blood pounding in his ears.

'DCI Churchill. Hello.'

'Er – hello.' His fingers fumbling, Bob placed a tissue across the mouth of the receiver. This is stupid, his conscience screamed, you're a grown man, a head teacher, you can't play silly games like this. But it works, I've seen it on TV. With his voice muffled he said: 'You're investigating the murder of that girl, Jasmine Hurst, aren't you?'

'Yes, that's right.' Churchill sounded puzzled. 'Do you know something about it?'

'There's a man you should ask. He's called Archibald Mullen, number 17 Bramham Street. Have you got that?'

'OK, but what can he tell us?'

'Ask him if he saw Simon Newby yesterday. He'll tell you.'

'Can I have your name, please, sir?'

'No, sorry.' Bob crashed the phone down, and used the tissue to mop his brow. What had he done? It felt awful. The image of Judas Iscariot came into his mind – Judas hanging himself in the garden. He understood why now. *He had betrayed his stepson!* He had done it and it couldn't be undone. And it was worse to have done it secretly like this, not better. He could never explain his reasons or defend their morality, *because no one knew he'd done it.*

He slumped at his desk with his head in his hands, groaning softly.

'Bob?' Sarah came in, and ran her hands lightly across his hair and shoulders. He could feel the tension in her fingers, too, but at least she was making an effort. 'Come on. It's been an awful couple of days, but at least we've got Emily back now. If we stick together we'll come through all this.'

He said nothing. Surprised, she cradled the back of his head against her breasts. It was the sort of gesture he loved, that had become all too rare in their busy lives. He tried to relax, but his body was rigid, frozen.

'Bob? What's the matter? Talk to me.'

Now or never. But he couldn't talk. He turned, put his arms around his wife, and held her silently. Feeling the soft feminine strength of her body. Seeing the image of Judas, swinging on a tree in the garden of Gethsemane, behind his closed eyelids.

Will Churchill was delighted. The informant's voice had sounded odd but it confirmed Terry's suspicion that the murder was connected with this boy Simon Newby. He collected Harry Easby, Tracy Litherland and Mike Candor and went straight round to Bramham Street. He pounded on Simon's front door. No answer.

'All right. Let's find this neighbour at number 17.'

Archibald Mullen greeted them eagerly, his yellow teeth parted in a knowing smile. 'You're late, young man. The lad's gone long since.'

'Who do you mean, Mr Mullen?'

'Simon Newby – him over't road. His car's not been here all day.'

'Do you know where he's gone?'

'Me? No, lad. But he went out last night after he hit yon lass in the street, that I do know. He drove off after her. This morning his car were gone and I've not seen him since.'

After he hit yon lass in the street. That was the key phrase. When Churchill and DS Litherland took his statement, the point became clearer. Simon had driven away in a blue Ford Escort about ten minutes after hitting the girl. When they presented Mullen with a photograph of the dead girl he unhesitatingly identified her as the one Simon had hit.

'Grand-looking lass – and she's dead, you say? By, there'll be a to-do about that, then. Pictures in the papers, no doubt!'

Outside in the street Will Churchill rapped orders as though he had a plane to catch.

'Harry, get on to DVLC and trace this car. Blue Escort, registered keeper Simon Newby, 23 Bramham Street. Got that? Mike, watch the house – if the lad turns up, pull him in. Tracy, get round to his parents' home, see what you can pick up there. I'll get a search warrant.'

*   *   *

117

After she had identified the body, Miranda Hurst sat on the green plastic sofa, pale and stunned. A WPC gave her tea.

'Is there anyone who might want to do this to your daughter, Mrs Hurst?' Terry asked.

'No. Of course not! She doesn't know anyone as monstrous as that, how could she?'

'I believe she knew a young man called Simon Newby?'

She looked up, tears smudging her mascara. 'Simon? Yes, she lived with him until perhaps . . . six weeks ago, something like that. You don't think *he* could have done this?'

'We don't think anything at the moment, Mrs Hurst, we're just trying to find out. Did she quarrel with him at all, as far as you know?'

'She did, yes. That's why she left him.'

'I see. And there was another boyfriend, later?'

'Yes, David. Brodie I think his surname is . . . I'm sorry, can I go now?'

'Yes, of course, Mrs Hurst. If you just happen to have this David Brodie's address?'

She wrote it down for him. Terry nodded at the WPC, who had seen him inflict a similar pain on Sarah Newby earlier that day. 'Call a car to take Mrs Hurst home, will you?'

As the pair walked slowly out he ran his hands through his hair and thought, How many more times? God. How many more?

'Mrs Newby? DS Tracy Litherland, police. I'd like to ask you a few questions, if I may? About your son, Simon. It might be better if we went inside.'

So it had begun, already. Grimly, Sarah led the way into the living room. 'My husband's asleep, I think. You may not know it, but we've had a hard couple of days.'

Bob was indeed asleep upstairs, and Emily had gone for a walk with Larry along the river bank, of all places. But they weren't worried about her now; she would come back. The four of them had spent the afternoon coming to an agreement which Sarah fervently hoped would work. Probably Emily and Larry were discussing it now.

The agreement was simple. If Emily would stay at home and complete her GCSEs, Larry could visit her as often as he wanted. He could help her with revision if he liked – but it had to be genuine revision, Bob had warned, with the bedroom door unlocked. Her mother is a real barrister and the law means what it says about girls under sixteen.

Sarah had winced, but to her relief Larry and Emily had agreed. It wasn't that much of a threat because the GCSEs started quite soon and Emily's birthday was a month later. But the great thing was that this Larry genuinely appeared to care for Emily and appreciate a little, at least, of their concern. Sarah rather liked him, too. He seemed naive and passionate but that is how the young are supposed to be. He wasn't bad-looking either; if she washed some of the dirt off, she could imagine how the lithe, skinny body under the ragged clothes could be quite appealing. Certainly Emily seemed to think so; but then she *knew*. And whatever she herself had done, Sarah had not wanted her own daughter to *know* boys in the biblical sense quite yet.

But if the boy stuck by Emily and gave her some emotional support, it might be the best thing that could happen. Neither she nor Bob had done enough of that recently; and now, with this disaster about Jasmine and Simon, it was going to be even harder. Sarah wasn't surprised that Bob was asleep; she herself had been sitting in an armchair for the past hour, thinking.

This detective was unwelcome. 'What do you want to know?'

'Did your son, Simon, have a relationship with Jasmine Hurst?'

'Yes. He loved her. I was about to go and break the news to him, when you came.'

'Well, I'll try not to keep you long,' Tracy said, diplomatically. 'Would you tell me about their relationship, please?'

Slowly, choosing her words with care, Sarah described her son's relationship with this young beautiful woman who now lay in the mortuary. Simon had met Jasmine a year ago, and brought her to this house several times. She had been a strikingly attractive girl, lithe, athletic, and Simon had been besotted with her. Sarah had been less impressed. The girl seemed to treat her son with quiet disdain, as though it amused her to have him running around her like a puppy. But Simon loved the girl, she repeated; he worshipped everything she did.

'Did they never quarrel?'

Sarah shrugged. 'Yes, they split up, about six weeks ago. She moved out of his house, went off with another boy.' She closed her mouth abruptly. She had no intention of telling this woman what Simon had confided in her, that Jasmine still visited him for occasional sex.

'Do you know where your son is now?'

'At his home, I suppose. I was going to see him. Some things you can't say by phone.'

'Before you go, Mrs Newby,' Tracy Litherland said, 'you should know that we have evidence that he was seen with a girl answering Jasmine's description last night, and that later he left home and hasn't been seen since.' Tracy briefly explained what the old man had said. 'Do you have any idea where he might have gone?'

'No.' This news shook Sarah considerably. 'Who told you about this old man?'

'I'm not at liberty to say.'

'You *are* treating him as a suspect, aren't you? The poor boy probably doesn't even know Jasmine's dead yet!'

'In that case we need to talk to him,' said Tracy carefully. 'He may have been the last person to see her alive, and he doesn't seem to be at home. Does he have grandparents, relatives, friends that he sometimes visits?'

Reluctantly, Sarah gave Tracy her parents' address, and a framed photograph of Simon. As she took it down she thought, First Emily, now Simon; I never knew it hurt so much.

'I want that back when you've copied it, please. And – what did you say your name was?'

'Detective Sergeant Tracy Litherland.'

'Yes, well, DS Litherland, I hope you're looking for other suspects too. Simon didn't kill this girl. He couldn't – he's not a murderer.'

Tracy had heard all this before from parents, many times. She responded with a detached professional compassion that Sarah recognized only too well from her own work.

'I hope you're right, Mrs Newby. I hope you're right.'

With a search warrant in his pocket, Churchill watched Mike Candor smash the lock.

Simon's house had a kitchen and living room downstairs, two bedrooms and a bathroom upstairs. The sagging armchair and sofa were strewn with magazines, socks and towels. There was a pyramid of empty beer cans in a corner, under a Manchester United poster and an old Pirelli calendar. The smell suggested that not all the beer cans had been empty when added to the decoration, if that was what it was. On some shelves in an alcove were a TV, video and CD player, all fairly new and in good order.

'I thought this lad was a part-time brickie,' said Churchill, staring at them in surprise. 'Where'd he get all this?'

Mike Candor shrugged. 'His parents, maybe? They're not short of a bob or two. Kids today, they take this stuff for granted, you know.' He was exploring the kitchen when Harry Easby gave a shout from upstairs.

'Sir! Come and have a look at these!'

He was in the smaller bedroom, not one dedicated to sleeping. The main piece of furniture was a padded exercise bench. Scattered around the floor were a weight-lifter's bar, a selection of weights, a skipping rope, some elastic stretching gear, a crumpled tracksuit, socks and trainers.

'Quite the fitness freak,' said Churchill, admiringly. 'So what's suspicious, Harry?'

'These, sir.' Carefully, Harry picked up a trainer by its lace. Will Churchill looked, and saw what he meant. The trainer was old and scuffed and muddy. As it twirled slowly in the air they saw little bits of grit and mud embedded in the sole, and the top of the shoe was stained green and brown, from mud and grass. The tread on the sole looked familiar.

'Weren't there some footprints near the body, sir?'

A slow smile crossed Churchill's face. 'There were, Harry. There were indeed.'

'Bob? Wake up, I've brought you something.'

He sat up in surprise. It was a long time since Sarah had done anything as domestic as bring him tea in bed. 'Oh, thanks.' He ran his hand through his tousled hair. 'What time is it?'

'Five thirty. In the afternoon.' She put the cup on a bedside table. 'Have a good sleep?'

'I suppose so, yes.' He had slept fully dressed – it was years since he had done that, too. He took his tea gratefully, then winced as memory flooded back. 'God, what a mess.'

'A policewoman came.'

'Why?'

'To get a photo of Simon, and ask about his relationship with Jasmine. They're treating him as a suspect, Bob.'

Bob sipped his tea and avoided her eyes. 'Why?'

'A witness claims he saw Simon with a girl like Jasmine. He hit her, this man claims.'

'Oh.'

She walked to the window. The wind was rustling the willow leaves in the garden. In the distance, she could see Emily and Larry, arm in arm on the river bank.

'Yes, *oh*. God knows where they found that out.'

She doesn't know I told them, Bob thought. *Thank God.* 'Do you think it's true?'

She hesitated. 'She did go back to him, sometimes. He *loved* that girl, Bob. I wish he hadn't, but he did. Maybe someone saw them together.'

'But the old man says he hit her. People do kill for love, Sarah.'

'Not Simon.' She turned, blood draining from her face. 'What are you talking about, *the old man*? Bob, do you know something about this?'

Nervously, Bob put down his cup. He felt ridiculous and vulnerable, sitting on the bed in his shirt and socks, with those bright hazel eyes glaring at him like a tigress. I should never have tried to deceive her, he thought, I have no gift for it.

'Look, I met this old man outside Simon's house when I was searching for Emily. He told me he'd seen Simon quarrel with a girl in the street. She was wearing Emily's coat, remember! I thought it was her!'

'So it was *you* who told them! For Christ's sake, Bob! Have you any idea what the police will make of this? What have you done?'

'The girl's dead, Sarah, this is deadly serious.'

'I know that – I saw her, damn it! But Simon's *our son*!'

In Bob's eyes Sarah read the cruel message: *Your son, not mine. Yours and Kevin's.* 'That doesn't mean he didn't do it. How much longer can you

121

blind your eyes to what he's like? Get real, Sarah – he's not your misunderstood little boy any more. He's a grown man.'

'*You rang the police and told them, Bob?* Without talking to me? *He's my son!*'

'That's exactly why I didn't discuss it with you. And because that poor girl Jasmine is somebody's daughter too. Was.'

'Don't preach to me, Bob, I'm not your school assembly.' She paused, then continued relentlessly. 'Would you have done this if he'd been your own son? If it had been Emily?'

'I think so, yes.' He wondered if it was true. 'I *have* tried with him, Sarah. You know that.'

'Over the years, yes.' Her first flood of rage ebbed, leaving a grey meaningless silt of despair. Is this what my marriage has come to? 'But we've given up, since he left home, haven't we? Both of us.'

'Maybe. He's nineteen years old, Sarah. He's a grown man.'

Sarah walked to the window, stared out unseeing at the willow tree and the river. She leaned her forehead against the glass to cool it. 'I thought we'd succeeded, in a way,' she said quietly, watching a heron lift itself laboriously into the air. What was the point of striving every hour God gave to live in an expensive environment like this if your son turned into a murderer? And your husband a Judas.

'You *shit*, Bob!' She whipped away from the window suddenly, slapping her palm against the wall in a second outburst of fury. 'By Christ, I wish you'd never met that old man! What were you doing there anyway?'

'Looking for Emily, I told you.'

'Yes, yes,' she said sarcastically. 'Always Emily. Would you have gone to look for Simon if he'd run away at fifteen? Or is that when you began to give up?'

'We both gave up . . .' Bob began, but Sarah shook her head decisively.

'No. Not me. Not now, not ever. Look, Bob, I've got to find him. Whether he did this or not he needs help now. You stay here with Emily, will you? Tell her where I've gone and why, if you can face it.'

'But we're supposed to be giving her support.'

'You do it.' She turned and was out of the bedroom door as she spoke.

'When will you be back?'

'When you see me.'

The words floated up from the hall below. The front door closed on her last word.

'If . . .'

'Yes, of course we have a search warrant, madam.'

Churchill held it out, and Sarah examined it meticulously, while he took in the incongruous sight of this slender woman in black motorcycle leathers, confronting him on the upstairs landing of Simon Newby's house. With her neat black shoulder-length hair, the leather jacket and trousers gave her an attractive boyish look, he thought, really quite fetching. But her brusque manner, the determination in her face and the tiny wrinkles around her keen cat-like eyes warned him that this was no child, no messenger girl to be brushed aside. This was the woman, after all, who had ruined Terry Bateson's case against Gary Harker.

'It's less than twenty-four hours since the girl was killed, isn't it?' she said sharply, handing the warrant back. 'Isn't that rather early to be smashing someone's door and making all this mess? Who's going to pay for it?'

'This is a murder enquiry, madam. The sooner we interview all suspects the more likely we are to get a result.'

'A result, yes, but maybe not the right one. This is my son you are talking about, Chief Inspector. He loved Jasmine Hurst, he'll be devastated by the news of her death. He doesn't need all this hassle as well.'

'We need to find him, madam. Do you know where he is?'

'No. I gave your detective the names and addresses of some relatives, have you enquired there yet? If he knows she's dead, perhaps he's gone away to grieve somewhere. He could be with friends, in a pub – how should I know?'

'You're his mother, wouldn't he come to you, if he was unhappy?'

'He might, but he hasn't. That's why I'm here.' She pushed past him, into Simon's bedroom where Harry Easby was indiscriminately throwing clothes on to the floor. 'Great God Almighty, what the devil are you doing?'

'Looking for evidence, madam,' Harry said.

'What evidence? Clean underwear? Who's going to clear all this up when you've gone?'

'It wasn't exactly tidy when we arrived,' said Churchill smoothly. 'And as you will know since you've seen the body, the young lady's throat was cut and there was a great deal of blood. So if we find bloodstains on your son's clothes, for example . . .'

'You'll be very lucky. Unless she cut herself or had a period while she was living here. That won't get you very far, will it?'

'Would these be your son's trainers?' Churchill asked, holding the old, muddy shoes in a plastic evidence bag.

'I've no idea,' said Sarah, looking at them scornfully. 'Anyway, where's the blood?'

'We'll leave that to forensics. All we're doing is looking for evidence at the moment, madam. Now I'm afraid I must ask you to leave.'

'I don't think so,' said Sarah coolly. 'This is *my* house.'

'What?'

'My husband and I paid the deposit on it, my son only pays the interest on the mortgage. So we're joint owners, as you could have found out if you'd asked before smashing the door down. I even have a key.' She took it out of her pocket and dangled it under his nose. 'I believe I have a right to stay in my own house while it's being searched?'

Churchill swore under his breath. 'So long as you don't impede our enquiries. But you may have a long wait. This is a serious investigation, we have to be thorough.'

'I'll survive. You get used to hanging around at the Bar. And perhaps you can tidy up and write out an acknowledgement for the damage to the door, before you go?'

She scored a few points but, after the other shocks of the day, it had an appalling emotional effect on her. When the police eventually left, making rudimentary attempts to stuff clothes back into drawers, an immense aching weariness flooded through her. She made herself a cup of strong coffee in the small, grubby kitchen and slumped on a stool to drink it.

It had been a dreadful few days – the disappearance of Emily, the death of Jasmine, and now this. *Simon, what have you done?*

She remembered the last time she had seen him, at court. He'd seemed angry then, but he was often like that. He felt he had failed in life, been betrayed by everyone. Abandoned by his father, Kevin, unable to live up to the expectations of herself and Bob. Christ! Was it *her* fault then, Bob's fault? God knew they had both tried, but the boy was so difficult, always wanting to do everything his own way, and always making a mess of it – no wonder he was so full of rage and resentment.

Or at least he had been until he met Jasmine. Sarah had never liked the girl but she'd made Simon happy, and proud, too, for a while. For Jasmine had been a stunning, drop-dead beauty – her son had strutted beside her like a bantam cock with two tails; worshipped the girl like a slave.

And Jasmine had known it. Known she could leave him and still come back, whenever she chose.

Was that enough to make him kill her? Had he finally realized what a bitch the girl could be, and turned on her in a jealous fury? It was possible, Sarah supposed. But actually cut her throat with a knife – Simon? Her baby whom she had bred in her body, fed with her own milk, taught to smile and walk and laugh – *could he do that?*

She imagined Jasmine's terror as she realized what was going to happen to her. Sarah remembered her own terror, when Kevin had beaten her before he left. Kevin, Simon's natural father. It hadn't been just the beating, the sense of betrayal; the really frightening part had been the way Kevin had seemed to *enjoy* her own fear. Like father, like son, she thought – is there a trait for murder in Simon's genes?

But half his genes are mine, so what does he inherit from me? They say I'm aggressive, single-minded, intolerant of failure, desperate for success at all costs. It's true; but those are virtues too. How else could a teenage single mum, a battered wife, progress from a run-down council estate to the Bar? It's Simon who's had the back hand of them; the neglect, the lack of time, the impatience, the impossible example to follow.

And so he left me for Jasmine – his living pin-up, his angel – and she betrayed him too. When he cut her throat, was it *my* memory that he was murdering?

If he murdered anyone.

I won't believe it, she told herself, I can't. Not my son.

17

Next morning Churchill called a meeting to assess what they'd got. Harry had bullied the car registration out of DVLC Swansea, and circulated it throughout the country. Tracy described her meeting with Sarah Newby. 'I got this photo and some addresses, sir. But she wasn't particularly co-operative – all right, what's so funny?'

A rash of grins and nudges spread amongst the men.

'She savaged us last night, Trace,' Churchill explained. 'Didn't you notice Mike clutching his balls just now? She-wolf in defence of her young.'

'Oh . . .' Tracy smiled sympathetically. 'Well, she probably saw what a load of wimps you are. Anyway, look at this.' She put the photo of Simon beside the photofit of Helen Steersby's assailant. 'What do you think?'

In the photo, Simon's red-gold hair was cut very short, the neat, round face clean shaven with a broad, pugilistic nose and light brown eyes. The skin was pink and healthy, the smiling mouth showed strong white teeth. The left ear was small and close to the head, with a gold ring in it.

The hair of the man in the photofit was hidden by the black woolly hat. His jaw was shaded with black stubble, his eyebrows darker than those in the photo, the eyes smaller and wider apart. The mouth was small, grim-looking. There was a ring in the left ear, which stuck out prominently. The unusually broad nose and round, neat shape of the face, though, were the same.

'Not identical twins, are they, Trace?' Churchill said doubtfully.

'But look at that hooter,' Mike Candor pointed out. 'And the ring in the ear.'

'That's the fashion,' Churchill said. 'Terence – you've met the lad. What do you think?'

'I think we should be cautious, sir,' Terry said, frowning at Tracy. Why hadn't she told him first before making this public in front of Churchill, of all people? 'Assault victims are pretty unreliable about facial identification, are they?'

Churchill laughed derisively. *'Cautious, unreliable?* This is the guy, ladies and gents, who took Gary Harker to court when his victim claimed to recognize him with a hood over his bonce!'

'That was different, sir. Anyway it was his voice she recognized, not his face.'

Churchill waved this away. 'Look. This is a lead for that attack on Helen Steersby, and you're rubbishing it already. We've got an attempted assault in the same area as this murder, by a guy with a striking feature like that nose. What more do you want? Well spotted, Trace.'

He turned back to Terry. 'What sort of lad is he?'

Terry thought back. 'Strong. Fit. Short-tempered, maybe. But no record, sir – I checked. And if he had this girlfriend, Jasmine, a real beauty by all accounts, why on earth would he go round scaring schoolkids? It doesn't add up.'

'Yes, but she'd left him,' Tracy said. 'Six weeks ago.'

'So what are you saying?' Terry persisted. 'That he got frustrated and started dragging schoolgirls off their ponies? We're looking for a nutter for that, a psycho. This lad seemed quite normal to me.'

'Normal? This is your impression when – Thursday morning?' Churchill's contempt was blatant. 'But on Thursday evening, this *quite normal* young lad seems to have raped his girlfriend in the woods and cut her throat. Maybe your judgement's not what it was, old son.'

Terry was silent. However cruelly put, Churchill had a point. Gary Harker was free, and now this. Maybe his own skills were waning. The others avoided his eyes. Once he'd been the blue-eyed boy with the sharp brain, on the fast track for promotion. Now his colleagues' respect was changing to pity. Probably he still hadn't got over Mary's death; perhaps he never would.

Churchill flipped a cigarette into his mouth and lit it with a snap of his lighter. 'Let's run through the rest. What have we got from the crime scene, Jack? We know her throat was cut and there was blood everywhere. What about footprints? That's what we need to know.'

Jack Middleton pointed to a photograph. 'Look here, sir. This is the best print we've got so far. It looks like a trainer, just a couple of feet from the body. I've taken a cast, but I haven't identified it yet.'

'Well, have a look at these, then.' Triumphantly, Will Churchill held up the evidence bag with Simon's muddy trainers in. 'Will they match it, do you think?'

'What size are they?'

'Ten. Nikes.'

Jack Middleton turned the bag over to look at the soles. A cautious smile spread on his face. 'Maybe, yes. I'll scan these into the computer. Is there any blood on the shoes?'

'Not obviously, but there are a lot of stains. If forensics find something, then we've got him. We found this, too.' He held up a second bag for every to see. Inside it was a large strongly made breadknife with a black handle.

'The pathologist says the cut was so deep it almost took her head off. Now in order to do that you need a weapon that's big, sharp and very strong – an ordinary blade would snap under the pressure. But this isn't an ordinary breadknife, it's an expensive one – tempered steel nearly two millimetres thick, from young Newby's kitchen. It looks clean, but if forensics find something . . .'

'Then we've got him,' Tracy Litherland said softly.

'Exactly,' Churchill agreed. 'Anything else from the crime scene, Jack?'

'Not so far, sir. We're combing it carefully for hairs and fibres, but that'll take time.'

'Never mind. The key evidence is in the body, not the grass.' Churchill surveyed the room triumphantly. 'Our man left his calling card, in the proper place. Semen, for us to identify him by. So if we catch him, boys and girls, that's it. Tracy can take a sample of his sperm . . .'

'You what, sir?'

'Joke, Tracy, joke. And if the DNA matches we lock him up for life. Even his clever barrister mummy won't be able to break a case like that, eh, Terence?'

Terry Bateson rang the bell of a small terraced house to the south of the city. The front of the house was fifty yards from the tree protest at the new shopping centre, the back looked over fields to the river bank where Jasmine's body had been found. A slightly built young man in a dressing gown peered out. 'Yes?'

'David Brodie?' Terry showed his warrant card. 'It's about Jasmine Hurst, I'm afraid.'

'Oh . . . yes. You'd better come in.'

Terry followed him into a small but immaculate kitchen. All the surfaces were clean, the cups on hooks, the knives in a wooden block screwed to the wall. 'She's dead, isn't she? Her mother rang me last night. I've not had much sleep.' He sat down at the table, his eyes red-rimmed with tiredness.

'I'm sorry, Mr Brodie. Would you rather I came back at another time?'

'No, it's OK, let's get it over with.'

'You have no idea who might have done this?'

Brodie shook his head. 'No. He'd have to be a madman, wouldn't he?'

'I understand Jasmine lived here with you. Is that right?'

'Yes. Most of the time. Except when she's at the protest. She sleeps . . . slept there sometimes. I go there too when I have time.'

'Really?' Terry looked at the young man in his neat, comfortable kitchen, and tried to imagine him in a treehouse.

Brodie smiled. 'Doesn't seem likely to you, does it? Well, I agree, I hate the mess and the dirt, so I don't sleep there. But it's a principle those people are standing up for. So yes, I support them when I can.'

'What about Jasmine? Did she sleep there this week?'

Brodie hesitated. 'Once or twice, yes. I'm on the late shift, you see. I leave here about one and don't get back until about eleven at night.'

'So when you got back on Thursday night, and she wasn't here, were you worried?'

Brodie looked away, out of the window, his eyes filling with tears. 'Not really. I just thought . . . hoped . . . she was at the protest. My mistake, I see now.'

'So when was the last time you saw her?'

'Thursday morning. We . . . had a row, you see. She walked out.'

'What was the row about?'

Brodie shook his head sadly. 'I can't really say. I'm sorry, this probably sounds stupid, but it was just . . . one of those emotional things where you think everything's fine, and then find it's not, you know? It started about *cleaning*, for heaven's sake; she said I was too fussy, but . . .'

'Was it about her other boyfriend, Simon Newby?'

Brodie's eyes widened in surprise. 'Part of it was, yes. How do you know about him? Oh, I suppose her mother told you.'

Terry remembered the Simon Newby he had met two days ago. A fit, muscular young man, quite unlike the slight, almost delicate boy he was talking to now. There was something about this young man that repelled him slightly. Too clean, too sensitive somehow.

'So what did she say about Simon?'

'She said – oh, stupid things – that I wasn't tough or strong, that I wasn't a man like him. Well, we knew that already – he's a yob, isn't he, a lout. That's why she left him in the first place, because he used to beat her up. I said if that's what she wanted she could go back and welcome – to live in a pigsty with a yob instead of a decent house where somebody cared for her.'

'He used to beat her up?'

'Yes. He even hit me, once, for Christ's sake.'

'When was that?'

'Oh, I don't know, six weeks ago. When she first left him. He saw Jasmine outside this house and when I told him to leave her alone he just hit me. Punched me in the face, the sod.'

'Then what happened?'

'He went away. But it was weird. He used to follow us around.' He paused, staring at Terry with those pale, red-rimmed eyes. 'Sometimes we couldn't see him but we could feel it.'

'You could feel it? How do you mean?'

'It's hard to describe. We just knew. Or we'd see a jogger in the distance and she'd say it was him. She often felt she was being followed. I wrote down some of the times.' The young man took out a diary. 'There, see. On a Monday. And then again the next Sunday.'

Terry leafed through the pages. There were five or six entries: *Simon outside house. Jogger near protest, Simon? Simon(?) near river.* And so on. He thought of Helen Steersby, and shuddered. 'Do you mind if I borrow this?'

David hesitated. 'It's . . . got some private entries in too.'

'I'm sorry about that. But this is important. I'll photocopy it and give it back to you. It must have been very frightening for you, all this.'

'It wasn't very pleasant, not for me anyway. But you know, Jasmine was never scared of him. I even think she enjoyed it, in a way.'

'*Enjoyed* it?'

'Yes. I mean, having two men to choose between. That was what our quarrel was about. She'd seen him again and I called her a bitch – God help me! I didn't know she was going to die!'

'Jasmine went back to Simon? When was this?'

'Last week. I didn't think she'd go again but it seems she did. If I'd stopped her she'd be alive now, wouldn't she?'

Terry looked at him thoughtfully. 'So, when she wasn't here on Thursday night, where did you think she was?'

'At Simon's, of course. Either there or at the protest.'

'Did you look for her?'

'Not that night. Yesterday morning, yes. I went to the protest, but she wasn't there. Then I went to Simon's house but she wasn't there either.'

'You didn't think of informing the police?'

'No. She's an adult, after all. I went to work, hoped she'd be here when I returned. Then her mother rang.' He wiped his eyes with a tissue, and blew his nose. 'It's hard to come to terms with, really . . . I'm sorry.'

'I understand, Mr Brodie. But if you could write all this down in a statement . . .'

Sarah was defending in a shoplifting case. Her client was an old lady who had been stopped by a store detective outside a small supermarket. Inside her shopping bag was a packet of bacon which had not been paid for. Also inside the shopping bag were eggs, milk and bread, all of which *had* been paid for. Sarah's client claimed that she had taken the bacon by mistake, in a fit of absent-mindedness. The supermarket, however, disagreed.

It was the prosecution's case that the bacon had been found *concealed underneath the old lady's library book,* this being clear evidence of *mens rea* in a deliberate, malicious and diabolically cunning criminal act in direct contravention of the Theft Act of 1968. The supermarket had been as stubborn and bloody-minded in bringing the charge as Sarah's client had been in refusing to have it dealt with by the magistrates, and so the packet of bacon now rested in lonely splendour on the exhibits table while the matter was disputed at a cost to the taxpayer in excess of a thousand pounds.

Normally Sarah would have enjoyed this farce, playing the well-paid battle of wits like a game of tennis, but today, with Simon missing, she found it hard to concentrate. Her attempt to establish that the old lady was confused by her medication was skilfully countered by the prosecutor, Savendra, whose devious smile and exquisite good manners charmed Sarah's client into admitting that she mistrusted her doctor, had poured her pills down the sink, and had hated the mini-supermarket ever since it had driven her corner shop out of business ten years before.

The jury, being thus convinced that she was of sound mind and evil intent, convicted. The judge sighed, gave her a conditional discharge and told her not to be so silly in future. Sarah made her way moodily back to her chambers.

'Buy you lunch?' Savendra offered, catching her up. 'Bacon sandwich, on the house?'

'Savvy, I'm not in the mood. I've got a son suspected of murder, in case you've forgotten.'

'Yeah, I know, I'm sorry. They haven't caught him yet, have they?'

'Not yet, but they will. They always do.'

'No they don't.' Savendra darted in front of her, forcing her to look at him. 'They *don't* always catch them, Sarah, you know that.'

'Well, that isn't the point, is it? We're not talking about some professional crook here, on the run to Bolivia, we're talking about my son, Simon! They think he's a murderer. And just to convince them, he's run away!'

'It doesn't look good, does it?'

'No.' Sarah shook her head wearily, as though bothered by a fly. 'So don't make jokes about it, Savvy. It's tearing me apart.'

He fell into step beside her. 'Seriously, come and have lunch. You look like you're wasting away. Come on. Somewhere quiet where we can talk.'

At the forensics department Will Churchill met Dr Theobald Brewer, a slow-moving gentleman in his mid-sixties for whom retirement and a life devoted to growing the perfect Brewer rose was only a few months away. He contemplated the young DCI with benign detachment.

'Yes, we've had some success with your trainers,' he said. 'There were traces of sandy soil consistent with the crime scene. And a number of grass seeds. Laila is working on them at the moment.' He indicated a tall young woman with clear black skin and dreadlocks, elegantly perched over a microscope. 'Oh, excuse me a moment, would you?'

Dr Brewer leaned out of the window, where a gardener was spraying roses. 'Hey, young man! You missed the Princess Mary on the left. It was infested with greenfly yesterday . . .'

Exasperated, Churchill caught the gaze of the young scientist, who was smothering a grin.

Dr Brewer was incensed. 'Look, I'll have to go outside and deal with this, Inspector. Laila will take care of you.'

Relieved, Churchill approached the young woman. 'Is there any blood on the trainers?'

'A few small stains, Inspector, yes.' She smiled, perfect white teeth and twinkling olive-brown eyes. 'Several in between the indentations on the sole of the left shoe, and five drops on the upper surface. They look just like tiny spatters of mud, but it's blood nevertheless.'

'*Yes!* You beauty!' Churchill enthused. 'And do they match the victim's DNA?'

'That takes time, sir,' Laila murmured, fitting a slide delicately under the microscope. 'We've sent samples away to Manchester. But the blood group is consistent with that on the breadknife.'

'There's blood on the breadknife too?'

'Yes. Just a few stains, in the groove where the blade fits into the handle.'

'That's it then! All we need is for those samples to match the victim and we've got him!'

Dr Brewer was berating the gardener outside the window. Churchill grinned at the young black woman, who favoured him with a conspiratorial, bewitching smile. There was no doubt which of the two scientists he needed to work with, to move this case forward quickly.

Perhaps he should drop by tomorrow, to see how things had progressed.

'So where could he have gone?' Savendra asked. He and Sarah were sitting upstairs at the quiet corner table of an expensive Indian restaurant overlooking the River Ouse. Sarah picked sparingly at her korma, but it and the champagne earned from Savendra's victory in this morning's farce had warmed her nonetheless; she had eaten little for the past few days.

'Even if I could tell you I wouldn't,' she said. 'Much though I respect your discretion.'

'This isn't a professional consultation,' said Savendra, twirling the stem of his wineglass. 'Just friends, that's all.'

'I know, and thanks. But I don't know where he is anyway. In one way I'm glad of it.'

'Do you think he could – you know, have done it?'

For a long time she didn't answer. So long, he thought she wouldn't.

But he could detect no hostility in her silence; just something reflective, silent, thoughtful. A loss of words.

At last she stirred. 'Do you want to have children one day, Savvy?'

He smiled, remembering, as he often forgot, that she was seven years older than him. 'When I meet the right woman, yes, I suppose. It happens, doesn't it?'

'It happens, yes. And is Belinda the right woman?'

'She thinks she is. I'm . . . *almost* convinced. But you haven't answered my question.'

'If . . . *when* you marry your Belinda, Savvy, as I'm sure you will, if she wants you to, and you have children, your life will change for ever. You will no longer belong to yourself – this happy, charming, carefree young barrister that I see before me, with no allegiance to anything but his fees and his motorbike – he will disappear, and part of him will belong to Belinda, and part of him, perhaps more of him, I don't know, to those children. Sometimes you will love them and sometimes they will make you angry. More angry than you can easily believe. And of course in your anger you can betray them, and they can betray you, but you won't let that happen if you possibly can . . .'

She stopped, running one finger softly round the top of her wineglass. She looked in his eyes, then away out of the window. He waited, but nothing more came.

'So even if you thought he did it, you wouldn't say?'

She smiled, and as she did so the tears came involuntarily to her eyes.

'That's it, Savvy, exactly. I couldn't possibly say. Lesson one in parenthood. You pass.'

She reached out to touch his hand, and for a moment his fingers entwined with hers, supportively. As friends.

18

The phone call came in the middle of the night. A few days after Simon had disappeared, an alert police constable in Scarborough noticed a blue Ford Escort, with the right registration number, parked outside a guest house. The message reached York at 2.15 a.m., and the duty sergeant phoned Will Churchill at home with a certain sardonic glee, which rose to pure sadistic delight when the new Detective Chief Inspector's phone was answered by a sleepy young woman.

'Hello . . . yes?'

'This is Fulford police station, madam. Is DCI Churchill there, please?'

'Who?'

'Detective Chief Inspector William Churchill, madam. It *is* urgent.'

'Oh, you mean Willy? Yes . . . Christ . . . it's for you.'

'Hello? Who the hell's this?'

'Chief Inspector Churchill?'

'Yes.' *Don't be long, Willy,* murmured a voice in the background, or so the sergeant would tell his friends in the canteen later, to predictable guffaws. *Was he long, sarge? How long exactly – did she say?*

'Duty Sergeant Chisholm, sir. Sorry to disturb you, but a car registered to Simon Newby has been found in Scarborough – a blue Ford Escort.'

'Right. I'm on my way. Have they made an arrest?'

'No, sir. They're keeping the car under surveillance.'

'Good. Put me through to the crime desk, will you? I'll need someone to come with me to Scarborough right away.'

'Right, sir.' Sergeant Chisholm transferred the call, grinning at PC Burrows who had just brought him a welcome mug of coffee.

'That's something you'll learn, son, when you've been here a while.'

'What's that, sarge?'

'A keen detective's always on the job.' He winked, and sipped his coffee happily.

It was a windy morning in Scarborough when Churchill and Harry Easby arrived shortly before four, with the breakers bursting white in their head-lights along the esplanade. The blue Escort was parked outside a peeling establishment called Seaview Villas. The only things moving in the street were a few used fish and chip wrappers, whirled in eddies by the wind.

DS Conroy waited at one end of the street, a uniform car at the other. 'We've made enquiries, sir, and your man's in room 7. DC Lane's getting a key from the landlady now.'

'Right. Send your uniform lads round the back, and we'll go in.'

Three minutes later the four of them pounded up the worn stair carpet, surprising an old man tottering towards the loo on the landing. Inside room 7 lay a young man, sleeping peacefully. Churchill held the photo-graph next to the face on the pillow. There was no doubt at all. They matched. He shook the boy roughly by the shoulder and he started up in shock.

'Simon Newby, I am arresting you in connection with the murder of Jasmine Hurst. You do not have to say anything, but it may harm your defence if you do not mention when questioned something which you later rely on in court. Anything you do say may be given in evidence.'

'What? Who the hell are you?'

'Come on, lad, we're off to York.'

* * *

Simon was handcuffed and bundled into the car in his pyjama trousers and a coat before he fully realized what was happening. Harry Easby waited with him there while Churchill and the two Scarborough officers searched his room and sealed his clothes in plastic evidence bags.

'What's going on?' Simon asked desperately.

'You're under arrest, son, didn't you hear? For the murder of Jasmine Hurst.'

'For the what? *Jasmine?* You're out of your skull!'

'Not me, son. We think you killed her.'

'You mean she's *dead? Jasmine?* Where? How?'

'You tell me, son.' The boy was in a panic, thrashing about. But he couldn't get out because his hands were cuffed behind his back and he was held in place by the seat belt.

'She can't be dead! What are you doing – let me out of here!'

Easby watched him with a quiet, satisfied smile. The wild eyes, the tears, the desperate thrashing movements. He had seen them all before. They might mean either guilt or innocence – most likely just panic. As Simon struggled, he watched, and said nothing.

Churchill returned to the car with two bags of clothes which he flung into the boot. He opened the back door and glanced at Simon with a fierce, triumphant smile. 'Gotcha!'

'I didn't kill her. Let me out – where are we going?'

'To York, my son. Remember anything you say may be used in evidence. Sit still now.'

'But how did she die? What happened, for Christ's sake?'

As Harry drove Churchill examined his prisoner with a long contemplative stare. He looked a mess – unshaven, his short hair tousled with sleep, his eyes wide with shock and panic. As he twisted angrily in his seat Churchill could see the muscles that he and Harry had felt as they bundled the lad downstairs. More than enough to subdue a girl, however tall and fit.

'You can't just break in and tell me Jasmine's dead, for Christ's sake! It's not true!'

'When did you last see her?' They weren't supposed to interview a suspect in the car but if the boy was going to talk anyway they couldn't very well gag him.

'I haven't seen her for days – weeks. What happened – how did she die?'

'She was raped, and someone cut her throat with a knife.'

'*Oh no.*' The bald statement seemed to shock Simon, and dissolve his rage and panic into grief. He slumped sideways on the seat and began to weep. It was a human reaction that in a normal person might mean innocence, Churchill knew; but in his experience rapists and murderers were not normal people. They were *normal-looking* people whose emotional wires had got horribly crossed. It was perfectly possible for a murderer to weep at the injuries he had himself caused, either out of remorse or schizophrenia or self-pity because his own guilt had been discovered. So all that mattered was the evidence.

'It made me puke, seeing that girl's body,' Harry said. 'People like you should be hanged, slowly.'

'But I *didn't kill her!*' The car swayed with the violence of Simon's response. 'So shut your fucking trap!'

'Stow it, Harry,' Churchill ordered. 'Questions at the station.'

'Sir.'

Several more times during the journey Simon protested his innocence, but when Churchill made no response, he lapsed into silence. As they entered York he asked: 'What happens now?'

'You go into a cell and the custody sergeant gives you breakfast, and then we'll have a proper recorded interview.'

'I can have a lawyer, can't I?'

'If you want. I'll call the duty solicitor.'

'No. My mother's a barrister, she knows who's best. I want to call her.'

Churchill sighed. 'All right, it's your choice. But I suggest you tell the truth, son. That's my advice to you.'

It was a rare event for Sarah and Emily to eat breakfast together; usually everyone grabbed their own in a headlong rush. Now both of them, shattered by the last few days, were attempting to restore their relationship. Out of consideration for Sarah, Emily had switched on the pop music station more quietly than usual; out of consideration for Emily, Sarah had refrained from switching it off.

'Which exam are you most worried about?' Sarah asked tentatively.

Emily frowned, and instead of dismissing the question as Sarah had expected, considered it. 'History, I think.'

'Why?'

'Well, there's such masses to learn, far more than any other subject; and then you don't get proper essay questions which let you explain it. It's all "What does this cartoon of Adolf Hitler prove" – stuff like that.'

'Is there anything I can help you with?'

'Mum, it's better if I do it on my own, honest. We'd only quarrel.'

'Well, maybe Larry knows some history. Are you going to see him today?'

As Emily nodded, the phone rang. She got up, a slice of toast in her hand. 'I bet that's him. Hello? Oh, *Simon!* God, where are you? Yes, she's here.'

As she passed the phone over Emily noticed her mother sway for a second in shock; but the hint of weakness was gone as soon as it came. With a recovery so complete it was almost a change of personality, Sarah's voice became crisp, sharp, businesslike.

'Yes. Right. I'll get someone down there right away. In the meantime say nothing to anyone. Do you understand? Just say your solicitor's coming and you can't answer any questions until you've spoken to her. And you're entitled to food and rest and decent treatment so if you don't get it, ask to see the custody sergeant. Say if you're not treated properly there'll be a complaint. And Simon – I'll be coming too.'

As Lucy Sampson entered the main police station, she was relieved not to see a reporter. But it was only a matter of time. Few of her clients came from middle-class families, and when they did, in a small city like York, there was enormous potential for social embarrassment. The *Evening Press* would be delighted – a local barrister's son charged with murder! It would be the talk of the legal circuit for months; it might ruin Sarah's career.

'Yes, madam?' The young desk constable looked up reluctantly from the *Sun*.

'I'm a solicitor. I've been called to a client in custody here – Mr Simon Newby.'

'Mr' was an important touch. Despite the safeguards of the Police and Criminal Evidence Act, the processes of arrest still stripped the accused of freedom, dignity and sometimes their clothes as well; it was her job to get all of these back, if she could.

'Right, madam, if you'll wait there.'

'I need to see the officer in charge of this case, right away. My client is facing a murder enquiry, young man; I don't intend to sit around like a spare piece of furniture.'

'I dunno . . .' The constable met her eyes. 'I'll see what I can do . . .'

A faint grin crossed Lucy's face. She had that sort of effect on young men nowadays; Savendra had once suggested, unkindly, that she reminded them of their mothers when they were being potty trained. Not flattering, perhaps, but it had its uses. Lucy was a large woman who had abandoned the struggle with diets and corsets years ago. She disguised her bulk in a long voluminous black skirt, white blouse and loose jacket with many useful pockets. Her feet spread comfortably in Doc Martens boots, a fashion she had adopted from her teenage son. When her hair had started to go grey she'd had it bleached pure white in an anti-ageist fashion statement.

The constable returned with Will Churchill, who held out his hand.

'Mrs Sampson? I'm the officer who arrested Simon Newby.'

Lucy nodded, ignoring the hand. 'Then I'd like to see him straight away. And I'll need the custody file.'

'Certainly.' Churchill showed her into a room with a table bolted to the floor, two chairs, and a buzzing neon light. As Simon came in she saw a tall, well-built young man with hazel eyes which reminded her irresistibly of his mother. His face was bewildered, sullen and defiant.

'Did my mum send you?'

136

'She did. She's outside. We've worked together a lot, your mother and I.'

'Well, you'd better be good. You've got to get me out of here.'

'I'll do my best.' Lucy smiled cautiously.

'I didn't kill her, you know.'

'Then that's what matters. I'm on your side, Simon. That's why I'm here.'

'Thank Christ for that. Nobody else is. They don't believe me.'

'Have you said anything to them so far?'

'I told them I haven't seen Jasmine for weeks.'

Lucy frowned. 'That's not what your mother told me. She said you'd been seen quarrelling with Jasmine outside your house, the night she was killed.'

'Oh, God.' Simon sat down abruptly. 'How did they know that?'

'A neighbour saw you. An old man apparently.' Lucy pulled a pad of paper from her briefcase. 'So you'd better tell the truth about that, Simon. Come on, I can't help you unless I know the full story. Let's start from the beginning, shall we? Tell me about you and Jasmine.'

Simon scowled and turned away, facing the wall. It was a response Lucy had seen many times before and it was not, she knew, a good sign.

'Why do you need to know about that?'

She spoke very gently. 'Because she's dead, Simon, and if I'm going to help you I have to know your story. Will you tell me? Simon?'

After a long, sullen silence Simon sighed, leaned forward, and began to talk.

'Right. It's now 11.15 a.m.,' said Churchill, with a meaningful glare at Lucy, who had delayed the interview for nearly two hours. 'We are at Fulford police station in York. Present in the room are Simon Newby, his solicitor Mrs Lucy Sampson, DCI William Churchill and DC Harry Easby. This interview will be recorded and a copy of the tape will be made available to Mr Newby's legal representative. Now then, Simon. Let me repeat the words of the caution . . .'

As he did so Simon avoided his eyes. He seemed tired, nervous, jumpy, Churchill thought. Guilty, almost certainly.

'Right. First I have to show you my notes of what you said in the car. If you agree they are a correct record, you should sign them at the bottom.' He passed over a sheet of paper.

At 3.47 a.m. on Tuesday 18th May, DCI Churchill of York police, accompanied by DC Easby of York police and DS Conroy and DC Lane of Scarborough police, entered room 7 of Seaview Villas in Whitton Street, Scarborough where Simon Newby was found to be asleep in bed. DCI Churchill woke Mr Newby and informed him that he was being arrested on suspicion of the murder of Jasmine Hurst. He was cautioned that he need not say anything, but that it might harm his defence if he did not mention when questioned something which he later relied on in court, and that anything which he did say might be given in evidence. Mr Newby was then escorted to a police car and driven from Scarborough to York.

After being cautioned, Mr Newby stated that he had not killed Jasmine Hurst, and that he had not seen her for weeks. He repeated this statement several times.

Churchill passed Simon a pen. 'Here. If it's a true record sign at the bottom.'

'No, wait . . .' The text terrified Simon. 'No, I didn't say that.'

'You did, son. I heard you – we both did. Several times.'

Simon turned to Lucy in panic. 'Well, I didn't know what I was saying, I –'

'Mr Churchill, did you interview my client in the car?'

'No, Mrs Sampson, of course we didn't. This is a record of voluntary statements made under caution.' He gave her a brief, dismissive glance, then focused his attention back on Simon. 'You told us you didn't kill Jasmine, and you hadn't seen her for weeks. Those were your own words, Simon. Are you now saying they aren't true?'

'Yes. No. No, it isn't true.'

'Which part isn't true?' Churchill asked silkily. 'That you didn't kill Jasmine?'

'No! Of course not that.' Simon hid his face in his hands, confused. 'I . . . I *had* seen her.'

'When?'

'The day before I went to Scarborough.'

'Last Thursday night?'

'Yes.' Simon glanced at Lucy. 'Tell him.'

'Before we go any further, Detective Chief Inspector,' Lucy intervened, 'my client has a statement to make.' She passed a piece of paper across the table. 'He wrote this a few minutes ago. I think it will help explain things.'

Will Churchill picked the paper up and began to read aloud.

'I met Jasmine Hurst a year ago and became very fond of her. In October she came to live with me at 23 Bramham Street and she stayed until March, when she left me. She said she was tired of me and had a new boyfriend. His name is David Brodie and he lives with her at 8a Stillingfleet Road. I went there once to ask Jasmine to come back and live with me but she wouldn't. I've met her a few times since then but only briefly. On Thursday 13th May I met her by the river and she came back to my house for a meal. I asked her to come back and live with me but she wouldn't. We argued about this and then she left. When she left I was upset so I decided to go to Scarborough for a holiday, to try to get over her. I drove to Scarborough that night and didn't see Jasmine again. I had no idea Jasmine was dead until the police arrested me this morning. I did not kill her and I don't know how she died. Simon Newby.'

Churchill looked at Harry and laughed. 'That's not what you said in the car, is it?'

'No, well, I was scared. I didn't even know she was dead until you told me. What am I supposed to say?'

'The truth, son.'

'Well, I have now. That's it, there on that paper.'

'So if you have no evidence against my client,' said Lucy, 'I would ask you to drop this mistaken charge and release him now.'

'Oh, you would, would you?' Churchill put a plastic evidence bag on the table. Inside it were a pair of muddy trainers. 'Well, we do have evidence, Mrs Sampson.' He spoke clearly so the tape would catch his every word. 'I'm showing Mr Newby a pair of men's Nike trainers, size 10. Do you recognize these, Simon?'

'No.'

'They were found in your house. They're yours, aren't they?'

Simon shrugged. 'Maybe. Lots of people have trainers like that.'

'Well, these trainers were found in your house, and they have mud and grass on them similar to the mud and grass found near Jasmine's body. There were also footprints there which appear to fit these trainers.'

'So? Like I said, thousands of people have trainers like that.'

'And the mud and grass?'

'I go running. That's what they're for.'

'Yes, sure.' Churchill leaned forward, watching Simon intently. 'And the blood?'

'What blood?' Simon's face paled. 'Where?'

Churchill pointed, to a group of faint, unremarkable brown stains on the toe just below the laces on the left shoe. Then he turned the shoe over and pointed with a pen at the indentations on the sole. 'Here, and here. They don't look much, but they're going to send you to prison for a long time, my son. Because the forensic scientists have examined these stains, and they're group AB negative, which is the same group as Jasmine Hurst. It's her blood, Simon, isn't it? You got it on your shoes when you killed her.'

'But I didn't kill her!' Simon half rose to his feet, shouting. 'Give me those shoes! They're not mine!'

Churchill held the shoes away from him, smiling. 'They *are* yours, Simon. They're the shoes the murderer wore, and they were found in your house, in your bedroom, with her blood on. Does anyone else live in your house?'

'No.' Simon sat down slowly.

'Anyone else keep their training shoes there?'

'No. But . . .'

'Well then. What about this?' Churchill produced another evidence bag. 'I'm showing Mr Newby a breadknife with a black handle. We found this in your house too. Is this yours?'

'No. How should I know?'

139

'There are fingerprints on here, Simon. We'll be matching them with yours later.' He paused, savouring the moment, staring intently into the eyes of the boy and his silent solicitor. 'This knife's got Jasmine Hurst's blood on, too!'

'It can't have! You're lying! Look, the blade's clean anyhow!'

'I didn't say it was on the blade, did I? No doubt you cleaned the blade after you killed her, and thought that was enough. But our cunning scientists have looked here, in the crack where the blade joins the handle, and they've found blood there, you see. Same blood group, AB negative. Jasmine Hurst's blood group. Blood from when you cut her throat.'

'I didn't! Say that again, you bastard . . .' Once again Simon half rose, but Lucy put her hand on his arm and, to her great relief, he sat down.

'Just listen to them, Simon,' she said. 'You don't have to answer, if you don't want to.'

'But it can't be her blood! I didn't kill her, I tell you!'

'Well, we'll see.' Churchill smiled patronizingly. 'Ever heard of DNA, Simon? We've sent samples of this blood away for DNA analysis and then we'll see for certain whose it is. That'll prove it one way or the other.'

'It'll prove it's not hers, then.'

'Will it? We'll see. You didn't rape her either, I suppose?'

'What? Of course not.'

Churchill gave a cold wolfish grin. 'So you won't mind giving a DNA sample, will you?'

Lucy could feel cold sweat trickling under her blouse. 'I'd like to consult with my client again . . .' she began, falteringly. But Churchill overrode her. 'In a minute, in a minute. First let me tell your client what we need the sample for, OK? You see, Simon, the man who killed Jasmine – the man who wore these trainers and used that knife – he didn't just kill her, he raped her first. And when he raped her, he left certain intimate body samples which will help us identify him. So if you don't mind, we need to take a DNA sample from you to compare with the DNA that the murderer left in her body. If you're innocent it may help to prove it. But if not . . .'

Will Churchill paused, letting the silence hang heavy in the room. Simon had his head in his hands, sobbing quietly. In a quiet, relentless voice Churchill continued. 'This means taking a swab from your mouth and a few hairs from your head. It won't hurt. But I must warn you that if you don't offer these samples voluntarily I can obtain them forcibly. Do you understand?'

Simon nodded, still weeping. The interview had lasted scarcely ten minutes but Churchill was sure the damage had been done. If the boy was going to confess, now was the time. Lucy Sampson tried to catch his eye. 'I really must insist, Chief Inspector . . .'

Simon muttered something which Churchill couldn't hear. 'What was that, lad?'

Simon looked up, his face, red, tear-stained. 'I said the semen will be mine!'

'Yours?' *Yes!* Churchill thought. *We've got him!*

'Simon, wait.' Lucy touched his hand but he ignored her, looking directly at Churchill.

'You heard. That's what I said.'

Churchill tried to hide the surge of triumph singing through his veins. 'All right. Do you want to tell me about it, lad?'

'Yes. Yes, I do.'

This is where he convicts himself, Lucy thought. If he really wants to confess, nothing I can say will stop him. But what will I tell his mother, waiting outside?

When Lucy came out Sarah thought she looked shattered, as though she had walked into a wall in the dark. But when the big woman came closer she realized that the familiar fighting spirit, the determination, were still there beneath her exhaustion.

'Well, what is it? Can I see him?'

'No. They won't let you, Sarah, I'm sorry. He's been charged and remanded to Hull. You can see him there.'

'But . . . *charged*? They think he did it then?'

'Obviously.' Lucy looked at her friend and thought, what a question for a barrister! But this woman in front of her was no high-powered lawyer, she was a mother, anxious for news of her son. She took Sarah gently by the arm.

'Come on, it'll be easier outside. We'll talk in my car.'

In the car Lucy went through the evidence slowly. First the footprints, the Nike trainers, the knife and the tiny stains of blood. 'AB negative. That's not Simon's group, is it? He might have cut himself.'

'I don't think so. I think he's O, like me. I'll ring the doctor to check.'

'They're sending it for DNA analysis anyway, so that'll prove it one way or the other. But Sarah, that's not the worst thing.' She looked at her friend sadly. 'The big thing is the semen. That's what we spent most of the time talking about.'

'What? She was raped, you mean?'

Lucy nodded. 'You didn't know?'

Sarah shook her head, and groaned. 'No. No, they never told me that. Trying to spare my feelings, I suppose. *Dear God!* Is there no end to this?'

'I'm sorry, Sarah. I thought you knew.'

'Yes, well, I had to know sometime. What are they saying? Simon did this too?'

'Not necessarily. They've taken a DNA sample from him, of course. But Simon's done himself a service there, thank God.'

'What do you mean? How?'

To Sarah's astonishment, a faint smile flickered on Lucy's lips. She laughed – a soft appreciative chuckle that gave Sarah the first tiny ray of hope she'd had that day.

'You should have seen that detective's face! He was sure Simon was going to confess and so was I, believe me. Simon said the semen was his – I tried to stop him but I couldn't, and I thought that's it, it's all over, but it wasn't. Because his story is that he and Jasmine made love that afternoon, inside his house. No rape, just sex. That's why she came there, according to him – that's what she wanted. It wasn't the first time, either – apparently she's been back several times, since she left him, poor lad. Do you think that's likely?'

She glanced at Sarah, instantly regretting the question. What could Simon's mother say but . . . 'As a matter of fact, yes. He told me that before. He was besotted with her, and . . . well, I shouldn't say this now she's dead, but she had him wrapped round her little finger. She liked teasing him; maybe she did the same to her new boyfriend too.'

'Well, there we are then. So he's given himself a chance, at least, with this story. The trouble is, they still insist she was raped.'

'How can they prove that?'

'Bruising to the vagina, according to young Winston in there. He went on and on – how did Simon account for that? Did he like to hurt her when they made love? When he said they made love did that mean rape? On and on until I said he was harassing my client. He's a nasty piece of work, I tell you.'

'I've met him. But did Simon admit rape?'

'No. He was quite clear about that and I don't think he'll change it. And of course, if he's telling the truth and she *was* raped, later, by someone else, the DNA analysis ought to show the real rapist's semen too. In which case, with the story he's told now, I'd say your boy might just be in the clear.'

'Yes. Maybe. *If* . . . and if that blood is his or at least not hers.' Sarah took a long, shuddering breath. 'So I suppose all we've got to do is wait.'

Lucy smiled, touched Sarah's shoulder gently. 'When was it ever any different?'

'It was always different, Lucy. Always, every time before this. Because before, it happened to other people. Not to me.'

19

Sarah had been to Hull prison many times before, but today it was a different place. The great black-studded gates seemed larger; the echoing corridors louder, filthier; the cat-calls and wolf-whistles more threatening. She had to queue with other visiting mothers; have her handbag searched by a contemptuous prison officer.

She came with Bob, too, which made it worse. As they were herded through the prison yard he shuddered at the packets of excrement thrown from cell windows overnight, and shrank from the other visitors.

Simon sat opposite them and looked down at the table, ashamed.

'You came then.'

'Of course we came, Simon,' Sarah said. 'As soon as we could.'

For a while none of them spoke. Simon resumed his nervous scrutiny of the table; Bob stared at his stepson coldly, as though at a delinquent he was being forced to accept into his school. In the end Simon began.

'You've spoken to that solicitor woman?'

'Lucy? Yes, I've talked to her, Simon. It . . . doesn't look brilliant.'

'Not brilliant? They think I killed her, Mum!'

'And did you, Simon?' Bob's voice was hard, like a slap in the face.

'What?'

'Did you kill her?'

Simon began to shake his head, slowly at first, then faster and more violently. '*No!*'

'Not rape her either?'

'No, I bloody well did not!' He got up abruptly, leaning over the table directly into Bob's face. 'How dare you come here, asking me questions like that? If you don't believe me don't come, you're not bloody wanted!'

Heads turned in the room. A girl at the next table sniggered. The guard folded his arms.

'You were the last one to see her, Simon,' Bob persisted. 'You hit her. A man saw you.'

'What are you, a bloody policeman? Just shut up, will you!'

'I need to know, Simon. We both do.'

Sarah thought, Bob's going to get hit, and he'll deserve it too; but instead Simon pushed his face close to his stepfather's and said: 'Well I didn't do it, OK? So now you know. If you don't believe me you can go fuck yourself.'

Everyone was watching now. Here in a prison visiting room, my son swearing at my husband. From a deep well of sadness, Sarah spoke. 'Simon, it's all right. Sit down. Please.'

For a second he glared at her, as if trying to decide who she was and whether to spit in her face. Then the rage left him. He sat, running his hands through his hair. 'I didn't do it, Mum, whatever he thinks. Whatever anyone . . .'

'It's all right, Simon, I believe you.'

'. . . I mean I don't even know where it happened, so . . . *you believe me?*'

'Yes.'

'Yeah, well. At least there's one of you.' He reached for her hand, across the table. She felt the tension in his fingers, and clasped his hand in hers, for comfort. He turned to Bob.

'What about you then?'

'I don't know, Simon. I'd like to . . .'

'Oh yes, you'd *like* to believe me,' Simon sneered. 'Only you can't manage it, right? You'd *like* to believe your stepson isn't a filthy murderer who raped his girlfriend and cut her throat, only you're not absolutely sure so you'd rather think about it first and check in the *Guardian* to see what their opinion is this week, is that it? Then maybe you'll let me know!'

'Simon, stop it!' Sarah clung tightly to his hand, partly to comfort him but mostly because she feared he might seize Bob by the throat. She should never have brought Bob; he just provoked Simon. And he wasn't finished yet.

'Sneer if you like, Simon, but that girl was raped before she died and you admit you had sex with her.'

'Yes, well, so I did, but it doesn't mean I raped her!'

'They've found her blood on your trainers.'

'It's not her blood. They may not be my trainers for all you know!'

'Oh come on, Simon, give the police some credit!'

Simon shuddered. 'So you think I did it, then, do you? That's all the proof you need?'

Bob shook his head sadly. 'What else could any reasonable person think?'

'Well, you're wrong, that's all! I didn't kill her and that's it! It wasn't me!'

For a moment none of them spoke. A tiny amount of Simon's anger subsided and he said: 'I loved that girl. You wouldn't understand that – you hated her, both of you!'

'*I* didn't hate her, Simon,' Sarah said.

'Yes, you did! You drove her away! Not *educated* enough for you, was she?' He snatched his hand away. Tears came into Sarah's eyes.

'This is hard for us all, Simon,' said Bob. 'Your mother had to identify her body, you know.'

Simon was shocked. '*You* had to do that? Mum? See Jasmine's body?'

Sarah nodded. 'In the mortuary.'

'But . . . why you?'

'They thought it was Emily.' Sarah explained, briefly, the events of that awful day, and how Emily had given Jasmine her jacket at the protest. 'She must have been wearing it, Simon, when you saw her.'

'Probably. I didn't think.' Simon looked down again at his hands, and for a while none of them spoke, an island of silence in the noisy, crowded room. 'What did she look like?' he asked at last. 'Jasmine. When you saw her?'

How do I answer that, Sarah wondered? None of this is easy. When she thought back to the mortuary all she could remember was the fear, and the appalling flood of relief afterwards. The body's appearance had mattered less than who it was. And who it wasn't.

'I only saw her face. It was very pale, I think. Pale, with a bruise on her cheek, and . . . some marks of twigs on her skin. Her eyes were closed. She was . . . a very beautiful girl, Simon.'

'Oh, I know that. Too damn pretty for her own good.' He brushed the tears away roughly with the back of his hand. 'And I hit her. *God!* I didn't know I'd never see her again, did I?'

'Did you cut her cheek when you hit her?' Bob intervened, in a more conciliatory tone.

'Oh come on, what are you talking about now? It was just a slap. Why . . .?'

'I thought maybe that's how her blood got on your trainers.'

'No. Christ, what are you tormenting me with this for? How did you get blood on your shoes, all this! I don't bloody know, is the answer!'

'I'm only trying to help . . .'

'Well don't. I don't want you here, go home!'

Sarah grasped her son's hands again, across the table. 'Don't give up, Simon. *I* believe you. I'm your mother.' *But mothers don't really count.* She saw it in Simon's eyes.

'Yeah, but that's just it, in't it? It's all these other bastards – Bob, the police . . .'

'We'll convince them too. You're innocent until proven guilty. Remember that.'

'That's just lawyers' talk, Mum. They don't think like that.'

'I *am* a lawyer, remember? And it *is* true. It's a lawyer's job to *make* it true.'

'Well, I hope to Christ you're right, because it doesn't look like that from here. And that other lawyer, that Lucy woman, she's no friggin' good, is she?'

'She's a good solicitor, Simon. She's doing her best for you.'

'Why am I banged up in here then? All day with nowt to do, and no room to move.'

'Because it's a serious charge. You don't get bail for murder.'

'I could get locked up for life, couldn't I?'

'Not if they can't prove it. If you're not guilty they won't be able to.'

As she answered, Sarah realized that people were getting to their feet. A prison officer was coming straight towards them.

'That's not true, Mum – innocent people get locked up, all the time. You've told me!'

The prison officer had his hand on Simon's shoulder. 'Time's up, son.'

As Simon stood up, his eyes still fixed on his mother's, she said: 'Not this time, Simon. I won't let it happen.'

She regretted those words all the long drive back to York. It was a promise too great to keep. She had meant to leave him some hope, but what hope was there, really? The evidence seemed too strong. Simon had been the last person to see Jasmine alive, he'd had sex with her, quarrelled with her and hit her. Then he'd run away to Scarborough. If the blood on his trainers and breadknife were hers too, there was enough evidence for any court to convict him.

But I don't believe it. I *can't*.

Don't. *Can't*. Don't. *Can't*.

Well, which is it, she asked herself, as Bob drove the Volvo along the long undulating roads to York. Do I *believe* he's innocent, or just *hope* he is because he's my son?

I wouldn't normally ask questions like these. If he maintained his innocence I would defend him, and what I believed wouldn't matter. But I'm not his barrister now, I'm his mother.

Bob drove silently beside her. The tension in his manner had grown worse since they left the prison. Sarah ignored it, focusing her thoughts on Simon. Her son had always liked to be active, outdoors, involved in sports. What was there in the prison – a snooker table, perhaps, shared by a hundred young men? And most of the time shut up in a tiny cell. What would he do – press-ups on the floor, pace up and down, two paces north, two paces south, again and again . . .

'I shouldn't have come,' Bob said.

'What?'

'He didn't want me; I only made things worse. Anyway if he is guilty as it seems then . . .'

'Bob? What are you saying?'

'Just look at the evidence, Sarah. How could you say you believe him? He was the last person to see her, he hit her . . .'

'Listen, Bob, there's still a case to defend. There must be. There's no evidence that puts Simon anywhere near this crime. He hasn't confessed, and your horrid old man only saw him hit her in the face, nothing else. And you may not be aware of it, but the police are searching for a serial rapist in the York area. You're not telling me that's Simon too, are you?'

'Not so far as I know, no, but –'

'For Christ's sake, what's got into you? *Not so far as you know!*'

'I'm sorry, but he did lie, Sarah, like he's lied to us, lots of times. Especially to me . . .'

'What about? Homework, drugs, pocket money? All teenagers do that, Bob. Look at your precious Emily, running off for days without a word! It doesn't make her a murderer, does it?'

'I'm just looking at the evidence straight, Sarah. We know he was the last to see her, we know he lies, we know he hit her . . .'

And so it went on; Bob's voice clanged like a relentless bell in her ear. As they entered their drive she made a decision. 'Look, Bob. You don't believe Simon but I do. I have to. I need some time on my own to think this through, and get some rest.'

'On your own where?' Bob turned, puzzled, the front door key in his hand.

'Simon's house. I'll spend tonight there – maybe two nights. You can look after Emily, and we won't quarrel. It'll be best for everyone.'

'But you can think *here*!'

'No, not with you in this mood. It's serious, Bob – you think Simon's guilty of murder!'

'All I said was the evidence points that way. For God's sake, Sarah! Emily needs you here, even if I don't!'

'She doesn't need to hear us quarrel. Just a couple of nights. We're under a lot of strain. I need space to think.'

'Well . . . if you'll be all right?'

'I'll be fine. Just leave me alone, OK? That's all I need, right now.'

And it was easy, really. When she explained to Emily, the girl simply shrugged and turned back to her books. So she packed a few clothes and cosmetics into the motorcycle panniers, climbed into her leathers, and rode away. Feeling strangely lightheaded, as though her wheels didn't touch the ground. Exhaustion, probably.

So easy to walk out of a marriage. Is that what I'm doing?

For a few nights. That's all.

It was dark by the time she got there. She wheeled the motorbike through a narrow archway off the street into Simon's back yard, a small area eight yards deep by five across, divided from the neighbours by brick walls seven feet high. A door at the back of the yard led into an alley, beside a substantial brick shed made of the old outside loo and coal store.

She pushed the bike into the cluttered darkness of the shed. The front wheel clashed against a paint can and a plastic bag fell across the saddle. Working by feel, she padlocked the rear wheel. Then she found her key to the back door and went into the house, carrying the fish and chips she had bought on the way.

The house was cold, dirty and untidy. It reminded her of the council house she and Kevin had moved into nineteen years ago, before Simon was born. Basic, battered, grimy, but a home for all that. Somewhere you could make a start. Which was what Simon had tried to do, she supposed. When he'd met her outside court he'd talked of new shelves and decent furniture . . . and now this. A half-painted wall, a heap of beer cans in the corner, *Loaded* and *GQ* magazines on the floor, a mouldy curry container beside the CD player.

No wonder Jasmine hadn't wanted to stay. They surely had something to argue about, if he asked her to live in a tip like this. But that doesn't mean he murdered her, though.

She put the fish and chips in the oven to warm up. Then she slung the curry container into the bin with the magazines. She found a mop, bucket and unused bottle of bleach in a cupboard, and got rid of a series of stains on the floor and worktop. Then she sat at the kitchen table, eating the fish and chips while the floor dried around her.

He *is* like his father Kevin, she thought. Our house in Seacroft had a chance because we moved in together. And so Kevin expected me to start nest-building, to make it neat and tidy and a proper home. That was my role, and he had a place in it too, the wage-earner and handyman. So he played along, until the baby got too demanding and I was too boring and we were too poor, every day scrimp and save without end.

And we were both too young – he was anyway. He wanted to be out with the lads, spending his money on himself instead of me and the baby.

Now what? Sarah washed up her plate and sat in the battered, filthy armchair, staring at the video and expensive CD player underneath. Simon's priorities. Several of the videotape covers, she saw, were quite blatantly pornographic.

Like father, like son. Kevin would have fitted in here well, she thought. The Kevin she remembered, the seventeen-year-old boy with the beautiful silky hard body, the best lover she'd ever had, the toughest little gamecock on the street, the most selfish bastard she'd ever shared a house with. If he'd lived alone, his house would have been a tip like this. And if I'd come later and tried to clean it up he'd have hit me; he was like that.

But he would never have killed me, surely?

In her mind she replayed the times Kevin had hit her. She remembered her fear, the sudden explosion of his anger, the sadistic pleasure in his eyes. And then it had been over, a minute or two of horror, then done. Perhaps, if he'd gone on . . . but he never had. His rage had died, he'd flung her contemptuously on the floor, and left. The last time, for good.

The memory frightened her. In the corner, she saw a bottle of whisky. It's been a terrible day, she thought; I need some comfort. She found a tumbler in the kitchen and half-filled it. I came here to think, she remembered, that's what I told Bob. What is there to think about?

Is my son a killer?

The whisky burned its way down her throat and she thought, *No, of course not*, it can't be true. I didn't carry a killer in my body for nine months. Things like that can't happen. Not to me. It's true his father was a sadist, but that doesn't make him a murderer, does it?

You wouldn't want to tell a jury about that, would you?

No. Nor would you want a jury to think about the pain and jealousy which must have consumed this violent, unpredictable youth after this exquisitely beautiful girl had lived with him, rejected him, come tantalizingly back into his life, and then rejected him all over again. That's the oldest motive in the world.

Yes, maybe, but it's all circumstantial. To convict him we need *evidence*, hard irrefutable evidence that it was really Simon who cut her throat, raped her and left her there for the insects and dogs to eat. Not someone else.

His semen was in her vagina.

Did he rape her here and then murder her later? Is that what happened?

The police think it all happened on the path by the river.

She could picture that more clearly. In her mind she saw a girl walking alone on the river path, a dark figure following a short distance behind her. Suddenly the girl saw him and tried to run – but it was too late, he knocked her down, pinned her beneath him. She fought, but he twisted her arm, and a knife blade gleamed in the moonlight, paralyzing her with fear. He hauled her up, and shoved her in front of him into the trees, her arm twisted behind her, the knife at her throat.

And then in her imagination they were gone, mercifully hidden from sight, and she didn't want to see what happened next, what he did to her, how long it took, how it hurt. But later in her mind she saw him come out on to the path, a dark figure in the moonlight, and she tried to see his face, to see if this monster could be her son – but the face was invisible, black as the night.

Sarah shuddered, and groped for the bottle. She seldom drank much but tonight the whisky seemed essential. Could it have happened like that? The vision had seemed so real, until the crucial moment when she'd been unable to see the murderer's face. Could the murderer have sat in this grubby armchair like me? Been in my body as a baby?

She stared at her empty glass solemnly. Then poured herself another.

In the morning she was woken by bright sunlight pouring though the bedroom curtains. She sat up, and a lump of pig iron lurched sideways inside her skull. She fell back, stunned, and for a while – a few seconds, half an hour, a week – watched the birth of the universe, from big bang to supernova, unroll behind her eyelids. Then she became urgently aware that her stomach wished to leave her body and reached the loo just in time to help it on its way. Sometime later she gazed with horror at the pale, trembling face of a sick woman in the mirror on the wall.

She hadn't felt this bad since she was pregnant. Not even then. Slowly, taking several aeons to complete the task, she opened a bottle of paracetamol, crawled to the kitchen to whisk up an egg in warm milk, then crept upstairs on her hands and knees, and went back to sleep.

Hours later she awoke to discover that the pig iron in her head had shrunk to a musket ball behind her right eye. Cautiously, so as not to dislodge it, she sat up, swallowed some more paracetamol, and crept to the bathroom for a cold wash. By twelve o'clock she was dressed, and eighty per cent conscious. Disgusted with herself, she slung the empty whisky bottle into the bin.

So this is how I behave when I try to sort myself out. Bob would be appalled. *I'm* appalled. I'm a mother, a wife, a barrister. Get a grip, woman. Get out of here.

She went out to the Kawasaki in the shed. The bike gleamed comfortingly. She patted its saddle and looked around. She was not surprised by the mess; if Simon couldn't tidy his own bedroom he was unlikely to make a fetish of an outside shed. There was a battered table under the window, a broken chair, a pile of half-empty paint tins, brushes with rock-hard heads jammed into a saucepan, some plastic chairs, several bin bags, and a pot with a brown, dead plant in it.

She picked up the bin bag which had fallen as she wheeled the bike in last night. A woolly hat dropped out, and something clattered down the side of the bike and lodged between the exhaust and the chain.

Cautiously, trying not to revive her headache, Sarah searched for it with her fingers. What was it – a coin, a metal washer perhaps? Whatever it was, if she left it there it would jam up the chain somehow and wreck the bike; that always happened with her and machines.

After several attempts the thing fell out. She picked it up and brushed off the dirt. It was a small golden ring, set with tiny stones in the shape of a snake, or an S. Sarah held it up to the light. A woman's ring, an engagement ring perhaps. S for what?

Simon?

She slipped it on her finger. Who would have a ring with S for Simon on it? Jasmine, obviously. But why was it here, in a bag in this shed? Another of Simon's failures, perhaps – he'd proposed to her with it and she'd dumped him. Or . . . what else was in the bag?

She picked up the other thing, the black woolly hat which had fallen out at the same time, and laid it carefully on the table. It wasn't a woolly hat, as she had thought. Not quite. As she unfolded it she saw the two holes cut in it for eyes. Nothing for the mouth. The sort used by terrorists. And robbers. *And rapists.*

The sort of hood that Sharon Gilbert had described. Here – in Simon's shed. *Why?*

Sarah's knees felt suddenly weak. She grasped the edge of the table and stared down at the repulsive thing. The blank eye slits gazed back up at her. What did it mean?

Jasmine's ring. A hood. What else was in this bag? Trembling, she fumbled inside. A pair of black jeans, a jumper. Nothing else. She put on her motorcycle gauntlets and examined the clothes more closely. Would there be blood – *please no*. So far as she could see there was none but forensics, she knew, could trace specks invisible to the naked eye. The police should have searched this shed but they obviously hadn't. *What did it all mean?*

Her head was still fuddled with the hangover. She found it hard to think clearly. But one thing seemed obvious. This balaclava was found in Simon's shed with Jasmine's ring. It must be his. The police may say he wore it when he killed Jasmine.

No one said anything about Jasmine's murderer wearing a balaclava.

How could they? There were no witnesses. Only Jasmine, and she's dead.

It's not Simon's, this thing. I've never seen him wear one. Why would he?

It's here in his shed. At the very least it's evidence.

If the police want evidence they must find it for themselves. That's their job.

It doesn't matter, it's my duty to give it to the police. I have no choice.

No!!

But it's evidence, isn't it? And I've found it. If I'm caught concealing evidence I'll be struck off, I'll never practise as a barrister again. I'll just be a mother.

You're a mother first and last.

The lawyer's voice in her head was firm, insistent, rational, but the mother's was more persuasive. Sarah gripped the edge of the table, staring at the wretched balaclava and ring. Why did I ever come in here? If I hadn't looked I would never have found them. No one would.

If Adam hadn't eaten the apple he'd never have known good and evil. But he ate and I looked so we both know something, though God knows what it means. Probably Adam was confused, too. Who did he talk to? Eve? I know who I've got to discuss this with right now.

Sarah stuffed the hood into her saddle bag, unlocked her bike, and rode towards Hull.

It's not a question of being *just a mother*, she told the lawyer's voice in her mind. That's not a role or a career choice you can try out for a while. It's a life sentence.

The prison was as depressing, the queues and searches as long and humiliating as before. She left the balaclava with the bike, to avoid the search; the ring was on her finger.

'You came without him then?' He glanced at her warily.

'Without Bob? Yes. He's teaching today.'

'Yeah, well.' Simon shrugged. 'I doubt he wanted to come anyway.'

'It's difficult for him, Simon. He's not used to places like this.'

'You think *I* am? Christ, Mum! Do you know how small the cells are? They lock you in all night with a stranger and this stinking bucket. It's gross. It's fucking medieval.'

'I know, Simon, and I'm sorry. But there's nothing I can do about it. Really.'

He took a deep breath, to control himself. 'Look. I've been thinking . . . about that blood.'

Something in his eyes made her shiver. It was a look she had seen so often before – the infinitely cunning look of a rat caught in a trap, a criminal about to change his story because his life depended on it. 'The blood on the shoe and the knife, you mean?'

'Yeah. Look, *if* it's hers – they don't know for certain, do they?'

'Not yet, no.'

'Then I've remembered. There's a way it might have happened.'

She waited, a well of infinite sadness rising inside her.

'You see, it wasn't that day, it was earlier in the week. We spent most of that afternoon in bed too, making love. But one time she got up, to make tea and toast. Well, she wore my shirt – she often did that, she looked good in it. She wore my trainers too. You know, like slippers. Well, when she came upstairs she'd wrapped a tissue round her thumb because she'd cut it. It wasn't a big cut but it was bleeding. So I got her a plaster and put it on. That's it.'

He stopped. His mother said nothing.

'Don't you see? Maybe she cut herself with the breadknife and some blood fell on my shoes. That's why it's there!'

It was a remote possibility, Sarah thought. Either that or a good lie – hard to prove either way. 'Just a few days before? So the cut on her thumb must still be there?'

'Yeah.' He nodded earnestly. 'With a plaster on it. I put it there myself.'

'Well, I can check. We're not even sure it's her blood yet. All these things take time.'

'How much time? Until the trial?'

'Six months, at least. Maybe more.'

'Six months, in here? *No!*'

She sighed. 'I'm sorry, Simon, it's out of my hands. Look, there's something I came to say. I've . . . got some questions.' She glanced around cautiously, lowering her voice to ensure they were not overheard. 'This morning I found two things in your shed which I can't explain. One was a black balaclava hood. You know, the sort terrorists wear, that you can pull over your face, with two holes for eyes.'

'So?'

'*So?* Don't be stupid, Simon. *Is it yours?*'

'How should I know?'

'Simon! This was in a bag in your shed! How did it get there?'

'God knows. I haven't been in that shed for months, Mum.' He gazed at her, a puzzled frown on his face. 'You said there were two things. What else?'

'This ring. On my finger. Just look at it quickly, Simon,' she whispered urgently. 'Don't let the screws see. Do you recognize it?'

'No. Never seen it before.'

'It's not Jasmine's? It's got an S for Simon on it.'

'No. She didn't like rings. I told you, I never saw it before.'

'So how did it get in the bag with this balaclava hood, then?'

'Well, as to the balaclava, lots of blokes have 'em. Bit of a laugh, like, you can make your own with a pair of scissors, pull it down and give folk a shock.'

'Simon! Do you do that?'

'May have done, once or twice. For a laugh.'

A laugh, she thought. God save us all from young men. 'So it could be yours?'

'No. I've not done it since school, Mum.'

'There were jeans and a jumper in the bag too, Simon. What about them?'

'I dunno. Maybe old ones that I slung out.'

There was something very wrong here. Something he was not telling her. 'Look, how can these things be in your shed if they're not yours? Don't say you don't know – the police won't believe that!'

'The police? What's this got to do with them? What *is* this, Mum?'

'Simon, are you completely stupid? Don't you know there've been other attacks on women apart from Jasmine?'

His face paled. 'What attacks? Has someone else been killed?'

'No, no one else has been killed recently. But there was the murder of that Clayton woman last year, and that rape case I defended, and another attack on a woman called Whitaker. Surely you must have read about them?'

'I don't read that stuff. What's it to do with me, anyhow?'

'The police are looking for what they call a serial rapist. And now that they think you killed Jasmine . . .'

'They think I did these others too?' His eyes widened, he clutched his head between his hands. 'Oh come on, they can't be that desperate!'

'The police *are* desperate, Simon, that's exactly what they are. But so far they've got nothing that fits. Until you. So if they find this hood in your shed . . .'

'You're not going to show it to them, Mum? You can't!'

'No, I can't. But Simon, I need to understand –'

'Time's up, everyone! Come on now, hurry along!' The warder was coming towards them. Only a few seconds left. Simon leaned forward earnestly.

'You chuck those things away, Mum, right? Get rid of 'em quick!'

'Yes, Simon, but . . .' The warder had his hand on Simon's shoulder.

'You sort it, Mum, please. I trust you. You're a lawyer, you know what to do.'

No I don't, Sarah thought, watching him led away. I haven't got the first idea.

20

The coffee slopped into the tray as Sarah put it down on the Formica-topped table. She had stopped at a transport café on the way back to York. She slumped into a seat, sipped the lukewarm, viscous-looking liquid, then pushed it away in disgust. She leaned her elbows on the table and buried her fists in her hair, tugging at it until her scalp hurt.

What was she to do? Normally she thought of herself as a forceful, decisive person who took a grip on events and controlled them, but not now. What was going wrong?

She had told herself there was no evidence and then found some. She had confronted Simon with this hood and ring, hoping that he would provide an innocent explanation. But he hadn't, had he? Not really. He had said he knew nothing of the ring and blustered about the hood but what had really hurt her was his eyes, the way they had avoided hers the whole time. And at first he'd pretended it was a *joke*, for heaven's sake!

If he had been a hostile witness with an attitude like that, she would have crucified him. And that's the point, she thought desperately. He *will* be on the stand and this stuff is evidence. I wish I'd never found it.

'Is this seat free, love?'

She looked up and saw a man in a checked shirt with a tray of all-day fried breakfast grinning down at her. The café was fairly full, there were no spare tables near her.

'Yeah, sure.'

'Ta.' He sat down, propped the *Sun* against the ketchup bottle, and began to saw his way into the double eggs, fried bread, sausage, bacon and beans. Sarah stared away from him, out of the window.

The point was she'd not only found it, she'd contaminated it too. Her fingerprints would be all over the ring and although she didn't think you could get prints off a woollen hood the fact that she'd touched it and taken it to Hull would complicate matters horribly if it ever came to court. She felt an icy wave flow through her as she imagined the scene. 'Why did you do that, Mrs Newby? You are aware, are you not, that all criminal evidence should be properly examined by the police?' '*I did it because he was my son!*' 'Were you intending to hide the evidence or tamper with it in some way?' She closed her eyes and shuddered.

'You all right, love?' The lorry driver was staring at her over his newspaper, a forkful of food half-way to his mouth.

'What? Yes, fine, thanks.'

'You don't look fine. You went all pale like, I thought you were going to faint.'

'No, I'm OK, really. Just a bit tired and cold, that's all.' She took a second slurp of the coffee, or whatever it was.

'Cold, on a day like this? You on a bike?' He nodded at the helmet and gauntlets on the table, which made the answer obvious. Sarah nodded.

'Wish my missus had the figure to fit in them biking leathers. They suit you.'

Oh God. Not here, not now, please. 'Thanks. My husband thinks so too. He's a boxer.'

She favoured him with the ghost of smile, letting her eyes dwell on the paunch beneath his shirt.

'Oh, yeah. No offence.' He carried on feeding while she sipped the vile coffee and gazed into the car park. Even if Bob *were* a boxer he'd still be useless, she thought bitterly. He got us into this, betraying his own stepson to the police. How could he do that?

But then what am *I* going to do with this hood and this ring?

The ring was still on her finger: it felt unreasonably heavy, like lead. The balaclava was in a plastic bag in the pannier of the bike. *Were you intending to hide the evidence or tamper with it in some way?* Yes, she thought, *yes.* I wish I'd never found it, I wish it didn't exist.

She picked up her helmet and gauntlets and walked out, past the man who was polishing the sauce from his plate with a crust of fried bread. She felt strange, light-headed and slightly foggy in her mind, yet she had decided exactly what to do. She walked to the bike, opened the pannier, and took out the plastic bag. She glanced inside to reassure herself that the hood was still there; a crumpled eye slit seemed to wink at her conspiratorially. She slipped the ring off her finger and dropped it in. The weight disappeared; swinging the bag lightly from one finger, she walked across the car park to a large litter bin just outside the café entrance. It was shaped like a post box, with a slot near the top. She pushed the bag in the slot, and posted it inside.

Then she took a deep breath, turned away, and felt a smile twist her face. She took five strides towards the bike, hesitated, and burst into tears.

The tears were totally unexpected and utterly uncontrollable. Sarah never cried like this: she didn't know what was happening to her. She leaned over the metal bike rail, sobbing so hard she was nearly sick. The tears overwhelmed her like a flash flood in a desert, and through her mind like sticks in the flood came memories. Simon as a baby sucking her breast; Kevin telling her parents he'd marry her; Kevin leaving, with baby Simon in her bruised arms; her first kiss with Bob, so gentle and different to Kevin; herself studying inside the playpen while the toddler

Simon trashed the house outside; herself carrying Emily on her hip while Bob clumsily played football with Simon; opening her exam results – O levels, A levels, degree; going into court in her wig and gown for her first case, so proud; Simon arguing with Bob, their faces red, his school report torn on the floor between them; Emily's empty bedroom only a week ago, teddy bears on the bed and books still open on the table; Jasmine's pale bruised face on the mortuary slab with a twig embedded in the waxy skin; Simon in prison this morning, frightened and evasive; Simon maybe four years old, hitting his sister Emily over the head with a stick so that her forehead had to be stitched by the doctor; the contempt on the face of a judge she had once seen, sentencing a solicitor to jail for conspiring with his client to destroy evidence in a drugs case.

And then the pictures were gone and the tears with them, as suddenly as they had come. She clung to the bike rail in the car park, cold and trembling but able to stand upright again. She felt a hand on her shoulder.

'Can I help you, love?'

She turned and saw the man from the café. He was big, rather flabby, with a round friendly face in which her clear washed-out mind detected no sign of malice or danger.

'You were crying. I couldn't help but see. Is there owt I can do?'

She let go of the rail and swayed. His hands grasped her shoulders as though she might break. 'Nah then. Steady does it.'

'Yes. Just hold me like that for a moment, if you wouldn't mind.' She smiled at him faintly, clutching his arm to balance herself. 'It's all very silly, it's just . . . I can't really say why.'

'Would you like to come inside and sit down? Cup of tea maybe?'

'No, it's . . . there *is* something you can do to help me, though. If you wouldn't mind.'

'No problem, love. Just tell me what it is, and it's done.'

'It's over here.' She summoned up her strength and began to walk, rather slowly, towards the litter bin. He kept his arm round her shoulder and she leaned against him, this complete stranger, drawing warmth from the human comfort.

'I put something in here a few moments ago, in a plastic bag.'

'You did. I saw yer actually, from the window.'

'Did you? Well, it was a mistake. There's something sentimental inside . . . private . . . a ring and something else . . . I shouldn't have thrown it away.'

'You want it back? I'll get it for you then.' He reached inside the bin but his arm was too big, it was stuck. She tried too but although her arm was smaller she couldn't reach far enough.'It's got a lock on, look. You stay here and I'll go and get the key. You OK now?'

'Yes. Thanks. I'm fine.' This is ridiculous, she thought when he'd gone. I could do this for myself, I don't need a man to help. But he was so eager and the truth was that just now she was finding standing up and being polite quite enough to manage on her own.

He came back with a spotty young man and a key. This is a dangerous moment, she realized, I've made enough of an exhibition of myself already. When the boy unlocked the lid she pulled out the bag herself, forestalling him, and took out the ring.

'That's it. It was my mother's. I don't know what I was thinking.'

'Sentimental value, like?'

'Yes. You've both been very kind. I'm really grateful.'

'You'll have that cup of tea now?'

'No. Really, thanks.' She caught his hand and squeezed it. 'You've been very kind but it's best if I get home. I'll feel better there.' She began to walk away.

'You sure you're strong enough to ride that bike?'

'Yes. Oh yes, I'm used to it, I'll manage.' She needed to reassure herself as well as them. I'll have to manage, she thought. I can't make a fool of myself again. She felt them watching her as she put the bag in the pannier, unlocked the bike, sat astride and strapped on her helmet.

'Well, get that boxer husband to make tea when you get home, then!' the man shouted.

Sarah smiled and raised her hand in thanks. 'I'll do that,' she said.

As if.

When she got home Emily was in her bedroom revising. With a sense of disorientation, Sarah remembered that her daughter had sat her first GCSE exam that morning. In the midst of mayhem, other people's lives go on as normal, she thought. She remembered a poem by Auden in which Icarus plunged from the sky to his death while a farmer ploughed his fields below, impervious to the tragic drama above his head. She went upstairs to her daughter's bedroom.

'Hello. How'd it go?'

'Awful, thanks.'

'Why? What went wrong?'

'Fat lot you care.' Emily hadn't turned round. Sarah was forced to stare at the back of her daughter's head, rejected. She sat on the bed.

'What was it? Geography?'

'German – see what I mean? And if you really want to know, I couldn't understand the listening or translation either. So I've cocked that up. Anyway, why weren't you here last night? The night before my first exam, of all nights.'

'I'm sorry, Emily, really. I slept at Simon's house, I told you. I went to see him again.'

Emily turned, examining her mother intently. 'Are you and Dad breaking up?'

'What . . . no, I don't think so. What makes you ask that?'

'You running off. He seemed pretty cut up about it. It didn't help me.'

'Emily, I'm sorry.' Sarah thought she should probably give her daughter a hug but the girl sat so stiffly that she feared a rebuff. 'All this business with Simon, you know . . . it's going to be hard for a while.'

'It says in our social science textbook that families often break up when they're under a lot of strain from some – what do they call it? – traumatic event. Like that Lawrence family whose son was murdered. They split up.'

'Yes, well, you shouldn't believe everything you read in social science textbooks.' This time she did manage to reach out and hold her daughter's hands. It was the right thing to do; Emily leaned forward earnestly, listening for once to what she said.

'When I split up with Simon's father Kevin before you were born it was nothing to do with strain from a traumatic event. He caused the trauma himself by finding another woman – there wasn't one before. And . . . of course it's awful about what's happening to Simon but it's no good if we don't support him. That's what . . .' She hesitated, uncertain how to finish.

'That's what you were arguing about with Dad. Is that what you were going to say?'

'Well, yes, in a way . . .'

'There you are then. That's probably what the book means.'

'We're not living in a school textbook, Emily! This is your brother Simon, he's remanded in custody charged with murder!'

'I'm not a child, Mum. I don't need a lecture!' Emily snatched her hands away.

If I'm not careful I'll wreck this too, Sarah thought. I've got to get something right today. 'All right, I'm *sorry*, Emily, OK? You're right, this is a big strain for all of us. None of us needs it – especially not you with your exams.'

A sort of calm returned. Then Emily asked her big question. 'Do you think he did it?'

Sarah tried not to avoid her daughter's eyes. This was no time to lie. But how to answer?

'I suppose there's a difference between what I *think* and what I *believe*,' she began slowly, wondering if she understood herself. 'If I start out by *thinking*, as the police and their lawyers will, then yes, there's plenty of evidence to make it seem he's guilty. He was the last person to see her, he hit her, he ran away to Scarborough the night she was killed . . . and other things.'

Including the contents of a plastic bag in the pannier of my bike, she thought despairingly. I can't tell Emily about those; they're my burden.

'But if you ask me what I *believe*, then that's a different question. Do I believe that Simon – I mean, we all know he has faults because we've lived with him, but . . . do I *believe* that he could have killed that girl –

raped her and cut her throat with a knife, then the answer has to be no. Doesn't it, Emily? Whatever the evidence seems to say, there must be something wrong with it.'

Emily considered the answer she had been given. 'You *have* to think – I mean, believe – that, don't you, because you're his mother?'

'Yes. And you're his sister.' How often have I seen families in court, Sarah thought. With no idea how it must feel.

Emily nodded. 'I don't want him to be guilty either. But . . .'

'But there's a lot of evidence. That's what Lucy, his solicitor, is looking at right now. And when it comes to court he'll have the best barrister we can find – a QC, I hope. That's what lawyers are for.' They sat for a while in silence, then Sarah got up. 'You get on with your revision, now. Be grateful these aren't decisions you have to make.'

But as Sarah reached the door, Emily said: 'If he *did* do it, though, I'd want him to be locked up for ever. He'd deserve that, even though he's my brother. I wouldn't want any clever lawyer to get him off when he's guilty, like you do sometimes.'

Bob showed no surprise to find her at home. She was slumped in an armchair, staring out at the weeping willow in the garden. There was a plastic bag on the carpet beside her. Classical music was playing softly, and she had a glass in her hand, as she occasionally did after a hard day at work. He crossed the room and poured a small whisky for himself.

'Where's Emily?'

'Upstairs, working. She's going out with Larry in half an hour.'

'In the middle of her exams? Is that wise?'

Sarah shrugged. 'She's been working all afternoon, Bob. Anyway there's something I need to talk to you about and it'd be better if she weren't here.'

Bob frowned. 'Sounds ominous.'

'What isn't, these days?'

'I'll go up and talk to her now, then. See how she got on.'

'OK.' As he went upstairs Sarah took her drink into the garden. At the end of the lawn was the gate leading into the field by the river. Only a week ago, she thought, I was out there wondering if Emily'd thrown herself into the water. Now I can imagine doing the same myself. How do people drown themselves, anyway? Do you just dive down and breathe water instead of air? It wouldn't work. You might want to die, but your body would panic and resist. You have to fight on, however bad you feel. That's just the way it is.

When Bob came down, she told him what she'd decided to say.

'Emily said something earlier that made me think. She said that families often split up because of the pressure of some traumatic event from outside. She'd read it in a book, poor kid, but it might be true for all that. The other day you told the police about Simon hitting Jasmine, and

I said you'd betrayed him. But . . .' She paused; it was so hard to admit this. 'You had to do it, I see that now. You had no choice.'

It was not what Bob had expected. All day he'd been thinking, this is how marriages end. First with a row about something fundamental in which both partners think they're right, followed by a physical separation, then a fight for the affections of your children, ending if you're unlucky with a complete loathing and hatred of the person you once loved. And it must be so lonely. So when he'd seen her there with a drink in her hand he'd been sure she had come to make a formal beginning of the process. Now this instead. He was hugely relieved.

'What . . . makes you say that?'

'I've thought about it. And – something's happened.' She picked up the plastic bag, and told him – about the hood and ring in the shed, Simon's response, and the decision she had made at the transport café. It was hard for him to take in at first.

'And this is why you came back?'

'Yes. Well, not the only reason. But you see, I thought the right thing to do – to protect Simon – was to chuck it in the bin, just as I thought the right thing for you to do was to keep quiet about that old man. But then when I tried . . . I couldn't do it. It's harder than I thought; it must have been like that for you too. So one thing is – sorry.'

He hadn't expected that either. It was not a word Sarah used often. And Simon, he knew, was very important to her indeed.

'I've been thinking too. I don't feel proud of what I did. I wish I'd never met the old sod.'

'But you did. And once you know a thing like that, you can't un-know it.'

'True. Especially when a girl's dead.' He sighed, staring out of the window. 'I suppose that's why I did it, really. Because of Jasmine's family. Suffering as we might have done if Emily had died.'

'Yes,' Sarah murmured. 'And if it *had* been Emily, I'd kill anyone who covered things up. That's all she has left now, Mrs Hurst – the right to know what happened.'

'So what are you going to do?' Bob looked at the plastic bag.

'Talk to you about it, first. If this thing isn't going to tear us apart, we've got to decide together. All right so far?'

'So far, so good. Yes.'

'Don't mock me, Bob, this is deadly serious. Now, there are three possibilities.'

Here comes the lecture, Bob thought. It's how her mind works.

'One, I take them to Lucy. She's Simon's lawyer, she can decide. But wouldn't I just be passing the buck to her, tempting her to conceal it as I was tempted myself?'

'Maybe. What's number two?'

'Two, I put them back where they were, and say nothing. Then the police either find the things for themselves or they don't. That way, if I've wiped my fingerprints off the ring, they don't know I've ever seen them.'

'And the third?'

'The one that scares me to death. I ring up the police and hand these things over myself.'

'I see.' Bob scratched his chin thoughtfully. 'And which do you think is right?'

'That's what I hoped you'd tell me. What would you do?'

'Well . . .' He hesitated. 'You've tried getting rid of them yourself, and failed. And if you give them to Lucy, I can see you're just passing the buck. Like you are with me.'

'You're my husband! *Bob!*'

'Yeah, OK, it's different. But if he really did these things, then haven't we got a duty to tell the police? I mean, Jasmine's dead – and there may be more girls. Kids like Emily.'

'You don't really believe he's like that, Bob. Do you?'

'We're not talking about what I believe,' he said desperately. 'We're talking about what to do with the evidence.'

'True.' She got up and strode distractedly round the room. 'Look, I can't hand this stuff over, I simply can't. Any more than I could throw it away this afternoon.'

'So you're going to put it back. That's all that's left, isn't it?'

Sarah ran a hand through her hair. 'Well, I can't just turn him in. He's my son. On the other hand I'm not hiding or destroying anything, I'm just putting it back where the police can find it if they do their job properly. That's all.'

'And if it goes wrong, and they find out?' Bob asked. 'I can see the headlines now. "York barrister hides evidence to save killer son." Is that what you want?'

'It's a risk I'll have to run, that's all. There are risks with all of this.'

'So if that's your decision, what do you want from me?' Bob asked slowly. 'After all, you've told me now.'

'I want your love and support, Bob.' Then she realized what was implied in his last words. 'And your promise to say nothing. You couldn't – you won't ring them yourself?'

'You said you wouldn't burden Lucy with this knowledge. But you've burdened me.'

The comment terrified Sarah, like a cold hand round her heart. She had come here for support, and now this. She stared at him bleakly.

'If you tell them, Bob, we really are finished. This is one of the hardest things I've ever had to do and it's tearing me apart. I'm risking my whole career for this, everything I've worked for since I was a kid. *But he's my son, Bob!* I need your support.'

Before he could answer, the doorbell rang and Emily came clattering down the stairs. They heard voices in the hall and then Emily came in with Larry, beaming happily. Emily looked pretty and flushed with excitement. Larry, in jeans, a black leather jacket and bootlace tie, had clearly made some attempt to improve his appearance. Sarah forced a smile.

'Hello, you two. Where are you going?'

'Out. To a meal at a place Larry knows.'

'In Larry's car?' Sarah looked dubiously out at a small rusty hatchback in the drive.

'Don't worry, Mrs Newby, I don't drink and drive,' Larry said. 'And she won't be back late either – I do know she's got exams this week.'

'But not tomorrow, so I've got all day to revise,' Emily said. She kissed Sarah on the cheek. 'Don't look so worried, Mum, I'm all right.'

'Yes, I'm sure you are. And you can trust Larry, I hope.' She glanced anxiously at Bob. 'Actually, I'm going out for a while, too. So I'll follow you down the road to check your driving, young man!' She went out into the porch for her leathers and helmet.

'Oh Mum!' Emily protested at this humiliation. Then a more serious thought struck her. 'You *are* coming back tonight, aren't you?'

'Just like you, young lady, *yes*.' She met Bob's eyes. 'I'll stay so long as we all trust each other. OK?'

Emily looked puzzled, not sure what her mother was talking about. 'If we have to trust each other why are you going to follow Larry down the road?'

'It was a joke,' Sarah said. 'I won't.' She smiled at them all – a tense, rather frightening smile – and stepped out into the night, alone.

21

It was dark by the time she got to Bramham Street. The sound of the motorbike echoed loudly from the terraced houses on either side. Sarah hadn't noticed it before; perhaps guilt focused her attention on it now. When she cut the engine it was quiet – the sound of television through windows, curtains drawn, no one on the street. She glanced around but there was no one watching from a window that she could see.

Anyway I have a right to be here, she told herself. It's my house, I have a key. I'll come whenever I choose. But for all her brave words she felt like a burglar.

She wheeled the bike through the archway into Simon's back yard. It was dark, but the streetlights lit different angles of the passage, so that Sarah walked through a kaleidoscope of shadows. She settled the bike on its stand, stripped off her gauntlets and helmet, and fumbled in the pannier for the plastic bag. Then she pushed open the door of the shed and stepped inside.

As she did so something seized her arm and she stumbled forwards on her face. To her amazement she was on her hands and knees on the shed floor. She tried to get up but something hit her on the rump and she fell forwards again, face down. Her right hand slipped inside the bag and got tangled up in the balaclava hood. She gasped, struggled to her knees, looked behind her, and saw –

A man blocking the doorway.

She could only see him dimly in the orange glow of the streetlight but he was a large, well-built man with thick arms and massive shoulders. She almost fell over a broken chair, recovered, and staggered to her feet. The intruder grabbed her arm, and slammed her against the wall. She pushed the balaclava hood into his face, blinding him for a second, her nails clawing at his cheeks. But a huge hand closed over hers, dragging the hood away from the side of his head and flinging it to the floor.

'Right then, what's this?'

The big, cruel face grinned into hers from a few inches away. As her eyes adapted to the faint orange light the features became clearer and the confidence in the man's face leaked away. They stared at each other, bewildered.

'Fancy Knickers Newby!'

'Gary Harker! Get off me!' She tried to free herself but as she wriggled his grip tightened slightly. He must be twice her weight, with the strength of a gorilla. 'What are you doing here?'

'What am *I* doing?' He still held her but less cruelly, more as though he had forgotten what his huge hands were gripping than anything else. 'Minding me own business, until you turned up. What you poking your nose in here for?'

He looked more annoyed than vicious, so far as she could tell in the gloom. But it was not a situation she intended to prolong. Was this how things had begun with Sharon? She had to get out of here, quickly.

'Let me go, you great oaf!'

'Let you go?' The hands still held her, a jeering smile twitching his lips. 'Why should I? Looking for me were you, Miss Fancy Knickers? Dressed up in all this kinky gear, too!' His right hand squeezed her breast, then slid down her waist to her hips. 'Fancied me all along, I'll bet. Well, now.'

A snake of fear slithered up her spine. She felt sure that if she struggled again she would provoke him more. She listened intently, hoping for some voice from the yard outside, but there was only the TV laughter far away, fainter than the soft hiss of his breath.

Very quietly she said: 'Gary, I know exactly who you are. You're not wearing a hood now. So if you touch me you'll have to kill me. Otherwise I'll see that you get sent down for rape with the longest sentence that's ever been passed. You'll be an old man before you come out again, your prick will dry up and shrivel off. Is that what you want? Twenty years inside?'

His hand moved thoughtfully across her buttock. 'Twenty years inside you, you mean?'

Dear God in heaven, she thought, what have I done coming in here all alone? She panicked, wriggling like an eel to slip from his grasp, but that was a mistake; his grip tightened and he slammed her against the wall, knocking the breath out of her. His breath was on her face, his huge hands pinning her arms to her sides, immobile like a vice.

'For God's sake, Gary, you're mad, I'm too old for you!'

She watched his face in the dim orange light as his mind lumbered to a decision. Her pulse was racing, she wanted to sprint away like a gazelle but she couldn't move. This is how I die, she thought, in a squalid scuffle in a shed. Then, to her surprise, his grip slackened.

'Old cow. Go on then, get out of it. I'm not that desperate, ta very much.'

Warily, she slipped past him, and stepped outside. An enormous urge to run surged through her but she took just three steps before turning round to face him. Three yards of pitch black shadows and orange glow between them. 'Right. Now do you mind telling me what you're doing here, in the first place?'

'What's it to you? You don't belong here.'

'I do, you know. This is my son's house. I own it, in a way.' It was amazing, she thought, how hard and insistent her voice could still sound, when her whole body was trembling like a jelly inside. Perhaps that's part of being *old*.

'Who – Simon? *Your son?* You're crackers.'

'No, I'm not. So you see, that gives me every right to be here, unlike you. What exactly are you doing in my son's shed, Gary? Thieving? You won't find much there.'

'That's what you think, Fancy Knickers. Shows how much you know.'

'What do you mean?'

'Your son – he's been nicked, hasn't he? For murder, I heard.'

Sarah's brain began racing along a new track. *What did this mean?*

'It's a mistake. The police *do* make mistakes, Gary, you ought to know that.'

'Oh right.' She could hear the mocking grin in his voice. 'So what did happen then?'

'I don't know, yet. My son isn't a murderer, Gary. If you've met him you'd know that.'

'Not a thief either, I suppose?'

'No, of course not. Look, you haven't answered my question. What are you doing here?'

As the silence lengthened she thought, Perhaps he knows about the ring, the balaclava. Could he have been looking for them – or something else?

His answer came as a joke, of all things. 'Cruising, o' course. Waiting for tarts. They drop in from time to time, tha knows. All done up in kinky leather!'

He smirked, delighted with himself. Then he stepped towards her out of the shed. She backed away nervously. 'That your bike, is it?'

'It is.'

'Fuck me.' He swung his leg astride the saddle, and turned the handlebars this way and that. 'Not bad. Fancy a ride?' He patted the pillion seat.

Sarah took a deep breath, and felt in her pocket for the key to the house. 'I'm going indoors now, Gary. If you don't get off that bike straight away and piss off out of here, I'll call the police and then we'll have you for TWOC as well as breaking and entering and stealing whatever you've taken from that shed. Otherwise I'll forget the whole thing. You choose.'

'Right then, I will an' all. Bitch.' Her last challenge had been a mistake. Before she could move he swung his leg off the bike and with one long stride across the yard grabbed her arm and yanked her towards him. The other hand smacked her hard across the face. It was like being hit by a wall. The blow filled her mind, there was nothing else, only the massive jolt, the pain, the sense that her jaw had been realigned by a concrete block. When there was room for other thoughts she realized she was sprawled face down across the saddle of the bike, one huge hand tugging her leather trousers down to her knees.

She screamed, a brief bubbling sound which was choked off by his other hand which clamped over her mouth and nose.

'Shut it, slag! I've always wanted to do this.' He was spreading her legs behind her, she realized, trying to get one either side of the back wheel but hampered by the trousers around her ankles. She tried to bite his hand but it was too big and all-enveloping, squeezing her nose so that tears ran from her eyes and she thought, *I'll die, he'll suffocate me!*

Then she fell sideways and there was a clatter and bang and a vast, immovable weight on her right thigh. There were men shouting, doors slamming. White light blazed in her eyes.

'Are you all right, love? Christ, she's under the bike!'

If the words had a meaning it didn't register with Sarah. There was swearing, a shout of 'Get in there and shut it!' Then what sounded like a radio crackling: 'Ambulance needed, 23 Bramham Street, urgent please.'

The weight lifted from her thigh and a man's voice spoke from the darkness. Calm, reassuring, not Gary's. 'It's all right, love, it's off now. Harry, get a blanket. You just lie still. *Sarah?* It's Terry Bateson.'

*   *   *

165

'Look, I wasn't raped, all right? Ooooh, my tongue!'

'I know you say that, but the officers say you were unconscious when they found you. So it's best to take samples to be sure. You might not know what happened.'

'I *know*.' Sarah's mouth felt as though it was about to fall apart like a rotten, bloated potato. 'It's my mouth that hurts, not . . .' She gestured to the other end of the couch, where the female doctor was preparing her swab. And my pride, she thought. What a fool I look now, with my legs in the air and my neck in a brace while that policewoman notes down what I say.

'You're lucky with your jaw. The X-rays show nothing broken, no teeth lost. The analgesics should kick in soon and you won't feel it any more. Just shift this way, please. There, that's it. Mmmm. No tears, no bleeding. Just these scrapes on your leg where you fell. You say he didn't penetrate you?'

'No!'

'Vaginally or anally?'

'*No!* Can I sit up now?'

'Yes, of course. I'm sorry, I do have to ask these things.'

Sarah swung her legs over the side of the couch. 'My mouth hurts and my leg aches but he didn't rape me, all right? I was lucky, the cabblly came in time.'

'Yes. The *what*, love?' The doctor looked up from her notes and smiled, cool and distant and professional. Checking my mind isn't deranged now, Sarah thought in despair.

'*Cav - al - ry*,' she said, as clearly and distinctly as she could through her throbbing, bloated mouth. 'The *cavalry* came in time. Joke.'

'Oh. Yes, I see.' The doctor smiled again, and squatted in front of her, looking directly into her eyes as though she were a child. 'Well, do you feel up to talking to the police now? Or would you rather they came back in the morning?'

'Talk now,' Sarah said. 'Get it over with.'

'All right, if you're sure. But if you feel bad just tell them to stop.' The doctor stood up and spoke directly to the detective, Tracy Litherland. 'No more than half an hour, maximum, all right? She's had a nasty shock and she needs to sleep. I suggest you just get the basic facts now and leave the rest until tomorrow.'

The basic facts, Sarah thought as she got carefully to her feet. Where do we start?

'Right, Harker, what's your story this time?' Terry noticed, with grim satisfaction, how stiffly Gary had manoeuvred himself into the chair, as though his ribs were hurting. The arrest had not been conducted with excessive gentleness. But his manner was surly, defiant.

'I dunno what you mean.'

'Oh, really?' said Terry derisively. 'We caught you in the act, old son. Four police officers saw you trying to rape this woman, Mrs Sarah Newby. You had her trousers down and your hand around her throat, for Christ's sake!'

'Not round her throat. It were her mouth.'

'Is that supposed to make a difference?'

'Yeah. Big difference.' Gary leered. 'She were kissing it.'

'You liar!' Terry rose from his chair without thinking, but Harry caught his arm, glancing pointedly at the two tapes running smoothly in the machine. Terry recovered himself, sat down.

'You were attempting to rape her. I saw you.'

A cunning leer came over Gary's face as he took in Terry's reaction. 'Got the hots for her yourself, have you, copper? Well, you're too bloody late, that's what. What you saw was just sex, no more and no less. She wanted it like that.'

The sheer effrontery of the idea stunned both detectives. Harry Easby recovered first. His tone, to Terry's irritation, contained a hint of amusement, as though he half admired the man for coming up with such a preposterous suggestion.

'You're saying, are you, that a respectable woman like that, a barrister, actually *asked* you to half strangle her and rip her trousers down across the back of a motorbike?'

'Summat like that, yeah.'

'For Christ's sake!' Terry was finding it hard to control himself.

'What were you doing there anyway?' Harry asked.

'Looking for young Simon.'

'Who? Simon Newby? Do you know him?'

'Yeah, a bit. He lives there, doesn't he?'

'Not in his back yard,' Harry smiled contemptuously. 'He lives in the *house*, Gary, not the back yard where we found you.'

'Yeah, well, I tried the door but he didn't answer, so I thought he might be in his shed.'

'Notice anything unusual about the front door, Gary, did you?' Harry asked, mockingly.

Gary thought for a bit. Then light dawned. 'Yeah, I did actually. There was a padlock on it. After you lot smashed the door, no doubt.'

'That's right, Gary. And can you think why we might do that? Any ideas?'

'"Cause you're a lot of friggin' hooligans, that's why. Smashing up property for no reason.'

'So you hadn't heard that Simon Newby had been arrested, is that what you're saying?'

'Arrested? For what?'

'For rape and murder, that's what! Oh come on, Gary, it was all over the *Evening Press* and on the telly! Don't tell me you didn't know!'

'All right. So what if I did?'

Gary was sweating, Terry saw. Harry was doing well, so far.

'So what you're saying is, you knocked on Simon Newby's front door when you knew full well he was in Hull prison. Is that it, Gary? Doesn't make an awful lot of sense now, does it?'

Gary stared at them, bemused. Like a rabbit caught in headlights, Terry thought. Harry laughed: 'Or are you saying you went there to meet his mother, for a bit of rough sex?'

God no! Don't put words in his mouth, Terry thought. Gary seized on the excuse eagerly.

'Yeah, right. That's it. She'd asked to meet me there. When she didn't answer the door I thought I'd wait in the back yard. I knew she'd put her bike there, didn't I?'

'I see. So you thought you'd wait in the shed, in the dark, so you could spring out and rape this woman when she arrived?'

'I told you, I didn't rape her. When she came in the yard she was hot for it.'

'Hot for sex with you, you mean?' said Harry incredulously.

'Yeah. Some women are like that, you know.'

'Oh yes.' Harry paused. 'Talk to her at all first, did you? Or just go straight at it?'

'We talked for a few minutes, yeah,' Gary said cautiously.

'And then she asked you for sex?'

'Yeah.'

Harry laughed. 'So we just spoiled a nice private party?' Beneath the derision in Harry's tone there was still that faint hint of admiration, as though for a good spicy story shared between boys. Gary responded to it.

'You could've joined in, if you'd asked. She'd like that. Four big coppers and me.'

Terry was consumed with loathing. This was the man he was sure had raped Sharon Gilbert, and probably murdered Maria Clayton too. Now he was denying what they'd seen with their own eyes. It wasn't funny, it wasn't funny at all.

There was a knock at the door. A uniformed constable passed in a note. It read *Interesting finds in the shed at Bramham Street. May be relevant to your interview. Mike Candor.*

'All right,' Terry said. 'Interview suspended at 11.35 p.m. We'll resume in the morning.'

'In that case,' Gary said, 'I want a lawyer.'

Sarah had hoped to be interviewed by Terry but Tracy Litherland ushered her into a room with Will Churchill. 'Where's . . . DI Bateson?' she asked.

'He's interviewing your assailant,' Churchill answered. 'He knows a lot about him, as I'm sure you'll understand. Whereas I have a particular interest in 23 Bramham Street.'

My son's enemy, Sarah thought. And now this.

Tracy Litherland began. 'Can you tell us exactly what happened tonight, from the moment you arrived at the house?'

Sarah told them, speaking slowly and carefully so that her bruised tongue and jaw did not slur the words. The doctor was right, the painkillers were beginning to do their stuff. But it was quite useful, having this temporary problem with speech. It meant that she could use a minimum of words without seeming evasive. But her mind was working slowly too and she knew there was something about being in that shed that she mustn't tell them.

Churchill was persistent. 'He didn't try to rape you in the shed, then?'

'No. He was surprised when he saw it was me, I think.'

'I imagine the surprise was mutual.' Churchill assessed her thoughtfully. As though I were more of a suspect than a victim, Sarah thought. But then in a way I am.

'You didn't expect to meet him there?'

'No. Certainly not.'

'Has he ever been there before, so far as you know?'

Sarah shook her head, to avoid using her jaw.

'All right. So when you saw who it was, were you afraid, or did you feel reassured?'

It was a cruel question – almost a copy of one of her own questions to Sharon Gilbert during the trial, Sarah realized. *Were you more or less afraid when you began to think the man in the hood was Gary?* Perhaps this man was in court when I asked it and wants me to know how it feels. Well, it feels awful. She glanced at Tracy for female support.

'I was frightened, of course. Any man who grabs me in a dark shed . . .'

'But he let you go?'

'Mm. But he grabbed me again outside. Then you lot came.' However unwelcome these questions she was enormously grateful for the rescue. 'Thanks.'

Churchill smiled. 'Just doing our job, Mrs Newby. Protecting the public, you know.'

Sarah frowned, puzzled. 'But why did you come just then?'

'Ah well.' He looked very smug now. 'The old man across the road – the one who saw your son hit Jasmine Hurst? Well, he keeps an eye out – phones us several times a day. Told us how you stayed there last night, when you arrived, when you switched the light out, what time you came out in the morning . . .'

What time I went to the shed, Sarah thought – *oh my God, did he see that bag?*

'. . . so when he told us Gary was there, and then you, I mobilized the troops and hared round pronto, to see what was going on. We hardly expected to find friend Gary demonstrating some of the finer details of the Gilbert case to his learned counsel, though, did we?'

Dear God, get me out of here, Sarah thought. 'Sir!' Tracy Litherland protested, shocked. But Churchill laughed, gripped by a manic desire to punish Sarah with mockery.

'Still, it's an ill wind that blows no one any good. It looks as though we're going to have the pleasure of charging Mr Harker with sexually assaulting the barrister who got him off his rape charge, doesn't it?'

Fuck you. Sarah glared at him without straining her jaw to answer. First you arrest Simon and now you bully me. She tried to think of a protest but for once no words came. Then suddenly she decided she was too tired to care. The doctor had been right, she realized, half an hour is quite enough. In a minute I'll fall asleep in this chair.

She glanced despairingly at Tracy, who responded quickly.

'Sir, the MO said just half an hour. I really think Mrs Newby's had enough.'

Disappointed, Churchill pushed his chair back. 'Yes, of course. Very well. We'll take a full statement tomorrow when you're feeling better.' He got up and opened the door. 'Your husband's waiting outside.'

'So he didn't actually . . .'

'He didn't actually rape me, no.' Slumped in the passenger seat of the Volvo, Sarah studied Bob wearily. 'Christ, is that all that matters to you?'

'No, of course not.' His left hand hovered in the air for a moment between them, as though to touch her, then landed instead on the gear stick as he changed down. 'I'm just trying to understand, that's all.'

'Are you?'

'Yes. I mean, why was he there?'

'I don't know, Bob. He di . . . didn't say.' Her bruised jaw throbbed, and the precise articulation of some words hurt more than others.

Bob glanced at her thoughtfully. 'God, I should have come with you, at least.'

'Mmm.'

'Though if you hadn't gone into the wretched shed in the first place, if Simon hadn't –'

'It's nothing to do with Simon, this . . .'

'Isn't it? Then why were you there? He's at the root of this somehow. I know he is.'

'*It wasn't Simon, Bob!*' Sarah screamed, then stopped, checked by the pain. More quietly, but with equal intensity, she continued. 'It was Gary Harker. I defended the bastard, remember? Laugh at that if you like.'

'For God's sake, I'm not laughing, Sarah. Come on, let's get you home. Tuck this round you.' He stretched out his left arm to adjust the blanket which a policewoman had wrapped around Sarah's shoulders. She shrugged it off irritably.

'I'm not an invalid.'

'You're a victim, though. Let's get you home to a warm bath and a whisky.'

'That sounds more like it.' Sarah gazed idly out of the window as the car swung over the River Ouse, with the lights of the Archbishop's Palace on their left. So peaceful it looked, so far removed from the cramped violence of Simon's back yard. Or was it? Down to her left, in the bushes by the footpath fifty yards south of the road, Jasmine's body had lain all night, with a fox gnawing at her throat. Sarah groaned.

'Not far now,' Bob murmured encouragingly. 'Did they give you any painkillers?'

'An injection, I think. Bob?'

'Yes?'

'Don't tell Emily.'

'What? She'll have to know sometime.'

'Yes, but not tonight. It's too late.'

Bob drove on for a while in silence, round the ring road to their country home. He pulled into their drive, and – a first for him – got out and opened the passenger door for her while she was still fumbling with the blanket. She thanked him with a faint, ironic smile. 'I should be raped more often.'

'Never again.' He put his arm round her and she leaned against him gratefully. 'Now, inside with you. Come on. What do you want first – a bath?'

'Oh God, yes please.' Only now as she walked through her own front door, did the trembling begin. Her knees started shaking and her legs felt like jelly. She collapsed into an armchair. 'Go upstairs and run it for me, would you, Bob? A deep hot one with bath salts if you can find any. Then bring a whisky and some candles, too.'

'Candles?' At the foot of the stairs, Bob hesitated. 'Why?'

'For the bathroom. I want it to be warm and comfortable and womb-like. Bring up a CD with some Mozart as well.'

'Anything you say.'

I don't want to see anything clearly tonight, she thought as he went upstairs. Tomorrow will be a day for decisions, rows of them waiting for me in the sun. Tonight I want to close my eyes, lie there and get clean.

22

When she returned the following morning Sarah was met, to her great relief, by Terry and Tracy Litherland. 'Where's your famous male chauvinist, then,' she asked. 'DCI Churchill?'

'Senior management meeting,' Tracy shrugged. 'I thought if DI Bateson . . .?'

'Yes, that's fine. Thank you,' Sarah twitched her sore mouth, hoping it looked like a grateful smile. All the muscles of her jaw were stiff.

Terry sat down opposite her. 'I hope you got some sleep.'

'Yes, thanks.' She experimented with a second smile, which hurt less. She had no idea what it looked like. She had tried to cover her bruised jaw with make-up, but she could do nothing about her half-closed eye.

'Well, I'm glad you're well enough to come in.' Terry slid a pad of paper across the desk. 'This shouldn't take long. We just need your statement, to confirm what you said last night.'

'Yes. I've been thinking about that.' Sarah bit her lip. 'I don't want to press charges.'

'What?' Terry stared at her. 'But Sarah, this was a serious assault.'

'I know. But I'm still alive.' Sarah was so glad it was this man, not the bumptious fool who had insulted her last night. She tried to speak as clearly and persuasively as she could. 'Look, Terry, I'm grateful to you all for rescuing me, of course – very. But *because* you came, nothing really bad happened. I mean, I wasn't raped and in fact I'm hardly hurt at all apart from this eye and my jaw, and that's just bruised, not broken. It's my pride that's hurt most, and a trial won't help that. Quite the opposite, in fact.'

'But . . .' Terry was bewildered. 'We caught him in the act! I was there; four police officers saw what happened. It's an open and shut case!'

'So he's admitted it, has he?'

'Well, no, not yet. But he'll have to, he's got no choice.'

'He can still plead not guilty, Terry. And that's what he'll do, just to humiliate me. Believe me, I know this man. I defended him. Remember?'

There was a stunned silence. Neither detective had expected this. Unpleasant questions stirred in Terry's mind. He liked this woman, but what was it all about? Had she *known* Gary was guilty in that trial, and been able to live with it? Why *had* she gone to her son's house last night?

Sarah broke the silence. 'So what *did* he say? You might as well tell me.'

'He . . . claimed it was consensual. He said you'd arranged to meet him there and you liked . . . rough sex.' Terry was embarrassed, but the words did not seem to shock her. Was there something in Gary's story, after all?

'And you said?'

'That I didn't believe him, of course. I saw what was happening, Sarah! We all did.'

'Yes. And I'm very – deeply – grateful that you came when you did.' Sarah studied him thoughtfully. 'But there's that tiny doubt in your mind, isn't there, Terry?' She turned to Tracy. 'Maybe in yours too. You don't want to admit it, because you're decent people, but when a man says that sort of thing you wonder, don't you?'

'Not me, Mrs Newby,' Tracy Litherland insisted. 'I can see the bruises on your face. He hasn't got a hope. No one's going to believe a daft story like that!'

'Aren't they?' Sarah sighed. 'Look, if he pleads not guilty I have to go in the box and give evidence, which is hard enough for any woman in a case of sexual assault. But this isn't just *any* case, it's a sensation! I was his barrister, remember! Normally a rape victim's name can't be published but in this case no one could hide it from the newspapers: after all, I previously defended this man on a rape charge in open court. And his counsel is going to ask me if it's true that I had secret meetings with him for – what did you call it? – rough sex! *Jesus*, Terry! It'll be like dropping meat in a shark pool; the press will have a feeding frenzy. And then they'll find out that my son is charged with rape and murder as well. It'll be the crime story of the millennium! I'll be all over the tabloids, they'll be camped outside my front door twenty deep asking me to pose in a wig and gown and my underwear! Do you really think that's what I want?'

'Do you want Harker to go free? Again?'

'Right now, Terry, I'd like to chop his balls off. But the fact is I have to think of *myself* in this situation. I'm the victim, remember? In cases of sexual assault the police are supposed to consider the victim's feelings. So I'm telling you now, *I don't want to press charges*. OK? Just forget it.'

Terry tried again. 'Look, Sarah, it may not come to that. His story's absurd, we'll break him in questioning and get him to plead guilty. Then you won't have to give evidence.'

'It's still a sensation, though, isn't it? Even with a guilty plea. Reporters aren't stupid.'

'Maybe not, but at least he'll be locked up. Otherwise he'll do it again to some other innocent woman. Just as he did to Sharon Gilbert before you. And the others.'

'We don't *know* he raped Sharon, Terry.' Sarah met his disbelieving eyes and sighed. 'All right, I admit it's likely and what happened last night makes it even more likely, but the fact is the evidence didn't convince a jury. That's why he got off. It wasn't some sort of wicked trick that I pulled, you know. You didn't have the proof.'

'Maybe. But I've got it now, Sarah. I can show you.'

'Proof that he raped Sharon?'

'Yes.'

It was Sarah's turn to look astonished. 'How come you've got it now and not before?'

'We found some things last night. In that shed.'

'*Oh.*' Although Sarah had been afraid of what they would find in the shed, in all the trauma it hadn't occurred to her that they had anything to do with Gary. 'What things? Tell me.'

'Come back this afternoon and I'll show you.'

'Why not now?'

'Harry's getting them identified. As soon as he comes back we'll confront Gary with them. Then I can show them to you and tell you his response.'

'Is your mum at home, sonny?'

'Yes.' The small boy stared up at Harry Easby. 'She's upstairs, working.'

'Could you tell her a policeman's here, to talk to her?'

The question seemed to pose more difficulties than Harry had expected. The child's face – a surprisingly strong, determined face for a seven-year-old – puckered with a frown. 'She's upstairs, working,' he repeated, surprised he hadn't been understood. 'Come back later.'

'No, wait.' Harry put his foot in the door just in time. 'I'm a policeman, son, all right? You just go upstairs and tell your mum I'm here. I'll wait inside, OK?'

'You can't . . .' But Harry already had come in. There was an awkward confrontation in the hall, when he actually thought the small boy was going to try to push him out, but Harry sidestepped him and went into the front room, where a four-year-old girl was playing with dolls.

'Hello. What's your name then?'

'Katie.' The child favoured him with a brief glance and returned to wrapping sellotape round a doll's forearm.

'And your brother?'

'Wayne.'

'I see.' Wayne glowered at him from the doorway. He showed no inclination to go upstairs. Harry was about to try again when he noticed a sound. It was rhythmic, repetitive, and came from the ceiling overhead. The nature of their mother's work suddenly became clear.

'I'll just wait here then, till your mum's finished,' he said, sitting on the sofa. 'OK?'

The rhythm of the bedsprings began to be accompanied by cries and groans. 'Does your mum do a lot of work?' Harry asked.

The little girl ignored him. Wayne frowned, still apparently wanting to throw this stranger out. 'You should ring up before you come,' he said accusingly.

'I will next time. What's the number?'

'479386.' Harry wrote it down.

This having exhausted the conversation, they sat in uneasy silence. After a while a man came downstairs and went out of the front door. A moment later a woman in a purple satin nightdress walked into the room. She stopped when she saw Harry Easby.

'Did you make an appointment?'

'No.' Harry grinned. 'I will next time. How much?'

'Not in front of the kids.' She ruffled Wayne's hair and smiled at little Katie. 'You OK, you two?' Seeing they were in no urgent need of anything she looked at Harry again, weighing him up. 'Well, I'm not busy. You can come upstairs if you like. I can tell you the prices there.'

In her bedroom Harry listened with interest to her prices and the range of services she offered. She was a tall, slender woman with elaborately curled peroxide-blonde hair. When she had recited her menu she smiled at him provocatively, one hand on her hip, the other brushing a lock of hair along her cheek. 'Anything you fancy, cowboy?'

'Another time, perhaps,' said Harry. He showed her his warrant card.

'Bloody hellfire!' She turned away angrily. 'I've done nowt wrong!'

'Oh no? Social Services might see it differently.'

'My kids are happy, aren't they?' A shadow of fear flickered across her face. 'Do they look neglected to you?'

'They might, if I wanted something,' said Harry nastily. 'But as it happens I don't – not for the moment anyway. You *are* Sharon Gilbert, I presume?'

'No, I'm Dr Livingstone. 'Course I am, you knew that before you came in.'

'All right.' He began to take things out of his plastic bag, and lay them on the double bed. 'There, Ms Gilbert. I need to know if you recognize any of these.'

'Interview resumed at 2.37 p.m. Present in the room, Gary Harker, his solicitor Mrs Lucy Sampson, DC Harry Easby and myself, DI Terry Bateson.' Terry checked the tapes were spinning smoothly in the recorder, then leaned both elbows on the table and stared at his suspect.

'Now then, Gary, I want to check a few details of your story. You said you were in this shed for about five minutes before Mrs Newby arrived. Is that right?'

'Yeah. More or less. I wasn't exactly counting the time.'

'I understand. You didn't, er, look at your watch before you went in?'

'No. Why should I?'

This question, Terry was pleased to see, brought out signs of anxiety on Gary's face. Skin a trifle paler than before, tiny beads of sweat around the temples. 'Oh, I don't know. Perhaps you wondered if Mrs Newby was late?'

'I didn't say I had an appointment.'

'Didn't you? I thought you went there to meet her. Or was it her son?'

Gary said nothing. He glanced briefly at Lucy, his solicitor, who refused to meet his eyes. Lucy hated being there. If she had not already been Gary's solicitor she would have refused to come. She was prepared to see that the police behaved within the law, and no more. Apart from that, Gary could drown in his own lies.

Terry noted the exchange of looks with satisfaction.

'You didn't really go there to meet Mrs Newby at all, did you, Gary?'

'I did. I told yer.'

'What for?'

'To thank her. She was my barrister, remember? Chewed *you* up in court, didn't she?'

'She did.' Last night Terry might have lost his temper. Today he felt in control. 'So why did you need a torch, Gary?'

'What torch?'

'This one.' Terry put it on the table. It was a pencil torch which would throw a strong, narrow beam. 'It was in your pocket when you were arrested last night.'

'So? I often carry a torch.'

'Sure. Useful tool for a burglar.'

'I told you –'

'Yeah, yeah, we know. You were waiting for your mistress. Find anything interesting in the shed while you were waiting, Gary, did you? A quick flash around with the torch maybe?'

'No.'

'Well, that's a pity, because we did. We searched that shed quite thoroughly, in fact. D'you want to know what we found?'

Gary shook his head, but Terry was delighted to note that the sweat was still there. The bastard knows what's coming all right, Terry thought. He put a small plastic evidence bag on the table. 'For starters, there was this ring.' He held it up a few inches from Gary's nose. 'For the tape, I'm showing Mr Harker a woman's ring, decorated with precious stones in the shape of the letter S. Ever seen that before, Gary?'

Gary shook his head. Terry smiled, and put another bag on the table.

This one contained a black balaclava hood, with slits cut for eyes. Gary shook his head again.

'Or these?' He showed Gary a pair of dark trousers and a black pullover.

'I never seen 'em before.'

'Sure.' Terry sat back, and Harry Easby took over.

'Well, that's strange, Gary, isn't it? Because I showed all these things to Sharon Gilbert this morning. What do you think she said?'

Gary said nothing. But the person who was really staring at the things on the table, Terry noted, was Lucy Sampson. She looked as though she were about to be sick.

'She said that this ring . . .' Harry dangled it in front of Gary's face. '. . . was *her* ring, stolen from her house by the man who raped her. The letter S stands for Sharon, she says. And the hood, the trousers and jumper look exactly like the ones the rapist was wearing, too.'

'Don't prove nowt,' said Gary truculently. 'I never seen them before.'

'Did you touch them?' asked Terry swiftly.

'No. 'Course not.'

'Are you sure about that, Gary? Think carefully, now. Because if we get these things examined by forensic, and they find your hairs or your fingerprints, that's going to prove you're lying, isn't it? Are you sure you didn't touch them?' As he had expected, Gary hesitated. He glanced at his solicitor, who ignored him.

'Well, not unless it were an accident, like. It were dark in that shed.'

'I see. But you didn't put the balaclava on your head, for example, or step into these trousers and jumper because it was cold, did you?' Terry asked mockingly. 'Just for five minutes, maybe, while you were waiting for Mrs Newby?'

'No, 'course not.'

'And they're definitely not your clothes?'

'No.'

'So if the forensic scientists happen to find your hairs, or your skin or whatever – your *stink*, Gary – inside this balaclava hood or these trousers or this jumper, then it will be a fair assumption that you wore them, won't it?'

'You won't find that.'

'No, Gary? Well, for your sake, I hope not, because these forensic scientists, they're devilish clever these days, you know. They might find hairs from Sharon's body or fibres from her clothes. And then where would you be, Gary old son? Eh? Tell me that?'

'You'll find nowt,' said Gary defiantly. 'Anyhow, how did they get there, in that shed?'

'True, that's the problem,' Terry said. 'Good question, Gary, I'll grant you that. But you know, I've got an answer now. Do you know what I think happened – are you listening to this, too, Mrs Sampson? You who defended this man and told me he was innocent? Listen now. I think you raped Sharon just like she said, Gary, I've always thought that. But afterwards you didn't go straight home, you went back to this shed. It's only a couple of streets away, and you know it because your mate Simon lives there. Why did you go there? Because Sharon had recognized you, and you knew that if she reported this rape to us we'd come looking for you. Then we'd take your clothes and get them examined by forensics.

'So what did you do? You changed into some of Simon's clothes – either you got them from his house or his shed. You dumped your own clothes in his shed, with this hood and ring, too. That's what happened, isn't it, Gary? That's why we found no forensics on the clothes from your flat. Because they weren't the ones you did the rape in. You left your clothes in the shed, until yesterday when you went back to get them. Clever scheme, Gary. Not bad at all. And it would have worked, too, if you hadn't been unlucky enough to be found there by Simon's mum.

'You weren't expecting her at all, were you? You went there to get back your clothes and this ring you took from Sharon Gilbert! That's why you were there.'

There was silence in the room when he had finished. The droplets of sweat on Gary's forehead had increased, Terry noted with satisfaction. Lucy was staring with intense disgust at her hands, as though she had touched something foul.

'You can't prove none of this!' Gary said defiantly. 'Anyhow I never took owt!'

'No, Gary?' Terry smiled as he produced his final piece of evidence. A plastic bag with a man's watch inside. An expensive-looking watch. 'Recognize this, Gary?'

Gary's face went a shade paler than before. Terry guessed that he'd been hoping the watch had been overlooked. He made a pretence of examining it closely.

'Beautiful watch, this. Waterproof to fifty metres, date, international time zones – do a lot of world travel, do you, Gary? And the initials G.H. engraved on the back, too. Nice piece of kit. It was in your pocket last night, Gary, when you were arrested. I thought that was funny, too. I mean, a watch like this, I'd expect a man to be proud – flaunt it on his wrist for the world to see. Not stuff it in his pocket as though he'd just, well . . . picked it up in a shed somewhere.'

He turned to Harry. 'Did you show this to Sharon, too?'

Harry nodded. 'I did, yes. She recognized it at once. She said it was the watch she quarrelled about with Gary Harker in the pub on the night before the rape. The man who raped her took that watch, she said. She was positive about that, too.'

'It was found in your pocket, Gary,' Terry continued. 'After you'd been in that shed. So would you like to tell us how it got there?'

The sweat on Gary's face was quite impressive now. Again he looked to Lucy Sampson for support, again she ignored him. Desperately he said: 'I found it.'

178

'Where?'

'In the shed. It was just there, in this bag in the corner, so I picked it up and put it in my pocket. I didn't have time to check it were mine for sure, I just thought it looked the same. I don't know how it got there, ask Simon about it. Maybe he raped Sharon as well.'

'Oh, sure. And you still say you didn't? After all this?' Terry gestured at the pile of evidence bags on the table.

'I were found not guilty, copper. In court. Think on that.'

Reluctantly, Lucy Sampson bestirred herself. Looking deeply uncomfortable with the whole business, she said: 'I'm afraid that *is* unfortunately the point, Detective Inspector, as you must surely know. Whatever evidence you may have found now, it's simply too late. My client has already been tried and acquitted of this crime. He cannot in law be tried for it again. Even if he were to admit to you now that he did it, that principle still applies. Unfortunately.' She looked at Gary for the first time. 'You don't have to lie any more, Gary, it doesn't matter. You can tell them the truth if you like.'

'And they can't do owt?'

'No. Not on this charge.'

Terry sighed. It was a bitter triumph. 'Unfortunately she's right, Gary. You've been found not guilty and that's it. But just for the record, tell us. You did rape Sharon, didn't you?'

A devious, cunning smile twisted Gary's face. He looked at the three of them, relishing his moment of victory. He waited.

'No,' he said at last. 'I didn't.'

23

'You're going to do what?' Churchill asked.

'Release him, sir. We have to. We've got no choice.'

'But we caught him in the act! I saw it – so did Tracy, didn't you? Tracy?'

'I saw it, yes, sir.'

'Then what . . . Terry, can't I leave you here for a single afternoon without some monumental fuck-up? What the bloody hell have you done this time?'

'It's not me, sir, it's Mrs Newby . . .' Grimly, Terry described their interview with Sarah. It had not ended when Sarah had wanted it to: for a good half-hour afterwards Terry had pressed her to change her mind. But she had not changed. It had been like arguing with a computer hologram that looked and moved like a human but was programmed beyond the reach of persuasion. And she *was*, after all, the victim; whether Terry liked it or not her feelings were neither illogical nor unclear. If that meant letting Gary go free, then tough. Let him go.

'So that's it?' Churchill asked incredulously. 'After what we all saw, *and* the fact that you're now certain he raped Sharon Gilbert?'

'Ninety-five per cent certain, yes, sir. We'll be completely sure if anything comes back on the hood and clothes from forensics. Not that it matters anyway. We found it all too late.'

Churchill slumped on to a desk in the corner of the incident room. On the wall behind him were photographs of the unsolved murder of Maria Clayton, nine months ago. A few feet to his right, a similar collage of the assault on Karen Whitaker. Churchill thumped the wall in frustration. 'You thought he did both of these, too, Terry, didn't you?'

'He's still a possible for Clayton, yes, sir. But not Whitaker – the DNA didn't match up.'

'Nevertheless, you believe this man Harker may have killed Clayton as well as raping Gilbert. You told this Newby woman that, did you? That if he's killed and raped already, he's likely to do it again? You did mention that?'

'I told her, yes, but it didn't make any impression.'

'What kind of a bitch is she?' Churchill muttered. 'I've never heard anything like it.'

Tracy Litherland intervened. 'I think she's a very determined, focused lady, sir, who's under a lot of stress but won't let anyone slap her down.' Terry had always suspected that she shared his dislike for their new chief, but never before had she made it so plain.

Churchill rolled his eyes. 'Thanks for the feminist perspective, Trace. But that's precisely what we *did* see last night – Harker slapping her down. And now she won't stand up to him.'

Stubbornly, Tracy repeated Sarah's reasons; the very reasons that she and Terry had spent so much time arguing against, only a few hours ago.

Churchill sighed impatiently: 'Yes, Trace, but there is such a thing as the public interest, or had you forgotten? You know, keeping murderers and rapists off the streets, that sort of thing. Aren't lawyers supposed to be interested in that, too?'

'Lawyers, sir?' Tracy shook her head.

'No.' Churchill answered his own question with a grim laugh. 'For them it's all just a game, ain't it? Just a sodding game.'

It hardly seemed like a game to Sarah and Lucy, just then. They had spent the afternoon in Lucy's office, discussing Sarah's decision not to give a statement. Sarah was relieved that Lucy seemed to understand; Lucy was wondering just how much more her friend could take.

Sarah, she thought, had already suffered too much in the past few days. She was pale, with a bruise along her jaw and her eye half closed. She looked exhausted too, which was hardly surprising. Not only had her son been arrested for murder, and she herself nearly raped, but Emily had run away from home and been feared murdered. All this in addition to the almost routine discovery that she was responsible for the acquittal of a guilty man.

All Lucy could offer was tea, talk and sympathy. To her surprise it seemed to work quite well. Sarah still seemed able to talk and think and lift a teacup without screaming and hurling it against the wall. Which helped, because they had serious questions to discuss.

Such as how to defend Simon. And his apparent connection with Gary Harker.

Sarah closed her eyes, and a childhood memory came to her, of a trip to the beach at Blackpool when she was small. She had been exploring a rock pool with her father and they had seen a small crab scurry for shelter under a stone. Sarah had been afraid to pick up the stone and so her father had lifted it for her. But under the stone, instead of the tiny crab which she expected, was a much, much bigger one. A huge crab, its shelly body as wide as her face, its vast serrated pincers raised in fury, its eyes on stalks swivelling intently towards her pink little toes, six scaly legs clattering sideways towards her while she screamed and screamed . . .

She shuddered at the memory, then glanced at Lucy doodling on a pad of paper. Outside, the evening rush hour was beginning.

'I'm sorry, I've kept you. You'll be wanting to go home,' she said.

Lucy smiled. 'Why now? I'll just sit in a jam. They won't expect me till seven.'

Sarah took a step nearer the stone in her mind. 'The only thing I'd regret about Gary, would be if he'd really committed all these attacks, as Terry Bateson thinks he did.'

Lucy considered this. 'There's evidence to disprove that.'

'In one of the cases, yes. They found some DNA on a hair from Karen Whitaker's attacker that wasn't a match for Gary.'

'There you are then. It wasn't him.'

'He could still have murdered the first one. The prostitute, Maria Clayton.'

'*Could have.* But there's no evidence. Come on, Sarah, you know this. They wanted to charge him with that before, but the CPS turned them down. They couldn't prove it then and they can't now. A hundred men *could* have done it.'

'Including my son? Simon?'

This was the sort of remark that Lucy feared. She studied Sarah cautiously before answering. An answer that was intended to rebuild confidence.

'Including your husband and my husband and any man without an alibi, if it comes to that. Come on, Sarah – suspicion and innuendo isn't any sort of proof.'

But Sarah had her hands around the stone now. She was going to lift it. 'The thing is, Lucy, Terry Bateson has always thought that these attacks are the work of one man; the Hooded Killer the *Evening Press* writes about. But he can't prove it, because for a start, one of the attacks – the one on Whitaker – was definitely committed by someone else. So he's wrong.'

'So he's wrong, yup,' Lucy nodded. 'Not the first time a policeman's been wrong.'

'He's wrong about the idea that it was *one* man, Lucy, yes.' Sarah's next words came out in a whisper. 'But what if it was *two*?'

'Two?' Lucy wasn't sure she'd heard correctly. 'Two men raping together?'

'Not necessarily raping together, no, but . . . co-operating. You know, maybe one does it one time, the other the next. One acting as lookout for the other, that sort of thing?'

Not just one huge crab under the stone, but two.

'Oh come on, Sarah! Now you're really in the realms of fantasy.'

'Am I? Probably, I hope so. But look at what we know. We know – so long as the forensic examination supports it – that Gary raped Sharon Gilbert. We know he claims he was with someone else that night, this fellow called Sean whom no one could find . . .'

'We proved he existed, remember? That was one of our better moments.'

'True. But even if we accept that this Sean exists, it doesn't mean it was him who was with Gary that night, does it? *What if it was Simon?*'

'We don't know that anyone was with him, Sarah.' This was just the sort of reaction Lucy wanted to suppress. But Sarah's imagination was in full flight.

'Well, he *said* someone was, didn't he? And it seems Gary went into a shed – Simon's shed – to change his clothes and dump his hood before he went home. How did he know there'd be clothes in that shed if Simon hadn't told him? How did he know the shed even existed?'

Will Churchill strode back and forth, like a maths teacher Terry had once known. 'Look, there's still one question that hasn't been answered by any of you lot.' He tapped his teeth with a pencil. 'And that is, what exactly is the connection between this woman's son and Gary Harker? I mean, I know what you think he was doing in that shed, Terry, changing his clothes after the rape – but *why there*? Did the boy know what Gary'd done, or didn't he? Was he an innocent in all this, or an accomplice?'

'What about the other way around, sir?' Tracy suggested. 'Was Harker completely unconnected with the murder of Jasmine Hurst? Or was he an accomplice there too?'

A tremor of excitement passed around the room. The three men – Churchill, Terry and Harry – shivered as though someone had walked over their graves. Churchill waved his pencil at Tracy in a chauvinist compliment. 'Not just a pair of pretty legs, eh, sergeant? There's a brain behind that beauty, gents!' Then before Tracy had time to take offence, he continued: 'And that, of course, could be another reason why Mrs Barrister Newby won't sign a statement against Harker! Because he knows something about her son which he might blurt out in court!'

'Oh, wait a minute, sir,' Terry protested. 'She must hate him more than we do – it's not Harker she's trying to protect, it's her own reputation!'

'She still has one, does she? I'm not so sure, Terence. She got him off the rape charge, she met him in that shed in the middle of the night – how do we know there isn't something in Gary's story after all? I mean, what was she doing there? Not looking for sex maybe but what about the balaclava and those clothes and the rest of it? Maybe she was doing a deal with Harker to get rid of them. In which case she'd be an accessory after the fact.'

'Accessory to what, sir?' Tracy asked. 'The rape of Sharon or . . .' Her sentence hung unfinished in the air. They tested the extraordinary possibilities in their minds. More than one crime might be linked by the events in this shed. A keen, hungry grin began to play around Will Churchill's lips – like a wolf sighting his prey.

'Her *reputation* she's trying to protect, you said, Terence? She'll need to, won't she, if it turns out she not only knew Harker was guilty of rape, but that her own son helped him, *and* that son's guilty of murder! The Bar Council won't look too kindly on that, will they?'

'It's not possible,' Terry said. The whole idea shocked him. 'There's no proof, nothing to connect her with either the rape or Jasmine Hurst's murder . . .'

'Only the fact that Gary did the one and her son did the other; Gary and Simon seem to know each other; and she met Gary in her son's shed!'

'Yes, but she didn't *choose* to meet him there,' Terry insisted. 'It was an accident. She went to park her bike, and there was Gary getting his watch back.'

'Just a coincidence, eh, Terence? That's not what Gary said.'

'The man's a nutter! A fantasist! Anyway we saw what he was doing.'

'Then why won't she press charges?'

'To avoid publicity, sir,' Terry repeated. 'You understand her, don't you, Trace?'

Tracy frowned. 'I understand, sure, but there are other explanations. What we need to know, surely, is what the connection between Gary and Simon actually is. Until then . . .'

'Right.' Churchill stood up. 'We'd better be quick. You haven't released him, have you?'

'No, sir. We've got him till ten thirty tonight, unless we charge him.'

'Right then. Come on, Terence; let's you and me go and see this thug, shall we?'

As they were leaving Sarah sighed and said: 'If only it could be Gary that killed Jasmine. But the pig was on remand, wasn't he?'

'Yes,' Lucy said putting on her coat. *'No!* No, he was free then, surely?'

'I thought it was the day the trial ended?'

'No. Your memory's playing tricks.'

They stared at each other in shock. A wild hope lit in Sarah's eyes. 'What are the dates?'

Feverishly, they scrabbled in Lucy's desk diary. 'There, I was right! Last day of trial, Thursday 13th. Gary was released at what? Three, four o'clock. And Jasmine's body was found next morning, the 14th. She was killed around midnight on the 13th.'

'So he *could* have done it!' Sarah breathed.

'Yes, but what motive would he have? What reason?'

'That man doesn't need a motive, Lucy. He's a monster. He raped Sharon and he attacked me. He ought to have been grateful to me if anything – I'd got him off, for Christ's sake. But when I met him in that shed I was just there, I was a woman, I asked him what he was doing and he snapped. Did what he's good at. He might have killed me if the police hadn't turned up.'

'Yes, but how would he have met Jasmine?'

'I wish we knew,' Sarah breathed quietly. 'I wish we knew.'

24

'Now then, Gary,' Terry began. 'How well do you know Simon Newby?'

Gary shrugged. 'I've met him around. On building sites and such.'

'All right, tell me about him. What do you know?'

'His mum's got a juicy arse.'

'Apart from that, Gary. We've been through all that.'

'Been through it, copper? You wish!' Terry tried to keep his face neutral, but Gary could see the effect his words were having. Churchill intervened, in his sneering southern accent.

'What about her son, then, Gary? D'you fancy him too?'

'You shut your filthy mouth! Anyhow, he's got his own bird. The dead one.'

'Oh yes. Justine.'

'Jasmine.'

'Jasmine, sorry.' Churchill corrected himself slyly. 'You met her then?'

'Yeah. So?'

'Fancy her, did you?' Terry resumed, intrigued by this discovery.

'She was all right. Better'n he deserved.'

'What did she look like, Gary?' Churchill asked. 'Describe her for us, will you?'

Gary thought for a moment. 'Well. Quite tall for a girl. Stunner to look at. Long brown hair, pretty face. Big tits.' He laughed, making a squeezing motion with his hands. 'Like melons.'

A little worm of excitement woke at the base of Terry's spine, and began to crawl up towards his brain. 'Did you touch them, then, Gary?'

'No chance. The lad would have killed me.'

'But you'd have liked to touch them?' Terry persisted. 'If you could?'

Gary eyed him pityingly. 'Not getting enough, are you, copper? I could take you places . . .'

Smoothly, Churchill took over. 'You say young Simon would have killed you. Is that how he behaved then, when she was around? A bit violent, protective, perhaps?'

'Him, violent?' Gary laughed scornfully. 'Say boo to him and he shits his pants. I've seen it. Girls might be scared of him but no one else.'

The two detectives were silent for a moment, each, from their different perspectives, taking this in. It said as much about Gary as Simon, Terry thought. The casual menace in the villain opposite them came from his sheer muscular bulk. How would a woman feel, confronted with such brutal, overwhelming force? A woman like Sarah, Sharon, even Jasmine Hurst perhaps . . .

'So how often did you meet Jasmine, altogether?' Terry asked.

Gary shrugged. 'Three, four times, perhaps. Can't remember.'

'Always at Simon's house?'

'Think so. Yeah.'

'Think hard, Gary. You never met her anywhere else? Didn't follow her home, maybe, try to get your hands on those breasts like – what was it – melons?'

'You're obsessed, you are,' Gary jeered. 'You need help. And no . . .' He spoke directly into the microphone. 'I did not follow Jasmine home. Nor did I shag her. Or murder her. How could I – I was in court!'

'Nobody's accused you of murdering her, Gary,' Terry said smoothly. 'But in fact you *weren't* in court when this girl was murdered. You were released that afternoon, and she was killed between nine and midnight that night. So where were you for the rest of that day?'

Gary's jaw fell open. 'You're not accusing me . . .'

'You brought the subject up, Gary. Not me. Answer the question.'

'I . . . well, I went home, to get changed and have a wash. Then I went out for a few jars.'

'To which pub?'

'The Lighthorseman, if you want to know. They had the football on the big screen. Arsenal versus Real Madrid.'

'Who won?'

'Real, 3–2. There were half a dozen lads there who saw me.' He gave Terry the names, sneering triumphantly. 'I stayed till closing time, then went home to bed.'

'Did you see Jasmine that night? Or Simon?'

'No.'

'All right, Gary, that's very helpful.' Churchill intervened impatiently. 'Now let's get back to why you're here, shall we? This business of sexually assaulting Simon's mother – your own barrister, for Christ's sake, the woman who got you off! Come on, son, help me out a bit. I've not come across this sort of thing before.'

'I told your mate there,' said Gary stubbornly, nodding at Terry. 'She asked for it.'

'Yeah, yeah, and I'm the King of China's grandmother. Listen, Gary, what I want to know is, why you were in that shed in the first place. Simon Newby's shed.'

Gary stared back, bemused. No sensible answer seemed to occur to him.

'You found a watch, Gary, I believe,' Terry prompted helpfully. 'And a ring, and some clothes which we've sent for forensic analysis.'

'Did Mrs Newby see these things?' Churchill asked. 'Or talk to you about them?'

Gary looked confused. 'What would she do that for?'

Churchill leaned forward, staring intently into Gary's face. 'Well, think about it, Gary. This woman, your barrister, meets you in this shed at night. It's a surprise to both of you. You have an argument, and you resolve this argument by trying to rape her, like the dickhead you are. So what was this argument about? She saw you trying to get rid of the evidence, was that it? She realized for certain that you were guilty, and –'

'No!' A cunning grin crossed Gary's face. 'I wasn't trying to get rid of that stuff. *She* was.'

'What?' This time, even Churchill was taken aback. There was a stunned silence, from which Terry recovered first.

'You're talking out of your arse again, Gary.'

'Am I? You prove it then.'

'I don't have to. It's as big a load of crap as you told us yesterday.'

'Are you going to charge me with raping her then?'

If there was such a thing as low criminal cunning, this bastard had it, Terry thought. He wasn't bright, he was a common violent thug who'd spent a large part of his adult life in prison and yet, when he was confronted with seemingly irrefutable proof of his guilt, his mind instantly homed in on the one route of escape. No one had told him that the charge of attempted rape was likely to be dropped, but he had guessed nonetheless.

Churchill tried to cover it up. 'Just answer the questions, son, then we'll see. Look, with you in that shed was all the evidence we needed to convict you of raping Sharon Gilbert, right? Are you seriously trying to tell us that *your barrister* was trying to hide it, not you? Why on earth would she do that?'

'I were found not guilty, remember?'

Churchill gazed at him wearily. 'Yeah, sure. The courts get it wrong sometimes. But come on, Gary – all that stuff in the shed *proves* your guilt, for Christ's sake! The watch, the ring, the hood – Sharon Gilbert's identified the lot, you know.'

'So? It doesn't mean *I* put them there, does it? I just found them – my watch, anyhow.' Gary hesitated, looking from Churchill to Terry, who smiled mockingly, not believing a word. 'And then she comes in and says . . .'

'Yes, Gary, what did she say? Come on now. Make it up quick or we won't believe you.'

'She says get rid of it quick, my son did it.'

Terry burst out laughing. 'Oh, very good, Gary, well done! Brilliant. You're saying your barrister came into the shed, saw you pawing all this evidence that proves your guilt, and said get rid of that quick because my son raped Sharon Gilbert. Is that it?'

'It was in his shed.'

'Yeah, sure. But instead of helping her get rid of it, you tried to rape her, remember. Is this an example of your social skills, or what?'

'It's not bloody funny, copper . . .'

'Not good manners though, is it? Your idea of etiquette?'

'I could go down for eight years . . .'

'And so you should.' Terry was still smiling at the sheer effrontery of it all, but Churchill, to his surprise, put a hand on his arm.

'Just a minute, Terence. Gary, are you seriously asking us to believe that your barrister, the woman who defended you, told you that her son, Simon Newby, raped Sharon Gilbert?'

Gary nodded defiantly. 'That's what I said, yeah.'

'And you're prepared to make a statement to that effect?'

'I might.'

The room fell silent. Terry was appalled. *What was Churchill playing at?* A pulse began to throb violently in his ears. 'Come on, Gary, this is total crap and you know it. Sharon identified *you*, not Simon – and so did her little kid, remember? The little boy who tried to protect his mum when you were raping her in front of him –'

'I were found not guilty!'

187

'Yes, but you *were* guilty, weren't you? Everyone knows that – even your barrister, who actually got you off. And how do you reward her? By trying to rape her and then accusing her son of your own filthy crime! You make me sick, you do!'

'I don't give a fucking toss –'

'Shut up and listen! Let me tell you what happened when she came into that shed, shall I? She saw you fumbling with that watch and hood and ring and all the rest of it, and she realized for certain that you were guilty, where before perhaps she'd given you the benefit of the doubt. And so maybe she did say get rid of it, I don't know, but if so it was to save *you*, not her son! Or more likely she just said what she really thought of you, you filthy slob, and that's what triggered your anger. What would you have done if we hadn't turned up when we did, eh, Gary? When you'd finished your rape? Would you have strangled her and left her for dead like you did with Maria Clayton, is that it?'

Gary glowered at him, menacing, furious. 'You weren't there.'

'I bloody well was, and so was DCI Churchill here. We saw exactly what you were doing to that woman . . .'

'Why don't you charge me then?'

The question stopped Terry dead, like a glass door he'd walked into. It was the one answer they couldn't give. Gary was going to get away again, and he knew it. Bitterly, Terry stared at Gary, so safe behind the glass door, and said: 'You murdered Maria Clayton, didn't you, Gary? You followed her on to Strensall Common and then you raped her and throttled her to death, just like you were doing with Sarah Newby. Isn't that right?'

Gary shook his head, sneering and contemptuous. 'Who?'

'You know who. And for all I know you did the same to Jasmine Hurst as well!'

'You're a madman.' Gary turned to Churchill for help. 'Is that who you employ now, madmen like him? I don't know who he's talking about.'

Churchill spoke to the microphone on the wall. 'Interview suspended at 9.27. DCI Churchill and DI Bateson leave the room. Come on, Terence. I want a word. *Now.*'

'My office!' Churchill snapped, compelling Terry to follow his short, stocky, visibly furious superior upstairs to the room which he had once hoped would be his own.

'Do you mind telling me what the bloody hell you think you're playing at?'

'I might ask the same of you, sir.' Terry was six inches taller than Churchill and almost equally angry, though for a different reason.

'Well, you might but you bloody well won't. Do you have a single shred of evidence that that man could have killed Jasmine Hurst?'

'Not at the moment, sir, no, but –'

'No, of course you don't! And the reason, as even a blind man in a box could see, is that Simon Newby did it. We have blood, semen, motive, opportunity, even the goddamn knife, for Christ's sake! Where have you been all these days? Lost in a dream?'

'Yes, OK, but you've seen what the guy's like, haven't you?'

'Oh great, so we're judging by appearances now, are we? Gary looks like a thug so he must be guilty, is that it? We're back in Victorian times now?'

'Well, it's more sense than saying Simon raped Sharon, anyway,' Terry said furiously. 'That's just utter crap – surely even you could see that? Sir.'

The antagonism between them was open now. Churchill met Terry's eyes coolly, making it clear that he, by virtue of his rank and the way he controlled his temper, was in the ascendant.

'Maybe it is, maybe it isn't. Where's your interrogation technique, Terence? You'll learn nothing by blurting out wild accusations like you did just now.'

Terry took a deep breath, trying to control himself. 'In my view, sir, the only wild accusation is to suggest that Sarah Newby, who we saw being assaulted yesterday in front of our own eyes, would conspire with a thug like Harker to conceal evidence about her son. She's got enough to deal with as it is, for God's sake!'

'Oh, I get it now.' Churchill smiled knowingly. 'So that's why Harker was needling you – you're soft on the woman, aren't you? Even though she chewed you up in court you're carrying a torch for her!'

Terry's silence only confirmed Churchill's suspicions, and as he rejoiced in his discovery his anger subsided. He had a new weapon to use now.

'Well, well,' he mocked. 'Terence in love! Better watch out, old son, she looks a dangerous bird to me – married too. But try not to let your emotions cloud your judgement, eh? At least when you're at work.'

'I didn't think I was, sir. I thought I was seeing things exceptionally clearly.'

'That's one of the delusions of love, old son. Come on – is it seeing things clearly to accuse Gary of killing Jasmine when we know Simon did it? And then accuse him of killing Maria Clayton, too – what's the evidence for that?'

'Only the evidence we've always had – he worked on her house, he'd boasted about having sex with her, he wore trainers similar to a footprint we found near the body, he has no alibi and a record of violence to women. It seemed like a good enough case to me . . .'

189

'But the CPS said it was too thin, right?' A pitying look crossed Churchill's face. 'And they were right, Terence, it is. I'm sorry, if you've nothing stronger than that we'll have to let him go.'

'Again.'

'Yes, again. However much you hate him, we follow the rules. If you think he did this Clayton murder, dig up the evidence and charge him. But until then . . .' He shrugged. 'I'm sorry.'

'We let this violent rapist back on to the streets?'

'If you choose to put it like that, yes.'

'So he's free, then?' Bob asked.

'Probably, by now.' Sarah lay back in the armchair, an icepack over her face. Bob had bought it this afternoon; it relieved the throbbing slightly. 'Things don't always go to plan.'

'But if you think he killed Jasmine, Sarah . . .'

'There's no proof of it, none at all. It's just that he was free and he's like that. For all I know it could have been a wandering maniac from Outer Mongolia. I just don't believe it was Simon, that's all.'

Bob said nothing. The question lay between them, like a huge unbridgeable canyon. Since the assault he had been kindness itself, ringing her at work, having a meal and this icepack ready in the evening, her favourite CD on the hi-fi. He hadn't questioned her decision not to give evidence against Gary. But he hadn't expressed faith in Simon.

They could hear Emily and Larry talking quietly in the kitchen. A nightjar shrieked outside the window. The silence between them lengthened.

'It makes me so angry, Bob,' Sarah said at last. 'Angry with Gary and the police but most of all angry with Simon for getting himself into such a stupid, stupid mess. When I asked him in prison he said the hood might have been used for a *joke*, for Christ's sake! Either that or he was lying. And yet he expects me to wave some magic wand and get him out.'

'You're too involved, Sarah. For your own health you should back off, leave it to Lucy. She's a professional –'

'And I'm not? Is that what you saying?' She pulled off the icepack and sat up, irritably.

'Not in this case, Sarah, you can't be. You're too emotionally involved.'

She got up and walked slowly across the room, resting her forehead against the cool glass of the window. 'It's for my own health that I *am* emotionally involved, Bob. If I don't feel I've done the best for Simon, then I will crack up, really. And you wouldn't want to know me then, Bob. No one would.'

25

Next morning Terry found himself back in front of Churchill's desk. The animosity was still there, smouldering under the ashes of a night's sleep.

'No hard feelings, I hope, Terence? A few harsh words are natural in a job like this. I've always encouraged blokes on my team to speak their minds, you know.'

'Sir.'

'Listen, Terence, I didn't get much sleep last night, I was thinking. It was one of your mistakes which set me off, matter of fact. But then nobody's perfect. It sometimes takes fresh eyes to come in and see what was there all the time.'

It was years since Terry had hated a senior officer so much. 'I don't understand, sir,' he said woodenly. Except that you're younger than me, and took my job.

'No, I know.' Churchill studied him with deep satisfaction. 'But look at the evidence, old son. We've got six assaults on women – Clayton, Whitaker, Gilbert, Steersby, Hurst and now Sarah Newby. Your original idea was that they were all committed by the same lad – Gary Harker. But that won't work. The DNA proves he didn't attack Karen Whitaker. He couldn't have attacked Helen Steersby because he was in custody at the time, and Jasmine Hurst was murdered by Simon Newby. So the only assault we know he committed was the one on Sarah Newby, because we saw it with our own eyes.'

'And Sharon Gilbert, sir.'

Churchill nodded sagely. 'I agree Sharon *claims* he raped her and there's evidence to support her claim, but not all of it does, even now.' He smiled enigmatically at Terry. 'Unlike you I examined that hood, when I took it down to forensics. What do you think I found?'

Terry refused to answer. Churchill delighted in his hostility.

'*Fair hairs*, Terence. With a tinge of red. Quite short ones . . .' He held his finger and thumb a millimetre apart. '. . . *inside* the hood, so they must have been left by the wearer. See what I mean now, about looking carefully at the evidence? Your friend Harker has brown hair. Whereas Simon Newby's hair is – go on, tell me?'

'Fair, sir,' said Terry bitterly. 'But –'

'And very short, too, as I recall. What my father used to call a crewcut, right?'

'But he couldn't have done it! All the evidence points to Harker –'

'Not this evidence, Terence.'

'Sharon identified him, for God's sake! Her son did too!'

'He was masked, Terence! Wearing a hood!'

'But . . .' Terry stuttered, trying to put up reasons for something he thought was obvious. 'But Simon didn't even know her!'

'Didn't he? All the rapist's stuff was found in his shed.'

'Yes, but the watch! The rapist took Gary's watch.'

Churchill nodded. 'I agree, that's a key point. But even so, where was this watch found? In *Simon's* shed, where Gary had gone to look for it. What does that tell you? Maybe he'd asked Simon to get it back for him, and Simon interpreted his instructions a little enthusiastically –'

'That's absurd, sir, it has to be.'

'Is it? It's only a possibility, true, but look what happens next. Gary has an argument with Simon's mother, and assaults her – a serious assault that she won't bring up in court. Why? Fear of what Gary might say about her son? About herself, perhaps? About what they both knew?'

Terry's baffled silence seemed to gratify him.

'You've always believed these attacks were the work of one man, haven't you, Terence? The Hooded Killer, as the *Evening Press* called him. Well, maybe your idea was right, but you got the wrong villain, that's all. What if our serial rapist isn't Gary at all, *but Simon Newby?*'

Terry shook his head. 'I just don't see it, sir.'

'Well, look more closely. I've sent Simon's hair for DNA analysis, and asked forensics to compare it with the fair hairs in the hood, right? I've also asked them to compare the Whitaker hair with both of those. If all three match, then presto! We've got him for three of your five assaults – Sharon Gilbert, Karen Whitaker and Jasmine Hurst!'

'And if they don't?'

Churchill shrugged. 'If they don't, we still prosecute Simon for Jasmine's murder, and look again at the rest. But I think they *will* match, Terence old son. For two reasons. One, Whitaker's attacker had fair hair too. Fair hair with a faint tinge of red, no less – under my pretty forensic scientist's microscope they look exactly the same. And two, the photofit that Helen Steersby gave us. Remember that?'

Terry nodded glumly. He could see what was coming.

'It didn't look like Gary, did it? Of course not, he was locked up at the time. But it *did* look like Simon, remember? Especially about the nose. If Steersby picks him out at an ID parade, there's another one crossed off our list. Which only leaves Maria Clayton.'

Churchill considered Terry thoughtfully. 'Did Simon have any connection with her?'

'None that I know of, no.'

'But you've had no reason to look, have you? Well, now you have.

I want you to go through that file again. Check it carefully, piece by piece, for anything, anything at all, that links to Simon Newby. If there is something, then your original idea about a single attacker will begin to make sense again, won't it?'

He smiled expansively. 'You were just focusing on the wrong man, old son. Gary instead of Simon. So this last one, the murder of Jasmine Hurst, may not be the crime of passion it first appeared, but the work of a guy who's been practising for some time.'

The door opened and a small boy peered out. Harry Easby smiled.

'Hello, Wayne. Is your mother working now?'

'No. She's on't loo.'

'Oh, right.' Harry hesitated, digesting this unusually frank admission. 'Well, er . . .'

'Who is it, Wayne?' A woman's voice called down the stairs, followed by the sound of a toilet flushing and feet descending.

'A feller, Mum. He's . . .'

Sharon Gilbert's smile of welcome faded as she recognized Harry. 'Oh, it's you.'

'Don't be like that, now. I've brought your ring back. Can I have a word?'

'If you must.' In the living room, she sat down and Wayne climbed on to her lap, from where he glared at Harry suspiciously.

'Where's the little lass?'

'Asleep, upstairs.' She frowned at him. 'How did it go then? Did you get him?'

'Gary? We made him sweat.' Harry passed her the gold ring with the letter S engraved on it. She looked insulted.

'Won't you be needing it for evidence?'

'We had it dusted for prints but there weren't any, I'm afraid.'

'So what have you charged him with?'

'Nothing, I'm afraid, love. He –'

'Nothing! But he raped me – I told you!'

'We know that, Sharon –'

'And this ring and that watch prove it. The trial was all wrong.'

'*I* know that, but the law says we can't charge him with the same crime twice.'

'So he's got away with it again, the bastard.'

'Yes, I'm sorry.'

For a moment he thought she was going to cry. Wayne thought so too; he put his arms up and hugged her. She hugged him back, fiercely. Then they heard Katie grizzling upstairs. She put Wayne down. 'There's a bottle of orange in the kitchen. Take it up to her, will you, Wayne.'

As he left the room Harry smiled. 'He's a little prince, that lad.'

Sharon opened her handbag for a cigarette. Her hair hid her face as she lit it. When she looked up Harry noticed again how attractive she was. She was also, he realized, very angry.

'So Gary's walking round, free as a bird. What am I supposed to do if he comes here? He might, you know!'

'Phone the station. Ask for me if you like.'

'Oh aye.' She gave him a brief, pitying glance. 'Gary eats lads like you for breakfast.'

'He didn't look so tough earlier. Like I said, he was sweating.'

She took a long drag on her cigarette. 'What are you, my personal bodyguard?'

That hadn't been his idea, but Harry suddenly saw possibilities in it. After all, officers were encouraged to use their initiative. 'Well, if you feel you need protection . . .'

'You'd offer it?' She laughed, a mixture of anger and contempt. 'And that's it, is it? That's all I get for being raped, screwed by the police and the bloody lawyers – *you*! What are you going to do, then, sunshine? Come round here on your night off?'

'I could do,' said Harry softly.

There was a silence. She sat down on the arm of a chair, crossing her legs slowly and flicking ash into the fireplace. A cool, knowing look came into her eyes. 'Oh yes. Fancied what I told you last time, did you?'

'I could be useful to you,' Harry said.

She laughed again. 'I can get plenty of fellers who are useful like that.'

'I'm sure you can. I meant, other sorts of protection.' He nodded towards the sound of the children's voices upstairs. 'From Social Services, for instance. Someone gives a bad word to them, they'll be round here like a shot. Place of safety orders, child protection, foster homes – you don't want that.'

'You rotten bastard! Get out of here – now!'

Harry stood. 'I don't want that either, Sharon. I think they're fantastic kids. You're not so bad yourself.' He put his hand on her arm. She shook it roughly away.

'Piss off!'

'You don't mean that, Sharon. I'm sorry, I shouldn't have said that about the kids. It was just an example, that's all. I could be useful to you, you could be useful to me . . .'

He touched her hair, very gently; ran a finger along the line of her jaw. There was still anger in her face, but also – resignation.

'Just how could I be useful to you, you young bastard?'

He tilted her chin up towards him, savouring the thrill of power. 'I think you know that well enough, darling. Don't you?'

The work of a guy who's been practising for some time. Churchill's words echoed in Terry's brain. He was shaking, not just with anger at his humiliation, but also at the awful possibility that Churchill might be right. Terry didn't think he could bear that. If this wretched man could waltz in from outside, take a brief look at these cases and instantly see a truth which had eluded Terry for months – well, what did that say?

And his argument was quite persuasive. The evidence of the hairs and the DNA might implicate Simon in the Whitaker case and even, astonishingly, in Sharon Gilbert's rape. Helen Steersby might pick him out in an identity parade too. Which would leave only the murder of Maria Clayton for Churchill to collect a full house. A glorious triumph for a newly appointed Detective Chief Inspector.

And yet, and yet. The boy was the wrong type, Terry thought. Every serial killer he knew of had begun with minor crimes – burglary, petty theft, minor violence – building up gradually to something more evil. Gary Harker had a long profile like this on the police computer. Simon Newby had none. He was a criminal innocent.

Unless we've missed something. *Go through it carefully, piece by piece . . .*

He felt an unexpected reluctance to touch the file on Maria Clayton. At first he couldn't understand why; then it came to him. It brought the image of his wife, Mary, into his mind. This was the first major crime he had worked on after her death. He'd forgotten how hard it had been to face. Several colleagues had suggested that he didn't need to take on a murder enquiry so soon, but he'd been determined. He wanted to get revenge on Maria's killer just as he hoped the courts would take revenge on the boys who had killed his wife.

But of course neither had happened. The boys got two years' youth custody, and were out in less than a year. And Terry had failed to find Maria's killer.

A few months later, he had been passed over for promotion, in favour of the outsider, Churchill. A man ten years younger than himself. A man with all the energy and ambition which he had lost. A man determined to humiliate him on the path to success.

He sighed, and opened the Clayton file. It doesn't matter who catches the villains, he told himself, what matters is that they *are* caught. But he didn't believe it.

He's wrong, and you can prove it, a different voice inside him said. It was the voice of another, younger Terry; the man he had been before Mary died. The man who sometimes worked all night and weekends too, the man who, with only a couple of months' practice, had run inside the first fifty in the Great North Run.

Begin at the beginning, the voice told him. *Check everything. The answer's in there somewhere. And if it isn't, you've got to go out and find it.*

As he read, it came back to him.

Maria Clayton had been found dead on Strensall Common in August last year. She had been bound, strangled and raped. Her small dog, a Yorkshire terrier, was found with its throat cut a few yards away. She had been an upmarket prostitute who lived in a pleasant detached house in Strensall. She was in her mid-thirties, with a daughter at boarding school, which in itself proved how successful she was. Her business had been discreet and well organized. Her maid, Ann Slingsby, a widow in her fifties, had rung the police to report her missing.

One obvious group of suspects were Maria's clients, who were recorded, with notes of their preferences, in Mrs Slingsby's appointments book. Terry smiled wryly at the embarrassment he had caused to businessmen, social workers, airline pilots, even a headmaster and a sprightly old age pensioner, the customers of the service Maria advertised as 'sexual therapy'. Many had appeared to be happily married; some, he feared, no longer were.

None, though, were as young as Simon Newby; all, unlike him, had good jobs which enabled them to afford her fees. Many had been with friends or family at the time of her death; none appeared to have any reason to wish to kill her.

So there we are, thought Terry. A woman leading a quiet life with no apparent enemies. There was no motive, nothing to explain why *Maria* had been murdered, rather than any other woman who had been walking alone at that time in that place. Which, of course, made the crime more frightening to the public and the press. And harder for the police to solve.

His team had interviewed everyone they could find who had been on Strensall Common that evening. Several people had seen Maria walking her dog, but she had been alone and seemed perfectly happy. No one had heard any screams or barks. One man had seen what might have been a masked figure running near where the body was found. But the figure had been a hundred yards away, it might have been a black man rather than someone wearing a mask, it might even have been a woman.

With a sigh, Terry spread the photographs on his desk. They were horrific, as bad as those of Jasmine Hurst, as bad as those of any murder he had seen.

Maria had been bound, half-strangled and raped before she was killed. The only puzzling thing was that there was no semen. Given her profession, Terry had expected to find some, but Ann Slingsby had told him that all her clients used condoms and indeed there were traces of lubricant in her vagina.

In addition to the bruising caused by strangulation, there was a small cut in her throat, to the left of the windpipe, possibly caused by someone seizing her from behind and threatening her with a knife. Jasmine's throat had been cut, much deeper, in almost exactly the same place. But this woman had been strangled, and only her *dog's* throat had been cut. Some black cotton fibres had been found in its mouth. Probably it had barked, and fought to protect its mistress. A brave animal, this tiny

Yorkshire terrier, to attack a man twenty times its own size. But unfortunately, it had not drawn blood.

The other evidence was a footprint from a size 10 Nike trainer a yard from the body. Similar prints were found on a path fifty yards away, the pressure from toe and heel indicating that the wearer had been running.

And that was it. A man with a knife, wearing Nike running shoes and black cotton trousers. Probably a black top as well, and maybe a black hood. Did any of this point to Simon Newby? The shoes? Well, Simon had size 10 Nike trainers. So did Gary, and millions of other men. The hood? Well, it's not certain there *was* a hood, so unless forensics find some trace of Maria on that balaclava from Simon's shed, that's out too. The tracksuit trousers from the shed, were they torn, bitten by a dog? That *would* make a difference. He made a note to ask forensics. Otherwise, there was nothing.

Reading all this, Terry remembered what Ann Slingsby had told him about the builders who extended the kitchen two months before Maria died. The five workmen had been amused to discover that Maria was a prostitute but most had been fine about it, accepting that she was a decent lady who was out of their class. One, however, had been awkward and boastful. Maria had told Ann she'd had sex with him, and regretted it. He was a yob, who didn't know how to behave. His name was Gary Harker.

Terry had traced the other builders; all four remembered Gary's boasts of having sex with Maria, and had seen her shut the door on him smartly when he asked for another session. Gary had been humiliated and angry, and they had avoided teasing him about it because that sort of joke could turn dangerous, with him.

Gary told Terry that she'd been too expensive. He agreed that he had asked for sex free next time but said it was a joke, claiming that she wasn't worth the fifty pounds she charged. He admitted that he occasionally went running on Strensall Common, and had no convincing alibi for the night of Maria's death. But when Terry searched his flat he found a blue Lycra tracksuit, not a black cotton one. His size 10 Nike trainers were new, and there was no balaclava hood. So he had been released.

And then, three weeks later, Karen Whitaker had been attacked.

By a man with a knife, wearing a black tracksuit, black balaclava hood, and wearing size 10 Nike trainers, who had stolen her camera. Not only had Gary Harker been one of a group of workmen employed to repair the student accommodation where Karen Whitaker lived, but he had also found nude photographs of her in her room and shown them to his workmates. Two of the photographs in her room had his fingerprints on them.

It was enough for Terry. Letters were appearing in the *Evening Press* accusing the police of failing to protect women. He arrested Gary and charged him with both crimes.

Then, four weeks later, the DNA report on the hair from the tape used to bind Whitaker came back. Terry groaned as he remembered that day. The charges in the Whitaker case were dropped. Three weeks later, the CPS refused to proceed against Gary in the Clayton case either.

Gary was released and, Terry thought, immediately proceeded to rape Sharon Gilbert. As soon as he was acquitted of that, he assaulted his own barrister. And despite the compelling evidence against Simon Newby, Terry still suspected that Gary might have murdered Jasmine Hurst too. True, there were differences in method: Maria had been strangled, Jasmine's throat had been cut. But everything about Gary's character fitted this murder, just like Maria's.

Gary had known both women were sexually promiscuous, after all. He could easily have thought, in his primitive way, that this meant they should be available to him. And then there was the footprint they'd found beside Jasmine's body – size 10 Nike trainer.

Terry shook his head sadly. It isn't enough, given the weight of evidence against Simon. Maybe Churchill's right, I am obsessed. But then he hasn't been on Gary's trail as long as I have, he didn't react like I did to the attack on Sarah Newby . . .

He shuddered. Gary was going to get away with that, too. The thug seemed to lead a charmed life. Well, perhaps it'll take a detective who's obsessed to put him away.

Terry looked at his watch, and saw it was nearly six o'clock. Trude would have cooked for the children, and they would be asking her if he had rung, pestering to know if this was one of the nights they would see their dad. Well, they would. Today at least nothing need interfere with that precious time in the evening, when he could play with his girls, hear about their day, and read them a bedtime story. Perhaps that made him a less diligent detective than Churchill, who had nothing else to think about. But at least it gave him a life.

Afterwards, he thought, when they're in bed, perhaps I'll take another look at that shed, find something Churchill's missed. Or read about these cases some more.

He stood up, stretched, and slipped a file into his briefcase to take home That's *my* bedtime story, he thought. Perhaps I *am* getting obsessive again. Perhaps I have to. Whether it's good for me, or not.

26

Sarah was in Simon's kitchen, kneeling on the floor. The idea had struck her quite suddenly: if Simon's story about Jasmine cutting herself was true, then there might still be some of her blood on the kitchen floor. Even a single drop would do.

But the floor seemed surprisingly clean. Then the memory came, flowing from her arms and body into her mind, of the energy with which she herself had scrubbed this floor after the police raid. She'd been consumed by anger – at the policemen who had invaded her son's house, and at Simon too, for letting his life get into such a chaotic mess. And so she'd compulsively scrubbed the floor, cleaning up after him.

Embarrassment flooded through her, closely followed by despair. Even if Jasmine's blood had once been here to save him, she'd washed it away.

She got up and was dusting down her clothes when she froze. There was a sound outside – not from the street but nearer, in the back yard. What was it – a footstep, a door opening? Oh no. *Not Gary*, not again! She should never have come back here alone. She switched off the kitchen light and waited in the dark, as her eyes adjusted to the gloom. Cautiously, she peered out into the yard. Was that a torch inside the shed?

She leaned forward, clumsily, and a cup smashed on to the floor beside her.

Jesus Christ, what a fool I am! A car drove past, its engine echoing off the walls of the terraced houses; and underneath that sound, she thought she heard footsteps, moving out of the yard towards the street. Go away then, Gary, if it's you, good riddance, *leave me alone* . . .

The front door banged.

A scream rose in her throat; she swallowed it. Listened, waiting.

The door banged again. No, it didn't *bang*, she told herself sternly, that's not someone trying to smash it down, it's a knock. People do that at doors. Yes, but Gary knows that too. I'm not opening it to him.

'Hello? Anyone there? I saw a light.'

Not Gary's voice, unless he's a mimic. Sarah went into the front room. 'Who is it?'

'Police. Come on, open up.'

This time she recognized the voice. Relieved, she opened the door. 'Terry! Why on earth are you here?'

'Let me in and I'll tell you. Unless you want the whole world to hear.' He nodded at the old man, who was watching from his window across the road. Sarah pulled a face before shutting it out with the door.

'So. My question remains. Was that you I heard outside in the yard?'

'Yes. I'm sorry. I must have made you nervous. Especially after the other night.'

'Don't worry. I'm a tough cookie, you know,' she said, feeling anything but. 'Take a seat.'

He chose the sofa, she sat beside the gas fire. An awkward silence followed. 'Well?'

'Why am I here? Looking for evidence, I suppose. Anything we forgot.'

Terry hadn't expected to find her here, hadn't planned what to say. In front of him now was the same attractive woman he had admired, and thought was his friend; the woman he had hoped might become something more. But then she had humiliated him in open court, and he had hated her, wanted her punished in every possible way. To his astonishment, his wish had come true. Troubles had fallen upon her in biblical proportions, as if there was a vengeful God, after all.

Yet she did not seem broken, repentant or crushed. Nervous, perhaps, a little weary, her face bruised and yellow. But still that straight spine, that spark in the eyes, that defiant self-confidence that he had once so admired.

'There are some unanswered questions about that shed,' he began cautiously.

'Such as?' She raised an eyebrow, disguising a tremor of guilt. Did he know she had touched the hood, the ring?

'Whether your son knew what was in there. What do you think?'

'He says he didn't. So I believe him.' Sarah shrugged. But it was a key question, she knew.

'When did you ask him?'

'This morning. He . . . rang me from prison.' *Damn!* Already she was being forced to lie; the wretched man was sharper than she'd remembered. She had cleaned the ring too thoroughly for fingerprints, but they could check prison phone calls if they wanted to.

'He knew nothing about the balaclava?'

'No.'

'Does he know Gary?'

'I wish he didn't, but yes, he does.' She shook her head wearily, ventured a wry smile. 'You wait until your kids are older, Terry, see if you like all the friends they bring home.'

'He brought Gary to your house?'

'Good God, no! Come on, Terry, what do you think I am?'

Terry shook his head. The suggestion came from Churchill's suspicions, rather than his own. But how much of the truth was she really telling him? She seemed unusually defensive tonight, but perhaps that was natural, in the circumstances.

Once again silence fell between them, as each searched for a possible way forward.

'This can't be easy for you,' Terry volunteered at last.

'Tell me about it,' she snapped; then relented slightly. 'No, Terry, you're right, it's not easy. Every day someone like you accuses my son of murder, or rape, or some other barbarity, and I have to listen. None of it's easy, and as far as I can see, it's probably going to get worse.'

A lot of people think you deserve it, too, he thought. 'I can understand that. And I'm afraid you may be right. Forensics have found hairs inside the balaclava.'

He paused, watching her reaction carefully. There was no obvious sign of worry.

'Gary's hairs, I suppose?'

'Apparently not. They were a different colour.'

'What colour?' Her voice still sounded normal, but he thought an involuntary tremor passed through her, as indeed it did. Sarah was wondering, They couldn't be my hairs, could they? I didn't try the hood on but I handled it, one of my hairs could have fallen on to it. Oh God.

'Fair hairs. Like your son's.'

Not mine then. Absurdly, she felt a second's relief, followed by an even stronger burst of swiftly suppressed panic, as she realized what he'd said. *Like your son's.* Sarah was dark; she remembered how delighted she had been by the colour of her baby son's hair, red-gold like his shiftless father's. When he was a baby she had loved to brush it; as a boy he had worn it long and wavy; as a teenager he had trimmed it brutally short; and now that he was an adult a detective had found traces of it inside a rapist's balaclava. Or hair very like it, at least.

'You can't prove it's Simon's just from the colour.' The old combative Sarah.

'No, of course not. It's been sent for DNA analysis.'

'Oh.' For a moment she was struck dumb. This whole conversation was going the wrong way. She tried to recover some sense of initiative. 'Even if Simon did wear this hood, what could he have used it for? You're not suggesting *he* raped Sharon, are you?'

'Not me, no,' said Terry awkwardly. 'But . . .'

'But someone is? Is that what you're saying?'

'There have been . . . discussions. They're not particularly pleasant, I have to warn you.'

'Go on.' She glared at him grimly. 'I've heard so much already, I may as well hear the rest.'

'All right.' He stood up, and walked across the room, thinking. If Churchill found out he'd been here, having this conversation, there'd be one hell of a row. But right now he didn't care about Churchill. His theories were wrong, they had to be. He sat on the arm of a chair.

'Look, I'm running a risk telling you this, you know. I wouldn't do it if . . . well, never mind. You asked if I thought your son raped Sharon and I said no. But that's just my view, not everyone's. You see, because of those hairs, there is now another, quite different theory about that rape. And it doesn't just relate to Sharon, it relates to several other assaults as well.'

Briefly, Terry explained Churchill's belief that Simon, not Gary, might have raped Sharon and assaulted Karen Whitaker and Helen Steersby. '. . . It's not certain, of course, but that's the way his enquiry is going. And the final possibility, for which we have no evidence so far, is that Simon may have murdered Maria Clayton as well.'

For the first few sentences Sarah tried to interrupt and argue, but as he went on she fell silent. She sat very still, on the edge of her seat, trembling slightly as each new detail was explained. When he had finished, silence fell. She sat like a woman of stone, her face lit by the single lamp to her right. He expected tears, but none came.

'*He thinks my son is a serial killer?*' Her voice was high, slightly strained.

'It's a theory. But he believes the evidence will support it. These hairs in particular.'

'Hairs? My God.'

She began to laugh, and he thought, I should never have told her, what'll I do if she breaks down in hysterics now? But she didn't. The laughter choked in her throat as swiftly as it had come. 'You said not *much* more. What other evidence has he got?'

'Not a lot, so far. That's why the DNA will be so crucial. If Simon's sample matches the hair in the Whitaker case, then Churchill's theory holds water. Especially if they both match the hairs he found in the hood. But if not, not.'

'And how long do we have to wait to find this out?'

'It could be quite a while. It depends on the backlog at the lab. But you know as well as I do, these results could prove him innocent as well as guilty. We just have to wait, that's all.'

He watched her in silence, as she sat sightlessly fiddling with her wedding ring. Then she looked up. 'So this is Churchill's theory, you say. What about you, Terry? Do you believe it, too?'

'It's not really a question of belief. The DNA evidence will prove it, one way or the other. And my opinion isn't worth very much at the moment, in the service . . .'

'Come on, Terry! You can at least have the guts to tell me what you think!'

'In this job, it isn't very wise to give an opinion . . .'

'I thought you were more than just a job, Terry. You're a man, too, aren't you? A father, with kids?'

In her anguished, desperate face Terry recognized something of himself. *I* was like this, he thought, in those terrible days after Mary's death. Everyone was fobbing me off with caution, procedures, platitudes, when all I wanted was to *know*.

But all his training went against it, for good reasons. You could commit yourself and be so terribly wrong. He looked at her and thought the hell with it, maybe I *want* to commit myself.

'All right, then. Well, for what my opinion is worth . . . *No*, Sarah, I don't think your son did commit all these crimes.'

'You don't?'

'No. I still think most of them were committed by one person. I just don't agree that it was your son.'

'Despite these hairs?'

'They may prove me wrong. I've been wrong before. I thought Gary attacked Karen Whitaker but he can't have done. Nor Helen Steersby. But for the rest – Maria Clayton, Sharon Gilbert . . . I still think he may be responsible for those. And they're more serious. More like the death of Jasmine Hurst.' Now I've said it, he thought. Trouble will come of this. But it's what I believe and if it's true then that young woman is a victim as surely as anyone else.

Hope can be as painful as despair. The cold distrustful anger evaporated from Sarah's voice. 'You're saying you think *Gary* may have killed Jasmine?'

'I've no evidence for it, you understand. None. But his record of petty crimes, theft, violence against women – it fits the profile of someone building up to serious crimes like this. I'm sure he raped Sharon, despite the hairs in the hood – and we know he attacked you.'

'That doesn't prove he murdered Jasmine, though, does it? What proof is there of that?'

Terry swallowed, aware of how unprofessional this conversation had become.

'None, I told you. Just a suspicion; the knowledge of what he's like. The fact that he knew Jasmine through Simon, that he fancied her – he admitted that – and that when he fancied a woman he thought he could do what he liked. And he *was* free that night: he'd been released for several hours. He was watching football in a pub until ten – that part checks out. After that, he says he stayed on, drinking in a private room. It's not clear when he left. His route home from the pub doesn't exactly take him near the river, but it's not far out of his way, either. He could have walked up there, for whatever reason, met Jasmine going home, talked to her – because he knew her, after all – and then . . .' Terry shrugged. 'It could have gone on from there.'

'He asked her for sex, she refused, so he pulled out a knife, raped her, and then cut her throat,' said Sarah softly.

'Exactly. It could have happened like that . . .'

'But there's no evidence to support it.'

'None.' Terry shook his head. 'And a lot to suggest it was your son.'

Silence fell between them again. Terry thought how little surprised she had seemed at what he was saying. Almost as though he were voicing her own thoughts.

A cocktail of emotions – relief, joy, terror, foreboding and guilt – effervesced inside Sarah. She smiled. 'If you think like that no wonder you're in the doghouse with your colleagues.'

'They don't listen; they've got their case.' He shrugged. 'Maybe they're right; I've lost the plot. I shouldn't be talking to you like this; it's not professional.'

'It's a comfort, though.' Sarah tried to smile again, and failed. 'I appreciate that. You must be the first . . .' She felt her voice falter, paused, took control of it. 'You *are* the first person except for Lucy – you know, his solicitor – who has actually said anything to suggest Simon might not have done it. And you don't even know him!'

'I've met him once, but it's not because of that,' Terry admitted. 'But I *do* know Gary, and I've got this obsession about these other cases. The only judgement I have about your son is that he wouldn't have done all these things. He has no record and he didn't strike me like that.'

'Thank you, Terry.'

Terry met her eyes, wondering. Her tone was passionately sincere and ironic at the same time; sincere because he had expressed belief in Simon, ironic because he had felt it necessary to reassure her that her own son was not a serial murderer. He felt embarrassed, conscious that he had gone too far. But he was tired – tired of professional discretion, tired of the rules, tired of Churchill and being treated like a rookie cop. It would bring a little comfort after all, and do no harm that he could see.

She shuddered, looked up at him again. 'There is another possibility, Terry.'

'What's that?'

For a while she didn't answer. She looked down at her hands, fiddling with her ring. 'I'm sorry, I can't say. There's probably nothing in it anyway.' She looked up. 'You've been very honest with me and I appreciate it.'

'You do understand why I've told you all these things? To help you and Simon, if I can. I'm taking a risk for you, but if you're going to hold out on me . . .'

'It's my son's life we're talking about here, Terry.' She got up from her chair, walked distractedly up and down the room a couple of times. 'All right, let me put it like this. Simon says he had nothing to do with Jasmine's death and I . . .' She hesitated, then continued firmly. 'I believe him. That will be his defence in court, if necessary. As for these other offences, no one's even asked him about them yet, but I can't believe he's a serial rapist. That has to be absurd. But there's a problem about these hairs, which may or not be his, and the fact that the hood and the other things were found in his shed. That's what your boss Churchill is focusing on. Now all I can say is that if – *if* – those hairs are his, and there's more to his relationship with this thug Harker than either of us know about, then, well . . .'

She paused again, a catch in her voice, and for while he thought she wasn't going to go on. But the voice resumed, cool, very controlled really for a woman under such monumental stress.

'. . . then what you have to realize is that he's only a kid really, just nineteen, while Gary Harker is ten years older and as you say, steeped in violent crime up to his eyeballs. So if Simon did try on this hood – for a laugh maybe or to try and impress his new friend – it was only that and no more. He'll have been following where the older man led.'

'Not if he attacked Karen Whitaker,' said Terry softly. 'That was just one man on his own.'

'I'm sure he didn't, Terry. But *if* – just for the sake of the argument, *if* those hairs in the hood are not only his, but match those found in the Whitaker case, then . . . then it could only be that he was put up to it by someone like Gary. Simon may be stupid but he's not cruel or misogynistic – he couldn't even think of doing a thing like that on his own.'

When she finished Terry didn't speak for a while. He let her words fall gently into his mind, wondering how they would settle on the suspicions already there. Hers was hardly an objective assessment – the words of a mother, spoken with the persuasive fluency of a barrister used to pleading in mitigation. But then how else could she speak, about her own son?

'Have you asked him?' he said at last. 'About his relationship with Gary?'

'Not yet. But I will.'

'If you could tell me what he says, it might help.'

She considered this. 'If it helps to convict Gary, then of course I will.'

I could hardly expect more, he thought. He stood up. 'I think we've said all we can, for now. I should go.'

At the door she put her hand on his arm. 'Terry, wait! Can I ask you one more thing?'

'What's that?'

'Let me know the DNA results, as soon as they come in. I don't want to wait, or hear it from that swine Churchill. Just give me a ring when you know. Please.'

'I'll do that, certainly. It probably isn't him, Sarah.'

'No,' she agreed numbly. 'It probably isn't. But tell me anyway, will you, Terry?'

'Yes.' As he left, he looked back, and saw her standing, a slight woman in the doorway of a terraced house, and thought, that's how she'll be if this all goes wrong. She'll grow old like that, no career, no family, all alone.

27

'I've told you all this,' Simon growled sulkily. 'I've told Mum anyhow.'

'Yes, but the answers weren't good enough,' said Sarah quietly. Lucy nudged her under the table to stop her saying more.

'Tell *me*, Simon, will you?' Lucy asked, in a reassuring, businesslike voice. 'We need to get all the facts straight before the police try to trip you up. Now, when did you first meet Gary?'

Simon stared at a spot on the wall. Lucy waited patiently. She was used to this sort of awkward behaviour from clients; the only difference today was the presence of the boy's mother, who also happened to be her friend.

On the way to Hull they had discussed whether it was a good idea for Sarah to be present at this interview. Her presence might either embarrass Simon or reassure him, loosen him up. Finally they had decided that Sarah should be present, if Simon agreed, but say as little as possible. That way Lucy could preserve something of her normal client-lawyer relationship, while at the same time assuaging Sarah's enormous emotional need to be involved.

But now, as Simon sat silent, Lucy wondered if this scheme was going to work.

'Would you rather talk to me on your own, Simon?' she asked at last. 'Your mother doesn't have to be here, if you find that difficult.'

Simon snorted scornfully. 'It's not her that's difficult. It's you and your daft questions. What's it matter, whether I knew Gary or not?'

'It matters because you may be asked about it in your trial,' Lucy explained patiently. 'His watch, and the ring and the hood, were found in your shed when he was there apparently looking for them. If I'm going to defend you, I need to know why those things were there. So let's start at the beginning, shall we? When did you first meet him?'

'I dunno. A year ago, maybe. Year and a half?'

Reluctantly, with gentle prodding from Lucy, a picture began to emerge.

Two years ago, he had been at college gaining NVQs in building skills and bricklaying. When he left he joined a pool of semi-employed labourers, working as demand rose, unemployed when it fell. Gary had been an older man in a similar position. Simon had been impressed and intimidated by him. He used his undoubted strength to work hard at times, and his cunning to deceive or scare his employers at others.

'You knew he was a criminal then?' Lucy asked softly.

Simon shrugged. 'He boasted about it. Said he'd been a right hard case in prison. Not many dared cross him. I tried to keep away.'

'So how did he come to visit your house?'

Simon stared at her, surprised that she knew about this; but he didn't deny it. 'He just came, that's all. Lots of lads did. I'd go to their place, they'd come to mine.'

'They didn't all use your shed though, did they?'

'No.' Simon looked down.

Lucy probed gently: 'What did he use it for, Simon?'

'To keep stuff he'd nicked.' Simon's voice was sharp and defiant, but he avoided Sarah's eyes. Lucy pressed her friend's hand under the table, to ensure she remained quiet.

'How did that come about, Simon?'

Reluctantly, Simon explained. As she watched, Sarah felt he seemed more ashamed of this than about the much more serious matter of Jasmine's death. Maybe that's a good sign, she thought. He feels guilty about this because he did it; he doesn't feel guilty about Jasmine because he didn't kill her. Or is it all bluster, an act put on for my benefit?

At many building sites, Simon said, there was a problem of petty theft. Tools disappeared, building materials were siphoned off to the labourers' own uses. It was more rife at the bigger companies because low-paid workers, like himself, felt they were being ripped off. So it became a challenge to redress the balance by nicking something for yourself. Or so Simon had seen it.

He had taken a few things – a still saw, some carpenter's tools. But he'd not known how to find a buyer, and asked Gary, showing him the tools in his shed, which had been a mistake. Gary had offered to find Simon a buyer if Simon helped him hide more stuff. At first Simon went along with it; then, when he tried to back out, Gary turned nasty.

Simon was caught in a classic piece of petty blackmail: if he refused to let Gary use the shed, Gary and his friends might beat him up, inform on him, or both. If he allowed Gary to carry on, he was paid a share of the proceeds. Simon took the money, and said nothing.

'They stored stuff until they could sell it,' he said. 'I never looked in there.' He glanced at his mother, embarrassed. 'OK, it was wrong but it doesn't mean I killed anyone, does it?'

Sarah shook her head, wordlessly. *It just means you were stupid, Simon. Again.* He read the message in her eyes.

'So Gary used your shed to hide stolen property,' Lucy confirmed. 'So what about this balaclava your mother found there? And the watch and the ring?'

'I told you, I was sick of it! I don't know nowt about them!'

Sarah spoke for the first time. 'You told me you might have made a hood, Simon. Don't you remember? For a laugh, you said.'

'I was just winding you up, Mum. Forget it.'

'Winding me up! For Christ's sake, the police think that hood was used in a rape! And they say it's got your hairs in it!'

'What?'

Lucy squeezed Sarah's arm hard under the table, but it was too late. The diplomatic approach had ended. Sarah explained what Terry had told her about the hairs. 'They're the same colour as yours – red-gold – short like yours is, and they were found in your shed. Can you blame them for thinking it was *you* who wore that hood?'

Simon shook his head wordlessly, looking wildly around the room as if for exoneration from some invisible audience. Sarah continued, remorselessly. 'So if you did make it and wear it as a *joke*, Simon, you'd better tell Lucy how it happened, because otherwise –'

'It was a stupid joke, Mum. I didn't mean it.'

'What was the joke? Wearing the hood or telling me you wore it?'

'Telling you I did. It's not true, OK? I didn't even know the bloody thing was there!'

'Oh, Simon, Simon.' Sarah shook her head sadly. 'How am I to believe you?'

'If you don't believe me, Mum, I don't want you here. You just make it worse.' He looked at Lucy. 'Maybe she should go.'

Lucy compromised. 'Your mum's almost the only person who does believe you, Simon. Without her you'll have no friends left. But you did promise to be quiet, Sarah. Remember?'

'OK, OK.' Sarah held up her hands. 'Fine. You talk, I'll listen. But remember, Simon, Lucy can only defend you if you tell her a story that makes sense, and is preferably true. So no more stupid jokes, for God's sake, now.'

'Do you see me laughing?'

'Simon, just let me get this right,' Lucy continued. 'You're telling us that you never wore the balaclava, so the hairs inside it can't possibly be yours. Is that it?'

'Yes.'

'OK. Well, the hairs have been sent for DNA tests, so when the results arrive we'll know whether they're yours or not. They can tell to within one probability in several hundred thousand, which makes it virtually certain. Do you still say they're not yours?'

However gently put, it was a killer question, as both Sarah and Lucy knew. They watched keenly for his response. To their surprise it came swiftly. 'Yes, sure. They can't be mine, I never wore it.' When they didn't react immediately he looked at them in astonishment. 'OK?'

Lucy recovered first. 'Good. If you're right then the test will prove you're innocent of any crimes connected with the hood. That's the great thing about DNA testing; it works both ways.'

A brief, nervous smile crossed Simon's face. 'Good news at last, then. So what are you two getting your knickers in such a twist for?'

'Because we're worried for you, Simon. The police are trying to use the evidence of this hood, and the things in your shed, to pin more crimes on you. It's only because your mum found out what they're thinking that we're able to ask you these questions now, before they do.'

Simon looked dazed. '*More* crimes? Like what?'

'Do you know Sharon Gilbert?'

'Who?'

'The woman who was raped. Your mum defended Gary. Remember?'

'Oh, yes, her.' Simon's look of confusion turned to incredulity. 'No, of course I don't. I saw her in court, that's all. Right slapper, I thought.'

'So you've never met her or talked to her in any way?'

'*No!*' He stared from one to the other in astonishment. 'And I didn't rape her either, for heaven's sake! I thought Gary did it.'

'He was acquitted.' Lucy shifted in her chair, uncomfortably. 'This all stems from the hairs in that hood, Simon, you see. If they're yours, they may try to prove that you raped that woman. Whoever did it was masked, after all, with a hood like the one found in your shed. From their point of view it'll clear another crime off their books. So if they *are* your hairs –'

'Well, they're not and I didn't. For Christ's sake! Isn't it enough that I'm charged with murdering Jasmine?'

'That's not the end of the story, I'm afraid. Last year, did you do some building repairs at the university?'

Sarah studied the expression of shock and confusion on Simon's face closely. It seemed genuine, but she no longer trusted her own judgement. Nothing seemed real any more. Was he really perplexed, or had he become, as so many people did, a consummate actor under the pressure of the fight to preserve his freedom?

If I no longer believe him, what will I do then?

'A bit, yeah. Some pointing, refixing window frames, and a wall to rebuild. Why?'

'You remember the police coming round? About a student called Karen Whitaker?'

'I remember the girl,' said Simon slowly.

'What do you remember, Simon?'

'She was attacked in the woods – oh God!' He stood up abruptly. 'They're not saying I did *that* too? This is bloody ridiculous!'

'What the police say, Simon, is that Gary saw some nude pictures in her room, and showed them to his mates. Like you. You all had a laugh about them. Do you remember that?'

Simon's face was flushed, there were beads of sweat on his forehead. 'Yeah, OK, yeah, I remember some nudey pictures. They were all over her room. So what? It's not a crime, is it?'

'Not to look, no, Simon. But a few days later someone – maybe a man who saw those photos – attacked the girl and her boyfriend when they were taking some more pictures in the woods. And her attacker was wearing a black balaclava hood.'

'Oh, I get it. So they think I attacked this girl as well, because this hood was found in my shed with these hairs inside. Is that it?'

'Yes,' said Lucy patiently. 'And the main piece of evidence that they have is another hair. The attacker was trying to bind the girl with tape, and a hair from his arm got stuck on it. So they're trying to match the DNA from that hair to the DNA from the ones in the hood. And then compare the results from both of these to the sample they took from you.'

'My God.' Simon dropped his head into his hands for a moment, then looked up, shaking his head slowly. 'What's it like, Mum, to have a serial rapist for a son? Will they lock me in a cave with a glass wall, like in *Silence of the Lambs*? Jesus! The world's gone mad! They don't just think I murdered Jasmine, but . . .'

He paused, tears in his eyes, unable to go on. '. . . God, *Jasmine*. As if that wasn't enough. And now this! All because of the hairs in a hood that Gary must have left in my shed, the bastard!' An idea came to him suddenly. 'They must be *his* hairs, mustn't they? It's *his* hood, *he* did it!'

'No. His hair's brown,' said Lucy quietly. 'Anyway his DNA doesn't match Whitaker's attacker. They're not his.'

'Well, they're not bloody mine either!' Simon stared at them both furiously, trying to pierce through the masks of concern and sympathy to what they really thought. 'You've got to believe me, all right? *Mum?* Come on now, this is a load of crap, I didn't do any of these things!'

'OK, Simon,' Sarah said quietly. 'If that's what you say, I believe you.'

'Thank Christ for that.' He held her gaze, trying to reassure himself that what she said was really true. She gazed back, trying to do the same in return. Both wanted to believe the other, but neither found that they could quite, completely, manage it.

Simon turned away first, to Lucy. 'So, is that it, then? All my multiple crimes?'

Lucy sighed. 'Not quite, Simon, I'm afraid. There are two more they'll probably want to ask you about. Helen Steersby and Maria Clayton.'

Not for the first time, Churchill was castigating Terry. His ammunition had come to light during further investigations into Simon's background. Tracy had discovered it, but Churchill latched on to it with delight. Terry sensed the atmosphere as soon as he entered the room.

'At last! The man himself!' Churchill was perched on a table, with one foot on a chair and the other swinging free, beaming. Harry Easby and Mike Candor seemed to share his mood, but Tracy looked flushed, embarrassed maybe. She flashed Terry a look which he was unable to interpret – a warning, or a hint of pity, perhaps?

'You remember how convinced you were, Terence, that our Simon had no connection with any crime except the murder of his girlfriend? He couldn't possibly be our phantom rapist, you said, he doesn't have the right profile. No criminal record, and no connection with the first murder, Maria Clayton. Remember that, Terence old son?'

'Yes. It's true, isn't it?'

'Not any more it isn't, no siree! Wrong on both counts. Tell me, when you made your list of possible contacts with Maria Clayton, you checked all her clients, right? And then the building workers, of whom friend Harker was one?'

'Yes,' Terry agreed cautiously.

'But what you didn't check, old son, was who *delivered things* to those building workers. They needed bricks, sand, cement, all that kind of stuff. And they didn't collect it themselves, they had it delivered from a builders' merchant called Robson's. Who just happened to employ, for a period of three weeks, guess who?'

A sick, empty feeling flooded Terry's stomach. 'Not Simon Newby?'

'The very same, old son. The very same.'

'But . . . for three weeks, you say?' Terry floundered feebly. 'Was that the same period . . .' The triumph on Churchill's face told him the answer before he had finished the question.

'More or less, yes. We'll come to that. But first, Tracy here has charmed their manager into showing her all his delivery notes, and – you guessed it – the driver who delivered one load to Maria's house was none other than Simon Newby. We've got the sheet, look, with his signature.'

Terry took the pink sheet, stunned. The signature *S. Newby* was quite plain at the bottom. He looked up, catching Tracy's eye. He saw what the anguished expression on her face meant now. It was an apology, and underneath that an expression of pity.

Worse was to come.

'You haven't asked why he only worked for three weeks,' Churchill prompted gloatingly.

But you're going to tell me, Terry thought. 'All right, why?'

Churchill nodded to Tracy. 'Your discovery. You tell him.'

In a cool, neutral voice Tracy said: 'He was dismissed after a complaint from a female employee. She says he felt her legs, and sexually harassed her.'

'But why isn't this on the computer?' Terry asked. 'He hasn't got a record – I checked.'

'The manager didn't want a fuss. He gave young Simon his cards the same day, and said if he ever came back he'd call the police. So that was that.'

'My God.' Terry sank down on a chair. 'What day was that?'

'June 7th. Two days before they started work on the extension. But it still gives him a link to Maria Clayton, doesn't it?'

Terry nodded numbly. 'Have you got this woman's statement?'

Tracy passed him a sheet of paper. 'Here.' As Terry read, his nausea increased. The image of Sarah Newby came back to him, standing slim, upright and alone outside her son's house, protesting his innocence. Had she known about this, when they met? Had she already known her son had lost a job for – what did this statement say? *He touched my legs from behind when I was bent over picking something up, and when I protested he grabbed my wrists and asked if I'd let him fuck me.*

Wonderful! And he'd told Sarah that in his – Terry's – judgement her son couldn't have committed these crimes, because he just wasn't like that. How could his judgement be so wrong? Because – face it, Terry – you were infatuated by the boy's mother, so you *wanted* it to be true. You were trying to please her. But if she knew about this, she must have been laughing up her sleeve as I spoke, taking me for a sucker all along.

Dear God, Terry thought. I can't do this job any more. I've lost my touch.

With deep satisfaction, Churchill was watching Terry's reaction. 'Don't take it personally, old son,' he said, in his oiliest manner. 'The world is full of surprises.'

'I read about it in the paper, that's all,' said Simon firmly. 'No more than that.'

'You never met this woman, Maria Clayton, then?' Lucy asked, patiently.

Simon shook his head. 'Not that I remember, no.'

'Never went to her house, worked on any buildings there?'

'What's the address again?'

'47 Flaxton Gardens. It's in Strensall.'

'I've had that many jobs . . . but no. No, I never worked there.'

'And Gary didn't talk to you about her?'

'No.'

'All right.' Lucy made a brief note on her pad. 'Well, as far as we know, that's the only possible connection between you and Maria Clayton – the fact that you know Gary who did some building work there. It's not much, so let's forget it. But then there's Helen Steersby.'

'Another one?' Simon shook his head wearily. 'It's daft, all this.'

'DCI Churchill doesn't think so. It seems that a schoolgirl, Helen Steersby, was accosted by a man when she was riding her pony in the woods, not far from the shopping development. He tried to pull her off her pony, but she hit him with her riding crop and rode away.'

'What's this got to do with me?'

'Nothing, I hope. But the girl made a photofit of what she thought the man looked like. And since they claim it looks a bit like you, they want you to go in for an identity parade.'

'They're screwy,' said Simon, putting a finger to his forehead and turning it like a screwdriver. 'Totally screwless.'

'So you didn't attack a young girl on a pony? On . . .' Lucy checked her notes. '8th May?'

'As it happens, no, I didn't. It was only little lasses on elephants that day.' He laughed mirthlessly. 'Look, can't you just stop it, all of it? I didn't even know any of these bloody women, let alone rape them or murder them or drag them off their stupid ponies. I didn't hurt anyone except Jasmine. Christ!'

He got abruptly from his chair again and drummed his fists on the wall, hard, so that flakes of plaster floated down. Then he noticed that both women had fallen silent, staring at him.

'What?'

Sarah drew a deep breath. 'You said you hurt Jasmine, Simon.'

'Oh. Yeah, well, I mean I hit her, Mum. In the street, you know that.'

'And that's all?'

'Of course that's all! *Jesus!*' He kicked the chair aside with a crash, and leaned forward, both hands on the table, glaring into his mother's face. 'You said you believed me, didn't you?'

'I'm trying to, Simon. You're not making it easy.'

'Well, try harder, can't you? I've got no one else.'

Once again their eyes locked. All Sarah could see was the face of an angry, hurt young man, thrust deliberately forward a few inches from her own. The smack of the chair hitting the wall still rang in her ears, and the sense of rage and injustice radiated from him so palpably that if she had not been his mother he would have terrified her.

She wondered how Jasmine would have coped with this level of fury from her lover. Was this why she left? Or had she – arrogant, beautiful, self-centred young woman that she was – actually *enjoyed* the reaction she could arouse? Maybe she even got a thrill out of his rage and the occasional slap or blow that she received, because it proved that she, not he, had emotional control. Was that why she had behaved as she did with David Brodie and Simon, playing games with the jealousy of both? Perhaps she enjoyed the game and wanted to see how much rage and jealousy she could provoke. That was very like the Jasmine Sarah remembered. Had she simply pushed the situation too far, tested Simon quite literally to destruction – the destruction of her own life?

Sarah had never articulated this fear to herself so clearly before. Now it came all at once. It was the best explanation so far. And his own words had led to it. She gazed back at him coldly.

Lucy tried again. 'Sit down, Simon, please. We can't discuss these things in a rage.'

'I'm not in a bloody rage. I just want to be believed, that's all.' Slowly Simon withdrew from his aggressive crouch over the table, picked up the chair, and straddled it, still glowering at his mother.

'Thank you. Now look, if we're going to defend you, we have to do a number of things. Firstly, we have to be sure that you're going to plead not guilty. Because if you *did* kill Jasmine, we can mount a completely different defence, claiming that she provoked you and you didn't know what you were doing. You understand all that?'

'What?' Simon's rage switched to Lucy. '*I didn't bloody kill her.* How many times –'

'OK, OK . . .' Lucy raised her hands, but Simon was not propitiated.

'No, it's not OK, Mrs Parsons! Either you accept that I didn't kill her, understand? *I didn't bloody do it!* Or you can piss off out that door and I'll get someone else! Get it?'

'OK, Simon –'

'I'll defend myself! I could do it a sight better than you, any road –'

'*Simon!*' Sarah didn't move but there was something in her voice so sharp and hard that it stopped him short like a small boy. 'If you want Lucy to help you you'll keep a clean tongue in your head and listen to

213

her, all right? Because you've got no one else, no one better. If you even try to defend yourself like that, they'll give you life with a minimum tariff of twenty years, straight off. And make no mistake, that's what you're looking at, if this goes wrong. This is the most serious thing in your whole life. Believe me.'

'You think I don't know that?'

'Well, treat it seriously then. Listen to Lucy, *think*, and get a grip. Flying into a rage will get you nowhere at all.'

Except here, she told herself grimly. Maybe his rage was the cause of it all.

28

Sarah was in court. Lucy had suggested that she take a holiday, but Sarah found work therapeutic; after all, whatever happened to Simon, she told herself grimly, she would have a life afterwards, a daughter to support, and a career that she had struggled to achieve; she wasn't going to abandon that now. Not even for Simon.

She could accept sympathy, from her colleagues. But not pity, not from anyone.

This morning's case, however, had hardly boosted her confidence. The accused, a well-known thug, had been seen eating a chicken sandwich in a supermarket without paying for it. When the police arrested him they found, to their delight, a replica gun in his pocket. He was charged with going to the supermarket armed, intending to commit an offence. With his previous convictions for armed robbery, this was a serious matter.

Sarah, in defence, had argued that her client had been simply carrying the weapon, with no intention to use it. Her client had neither intended to commit armed robbery nor done so; he had simply eaten a chicken sandwich, and left the store peacefully. It was petty theft, no more.

The judge listened, smiled, and gave her client seven years for armed robbery.

She walked disconsolately back to her chambers, still in her wig and gown. God help Simon if he gets a judge like that, she thought. Or a barrister like me. Seven years for stealing a sandwich! As she crossed the road she saw Terry coming towards her on the opposite pavement. She smiled as he approached.

'Hello, Sarah. Can we talk?'

Something in his manner made her heart lurch unpleasantly. 'What, here?'

He looked around. 'Wherever. It won't take long.'

'There's a bench free by the river. Let's go there.'

They sat on the bench and watched a pleasure cruiser move upstream. For a while neither spoke, then Terry met her eyes. She saw no warmth, no sympathy.

'Terry, what is it? What do you know?'

'It's more what I *don't* know and what you *do*,' he said harshly. 'For instance about your son's previous jobs and how he lost one of them.'

'Terry, I don't understand. What jobs?'

'You really didn't know, when you spoke to me the other night? That he worked as a delivery driver for Robson's, the builders' merchants?'

'So? He's had dozens of jobs.'

'He was sacked from this one.' Terry studied her keenly. 'You know why, don't you?'

'No! Terry, *what is this?*'

'He stuck his hand up the secretary's skirt.'

'Oh my God. How do you know this?'

'Tracy found out. And what's worse, he delivered a load of building materials to Maria Clayton, the prostitute who was murdered. So he did have a connection with her, after all.'

'It doesn't mean he killed her.' Sarah's voice was faint, little above a whisper.

'Of course not, yet. But Churchill thinks it will. His theory is that Simon had sex with her, it went wrong somehow, and snap, something broke in his head and the first of these killings started. With the balaclava and the knife.'

He flew into a rage, Sarah thought. Like yesterday in the prison.

'All this because he delivered things to her house? Terry, really!'

'I'm just telling you how he's thinking.' Terry heard the strain in her voice and saw her fingers shaking. 'Sarah, are you really saying you didn't know?'

'I knew he had the job, yes, but not every delivery he made. Why should I?' *And why should I believe what he told me yesterday?* 'And certainly not how he was sacked. *Jesus*, Terry!'

In profile, he thought he saw tears in her eye. He got up.

'Well, that's it. I really shouldn't tell you any of this. I have to go.'

She stood to detain him. 'Terry, I thought we were friends.'

'I saw Maria's body, Sarah.'

'And I saw Jasmine's. You know that, you were there.'

'Yes.' He hesitated. 'Look, there are still the DNA tests. I'll let you know.'

Then he left, with that long, loping stride that would make it impossible for her to catch him without running and making herself look ridiculous.

*   *   *

215

'All right, let's go through this again. You stuck your hand up this woman's skirt.'

'It was a *joke*, Mum. She was a fat cow, she'd been giving everyone grief, and when she bent over she farted. The other drivers were pissing themselves.'

'And so you got the sack for molesting her.'

'She only had the job because she was the boss's moron sister. She deserved it.'

'Oh, Simon, Simon.' Sarah shook her head in despair. 'You realize what they'll make of this, don't you?'

'Mum, the woman's still alive . . .'

'But Maria Clayton isn't, is she? And you delivered building materials to her house.'

'I never met her, Mum. Honest. She wasn't there.'

'Two days ago you told us *you'd* never been there.' Sarah jabbed her finger at Lucy's notes. 'Never worked there, you said. Never saw her.'

'Yeah, well. There were that many deliveries . . .'

'You lied to me, Simon. Again.'

'I *forgot*, Mum. That's all.'

Sarah sighed, speechless. They had been in this dreary prison room for half an hour now. Simon gazed sulkily at the clouds outside the window. After a pause, Lucy resumed.

'All right. Let's leave that and concentrate on the murder of Jasmine, which is the only thing you've been charged with so far. We've agreed that you're pleading not guilty. So we have to establish several things. First, what exactly did happen on that day, the last day you saw her, and whether you have any witnesses to prove it. Second, we have to examine all the evidence that the police produce, and in particular why your trainers and breadknife have Jasmine's blood on.'

'I told you. She cut her thumb in the kitchen.'

'Yes. The pathologist's report confirms there was a small cut on her thumb . . .'

'I put a plaster on it,' Simon said.

'But he doesn't mention a plaster. I'll check that, though.' Lucy frowned, and made a note. 'Third – this is the least important but it would be wonderful if we could do it – we have to think about who *did* kill her if you didn't.'

'What do you mean, *least* important? It seems like the most important to me.'

'Of course it's *important*, Simon,' Lucy explained patiently. 'But it's not strictly our job. It's a matter for the police. All we have to demonstrate is that you didn't kill her. Or in fact less than that – simply that there's no evidence that you did. But believe me, even that's going to be hard enough. Finding out who *did* do it is another matter altogether.'

'Well, I can give you one name for a start. David Brodie. He should be locked up instead of me, the bastard! See how he likes it!'

'Why do you say that, Simon?'

'Well, isn't it obvious?' Simon snorted contemptuously. 'She was living with him but he was no good at sex – she told me. That's why she came back – treated me like a fucking stud! Well, he must have known that, mustn't he? She needed it too much, she'd have told him. So that would have driven him mad, even a wimp like him. And where was her body found? Quarter of a mile from his house. So why aren't they searching *his* place, eh? Looking for bloody knives in *his* cupboard?'

'I don't know,' Lucy answered cautiously. 'I can ask the police, though.'

'Well, ask then, will you? *Please?*' Simon glanced aside at his mother.

Sarah smiled faintly, encouraging his attempt at politeness. 'We'll ask, certainly. But while we're on this, Simon, what about another possibility? Gary Harker?'

'Gary?' he said. His face paled slightly. 'Why him?'

'Well, he's a violent man, as you know. He almost certainly raped Sharon Gilbert, and . . .' Sarah hesitated. She hadn't told Simon how Gary had attacked her, and she didn't want to tell him now. Partly because she was ashamed of the whole incident and wanted to block it out, but more because she feared Simon's response. He would be outraged by an attack on his mother, and she'd had enough of his rage already. No doubt the prison warders had too.

So she continued, rather feebly: '. . . and he has a record of petty crime and violence going back to his teens. In addition to which he had met Jasmine, hadn't he? At your house?'

'Yeah, I suppose he had, once or twice. But he had nowt to do with her, surely?'

'I don't know,' Sarah said. 'I wasn't there.'

'No, well, he didn't. She was always with me when he was there, and . . . Christ, I'll kill the bastard if he's touched her!'

'We don't know that he did, Simon,' Sarah said. 'It's just that, you see, he's the sort of man who *could* have killed her, isn't he? If he asked her for sex, perhaps, and she refused.'

'*Jesus.*' Simon banged his forehead with his fist, repeatedly. The thought of Gary with Jasmine clearly hurt him badly.

'So if you can think of any occasions, any incidents that might suggest his involvement, tell us about them and we'll pass them on to the police and if possible use them in court,' Lucy continued. 'Any suggestion that someone else may have killed her is good. But Gary's rather a long shot. He was only released from court on the afternoon of the day she died. You didn't see him at any time that day, did you?'

Simon looked at her blankly. 'No, how could I? I was with Jasmine all afternoon, in bed mostly. I didn't see him there.'

'He didn't come round to your house, ring you, anything like that?'

'No.' He swallowed nervously. 'Look, if he killed her – and you're right, Mum, he could have, he's the sort of bastard who could, no doubt about that – then I don't know why or how he met her. But – oh God . . .' He sank his head in his hands, and Sarah realized he was crying. '. . . it's bad enough that she's dead, but to think it might be *him* . . .'

They waited until he recovered his composure. Sarah remembered the suspicion she had voiced so unwillingly to Terry Bateson the other night; what if this series of crimes had actually been perpetrated by *two* men, working together, one perhaps under the influence of the other? Had Gary controlled her son, in some way?

When he looked up, wiping his eyes with his sleeve, she asked gently: 'Why do you hate him so much, Simon?'

'Because . . .' He shook his head. 'No, I can't.'

'Because what? Tell me.'

Still no response. He looked away from her, at the wall, but found no comfort there.

Lucy added her voice. 'Come on, Simon. We can't help you if we don't know.'

'Oh God!' He put his hands flat on the table, looked at the two women desperately. *'Because I'm afraid of him,* that's why, if you really have to know. So if he can scare *me,* what he might have done to Jasmine . . .'

'What did he do to you, Simon?'

'It wasn't just him.' He took a deep breath. 'Him and that bastard Sean. They beat me up in the toilet and . . . I shit myself.' He shook his head violently from side to side, as though to escape the memory. 'They stuck my face down the toilet . . . That's why I let them use the bloody shed! I don't want to talk about it, Mum, I'm sorry.'

He got up and turned away from them again, banging the wall repeatedly with the flat of his hand, and then his head, thump, thump . . .

Sarah stood up and held him, put her hand on his forehead so that he would have to bang that if he wanted to bang his head. She could feel him sobbing, her big strong son . . . She put her slim arms around him but how could they protect him, if his own strength had been destroyed? She met Lucy's eyes and they both thought, We're Gary Harker's defence team, we got him off . . .

At last Simon sat down. Ashamed and embarrassed, he tried to regain his dignity. 'I'm sorry, it weren't that bad really, just their idea of a filthy joke. But no one's ever done owt like that to me before and if they tried I could always stop them. But not these two. And the thought of him, either of 'em, having to do with Jasmine, it's . . . I don't want to think of it.'

Two of them, Sarah thought. But not Simon and Gary, after all . . .

Terry was at home, in his living room, reading. His daughters were, he hoped, asleep. He was reading Maria Clayton's diary. Rereading it, rather; he had read it several times before. It was an odd mixture of

218

personal appointments, notes, lists, philosophical reflections and comments on her clients.

It was the latter, naturally, which interested Terry most. They had a wide number of preferences, some of which, clearly, Maria had found amusing. Terry sympathized with her. Why, for example, would a salesman, married with two children, want to dress up as a French maid and have his bottom spanked if he spilt Maria's drinks? No wonder some of these men had been reluctant to help the police enquiry. Still, Terry thought, such activities were harmless, if absurd. Whatever the men who indulged in them were, they were not dangerous psychopaths.

So it was the other details Terry was checking on now. The appointments, the notes. He checked them all, one by one, against a timetable of the last two months of Maria's life. It was a slow, painstaking search for the one vital clue which would throw everything else into place.

But not tonight, it seemed. He yawned, his mind wandering, then leafed backwards to an entry that had puzzled him earlier. It seemed to refer to one of Maria Clayton's clients. He read it again.

S big promise, no result. Gets it up but can't get it out. V frust for him, poor lamb, blames me. Outside? No way, José, I say.

What did it mean? Like many entries it seemed to refer to a client with sexual difficulties. But Maria's attempts at therapy had caused more frustration, which he apparently blamed on her. *Outside?* was a little more puzzling. Was the man waiting for her outside the house, and she had told him to leave – *No way, José, I say?* Or had he, perhaps, wanted to have sex outdoors?

Either way, it was interesting. Maria had refused, leaving the man frustrated; so he might have returned to force himself upon her. And his name, apparently, began with S. Well, there were millions of Samuels and Sidneys and Stephens in the world, and no doubt several had come to Maria. Simon began with S, too. Could he be the client Maria was referring to here?

On reflection, Terry doubted it. Firstly, the diary entry was dated 18th July, a fortnight after Gary and the others had finished the extension, and six weeks since 5th June, Simon's only recorded visit.

And what about *big promise, no result?* It seemed to suggest some sort of impotence in the man. Yet everything Terry had learned about Simon suggested a vigorous, healthy, red-blooded young male, violent and aggressive perhaps but hardly someone who, in bed with Maria, would have the slightest difficulty in getting it up. And yet, and yet . . . what other sexual problems were there? It wasn't a subject Terry was expert in.

Most of Maria's clients, he reflected, had been middle-aged men like, well, himself. The ones he felt least sympathy for were those with a wife and children at home, but others had reached their early forties to find themselves single, or divorced, or widowed as he was. Their need for discreet sexual gratification was easy enough to understand.

Easier, at least, than a desire to rape and murder.

He yawned again. Then he climbed the stairs quietly to the landing, crept into his daughters' bedroom, and listened for the reassurance of their quiet steady breathing. Trude's light, he noticed as he came out, was still on under her door. Writing to her boyfriend, perhaps.

He went into his own room, undressed, put on his pyjamas, and climbed wearily into bed.

29

The Inspector smiled. 'You must be Helen Steersby?'

The girl nodded, and Lucy thought how young she was. Like many fourteen-year-olds she was long-limbed and gawky but still obviously a child, even if she was tall enough to look adults in the eye. Lucy imagined her being assaulted by a burly young thug in a mask, and shuddered.

Inspector Harvey, in charge of the identification parade, introduced Lucy to the girl and her mother, then explained the procedure. 'Through that door you'll find a long window in one wall. Behind that window you'll see ten young men. They can't see you, because the window is made of one-way glass. Do you understand that?'

'Yes,' Helen said quietly. Her expression, Lucy noted, was anxious, determined and deeply serious. If she does pick Simon out, she'll make an impressive witness.

'I want you to look at each man very carefully, at least twice. There's no hurry, take as long as you want. It's quite possible that the man who attacked you isn't there at all. If he isn't, just say so.'

'OK.'

'But if you do recognize him, tell me the number. Nothing else, just his number. OK?'

'Yes.'

'Right then. Mrs Parsons, are you satisfied?'

'Yes.' Lucy was here on Simon's behalf to ensure that everything was done correctly. They went through the door, and saw a row of young men behind the glass, quite unaware of their presence. Each young man wore a black woolly hat. Several wore earrings but not Simon; Lucy had persuaded him to remove his. Helen peered at them nervously.

Inspector Harvey spoke into a microphone. 'Would you all stand up, please. Look straight ahead, until I tell you to move again.'

As Helen moved along the line Lucy recalled the photofit that she and Simon had been shown that morning. Only when he had put the woolly hat on, had the likeness become really close. She looked at him now and thought, It's the nose. That flat, prominent nose will give him away. She drove her fingernails into her palm and watched silently.

Helen paused at number 2, Simon's position. She studied him for a long, long time before moving on. It's all over, Lucy thought, she's recognized him. But the girl was very conscientious. She spent almost as much time on each one. When she reached the end she looked questioningly at Inspector Harvey.

'Look again carefully, Helen. We've got all the time in the world.'

Helen walked slowly back along the line. She looked long and hard at Simon, but equally long and hard at number 7 who also had a large nose, and at two others whose noses were not prominent at all. Then she looked a third time, and turned to Inspector Harvey.

'He's not here.'

Lucy breathed a silent sigh of relief.

'You can't identify any of these men as the one who attacked you?'

'No. I'm sorry, but you did say . . .' The girl looked crestfallen, on the verge of tears.

'Yes, of course, Helen, that's fine. It's very sensible and honest of you.' Despite himself, he sighed. 'That's it, then. If you'd like to come this way . . .'

'She didn't pick any of them?' Churchill asked incredulously.

'Sorry, no.' Inspector Harvey dropped his report on the desk. Churchill ignored it.

'Oh well. You did your best, I suppose.' He glowered out of the window.

'I carried out the identification parade in the correct manner, if that's what you mean.'

'Of course that's what I mean.'

There had been an edge to Harvey's voice which Churchill didn't care for. By rights Harvey, a uniformed inspector, should have called the new DCI 'sir', but he hadn't. Churchill wondered whether to make a point of it. Harvey was a well-respected officer old enough to be his father. He decided against insisting on his rank. Instead he snatched up the report from the desk and skimmed swiftly through it. A copy of the photofit was attached.

'Was he wearing this?' Churchill jabbed his finger at the earring in the photofit.

'I didn't notice one, no.'

'So did you say anything about it? Offer him one?'

'We'd have had to fit earrings to all ten in the line up. We can't do that. They all wore black woolly hats, though.'

'Yes, well. Did she even *look* at Simon Newby?'

'Very carefully, three times. But she was quite definite. Her attacker wasn't there.'

'Oh well. She's only a kid, I suppose,' Churchill said dismissively. 'Thanks, Bill.' As Harvey left Terry Bateson came in. Churchill thrust the report into his hands.

'Here. Look at that for a load of useless gibberish.'

Terry read it carefully. 'I see.'

'Total waste of time,' Churchill muttered irritably. 'I'll bet Mrs Solicitor Parsons told him to take his earring off, and Dixon of Dock Green there never noticed. It seems this city's full of smartass lawyers and half-witted policemen. Tourist attraction, is it, Terence?'

The young woman had a thin face, no hair at all, and a line of studs like a scar in her right eyebrow. She wore baggy jeans and a purple T-shirt, and her hands, like her clothes, were strong, practical and stained with dirt. A strong whiff of dope hung around her like a miasma. She draped herself luxuriously across Sarah's armchair, her left leg dangling over the arm, her right hand waving in the air as though in search of a joint or cigar, and talked.

She explained how global capitalism was destroying the environment, not just the physical environment like trees and fields and rivers, but the social environment too and the way people related to each other, and how much of this was supported by the traditional family which was really just a nursery producing children to feed the educational factories and workplaces of the exploiting classes, and how if anything was going to change this would have to change too, which was why it was vital that people on the tree protest came together to form new and ever-changing kaleidoscopic forms of social evolution . . .

Sarah finally interrupted her. 'You came to tell me about Jasmine.'

Larry and Emily, who had brought this motormouth into her living room, watched from the sofa, nodding wisely as the diatribe continued. Had there been a twitch of amusement on Emily's lips, Sarah wondered, or was she swallowing this tripe whole like medicine?

'Yes, well I was coming to that, Sacha . . .'

'Sarah.' Or Mrs Newby to you, child, Sarah thought irritably.

'Sarah, sorry. Well, I mean, like that's what Jasmine was after, attempting to liberate herself, I mean free her whole psyche from the socio-economic forces of repression. She was working on herself through direct action against the chains of how she'd been brought up.'

'What I'm really interested in,' Sarah insisted tediously, 'is who might have killed her.'

'You said someone was following her,' Larry prompted. It was kind of him and Emily to find this potential witness, Sarah thought; but surely they could have found someone a touch more focused.

'Yeah, she said. It seemed like a joke at first, but in her case –'

'Did she say *who* she thought was following her?' Sarah asked.

'Well, Sarah, I'm sorry to say this but you've got to face that it might have been your own son. I mean like there were two of them but . . .'

'I've only got one son,' Sarah pointed out.

'Two men in her life that were serving her, but I only met one, that Dave Brodie. He came to the protest but more to follow her, the way I saw it, and also because he thought the trees were *pretty* rather than important. I mean he was a typically repressed, anally retentive little shit, God knows what she saw in him but what she didn't see was the real anger in him too, I mean he could easily have been on the other side of the barricade with a helmet and a chainsaw, I dunno what he was doing with us really, probably just trying to get into Jasmine's knickers. Which he did, matter of fact.' She laughed, and swung both feet over the arm of the chair.

'You said he was angry?'

'Yeah, sure, jealous of the other guy, your son. Basic male hang-up, ownership thing.'

'Did he ever threaten her, anything like that?'

'They had rows, sure. Screaming matches in the camp. We watched. Liberation theatre, let it all hang out.'

'When?'

'Couple of times. Once . . .' She glanced at Emily. 'The night before you came, it was.'

'That would be what – the 11th?' Sarah made a note. 'What happened exactly?'

'Just bitching and screaming. He asked her to come home and she wouldn't. She said she was tired of him and the protest mattered more than his kitchen floor, and if she did go anywhere it'd be to her mum. He said he knew where she went because he followed her and it wasn't her mum, and if she ever went there again he'd do something.'

'What did he say he'd do?'

'That's just it.' The girl laughed. 'She asked him straight out and he couldn't say, could he? I mean he's just a little nerd, really, a nice guy if you fancy that sort of thing but he couldn't hurt anyone, could he? He's not big enough.'

'So what happened?'

'He went home and she stayed. Then next day you came, I think.' The girl nodded at Emily. 'You swapped coats with her, and . . . I think she took pity on him and went back. Probably thought he'd be all over her with gratitude, poor little prick.'

'On the 12th?' Sarah said. 'The day before she died. Did you see her again on the 13th?'

'No, sorry. Saw *him* though.'

'You saw David Brodie that day?'

The young woman frowned, the studs along her eyebrow writhing grotesquely. 'I think it was then – yeah, right. I was having a wash that morning when he came in and asked where she was, was she back in camp. Seems they'd had another row at breakfast. So I said no, she'd probably gone to look for a real man in town. He's such a little jerk, I couldn't resist. Well, he marched off with steam coming out of his ears. But I dunno if he ever found her . . .'

'Did he say anything before he left?'

'Just bullshit really – like he knew where she was, and if she wasn't back that evening he'd sort her for good. It was a joke, really, macho crap like in the mouth of a wimp like him . . .'

Her voice trailed away as the implication of what she had said became clear. Sarah made a hurried note. 'In that case we may need you, Ms – what was your name again?'

'Mandy. Mandy Kite.'

When at last Mandy had gone Sarah sat with Larry and Emily. Bob, who had refused to have anything to do with the woman, was making a curry in the kitchen.

'Well,' Emily said. 'What do you think?'

Sarah looked up from her notes. 'I think,' she said slowly, 'that it's promising, but it may mean nothing at all.'

'Mum?' Emily frowned, puzzled. 'What's that supposed to mean?'

Sarah chewed her lip thoughtfully. 'What you want it to mean, is that this David Brodie killed Jasmine, not Simon.'

Emily nodded energetically. 'Yes, exactly. You heard her, Mum – he had a row with her, he was furious, he marched off to look for her and sort things out . . .'

'But we don't know if he found her, do we?'

'Well, he was looking.'

'According to Mandy. Not according to his statement to the police, though. I've seen it.'

'So he's lying!' Emily burst out. 'Of course he would if he killed her, wouldn't he?'

Sarah studied her quietly. 'It's exactly what they say about Simon, isn't it? That he killed her because he's jealous, and then lied?''

Emily looked crestfallen. 'Yes, but . . .'

'But like me, you don't want to believe it. You want to blame someone else. But to do that we need proof. Look, Emily, I've made notes and we'll get a proper statement from her in Lucy's office tomorrow. Then Simon's barrister can decide what to do with it. It may be useful but an allegation like that can also be very cruel.'

'Why?'

'Well, just think, Emily. What if this David didn't do it and a lawyer says he did, how would that feel?'

'It's what your mother calls the game of proof,' said Bob tactlessly from the kitchen door. 'Other people call it lying to save your skin.'

'Dad!' Emily flared angrily. 'We're trying to save *Simon*!'

'Which is all very well,' said Bob gently, 'if you don't ruin other people's lives in the process. We all want to save Simon if he's innocent, but . . .' He paused. A silence, electric with bitter unspoken arguments, crackled between them.

Carefully, to avoid an explosion, Sarah said: 'There's a lot of evidence which seems to suggest Simon's guilt, but when it's examined in court it may look rather different. And apart from this David Brodie, there's at least one other possible suspect. A man called Gary Harker.'

'The man you defended?' Emily asked.

Sarah nodded. Her eyes met Bob's in an unspoken compact. Emily didn't know that Garry had assaulted her. She'd explained her bruises as an accident with her bike – there were scratches on the petrol tank to prove it. She didn't want Emily to know. Bob, for once, supported her.

'That's just a coincidence,' he said. 'Obviously when your mother defended him she had no idea he might do this, if he did. Now come on, sit up. I don't often cook but when I do I expect it to be treated with some respect.'

'Mum . . .' Emily's eyes were bright with anxious curiosity. 'Why do you think Gary Harker might have done it?'

As they sat at the table Sarah met her daughter's eyes, and sighed. This wasn't going to be an easy evening, after all.

30

'Oh, hello. Mr . . . Bates, isn't it?'

'Bateson. Detective Inspector.'

'Ah yes. Well, come in.' The slight frown that crossed the woman's face, Terry thought, was nothing personal. It was to do with the painful memories he brought back.

Ann Slingsby, a well-dressed, motherly woman in her fifties, had been Maria Clayton's maid until her death last year. Her duties had been to answer the phone, make appointments, clean the house, and when necessary make tea for Maria's clients when they arrived early, like a receptionist at a private clinic. She showed him into a living room furnished with comfortable flowery armchairs, lovingly polished china ornaments, an array of family photographs and a widescreen television. She poured tea into bone china cups, chattering cheerfully about her recent trip to the United States.

'But enough of my holiday stories. Have you caught that evil man yet?'

'Not yet, no. So I'm checking every detail, to see if there's anything we missed.'

'Well, you're lucky to find me, Inspector. Next week I start with an acupuncturist. He rang when I got back. One of Maria's old clients, you know. Milk?'

'Please.' Terry sipped his tea appreciatively. Then he pulled a pink form out of his pocket, with the signature, *S. Newby*, at the bottom.

'Now, I believe Maria had a delivery of building materials on 5th June last year . . .'

An hour later, two things had become clear. In the first place, Ann Slingsby *did* remember the young man who had delivered building materials on 5th June. A fair-haired young man, she said, quite handsome but a bit uncouth in his manners. She remembered because there had been a problem about where to dump the materials. Maria had been away and left no instructions.

'Away where?' Terry asked.

'Venice, with her daughter. They came back on the 10th. Surely I told you before?'

'No,' said Terry, astonished. How could he have missed such a vital point? Presumably because no one had asked about these dates earlier; they hadn't been important. But if Maria had been in Venice on the 5th, she couldn't have met Simon. And he was sacked from his job on the 7th, three days before she returned. His connection with Maria's death, so vital to Churchill's suspicions, collapsed. So Sarah was hiding nothing after all, Terry thought. Simon never met her.

The second discovery came when he showed Mrs Slingsby the entry in Maria's diary.

S big promise, no result. Gets it up but can't get it out. V frust for him, poor lamb, blames me. Outside? No way, José, I say.

'The first part seems pretty clear,' Terry said. 'A man with some kind of sexual problem, impotence of some kind. But she must have come across that more than once. It would be a speciality of hers, I suppose?'

'Oh yes, she had her ways, dear.' A friendly, knowing twinkle came into Ann Slingsby's eyes. 'And the last part probably means he asked her to do it outside and she wouldn't. She had the neighbours to consider, after all.'

'Yes, well, who do you think he could be, this S? It's dated 18th July, after the builders left but about a month before she died. I've checked through the appointments book for that day but there's no client whose name begins with S, or who admits to a nickname that does, either.'

'You asked them all, did you? Poor lambs.' She took the diary and appointments book, poring over them carefully. 'No, you're right. Anyway . . .' She looked up, thinking hard. 'It was around then that I was ill.

226

Didn't I tell you? Maria had to do all the reception for herself. Only a few days, but it could have been then.'

'So you can't guarantee who came on that day?'

'No. I had tonsillitis, I was feverish. But I remember . . . oh my goodness, I don't think I told you this. That delivery driver.'

'Who? Simon Newby?'

'No. Not him, I mean the one who came later.'

'There was *another* delivery driver? From the same firm?'

'Yes. Robson's, wasn't it? He brought the tiles for the roof.'

'You don't remember his name?'

'Sorry, love, no.' She clicked her lips. 'Heavens, I should have mentioned him before, shouldn't I? I never met him, you see, Maria dealt with him. But there was something she said.'

'What was it?' Terry asked patiently.

'Let me think. She made some sort of joke about him. That's all, really. I'm afraid we did that sometimes about the men, you understand. In a friendly way only.'

I'll bet you did, Terry thought, wryly. 'But what was the joke about?'

'Well, he came back, didn't he? After all the building work was done. And he had some sort of problem, maybe like it says there in her diary. I wasn't here, it was in the evening, but she told me about it. She said a workman had brought her another extension but this time she couldn't make use of it. Something like that.' She smiled apologetically. 'It was just a silly joke.'

So that's it, Terry thought. He'd missed the delivery driver in his first investigation, but Tracy had missed the fact that there'd been a *second* one, a replacement when Simon Newby lost his job. This man, it seemed, had sex with Maria – *and* had a problem. Terry sat silent, thinking.

'I'm sorry, dear, I've shocked you. But we were very discreet, most of the time. That was the key to the business.'

'I'm sure it was, Ann.' He folded his notebook and smiled, ready to go. 'I'm glad I wasn't one of your customers, though.'

'Are you? Oh no, don't say that, Mr Bateson, please.' She escorted him to the door. 'You'd have been welcome, any time at all.' And to his complete astonishment, as he stepped over the threshold she patted his bottom gently.

'So it can't be him, sir,' Terry said. 'When he delivered the stuff, she was in Venice.'

'You trust the old bird, do you?' Churchill asked. 'She knows what day it is, and so on?'

'She's as sharp as you or me, sir. Sharper, probably.'

He couldn't prevent a silly grin from playing around the corners of his mouth. The day was starting out well. The pat on the bottom had been good; Churchill's scowl of frustration was even better. It was a while since he'd felt so pleased about something at work.

The look on Tracy's face was gratifying too. She had shown him up before; now the tables were reversed. She hadn't checked the dates; he had.

A uniformed constable, PC Burrows, came in. 'Fax for you, sir,' he said to Churchill. 'From the forensic lab. Sergeant Chisholm said you'd want to see it straight away.'

'Yes, thank you.' Churchill scanned the papers greedily. As he did so the expression on his face changed. The eager wolf-like grin faded. He frowned, flushed, and peered at the words more closely. Then he turned abruptly to the second page as though he wanted to rip the information out of it with his fingers. Offensive information which ought not to be there at all.

The others watched him silently. Mike Candor spoke first.

'Bad news, sir?'

Churchill looked up at the ceiling, ignoring them all.

'Wonderful,' he said at last. 'Don't these blasted scientists always let you down just when you need them most!' He thrust the paper at Mike. 'Here. Read it for yourself.'

Mike read the sheets carefully, and then passed them to Harry. 'It's the DNA analysis of those three hair samples – you know, the ones from inside the balaclava; the one left by Karen Whitaker's attacker; and the ones we took from Simon Newby.'

'Yes,' Tracy prompted. 'And?'

'Well, the good news is that the hairs in the balaclava match the one left by Whitaker's attacker with a certainty of several million to one. Which proves that whoever attacked Whitaker wore that hood. The bad news is that neither the Whitaker hair nor the ones in the hood match the sample we took from Simon.'

'Simon didn't attack Whitaker?' Tracy's voice reflected her surprise. 'So who did?'

'Well, there's the mystery,' said Harry. 'We said it wasn't Gary Harker because we checked that already, but get this! There were *two* sets of hairs in the balaclava, not just one!'

'Two?'

'Yes. A lot of fair hairs and some brown ones. And the brown ones match the sample we sent them from Gary last year. They're his! Only it was a *fair* hair we found on Whitaker's tape, wasn't it?'

Tracy nodded. 'Which meant Gary couldn't have done it. So we dropped the charges.'

Terry turned to Churchill, who was pacing up and down morosely, his hands in his packets. 'You never told me there were any brown hairs in that hood, sir.'

'No, well, I didn't know, did I? All I saw were fair hairs.'

'So what this does prove,' Terry continued belligerently, 'is that all this about Harker not raping Sharon is a load of cock. He *did* rape her, after all. Wearing that hood.'

'Yes, well, it's a pity you didn't get a conviction then, isn't it?' Churchill scowled.

'Let me look at that,' said Terry, taking the report from Harry. 'It seems to me this, together with Mrs Slingsby's evidence, puts Simon in the clear, doesn't it? At least as far as Maria Clayton and Karen Whitaker are concerned. He had no connection with either of them.'

'No,' Churchill agreed gloomily. 'There's more than one villain after all, it seems.' He thumped the wall, sending several sheets of paper fluttering from the noticeboard. 'Shit!'

In his office, Terry put his feet up and thought. Both he and Churchill, it seemed, had been wrong. They had both believed that all these crimes were committed by one person. He had believed that person was Gary, Churchill that it was Simon. But the evidence supported neither of them.

Gary must have raped Sharon – his hairs in the hood, added to all the other evidence, made that more certain than ever. But the reddish *fair* hairs in the hood suggested that someone else had attacked Karen Whitaker; someone who was neither Simon nor Gary. And the evidence for Gary murdering Maria Clayton was no better than it had ever been. And the idea that Gary had killed Jasmine seemed even more remote; he had no motive, there was no evidence that he'd been anywhere near her that night.

And it seemed neither Gary nor Simon had attacked Helen Steersby.

On the other hand there *was* compelling evidence that Gary had raped Sharon and that Simon had murdered Jasmine. Both were, in a sense, crimes of passion – the assailants well known to their victims, the motive a form of violent vengeance.

Three facts still worried Terry. The fact that Gary and Simon knew each other. The fact that at least one, and possibly two assaults had been committed by neither of them. And the fact that the evidence which proved this had been found in a shed owned by one of them, inside a balaclava hood used by the other.

He puzzled over this for an hour without getting anywhere. Then he remembered his promise to tell Sarah when the DNA results came in. For her, clearly, it would be a kindness, but it was risky, all the same. It was Churchill's case; for Terry to anticipate him might well be construed as a disciplinary offence.

But there was such a thing as compassion, too. He decided to ring her from home tonight.

'So he's out of the frame for all these other cases. You should be pleased.'

'Because my son's no longer suspected of being a serial killer? Oh, I am, Terry, I am.'

The ironic edge to Sarah's voice couldn't disguise her relief about the DNA results, and the result of his interview with Ann Slingsby. But as usual, her mind was on to the next thing.

'So if you admit you were wrong about this, maybe you're wrong about Jasmine, too?'

'That's not my case, Sarah.'

'Well, your DCI Churchill, then. Is he having second thoughts?'

'Not about that, no. Like me, he thinks we may have been mistaken to see these crimes as part of a series. But he still thinks he has enough evidence to convict Simon for the murder of Jasmine. I imagine he's treating it as a crime of passion again, just as he did at the beginning.'

'So the prosecution's still going ahead?'

'Yes.'

'Even though it could have been Gary? You said so yourself, remember?'

'Yes, well, that's the other piece of bad news, I'm afraid. I've checked his alibi for the night of Jasmine's death and for once it seems to add up. Five witnesses saw him in the private room of the Lighthorseman until after midnight, celebrating his acquittal. I'm sorry, Sarah.'

'Oh.' There was a pause. In the lounge, Terry could hear Trude reading to his daughters. 'But you say Gary's hair was in the balaclava too,' Sarah resumed thoughtfully, remembering the night he had attacked her in the shed.

'Yes. Which is more proof that he raped Sharon, if we needed it.'

There was a silence on the other end of the phone.

'The jury decided on the evidence presented to them at the time, Terry. Which is less than we know now.'

'And that's my fault, is that what you're saying?'

'I'm not saying anything. Look, we're neither of us perfect, but what concerns me is Simon's defence. You said yourself you didn't believe he could have killed Jasmine.'

This time, the silence came from Terry's end. With every second, Sarah's pain increased.

'Terry?'

'What I think I said was, I didn't believe he was the type to attack a range of women. I've been proved right on that. But for a single attack on his girlfriend, perhaps in a jealous rage . . .'

Moments like this, Terry thought, are crueller over the telephone. Her voice came back at him tinny, bitter, distant. 'I thought you were on my side, Terry.'

'I'm on the side of the truth. I have to be. That's my job.'

'And I'm just Simon's mother, which makes me blind, I suppose. Look, just because Gary didn't do it, it doesn't mean that Simon did. What about David Brodie? He had a motive – jealousy, because Jasmine was two-timing him with Simon. Dozens of times, it seems.'

'Have you met him, Sarah? He's a nurse – clean, house-trained, inoffensive . . .'

'So was Dr Crippen, probably.'

'Yes, but he used poison, not a knife. Jasmine was a big girl, athletic, probably stronger than him . . .'

'Jealousy can fire people up,' said Sarah desperately. 'What if I told you I had a witness who saw this David Brodie full of anger, stalking off to find Jasmine a few hours before her death?'

'Then I'd suggest you investigate further,' said Terry slowly. 'Tell Churchill, if you're sure it adds up to something. In the meantime he's still got the blood on the shoes and the knife, and the semen, and the fact that Simon was the last person to be seen with her before he ran off to Scarborough. He's dead set on it, Sarah. It's a strong case to upset with a little bit of incidental jealousy.'

'But if it's all I've got, Terry?'

'Then I wish you luck. If it leads to the truth, at least.'

And that, Sarah thought, was the difference between them. He, as a moderately decent policeman, had the moral luxury of an objective search for the truth, whatever it might turn out to be; she, on the other hand, was committed to Simon's innocence.

There had been many moments over the past couple of weeks when she had doubted him; but as a lawyer she was used to that. You don't ask clients if they're innocent; you ask how they wish to plead. Then you present their case to the best of your ability. The search for truth is conducted by the court and the jury; the lawyer is *supposed* to be biased.

But when the lawyer is a mother too – well, that's just more of the same. Simon may be a liar, she thought, violent, unstable, and downright stupid at times – but he's not a murderer, he can't be.

I couldn't live with that.

The more Terry thought about his meeting with Ann Slingsby, the happier he felt. It wasn't the exquisite tea or the pat on the bottom which cheered him, though both were welcome; it was the priceless jewel of information which had not only confounded Churchill but might also, with luck, solve the Clayton murder, all in one go.

There had been a *second* delivery driver! And not only had this man delivered tiles to Maria's house when she *was* at home – unlike Simon Newby – but he also, apparently, *had a sexual problem!* If that wasn't a suspect, what was?

On the way to the builder's merchant, Robson's, a second thought struck him. What if this same driver had delivered building materials to the university lodgings where Karen Whitaker lived? Might as well check those dates too.

The receptionist at Robson's was uncooperative. A burly girl with fat legs and a hint of a moustache, she kept him waiting for nearly five minutes while fiddling with some paperwork. The employment clerk in the back office seemed brighter, but worried somehow. He checked the addresses and dates Terry gave him, and fished some delivery notes out of the files. He laid them before Terry reluctantly.

'There you are, that's them.'

The handwriting on each was identical. So it *was* the same driver, Terry noted with a pulse of excitement. 'What's this signature at the bottom? The driver's name?'

The man inspected it in surprise, as though wondering why it was there. 'Hard to read, isn't it? Just a scrawl. Some of these lads are barely literate, you know.'

Terry had met this sort of response before. 'Look, I'm not from the DSS or the Revenue, OK? This is a murder enquiry. So if you're going to be obstructive . . .'

The scales seemed to lift from the man's eyes. 'Irish fellow – name of Sean . . . something.'

'Sean what?'

'Ah well, he'll have wanted to avoid tax, you see . . . we wouldn't keep a record.'

'You pay them under the counter, no questions asked?'

'Your words, not mine. No address, no phone number, nothing.'

'But you let this man drive. You must have seen his licence!'

'Oh, yes, of course, but . . .' The man shrugged. 'I didn't keep it, did I?'

Terry sighed. 'Well, at least you can give me a description. Or I *will* tell the Revenue.'

The man held up his hands. 'Look, in a murder case, no question. I'll get some lads too. There's several knew him. When he left us he worked for MacFarlane's, I think.'

At MacFarlane's he was embarrassed to meet Graham Dewar, who had given evidence that the man Gary had claimed to be with *did* exist after all. A man called Sean.

'If you'd asked me before I'd have told you,' Graham Dewar said reprovingly. 'But . . .'

'Yes, well.' Terry sighed. 'He wasn't on site back then, was he?'

Dewar shook his head. 'Lads like him don't stay long. We were well rid, at that.'

Two other labourers also remembered this Sean. Their information confirmed what Terry had learned at Robson's. Sean was a big man, everyone agreed, strong and exceptionally fit. He could carry a hod of bricks up ladders for eight hours a day, before going out in the evenings for a run. He had done some boxing, apparently, and had the face to show it.

But none of this accounted for the informants' clear dislike of him, or the anxiety some showed when Terry's questions began. One problem seemed to have been his unpredictable temper. He could be calm one minute, in a violent rage the next. Anything could set it off, and the result was frightening. Two men had left, rather than work alongside him. His one friend was Gary Harker, who seemed to have known him before, in prison.

The day Sean left MacFarlane's, a number of tools went missing. Sean's name was mentioned to the police as a possible suspect, but the investigating officers, like Terry, found no address or surname. MacFarlane's, like Robson's, had no record.

So, what did this add up to, Terry wondered, as he drove home. On one level the man seemed just a petty thief. One of many casual Irish building workers avoiding tax. A fitness fanatic with an unpleasant, somewhat obsessional character.

But this was also a man with a sexual problem which Maria Clayton had joked about with her maid. What if she had mocked him to his face – this ex-boxer, this fitness fanatic who perhaps trained to compensate for his sexual inadequacy, whatever it was? There was his motive all right – a hatred of women, a sudden violent loss of control.

And this same man had delivered building materials to Karen Whitaker's lodgings. And, like her attacker, had fairish hair. So, how to find him? The Irish passport office couldn't help without a surname, passport number, or address in the Republic. Not even a record of a driving licence, for God's sake – what if he'd had an accident driving Robson's lorry?

But he knew Gary Harker, an ex-convict. A friendship possibly made in prison. So this Sean, too, must have previous convictions. He could check the court and prison records – particularly where Harker had served – but without a definite surname, that would be difficult too.

31

Time passed. Summer came and went. Simon sweated, played endless games of pool, and paced the prison landings. At night he dreamed of Jasmine's face, cheek bruised, throat cut, her blackened lips opening silently. She wanted to tell him something; but what, he never heard.

Sarah worked, defending shoplifters and petty thieves during the day.

In the evenings she sat up late, poring over the details of Simon's case. She talked to Bob when she could, and Lucy several times a week.

Emily's GCSE results came through, and she began her A levels at the sixth form college. She and Larry spied on David Brodie, passing on snippets of information to Sarah.

Terry Bateson continued his slow, painstaking attempt to solve the Clayton and Whitaker cases. Forensics confirmed that the black trousers found in Simon's shed were torn, and their fibres were consistent with those found in the mouth of Maria Clayton's Yorkshire terrier; but there was nothing to show who had worn them. Terry's attempts to trace the Irishman were equally frustrating. No one had seen him for months; it seemed unlikely he was still in York.

A judge was chosen for Simon's trial, a date set. Lucy received copies of the prosecution evidence and, in agreement with Sarah, chose a barrister. He was the best they could get, a highly respected criminal silk, Sir Richard Haverstock, QC.

She met him and his junior in Hull prison, two weeks before the trial. Sarah had wanted to come, but she was defending a car thief in Newcastle. It didn't matter, Lucy had told her, things might go better without her. Sir Richard was a perfectionist, renowned for his analytical skills, but known to detest lawyers who became emotionally involved with a case. He was a great catch, but his status made it hard to arrange a meeting. He could manage today only because of an adjournment in the multi-million pound drug-smuggling trial he was defending.

The two barristers wore expensively tailored mohair suits with a casual assurance which suggested that they never wore anything else. Lucy was dressed in her semi-formal clothes – clean blouse, black jacket, long black skirt to conceal her generous lower body, and Doc Martens. They shook her hand patronizingly.

Simon had got thinner, Lucy thought as he walked in. The blue prison overalls hung off him loosely; she wondered if he was eating at all. He slumped into a chair and stared at the blue sky out of the window.

'So, Mr Newby.' Sir Richard began. 'I've come to defend you. I need to hear your side of the story.'

'Hasn't Lucy told you that, already?'

'Yes, of course. I have it all here in this file. But I need to hear it from your own lips, too.'

'Why? To see if I'm lying?'

'Not at all. Please understand, I'm not a policeman, Simon. I'm on your side. But I need to know what happened, exactly as you experienced it. It makes it easier for me to defend you.'

'For the hundredth time.' Simon sighed, and began to tell his story. But he wasn't really concentrating. He kept gazing out of the window, away from the two elegant men who listened, making notes on their pads. What's the matter with him, Lucy wondered? It's as if he doesn't care.

Several times he missed out important details, and she had to prompt him.

Sir Richard asked questions, teasing out aspects that Simon had skimmed or forgotten. But still Simon ignored him, as though he were unimportant, an irrelevance compared to the sunlight streaming through the window. It was a particularly bright day, and a sunbeam reached the foot of Simon's chair. It fascinated him. He dabbled his foot in the pool of brilliant light.

Sir Richard's questions ended. He tapped his pencil thoughtfully against his notes, and looked up. 'It has to be said, Mrs Parsons, that the prosecution do have a strong case. In the circumstances I'd be failing in my duty if I didn't warn our young client that at first blush, his hopes of outright acquittal are not particularly promising. Whereas for a plea of manslaughter, with diminished responsibility due to sexual jealousy, I could hold out far better hopes. But for that you would have to change your story, young man. Do you follow what I'm saying?'

'No, sorry.' Simon dragged his attention away from the sunbeam. 'What do you mean, manslaughter?'

'I mean, given the circumstances of your relationship with Jasmine Hurst, it would be easy to make a jury understand how upset and angry you were about her and this . . .' he checked his notes '. . . David Brodie. Especially given the way Jasmine kept coming back and, as it were, teasing you before going away again. I could play on the jury's sympathy quite a lot with that. Then if you were to say, for instance, that you had an argument – that you asked her to come back but she refused, and as a result of that refusal you experienced an uncontrollable rush of emotion, a sudden violent loss of control in which you killed her without intending to do it or even knowing what you were doing, well . . .'

He threw open his hands, as though the conclusion was obvious. '. . . I could plead manslaughter, which carries a much lesser sentence than murder. In fact, the trial could be over in a day, with no jury at all. But that's not possible with this story you're telling at the moment, you see.'

'What?' Simon shook his head, bemused.

'With the story you are telling now, I must warn you that our chances are not particularly good. And if you are convicted of murder you will go to prison for life. Whereas if, on reflection, you were to tell a different story, that you suffered a sudden loss of control and killed Jasmine in a moment of jealous passion, without meaning to, then everything changes. We can plead diminished responsibility. Do you see?'

'But I didn't kill her.'

'I know you say that, Simon, I understand that fully, I assure you. But let me put this to you – I want you to think about this very carefully before we meet again, because it's very important. There is such a thing as suppressed memory. There have been several cases recently where a psychological examination has established that a person who committed

235

a terrible crime – a murder like, for example, this murder of Jasmine – remembered nothing about it at all. It was like a car accident, the shock erased the memory. Do you follow what I'm saying?'

Simon nodded slowly, his face sullen, hostile, confused.

'So they could quite truthfully tell a story – as you have done – saying that they didn't do it, when in fact they *had* done it but couldn't remember. Often these people went wandering off after the crime just like you disappeared to Scarborough. But later when it was proved they had suffered such mental trauma it was easy to claim diminished responsibility. Their barrister explained that their earlier stories were not lies at all, but simply the truth as they saw it because part of their memory was missing. Now I know a number of eminent psychiatrists and what I would like –'

'Fuck off.'

'I'm sorry?'

'Fuck off, you slimy cunt.' Simon leaned forward over the table, his face a few inches from Sir Richard's. 'Get the fuck out of here now, before I push your nose down your throat. Do you hear me? *Go!*'

'Wait, just a minute, let's calm things down . . .' Sir Richard sat back, waving his pen in Simon's face. 'OK, I see you don't agree –'

Simon knocked the pen, spinning, out of his hand. Then he pulled Sir Richard's nose, so that the barrister fell sideways, on to the floor. Simon spat and the phlegm landed in his ear.

Then Lucy caught hold of Simon, wrapping both her arms around his so he couldn't attack further, enfolding his slim hard trembling body in a massive soft motherly embrace. The junior barrister hit the alarm button and two warders came in. Simon was led away in handcuffs.

On the way to the car park Sir Richard, dusting down his expensive mohair suit, said little. He touched his keys and the lights of his Jaguar lit up like a faithful dog. He favoured Lucy with what he hoped was a wry smile.

'I seem to have hit the wrong note, rather. But put it to him again, Mrs Parsons, will you? When he's in a calmer mood. It was a serious point and may prove to be his only real defence. If he chooses to adopt it, that is.'

He opened his car door, then another thought struck him.

'Oh, and don't worry. I've never yet stooped to suing one of my own clients for assault. Wouldn't be very good PR now, would it?'

'He did what?'

'Pulled the man's nose, dragged him to the floor, and spat in his ear.'

Lucy struggled to keep her voice neutral, but her emotions bubbled beneath the words. Officially she was, of course, appalled; but underneath she could not disguise her guilty delight. Lucy had always loathed being patronized by plummy QCs like Sir Richard; never before had she seen one so swiftly, comprehensively humiliated.

'Sweet mother of God, Simon, what have you done now? Oh dear me.' Sarah began to shake. At first Lucy couldn't identify the reaction, then she realized it was laughter. A wild, hysterical kind of laughter, but laughter all the same. And once Sarah had begun to laugh Lucy started too, as she'd been longing to do all morning. The two of them rocked back and forwards in their chairs, hooting helplessly.

'So what now?' Sarah asked, sobering suddenly. 'Will he still take the case, d'you think?'

'He was still speaking of Simon as his client, when he got into his Jaguar.'

'Well, that's something, I suppose. But it's hardly likely to increase his level of commitment, is it?'

Lucy frowned. 'His feelings ought not to come into it. Sir Richard Haverstock is a *professional*, Sarah.'

'Yes, he is, isn't he?' Sarah met her friend's eyes with a deadpan grimace. 'A Queen's Counsel, no less. Not a spittoon.'

'Look, I've spoken to him and he doesn't hold it against you. He understands that you're under a lot of stress and he'll forget all about it and give you the best defence he can.'

'How can he?' Simon asked angrily. 'He wants me to plead guilty. He thinks I did it.'

'He wasn't saying that exactly, Simon. He was saying the prosecution have a strong case.'

'So he's given up already. That's it, isn't it?'

Simon, Lucy and Sarah were back in the interview room in Hull. It was less than a week before the trial was due to start. Sir Richard had not been back to see Simon again, but Lucy had had several long phone conversations with him. The man had been smooth, urbane, reassuring.

'It's his duty to give you the best advice he can. He said if he could present you in a sympathetic light, you might get eight years and be out in five. Which is a lot less than life.'

'*Eight years?* Christ.' Simon stared out of the window, while a warder watched through the door. Since his assault on Sir Richard, Simon was handcuffed during visiting.

'Is that what *you* do, then, Mum? Tell people to plead guilty when they didn't do it?'

'Sometimes, Simon, yes. If the prosecution case is very strong, I might advise a client to do that in his own best interests. But it's always the client who decides, not the lawyer.'

'Yeah, well I'm the client and I'm pleading *not* guilty, OK?'

'I think you made that clear to Sir Richard when he was here,' said Lucy. 'And I've told him that over the phone. Naturally he'll defend you on that basis if you insist, he said.'

Simon looked down at his manacled hands. He was thinner and more subdued than she remembered, Sarah thought. She wondered if they were giving him some sort of calming drug. Or more likely, the impending urgency of the trial was getting to him.

'Yeah, but what does he actually *know* about my case? He's only met me once.'

'I've sent him the papers,' Lucy answered. 'Four box files. He's had them a week now.'

'*A week?*' Simon stared at her, anxiously. 'Is that long enough?'

Lucy hesitated. The truth, she knew, was that Sir Richard had probably not given the papers more than a cursory glance so far. His massive, complex and highly lucrative drug-smuggling case was due to finish tomorrow, and had certainly occupied all his mental energies for the past month or more. By comparison, Simon's case was small beer. But if the drug trial did finish on time Sir Richard and his junior would still have a long weekend to familiarize themselves with the evidence.

This was not unusual. Barristers prided themselves on assimilating large amounts of complex information swiftly. They were used to it. It was how the system worked. It was clients, rather than lawyers, who were unhappy with it.

She explained all this to Simon, who began to sway his head from side to side, in a panic.

'You mean, they still don't know shit about my case? They're going to read all this stuff that you and Mum have spent months on in just *three days*?'

'They've already read some of it, Simon, obviously. Otherwise they wouldn't have been able to talk to you about it last week.'

'He didn't talk to me, the ponce – he told me to plead guilty!' Simon got up, walked to the window, and rested his manacled hands on the bars. The guard peered in anxiously. 'Christ! The miserable sod advised me to plead guilty and he hadn't even read the case! I thought at least he'd done that!'

'Simon, he knew the main facts –'

'Sod the main facts! He's supposed to know *everything* about it, isn't he? Specially if he tells me to plead guilty!' Panic was clear on his face. 'This is the guy you chose to defend me? *Why?*'

'Because he's a top criminal QC, Simon,' Lucy insisted. 'We were very lucky to get him.'

'And that's your idea of luck, is it? A guy who tells me to plead guilty before he's read the papers? A guy who wants me to rot in here for five long years?' He gazed for a while at the windblown clouds racing freely over the rooftops. Then he took a deep, sobbing breath and turned back into the room. 'Well, I don't want him.'

'What?'

'You heard, I don't want a turd like that defending me. I'd rather defend myself.'

'You can't do that, Simon,' said Sarah coolly. 'Be sensible. You don't know the first thing about the law.'

'Maybe not.' He focused on her for the first time. 'But *you* do, don't you, Mum. Why don't *you* defend me?'

'*Me?* I can't, Simon.'

'Why not? You're a barrister, aren't you? And at least you know about my bloody case. You know everything about it, you do. You even saw Jasmine's body.'

'Which is exactly why I can't defend you. I'm too closely involved. I'm your mother, after all . . .'

'True. And you believe I'm not guilty, as well.'

'Yes.' If there was a hesitation in her voice it was the tiniest possible one, so tiny that Sarah hoped only she herself heard it. 'Yes, I believe you're not guilty.'

'Well then. That's a thousand times better than Sir Richard Pissface. *You* should do it.'

'I understand why you think that, Simon, but I can't. I told you, I'm too closely involved. The whole point of hiring a barrister is to hire a professional, an expert in the law who can put forward your arguments in the best way possible without the liability of . . .'

She hesitated, words unexpectedly failing her for a moment.

'Without *what*, Mum? Without the liability of actually *caring* one way or the other, is that what you were going to say?'

'Something like that, Simon, yes. It's how the system works.'

'Then the system stinks. It's a load of shit.'

For a while no one said anything. The three of them thought hard. Simon's eyes were locked on Sarah's. Lucy watched, afraid to speak. This wasn't just a matter of legal advice now, she thought. It was between Simon and his mother.

'Is that true, Mum? You're not allowed to defend me, really? There's a law against it?'

Sarah's mind was racing – through everything she'd learned since she began to practise law. Simon had raised a question which, in all those years, had never actually come up.

'I don't think there's a law against it exactly, Simon,' she said falteringly. 'It's just the way it works.'

'And you're happy with that, are you?'

'I didn't say I was happy with it . . .'

'Mum, listen to me. All the time I was a kid, you were studying. You couldn't go swimming with us, you couldn't play football, because you had an essay to write or a book to read. Always. Then when you passed your exams and we thought it would get better, you got more exams, more essays. Remember? You were away for weeks, months on end. Study, study, study, that's all you ever did. I never saw you. Your studying was more important than games and housework and cooking, you said, I'd understand that some day. You'd be a lawyer and I'd understand.

'Well, now you *are* a lawyer and I'm stuck in this stinking cesspit of a jail, accused of a murder which I didn't do – and I *don't* understand. *Why* can't you defend me? You're a barrister, aren't you – just as good as Sir Richard Filthy Ponceface – and you actually *know* all about my case, which he doesn't and no other barrister does. I'm just asking you to use what you know. And you say you can't because you're my mother. *Christ!*'

He turned away, gazing blindly at the clouds outside the window. Sarah was shocked. It was the longest speech she had ever heard him make.

'That's just cruel, Simon,' she said faintly. 'I didn't abandon you when I studied –'

'You may not have meant to, Mum –'

'I didn't mean to and I didn't do it! You know I didn't! You were fed, you were clothed, you had friends and a father – Bob, he spent hours with you . . .'

'So why did you always have your nose in a book, then?'

'Because I wanted to get out of the filthy slum where we lived. Because I wanted to make a life for myself and for you and all of us. A life in which we could be proud to hold our heads up and not scrounge around like victims blaming society for everything. That's why, Simon. And I did it, too, didn't I? Only you . . .'

'Only I what?'

She shook her head, despairingly. 'Only you didn't understand, Simon. You still don't understand, do you? I wasn't doing it just for me, I was doing it for all of us, for you most of all! And now look . . .' She waved at their drab, dirty surroundings. 'What are we doing *here*?'

'Do you think I want to be here?'

'No, but you got us here. No one else . . .'

'Well, now I want you to get me out! That's what I'm asking, Mum. *Please*. You know how to do it, no one else does.'

'You shouldn't have such faith in me . . .'

'Why not? I've seen how hard you work. What else was it for, all that study?'

'God!' She slammed her hand hard on the table. 'You still have no idea, do you? If only you knew, if only you understood what it was like having you there all the time. Holding me back, and yet being the reason, the only reason I did it all . . .'

'So are you saying you *can't* do it because the law won't let you? Or are you saying you *won't* do it because you don't care? Which is it, Mum? Tell me.'

Sarah's anger left her as suddenly as it had come. She couldn't answer; she didn't know what to say. She looked at her tall, desperate son, his hands manacled in front of him, and was struck dumb.

'Or did you do all that work, all that study, just so you could defend druggies and burglars who you don't know and don't give a shit about? Is that it, Mum? Is that your great profession which you studied so hard for all these years, to get us out of the slums?'

'Simon, you don't understand!' She reached one hand tentatively towards his. 'You need a cool head to defend you, not someone who loves you and –'

'Love, my arse!' He snatched his hands away. 'If you loved me you'd defend me, that's the truth of it.'

'You're just trying to make me feel guilty, Simon. What you really need is someone much, much better than me.'

'What I want is someone who *cares*, Mum. Don't you care about me?'

'Of course I care. That's the whole point. That's why I shouldn't do this. If I messed it up I'd never forgive myself.'

'That's exactly the point, Mum – don't you see? No other lawyer in the world – not even Lucy – cares about this case as much as you. That's exactly why I want you to defend me.'

For once in her life, Sarah felt herself losing the argument. Losing, and despite herself, wanting to lose. She drew a deep breath. 'You really want this? Even though I tell you it's unwise?'

'If I say I want it I do, Mum. Trust me.'

'It's you who'll be trusting me, more like.'

'Yeah, OK.' A nervous smile flickered on his lips. 'You mean you'll do it then?'

She hesitated, struggling to maintain some detachment. 'If you really want me to.'

'Mum!' He laughed aloud with relief. '*I want you to*. OK?'

'All right, Simon.' She felt like a priest giving a blessing. 'I will.'

Only she wasn't a priest, she didn't believe in miracles. Especially not miracles performed by her.

'Sarah . . .' Lucy's voice warned. 'I'm not sure you can . . .'

'I will if I *can*, Lucy, that's what I'm saying. Simon, look, there are laws and precedents and the judge will have to decide about those. If he won't let me I can't do it. But if you really want me to defend you and the judge allows it then I will.'

32

The judge, His Lordship P.J. Mookerjee, frowned at the two barristers in front of him. On his desk was a letter from Sarah, briefly outlining her position. She was the mother of the defendant, who wished her to represent him in court. She was aware of no statute or regulation which specifically prohibited such a choice. Nonetheless, it was an unusual situation, which she would like to discuss in chambers before the trial began.

Judge Mookerjee was young for a judge. Sarah guessed he was in his late forties, ten years older than herself. He was a short, chubby man of Indian descent, with a luxuriant black moustache and gold-rimmed glasses through which he peered at Sarah keenly.

'Well, Mrs Newby.' He smiled briefly, a gleam of perfect white teeth in his dark face, an attempt perhaps to put her at ease. 'Do you mind if I ask whose idea this was in the first place? Yours, or your son's?'

'My son's. I advised against it, but . . . he was very insistent.'

The judge nodded. 'As children sometimes are. Don't you find, Mr Turner?'

'Indeed,' Phil Turner answered non-committally. 'Though mine are still too young to face me with dilemmas like this, thank God.'

'Let's hope they never do,' the judge replied smoothly.

Sarah had a sense, not unfamiliar to her from judges' conferences, that the agenda was already slipping away from her and being redefined according to some male world-view from which she was forever excluded. Or was she too sensitive, overreacting to what was simply good manners, the public school veneer never acquired in Seacroft?

She studied the men keenly. The more she could learn about their ideas and prejudices now, the better. Whatever happened, these men would affect the future of her son. If her request was granted, she would face them in court. If not, she would watch from the public gallery, able to see everything but influence nothing. I would hate that, she thought. She hadn't wanted to represent Simon at first, but the idea had grown until now she wanted it passionately. She wanted to be in there, fighting in every way she could. Even if she failed, at least she would have tried.

The prosecuting barrister, Philip Turner, was a big, bluff Yorkshireman, well known and respected around the northern circuit. Still a junior like herself, he had years of experience and a success rate second to none. Part of this, Sarah believed, was due to his straightforward, honest manner. There were no airs and graces about him, despite his education at St Peter's School and Merton College, Oxford. He was a farmer's son who had retained a Yorkshire accent, and it was easy to imagine him, with his powerful build, battered nose and cheerful grin, at the wheel of a tractor, the bottom of a rugby scrum, or supping a foaming jar of Sam Smith's ale.

Juries, in short, liked Phil Turner and trusted him. So from Simon's point of view, he was the most lethal prosecutor possible.

Judge Mookerjee, on the other hand, was an unknown quantity. Sarah had never appeared before him. She had consulted Savendra, who'd said only, 'Decent enough chap, very sharp, Cambridge cricket blue, I believe. Rumoured to be a bit challenged in the sense of humour department, though.'

She smiled inwardly. No flip jokes, remember. Not that any sprang to mind. This was far, far too important for that.

'There are several issues, it seems to me,' the judge began. 'Firstly, the straightforward point of law. I, like you, Mrs Newby, have found no statute which prohibits a member of the Bar from representing a member of her own family. The choice of legal representative rests with the accused. Would you concur with that, Mr Turner?'

'I agree, yes,' said Phil Turner. 'There's nothing against it in law.'

'Very well, then.' The judge leaned forward on his desk, lacing his fingers under his chin. 'First point, and perhaps the vital point, to you, Mrs Newby. However . . .'

Sarah's heart sank. He's thought of something I haven't, she told herself.

'. . . there are other points to be considered. Most importantly, is this a wise choice, in the interests of justice and your client? It's not difficult to find reasons why it might be against those interests. Several spring instantly to mind. Lack of objectivity, emotion getting in the way of reason, and so on. Have you considered it in that light, Mrs Newby?'

'I have, my lord, yes. As I said, I advised my son – my client – against this in the first instance. But he was insistent – very – about his right to choose.'

'Which is enshrined in law, I agree. But just because he asks you to represent him does not mean you have to agree. You can decline a case, you know.'

'I know, my lord. But I now wish . . . I mean, I am happy to accept the brief.'

She remembered Simon's earnest, desperate face in the prison room in Hull, and her own rush of strong, protective emotion when she had agreed.

The judge nodded. 'Very well. But I have two conflicting responsibilities here, it seems to me. On the one hand, I will of course uphold your son's rights in law. On the other hand, I must put it to you – I will say it no stronger than that – that your own emotional involvement in this case may – and I only say *may*, I have no experience of this – *may* mean that you quite inadvertently give a less good service to your client than would be given by a disinterested advocate. And therefore that your son would not receive as fair a trial, as in the interests of justice he is entitled to receive. Have you considered that too?'

'I have, my lord,' said Sarah solemnly, ignoring the implied insult that she, as a mother, was not up to the job. 'I put this point to my client and he strongly felt – he *believes* – that it will work the other way. Because I care so much about the case, he thinks I will do a better job.'

'I see.' Judge Mookerjee gazed at her silently for a moment. Sarah wondered about the expression on his face. Was it sympathy, or mere curiosity – the sort of detached curiosity that all lawyers feel from time to time at the parade of human oddities which pass before them? Was this how everyone would look at her, when the trial finally began? She felt an unwanted prickling of tears at the corner of her eyes.

'Let us hope your son is right in his judgement,' the judge said eventually. 'I wish my children may trust me as much. But there is one other point; the reaction of the jury. On the one hand, they may feel sympathy for you, and therefore for your son. It's a natural enough human reaction. On the other hand, and I feel bound to point this out, things might go the other way.'

'How do you mean, exactly?'

'Well, look at it this way. Were you merely a paid advocate, as you would be in any other case, then the jury may think that you retain, paradoxically, a certain independent reputation. In other words, if a defence barrister says something, we expect the jury to consider it seriously. But if you, as the accused's *mother*, say something, the jury may not give it the same weight. Do you see my point? They may think, well, she's the boy's mother, she *would* say that, wouldn't she? It's not an independent barrister who's saying that, it's only the boy's mother.'

Sarah hesitated, uncertain how to respond. This idea had not occurred to her. Then Phil Turner laughed.

'I think, my lord, that you attribute too sophisticated an understanding to the ordinary juror. They don't have a very high opinion of us, you know. Specially not of defence lawyers. The public just see us as whores, paid to tell lies for a fee. So the fact that in this case someone may think Mrs Newby's telling lies because she's the lad's mum . . .' He shook his head slowly. 'It makes no difference, in my view.'

He smiled at Sarah apologetically. 'That's how folk see me, anyhow.'

'So I'm a liar whether I'm his mother or not?' Sarah snapped. 'Thanks for nothing, Phil.'

Turner looked hurt, but Sarah didn't care. It was not his words that had irritated her. It was his bluff male self-confidence, the way he'd made his point appear such straightforward common sense. It terrified her. This man's job was to send her son to prison for life. And if he spoke that way in court, everyone would be bound to trust him. They would know he had no reason to lie.

And then they would look at her.

Sarah shuddered. The judge was right. The jury would despise her because she was Simon's mother. They'd wonder how any woman could bring such a monster into the world. They would feel pity, and scorn, and not listen to a single word she said.

Judge Mookerjee watched her. 'Have you considered this, Mrs Newby?'

'I have, my lord, yes,' she lied. *I can't back out now. I won't.*

'Very well. Then this court has no objection to your representing your son, Mrs Newby. It is a matter entirely between you and him.'

Too right it is, Sarah thought grimly. 'Thank you, my lord.'

Phil Turner smiled politely. 'I hope we can maintain a professional relationship, Sarah. Whatever I say in court, there'll be nothing personal in it, believe me.'

Sarah glared at him. His bluff, honest looks must have been given him by the devil, she decided. She was going to have to learn to hate this man.

'Oh yes, there is, Phil,' she said firmly. 'Every last bit of it's personal, for me. Whatever you say in there, hurts my son. So don't you ever forget that.'

She walked smartly out of the room, alone.

33

Lucy had warned Sarah about the press, but the message had not really sunk in. She had been too busy preparing her case. It was not until she left her chambers, and walked the short distance across Castle Street to the court, that she saw what Lucy had meant.

Outside the Crown Court was a wide circle of grass, the Eye of York, with a circular road running round it. The eighteenth-century court building, with its stone pillars and the blind statue of Justice with her spear and scales, faced in towards this grassy circle. On two more sides was the old prison, now the Castle Museum. On the northern side, on a high mound, was the keep of the Norman castle, Clifford's Tower.

On a normal morning this area was largely empty. Schoolchildren might queue for the museum; the black-windowed prison bus would park outside the court; the judge's limousine would pull up smoothly at the court steps. Witnesses and jurors would mill uncertainly in the entrance. And that was all.

But today, Sarah saw in horror, the Eye of York was packed. There were four TV vans, each with camera crew, news reporters and fluffy microphones on sticks. The court steps and terrace swarmed with reporters, with microphone or cameras in their hands. Cars were parked indiscriminately all around the grass; the outnumbered security men had retreated, trying only to control entrance to the court itself. Sarah paused, stunned at the sight.

'Mother of God, Luce, why didn't you warn me about this?'

'I did, lovey, I did,' Lucy muttered, awestruck. 'But I never thought it would be this bad. Come on, heads down, let's get through it quick.'

'But why are they here?'

Sarah found out soon enough. They were twenty yards from the entrance when the first reporters rushed towards them. Cameras flashed and questions battered their ears.

'Mrs Newby, what's it like to defend your son?'

'How do you feel about this murder? Did you know the victim?'

'Had she ever visited your house?'

'Do you feel guilty, Mrs Newby? Isn't it a bit like defending yourself?'

Lucy gripped her friend's arm firmly, dragging her forwards through the scrum.

'Don't say a word, just keep walking. Come on, we're nearly there.'

As they got to the foot of the steps two security men reached them, elbowing media people out of the way. But to Sarah it seemed an age before the assault from cameras and questions ceased, and they were safe inside.

'My God! I never expected that. Those questions were so *personal*.'

'Yes, they were, weren't they?' Lucy looked at her anxiously. 'But it doesn't matter, Sarah, you don't have to answer them.'

'No.' Sarah breathed deeply, then smiled. A shaky, nervous smile, but a smile for all that. 'Anyway, this trial isn't about me, it's about Simon. Come on, we've got work to do.'

Simon was in a cell below the court, dressed in the ironed shirt, suit and tie that Sarah had bought for him. The sleeves were tight over his biceps, and a little too short. Sarah tried to tug them down, but he drew back irritably.

'Mum, I'm fine. It's OK.'

'Yes. You look great, Simon. Anyway, all you've got to do is say you're not guilty, and then sit there, looking sensible.'

'Yeah, OK, I'll try. But it's shit scarey, Mum. What if the jury's crap?'

'This isn't America, I can't choose the jurors for you. But don't worry.' She looked at him firmly. 'You're not guilty and that's it. Say it loud and clear and look the judge straight in the eye. We're going to *win*, Simon.'

'Yeah. I bloody well hope we are, anyhow.'

'We are. But don't swear – not if the jury can hear you. These things matter now, Simon.'

'Yeah, OK. I'm sorry.'

'I'm going upstairs to put on my battle gear now. Lucy will stay with you. See you in court.' She smiled, and banged for the guard to open the door. Lucy was patting a spot under Simon's chin where he'd cut himself shaving. Oh no, not blood on his throat, please, Sarah thought. Then the door opened and she walked briskly upstairs to the robing room.

Where her opponent, the bluff, charming Phil Turner, was waiting for her.

The court was, as she had always known, a theatre. Usually, however, they played to a few relatives, idlers and an aged court reporter sleeping off his liquid lunch. Today the public gallery was packed. Not a single seat was left free. A buzz of conversation echoed from the stucco pillars and the decorated ceiling of the dome. Sarah had to bend her head to catch what Lucy was saying.

'. . . like a football match . . .'

'Yes,' she nodded. 'Why are they here?'

Lucy jerked her thumb towards the crowded press bench. 'Because of them. And you. A dreadful murder, a mother defending her son . . .'

Sarah shuddered, then stiffened herself instantly. It was not the eyes of the press and public that mattered, but those of the prospective jurors, seated immediately behind the dock. She must try to look confident for them.

And for Simon.

There was a hush, then a further swell in conversation as Simon entered the dock, with two security men beside him. He looked around, amazed, and everywhere conversations died, then rose again as his look passed on. Sarah walked back, stood on a bench and leaned in over the side of the dock.

'You never said it would be like this, Mum.' His face, already pale from months on remand, had gone, if anything, even whiter.

'It isn't, usually. Probably they'll lose interest after an hour or two. Court proceedings are very slow, you know, and often boring. Just try to look calm and serious. And remember, the jury are the important people. If they like you, that's half our case won.'

As she regained her seat the clerk called out, in her loudest voice: 'All stand!' Judge Mookerjee entered from the door beneath the royal coat of arms, bowed to Sarah and Phil Turner, and sat down. The audience did the same.

'Her Majesty's Court of York is now in Session, His Lordship P.J. Mookerjee presiding. All those who have business with this court are hereby required to draw nigh and give attendance!' the clerk proclaimed. 'Is Simon Newby in court?'

Sarah rose to her feet. 'He is, my lord.'

The clerk directed her gaze to the dock, behind Sarah. 'Stand up, please.'

Simon stood, nervously clasping his hands.

'Are you Simon Newby, of 23 Bramham Street, York?'

'Er, yeah.'

Sarah groaned. *Make a better effort than that, Simon, please.*

'Simon Newby, you are hereby indicted before this court on one count, namely: on count 1, on the night of 13/14th May this year, you did murder Jasmine Antonia Hurst, of 8a Stillingfleet Road, York, contrary to Section 1 of the Homicide Act 1957. How do you plead? Guilty, or not guilty?'

There was a pause. Not a long pause, perhaps, but to Sarah it seemed to last for ever. Lucy was supposed to have coached him in this but probably like many first-time defendants he was overwhelmed by the high-flown language, the sheer terror of a public trial for murder.

'Not guilty.' There was a sigh from the public gallery, who had collectively been holding their breath. Sarah turned round to smile encouragement.

'Very well,' said the clerk smoothly. 'Sit down, Simon. We will move to empanel a jury.'

Seven men were chosen as jurors, and five women. A minuscule advantage to Simon, Sarah thought speculatively, watching them take the oath. Two were young men with short hair like her son. One wore an earring. But three others wore suits and ties, an unusual proportion nowadays. The women, she noticed – two over thirty, three under – all studied Simon intently. None of the looks were friendly.

In America, she thought, Lucy and I would have spent hours interviewing these people to ascertain their views and suitability to serve. As it is I have to take pot luck. I can object to no one without cause, and since I know nothing about any of them the only possible cause is if one of them can't read the oath or admits to being Jasmine's best friend.

Oh well, justice is blind, like the statue outside.

Phil Turner rose to his feet. In his old wig and gown, he looked just as Sarah had feared. The ancient wig was shoved back a little and to the side, like the flat cap of a farmer. His gown and suit were comfortable rather than smooth or ostentatious. He turned his rugged, dependable face towards the jury, and began.

'Ladies and gentlemen, the case you are to try is a murder. All murders are serious, but this was a particularly horrible and brutal one, and it will be my duty to present you with some very unpleasant and upsetting evidence. I am sorry for that, but it cannot be helped. It is my duty to prove that the man who committed this awful crime, the murderer, is the young man whom you see sitting in the dock – Simon Newby. It is the job of my learned colleague Mrs Newby here – who, most unusually, you may think, happens to be Simon's mother – to defend him against this charge.'

He paused, while the jury examined Sarah with interest. A hushed murmur came from the public gallery.

'And it is your job – the most important job of all – to listen carefully to all the evidence put before you, and then to decide on one simple question: does this evidence prove, beyond all reasonable doubt, that Simon Newby committed this murder, or not?'

Wonderful, Sarah thought, as several jurors nodded solemnly. They're eating out of his hand already. The moment that man opened his mouth they had him placed; as a decent, dependable Yorkshireman, one of their own. And he's telling them my son's a murderer.

'It's as simple as that,' Phil Turner continued calmly. 'And my answer is equally simple: does the evidence prove that Simon Newby is guilty? Yes, it does.'

He lifted one foot comfortably on to the bench beside him, like a countryman leaning on a fence, telling a story to a group of friends.

'Let me outline it for you. Firstly, the murder itself. You will hear police officers and forensic scientists describe it all in great detail. But the basics are these. Early on the morning of Friday 14th May a man was walking his dog on a footpath near the River Ouse south of York, when the dog found something in the bushes. When the man looked he saw the body of a young woman. He called the police and later that day they identified the body as that of Jasmine Hurst, a young woman of twenty-three who lived with her current boyfriend David Brodie about half a mile from where her body was found.

'The forensic scientists will tell you, members of the jury, exactly how poor Jasmine was killed. But in simple layman's terms, she died because her throat was cut. Her throat was cut with a large, serrated knife by someone who was standing behind her, probably pulling her head back by her hair to expose her neck. Naturally, once her throat was cut, she died very swiftly.

'But her ordeal was not swift, ladies and gentlemen. The cuts on her arms, the bruising to her face and genital area show that before she was killed she was beaten and raped. This young woman suffered a prolonged, brutal attack in which her death was only the final stage.'

The jury watched him, riveted. He looked at each of them briefly, then resumed his story.

'So, how do we know who did it? Well, firstly, there were a number of footprints near the body. Footprints, in particular, of a man's training shoe, size 10. You will know that all training shoes have different patterns on the sole, and you will hear that there are forensic experts who make a study of these. You will hear, too, that in Simon Newby's house the police found a pair of training shoes whose size and make exactly matched these footprints by the body. And you will hear that one of those training shoes, the shoes found in Simon Newby's house, was stained with the blood of Jasmine Hurst.

'Secondly, you will hear evidence that Jasmine Hurst was raped, and that semen was found in her vagina. You will hear forensic evidence that the DNA in that semen matches exactly the DNA found in a sample taken from the accused, Simon Newby. Proof conclusive, you may think. Her blood on his training shoe, his semen in her body. That is what the prosecution believe.'

He paused, and looked down thoughtfully at Sarah. Long enough for the jury to examine her too. Sarah willed her face to show no emotion whatsoever.

'But Mr Newby pleads not guilty, as is his legal right, and so it is my duty to call all this detailed evidence before you so that his defence can question it.'

Which makes it my fault, Sarah thought. Well done, Phil. None of us would have to go through any of this excruciating torture if only I'd told my son to own up and plead guilty. That's what he wants them to think. That's what they *are* thinking, now.

Phil Turner's calm, reassuring voice continued, inviting the jury to trust him to lead them through this maze of guilt and evil.

'But why, you may ask, would anyone do such a dreadful thing? Was this a random attack or was there a motive? This is something the police always ask. Well, yes, there certainly was a motive – a very basic motive, jealousy. It's a simple, age-old story. You will hear that Simon Newby was a former boyfriend of Jasmine Hurst. They had lived together for several months. Then Jasmine met another young man, David Brodie, and went to live with him. No crime in that; it happens all the time. But it made young Simon jealous. A quite natural, understandable emotion. Except that, unfortunately, *his* jealousy got out of hand. He couldn't take no for an answer. You will hear evidence that he followed Jasmine around, pestering her to come back to him; and that he threatened her new boyfriend with violence.

'Then, the very day before she died, Simon met her again, and persuaded her to come to his home. But they didn't make up, as he probably hoped: they quarrelled, violently. You will hear a witness who saw them arguing bitterly in the street outside his home; a quarrel in which Simon punched his former girlfriend in the face.

'And finally you will hear what Simon did the day after this quarrel, after he had punched her in the face. Was he at home when the police came to question him about the body they had found? No, members of the jury, he wasn't. He had run away in the middle of the night – the same night that Jasmine was killed. No one knew where he had gone or if he ever intended to come back. It was only by good detective work that the police found him, a few days later, in Scarborough. And you will hear that when he was arrested and interviewed about Jasmine's death, the first thing he told the police was that he hadn't seen Jasmine for weeks. When in fact, a witness saw him hit her on the day of her death.

'So that, in brief, is the evidence I shall lay before you, members of the jury. Evidence of a terrible crime motivated by sexual jealousy. Evidence that Simon Newby was the last person known to see Jasmine Hurst alive, and that he was using violence towards her then. Evidence that he disappeared on the night she was murdered, and lied when the police interviewed him about her death. And most conclusive of all, forensic evidence that his training shoe, with her blood on it, matched the footprints found at the scene of the crime; and his semen was found in her bruised vagina.

'It's a terrible, damning story. However, you must not simply take my word for it. It's my task to prove that all this is true, and it is for you to judge, after listening to all the evidence, if I have succeeded. If I have not – if there is still any doubt in your minds about Simon Newby's guilt – then he gets the benefit of that doubt. Simon Newby does not have to prove anything. He says he is not guilty and that is all he is required to say. It is for me, representing the prosecution, to prove to you that he is.'

He paused, surveying each of the jurors in turn, drawing them into his confidence.

'And so now I would like to call my first witness.'

Why bother? Sarah thought gloomily, watching the jury. As far as they're concerned you could take him out and hang him now. You may say he's innocent until proven guilty but none of them listened to that. It's all over in the first half-hour. The rest is just going to be a charade.

34

Investigations had moved slowly over the summer. Terry brought the building workers into the station to create a photofit, and sent the results to the Garda Siochana. He went surfing in Cornwall with the girls. Then, with school holidays over, he took the photofits of the Irishman, Sean, to Helen Steersby. To his delight, the girl said, yes, her attacker had looked something like that. He played her a tape of men with different accents. She picked one from southern Ireland as nearest to the voice of her attacker. Hardly a positive identification, but a satisfying step nonetheless.

If Sean *had* been in York during Gary's trial, then he was a suspect for all three remaining assaults on women – Steersby as well as Clayton and

Whitaker. And, intriguingly, when his mate Gary had raped Sharon Gilbert, he'd claimed he'd spent the evening with Sean. What was all that about, Terry wondered? A competition to see which of them could treat women worst?

On his way to lunch, he heard a commotion around the custody sergeant's desk.

'He fucking raped me, he did! You all know that but you don't do nowt, do yer?'

'Ah, shut your trap, you daft cow! I want her prosecuted, I do, for assault.'

The voices attracted his attention. He recognized them both. Turning swiftly along the corridor, he saw two uniformed constables struggling to hold Gary Harker, while a WPC kept a firm grip on Sharon Gilbert. Sergeant Chisholm was booking her in.

'What's up, Nick?' he asked a constable holding Gary.

'Brawl in a pub, sir. She claims he hit her . . .'

'Oh yeah, right,' said Gary belligerently. 'And I did this to myself too, did I?'

Terry noted several trails of blood below Gary's left eye. The sight filled him with sadistic glee. 'Cut yourself shaving, Gary, did you?' he enquired.

The question enraged Gary, who elbowed one constable in the face, broke loose from the other, and was half-way to Terry before the two constables tripped him, smashed him face down on the floor and cuffed his hands behind his back.

'See what he's like?' Sharon screamed. 'You know what he did, Mr Bateson, don't you?'

'I know, Sharon, yes.' He turned to the constables. 'Book him for assault while resisting arrest. Then fill me in on this case, OK? In my office upstairs.'

An hour later he interviewed Gary with Nick Burrows, one of the arresting constables, while Harry Easby interviewed Sharon with the other.

'So how did this happen, Gary?'

'She just sunk her nails in, didn't she? Bitch!'

'And you were doing nothing to her, of course?'

'Have you seen them nails? You ought to do her for wearing offensive weapons.'

'Let's just take it from the beginning, Gary, shall we? Where did this argument start?'

The story in itself was simple. Gary claimed to have been in the Lighthorseman when Sharon came in with a girlfriend. Dressed, as Gary put it, 'for a day's work on her back'. He had approached her, he said, in a friendly spirit to buy her a drink and make up for the past, whereupon she had tried to tear his eyes out with her dagger-like nails.

'No excuse, she just went for me. I bet a dozen witnesses saw it. So do your job, Mr Bateson. I want that bitch charged with assault.'

Reluctantly, Terry ordered the constables to get witness statements. When they returned, Terry contemplated them gloomily. Two witnesses had seen Sharon scratch Gary's face. Neither had seen him hit her.

'It's quite monstrous, sir, I agree,' Nick Burrows said. 'But if he persists with this complaint we'll have to charge her with assault, won't we? We've no choice.'

'He assaulted you too, constable. I saw it. We all did.'

'Yes, but in a police station, sir. The lawyers will say we provoked him.'

Harry Easby had interviewed Sharon. He looked shattered by the whole experience; why, Terry could not at first understand.

'She says he was making offensive remarks and tried to put his hand up her skirt,' Harry said. 'That's as far as the physical stuff goes. She claims her girlfriend Cheryl will support her so I've sent a car to fetch her in now. But the real problem isn't that, boss.'

'What is it, then?'

'She's gone hysterical, she really has. What turned him up so much, was that she's getting a reporter from some TV programme – *Rough Justice*, I think – to interview her about her case. Apparently this reporter's up here to cover the Newby trial and Sharon went to meet her in that pub for lunch. She claims because you've got new evidence the CPS ought to go for a second trial. You know there's been talk about that in the papers recently – saying the prosecution ought to have a second go after an acquittal in serious cases where major evidence comes to light . . .'

'We should be so lucky.' Terry laughed bitterly. 'Hot air. It'll never happen.'

'Well, maybe not, but that's what journalists love, talk, isn't it? Anyway Sharon thinks hers could be a sort of test case on TV. You know – "The law needs changing to prevent injustice" – that kind of thing. Bad publicity for us.'

'Wonderful,' said Terry gloomily. 'And guess who's in the firing line. Did she scratch him on purpose, then, as a publicity stunt?'

'Could be,' Harry shrugged. 'I don't know.'

Terry could see the embarrassment, the hours of paperwork and media interviews, stretching ahead of him. If the case ever did appear on TV he'd be the joke of the nation.

An awful thought struck him.

'This reporter wasn't there in the pub? Filming the fight while Sharon set it up?'

'No, thank God. But she turned up soon after. She's got the story by now, for sure. The whole pub was buzzing with it.'

'Bloody hellfire.' Terry gazed at Harry in despair. 'And Harker wants us to charge her with assault, which makes me look dafter than ever. I'll be on telly as the dumbo detective who not only failed to get a rape conviction, but prosecuted the victim for assault.'

'And if you don't, Harker puts in a complaint.'

'Exactly. Well, let him. He assaulted you too, didn't he? Keep him in overnight.'

'And what about her, sir? She's, er, got kids you know.'

'Yes.' Terry contemplated Harry curiously. It was unlike him to be so concerned. 'Well, I can look stupid doing the right thing, at least. Get a statement from this Cheryl and send Sharon home. Will that persuade her to give up her chance of becoming a media superstar, Harry?'

'Not likely, sir.'

Terry sighed. 'Oh well. It was a good life while it lasted.'

Phil Turner began with the undisputed statement of the man who had found Jasmine's body. The grim facts, read out in Turner's calm, dependable voice, held the jury's attention.

'I was taking my dog for a walk at seven in the morning . . . the dog started barking in the bushes . . . a few yards off the track I saw the body of a young woman, the throat all covered with blood, and my dog barking hysterically at it . . .'

Sarah saw a middle-aged juror fumble for a tissue in her handbag, and a younger man dart nervous, vengeful looks at Simon in the dock.

PC Wilson, who had responded to the 999 call, had felt for pulse and breathing but found none. In his opinion the young woman had been dead for some time. Nothing that PC Wilson said was controversial and Sarah had no questions.

Dr Jones, the forensic pathologist, was a different matter. Sarah shivered as he took the Bible in his right hand. She vividly recalled the last time she had seen that smooth, sharp face. The memory became worse as the usher distributed a book of photos of Jasmine's injuries. Several jurors turned pale as they looked at them.

Sarah had seen these photos before but they still upset her. She remembered how she had been called to identify this very body – Emily's body, as she had expected. The smell of formaldehyde came back to her, and that cold, clinical room. This pathologist had been watching her, waiting until she could screw her courage that last turn higher and say yes, I'm ready now, let me look. And see that it wasn't Emily after all.

A hand touched her shoulder. Sarah turned to see Lucy watching her anxiously.

'Are you OK?'

'Yes . . . yes, sure.'

'Only you seemed upset.'

'I'm fine. It's OK. Thanks.'

The judge had noticed her distress too. God, how long did I lose it? A few seconds, a minute perhaps? To her relief she realized that Phil Turner was proceeding normally; her lapse had not upset him, at least. She sat up straight and focused her mind on the matter in hand.

'Dr Jones,' Turner was saying. 'What was the cause of Miss Hurst's death?'

'She died from a severe arterial haemorrhage caused when the carotid artery was severed by a sharp instrument. Death in such instances is fairly swift.'

'And what can you tell us about how this fatal wound was inflicted?'

'Well, I'm afraid the victim's throat had suffered some subsequent damage – after death – due to possible gnawing by a fox or a dog . . .'

Sweet Jesus, Sarah thought, I hope someone warned Jasmine's mother to avoid this.

'. . . but there was enough of the original wound remaining to indicate that it was inflicted by a sharp instrument such as a knife, entering the throat just below the left ear and travelling across to the right, severing the artery and windpipe on the way. It's the sort of wound that could easily be inflicted by a right-handed assailant standing behind the victim, holding her head back by her hair to expose her neck, while he cut her throat with the knife.'

'I see.' Phil Turner paused thoughtfully. 'And from your examination of the wound, were you able to tell anything about the nature of this sharp instrument?'

'Certainly.' This pathologist was a supremely confident young man, Sarah thought; not the sort who would react kindly to any questioning of his conclusions. 'It was a single cut, severing nearly half of the neck in one go. So it would have to be a relatively large and sharp instrument to do that. With a serrated edge.'

'How can you tell that? About the serrated edge?'

'Well, because of the marks made on her vertebrae. You can see that in photograph 15.'

Sarah studied the photograph carefully. It showed a number of small irregular marks which the pathologist identified as typical of a serrated blade.

'Dr Jones, did you find any other knife wounds on Miss Hurst's body?'

'Yes. Four cuts on the inside of her left forearm. You'll see them in photograph 17.'

'And how, in your opinion, were those cuts inflicted?'

'They are the typical wound that we see in a person trying to defend themselves from a knife attack. You naturally raise your arms up like this . . .' Dr Jones went into a defensive crouch in the witness stand. '. . . and as you see, the inside of your forearm is exposed. If the victim was attacked from behind, the cuts would go across the arm and slightly upwards, as these do.'

'And were these cuts also inflicted by a weapon with a serrated edge?'

'One appears to be. The knife marked the fibula – the smaller bone in the forearm. You can see that in photograph 18.'

Phil Turner picked up a knife in a plastic bag. 'My lord, could I ask the witness to examine this breadknife. Exhibit 1 for the prosecution.' The usher passed it forward. 'Do you recognize this knife, Dr Jones?'

'Yes. It's a breadknife given to me by the police to examine in connection with the wounds inflicted on the deceased.'

'And what was the result of your examination?'

'I tried to establish whether or not this knife could have caused these wounds. I did that in two ways. Firstly, I made quite careful measurements of the blade and serrations, and compared these measurements to the marks on the victim's vertebrae and fibula.'

'And what was the result of that experiment?'

'The distances were compatible, to within a quarter of a millimetre or less.'

'So according to those measurements, it was quite possible that this knife could have caused these wounds?'

'Yes.'

'And for your second experiment?'

'I used the knife on the bones of a pig. A dead pig, of course.'

'And what results did that show?'

'You can see it in photographs 26 and 27, I believe. The marks are almost identical to those on the dead girl.'

The jury, Sarah noticed, were fascinated, examining the photographs and Dr Jones intently, with expressions which varied from open revulsion to excitement and even awe. Certainly he had captured their interest; perhaps if he allowed his scientific enthusiasm to go too far he might also repulse them, which would be a small advantage. But more likely, that repulsion would fall upon Simon.

And the gruesome, intimate details were far from over.

'Now, Dr Jones, let me take you to another subject. In your report, you claim that the victim was raped . . .'

'So we're not preferring charges, Sharon,' said Terry, as emolliently as he could.

'I should bloody well think not. It's him should be locked up, not me.'

'I know,' Terry sighed. 'But the law . . .'

'You can stick the bloody law up your backside. What good's it done me, eh? Sod all. But for brutes like him it's different. Not enough evidence to convict, my arse! Can I go?'

'Yes. Just try to stay out of trouble, if you can.'

'Me? Oh thanks very much. You've not heard the last of this, Mr Smarmy Bateson. There's telly as well as courts, you know.' She fished a cigarette out of her bag and lit up, trying to recover her dignity. 'I don't know how you lads can face yourselves in the morning, doing a shit job like yours. No one's so much as mentioned my kids, the whole time I've been in here.'

'How are they, Sharon?' Terry ventured feebly, remembering the brave little boy who had tried to protect his mother. A fine story for the cameras, that would be.

'With Mary, I sincerely hope. I should've fetched them hours ago. Don't I even get a lift home? Me a single mum, *and* a rape victim!'

'I'm going that way, sir,' Harry broke in. 'I'll see you find your kids all right.'

She took a long drag on her cigarette, and blew the smoke out, straight at him. 'Yeah, and that's all you're going to see, too, sunshine. All right, then. See you on telly, Inspector. They'll grind you into sewage, they will. You and Gary both.'

Terry accompanied her and Harry to the front door. It was nearly four o'clock, the end of his shift. He wondered what his children would be up to, and how the first day of Simon's trial had gone. There'd be reporters and TV journalists there too. But Churchill wouldn't mess *his* case up – he had too much luck. Unlike Terry. Or was he simply a better detective?

Terry watched Harry cross the car park with Sharon, and blinked. Had Harry squeezed her buttock as he opened the passenger door? Surely he must have imagined it. The mood she was in she would have raked his face with her nails and run screaming back for a complaint form. Anyway the lad would never be so daft.

The evidence which Dr Jones presented to prove that Jasmine had been raped seemed as clear and convincing as his evidence about the way she had died. He had found bruising to the walls of her vagina, and traces of semen within it. There were cuts and scratches on the backs and sides of her legs which were also consistent with a violent sexual attack.

As Sarah rose to cross-examine, she noted looks of pity and irritation from the jury. We've made up our minds already, the expressions said; Dr Jones has told us the truth. Going through it all again will be a pointless waste of everyone's time.

A few looked less hostile, though. She focused her hopes on a man at the back, and began.

'Dr Jones, I'd like to return to these cuts on Miss Hurst's arms. They were quite severe, noticeable cuts, I think you said?'

'It would have been very hard to miss them,' Dr Jones agreed smoothly. Sarah noticed once again how unusually well dressed he was, in an expensive charcoal suit, pale lemon shirt, light blue tie – quite a fop, really; proud of himself. Maybe she could provoke him into showing off, and lose some of the jury's sympathy that way.

'Yes. Just so that we're clear about these cuts, Dr Jones, how big were they? How deep and wide, and so on?'

'They varied. The shortest was about an inch, the longest about three inches long, on the inside of her left arm. As for depth, one went into the bone.'

'And from these marks on the victim's bones, you deduce that all the cuts were inflicted by a weapon with a serrated edge, like the breadknife Mr Turner showed you?'

'Exactly, yes.'

'Yes. But that doesn't prove that these wounds were inflicted by that particular breadknife, does it? I mean, there must be hundreds, probably thousands, of breadknives of the same model manufactured by the same company as the knife Mr Turner showed you, and every one of those knives could have inflicted exactly the same injuries, couldn't it?'

'Obviously.' Dr Jones shrugged. 'But none of those other knives were found in the defendant's home, were they?'

'Weren't they?' Sarah stared at him witheringly. 'You visited my son's home then, did you, Dr Jones?'

Dr Jones blushed, seeing his mistake at once. 'No, no, of course not. I was simply given the knife by the police. I have no first-hand knowledge of where it was found.'

'Exactly. So let's stick to what you *do* know, shall we? I'd like to draw your attention to another cut on the body. Would you tell the jury what you can see in photograph 36, please?'

'It's a photograph of the victim's left hand.'

'And is there a cut on that hand?'

'Yes, there is. A very small cut on the thumb.'

'Did you examine that cut?'

'I . . . examined it briefly, yes.'

'Only briefly, you say. Why was that?'

'It seemed a very minor wound in the overall context of her injuries. It certainly didn't contribute to her death.'

'Quite so. But your job is to examine *all* injuries to the victim's body, isn't it? However minor. Could you tell the court, please, did this cut exhibit similar characteristics to the other cuts we've been discussing? In terms of depth, age and so on?'

'I'm not sure. May I consult my notes? . . . I'm afraid I couldn't be certain about that. I've simply noted it here as a minor cut to the left thumb.'

'Was it healed?'

'I'm sorry?'

'This minor cut on the thumb. Had the blood in it clotted and begun to knit together? In the natural way that cuts heal?'

'I, er . . .' Dr Jones looked carefully at his notes. 'I'm unable to say. As I say it was a very minor injury.'

And you didn't examine it, Sarah thought with vindictive glee. Got you, you smug bastard!

'Do you notice a black mark around the cut? Signs of a sticking plaster that's fallen off?'

He frowned, and looked closer. 'It might be that, yes.'

'So it is possible, then, that unlike all the other wounds on the body, this cut had begun to heal? In other words, that this cut had been inflicted some hours, even days, beforehand?'

Dr Jones shrugged, as though the matter was unimportant, a trifle. 'It's possible, yes.'

The shrug irritated Sarah. She had offered him a way out and he had spurned it. Her concluding question, spoken with perfect politeness, crackled with concealed contempt.

'So there's nothing in your notes, or your thorough, detailed and professional examination of the body, to exclude that possibility?'

'No.' Dr Jones glared back at her coldly. But he'd got the point, Sarah thought. So had the judge. It wasn't a minor detail that he had missed. Nothing ever was, in a murder case.

It was after four o'clock. Sarah was not tired, but she sensed the jury's attention flagging.

'My lord, I have quite a number of further questions for this witness, but time is getting on, so might this be a convenient point to pause?'

The judge agreed instantly. 'Very well, Mrs Newby. Until ten tomorrow morning, then.'

The clerk called, 'All stand!' The judge got to his feet, bowed, and left the court. A buzz of conversation broke out. Sarah rushed back to the dock, where a security guard was handcuffing himself to her son's wrist.

'All right, Simon? That's it for today.'

'Yeah. Back to my cell, then?'

'I'm afraid so. But so far, so good.'

'You think so? Really?' The anguish in his eyes burned into her own. Whatever she said now would stay with him through the night.

'Yes, really. Nothing went wrong today. We gave as good as we got. And I've plenty more questions for that pathologist tomorrow.'

'You've got to do this, Mum. You've got to get me out of there, you really have.'

'I know. And if I possibly can, I will.' Tiptoe on a bench, she reached into the dock and grasped his left hand, the one that was free. 'Have a good meal and a sleep, and *don't worry*. You've got me and Lucy to do that for you.'

And we will, she thought, as she watched him led away. Late, late into the night.

*   *   *

Harry swung the car out into the Fulford Road. Beside him, Sharon was examining her face in the courtesy mirror.

'So where'd you get this idea of the reporter, anyway?' he asked irritably.

'That's for me to know and you to find out.'

'Well, I'm trying to find out. That's why I'm asking.'

'And I'm not telling.' She sucked in her cheeks, brushed back an eyelash, and flashed him an impudent smile.

Harry drove silently, controlling his temper. He had thought he was set up nicely with this woman. He kept the social services and vice squad off her back, while she gave him free, regular sex and occasional nuggets of useful information. So far these had led to two arrests – of a minor drug dealer and a burglar posing as a window cleaner. It was exactly the way an informant should operate, in his opinion. But it all depended on his remaining in control, while she gave information to him, and no one else. Certainly not to national TV.

'What exactly do you think you'll achieve?' he asked after a while. 'However much publicity you get there can't be a second trial, you know. The law forbids it.'

'Then they should change the sodding law, shouldn't they? Like it said in the paper.'

'Not soon enough for you, Sharon. That'll take years – if it ever happens.'

'That's what you think. I got my sources.'

He drove on, thinking hard. Harry wasn't overly concerned about anyone apart from himself, but he could see that if this scheme of Sharon's caused trouble for the police, then it wasn't just Terry Bateson who was likely to be involved. Whatever scandal she managed to stir up, the camera's unblinking eye might focus on him. How would that help his future career? The idea made him squirm.

'Look, Sharon, you're making a mistake. I mean, guys like this reporter, they're not interested in you for yourself. He'll just exploit you for what he can get . . .'

She laughed. 'Tell me about it, lover boy. Anyhow, it's not a guy, it's a woman.'

'This woman then. She'll come up from London, milk your story for what she can get, splash it all over the papers, and leave. You'll be a star for a day and then left on your own. It won't change a thing.'

'It will for me. I want everyone to know the truth.'

'About what? How Gary raped you? That's been in the papers already, only the jury didn't believe you. How will this be different?'

'Because it won't be just about Gary. It'll be about you lot too, and how you screwed it up. You don't like that, do you? Well, that's what I want and that's what I'm doing.'

'And what about Gary? What if he comes looking for you again?'

'Then I'll scratch his other cheek, the bastard!' She took a deep drag on her cigarette, then turned her head and deliberately blew smoke all over his face. 'Why didn't you charge him this time, eh? I told you, he stuck his hand up my skirt.'

'That's not what the other witnesses said. There were two of them.'

'And you listened to them, of course, like you always do. Not to me. Well, I'll find someone who *will* listen. Drop me here, will you?'

Harry pulled the car into the kerb, and watched her go into the house where she had left her kids. He knew she didn't like him much, but he didn't care. To an extent it only added to the excitement, the sense of being able to control and exploit her that he'd had. Until now.

He scowled, and drove slowly away.

35

Next morning, the reporters were still there. But this time, Sarah walked straight towards them. The questions came from all sides.

'Mrs Newby, is the trial going well?'

'Why are you defending your son yourself?'

'Could you give us a few words, please?'

At the top of the steps she paused and turned. She had never heard this done by a British barrister but she knew of nothing against it in law. Every newspaper, TV and radio station had reported Phil Turner's opening speech. If I'm going to suffer this publicity, she thought, I may as well make use of it too.

A TV cameraman focused his lens on her face. Lucy tugged discreetly at her elbow, but Sarah ignored her. 'I just want to say that I took this case at my son's request. He assures me he is innocent and I believe him. That may be unusual for a barrister but it's perfectly legal. I intend to fight this case to the best of my ability and prove his innocence.'

Pens scribbled in notebooks, microphones were thrust in her face.

'The victim was your son's girlfriend, wasn't she, Mrs Newby? Did you know her?'

'I knew her, yes.' Sarah hesitated, feeling Lucy's tug more insistent than before. She hadn't planned to answer any more questions, didn't know quite what to say.

'Did you like her, Mrs Newby?'

'Do you feel sorry for her parents?'

The TV camera zoomed closer to her face. This is why we don't do this, she realized, it needs planning and preparation. She took a deep breath. 'Jasmine Hurst was a very beautiful girl and my son was in love with her.

261

Her parents have all my sympathy at this terrible time. But my son did not kill her.'

Her voice faltered and she thought, God no, the whole world is going to see this.

'So who did kill her, Mrs Newby? Do you have any idea about that?'

'No, I'm sorry. That's all. Thank you very much.'

She went inside, feeling her whole body trembling. 'For heaven's sake, Sarah, what are you doing?' Lucy said. 'We're not in California now. What if the judge says you've unfairly prejudiced the case?'

'Then he does.' Sarah smiled shakily. 'How did it look? Did my voice break?'

'Keep the day job, love, leave Hollywood to the experts.' Relenting, Lucy gave her a brief, motherly hug. 'The real jury's in here, not outside.'

To Sarah's relief, Judge Mookerjee ignored her remarks outside court. Dr Jones took the stand in a dark suit with yellow tie and matching silk handkerchief. Sarah stood.

'Now, Dr Jones, let us turn to the semen from Miss Hurst's vagina. You have described how the DNA in this semen was an exact match for the DNA which you took from my son.'

'I have, yes.'

'Very well. You may know, Dr Jones, that the defence does not dispute that the semen is indeed that of my son, Simon Newby. He will give evidence that he and Miss Hurst made love earlier that day at his house in a consensual, loving fashion. That's why the semen is there, he says. So may I ask, Dr Jones, is there anything about the sample that would contradict this story?'

'Simply the fact that it was there. In the body of a girl who had been raped and murdered.'

Sarah frowned. 'Dr Jones, I'm not sure you understand my question. Let me make it clearer. I want you to put aside the vaginal bruising, and the victim's death, and concentrate solely on the semen which you examined. Was there anything about the age or condition of the sample which would tell you when, precisely, it entered her body?'

The pathologist shrugged, as if the question was of minor academic interest. 'Well, if you concentrate on that alone, then I suppose the answer is no, not precisely. By the time I analysed the sample, it was already some sixteen hours old. There is no test that could precisely determine whether it was deposited at the time of death or a few hours earlier.'

'So it is possible that Miss Hurst had sexual intercourse several hours *before* her death?'

Dr Jones frowned, as though correcting an errant pupil. 'If she did, then the vaginal bruising would suggest it was more like a rape than the loving consensual activity you describe.'

'Very well, let us come to that.' Sarah was determined not to be patronized by this man, but every time she looked at him she saw him in his white coat, about to show her Emily's body. He had seemed the ultimate figure of medical authority then, the gatekeeper to life or death.

Resolutely, she thrust the memory aside. Now he was a threat to her son.

'In your report you describe some bruising. When do you believe this bruising occurred?'

'Immediately prior to the victim's death.' He shrugged, as if the answer were obvious.

Sarah contemplated the witness coldly. 'Can you be more precise about that, Dr Jones? Do you mean ten seconds before death? Five minutes? Half an hour? Two hours? More?'

'Probably a few minutes before. Depending on the severity of the actual trauma, it could theoretically have been longer, I suppose. But you'd have to consider this along with the evidence of the crime scene to decide when the rape actually happened.'

'Very well. But I'm interested in your phrase "depending on the severity of the trauma". Can you explain that a little further?'

'Well, these bruises appeared relatively minor. The most likely explanation of that is that the victim was raped only a few minutes before her throat was cut, and therefore although the vaginal trauma she suffered was quite severe, the bruising did not have time to develop fully before the blood flow was cut off.'

'And the other explanation?'

'I suppose . . . a theoretical alternative explanation could be that she suffered a milder vaginal trauma sometime before, and that the bruising had in fact fully developed.'

It was a key admission, reluctantly given. 'So how long before could this much milder vaginal trauma have occurred, doctor?'

'Well, it's hard to be precise. If it was very mild, two or three hours, I suppose. But . . .'

'Thank you. So it *is* possible that this bruising was caused up to two or three hours before death. And in that case, the trauma that caused it was much milder than the brutal rape which my learned friend has attempted to describe?'

And so my son didn't rape her. Or at least, not very roughly. Oh Simon, Simon!

'It's a theoretical possibility, yes. But only if you treat these injuries in isolation from all the others, which indicate a violent, sexual attack. There were scratches to the backs and insides of her thighs, which would indicate a violent sexual assault.'

'You put the prosecution case very well, doctor. But it remains true, does it not, that there is a completely different and credible possibility – that the semen and bruising in the vagina were the result of a very much

263

milder and less violent form of intercourse which may have taken place up to three hours *before* the violent attack which led to her death? That's what you said, isn't it?'

It was a vital point. Sarah fixed the witness with a basilisk stare.

'It's a theoretical possibility, yes. But only if you disregard the rest of the evidence.'

'Or if the rest of the evidence can be explained in a different way,' Sarah persisted. 'In which case, although she was murdered, she may not have been raped at all?'

Dr Jones hesitated, then shrugged. 'That is a possible interpretation, yes. Although even if I accept your premise, I wouldn't call this sexual activity *mild*, exactly. Loving, consensual sex doesn't usually cause trauma or bruising of any kind.'

It was a damaging reply, Sarah knew. Even if Simon's story were true, how had he treated this poor girl? She remembered how tantalizing and aloof Jasmine could be; and Simon's intense, frightening rage. What had really happened between them that day?

'But mild or not, these bruises do not necessarily indicate rape?'

Dr Jones hesitated, making a conscious effort to be fair. 'If intercourse took place some hours before death, then . . . the physical evidence does not necessarily indicate rape, no. But at the very least it does indicate vigorous penetration. If Ms Hurst had been alive and complained of rape, these bruises would certainly have supported her claim.'

'But it is also possible that this bruising was caused by sexual intercourse which was vigorous, as you say, but still consensual. Not a rape?'

'Possible, yes.'

'Thank you.' Sarah glanced at the jury. She had established this vital point; now was the time to develop it further. 'So, Dr Jones, if we accept that sexual intercourse took place some hours before death, then there is no *physical* proof that the man with whom Jasmine Hurst had sex, was the same man who cut her throat and killed her, is there?'

The silence in court was electric. Reluctantly, he sighed. 'If we accept your premise, no.'

Was it enough? Did the jury understand how vital this was? Sarah was not sure. When in doubt, she had learned, you must drive your point home, by repetition if necessary.

'So from your evidence, Dr Jones, is it possible that Jasmine Hurst had sexual intercourse with my son in his house that afternoon, as he says, and that her throat was cut by a quite different man several hours later?'

Dr Jones sighed. 'It's possible, yes.'

'Thank you. That's all I have to ask.'

She smiled, and sat down.

*   *   *

After a night in the cells Gary slouched into the interview room, surly and unshaven. He slumped into a chair, his heavy forearms on the table. 'Have you charged her then?'

'Not yet, no.' Terry studied him contemplatively, pleased to see that his scratches were inflamed and angry. 'You assaulted a police officer.'

'Did I fuck! He attacked me. You all did!'

'It's a serious charge, Gary. The magistrates hate that kind of thing.'

'You're joking. I'd get a jury, anyhow. It were police brutality – four of you beat me up!'

Terry was not surprised. Gary knew the system well enough to work it to his advantage. With legal aid, he would be much better off avoiding magistrates and opting for trial by jury. His defence lawyer would claim that Gary had been assaulted in police custody. There were stories like this in the press all the time.

Even if a jury did convict, he'd get six months maximum, out in three. Terry decided to cut his losses and go for a deal. He studied the big man coolly.

'Funny thing, Gary, that's exactly what Sharon says. She was sitting peacefully in the pub, when all of a sudden she was assaulted, by a man twice her size.'

'That's crap, that is. She went for me. Everyone saw it.'

'Not everyone, Gary. Some did, some didn't. But what happens when we charge her with assault, Gary? Think about it. The magistrates look at you, fifteen stone of solid brawn, and then her. Who are they going to believe, do you think?'

'It won't be magistrates. It'll be a jury.'

'Ah no. This time she gets to choose, not you. You'd have to pretend to be the victim. The trouble is, not many victims look like you.' Terry smiled, savouring the moment. 'What I'm saying, Gary, is this. I can charge you with assaulting a police officer, and oppose bail on the grounds that you're a danger to the public. That way you'll serve a couple of months on remand, whatever happens at the end of it. Maybe you like being locked away, I don't know?'

The threat, he guessed from Gary's silence, was going home. He continued in the same calm, reasonable voice. 'On the other hand, if you drop your charge against Sharon, a lot of police time and money would be saved. We'd look at it in that light.'

'You wouldn't charge me with assault?'

Terry smiled thinly. 'You choose, Gary. You go home now, or you don't. Up to you.'

Gary was silent for a moment. It was a mistake to regard this man as stupid, Terry thought. He might not be great at nuclear physics but he had an instant, unerring regard for his own self-preservation.

'All right,' he said at last. 'It's just scratches anyhow. Women's stuff.'

'You're dropping the charges?' Terry asked formally.

Gary nodded sullenly. He hadn't got what he wanted but had only lost a night in the cells.

'OK. There's this form to complete.' Terry watched Gary sign in solid, careful writing. 'Oh, just one other thing, before you go.'

'What?'

'These pictures.' Terry spread the photofits of Sean which he had got from MacFarlane's staff on the table. 'Anyone you know?'

Gary scowled. 'No, don't think so. Who are they?'

Terry watched him closely, not believing the denial for a second.

'No? Oh come on, Gary, try harder. He worked for Robson's, delivering tiles to Maria Clayton's house. And to the university lodgings where that girl Karen Whitaker lived. You worked with him at MacFarlane's too, remember?'

'Sean.' Gary shrugged. 'These aren't supposed to be him, are they?'

'Yes, they are. Don't they look right?'

Gary smiled contemptuously. 'Not really.'

Oddly, now he'd acknowledged who the photofits were meant to represent, he seemed unable to take his eyes off them. Terry watched while Gary examined each picture in turn.

'Maybe you could help us make some better ones?'

Gary didn't dignify this with an answer. Instead, to Terry's surprise, he asked: 'Who helped you with these? That bitch Sharon?'

'Sharon? No. Why? Should she?'

'She'd do owt to cause trouble, that one.'

'*She* knows him, then, does she?'

Gary got abruptly to his feet. 'I'm free to go, you said?'

'In a minute. When did you last see this Sean, Gary?'

'God knows. Years ago.'

'Really? Then why did you cite him for an alibi, at your trial?'

Again, Gary didn't bother to answer. Something was eating him up, Terry was sure of it. 'Can I go now, or what?'

'For the moment. If you do see your friend Sean, tell him I'd like a word, will you?'

The forensic scientist, Laila Ferguson, was tall, with clear black skin and a strikingly beautiful face. She gave her evidence in a pleasant, husky voice. The seven men in the jury paid her rapt attention.

Yes, she had examined a breadknife, exhibit 1, and found minute traces of blood under the handle. And a pair of size 10 Nike training shoes, exhibit 2, on one of which she had also found blood – two stains in the crevices of the sole, and five on the upper surface, near the toe. DNA analysis had proved that all these stains were identical to the blood of the victim, Jasmine Hurst. On the trainer she had also found grass stains and sandy soil consistent with samples taken from the crime scene.

Phil Turner sat down with an air of quiet contentment. Sarah rose slowly.

'Ms Ferguson, let's take the minor details first. These bits of grass and soil which you found on the trainer, they were consistent with samples from the crime scene, weren't they?'

'Yes, they were.' Ms Ferguson nodded calmly.

'But – to make this quite clear for the jury – "consistent with" doesn't mean that the samples on the shoe actually came from the crime scene, does it?'

'No . . .'

'It just means that they *could* have come from that area. But they could have come from other places on the river path, couldn't they? Half a mile away, perhaps?'

'If there was the same sort of soil there, yes. And grasses.'

'So if someone had been jogging regularly along that river path, would you expect to find the same sandy soil and grass seeds on their shoes? Even if they hadn't been within half a mile of the crime scene?'

'Possibly, yes . . .' The young woman could probably explain the matter further, but Sarah had no intention of letting her do so. Her calm beauty and assured scientific competence had impressed the jury too much already this morning; she needed to be rattled, have some of her flaws exposed.

'So this phrase "consistent with" doesn't take us very far, does it? What about blood?'

'I'm sorry?'

'The only thing that really connects either of these shoes with the crime are a few tiny stains of blood that you found on one shoe – the left one, I think. Two stains on the sole, and five on the upper surface near the toe. Let's examine the stains on the sole first, shall we? How large were they?'

'Not large. One was about half a centimetre across and the other a bit less.'

'And they were both hidden in the patterns of the tread?'

'That's right, yes.'

'Where you found traces of sandy soil and grasses.'

'I did, yes.'

'All right. Tell me, Miss Ferguson, did you find traces of anything else in the tread of these shoes? Things not obviously connected to this crime?'

Laila Ferguson frowned, trying to remember. The frown did things to her face which entranced the younger men in the jury. 'Yes, I think so. There was grit – from pavements and roads, probably. Household dust. And traces of mashed potato chip, on the heel of the right shoe.'

Someone laughed, and Sarah smiled, glad to ease the tension. 'So these trainers had quite an eventful life, it seems. They hadn't been cleaned recently, then?'

'No,' Laila nodded emphatically. 'They were fairly dirty.'

'All right. Now tell me, Miss Ferguson, the blood on the sole of this shoe – was it mixed up with any grass, at all?'

'Some of it, yes. Several fragments of grass had blood on them.'

'And does that mean that the grass and the blood got on to the shoe at the same time?'

'It . . . could mean that, yes.'

'But it doesn't necessarily mean that, does it? I mean, if the grass was already lodged on the shoe when the blood fell on it, the blood would still stain the grass, wouldn't it?'

'Yes, I suppose so,' Ms Ferguson agreed hesitantly.

'So, from your evidence, it's not possible to say whether this grass got on to the shoe at the same time as the blood, or at a completely different time, is it?'

'No . . .'

'Nor is it possible to say *when* this blood got on to the sole of this shoe?'

'No.'

'Or *where*, either, surely. I mean, the blood could have got on to the sole of the shoe in the house, when the household dust got there; or out in the roads, when the road grit got there; or perhaps on a path where there was sandy soil. Is that right?'

'I suppose that's right, yes,' Ms Ferguson agreed, frowning thoughtfully. 'I mean, all I can say is that the blood was there. I can't tell you when or how it got there.'

'Exactly.' Sarah let the words hang in the air, and looked at the young woman with some warmth. 'Now let's think about these drops of blood you found on top of the shoe, if we may. How big were they?'

'The largest was two millimetres across.'

'Big enough to see with the naked eye?'

'Oh yes. The size of a small drop of ink.'

'I see. And the others?'

'One was about the same size. The rest were smaller. The size of a large grain of dust.'

'Five drops of blood, three of them the size of a grain of dust. But you examined the shoe very carefully, I suppose? The top and the sides, the laces and the tongue, you looked inside too? With special scientific equipment, I take it?'

'Yes, of course. I spent hours examining this shoe. There were plenty of other marks, mud and grass stains chiefly, and some paint and coffee; but there were just these two bloodstains on the sole and five on the upper surface near the toe.'

'And the other shoe? Any blood on that?'

'None at all, no.'

'No blood anywhere on the left shoe. Very well. Would you turn to photo number 3, Ms Ferguson, and tell the jury what you see there, please.'

'It's . . . a photograph of a dead body.'

'Yes. It's a photograph of the murder victim, Jasmine Hurst. It was taken at the crime scene, where she was discovered. I want to draw your attention to the blood in the photograph, Ms Ferguson. Is there a lot of blood?'

'A lot, yes.'

'I'm sorry if this is distressing, but could you describe to the court, in your own words, just how much blood you see in the photograph, and where it is?'

'Well . . . there's a lot on her throat, where it's been cut, and . . . all over her chest and upper body. It's on her arms too . . . her left arm seems to be cut and there's blood on her legs too.'

'Is there blood on the grass beside the body?'

'Yes. Some of the grass looks a reddish colour.'

'There was blood on the grass; the scene of crime report confirmed that. Now, Ms Ferguson, when someone's throat is cut, the blood doesn't just leak out, does it – it sprays out everywhere, pumped out by the heart because an artery has been severed. Is that right?'

'Well, I've never seen it . . .'

'You're a scientist, aren't you? A forensic scientist – you know how an artery works?'

'Yes, of course. You're right – the blood would spray everywhere.'

'Yes. And we can see that in the photo, can't we? Blood on the victim's chest, blood on her arms and legs and all over the grass. A lot of blood, you said. Blood everywhere. Am I right?'

'Yes, that's right. There's a lot of blood in this photo.'

'Very well. Now you're a forensic scientist; so what would you expect to find on the shoes of the person who committed this horrible crime? Someone who struggled with the victim, stood close enough to cut her throat?'

'Blood . . .'

'Yes, of course. You'd expect to find blood on those shoes, wouldn't you? Not just blood on the top of the shoes, from the spray you've described, but blood on the soles too, from that bloodstained grass. You'd expect to find blood in all the little cracks of the soles, wouldn't you? The soles of both shoes?'

Laila Ferguson hesitated. The girl was far too intelligent not to see where this was going. Sarah had noticed her talking quite intimately to Will Churchill outside the court; she must know how vital her evidence was to his case. What would she do? Prevaricate and attempt to spin the evidence to support the police? Or value her own reputation as an independent scientist? She was very young – it could be the first time she had been in a situation like this.

She fiddled with the plaits of her afro haircut, then looked directly at Sarah.

'If the shoes had walked in that grass, yes, I would.'

Good girl, Sarah thought. 'The only way to get the blood out of the soles would have been to wash them, wouldn't it? I suppose you'd have to wash them quite thoroughly?'

'Yes, you would. Blood is notoriously hard to get rid of.'

'Did these shoes look as though they'd been washed?'

Laila Ferguson smiled – a flash of white teeth in her striking black face. 'Not recently, no. They were filthy.'

Sarah smiled back. She was getting to like this girl. 'All right. What about the upper surface of these shoes? Given the amount of blood we saw in those photographs, most of which came from the victim's throat, wouldn't you have expected to find some of that spray on top of murderer's shoes, too? Not just five tiny drops, but quite a lot of it?'

'If the victim was standing up when her throat was cut, certainly. I suppose it's possible she might have been lying down. Or the murderer stood behind her.'

There's such a thing as being too clever, Sarah thought grimly. Or in my case, not clever enough. I should have thought of that first.

'Even then, he would have to step carefully to avoid it, wouldn't he? Given how much blood we can see.'

'There's a lot of blood in the photo, yes. It would probably get on the killer's shoes.'

'And yet there was no blood at all on one shoe you examined, isn't that right?'

'Yes.'

'And on the other one, just two tiny stains on the sole and five drops, two of them the size of – what did you say? – a grain of dust on the upper surface. That's all you found, isn't it?'

'That's all the blood I found, yes.'

'Very well.' Again Sarah paused, looking at her notes, to let the impact of the last few questions sink in. She had a clear sense that the jury was interested, and intrigued. This had been her best morning so far. She looked at Laila Ferguson again.

'Now, what about the blood on the breadknife. Were these stains any bigger?'

'No. There were just a few small specks, trapped in between the blade and the handle. There isn't much room in there.'

'What about the rest of the knife? Were there any stains on the blade, or the handle?'

'No. The knife was quite clean; it looked as though it had been washed recently.'

'Very well. But that's a normal thing to do with a breadknife, isn't it?'

Laila Ferguson shrugged. 'Yes, I suppose so.'

270

'What was the handle made of?'

'Plastic.'

'Did you find any blood on the handle? Anything to suggest that a person with a bloodstained hand had gripped it, for instance?'

'No. But then blood wouldn't stain plastic, if it was washed soon enough.'

'I see. Now, what can you tell us about the age of this blood?'

'I'm sorry?' The question clearly came as a surprise to Miss Ferguson.

'How old was it?'

'I . . . it's impossible to tell. It was dried blood, so obviously it was more than a few hours old, but beyond that there's no way of saying.'

'You can't say if the samples were a week old, two weeks old, a month old even?'

'I'm afraid not, no.'

'If you can't say how old it is, you can't say *when* the blood got on to the knife, can you?'

'No.'

'Or on to the shoes?'

'No.'

'Very well. So you have no way of saying that this blood got on to the shoe or the knife at the time of Jasmine's death, have you?'

'Well, I can't say that, no.' Laila Ferguson looked surprised at where the questions had led her. 'I can only tell you definitely that the blood came from Jasmine Hurst. That's all.'

'Yes, I understand that,' said Sarah patiently. 'But as far as you're concerned it's possible that all of these bloodstains could have got there as the result of an incident that occurred several hours *before* Jasmine's death? Days earlier, even?'

'Well, yes, I suppose so.' Whether Laila Ferguson had anticipated the direction these questions were leading or not, she seemed unable to resist it.

'A quite different incident, nothing to do with murder at all.'

'Perhaps.'

'Very well.' Sarah paused, to gather her thoughts and ensure that the jury were waiting for her next question, when it came. She had got as far as she could with this witness. If she were to build the basis for Simon's defence later, the next few moments were crucial.

'So if Simon Newby says, as he does, that this blood got on to the shoe and the knife when Miss Hurst cut her thumb in the kitchen, that is scientifically quite possible, isn't it?'

'I can't say what happened,' Laila Ferguson answered. 'I wasn't there.'

'No, of course not. But what I mean is, there's nothing in your scientific examination of the shoe and the knife and the blood to say that it *isn't* a reasonable explanation, is there?'

'No, I suppose not.'

'Even if this accident happened some hours or even days before-hand?'

'True. There's nothing to say it couldn't have been like that.'

'Very well. And given the very small, almost insignificant amounts of blood we're talking about here, compared to the massive carnage at the murder scene, don't you think that's a more likely explanation, Ms Ferguson? A minor accident in the kitchen, producing a few drops of blood on a shoe, and a tiny stain on a knife?'

Phil Turner coughed, looking meaningfully at the judge. Sarah knew she was perilously close to asking the witness to speculate about things beyond her competence. But the important thing was to plant the idea in the jury's minds.

Before the judge could react, Laila Ferguson answered. 'I suppose it's a theoretical possibility, yes.'

'Thank you,' said Sarah, and sat down. Wondering, with a small part of her mind, whether Will Churchill would be quite so entranced with the lovely young scientist now.

36

Every time she saw Will Churchill in court, Sarah experienced a fierce rush of hatred. It was not normally like this. In the past there had been a few police officers – like Terry Bateson – whom she liked, a majority whom she tolerated, and a few whom she despised. She had never hated one before. But then, no policeman had ever charged her son with murder before.

Churchill appeared to be enjoying the trial, patting his officers on the back, cracking jokes with Phil Turner, and trying to chat up the forensic scientist, Laila Ferguson.

When he saw Sarah watching, his laugh grew louder.

On the witness stand he explained why he had searched Simon's house and what he had found there, and how he had arrested Simon in Scarborough a few days later.

Phil Turner nodded. 'When you arrested Mr Newby, did you caution him?'

'Yes, we did.'

'So he was told, was he, that there was no need for him to say anything, but that anything he did say might be used in evidence?'

'He was told that, yes.'

'Did he appear to understand it?'

'Yes. He was fully awake and I spoke the words of the caution slowly and clearly.'

'Very well. And after he had been arrested and cautioned, did he in fact say anything?'

'Yes. He said that he hadn't killed Jasmine Hurst and that he hadn't seen her for weeks. He repeated those statements several times.'

Sarah glared at the judge. She had argued in chambers for this damaging evidence to be excluded. But Turner had played the tape of Simon's interview, arguing that although Simon had retracted the statements he had made in the car, he *had* admitted making them. To Sarah's disgust, Judge Mookerjee had agreed with him.

'Where was Simon Newby when he made these statements?'

'In the police car on the way from Scarborough to York. With DC Easby and myself.'

'How did you respond?'

'I said he would be interviewed at the police station. That's correct police procedure.'

Turner nodded approvingly. 'Nonetheless, it is also correct procedure, is it not, to make a note of any comments an arrested person may make after caution. Did you make such a note?'

'I did, yes.'

'Would you read it to the court, please?'

In his flat estuary English Churchill read: '*At 3.47 a.m. on Tuesday 18th May, DCI Churchill of York police, accompanied by DC Easby of York police and DS Conroy and DC Lane of Scarborough police, entered room 7 of Seaview Villas in Whitton Street, Scarborough . . . After being cautioned, Mr Newby stated that he had not killed Jasmine Hurst, and that he had not seen her for weeks. He repeated this statement several times.*'

'When you arrived at the police station, was Mr Newby given access to a lawyer?'

'He was, yes. Mrs Lucy Parsons.' Churchill eyed Lucy contemptuously.

'Was Mr Newby cautioned again?'

'He was, yes.'

Sarah shifted restlessly in her seat. In his slow, painstaking way Turner was walling Simon in. The more solidly he built his case, the harder it would be for her to tear it apart.

'Did you show Mr Newby this note?'

'I did. I asked him to sign it as a correct record of what he had said.'

'And what was his response?'

'He refused. At first he claimed he hadn't said those things at all. Then when I challenged him, he agreed he had said them but wanted to change his story. He admitted that he *had* met Jasmine Hurst on the day she was murdered, after all.'

'I see.' Turner paused, letting the words resonate in the jurors' minds.

He was making Simon look like a panic-stricken liar, who made up his story as he went along. And it was about to get worse.

'He changed his story *after* meeting Mrs Parsons, his solicitor, you say?'

'That's right, sir. Yes.'

'I see.' Turner gazed at Lucy, sitting stony-faced behind Sarah. His look was thoughtful, one eyebrow slightly raised. A brief glance, followed by a long pause, while the jury stared at Lucy too. Thinking, no doubt, she told him to change his story.

You devious old bastard, Sarah thought. Once she might have admired his court craft; now icy fury flooded through her.

'So what happened next?'

'Mrs Parsons handed me a statement which Simon had written himself.' Churchill read the statement aloud. '*I met Jasmine Hurst a year ago and became very fond of her. In October she came to live with me at 23 Bramham Street and she stayed until March, when she left me. She said she was tired of me and had a new boyfriend. His name is David Brodie and he lives with her at 8a Stillingfleet Road. I went there once to ask Jasmine to come back and live with me but she wouldn't. I've met her a few times since then but only briefly. On Thursday 13th May I met her by the river and she came back to my house for a meal. I asked her to come back and live with me but she wouldn't. We argued about this and then she left. When she left I was upset so I decided to go to Scarborough for a holiday, to try to get over her. I drove to Scarborough that night and didn't see Jasmine again. I had no idea Jasmine was dead until the police arrested me this morning. I did not kill her and I don't know how she died. Simon Newby.*'

'So this was quite different to what he had told you an hour before, in the police car?'

'Yes, it was.'

Turner rubbed his nose thoughtfully. 'Chief Inspector Churchill, you have many years' experience of interviewing criminal suspects, have you not? In your experience, is it usual for a defence solicitor to come into the police station, confer with her client, and then begin the interview by producing a written statement of this kind?'

'No, it's very *un*usual.' Churchill smiled. 'In fact, it's the first time I've seen it myself.'

This was too much. Sarah stood up. 'My lord, I really must protest. It seems that my learned friend is attempting to imply some form of professional misconduct on the part of Mrs Parsons, but there is no basis for this whatsoever.'

Judge Mookerjee raised his eyebrows. 'Mr Turner?'

Turner glanced at Sarah in mock surprise. 'My lord, I'm merely trying to establish how the defendant arrived at his version of events.'

'Which implies that he was influenced by his solicitor,' Sarah insisted. 'My lord, there was no impropriety whatsoever in my colleague's behaviour and on her behalf I most strongly resent the implication.'

'If there is such an implication of course I withdraw it.' Turner bowed to the judge. 'I am happy to agree that Mrs Parsons has behaved entirely within the law.'

Judge Mookerjee studied the two barristers. 'Does that satisfy you, Mrs Newby?'

Within the law, Sarah saw, was a stroke of genius. It was impossible to challenge and yet it suggested that Lucy had done something wrong, even if technically legal. Probably half the jury had missed Turner's subtle innuendoes; now she had emphasized them. Not for the first time in her career, she had been outsmarted. There was nothing for it but to back out as gracefully as she could.

'Indeed, my lord. For the present.'

'So, Chief Inspector Churchill,' Turner resumed. 'What was your response to this unusual written statement?'

'Well, Mrs Parsons said that if I had no evidence against Mr Newby, he should be released immediately. I said that we did have evidence. I showed him the trainers which we had found in his house, with the mud and grass stains and blood on them. I explained that they matched the footprints near the body.'

'And what was his response?'

'He said they weren't his trainers.'

'Did he suggest who else they might belong to?'

'No, sir. I asked if anyone else kept their trainers in his house, and he said they didn't.'

'Did you show him any other evidence?'

'Yes. I showed him the breadknife, and told him it had blood with Jasmine's blood group on it. AB negative. The same blood group as on the trainers.'

'What was his response to that?'

'He was very angry. He got to his feet and threatened me. At first he said it wasn't his knife at all. Then he said that it couldn't be her blood because he didn't kill her.'

'I see.' Again Turner paused, and the eyes of the jury strayed to Simon in the dock, imagining him threatening two policemen, and lying about the ownership of the knife. Sarah guessed what was coming next.

'At this point, did Mr Newby mention anything about Jasmine cutting her finger with the breadknife?'

'Nothing at all, sir, no.'

'Did he ever suggest that to you?'

'No, never.'

'So it's fair to say, is it, that this explanation for the blood on his knife and trainer is something that he now relies on for his defence, but which he failed to mention when interviewed?'

'It is, sir, yes.'

'Very well. Let us move on to another aspect of the defence case, if we may. Can I ask you to look back at that statement which Mr Newby wrote, after meeting Mrs Parsons. Does it say anywhere that Simon made love to Miss Hurst on Thursday 13th May?'

Churchill pretended to consult the document, then looked up. 'No, it doesn't.'

'What does it say happened that afternoon?'

'It says, *I met her by the river and she came back to my house for a meal. I asked her to come back to live with me but she wouldn't. We argued about this and then she left.* That's all. Nothing about making love.'

'So at what point did Mr Newby mention this to you?'

'When I told him that Miss Hurst had been raped before she died. I said we'd found traces of semen, and so DNA analysis would identify the man who raped and murdered her.'

'And what was his response?'

'At that point he said that the semen would be his. He claimed that he had made love to Jasmine earlier that afternoon.'

'Did he admit that he had raped her?'

'No, sir. I asked him about that and he said he had not.'

'I see. But again it's fair to say, is it, that in his original handwritten statement he made no mention of this act of sexual intercourse which he is now trying to use in his defence? He only came up with it when confronted with the evidence.'

'That's correct, yes.'

Phil Turner waited for a moment, rubbing his ear as though wondering if there were anything he had missed. Several jurors were scowling at Simon with unconcealed disgust.

'Thank you, Chief Inspector. Wait there, please.'

When Sarah stood up, Churchill faced her with a polite, contemptuous smile. The trick in situations like this, as they both knew, was to put the police in as bad a light as possible.

'Mr Churchill,' she asked, refusing to dignify him with his rank. 'What time of day was it that you arrested my son?'

'At 3.47 a.m., madam.' *Madam* was an exquisite touch. As he spoke he looked away from her towards the jury, to suggest that she was troubling him with trivialities.

'Why?'

'Why what?' Reluctantly he looked back at her.

'Why did you arrest him so early in the morning?'

A look of amazement crossed Churchill's face. 'He was the suspect in a serious murder case. I arrested him as soon as I could. The Scarborough police spotted his car late that night and I drove immediately to Scarborough to arrest him.' What's wrong with that, his look said.

'So he was asleep when you arrived, was he?'

'He was in bed asleep, yes.'

'And did you make the arrest alone, or with other officers?'

'With two Scarborough officers and DC Easby.'

'I see. So at quarter to four in the morning, Simon Newby was asleep in his bed. Two minutes later, four policemen burst into his bedroom and arrested him. You told him why he was being arrested and informed him of his rights. In a loud, slow voice, I think you said.'

'I spoke slowly. I didn't say my voice was loud.'

'While he was still in bed?'

'Yes.'

'And then you handcuffed him?'

'Yes.'

'And took him outside to your police car?'

'We did, yes.'

'What was he wearing at this time?'

'His pyjamas.'

'I see.' Sarah looked at the jury to see what effect, if any, her questions were having. Most looked reasonably alert, at least. 'So let me get this picture right. Here we have a young man, fast asleep in his bed at 3.47 in the morning, when suddenly he wakes up to find four police officers in his bedroom shouting at him. Before he can get out of bed they tell him his girlfriend is dead and that he is being arrested for her murder. Then they handcuff him, drag him downstairs and put him in a police car. Is that what happened?'

'Madam, he was being arrested on a *very – serious – charge.*' Churchill spoke slowly and clearly, as though explaining to a slow-witted child. Someone in the public gallery laughed.

'And then you interrogated him,' said Sarah coldly.

'I beg your pardon? When, exactly?'

'In the police car. You asked him questions in the police car, didn't you? On the way back from Scarborough.'

'No, madam, we did not. I've already explained that.'

'I think you did. My client remembers very clearly that you asked him questions in the police car.'

'No, madam, we didn't ask him any questions until we got back to York.'

'Well, *you* say that, but I put it to you that you *did* ask him questions in the police car.'

'No.'

'My client clearly remembers that you did. He will give evidence that you did.'

'We did not.'

'You see, this is a vital point, isn't it, Mr Churchill? I suppose even you can appreciate the feelings of a young man who has been dragged out of his bed by four strangers in the middle of the night, forced into a car, and told that his girlfriend is dead. How would you expect that young man to feel? Confused, perhaps? Terrified? Overcome by grief? All of those things?'

'He might be overcome by guilt.'

'Not if he was innocent.' She paused and glanced at the jury. 'Mr Churchill, there are rules to protect suspects in these situations, are there not? Do you remember what they are?'

Churchill sighed, and spoke in a monotone as though deliberately reciting something he had learned off by heart. 'A suspect who has been arrested should not be questioned further until he is in an interview room in a police station where the interview can be recorded on tape.'

'Exactly. And one of the purposes of those rules is to protect the accused, isn't it? From being unfairly harassed when he is handcuffed in the back of a police car, for instance.'

'That may be one purpose, yes. Another is to protect the police from false accusations by unscrupulous lawyers.'

Touché, she thought. But Sarah was playing the game for real today. 'I put it to you, Mr Churchill, that you knowingly and deliberately broke these rules in the most cynical manner. Not only did you arrest this young man quite unnecessarily in the middle of the night, in a way calculated to terrify him out of his wits; you then handcuffed him, told him his girlfriend was dead, and interrogated him *in your car* while he was overcome with grief and shock.'

'No . . .' Churchill shook his head.

'You did all this deliberately to confuse him and get him to say something to incriminate himself. And you were successful, weren't you?'

'He made these statements voluntarily. There was no interrogation in the car.'

'*Voluntarily,* you say? When he was dragged from his bed in his nightclothes, and handcuffed in the car with two strange men? How was he handcuffed, Mr Churchill? With his hands in front of him or behind?'

'His hands were behind him.'

'Was he restrained in any other way?'

'He was strapped into his seat, yes, for his own safety.'

'And you call this situation *voluntary*?'

'His situation wasn't voluntary, madam, no. He was under arrest. But he made his statements voluntarily, without any interrogation. As I have already said.'

'So you handcuff a young man, in his pyjamas, in the middle of the night, with his hands behind his back, drive him fifty miles through the countryside with two strange men who accuse him of murdering his girlfriend, and then you call his statements voluntary?'

'He made his statements voluntarily, and I recorded them in the normal way.'

'Most people would call that intimidation, Mr Churchill. So now of course we understand why he made this foolish mistake of saying he hadn't seen Jasmine for weeks. He lied because he was terrified out of his wits, because you had been bullying him ever since you woke him up at quarter to four in the morning –'

To her surprise, Phil Turner was on his feet. 'My lord, is there a question in all this?'

Judge Mookerjee peered at her. 'Mrs Newby?'

'I was coming to that, my lord. How long is the drive from Scarborough to York?'

'About an hour, at that time in the morning. But –'

'So for all that time, while Simon was adjusting to the shock of hearing his girlfriend was dead, you were interrogating him, accusing him of murder. No wonder he was terrified, no wonder he felt he had to lie to save himself!'

'We did not ask him any questions in the car. This arrest was conducted according to the rules, and his statements were recorded according to the rules as well. That's why I showed him a written record of his comments at the start of the interview in the police station.'

'When he immediately denied them, is that right?'

'After he'd had legal advice, yes.'

Churchill nodded at Lucy, to remind the jury of the implication that she had done something unethical. Swiftly, Sarah challenged him again.

'That's not true, though, is it, Mr Churchill? My son didn't have time to discuss your notes with his solicitor – he denied them immediately you showed them to him.'

'At first he did, yes. Then he agreed that he had made those statements, but changed his story to say that he had seen Jasmine Hurst on Thursday 13th after all.'

'Yes. So as soon as he was in a proper environment, where he had a solicitor with him as was his legal right, and he was no longer handcuffed in a car being shouted at by two men who told him his girlfriend was dead, he began to tell the truth. Is that what you're saying?'

Churchill smiled dismissively. 'He changed his story, yes. After he'd seen his lawyer.'

'All right. Let's look at what he did after he had spoken to his lawyer. Not only did he begin to co-operate with you, Mr Churchill, but he actually did something quite unprecedented in your experience. He volunteered a written statement of the truth, isn't that right?'

'He gave me a statement that was partially true, yes.'

'*Partially* true, Mr Churchill? Would you read the statement again, please, and tell me which parts of it you think are not true?'

To her delight Churchill fell into her trap. He picked up Simon's statement and began to read through it. The court fell silent, waiting. After nearly a minute, he looked up.

'I mean that the statement was incomplete. It missed a number of crucial details.'

'So there is nothing in his statement that is untrue. Is that what you are saying?'

'It's incomplete. For example –'

'But it's all true, isn't it? Every word of that statement is true?'

'True as far it goes, yes . . .'

'Thank you.' For a second, Sarah thought that she had him. But she was wrong.

'It doesn't say that he had sex with her, which he is now relying on for his defence. It doesn't say that he hit her in the street, leaving a bruise on her face. Those are pretty important omissions, in my view. It doesn't say that he spied on her when she was with David Brodie, and had a fight with him outside his house. That's true as well, Mrs Newby, you know.'

Shit! She'd had him on the ropes, but he'd winded her with three heavy blows to the body. Her mind froze and she reeled, eyes glazed, waiting for the knockout. Then she hit back.

'That doesn't alter the fact that everything in that statement was true. If I asked where *you* were last night, Mr Churchill, you might say you were with a young woman, but you wouldn't necessarily tell me what you did in bed with her. You'd be embarrassed, wouldn't you?'

As Churchill hesitated, surprised by the question, a smothered male laugh came from behind her in the courtroom. A look of fury crossed his face, followed, to her delight, by a faint but unmistakable blush. I've touched a nerve I didn't know existed, she thought, delighted.

'Perhaps I would, yes. But then no one's accused me of murder.'

'Nevertheless, that's why my son didn't write down that he had sex with Jasmine that afternoon. He had no idea it was important at the time, had he? He simply told you he'd been with her, which was true.'

'Possibly.' Churchill was looking daggers past her, at whoever had laughed. She longed to look round herself.

'There you are then. As soon as my son was at the police station, he gave you information that was entirely true. And in the course of that interview, when everything else he said was true, did he at any time admit to killing Jasmine Hurst?'

'No, he denied it.'

'Exactly. He's always denied that, hasn't he?'

'Yes.'

She had almost finished with Churchill. She glanced at her notes to remind herself how she had planned this last night. Surprise him now, keep him off guard.

'When did you first tell him that Jasmine was dead?'

'I . . . when we arrested him. We told him then.'

'Pretty shocking news, wouldn't you say? Especially when it's brought to you by four policemen in the middle of the night. How did he react to it?'

'He claimed he didn't know she was dead.'

'*He claimed he didn't know.*' Sarah let the words hang a little in the air. 'I suppose it never crossed your mind, Inspector Churchill, that this *claim* might actually be true? In which case your manner of breaking this terrible news was – what shall we say? Brutal?'

'I believed that he had murdered her.'

'You *believed* that, yes, but what if you were wrong? What if you were quite wrong and he really thought Jasmine was alive? What sort of reaction would you expect?'

Churchill shrugged. 'If he really believed Jasmine was still alive, I suppose he would have been shocked.'

'And how did he behave?'

'Well, he *appeared* to be upset, of course. He said he didn't know she was dead and started screaming at us. But in my view it was all fraud. He was shocked to be caught, that's all.'

'He *appeared* to be upset, you say. Did he ask you how she had died?'

'Yes.'

'Was this in his room, or in the car?'

'In the car.'

'When he was handcuffed and strapped to his seat. Did you tell him how she had died?'

'In general terms, yes. I told him she'd been raped, and had her throat cut.'

'And what was his reaction to this news?'

'He appeared to be upset.'

Again Sarah let the words hang in the air. The longer she waited, the more callous she hoped they might sound. But it was only a hope. The jury might equally well sympathize with Churchill's cynicism.

'Describe this *appearance* of being upset for us, Inspector, if you will. Did he seem shocked? Did he weep? What did he do?'

Churchill looked up at the ornate domed ceiling for a moment and sighed, as though to indicate his impatience. 'As I recall he fell silent for a while. Then he started shouting at us and saying he hadn't seen her for weeks.'

Damn! She had walked into that. I need an exit strategy, quick.

'So, to sum up your evidence, Mr Churchill. Four policeman woke my son in the middle of the night, handcuffed him and told him his girlfriend was dead. He *appeared* to be upset by this. You told him she had been raped and had her throat cut and he *appeared* to be even more upset by that. Correct so far?'

The mocking smile again. 'If you put it like that, yes.'

'Then, when he is handcuffed in your car and still appears to be upset by this truly shocking news, you accuse him of murder and start to question him –'

'No!' Churchill shook his head vigorously. 'We did not question him in the car.'

'All right. When you are *not* questioning him in the car but you are describing to him how she was killed and simultaneously accusing him of her murder while driving him through the darkened countryside in his pyjamas with his hands cuffed, and according to you he *appears* to be upset, at that point he starts to lie and say he hasn't seen her for weeks. Is that right?'

'It's your way of putting it, I suppose.'

'Is any of it untrue?'

He thought back over what she had said. 'Not in detail, I suppose, but –'

'Very well, then. You then take him to a police station where he is allowed to see a lawyer and has a few moments to take in this appalling news without feeling that he is being kidnapped by two strangers who don't believe a word he says, and at that point he immediately begins to co-operate and tell the truth. Is that right?'

'Not all the truth, no. He told us he didn't kill Jasmine.'

'Apart from that, what else did he tell you in that interview that you don't accept as true?'

Churchill paused before answering, searching swiftly through his mind for a detail she had forgotten. Then he grinned.

'He said he'd made love to her in the afternoon. I don't believe that.'

'You may not *believe* it but you've no way of *knowing* whether it's true or not, have you? The pathologist has already confirmed that it's possible.'

Churchill shrugged dismissively, without answering.

'You don't *believe* he was genuinely upset to hear of her death, but it's perfectly possible that he was, isn't it? If he didn't kill her?'

'If he didn't kill her, yes.'

'So, if we accept that he didn't kill her, Mr Churchill, everything that he did and said becomes perfectly comprehensible, doesn't it? He was shocked, upset and terrified in your police car, when he panicked and told you a lie; but after that he recovered and everything he told you was completely one hundred per cent true. If we accept that he didn't kill her, that is.'

Churchill spread his hands in exasperation. 'Well, if you accept that, Mrs Newby, yes. But I don't accept it, you see, not for a moment. I think he killed her.'

It was the best she could do. Quickly, to show she was not at a loss but was where she had wanted to be, Sarah smiled. 'Thank you, Mr Churchill. That's all I want to ask.'

She folded her gown about her, and sat down.

'You stitched him up, the sod.'

'Did I? I hope so, Simon. He's a difficult witness to shake.'

'You made him look like a thug. He is too.'

'Let's hope the jury agree with you.'

'They will. Anyone could see what a pig he is.'

'That was the plan, certainly.' Sarah paced the brief length of the cell and back again. The adrenalin was still flowing in her, making it hard to stay still. Churchill had shaken her as much as she had shaken him. 'It must be hard, watching all this.'

'Not when you're doing so well. You're brilliant, Mum – honest!'

The enthusiasm, even the choice of words, reminded her of the small boy he had once been. Before all the teenage rebellion and hatred and . . . this. The brief light in his face brought her a keen joy and regret for all that was gone. She squeezed his arm briefly.

'I wish all my clients were so grateful. But we've a long way to go yet.'

The cell door opened and a guard put a tray with pre-wrapped sandwiches, an apple and coffee on the bench beside Simon.

'Such luxury,' Sarah said. 'Lucy'll be down to eat with you. I've got some notes to check in my chambers. See you this afternoon, OK?'

Outside, there was the usual shock of sunshine, tourists, traffic and a warm autumn wind that caressed her face and played with her gown as she walked. It was always so strange to step out of the all-absorbing world of the trial into this sound, bustle and colour. Like stepping out of the programme into the adverts. She walked past children climbing the grassy slopes of Clifford's Tower, a French tour guide giving a lecture. She waited at the traffic lights, one hand clutching her wig to stop it blowing off in the wind. A man pressed the button beside her.

'How's it going, then?'

'Who – oh, *Terry*. Hi.' They crossed the road, squeezing through a line of German schoolchildren. 'It's, er . . . OK so far.'

'You had my boss on the stand this morning. He's not your greatest fan.'

Sarah grimaced. 'Nor I his. But I made a little progress, I think.'

'How's Simon bearing up?'

'He thinks we're doing well.' She looked at Terry thoughtfully, wondering how far she could go. 'But that's probably because he knows he's innocent. No one else does. What I really need, is to know who *did* kill her. David Brodie, for instance?'

Terry met her gaze seriously, knowing he didn't have the answer. 'I'm sorry, Sarah. But I'm afraid at the moment . . .'

Real life returned in the shape of Simon's neighbour, Archibald Mullen, who had dressed for the occasion. Instead of his old carpet slippers and cardigan he wore a jacket, shirt and tie. His sparse hair had been plastered to his scalp with Brylcreem. His pipe, which Sarah had seen him smoking in the foyer, had been extinguished and stuffed into his pocket.

Phil Turner took him slowly through his evidence – how he had seen Simon and Jasmine often, and recognized them; how he'd seen them arguing in the street on the night she died; how Simon had hit her and she had run off, crying; how Simon had gone back into his house and then come out later to drive away in his car. It was a crucial, damning part of the case against Simon.

Watching, Sarah thought, the old buzzard's giving the performance of his life. He must have been standing in front of the mirror practising this for weeks.

If Bob hadn't met him, Simon might never have been arrested.

When Turner sat down Sarah hesitated. She was debating with herself whether to ask the old crow anything at all. Foolishly, she stood up, and instantly his old dark eyes swivelled to find her, like a thrush focusing on a worm.

'Mr Mullen, you must have been watching this incident with great care.'

'I saw what happened, right enough.' The Adam's apple in his leathery old throat bobbed sharply as he spoke.

'I just want to get a picture of this,' Sarah probed cautiously. 'You were cleaning your teeth, when you heard a noise outside. A door slamming and people arguing, you said.'

'Aye. Shouting at each other, like.'

'So when you looked out of the window, the argument had already begun?'

'Aye. Going at it hammer and tongs, they were.'

'But you didn't see the start of the argument, did you?' This, really, was the only useful point Sarah had to make.

'I saw best part of it. I saw him hit her, any road.'

'Yes, I'm not disputing that. But you hadn't been watching the street all evening, had you? You'd been watching television.'

'True.' The old man squinted at her suspiciously.

'So when these two people slammed the door and started arguing, a minute or two passed before you started watching them. Isn't that right?'

'I saw him hit her,' he insisted stubbornly. 'You'll not change me tale on that.'

'Yes, but . . . Mr Mullen, which of these two slammed the door? Simon, or Jasmine?'

'Him, likely.'

'How do you know? Did you see him do it?'

'No, but it's his house, in't it? Stands to reason.'

'Women slam doors too, Mr Mullen.'

'Aye, but she came out first. *She* were leaving, not him.'

'But you didn't see either of them slam the door, did you, Mr Mullen?'

'I didn't have to. It don't really matter, anyhow, does it, lass?'

The jury probably agreed, Sarah realized. She was failing dismally to establish a rather unimportant point. She tried again. 'What matters is how much of the argument you saw, and how much happened before you started watching. Which of them started shouting first?'

'Nay, it were six of one and half a dozen of t'other. Both yelling at once, like.'

'So the fact is, you were cleaning your teeth when you heard a door slam and people shouting at each other. You put down your toothbrush, walked to the window, and looked out to see what was happening. That's right, isn't it?'

'Nay. I kept a good grip of me brush. Tha can watch a scrap and clean thi teeth at same time, lass.' He made the point with such delight that several people in the public gallery exploded with suppressed laughter.

Sarah sighed. This was going nowhere. 'I'm sure you can, Mr Mullen. The point I'm trying to establish, though, is this. You didn't see all of the argument, although you did see the young man hit the girl. But it's perfectly possible that she hit him first, before you started watching, isn't it? Which would explain why he was angry, and hit her back.'

'Nay, lass, I saw what I saw, and it were none of that. Tha'll not put words in me mouth.'

The old buzzard can go on like this all night, Sarah thought. With the jury happy to watch him, and no benefit at all to Simon. She sat down abruptly.

'No more questions, my lord.'

37

The man had been in the car for nearly two hours now. He sat and smoked and watched the windows. From time to time he ran the engine to keep warm. It was a cool night, and the streets were swept by showers of rain. The tarmac glistened under the street lamps, and he switched on the wipers, to maintain a clear view.

The woman would be out soon, he told himself. He had watched her go in, and identified her by the expensive camera round her neck, the jeans, the anorak. She was not the sort of visitor the house normally had. A young woman, he thought, about twenty-five, brisk, self-confident. Not the sort to worry about walking these streets late at night in the rain.

Someone who was used to big cities, who would not see York as dangerous. Someone who was here to get the story, make the most of it, and move on. Who would use people like himself as steps in the ladder of her career.

The door opened at last, a crack of reddish light in the darkness of the street. The woman came out, making her farewells, her short blonde hair framed for a second in the light from the doorway. Then she was coming down the street towards him.

She moved with a swift, jaunty, athletic step, her unzipped anorak folded across her chest by her arms against the sudden damp cold of the night air. She was within ten yards of him, five.

He thought, I could open the door now, shove it rudely across the narrow pavement to make her stop. And then in the same swift violent movement I could jump out and . . . what?

Nothing.

She had gone past his car, around the corner towards the light and safety of the main streets and the warmth of her hotel. And the man sat silent, his fingers tensing and loosening on his steering wheel. Thinking.

That's what it must be like. That's how it's done.

He got out of the car and walked towards the door from which the woman had left.

'You could come and watch,' Sarah said from the bed. 'Then I wouldn't have to repeat it all for you.'

'I've got a school to run, Sarah. Anyway, Emily and Larry tell me most of it.' Bob took off his jacket and hung it up.

'So why ask me now?' Sarah stretched her legs under the duvet, feeling the muscles relax. 'I've had enough, Bob. I'm tired.'

'I'm not surprised. You woke me four times last night, muttering away to yourself.'

'Go in the spare room then.'

'I can't sleep there. The bed's too small.'

'God!' Sarah groaned, thumped her pillow and sat up. 'Look, Bob, I'm sorry, I can't cope with this. I've got a murder trial to defend and tomorrow I'm going to ruin some poor boy's life in order to save Simon. So right now I need to sleep and if you can't manage the spare bed, I can. Just don't wake me before seven.'

She snatched up two pillows and stomped out of the room. Bob watched her go, listening to the lights snap on and off and the door slam along the corridor. Then he climbed into the warm, empty bed.

'Who the hell is it? Oh no, not you!'

'Yes. I've got to come in, Sharon.'

'Not now. For God's sake, I've just put the kids to bed.'

'Great. Perfect timing. Come on, shut the door, it's cold out there.'

'But I don't want –'

'I do, though.' He was inside, pushing her back along the hall. 'What you going to do, call the police?'

'You miserable bastard . . .'

'Compliments, compliments. Come on, Sharon, do you want to do it here or upstairs?'

She had her face averted but he was kissing her neck, her cheek, her throat. He could feel himself hard and her slender body trying to push him away, which only made him more eager. He pinned her against the wall, kissing and fondling her while he overpowered her with his weight. The scent of her neck and hair combined with the rank smell of fear to excite him. He felt her resistance weaken.

'Here, then?'

'No, come up, for Christ's sake. The kids.'

She wriggled out from between him and the wall and led him upstairs, his hand firmly clasped around her wrist. A bedroom door was open and a child's voice called from within.

'Mum? Has that lady gone?'

Sharon poked her head around the door. 'Yeah, it's OK, Wayne. Everything's fine.' Then, without looking at him, she led the way into her own bedroom. Her workplace. As he shut the door softly behind him, she kicked off her shoes and began unbuttoning her blouse. Her face was hidden by her hair. He stood and watched.

When her blouse and bra were off he hadn't moved. She looked up, questioning. 'What?'

'Go on. All of it. Then you can do me.'

'Pig!' She unzipped her skirt, stepped out of it and began to peel off her tights. There was nothing provocative about the way she did it. Her manner was sullen, angry, brusque. 'What the fuck you doing here at this time of night anyhow?'

He laughed. 'What the fuck is exactly it. I was working late so I thought you could too.'

When she was naked she began, sulkily, to unbutton his shirt. He ran his fingers down her back and sides as she did so. His caresses evoked no response. She undressed him as though she were changing a nappy. 'You're a right bastard you are, Harry Easby.'

'Am I?' When he, too, was naked he shoved her backwards on to the bed, and climbed on top of her. 'Then let's see just how much of a bastard I can be, shall we?'

Afterwards he lay on the bed beside her, watching the smoke from his cigarette drift upwards towards the ceiling. She was curled away from him on her side. He patted her rump.

'At least you give value for money.'

'What money? You pig, you don't pay.'

'No, but if I did.' He fished a fag from his packet and tossed it over to her. 'Here.'

Sullenly, she put on a dressing gown, and lit the cigarette. 'You staying long?'

'For a bit. I've got some questions to ask you. How'd it go with the reporter?'

'Her?' Sharon took a long drag on her cigarette and looked away, warily. 'All right. She asked her questions, I answered them.'

'So? What happens next?'

'She writes her story, I suppose. That's what journalists do, isn't it?'

'I wouldn't know, I've never had one.' Harry laughed at his own coarse wit. He got out of bed, put on his underpants and trousers, and took an envelope from his jacket pocket. Inside the envelope were two photofits. He spread them out on the bed. 'I wanted to ask you about these.'

She peered at them incuriously. 'Yeah, what about them?'

'Do you recognize the man in the picture?'

'They're the same feller then? Meant to be?'

'The same lad, yeah.'

Sharon looked more closely, comparing the two, and her initial lack of interest began to fade. Harry watched her long blonde curls slide across her shoulder as she moved her head.

'It is a bit like a feller I know, yeah.'

'Oh yeah. Who's that then?'

She considered him, cautiously. 'I don't know that I should say.'

He snatched her wrist swiftly, squeezing so that it hurt. 'Ah, but you should, you see, Sharon. That's why I'm asking.'

'Let go me hand, then.' She pulled, but his grip tightened.

'Who is it? Tell me.'

'A mate of Gary's.'

The grip loosened. 'Name?'

'An Irish lad, calls himself Sean Murphy. Nasty piece of work.'

Harry let go her wrist, and sat watching her intently. 'Good girl, got it in one. So tell me, Sharon. How do you know him?'

She laughed. 'Same way I know you, as it happens. All't bloody same, you men.'

'He's one of your clients?'

'Was, yeah. Not any more.'

'Why not? What happened?'

She got up, flicked her ash into a glass, and began to pace slowly by the window. 'If I were a doctor, I couldn't say, could I? They have *clients*, and they're supposed to keep it all secret, aren't they? Confidential.'

'Yes, but you . . .'

'I have clients too, even if some don't pay as they should.' She glanced at him scornfully. 'But anyhow, that feller in them pictures, I reckon he needed a doctor as much as he needed me.'

'Why? He wasn't diseased, was he?'

'No, not like that. But he couldn't do it proper. Unlike you, it has to be said.'

'How do you mean?'

'Well, there was something wrong with him. He could get it up, see, but he couldn't do it. No sperm, nothing like that.'

'He couldn't produce sperm?'

'No.' She tossed her head, drawing deeply on her cigarette. 'Believe me, I checked. He wore a condom, but it were empty. I gave him a hand job, and – nowt.'

Harry stared, then began to laugh. 'But . . . poor bugger!'

Sharon shuddered, and stubbed out her cigarette. 'Yeah, well, it wasn't so funny at the time, believe you me. That feller there . . .' she nodded at the photofits '. . . is built like Arnold bloody Schwarzenegger and he's got the mind of a fucking terminator as well. He could put *you* through that wall with one hand. Only there's one part of his body that don't work so well, see – his dick! It's just dry and hard and drives him mad. And guess who he blames for that?'

Harry was still laughing. 'His mother? Tony Blair?'

'It's not funny, Harry. He blamed *me*. I tell you, I thought I wasn't going to get out of this room alive. He's a fucking psychopath, he is.'

'He threatened you, you mean?'

'Threatened me? He had his hands round my throat.' She shook her head, upset by the memory. 'Anyway, what you after him for?'

'He's . . . a suspect in a murder case.' Harry sobered. 'So when did you last see this Sean?'

'About a year ago now. Thank God. If I never see him again it'll be too soon.'

Harry put on his shirt. 'There you are, Sharon, you see. I knew you had something for me that couldn't wait. That's why I came.' He stuffed the photofits back into the envelope and put on his jacket, favouring her with what he imagined was a triumphant, sexy grin. 'Thanks, kid. You made my night.'

Sharon watched from the landing as he went downstairs and out of the front door. Then she switched out the light, leaned back against the wall, and slid slowly down it to the floor.

David Brodie placed his hands on the edge of the witness box nervously, terrified to find himself the focus of so many pairs of eyes. Phil Turner began gently.

'Mr Brodie, how well did you know Jasmine Hurst?'

'Very well.' Brodie smiled at some inner memory. 'I was her boyfriend. I loved her.'

'How long had you known each other?'

'About . . . three months, I suppose.'

'And how did you meet?'

'At a party. She looked lonely and we got talking. She'd had a quarrel with her boyfriend, and had nowhere to spend the night. I said she could use my spare room if she liked. So she did.'

Sarah watched intently. He was speaking to the gallery, she thought, like Hamlet on stage. He hardly looked at Phil Turner at all.

'Who was the boyfriend she had quarrelled with?'

'Simon Newby.'

'Did you see any evidence of this quarrel?'

'She showed me a bruise on her arm where he'd hit her.'

'How did you feel about this?'

'Well, shocked. I couldn't imagine anyone wanting to hit her.'

'So she stayed in your spare room?'

'Yes.' He blushed, aware of a possible misunderstanding. 'I didn't try anything on; I mean I wouldn't. She just wanted someone to talk to, I think. I was a bit overawed, to tell the truth. She was a very beautiful girl.'

'So how did your relationship develop?'

'Well, next morning she went back to Simon to try to patch things up. I mean, they'd been living together for some time, and she had all her things there in his house. So I said fine, but if she needed to get away she was welcome to come back any time. I showed her where I hide the key in case I wasn't there. I'm a nurse, you see; I work late shifts at the hospital.'

'And did she come back?'

'Sure. One night, when I came home at eleven o'clock, there she was. She'd let herself in and had a meal ready for me in the oven, of all things. It was amazing. She said she'd quarrelled with Simon again and was moving out, for good this time. She asked if she could stay for a few days till she found somewhere else to live.'

'And you agreed?'

'Too right I did. I said she could stay for as long as she liked and she did. She . . . she stayed for the rest of her life, in fact.' His voice faltered, and his eyes strayed towards the jury to see if they understood what he meant. It's all a performance, Sarah thought. He's on stage.

'And you became lovers?'

'After a while, yes, we did.' He looked down modestly.

'Very well. Now during this time, did you ever meet the defendant, Simon Newby?'

'Yes, I saw him several times. He found out where she lived, you see, and he used to spy on us and make our lives a misery. He hit me once.'

'How did that happen?'

'Well, Jasmine was going out of the house. I heard shouting, and when I came out he had his hand on her arm. So I told him to leave her alone and he yelled at me to, well, fuck off, he said. Then he hit me.'

'How?'

'Just punched me in the face. It was bloody hard. He's strong, you know.'

Several jurors nodded, noting how much bigger and stronger Simon was than the witness.

'So what happened then?'

'Well, I fell over and Jasmine started screaming and kicking him. Then he ran off.'

'Did you report this assault to the police?'

'No. I wish I had now. If I had perhaps none of this would have happened.'

Again there was a slight, and to Sarah's ear suspicious, catch in his voice. Or was she just persuading herself, screwing up her courage for action?

'This harassment of you and Jasmine – did that continue?'

'Yes, it happened several times. I think because . . .'

'Yes, Mr Brodie? Because . . .?'

'Because she gave in and went back to see him sometimes. Just to talk, she said. I didn't like it but there wasn't much I could do. She seemed to think it was amusing. She said he was just a lovesick kid and she could handle him. Just shows how wrong you can be. I should have done something. But it's too late now.'

This time there really were tears. He struggled with a pack of tissues. This will impress the jury, Sarah thought gloomily. He loved her too, poor wimp.

'I know this is distressing, Mr Brodie,' Turner persisted, 'but could you tell the court, please, exactly when you last saw Jasmine alive.'

'It was on the Thursday, 13th May. She left about ten; she said . . . she was going to the protest. But I knew she wasn't. She was going to see him.'

'She was going to see Simon, you say?'

'Yes. I asked her not to go. But she went anyway.' He blew his nose.

'And was that the last time you saw her?'

'Yes. I worked from two till ten. When I got home, she wasn't there. I thought she was still with him, but she wasn't, was she? She was out there, dead on the river bank.' He pointed at Simon in the dock. 'Where he killed her!'

Phil Turner waited, allowing the moment its full effect.

'Thank you. Just wait there, please. Mrs Newby may have some questions.'

Too right I have, Sarah thought. And you're going to hate me for them.

As Harry came in, Terry glanced pointedly at his watch. 9.37.

'Yeah, OK, sir, I'm sorry.' Harry grinned. 'But I was out late last night on the job, to coin a phrase. And it *was* worth it, believe you me.'

'Oh yes? Tell me then.'

Harry spun a chair round and straddled it, eyes gleaming with triumph.

'Well, I saw Sharon yesterday, after her meeting with the journalist.'

'Oh yes. How did that go?'

Harry shrugged. 'She didn't talk much about it. But get this, boss. I showed her these.' He flung the photofits of Sean on Terry's desk. 'And she knows him. One Sean Murphy.'

'So we have a name at last.' Terry remembered Gary's question. *Who helped you with these? That bitch Sharon?* 'How does she know him, exactly?'

Harry laughed. 'As a man knows a woman, in the biblical sense. Only there's just one small and stunning difference, you see.'

Dwelling with great relish on the detail, Harry described what Sharon had told him, about Sean's behaviour and his unusual sexual difficulty. Terry listened, astonished.

'Is that possible? I've never heard of it.'

'I rang my doctor this morning. Apparently it's a one in ten thousand thing, the sort of weird example they put in medical textbooks to cheer everyone else up.'

'But . . . the poor bugger. It would drive you wild, wouldn't it?'

Harry nodded. 'That's what Sharon said too. She said he scared her shitless.'

'So what did he go to her for, if he knew that would happen?'

'Maybe he hoped it would work this time. I dunno. But what struck me, sir, you see – in the middle of the night I was thinking about this and I remembered. This lad, Sean, he's a possible suspect for Maria Clayton's murder, right? And one of the main problems in the Clayton case is that she was raped, but there was no sign of any semen. Well, if this guy did it . . .'

'He wouldn't have left any. Quite.' Terry stood up suddenly. 'And when it didn't work of course he'd be in a blind rage and might kill her for it. Where's that damn book?'

He scrabbled through the heap of files on his desk to unearth Maria Clayton's battered diary. The page he wanted was marked with a yellow sticker.

'Here it is. Look!' He held it out for Harry to see. *S big promise, no result. Gets it up but can't get it out. V. frust for him, poor lamb, blames me. Outside? No way, José, I say.*

Harry grinned triumphantly. 'By, it's got to be him, sir! *Blames me*, she wrote – that's exactly what Sharon said – *and* his name begins with S. We've got him!'

'Yes, but . . . where is he? That's the million dollar question now, Harry lad!'

*　　*　　*

The trembling began just before Sarah stood up. She often felt nervous before cross-examination; the adrenalin sharpened her performance. But this time it was different. Huge South American butterflies fluttered wildly in her stomach. She clasped her shaking hands behind her back, under her gown.

She had thought long and hard about this plan. Without real proof it could easily backfire. But if it worked, she could sow enough doubt to save her son. And that was how the game was played. Not to be fair or decent, but to win. She smiled briefly at her victim.

'Good morning, David. Now, you've told the court how Jasmine left Simon and came to live with you. When you first met her, did you have another girlfriend?'

'Not really. I'd been out with some nurses, but I didn't have a proper girlfriend, no.'

'No girlfriend living with you?'

'Oh no.' He shook his head vehemently.

'In fact, had you ever lived with a girl before Jasmine Hurst?'

'Well, no . . . not actually lived with anyone before, no.'

'So this was something really rather special for you?'

'Special? Oh yes, very special indeed. I loved her.'

'She was very beautiful, wasn't she?'

'Oh yes, she . . . could have been a film star, easily.'

'And she was a little older than you, I think?'

'A couple of years older, yes.'

She was surprised how comfortable he seemed with these personal questions. If she hadn't been his enemy, she might have felt sympathy for him. She pressed a little harder.

'Did you want to marry her?'

'If she wanted . . . yes, sure . . . I'd have been happy . . .' His eyes filled with tears. Hard to fake, Sarah thought. But it happens; fathers kill their own children and weep afterwards.

'You were deeply in love with her, is that right?'

'Yes.'

'In fact you'd have done anything, anything at all, to keep her?'

'Yes, of course.'

'So when she said she was going to leave you, you must have been deeply upset.'

'Yes, I . . . what do you mean?' For the first time a frown crossed his brow, as if he guessed where the questions might lead.

'You didn't only quarrel with Jasmine that Thursday morning, did you? You quarrelled two days before.'

'No, we . . . not really a quarrel, no.'

'You quarrelled at the protest camp. Isn't that right? You were screaming at each other.'

'It . . . we . . .' It struck him that she would only say this if she had witnesses. 'We did shout a bit, yes. But it was just a silly quarrel. Only words.'

'Only words.' Sarah let the implication sink in. 'I see. What was it about?'

'About? Oh, silly things . . . I'm a very tidy person, and sometimes that annoyed her. I don't see why, really, I mean that was something she *liked* about me at first. She said it was better than the filth in his – your son's house.'

'Anything else?'

'Well, of course I'm not as big as him, as crude. She said she liked strong guys, but she didn't really, she was just winding me up . . .'

'Did it make you angry when she said those things?'

'Well, more hurt than angry, I suppose. But it wasn't true. She loved me really . . .'

'But in this quarrel, she said she was tired of you and was going to leave. Isn't that right?'

'I don't remember.'

'Well, that's what other people heard. Are you saying they're wrong?'

'People say all sorts of crazy things in quarrels. They don't always mean them.'

'But they do sometimes. The truth is you quarrelled with her and you were afraid she might leave you. That's right, isn't it?'

'No, she couldn't – I loved her.'

'But she did though, didn't she? She went back to Simon and made love to him.'

As Sarah had expected, Phil Turner rose to his feet. 'My lord, I fear my learned friend is straying into fantasy. There is no evidence for any of this and she is harassing the witness.'

Sarah faced the judge firmly. 'My lord, I have witnesses to substantiate all these points. My son claims that Miss Hurst returned to his home and made love to him frequently, and I have a witness to this quarrel and to Mr Brodie's state of mind at the time. Since his own evidence makes several claims about my son's state of mind and alleged motivation, it would seem fair to question his also.'

Judge Mookerjee considered, then nodded. 'Very well, Mrs Newby. Continue.'

Sarah drew a deep, grateful breath. 'That's true, isn't it, Mr Brodie? She didn't just talk to Simon, she was unfaithful to you, wasn't she? She even teased you about it. She said Simon was more of a man, a better lover than you.'

'No, she didn't. She wouldn't do that.' He was very upset now. Pale, anxious, distressed.

'I suggest that's exactly what she did. Jasmine could be cruel, couldn't she?'

'No. Don't say that about her. She didn't mean it.'

'Did you follow her, after these quarrels? To see where she went?'

'I don't . . . I . . .' Clearly this question came as a shock. Sarah watched, and waited. 'I . . . did follow her once, yes. I saw her near his – your son's house. I watched her go in.'

'Only once? Or more than once?'

'I . . . followed her a few times, yes. I'm not proud of it.' He looked around court, afraid, suddenly; his performance was going wrong but the audience were still there.

'When she went into Simon's house, what did you do?'

'I . . . waited outside a bit, then I went home. I was upset.'

'Yes. So when Jasmine came home, what then? Did you tell her you'd followed her?'

'She found out. She saw me once. She . . . she laughed at me.'

'How did you feel then?'

'Hurt.' He looked down, embarrassed. 'I just wanted her to come back to me, that's all.'

'I see. And apart from following her, how did you try to make her do that?'

'I . . . the same as I always did. I'd try to be nice to her, make her feel secure and happy in my home. That's where she belonged. It was a safe place, clean and decent, not a pigsty like his . . . your son's home. I treated her decent.'

'So the more cruelly she treated you, the more you tried to please her.'

'Is that wrong? I loved her.'

'And she twisted you round her little finger. When she saw Simon following her, she wasn't frightened, she was amused. And she laughed when you did it too, didn't she?'

'You make her sound horrible. She wasn't like that.'

'She played with people, didn't she? She played with you both.'

'She wasn't playing with me. I was trying to make her see sense. I loved her.'

'Exactly. So it must have made you angry when you followed her and saw her going into Simon's house to make love to him. Were you angry?'

' Of course I was angry, but . . . I knew if she'd stay with me, she'd get over it in the end.'

'But on that day when you argued at the protest, Tuesday 11th May, she told you she was leaving, didn't she?'

'Yes, but . . . she'd said that before. I didn't believe her. I knew she'd come back – it was on her way back that he killed her!' The court was hushed, completely silent now.

'You say my son killed her, but you have no evidence to prove that, do you, David? It could have been someone else, who also had a motive. Couldn't it?'

'Well, who else could it be?' He looked around, desperate, astonished. 'For Christ's sake, you're not suggesting *me*, surely? That's crazy! I mean, *he* hit her, remember? I never did that.'

And so he'd said it himself, without her having to accuse him. The atmosphere in court was electric. She felt the crackle of attention all round her.

'On the morning she died, where did she say she was going?'

'To the protest. But it wasn't true. I went there myself to check.'

Sarah smiled grimly. 'So what did you do then, David? Did you go to Bramham Street to spy on her, as you'd done before?'

'*No!* I didn't. I wanted to, but I thought . . . there's no point. I went straight to work.'

'Really?' Sarah shook her head, disbelievingly. 'And while you were at work, you forgot all about Jasmine, did you?'

'*No!*' Once again, tears filled his eyes and he fumbled for a tissue. 'I was upset, of course I was.' Sarah thought of the pain she was inflicting, then instantly hardened her heart.

'So you were upset about Jasmine. What time did you leave work that night?'

'At the end of the shift. Ten o'clock.'

'What did you do then?'

'I cycled home.' He watched her warily again.

'But you'd been thinking about Jasmine all evening at work, you say. Did you go to Bramham Street on your way home?'

'No.'

'Didn't you, David? Why not? How could you resist the urge to stand outside, see if the bedroom light was on, see if you could hear her laughing with him?'

'I told you, I didn't go. Anyway I thought she might have come home.'

'But she hadn't, had she? Did you go out again, to look for her?'

'No. Of course not. There was no point.'

'Because you knew where she was?'

'I thought I did, yes.'

'You didn't go back along the cycle path by the river, where Jasmine's body was found?'

A soft indrawing of breath ruffled the air as the point of Sarah's question became clear.

'*No!* I wish I had, I might have saved her!'

'Did you cycle home that way?'

'No. Not that day.'

'Why not?'

'It was dark. I don't go that way when it's dark.'

'But it's a route you know well?'

'I use it sometimes, yes.'

'And Jasmine used it too?'

'She did, but I told her not to use it after dark, for that exact reason. Anyone could be hiding in the bushes. A monster like him!' He glared at Simon.

'I see. So you knew that this was a route that Jasmine used, and you thought it was exactly the sort of place where a murderer or rapist might attack her. Is that right?'

'Yes.'

Sarah drew a deep breath. Almost there. 'So if the idea had come into your head to murder Jasmine, you'd have known exactly the right place to choose. Wouldn't you, David?'

His face paled in horror. 'You're mad! I didn't kill her! Simon did!'

'So you say. But there was no one with you, was there, David? No one who can support this story that you didn't use the cycle path, or go out again to look for Jasmine late that night?'

'No. But it's all true. For Christ's sake!'

Turner was back on his feet. 'My lord, I really feel that this has gone far enough. My learned friend is badgering this witness without a shred of evidence to support these allegations. She is causing great distress to no purpose.'

Resolutely, Sarah faced the judge, on whose face was a clear expression of distaste. 'I have made no allegations, my lord, none. I have accused this witness of nothing; he has accused himself. I have merely sought to establish that he has the motive, the opportunity, and the lack of alibi, precisely that which is alleged against my son.'

Judge Mookerjee contemplated her, considering the situation before him. But before he could decide, Sarah resumed. 'Anyway, my lord, I have no more questions for this witness. So if I am causing distress, it is ended.'

The judge nodded, relieved. 'In that case, Mr Brodie, you may stand down.'

David Brodie stood there, irresolute, shaking. He half turned to go, then changed his mind and faced Sarah again. His hurt, bitter voice carried clear across the court.

'I loved Jasmine, and your son killed her. You know it, too, don't you? Bitch!'

Amid the excited buzz of conversation, Sarah turned to look at Simon. Directly above him, watching from the public gallery, was her husband, Bob.

38

Since the start of the trial Sarah had felt stared at. It was not just the cameras outside – everywhere within the building people were aware of her, either watching her openly or from the corners of their eyes. She was on public view. But today was worse than ever. As the court emptied for the lunchtime recess, she could feel the eyes feeding on her, hundreds of them.

She shivered as she came into the crowded lobby, where journalists, security guards, students, police and witnesses were milling around indiscriminately. Lucy squeezed her arm.

'That was a tough thing to do.'

'Tell me about it. Oh Christ, look out. Left turn, quick.'

David Brodie was a yard away, speaking indignantly to his solicitor. When he saw Sarah he stepped impulsively forward. 'You're a bitch, you know that? A rotten stinking cow! I never killed her and you know damn well I didn't –'

'David, David, come on. You'll make things worse . . .' The solicitor caught his arm, while Sarah and Lucy slipped past them out of the front door straight into the huge black eye of a TV camera. A smartly dressed young woman thrust a microphone in Sarah's face.

'Mrs Newby, how did the trial go this morning?'

'No, sorry, not today.' Lucy dragged Sarah down the steps and away, the camera filming them but making no attempt to follow. It was then that Bob appeared.

'Sarah, can I have a word?' His face under the beard looked grim.

'We're just off to lunch, Bob.'

'Fine, I'll come too.'

'This is a surprise, Bob.' Sarah kept walking briskly. 'How will the school manage?'

'For a day, it'll have to. Sarah, what the hell were you doing in there?'

'Defending Simon, of course. How can you ask?'

They stopped by a bench on the quay. Lucy watched awkwardly.

'You were destroying that young man's reputation!'

'I'll do whatever it takes, Bob. That's the name of the game.'

'But *he* didn't kill her. You know he didn't. Christ, you could see how upset he was.'

'Guilty people get upset too, you know.'

He shook his head sadly. 'You don't believe it, though, do you? Not for a minute.'

She faced him grimly. 'Don't I, Bob? How many more times? It's not a question of what I believe, it's what I can do for Simon that counts. How much doubt I can raise in the minds of the jury. That's what this morning was about.'

'Well, you may as well know that you didn't raise any doubts in my mind with that performance. Just the opposite. If I were on the jury I'd be *more* likely to think Simon's guilty, if that's the best defence you can offer.'

And he was gone, striding swiftly away without a backward glance.

*   *   *

Phil Turner's last witness was Miranda Hurst, Jasmine's mother. The court fell silent as she made her way quietly to the witness stand. A tall blonde woman in a plain black suit and gloves, she took the oath in a soft voice with one hand on the testament. Despite her make-up there were dark smudges beneath her eyes. Turner began gently.

'Mrs Hurst, I realize how painful this is for you. I will ask as few questions as possible.'

'Thank you.'

'Would you say you had a close relationship with your daughter, when she was alive?'

'Fairly close, yes.'

'She was twenty-three, wasn't she? She'd left home some years before. Did she still visit you and discuss things from time to time?'

'Oh yes. She was a good girl that way. She came every week or so. Sometimes we'd meet for a swim and have lunch or go shopping after.'

As Sarah watched, she wondered why she had never met this woman while Jasmine was alive, and whether it might have made a difference, if they'd been able to talk. But then, she'd never really liked Jasmine, and she doubted if this woman had ever had much time for Simon.

'Did you talk about her boyfriends sometimes?'

'Yes, we did.'

'Did you meet them?'

'Yes. I met him.' She pointed at Simon, in the dock. 'And David. Both of them.'

'What was your attitude to Simon Newby? Did you like him?'

Here we go. Conscious of the eyes watching her, Sarah made her face a neutral mask.

'Bit of a layabout I thought. Nice to look at but no guts.'

'Did you tell Jasmine what you thought?'

'Yes. But she wouldn't listen, would she? Girls that age, they do what they want.'

'Indeed.' Turner smiled sympathetically. 'As you got to know Simon better, did your opinion about him change?'

'Changed for the worse, yes.'

'Why?'

'Well, his house for one thing. It was a tip. I'd brought Jasmine up proper, I didn't want to see her in a pigsty with beer cans all over the floor. But the worst thing was he beat her. I should have stopped it then.'

'When?'

'When I saw the bruises. We went swimming one day and she had a great black bruise on her arm. I asked her why and she said they'd had a fight. Simon had done it.'

A murmur, a vast collective intake of breath, passed through the court. There's another serious blow, Sarah thought.

'What did you do?'

'I said she should come home to me. But she just laughed. She wouldn't listen.' Until now Mrs Hurst's voice had been quiet, but it suddenly rose to a shout. She pointed at Sarah. 'It's *her* fault! His mother sitting there all prissy in her wig! If she'd spent more time at home bringing up her son decent instead of sticking her nose in law books, none of this would have happened!'

Another murmur, louder than before. This is a massacre, Sarah thought. She kept her face perfectly still, expressionless. Phil Turner glanced sideways at her, then continued.

'Were you afraid for your daughter, when you saw these bruises?'

'Of course I was. What mother wouldn't be?'

But did you ring me, Sarah thought? Did you tell me about all this when I might have stopped it? No. Did I see the bruises myself? No again.

'Very well. Her other boyfriend, David Brodie. What's your attitude to him?'

'A decent lad. A sight better than Simon. Better for Jasmine too, if she'd stuck by him.'

'To your knowledge, was he ever violent towards your daughter?'

'Who, David? No, never. He's not that sort.'

So there goes this morning's effort, Sarah thought. Wrecked in a single confident remark.

'Jasmine wasn't afraid of him, was she?'

'Her? No. She could twist him round her little finger.'

Now there's a true saying.

'To your knowledge, was Jasmine ever afraid of Simon?'

'Well, when she left him to move in with David, he was very angry. He came round, in a filthy rage, to see if she was with me. She hid upstairs and I told him she wasn't there.'

'What did Simon do?'

'He didn't believe me. He wanted to go upstairs but I wouldn't let him. I had a fair job to get him out the house, but he went in the end.'

'Were you afraid?'

'Angry, more like. I told him I'd clatter him with the broom if he stayed in my kitchen. I would have too!'

A woman in the jury nodded furious agreement.

'What about Jasmine? Was she afraid of him then?'

'She must have been, mustn't she, or she wouldn't have hid. But she wouldn't let on, she's not that sort. Wasn't, I mean . . .' For the first time, her voice broke, and she fumbled in her bag for a tissue. Turner waited while she blew her nose loudly.

'She had a good laugh about it after, the silly girl. If only she'd had more sense . . .'

'I'm sorry, Mrs Hurst. I do understand how you feel. I have no more questions, my lord.'

Judge Mookerjee nodded. 'Very well. Would you like a break, Mrs Hurst? I think fifteen minutes would do us all a lot of good, don't you? Then Mrs Newby may have some questions.'

Of all the witnesses Sarah had to cross-examine, this was the one she dreaded most.

Whatever Jasmine's failings – and there had been many – she had been this woman's daughter, and now she was dead. Sarah remembered her own feelings in the mortuary, expecting to find Emily under that sheet. It had been the worst horror of her life, but she had been rescued from it. This woman had not. She had gone to the same place, been confronted with the same body on a trolley, and when the sheet had been pulled back there had been the cold face of the child she had carried, nurtured and loved for twenty-three years.

And she believed Sarah's son had killed her.

As the court reassembled, Sarah stood up. There were no butterflies now; just a grey feeling of dread. I can't offer her sympathy, she thought. She would just spit it back in my face. I must be as quick and clinical as I can. Across the courtroom, she met Jasmine's mother's eyes.

'Mrs Hurst, when did you last see your daughter alive?'

'Two – no three days before.'

'Before she died?'

'Yes.'

'What were the circumstances of this meeting?'

'She came to my house for a cup of tea and a chat. She often did that. Kept in touch.'

As Simon didn't. Sarah understood the implied message.

'Was she there long?'

'An hour. An hour and a half maybe.'

'Time for a good chat then. In this conversation, did she say anything about Simon?'

'About your son? Yes.' Mrs Hurst's mouth closed shut.

'What did she say?'

'That she were still seeing him.'

'Did she say that she intended to move back in with him?'

'No. Thank God. Just that she were seeing him.'

'And did you approve of this?'

'*You ask me that?* You've got a nerve.'

The venom in the reply shook Sarah. For a moment she was lost for words. While she floundered, Judge Mookerjee leaned forward to speak to the witness.

'I appreciate how difficult this is for you, Mrs Hurst, truly. But please confine yourself to answering the questions, as straightforwardly as you can. You don't have to look at Mrs Newby. You can look at me if you prefer.'

Mrs Hurst nodded bitterly. 'Of course I didn't approve. I wish she'd never met him.'

'Very well.' Never had Sarah been more grateful for the gift of controlling her voice. Her knees were trembling like jelly and her feet wanted to run but her voice stayed calm. 'And did you give her that advice?'

'I'd told her before. She knew what I thought. It made no difference.'

'She was going to see him anyway?'

'She was. Sadly.'

'Did she seem anxious about this? Worried in any way?'

'About going to see him? No, not particularly.'

'Very well. Now you've told the court about bruises you once saw on her arm. Did she have any bruises on this occasion?'

'She had a jacket on. I wouldn't have seen, would I?'

'Did she tell you about any bruises she'd received?'

'No. But then she never had done. I only saw them by chance, like.'

'But that was only once, wasn't it?'

'So? Once is enough, in my opinion.'

'When was it exactly, that you saw these bruises?'

'Oh, three or four months before, maybe. When she lived with him, then she had them.'

'All right.' Sarah drew a deep breath. The first part of this ordeal was nearly over. 'Would it be fair to say, then, that when you last saw Jasmine, you saw no signs of bruising on her body; she didn't talk about being hit or beaten in any way; and she told you she was seeing Simon regularly, of her own free will. She didn't say she was afraid of him at all.'

Miranda Hurst glared at Sarah bitterly, then looked away, as she'd been advised, towards the judge. 'If you want to twist things you can put it like that, I suppose.'

'Is any part of it untrue?'

'Not in so many words, no.'

'Very well. The only other thing I want to ask you about is David Brodie. Did she talk about him on the last day you saw her?'

'She did, yes.' Mrs Hurst looked at Brodie sadly. 'She said she was going to leave him.'

'Did she say why?'

'She was tired of him, she said. She said he was too neat and . . . possessive.'

'Did she mention any quarrels they'd had?'

'She mentioned one or two, yes. Just words, though. Nothing violent. He couldn't hurt a fly, that lad. Not like yours.'

I'm losing it, Sarah thought. This could collapse into a cat-fight at any time. That's what this woman wants – to make me suffer. In her most neutral voice, she continued.

'So, to sum up, when you last saw Jasmine, she said she intended to leave David Brodie and had had several quarrels with him, and she was still seeing my son. Is that right?'

'Yes.' Miranda Hurst nodded cautiously, wondering where this was leading.

Nowhere, was the answer. She had arrived. Without a word, Sarah sat down.

After a moment, when she realized what was implied, Miranda Hurst began to shout angrily. 'But David didn't kill her, your son did! He's a filthy murdering sadist, whatever your lawyer's tricks in here! He killed her, the bastard, and you should be ashamed!'

There was nothing Sarah could do. She sat and waited for the judge to intervene, which he did, belatedly and with embarrassed reluctance. 'Mrs Hurst, I'm afraid that's all now. You really mustn't say any more, however upset you are. This court is grateful to you for giving your evidence but you should go with the usher and stand down now.'

As the usher took her gently by the arm and began to lead her away, the tears began to flow uncontrollably. In the well of the court, right in front of the jury, she looked across at David Brodie, and pointed directly at Sarah. 'You're right what you said, David. She's a first class bitch, she is, and everyone here should know it! Her son should have been drowned at birth!'

When she had gone, Phil Turner rose to his feet in the stunned silence.

'My lord, that concludes the case for the prosecution.'

'In that case . . .' Judge Mookerjee glanced at the clock, which stood at 3.25, then back at Sarah, sitting white-faced like a stone. '. . . although it may be a trifle early, in view of the somewhat emotional nature of this afternoon's evidence I think it might be best for all concerned if we were to adjourn until tomorrow morning. If that suits you, Mrs Newby?'

Sarah stood, stiffly. 'Indeed, my lord.'

'Then let us call it a day.'

The judge rose to his feet, the usher called, 'All stand!' and the hubbub began.

39

'I'm trying to establish reasonable doubt,' Sarah insisted. 'And it seems to me that these two witnesses, together with Brodie's own testimony, do exactly that.'

'Hm.' Judge Mookerjee listened thoughtfully, then turned back to the papers on his desk. Sarah and Phil Turner were in front of him, discussing the admissibility of evidence for the defence. The papers on the desk were an outline of the statements given to Lucy by two witnesses whom Sarah wanted to put on the stand – the eco-warrior, Mandy Kite, and a nurse, Ian Jinks.

Mandy Kite, after prolonged persuasion, had agreed to tell the 'pigs' court' about David Brodie's furious argument with Jasmine two days before she was killed, and that he had threatened to 'sort her out' on the morning she'd died. She would also say that once when she'd been with Jasmine they'd been followed by someone who might have been Simon but might equally well have been David.

Ian Jinks was a nurse whom Larry and Emily had found. He was prepared to testify about the change David's relationship with Jasmine had created in him; at first he had been delighted, ecstatically happy, then increasingly worried and anxious as he began to suspect that she was still seeing Simon. On the night Jasmine was killed Brodie, according to Jinks, had been angry and upset, unable to do his work properly. Just before he left he had said he would like to 'cut someone's head off' which was quite out of character.

'My lord, my learned friend intends to use these two witnesses simply to accuse Brodie,' Phil Turner insisted. 'There is no direct relevance to the guilt or innocence of her son.'

'That seems a reasonable interpretation,' the judge murmured. 'Mrs Newby?'

It was not only reasonable but accurate, Sarah knew. That was exactly what she wanted to do. Her problem was the second part of Turner's statement. What connection did these witnesses have to *Simon*?

'Their testimony is entirely relevant, my lord,' she insisted earnestly. 'This trial is about whether or not my son murdered Jasmine Hurst. If I can demonstrate a reasonable possibility that the murder was committed by someone else, then clearly that is evidence that the jury should consider. If it's possible that Brodie killed her, then it's possible that my son didn't. There is a reasonable doubt.'

Turner frowned. 'The doubt is only reasonable if you can create a credible case for Brodie's involvement. As it is, you have no witnesses who put him anywhere near the scene.'

'Neither do you,' Sarah retorted. 'No one saw Simon anywhere near the body. Whereas Brodie lives just a quarter of a mile away.'

'True, but we have forensic evidence. Semen, blood on his trainers and the knife –'

'I've accounted for the blood and semen in cross-examination, Phil. You know I have.'

'So you say.' Turner laughed drily. 'It depends whether the jury believe your story or not. Anyway why would Brodie kill her?'

'Jealousy, of course!' Sarah faced the judge eagerly. 'This girl was playing them both along, they both had equal reason to be furious with her. That's the motive – the only motive – which the prosecution have to explain why Simon would kill her. Sexual jealousy. Well, these two witnesses give Brodie exactly the same motive – in fact, they show his jealousy was much stronger. The prosecution have no witnesses to say that Simon threatened to cut her head off.'

'He hit her, though, didn't he?' Turner interrupted. 'In full public view.'

'Yes . . . all right, he hit her, but Brodie was seen to scream at her and make threats.'

'Not necessarily against Jasmine though,' the judge pointed out. 'As I read Mr Jinks' statement it seems he was threatening to cut *Simon's* head off. If he meant it at all, that is.'

'It's not clear who he was threatening, my lord,' Sarah said despairingly. 'All I am asking is to put this witness on the stand, then Phil can cross-examine him as much as he likes. Let the jury decide.'

'Mr Turner?' The judge leaned back, folding his arms.

'I understand my friend's passion, my lord. But on balance, I believe her argument is flawed. This trial is to establish the guilt or innocence of *Simon Newby*, no one else. If there were a single shred of evidence to put Brodie near the body, then I would say yes, in the interests of justice it must be put before the jury. But there isn't. All she has is this suggestion of motive which, quite frankly, isn't good enough. As I see it, Brodie probably *was* in love with the girl and is genuinely heartbroken by her death. To allow further suggestions that he's the murderer, with no evidence to back it up, would seem to be an abuse of process. And rather cruel, too.'

Sarah shrivelled inside. 'But there *is* evidence, my lord. The evidence of these witnesses and his own cross-examination . . .'

Judge Mookerjee waved a hand to silence her. 'We've been through all that, Mrs Newby. And I agree with the prosecution. The evidence of these two witnesses sheds no light whatsoever on the actions and culpability of the accused, Simon Newby. So I shall exclude them.'

There was no more Sarah could do. She rose, and walked across the street to her chambers. Where she met Lucy, with a pen in one hand and a cheese sandwich in the other.

'Any luck?' she queried.

'No.' Sarah flung her wig down in disgust. 'We just lost half the defence before I've even started.'

Terry and Harry were in the car outside Gary's flat. When he arrived, they got out and followed him to his door. He turned and saw them. 'Oh no, not you again.'

'This isn't an arrest,' Terry said. 'For once. Just a few questions. Can we come in?'

'What if I say no?'

'We'll do it down the station.' Terry smiled. 'You choose.'

Gary scowled, and led them into a room decorated with beer cans and old plates of curry. 'That cow Sharon been complaining again, has she?'

'No.' Terry chose a seat carefully. 'It's about those pictures I showed you in the station. Of your mate Sean.'

'He's not my mate.' Gary opened the fridge for a can of export. 'Who says he is?'

'Well, quite a lot of people, as a matter of fact. Sharon, for one.'

'What does she know about him?' He supped his beer truculently.

'More than you'd think.' Terry studied the man's face, on which he thought he detected a sheen of anxious sweat . . . 'Oh come on, Gary, don't mess me about. This lad was your so-called alibi the night you raped Sharon. Remember?'

'I were found not guilty, copper.' Gary slammed the can down on his chair, bringing froth through its top. 'Christ, how many times? I did not rape Sharon. OK?'

'Yeah, yeah.' Terry sighed. 'And you weren't in prison with Sean either, I suppose?'

'I were locked up with five hundred and odd lads. Doesn't mean I knew 'em all, does it?'

'You shared a cell with this one. Sean Patrick Murphy. It says so here – look, on the prison records.' Terry held out a paper which Gary ignored. 'With his photo.'

'All right, so I did. What's that to do with you?'

'I need to talk to him, Gary. About some serious sexual assaults. That's why we're here.'

'We need your help to find him,' Harry put in.

'You must be bloody daft, the pair of you.' Gary shook his head in derision. 'You couldn't pin owt on me, so now you want to pin it on him. That's it, isn't it?'

'We'd remember your help,' Harry offered. 'Next time you were in trouble.'

'Yeah, right.' Gary took a long swig of his beer. 'As if I'm a stinking snitch. Which crimes, for instance?'

Was he going to bite, Terry wondered? As neutrally as he could, he said: 'You remember that woman who was murdered? Maria Clayton? You did some building work on her house.'

'And you thought I killed her, didn't you, Mr Bateson? Only I didn't, see.'

'Yes, well.' Terry looked at his hands. 'Sean delivered some tiles there, for Robson's.'

'So?'

'And he screwed her too, Gary. Same as you did. Almost.'

'She'd screw anyone, for money. Except you, maybe.'

Behind the routine insolence the man was interested now, Terry could see.

'It doesn't surprise you, that?'

'No. Why should it? That's what tarts are for.' There was no sign of surprise, Terry noted, no apparent awareness of Sean's sexual disability.

'And he delivered some more building materials to the student lodgings where Karen Whitaker lived. Remember her, Gary?'

'Her with the nudey pics? Yeah – you thought I chased her in't woods, didn't you? Prat!'

'Sean delivered on the day you found those pictures, Gary. Did you show them to him?'

'Might have done. So?' A look of devious cunning spread across Gary's face. 'Oh, I get it. You're after him for that, too, are yer? And the murder – is that it?'

'Maybe,' Terry admitted cautiously. 'Some evidence points that way.'

'Like the evidence that said I did it, eh?' He laughed bitterly. 'Where's that now, then?'

Terry hesitated. There was no easy answer. But if he had nothing to say Gary suddenly had plenty. His face flushed with anger as he realized what Terry was admitting.

'All these months you've been after me for them two and now you change your mind, just like that? What about a fucking apology then? And while you're about it you can drag that bitch Sharon in here to apologize too, instead of scratching me fucking face when I go to buy her a bloody drink!'

'Oh, come on, Gary, you did rape her! I've not changed my mind on that, no one has!'

Gary glared at him. 'You daft pillock! You don't know shit, do yer?'

This was going as badly as Terry had feared it might. He was glad he had Harry with him. 'Look, Gary, all I want is a bit of help to find this lad Sean. These are serious crimes we're investigating. If he's innocent, he's got nothing to fear. Where is he? Is he in York now?'

'Even if I knew, which I don't, you're the last person I'd bloody tell.' Gary supped his beer contemptuously. 'So if that's it, Mr Bateson, I suggest you take yon poodle and clear out of here. All right?'

Sarah's spare bedroom overlooked the drive, where Larry's old hatchback was parked. She could hear music in Emily's bedroom. The judge's ruling had upset the young people badly. They had found Ian Jinks and Mandy Kite, and believed that Brodie was Jasmine's killer. Sarah knew she should spend time talking through their disappointment. But time was something she didn't have, any more. Tomorrow she would put her only witness, Simon, on the stand. They had only one chance. If they messed it up, they would lose, for certain.

This room had once been Simon's. She sat at the desk they had bought for him to do his homework, checking her questions for tomorrow, imagining his answers, puzzling over the most effective way to present his case. She made notes, pressing the pencil hard into the paper.

Annoyingly, the lead snapped. She searched the desk drawers for a sharpener. Nothing useful, of course. The first drawer was empty, the second contained motorcycle magazines – the sort where the female riders wore boots and nothing else – the third contained an old brown envelope. Idly, she emptied the contents on to the desk.

It was full of old photographs. Surprised, she spread them out. They were almost all of Simon as a child. Simon aged five, going to school; Simon playing football in the park at Seacroft; Simon with bucket and spade in Blackpool, on a rare family holiday; Simon in Bob's mother's kitchen with his face covered with chocolate, trying to bake a cake. They were photographs she hadn't seen for years.

The door opened softly behind her and Bob came in. 'What are you doing?'

She sighed. 'I was writing my notes. Then I found these.'

'What are they?' He came to look, over her shoulder.

'They were in Simon's drawer. He must have put them there, once upon a time.'

'Are they all of him?'

She sifted through some more: Simon holding baby Emily in his arms; Simon and Bob reading a book; Simon in a Leeds United football shirt.

'It looks like, it, yes,' Sarah said. 'I didn't know we had so many.'

'That's because he's put them here. They must have meant something to him, at the time.'

'Yes.' A painful thought struck her. 'There don't seem to be many of me.'

It was true. There were plenty of Simon alone; a few of him with grandparents or Bob; but only two of him with Sarah. One was of Simon as a baby, clutched in the arms of a miniskirted Sarah who looked younger than Emily was today; and the other was of a gangly teenager, standing sullenly beside a beaming mother in mortar board and gown receiving her law degree.

'Where are the rest?' she murmured, distressed. 'Surely there are more than this?'

'Maybe he took them with him.'

'Or maybe there weren't any. I was always so busy studying, I didn't have time. He said that to me in prison, a while ago.'

'Well, you're making up for it now,' said Bob softly.

'Yes, years too late.' She shovelled the photos back into the envelope and picked up her pad, then threw it down in disgust. 'What does it matter? I'm as ready now as I ever will be.'

She saw a stray photo under the pad, and pulled it out. It was of Bob, lying on the ground between two goalposts, having failed to save a shot from a triumphant ten-year-old Simon.

'He was your project, in those days.' She turned to face him. 'What happened, Bob?'

'He grew past the point where I could help him. Now only you can.'

'*If* I can,' she muttered, feeling the grey despair leak into her soul. 'Bob, about today . . .'

'Let's not talk about it. I shouldn't have poked my nose in.'

'I only did it for Simon.'

'I understand that. You're the lawyer, I'm not. Only . . .' He shook his head.

'Only it was a cruel thing to do to David Brodie. Is that what you were going to say?'

'Sarah, please. I don't want to quarrel.'

'Of course you're right. I'm not so stupid that I can't see that, Bob. The trouble is that being a lawyer makes you see morality . . . in a more complex way than you probably do.'

For a while they sat silent. Emily's bedroom door opened and footsteps went downstairs.

'Well, there's an admission. You mean you don't really think Brodie did it at all?'

'There's no proof that he did, Bob, is there?'

'So who did it then, if Simon didn't?'

'God knows. But all that's left, now, is his assertion that he didn't. Tomorrow he's going to try to make the jury believe him. If he can't do that, he's finished.'

There was another, longer silence. Outside the window, they heard Larry and Emily talking quietly. Then Larry's car door slammed and he drove away. Emily came upstairs and went into her bedroom.

Bob put his hands on her shoulders, kneading the tense muscles gently. 'I'd hate to do what you do. You carry the whole world on these, don't you?'

He used to be good at this, she remembered. Before they both became so busy, and the children tore them apart. She leaned into the massage, letting her arms relax.

'You don't have to sleep in here, you know,' he said after a while. 'It makes me lonely too. Why not come back and join me?'

'All right, maybe I will.' She touched his hand to stop him, kissed his fingers and straightened up. 'I'll come when I've finished this.'

Two hours later, she crept into bed beside her sleeping husband.

40

Simon walked quite calmly to the witness stand. His face was pale, but that was a prison pallor due to months on remand. He read the oath in a clear, slightly subdued voice. Then he looked up, taking in the crowded public gallery, full of eyes that had been above him in the dock, and focused his attention on his mother.

She began at the heart of the matter.

'Simon, you have heard the prosecution claim that you murdered Jasmine Hurst. Is that true? Did you kill her?'

'No, I did not.' The voice was firm, a little louder than before. The jury, she knew, were watching and listening intently; not so much for what he said, but for the conviction with which he said it.

'Do you know who killed her?'

'No. How could I?'

This was the answer she had planned and rehearsed with him. Simple, and true. But then, to her surprise, he glared pointedly at David Brodie. 'I've got my ideas but no proof.'

They had already discussed this idea and rejected it. Sarah feared that any further attempt to accuse Brodie was likely to backfire. She thought Simon had been convinced. Clearly not, however. They'd planned everything and here he was already striking out on his own.

'Did you love Jasmine?' she continued coolly.

'Love her? Yes.' He appeared to consider the idea for a moment, then repeated himself with more emphasis. 'I did. Yes.'

Careful, Simon, she thought. Don't start acting now. She had warned him against this, but the witness stand did strange things to people, particularly those facing life imprisonment.

'Would you tell the court, in your own words, exactly what happened on Thursday 13th May. From the beginning.'

Simon drew a deep breath, and faced the jury, as she had suggested. 'Well, I was off work, so I had a lie in, like, until about nine thirty. Then I got up and went for a run.'

'Where did you go for your run?'

'Where I often go. Down the river opposite the Archbishop's Palace. Past where she were found that night. So if there were mud and such on my shoes, that's where I got it, see?'

She sighed. His fake worker's accent had become stronger. *Idiot!*

'You were wearing these training shoes that were shown in evidence, were you?'

''Course I were. They're my shoes, aren't they? What else would I wear?'

For Christ's sake, Simon, she wanted to scream, I'm not arguing with you, I'm here to help you. 'All right. What happened then?'

'Well, when I got back, I met her. Jasmine. She was by the river not far from my house.'

Better now. Less accent, less truculence. Perhaps it had just been stage fright. She nodded encouragingly. 'Were you expecting to meet her?'

'Not exactly. She came to see me sometimes but I never knew when.'

'Was she coming to see you then?'

'She said she was. Yeah.'

'How did she look?'

'Stunning, like always.' He glanced at the jury, then realized he'd misunderstood the question. 'Oh . . . well, a bit angry, or upset. I asked what's up and she said she'd had a row with David, like. Anyhow, she came in.'

'What happened then?'

'I had a shower, she made some tea, and we talked for a bit. Nothing special, really.'

'Had she visited you like this before, while she was living with David?'

'A few times, yeah.'

'What usually happened on these visits?'

'Well, we'd chat for a bit, maybe have a meal, then we'd go to bed together, and sometime later she'd . . . leave.'

A shaven-headed male juror, she noticed, was nodding approvingly. This sounds normal to him, then, at least. 'Is that what happened this day?'

'Yes. We had a bite to eat, and then . . . she took her clothes off . . . you know.'

'You had sexual intercourse?'

'If that's what you call it, yes. I shagged her.'

There was a snort of suppressed laughter. *Jesus*, Simon! Of all the words to use, why pick that one? The point of this is not to shock your mother, but to ingratiate yourself with the jury. The younger jurors, she saw, looked amused, but several others looked distinctly disgusted. Phil Turner smiled ironically.

Now another key question. 'So, to be quite clear, Simon, was this sexual intercourse something you both wanted? Or did you force it upon her?'

'No, of course not. She wanted it – why else did she take her clothes off like that? That's why she came. She knew what was going to happen.'

'So you didn't rape her?'

'No, not at all. Nothing like it.'

She could almost hear the jury's minds working. Is this man lying or not? All they had to go on was their experience of life – similar situations, similar young men to Simon.

'The forensic pathologist has described some bruises which he found inside her vagina. Can you account for those?'

'Not really, no. I mean, I didn't hurt her, if that's what you're saying. She liked it, she always did.' He hesitated. 'I mean, maybe it bruised her when she got excited but I wouldn't know that, would I? She didn't complain.'

'Did you wear a condom?'

'No. She were on the pill. She said.'

Such questions for a mother to ask her son, in public. Sarah remembered the childhood photos she had found last night. 'All right. What time of day was this?'

'Early, mid-afternoon maybe. Hard to say. We went to bed and I fell asleep. Maybe she did as well. Then we went for a walk, bought some Chinese. I thought . . . I thought it was a real good day. Then when we came back it went wrong.'

'What went wrong?'

'Well, like I say we were getting on fine. She was saying what a pain David was with all his tidying and fussing, and I *knew* he couldn't screw her like I did, she told me that every time, it was quite a joke with her really . . . so I thought she might leave him and come back for good. She said she would, too; I remember it clearly. I was really happy.

'But then, after the Chinese, she looked at her watch and said she'd have to go. So I said "Go where?" And she said, "To David, of course. You don't think I could live in this pigsty, do you? He'll have the bed made and the house all nice" – you know, stuff like that. And I was so angry, then. It was like she'd kicked me right in the guts. So I yelled at her. I said she'd promised to stay and we'd had a great time, but she just laughed. She said that was part of the game, something like that, it would make it even better next time because I'd want her even more. And that made me sick because I saw she'd been doing this all the time and probably did the same to David too, she was just a bitch, I said that . . . I wish I hadn't now but I did . . .'

For part of this speech he had been talking to the jury, then turning back to her and even the judge and the people in the well of the court, as though he wanted to convince everyone of what he was saying. For the first time Sarah felt it might work, that people might really believe her son and understand him. But they might also realize he had just described a perfect motive for killing Jasmine. They had seen her mutilated body. Now here he was calling her a bitch. Pray God Jasmine's mother's not here. 'And then what happened?'

'She just walked out. I tried to stop her but she was too quick, she was outside. That's probably when that nosy old git was cleaning his teeth and heard us shouting. Anyway I tried to pull her back in and she clouted my face with her bag – he didn't see that, did he? But that's why I hit her back, because it hurt. Anyway she was such a bitch, to go like that after all she'd said. So then I went back in and . . . that's the last I saw of her.'

'You never saw her again?'

'No.'

There was a collective relaxation around the court, as though a key moment had passed. But what conclusions had people drawn, Sarah wondered? That was the mystery.

'So what did you do then?'

'Nothing special. I just mooched around indoors thinking about how she'd behaved. I was all, like, churned up inside. Then after a while I went out and got in the car.'

'Why did you do that?'

'Well, I couldn't stay there. I had to go somewhere.'

'Where did you go?'

'Scarborough, in the end.'

'Why Scarborough?'

'Why not? It just happened, really. I turned left out of York and that's where I ended up. I went for a walk on the beach in the middle of the night. Quiet, it was. Just me and a pair of seals in the dawn. I'd never seen a seal before. I didn't know they had them in Scarborough.'

'What did you do in the morning?'

'Got breakfast, found somewhere to stay. Did a lot of thinking.'

'What were you thinking about?'

'What a mess my life was. How I could make a new start.'

'Did you think about Jasmine?'

'Yes. 'Course I did.'

'What did you think?'

'How I loved her. How beautiful she was and what a bitch she was to me and probably every other man she'd ever met, and what could you do if you loved someone like that. Whether I could break the habit of her like giving up smoking. Every day I stayed in Scarborough I thought I'd maybe won something. I thought I'd proved I could live without her and also maybe she was knocking on my door in York and feeling the same hurt I felt. I thought if I managed a month maybe I'd be cured of it. I could start a new life and never go back.'

'And you had no idea that she was dead?'

'No, of course not. No.'

'And you didn't murder her?'

'How could I? I was in Scarborough. I never saw her again after she left my house.'

Phil Turner glanced up, ready to cross-examine if she had finished. But she hadn't.

'All right, Simon. Let's examine a few details. You've told the court you wore your trainers to go running, and you've heard the forensic scientist describe how she found traces of Jasmine's blood on those trainers. Do you have any idea how that blood could have got there?'

'Well, all I can think is, it happened a few days before, on the Monday.'

'What happened then?'

'Well, the same thing, she came to my house then too. And after we'd made love, she was walking round the house in my shirt and those trainers – nothing else. Anyhow she was in the kitchen and I heard her call out, and when I went down she was swearing and sucking her thumb. She'd cut herself with the breadknife. So maybe some blood fell on to the trainers then.'

'Was there a lot of blood?'

'Not a lot, no. She ran it under the tap and I gave her a plaster and that was it really.'

'Did the blood get on the breadknife?'

'Yes. Some of it, anyhow. I noticed it next morning when I was washing up. There was a stain on the blade near the handle. I thought I'd washed it all off but obviously not . . .'

Pity about that, Simon, Sarah thought cynically. If you'd washed it off and put your shoes in the washing machine we'd never be here, would we?

'Why didn't you tell the police about this when they interviewed you?'

'I didn't think. I mean, it was nothing, just a tiny cut. I'd forgotten all about it. And then they were shouting at me and saying she was dead, for Christ's sake . . .'

'All right, let's talk about when you were arrested. What happened then?'

'Yeah, well. I was asleep, and then – in the middle of the night – there were these men in my room. It was like a weird nightmare. Men shouting and yelling over my bed.'

'What were they saying?'

'I don't know. I didn't get it, at first. Then one of them said Jasmine was dead but I didn't believe him. How could I?'

'Did they read the caution to you?'

'You're joking! They might have done, but I didn't know what was going on. I was terrified. I thought they were going to kill me at first, then they were saying Jasmine was dead and I'd killed her and they dragged me outside and shoved me in this car.'

Would the young men in the jury believe this? Sarah wondered. Surely some had had dealings with the police on a Saturday night. How well had they been treated? She continued with the standard questions with which a lawyer dissects a chaotic and confused situation.

'Did you understand that they were policemen?'

314

'They said they were but I couldn't believe it. I thought they were burglars or something.'

'Did they show you any identification?'

'No. They just handcuffed me and dragged me downstairs.'

'All right. What happened in the car?'

'They kept telling me Jasmine was dead and that I'd killed her. They were shouting, asking me questions – why was I in Scarborough, how did I kill her, where was I when she died?'

Lucy and Sarah had both insisted how important it was for Simon to emphasize this point. The lesson seemed to have gone home. The only danger was that he would overdo it.

'What was your state of mind at this time?'

'I was scared . . . I mean shit scared. I didn't know what was happening, it was like some awful nightmare. I just wanted to get out as fast as I could.'

'Did you answer those questions?'

'A bit, yeah. I said I hadn't killed her.'

'Did you say anything else?'

'Maybe. I don't know what I said, really, I was that scared. I was in a panic. I could have said anything; I just wanted to get out of there.'

'All right. What happened at the police station?'

'Well, Lucy – Mrs Parsons, my solicitor, came, and – I told her the truth. She told me to write a statement and sign it.'

Good, Simon, well done. Nearly there now. She risked a faint nod of encouragement.

'Did DCI Churchill show you another paper which he asked you to sign?'

'Yes.'

'Why didn't you sign it?'

'Because it wasn't true. His paper said I hadn't seen Jasmine for weeks and that wasn't true, I had. I saw her the day she died. But all I did was make love to her, I didn't kill her, for God's sake. I couldn't do that!'

That's all, then, Sarah thought. I can't end better than that.

'All right, Simon, wait there. Mr Turner will have some questions.'

She sat down, leaving him alone on the stand. Her hands began to tremble.

When Terry's phone rang, he didn't recognize the voice on the other end at first.

'Inspector Bateson?'

'Yes.'

'Miles Beelby, employment clerk at MacFarlane's. You remember, you spoke to me a while ago. About that Irish lad who once worked here.'

'Oh, yes.'

'Well, I was talking to a mate of mine at TransPennine, you know, the contractors for the designer outlet. He said a lad like that came in to him earlier this morning, asking for work.'

'What?' Terry sat up gripping the phone tightly. 'What happened?'

'Well, your luck's in. They need a bit of extra labour. So he's starting tomorrow.'

'Tremendous!' A smile began to spread across Terry's face. 'He didn't leave an address or phone number, anything like that?'

'No, sorry, usual caper. But if you ring this mate of mine he'll be able to tell you more. Frank Carrow, at TransPennine.'

'Right, Mr Beelby. Thanks for your co-operation. I'll ring him straight away.'

The usher took the paper from Phil Turner, and handed it to Simon.

'Do you recognize that, Mr Newby?'

'Yes.' Simon shrugged. 'It's something the police asked me to sign. In the station.'

'Would you read the last two sentences for me, please.'

Simon had never been a great reader. Somewhat laboriously, he read out: *'After being cautioned, Mr Newby stated that he had not killed Jasmine Hurst, and that he had not seen her for weeks. He repeated this statement several times.'*

'Is that true?'

It was an ambiguous question, Sarah saw at once. Presumably Turner intended it to confuse the witness and make him appear deceitful, whatever answer he gave.

'It, er . . . well, part of it's true. It's true that I didn't kill Jasmine. But the other part, no, that's not true. That's why I didn't sign it.'

Simon looked at Sarah, who nodded approval. Well done, you avoided the trap.

'So it's a lie?' Turner persisted.

'Part of it is, yes.'

Turner sighed ostentatiously, as though he were already weary of being deceived. 'To be clear, the part which you claim is a lie is where you say you hadn't seen her for weeks. Is that what you're saying?'

'Yes, that's right.'

'All right, Simon. But I'm still not quite sure I understand. Are you saying those words are a lie because you *didn't* say them, or because you *did* say them but when you got into the police station you realized they were untrue? Which is it?'

'I . . . I'm not sure.' The questions were like dogs running rings round a bull, Sarah thought, snapping at its heels to confuse and irritate it.

'Let me help you. You see, both detectives agree that you *did* say those words, but that in the police station you changed your mind and admitted that you had seen Jasmine on the day she died, after all. Is that what happened?'

316

'Yes, that's right.'

'Thank you. So your first response after you had been cautioned was to tell the policemen this lie. Then when you met your lawyer you changed your mind.'

'No, look, you're twisting things. I don't know what I said in the car, I was too scared. I don't know if I said those words or not.'

Simon flushed. Turner was deliberately trying to provoke him, Sarah thought.

'I think you *did* say them, Simon. I suggest that your very first response when the police arrested you was to tell them this lie. It was only when you met your lawyer that you realized that no one would believe it, so you changed your story. Only that story's a lie too, isn't it?'

'No, it's the truth.'

Turner was scarcely looking at Simon, Sarah realized. Much of the time he was watching the jury, or gazing above Simon's head, as though her son was beneath contempt. She felt his anger building, as Turner intended.

'All right, let's examine your second story, shall we? You say you went for a run by the river on the morning of the 13th, and that's why your trainers were stained with mud and grass. Did you meet anyone on your run?'

'Not before I met Jasmine, no.'

'So no one can confirm that part of your story. All right. Then you say you had a meal with Jasmine and went to bed together. There were no witnesses to this either, I suppose.'

'Of course not, no. We were alone, for fuck's sake.'

'For fuck's sake. Quite.' Turner smiled. 'And of course the only witness to this is dead. You say you made love and she enjoyed it. But that's just your word against hers, too, isn't it?'

'What?' Simon looked confused and angry.

'Well, you say she enjoyed it. But her body cries out that you're lying, doesn't it, Simon? Because her poor, murdered body has a bruised vagina. How did that happen, do you think?'

'How should I know?'

Turner shrugged. 'Well, you say you made love to her. Are you a brutal lover?'

'Bloody hell . . .' His face flushed, Simon gripped the stand in front of him. Turner waited, hoping that he would do something violent or stupid. Sarah searched for a reason to intervene, but could think of nothing.

'What does that mean? Yes or no?'

'It means . . . I don't know. I just made love to her, that's all.'

'*I shagged her* – I think that's what you said.'

'Yeah, well, whatever.'

'It sounds brutal to me. Do you mean you raped her?'

'No. I shagged her like I always did. It's what she came for – what we always did.'

'I suggest that you raped her. Either there in your house, or later beside the river path.'

'I've told you. *I didn't rape her.*'

'All right, that's your story.' Turner sighed, and paused for nearly half a minute, letting the jury think. 'But there was only one other person present, and her body tells a different story. *I have a bruised vagina*, her dead body cries out to us, *that shows you someone raped me.* Is Jasmine lying, then, Simon? Is that your story now? It's the evidence of her dead body that's lying, is it? Not you?'

'I don't know what you're talking about.'

'Don't you? Well, I think the jury do. They know that dead bodies can't lie. And they know that *you* can, because you lied to the police when they arrested you. The evidence from Jasmine's body says two things. It says you had sexual intercourse with her, and it says that she was raped. You're not claiming another man raped her, are you, Simon? Another man who mysteriously left no body samples, no pubic hair, no semen, no DNA? A man from Mars perhaps, who left bruises, and nothing else?'

'I don't know how she got the bruises.'

Sarah caught Simon's eye and smiled encouragement. Despite the incessant goading, he was doing better than she'd expected. He hadn't lost his temper, he hadn't shouted or screamed or taken refuge in some newly invented lie, which would have been the worst thing of all.

None of which altered the fact that Turner was doing very well indeed.

'All right. Let's look at another part of your story, shall we? You claim that the reason Jasmine's blood was on your trainers and your breadknife was that she cut her finger in your kitchen. Is that right?'

'Yeah. I think that's why it's there.'

'Were there any other witnesses to this accident? Apart from yourself and Jasmine?'

'No, of course not. We were alone in the house.'

'Again.'

'Yeah, so?' Simon sneered. 'That's just where it happened.'

'Very conveniently, the jury may think. You didn't mention this to the police when they interviewed you, did you? Although you're relying on it for your defence now.'

'No, well, I didn't think of it then. It was only a tiny cut. I didn't think it was important.'

'No. You came up with it later, when you needed to explain why Jasmine's blood could be on your trainer and your breadknife. The trouble is, once again all we have is your word for this fantastic story. Because the only other witness is dead.'

'I can't help that.'

'Nothing to do with you, you mean? The fact that she's dead?'

318

'No.'

'All right. Let's look at another aspect of your incredible story. What happened after you punched Jasmine in the face outside your house?'

'I didn't punch her. It was just a slap, for fuck's sake.'

Careful, Simon. Sarah frowned, hoping he would see her and keep the language clean.

'Just a slap, you say.' Turner tugged at his ear thoughtfully. 'Must have been some slap, to leave a great ugly bruise on her cheek like that.'

'It was a slap. After all, she hit me first, with her bag.'

'Oh, did she? Really. Did it leave a bruise?'

'No.'

'You didn't go to hospital to have it treated?'

'No . . .' Simon's answer was almost a growl.

'But for once we have a witness to this fight, Simon, don't we? Mr Mullen. And he doesn't agree with your story. He's quite clear. You hit Jasmine, he says. He didn't say anything about her hitting you.'

'No, well, he didn't see everything, did he?'

'So he's lying, is he? Not you, him.'

'I said he didn't see it all.'

'I see. Well, once again it's your word against his, isn't it? Because the only other witness is dead. With a bruise on her cheek from this slap of yours.'

This time, Simon didn't bother to answer. He simply folded his arms and stared silently at his tormentor. Turner avoided his gaze, looking down at his notes. Whatever the jury made of this, Sarah thought, it was unlikely to be helpful to Simon.

'All right, let's examine the rest of your story, shall we? After you slapped her, as you say, you got into your car, and drove away to Scarborough, all on your own. Where you arrived in the middle of the night, with only seals to see you. Correct?'

'The beach was empty, yeah.'

'So again, we have only your word for this too. And you stayed there for several days, without contacting anyone.' Turner put a foot on the bench beside him, and scratched his ear, as though he were genuinely puzzled. 'So remind me – why do you claim you ran away?'

Simon turned to the jury, as though this was something he *did* expect them to believe. 'After the quarrel with Jasmine, I was sick with the way she'd behaved. I couldn't take it any more. I wanted to get away, try to forget about her, make a new start.'

'You weren't sick of the way you'd behaved yourself?'

'Well, yeah, a bit. But she was teasing me, leading me on . . .'

'And that made you angry?'

'Yeah.'

'So when you went to Scarborough, did you contact anyone to tell them where you were? Your friends? Your parents? Your sister?'

'No.'

'Why not?'

'I wanted to be on my own.'

Turner scratched his head, rubbing a pencil under his wig. 'But you weren't angry with your friends or your family, were you? You were just angry with Jasmine?'

'Yes.'

'So why not ring someone and talk about it? Ring your friends, your sister, your mother here, your dad – tell them how she'd treated you, how you felt.'

Because my son's not like that, Sarah thought. Probably most young men aren't. As Phil Turner must know.

'I don't know. I was too angry. I didn't want to talk.'

'Jasmine had made you very angry then?'

'Yes. But I didn't kill her.'

'Didn't you?' If there had been any shred of irony or amusement in Turner's voice before, it had all drained away now. 'I think that's exactly what you *did* do, Simon. I suggest that your anger is the only true part of this whole story. Jasmine made you angry, all right. So angry that you couldn't control yourself. So angry that you punched her in the face in the street, and called her a bitch. So angry that you went to the river path where you knew she walked; and there you waited for her, raped her, cut her throat, and dumped her poor dead body in the bushes. That was the result of your anger, wasn't it?'

'No.'

The courtroom was utterly silent, a hundred eyes focused directly on Simon.

'After that you drove to Scarborough because you wanted to hide, to escape from this horrible thing that you'd done. And the reason you didn't phone your family or friends wasn't because you were still angry as you say. It was because your anger had turned to guilt and fear that you would be found out. That's the real truth, isn't it, Simon?'

'No, it's not. You've just twisted it all. I didn't kill her. I didn't even know she was dead until the police told me.'

Thank God, Sarah thought, he's not displaying any anger now. He's past anger, the moment is too serious. He's cold and certain and staring his enemy in the eye.

'Didn't you? And yet your first response to the police, your very first response, was to lie. Not to show grief about this girl you say you loved, but to try to save your own wretched skin. That's the truth, isn't it, Simon? You lied because you knew you were guilty.'

'I did show grief. I loved her. You don't understand that.'

'But you killed her.'

'No.'

'The evidence of her body says you killed her, Simon. Dead people don't lie.'

'Someone killed her all right, but it wasn't me. I didn't do it.'

'Oh yes, you did, Simon.'

'No.'

Turner sat down. The court was silent. The judge glanced at Sarah, who rose to her feet.

'That concludes the evidence for the defence, my lord.'

Simon had resisted as well as he could. There was nothing she could ask him that would improve matters, no further witness she was allowed to offer. Now everything would rest on the speeches from the lawyers.

'Very well. Mr Newby, you may return to the dock, if you will.'

As Simon walked past Sarah smiled at him encouragingly. The smile was partly for him, and partly for the jury. If you act as though you've won, people sometimes believe that you have.

41

It seemed ironic that it was such a beautiful morning. Sarah sat in bed, nursing a cup of tea and staring out at a clear blue autumn sky with wispy cirrus clouds high above. The river meadows were blanketed with silver mist, rising in wispy tendrils as the sun began to burn it off. A heron flapped lazily by, in search of its favourite fishing spot.

For Sarah, there was no comfort in any of it. As she got up, showered and dressed, her mind was running through her speech, as it had nearly all night. In her dreams the judge had dangled a hangman's noose with a ten-year-old Simon choking in it. The judge swung him to and fro as she stumbled and forgot her words.

Well, that's all rubbish, she told herself briskly. It's the jury that matters, anyway.

Bob groaned and sat up. 'How do you feel?' he asked blearily.

'Tense. On edge. Fighting fit.' She smiled at him in the mirror as she applied her lipstick.

'You'll do your best. You always do.'

'Yep,' she agreed. 'That's me.' It was like the day of her law finals, only ten times worse. She pulled on her motorcycle leathers. 'Wish me luck?'

'Yes . . . sure.' His hesitation hurt. 'May the jury make the right decision.'

'They will, Bob. They will.' Her eyes fierce and determined, she walked out into the beautiful, misty morning.

Terry's daughters were asleep when he left home that morning. Trude would take them to school. He reached the building site at half-past seven. It looked as if the eco-warriors had been defeated. Most of the trees had gone; there were big yellow machines and concrete foundations everywhere. The site manager met them at the gate, and Terry parked the car just inside. Terry and Harry accompanied him into the warmth of his office.

'You can sit by that window,' the man said, handing them tea in polystyrene cups. 'Anyway, he'll come in here first to punch his card. So you're bound to see him, aren't you?'

'Let's hope so,' said Terry, peering out through the grimy, wire-covered glass. 'We've been waiting long enough, after all.'

In the prison van, Simon sat in a tiny, claustrophobic cubicle. He hated it. Sometimes he felt his head would burst from the pressure of confinement.

But this would be his life, if he lost today. Confined for up to twenty hours a day in a room as big as a bathroom. And the nature of his crime would make it worse. Already he had been taunted and jostled by remand prisoners who knew what he was accused of, and being defended by his mother made things worse. If he was convicted, he could expect razor blades and excrement in his stew, beatings and rape in the shower. He would be on the special wing with paedophiles, rapists and other sex criminals, and if there was a prison riot – well, he would be one of the first targets.

Outside, the sun was burning the mists off the fields. He watched the cars and houses and people go by, as if they were in a foreign country.

Tracy Litherland sat in her car, fifteen yards from Gary Harker's front door. Terry had chosen her for this because she, unlike most of her colleagues, had no connection with Gary. She recognized him from the photographs but he, she hoped, was unlikely to recognize her. He would just see a woman in a car reading the *Daily Mail*.

Tracy feared that her car – a shiny blue Clio of which she was inordinately proud – might attract more attention. The car in front was a ten-year-old Sierra, the white van directly outside Harker's door had a wing rotten with rust. Several people had already peered inquisitively through her window.

And then, quite suddenly, Gary came out. He got straight into the white van, and drove away. Tracy began to follow him. It was probably pointless – he would go to work and that would be it. But Terry had insisted that they cover all angles and she, for once, had got the duff job. Ah well . . .

She kept the white van in view along the Fulford Road. It crossed the river by Skeldergate Bridge and headed into the warren of little streets by the Knavesmire. Tracy's interest began to rise. Surely he didn't work here? But she dared not get too close. She stayed back, and nearly lost him when he took a sharp turn down a back alley between the houses, designed for Victorian nightsoil men. If she followed down there he would definitely see her. But maybe . . .

She made a guess, turned left, and got stuck behind a bread van double parked outside a shop. She hooted her horn relentlessly until it moved, then turned left again into a street parallel to the one she had left. No white van. Damn! Where could he have gone? Sweating, she drove slowly along the street. Nothing. Then, in her rear view mirror, she saw the van pull out of the alley into the street behind her. Now *he* was following *her*.

Or rather *they*. As the van stopped behind her at a T-junction she saw two men in it. Staring directly at her. She studied them in the mirror. The man in the passenger seat turned to talk to Gary, and as he did so the sun lit his face clearly. That was him, surely – *Sean*, the man in the photofit! The shock paralysed Tracy so she didn't notice that the road was clear ahead. Gary hooted irritably.

Damn! Now I've really got their attention. Quickly, she pulled out into the main road. The white van followed close behind her.

Lucy adjusted Simon's tie critically. 'Not too bad. You look like a pop star.'

'A star with a prison record,' he muttered morosely. 'Great.'

'Come on, think positive.' She smiled encouragingly. 'You may be free tonight.'

'Do you think so? Really?'

Long experience had taught Lucy the raw earnestness of questions at a time like this. Simon was watching her intently as though a twitch of her mouth could determine his fate for ever. Her opinion was all he had, a liferaft in the storm. She smiled firmly.

'I think you have a chance, yes. Your mother's done a good job and you held up well against Turner yesterday. The jury must have some doubts.'

'Some doubts. That won't be enough.'

'It should be, if they play by the rules. But no one knows what goes on in the jury room, unfortunately. We're not allowed to ask.'

'There are some wicked old bats in the jury. That cow with the necklace hates my guts.'

'Well, whatever you do, don't scowl at her. Try to look innocent and unthreatening.'

'Yeah, sure. Oh Jesus!' He shook his head anxiously. 'There's one thing I should have said yesterday, but it never came out.'

'What was that?'

'That if . . . if they do get it wrong and convict me, then the guy who murdered her will still be free, won't he? He could do it again!'

Time passed. Nearly forty men had come into the Portakabin to punch their cards before going out to start up the massive machines. Several had glanced curiously at Terry and Harry watching by the window, empty polystyrene cups in front of them. But no Sean.

He'll come soon, Terry told himself, he must have just overslept. Nonetheless, as the flood of new arrivals slowed to a trickle, he began to feel not only conspicuous but foolish.

'You sure he starts today?' Harry asked the site manager, at his grimy desk.

'That's what he said.' The man shrugged apologetically. 'Maybe he's got a better offer, gone racing, or just overslept. Who knows? For a lot of lads like him, work's just an unwelcome interlude in a life of idle pleasure.'

'Has anyone else not come in?' asked Terry, peering at the rack of punchcards irritably.

'A few.' The man pulled out the unpunched cards. 'Adams . . . Greer . . . Harker, again . . .'

'Let me see that!' Terry took the card, which confirmed exactly what he had feared: Gary worked here! Gary, who knew they were looking for Sean! And *he* was missing today, too . . .

'What does Harker do here?'

'Labouring, mostly. Laying concrete.'

'Could he have overheard you when I phoned yesterday?'

'No, of course not. I was in the office!'

'I hope so.' Terry waved the card in his face. 'Because this man Harker –'

At that moment Terry's mobile rang. Tracy spoke in his ear.

In most of Sarah's cases, there had been a camaraderie between the barristers on either side. This was something that was frequently resented by clients but well understood at the Bar. Barristers were rivals, certainly, but not enemies. Friendly banter between them gave a veneer of civility to the contest.

But not now. Objectively, Sarah recognized that Phil Turner was a capable, honest man, good at his job and probably excellent company for his friends. All this simply made her fear him. If only he could have been smarmy, arrogant, callous – anything to make the jury distrust him. But he wasn't. He was an excellent prosecutor with a decent, down-to-earth manner that no juror could fail to like. He terrified her.

Recognizing this, Turner treated her with studious, distant politeness. They sat at the same large table in the well of the court, a frozen wall of silence between them.

He rose to face the jury for the last time, his ancient wig askew as always, and the court settled back comfortably to listen. Sarah shuddered.

'Members of the jury, as I said at the start of this trial, it is my job to convince you, beyond all reasonable doubt, that Simon Newby is guilty of this murder. And as I said then, if after listening to all the evidence you still have doubts, then Simon must get the benefit of them. If you're not sure, then you must find him innocent. You must only find him guilty if you are absolutely convinced, in your own minds, that he did commit this terrible crime.'

That's got the formalities out of the way, Sarah thought. Now he'll go for the throat.

'So, what would convince you of his guilt? Well, we've heard all the evidence, and examined it in exhaustive detail. Mrs Newby has cross-examined all of the prosecution witnesses and tried to cast doubt on their conclusions, as is her right. Simon Newby has told you his story. And what is the result, members of the jury?'

He paused, letting the silence build. Sarah watched the jury anxiously.

'The result, I suggest to you, is that Simon's guilt is clearer than ever before.'

Two – no, *three* – jury members nodded solemnly in agreement. A middle-aged lady with a pearl necklace, a man and a young woman. Sarah felt sick. If they do convict, she thought, I may actually vomit. People do, in extreme shock.

'Let's recall that evidence, shall we? Firstly, the forensic . . .'

Tracy had stayed in front of the white van all the way back across Skeldergate Bridge and along the Fulford Road. She had thought about turning off but then she would have lost them. She had feared they might overtake her and try to drive her off the road, but thank God, they had not done that either. To them, she hoped, she was just a dozy woman driver. Nothing more.

Then, without warning, they turned right into the streets by the river. Tracy had already passed the turning, but she swung into a garage forecourt, came out going in the opposite direction, and turned after them. Once again, the van was gone. She guessed and turned into a dead end. She did a U-turn, drove the other way in a panic, looking right and left, and then, to her great relief, came round a bend and saw the van parked outside a house. As she drove past she saw Sean get out and go up to the door. Gary stayed in the van.

Her heart pounding with excitement, Tracy drove about thirty yards beyond the van, and parked on the opposite side. She adjusted the mirrors to watch the van with her back to it. Gary hadn't noticed her yet, she hoped. Cautiously, she picked up her mobile and phoned Terry.

* * *

Turner dealt with the forensic evidence in comprehensive detail. The semen, the vaginal bruising, the footprints, the blood on the knife and the shoe. It was a formidable list, he said, all pointing in one direction. And what of Simon's story that the blood had got on the knife and shoe because Jasmine had cut her thumb in the kitchen? He looked each jury member in the eye.

'Well, he had to invent something, didn't he? So that's what he's done. A cock and bull story that a child could see through. I don't think we need waste any time on it, do you? It's a lie, members of the jury, pure and simple.'

Sarah seethed with anger. It was the most devastating response he could have made. This was a crucial part of her defence, but instead of engaging with her arguments and rebutting them he'd just dismissed it out of hand, as a lie. How could she revive it now?

'So what about Simon's story, his explanation of what happened? Well, members of the jury, you saw him for yourselves, in the witness stand. You know from your own lives how you judge whether someone is lying or telling the truth. What did you think of his performance? Let's look at it, shall we?' He hitched his foot up on the bench beside him, in the familiar manner of a farmer leaning on a gate, and rubbed his ear thoughtfully.

'He says he made love to her gently, but there are bruises in her vagina. He says he only slapped her, but there's a bruise on her face. He says he drove straight to Scarborough, but he didn't book in at a guest house until the following day. And he says he was upset about how Jasmine had treated him, but he didn't discuss this with anyone.'

Turner looked down cruelly at Sarah. 'He didn't go to his mother, did he? Or his father or his family or his friends. No one has come here to say, "Simon was upset about his relationship with Jasmine. He rang me to ask my advice." No. Because you can't ask someone's advice about what to do with your girlfriend when you've already murdered her, can you? And that's what Simon Newby had done. He'd murdered her, and gone to Scarborough to hide.'

Sarah remembered her nightmare about the judge swinging a ten-year-old Simon in a noose. That had been painful, but it was bliss itself compared to this.

Turner shuffled his notes as though he had finished. Then he looked up again.

'Oh yes, I nearly forgot. There's one other defence that was put forward. The idea that David Brodie murdered Jasmine, not him.' He paused, stacking his papers. 'Well, there's no evidence for that at all, members of the jury. None. It's just the panic reaction of a guilty child, pointing the finger at someone else, *anyone* else, saying it's not *me*, sir, it's not *me*, it was him.

'You saw Mr Brodie on the stand, members of the jury. You heard his evidence. And you saw Simon Newby, too. You choose. Who do *you* think raped and murdered Jasmine Hurst?'

Abruptly, he sat down. And even that was a *coup de théâtre*, Sarah realized. He'd done it before anyone expected. He hadn't bothered to sum up in a final peroration, inviting them to convict, as most barristers did. He'd simply treated Simon's story with contempt, as though neither he, nor any reasonable person, could be bothered with it any longer.

Follow that, she thought.

'Tracy?' Terry said. 'What's up?'

As Harry watched, Terry's face changed. 'You saw *who*? . . . But he didn't see you, did he? You'd better be right. So where is he now? The registration of the van? Right, stay there. Don't do anything, don't go near him until we get there. Understand? We're on our way.'

He switched off his phone and opened the Portakabin door, all in one movement 'Bloody hellfire! Come on, lad, quick!'

'Yes, sir. But what is it?'

Terry was already outside. As he ran, he shouted: 'I'll tell you on the way. The main thing is to get there before anything happens to that woman. Come on, lad, run!'

'Members of the jury, that was a pretty devastating speech, wasn't it?'

Sarah paused, surreptitiously gripping the table with her fingertips. Her voice had cracked slightly in that first sentence, and it shocked her. Her voice *never* let her down. She didn't intend to play for sympathy, not now, not ever. She was no good at it. The trouble was that the strength of her emotion made her feel dizzy. There is a difference between being properly nervous, to get your adrenalin going, and being so petrified that you can hardly speak. She tried again.

'According to Mr Turner my son is a compulsive liar, a rapist and a murderer. Presumably a coward too, since he ran away. Well, it's a point of view, and he's entitled to it. But there's another way of looking at the same events.'

She drew a deep breath, and let it out slowly, feeling the fear fade slightly.

'The other view is that Simon Newby stands before you falsely accused of this horrendous crime. That despite being bullied and harassed he told the truth to the police from the moment he arrived in the police station, and yet has suffered the horror of being shut up in a remand prison for months, while he is grieving for the girl he loved. And now he has come to this court and seen the prosecution build a mountain of evidence out of bricks without mortar, a mountain that will collapse at the slightest push with a finger.'

At least they were all watching her now. she noted. The strength was flowing back into her legs. Her voice had not cracked again.

'Let's look at the evidence again, shall we? And this time, perhaps we can do it without the bullying, the contempt and the cutting of corners which has been the hallmark of the police and prosecution throughout this case.' She turned deliberately to face Phil Turner, her face cold as winter. He ignored her, tying up his notes in red tape.

'First, let's look at the forensic evidence, on which the prosecution lay so much store. Look at it dispassionately, as it really is. The blood first, then. There was Jasmine's blood on Simon's shoe, and Simon's knife. The defence don't dispute that. Yes, it *is* Jasmine's blood, found in Simon's house. But then Jasmine had been in Simon's house many times; she even lived there for some months. And how much blood was it? You've seen the photographs of the body, and the crime scene. Horrific, weren't they? Blood, vast amounts of it, everywhere. It's a nightmare to think of the way she must have died. Whoever killed her, you would expect, would be covered in her blood.'

It was all right now. She paused, looking at each member of the jury in turn, and realized her nerves had gone. She was at the still centre of the court, in control of her voice and her thoughts, in control of what they would hear.

'So how much blood did the police find on Simon's trainer? Two tiny smears on the sole, and five small drops on the upper surface. Nothing at all on the other trainer. And a minuscule amount under the handle of the knife. It hardly fits with the photos of the crime scene, does it? Even the forensic scientist admitted as much.

'Nonetheless, it *was* Jasmine's blood. The defence admit that. So how did it get there? Well, there's a perfectly reasonable explanation. Jasmine cut her thumb earlier in the week, when she was in the kitchen wearing Simon's trainers. It was a tiny cut, so small that the pathologist, you remember, didn't examine it as thoroughly as he should. In fact he missed an important piece of evidence. But since a highly respected forensic pathologist missed this cut, it's hardly surprising that my son failed to mention it too, when he was first interviewed by the police. It was a tiny cut, the sort of thing that happens every day. He washed her thumb under the tap, gave her a plaster, and forgot all about it.

'And that's why such tiny, almost invisible amounts of blood were found on the shoe and the knife. Because the cut itself was tiny, insignificant, and nothing to do with a murder.'

She had their attention now, she noted, or the attention of most of them. The elderly woman at the back was fumbling in her handbag, looking for what? A tissue? A lipstick? This is my son's *life* we're talking about here!

'And yet this perfectly reasonable explanation was dismissed by the prosecution with contempt.' She glared at Phil Turner once again. 'That's what I mean by cutting corners. Bullying. Saying it's a lie rather than examining the evidence in detail.' She hoped he would stand up and object. But he simply sat there, his face composed, unimpressed.

328

'So at the very least there is reasonable doubt about the blood. I would go further. Based on those photos and the evidence of the forensic scientist, I would say it is almost certain that those trainers were *not* the ones worn by Jasmine's murderer.'

Now she'd said something. A murmur moved through the court, music in her ears.

'So what about the semen? The only other piece of forensic evidence that connects Simon with this crime. Well, there's a very simple explanation for that too, isn't there, ladies and gentlemen? The simplest possible. Simon admits that he made love to Jasmine that afternoon. It happened regularly, he says. That's why she came there. And we know she was in his house that afternoon, don't we, because a witness saw her leave. There is no reason at all to suppose that this part of Simon's story isn't true. They made love, and they quarrelled. It happens all the time. And then she left his house.'

She drew another deep breath, aware that she herself was skimming over crucial details now. The old woman had found her tissue and was listening, a disdainful expression on her face.

'The prosecution have no reason whatsoever to dispute this part of Simon's story. The love-making – even if it was rough, even if it caused bruising – almost certainly took place inside his house that afternoon. Several hours *before* Jasmine was murdered, ladies and gentlemen. The sexual intercourse has no necessary connection with Jasmine's murder.'

It was a risk, she realized. If they went for this explanation there was a possibility that they might acquit Simon of murder and convict him of rape. But she had their attention all right now. They were thinking.

And that was the first step towards creating reasonable doubt.

When Terry ran, not many detectives could keep up. By the time Harry reached the car, Terry had already started it. As Harry clambered in beside him, panting, the tyres squealed and the acceleration slammed him back into his seat.

'So what is this, boss? Who was on the phone?'

'Tracy, that's who.' Briefly, Terry explained. 'She followed Gary and guess what? He's driven our lad Sean to Sharon's! Sean's gone inside and Tracy's watching the door.'

'My God! What's the bugger gone there for?'

'Search me, but it doesn't feel good, does it? Not with Gary waiting outside. He's already raped her once, for Christ's sake!'

'But it's not Gary that's gone in, you say?'

'No. Not yet anyway. But you say Sean's visited her before, so maybe he's gone back for another try, to solve this sex problem of his. How's Sharon likely to respond to that, Harry?'

'Not well, sir.' Harry's face paled as he thought about it. 'She said he scared her shitless last time. She never wanted to see him again.'

'Exactly. And this is a possible murder suspect. Come on, come on! This is the time we need a blue light, for God's sake!' He swore at the traffic and pulled out to pass a delivery van, only to be stuck in a queue of vehicles waiting patiently for an old lady on a pedestrian crossing. 'I just hope they haven't spotted Trace. If they have, or if Sharon tells him about those photos you showed her, then . . .' He drew his hand across his throat, then slammed the car into gear.

'So from the forensic evidence,' Sarah said, 'in my view, you cannot convict. It simply doesn't prove what the prosecution want it to. There are too many doubts, and other perfectly reasonable explanations which you must consider.

'What about the rest of the evidence, then? The witness evidence that puts Simon on the riverside path that night when Jasmine was killed? Well, that's easily dealt with, isn't it? There isn't any. None at all. Nobody saw Simon on that footpath that night, nobody saw him within a mile of where Jasmine was murdered.'

This wasn't going down so well, she could see. Two men were frowning and a young woman whispered something to her neighbour. Yet it ought to be such an obvious, easy point to get across. Grimly, she persevered.

'Simon tells us he drove away to Scarborough that night and the prosecution have no evidence, no evidence at all, to show that's not true. So I suggest that in fairness to him, we must assume that it *is* true.'

They didn't like this, damn them. She'd done better with the forensic evidence, which should have been harder. It must be the impression Simon had created on the stand.

'And if you accept that, then you must also accept that when the police came to arrest him, bursting into his bedroom in the middle of the night in that brutal way, then he had no idea that Jasmine was dead. He wasn't just shocked and terrified, as anyone would be, to be snatched from his bed in the middle of the night – he was also overcome by grief. Suddenly, in the cruellest, worst possible way, he learns that his girlfriend is dead. Murdered by some maniac with a knife. And the police think it's him.

'Imagine that for a moment, ladies and gentlemen. Imagine yourselves in the same position. Can you be sure you would behave rationally and sensibly, when the world seems to have gone mad all around you? Isn't it possible that you might say something in a panic that you later realize was wrong, just to escape from this terrifying situation? Something like, "I can't have killed her, I haven't seen her for weeks"?

'The police have rules for how to behave in these situations, and that's why they are there. So that they aren't allowed to put unfair pressure on people which may amount to pyschological torture. That's why they're not allowed to interrogate suspects in police cars. Because there's no tape recorder there, no lawyer, nothing to see that everything is fair.

330

'And yet that's exactly what happened in this case, isn't it? The police interrogated Simon in the middle of the night in a police car, and trapped him in a lie. Bullying again, isn't it?'

Several heads were nodding in sympathy, she was pleased to see. One of the shaven-headed young men who'd seemed to dislike Churchill, and a fair-haired young woman. The old woman with the necklace and handbag was frowning, deep in thought.

'But if Simon did lie then, he changed his mind as soon as he reached the police station, didn't he? Of his own accord he made a full written statement, and everything in that statement was true. There's only one thing the prosecution claim is untrue, and that's why we're here today. He says he didn't kill Jasmine, they claim he did. But everything else in that statement *is* true.'

She paused, looking at her notes. The ending, which had been so clear in her mind last night, had temporarily escaped her. It had taken so much emotional energy to get to this point, she had forgotten how to go further. The confidence which had carried her so far had drained away, gone. She felt herself rambling.

'So . . . you may ask yourselves, if Simon didn't kill her, who did? Well, the sad truth is, I don't know. I don't believe Simon does either. Maybe you think it was rash of me to question David Brodie in the way that I did, but my point was to show that David had as strong a motive for killing Jasmine as Simon had . . .'

'My lord.' Turner was on his feet. The judge was looking at him, and the attention of the jury had switched away from her. 'My lord, we discussed this in chambers. In my view, it's improper for Mrs Newby to make such insinuations without evidence.'

The judge nodded. 'I agree. Mrs Newby, please. Members of the jury, I must ask you to disregard that last remark.'

And so she was destroyed. Right at the end of her speech she had not only lost the jury's attention but been publicly reprimanded. She felt a flush rising to her face, her fingers trembled.

Somehow, her voice struggled on.

'. . . and yet *motive* is the only thing the prosecution have to rely on. The forensic evidence is flawed, there is no . . . excuse me . . . no witness evidence to put Simon anywhere near the crime; he has made no confession, you see . . . and so all the prosecution have to say is that Simon must have killed her because he quarrelled with her. Well, I am sure we all quarrel with our partners all the time without killing them. It's absurd . . .'

It was no good. The interruption had thrown her. She had lost the jury completely. Some of them were still watching her out of politeness, some in pity, and several were looking at their hands in embarrassment. But she had to struggle on. She had to.

'. . . the police have cut corners in this case. They've gone for the easiest suspect, the person who saw her last. They bullied him in the police car, they've produced shoddy forensic evidence, and they have no witness evidence at all. In these circumstances, I suggest that you, the jury, have every ground for reasonable doubt. The prosecution have failed to prove their case. So you *must* find Simon not guilty.'

In that very last sentence, as in her first, her voice broke. It was almost, but not quite, a sob. Humiliated, she sat down, feeling smaller and more useless than she could ever remember.

The silence in the courtroom radiated pity.

After a long moment, the judge coughed, and faced the jury.

42

'Oh no, *no*. I don't want you. *Get out!*'

Sharon tried to slam the door in Sean's face, but he was too quick for her, too strong. He had one foot inside already and when she tried to shut it he shoved it back, slamming her against the wall. She swung her arm to hit him but he caught her wrist easily and held it back against the wall beside her head.

'Now then, Sharon, that's not nice, is it? No way to greet an old friend.'

'Old friend be fucked. What do you want?'

His face, a few inches from hers, darkened with anger. 'Be fucked you say, is it? Well, maybe that *is* what I want. Like last time.'

Only you couldn't manage it, thought Sharon. So you beat me half to death. Katie began crying in the living room. 'That's my little girl. Let me see to her, will you?'

'Just a second, then. Make it quick.'

He released her, and she scooped up the child hurriedly, trying to think clearly at the same time. This was one customer she didn't need. *Think.* 'It's all right, Katie, love, it's just a man visiting. Is it your teeth again?'

The child, as she had hoped, nodded tearfully.

'Look, it's her teeth, they've been hurting all night, I've got to get some Calpol from the chemist. If you come back later –'

'No. Now. If she's had the toothache all night another half-hour won't matter.'

'*I* choose who I go upstairs with, Sean. It's my body –'

'Put her down, woman.' To her horror he actually tried to lift the child from her arms. When she clung on, he took something from his belt. There was a pain, a *sharp* pain in her neck, below her ear. 'Put her down, Sharon. I don't want to cut the baby.'

Trembling, she obeyed. 'It's all right, Katie, we'll get the medicine soon, OK?'

When she had shut the living-room door she saw the knife clear in his hand. A long, jagged blade, the tip an inch from her throat. Her limbs were trembling like jelly.

'Please. What do you want?'

'Upstairs. *Now!*'

She stumbled up to her bedroom, the man with his knife close behind. 'Look, I'll do what you want but just don't hurt my kid, all right. Don't hurt my kid.'

'I won't hurt her. I don't care about kids.'

'All right, what do you want? I'll do it any way you like.' She began unbuttoning her blouse, her fingers clumsy like thumbs. She could see he had a hard-on but that wasn't his problem, was it? It was later.

'You've been a bad girl, Sharon, they tell me.'

'Who tells you? I don't know what you mean.' She dropped her blouse on the floor and began unfastening her bra, the knife still pointing at her throat.

'Our friend Gary tells me.'

'Gary?' She took off the bra and stood there, trembling. Somehow, she must gain control of this situation. 'What's he said about me?'

'You've been talking about him to the press. Go on. Don't stop.' She stepped out of her skirt. He took a sheet of paper from his pocket. 'He wants you to sign this.'

She took it and read, in Gary's big, clumsy handwriting: *I want you all to know, the press and TV too, it's not true when I said Gary raped me. I knew it were not him but I had got to get back at him one way or other. All what I said in court were lies.*

Astonishment overcame her fear. 'He really wants me to sign this?'

'He does so.' A faint, ironic grin appeared on Sean's face. 'Will you do it?'

'Is that what you're here for?'

'That's what Gary thinks I'm here for.'

'But you want something else?'

'Yes.' He waved the knife at her tights and panties. 'Them too.' When she stood before him naked he said, 'What I want is a lock of your hair.'

'My hair?' Somehow this frightened her more than anything else. The strange smile reappeared, as if he thought the demand might amuse her; but it didn't. It scared her witless. 'What do you want that for?'

'To add to my collection. Cut some off for me, will you?'

There were scissors on her dressing table, with her brushes and make-up. She sat down automatically in front of the mirror, as she did every day. But not like this, not naked with a knife at her back. She lifted the scissors to cut some hair.

'A good long bit, now. You've plenty to spare, after all.'

Suddenly it came to her. 'You're the one they want, aren't you? The one who killed that woman, last year. Maria something – Clayton.'

His voice lost its playful tone. 'How in hell do you know that?'

'Because they're on to you. The police have got photos of you, and I . . . saw them.'

Scared as she was, she realized too late what she'd said. But she'd said it because she needed something – words, objects, anything at all – to throw at him and protect herself. She got up, scissors in one hand, a lock of hair in the other, and backed away. Towards the bed, towards the *telephone*. If she could ring 999, perhaps . . .

'The police have shown you photographs of me?'

'Yes. They asked if I recognized you. Here.' She handed him the lock of hair. Anything to gain a little time, live a little longer. 'Did you kill her, really?' She made her voice sound as if it was some heroic, wonderful feat. The phone was only a foot away now.

He sniffed the hair, then slipped it into his pocket. 'Clever girl. But that's not all I did.'

'Not all?'

'No. Don't forget the others.'

'What others? Who do you mean?' Only a foot to the phone now, on the bedside table behind her. She could reach it easily. The problem was how to distract him long enough to dial. And then what?

'For example this girl they're having the trial about now. Jasmine Hurst.'

'You killed Jasmine Hurst?'

'With this very knife. Look at it, Sharon, I brought it specially for you. Sharp, isn't it?'

As she moved backwards, he stepped towards her, round the side of the bed. The knife was only an arm's length from her throat. If she picked up the phone, she'd be dead before she could dial. But if she didn't dial, she'd die anyway.

'I can see you trembling, Sharon. I like that.'

Her mind was racing so fast she was aware of everything, every tiny movement of his face and hands, even while she was thinking what to do. Everyone said you should humour people like this, make a relationship with them if you could. As long as he still wanted to talk to her she would stay alive.

'The papers call me the Hooded Killer, you know. But you can see my face.'

'The Hooded Killer? But he attacked other people, didn't he?'

'A few, so far. That girl Whitaker who had such a lucky escape. And you, the first time.'

'*Me?*' The phone was directly behind her now. She could feel it against her thigh. Very carefully, with her left hand, she began to shift the receiver off its cradle. Thank God the buttons were on the base of the phone, not the handset. If she was lucky she might manage to press 9 three times without him noticing. If only she could keep him talking.

'What do you mean, *me*, the first time?'

'You may as well sign the paper for Gary, you know. After all, it's true what it says. About him not raping you.'

'What?'

Yes, the handset was off now. He was mad, but she didn't care what he said, so long as he said something, to mask the dialling tone. Her fingers fumbled behind her. *Where was 9?* Bottom right, wasn't it? Or was that those star and hash things?

'Yes, it was me that raped you that night, Sharon. Not our friend Gary, as you thought. The joke was on him, don't you think?'

'*You?* But it wasn't you, I recognized him!'

'By his voice, right?' He laughed, and held his left arm in front of his mouth, so that the sleeve muffled his voice. To her astonishment he said, in a Yorkshire accent, very like Gary's: 'Wayne, go away.'

The memory of that night flooded back – *this man after all, not Gary.* He hadn't ejaculated then, either, had he? He just pulled out and hit me in the face.

More keenly she remembered the way her little son had fought back. A desperate surge of adrenalin rushed through her. Thank God Wayne was at school; but Katie was downstairs, and she was all they had, both of them.

'Oh God, help me.' She slumped down on the bed, making it look like a faint, though it wasn't really, not yet. Her hair fell forwards over her face and she glanced quickly under it at the phone. Nine wasn't at the bottom right, but the next one up. She leaned sideways and dropped her hand over the phone, as though accidentally, fumbling for balance.

'But why?' Her finger pressed 9 three times. 'Why did you do that?'

'For fun, that's all. For a bet, Sharon, because Gary was pissed with you, and didn't have the guts to do it himself. Just like now. Only now, you know all about me, don't you, Sharon? So you could tell everyone.'

He moved closer, the tip of the long, serrated knife flicking her left nipple. She clutched the scissors and stared at him, trying to think of something to say. Anything at all, to save her life.

'Emergency services. Do you need fire, police or ambulance?' the telephone asked.

Terry and Harry were stuck in slow-moving traffic. Terry edged the car to the middle of the road, to see if he could overtake. But there was a traffic island just ahead, and a steady stream of cars coming the other way. Frustrated, he drummed his fingers on the wheel.

'Ask Tracy what's happening now,' he said. 'Is Sean still inside the house?'

Harry dialled the number. The response stumped him.

'No signal, sir. Either that or she's got it switched off.'

'Hell's teeth! What the bloody hell would she do that for?'

'No idea, sir, I'm afraid.'

Sarah found it hard to listen to the judge's summing up. She had made such a mess of things, she had let Simon down. It had all been going so well, too – she had overcome her nerves, controlled her voice, had the jury's attention focused on her. She had made all the points she wanted to, and then . . .

She couldn't understand what had happened. She had choked, like an athlete in sight of the winning tape. She had forgotten her conclusion, lost all energy and conviction at that vital moment. She had never even meant to mention David Brodie and when Turner had interrupted her, she'd had no response. Simon would go to prison because she had let him down.

'And so, members of the jury, the guilt or innocence of this defendant is entirely a matter for you. It is a heavy responsibility which I am sure you will approach with the utmost seriousness. There is no hurry; you should consider the evidence thoroughly, and take as long as you need. Your verdict should be one on which you all agree. Now, the usher will conduct you to a room to begin your deliberations.'

As the jury left, Turner caught Sarah's eye. 'That's us finished. No hard feelings, I hope?'

'They're all hard, Phil. Always will be.' She turned away, cutting him dead. It was not the way barristers were meant to behave but then barristers were not meant to defend their own sons. She understood why now, better than she'd ever done.

As the court emptied, she walked back to the dock. 'I'm sorry, Simon. I blew it.'

'What? No, Mum, you were great.' His face was tense, but not downcast.

She frowned at the security guards. 'I'll talk to you downstairs, then.'

'Yeah, OK. We'll have one of those five-star lunches.'

The fact that he was cheerful, even hopeful, hurt her more. She watched him go down to the cells below, the way he would go when he was convicted in few hours' time. Then, dragging her wig from her head, she walked disconsolately out of court, with Lucy at her side.

At last the traffic cleared, and with some risky, assertive driving from Terry they reached the street. They parked a few spaces behind Tracy's blue Clio. Terry called her on her mobile.

'All right, Trace, we're here. What's happened?'

'Nothing much, sir, since I phoned in.'

'Nobody gone in or out?'

'No, sir. Like I said, Sean – if that's who it is – went in there about ten, fifteen minutes ago, and Gary's still in that van –'

'Not now he isn't,' Harry broke in, looking over his shoulder. 'He's got out, look! He's going up to the house.'

Terry looked, and saw Gary disappear through the front door. Now what, he asked himself. 'Do you think he's seen us?'

'Could well be, sir,' Harry suggested. 'After all he knows you and me well enough.'

'Damn,' Terry muttered. What to do now? It was bad enough Sean being in that house with Sharon and her kids, but Gary too? The question was, should he wait for them to come out, call for back-up, or go in straight away? If they didn't know they were being watched, he could wait, but if they did there was no sense just dithering about here any longer.

'Come on,' he said, opening the door as he spoke. 'We're going in.'

But as he did so Gary came out of the house, quickly followed by the other man, Sean. Gary pointed up the road, directly at Terry, and sprinted for the van, followed by Sean, who seemed to have something long, a stick or a knife in his hand.

Terry began to run, his long legs stretching over the ground as fast as he could make them go. But the van was twenty yards away, maybe more, and the two men were already inside it. Fifteen yards . . . ten . . . the van shuddered as the engine started and smoke came out of the exhaust. Terry knew Harry would be far behind him but he didn't care. He ran up to the van as it started to move, and with a final lung-heaving stretch grabbed the driver's door handle. He could see Gary's face inside. He pulled the door open, but he was still running and the van was accelerating faster, pulling him off his feet as it swerved deliberately close to a parked car which swept Terry's legs from under him and sent him slithering over the bonnet into the windscreen and down, loose and crumpled, on to the road.

There was a lime tree at the side of the road. Its leaves fluttered prettily in the breeze beneath a clear blue sky. It's funny I never noticed this before, Terry thought, it's such a nice picture on a lovely day. There was a ringing in his head and a face appeared between him and the tree, looking down.

'Sir, are you OK?' the face asked anxiously, in the voice of Harry, whom it resembled.

'Yes, I . . . what happened?' Terry heaved himself up on his elbows. The road pitched and heaved like a ship out at sea. He staggered to his feet and clung on to a parked car whose windscreen was, for some reason, shattered. There was blood on his hands where he had grazed himself and the sleeve of his jacket was torn. He remembered.

'Get after them, Harry. Call a squad car. Get their number.'

337

'Tracy's doing it now, sir. She's phoned in. I think . . . we should go into the house.'

As the ringing in his ears faded and the road settled down to something like normal behaviour Terry noticed a crying, a screaming like that of a child in distress. It seemed to be coming from Sharon's house. He walked as steadily as he could towards the front door.

The crying came from the top of the stairs. As Terry climbed them, following Harry, he saw a little girl inside a bedroom to the right. She was howling, her mouth wide open, tears streaming down her face, pointing with her pudgy right hand at something further inside the room. Harry walked straight past her. Terry stopped to pick her up.

Inside the room there were clothes strewn across the floor and on the bed, sideways across the pillows at the top end, lay a naked woman. It was Sharon. She lay face up, her long blonde hair spread out, her breasts flopping sideways, blood streaming from a wound in her stomach just below her ribs. One hand twitched and fluttered feebly near the wound, as though trying to find the blood and staunch it and take away the pain.

'Sharon?' Harry bent over her, swept the hair from her face, looked in her eyes and felt her wrist. 'There's still a pulse, sir.'

'Stop that bleeding, then.'

Terry fumbled for the phone in his pocket, but with the child on his hip, clinging to him with all the ferocious strength of utter terror, he couldn't reach it. Then he noticed a phone by the bed near Sharon's feet, only the receiver was off the hook, on the floor somewhere. He bent to pick it up and to his surprise heard a voice on the other end.

'Caller? Caller, are you there? Answer me if you can. Do you need police, fire, or ambulance?'

'The police are here already,' said Terry. 'Send an ambulance. Quick!'

43

'I thought it was unfair. After all, Turner talked about Brodie in his own speech, didn't he? That was what he closed with.'

Lucy's voice echoed strangely from the concrete walls of the corridors below the court. This place, which she knew so well, today seemed weird to Sarah, almost dreamlike. Perhaps they were taking *her* to be locked away, she thought. She was sure she deserved it.

'You're right,' she replied, with the part of her mind which was still functioning. 'I should have noticed that.'

'He took you unawares, that's all.'

'He did. But I should be ready for ambushes, damn it! That's my job.'

'Never mind. You did your best.'

'No!' Sarah stopped, while the warder opened the door of Simon's cell. 'That's just it! On this one occasion when it really mattered, I *didn't* do my best, Lucy! I let him down!'

As they went inside, Sarah saw that Simon had heard. He stood, pale and dismayed, as the door clanged shut behind them. 'What do you mean, Mum? *How* did you let me down?'

'I . . . didn't end as well as I could, Simon, that's all. You must have noticed.'

'Your speech, you mean?' She saw fear in his face as the blow hit home. 'You said everything, didn't you? I thought you did.'

'I said everything, yes. It was just . . . he tripped me up at the end with that reference to Brodie. I should never have made it. The rest was fine.'

She touched his arm and felt the tension in it. He shook her off abruptly and sat, head cradled in his hands. Then he looked up, eyes wild.

'But you had to talk about Brodie, didn't you? I mean, if *I* didn't kill her, who did?'

'That's what I wish we knew, Simon,' said Lucy softly.

The paramedics eased the stretcher gently into the ambulance. There was a small crowd on the pavement outside the house. A policewoman tried to comfort the little girl in the doorway.

'You go with her, Harry,' Terry said. 'Anything she says . . .'

A paramedic frowned disapprovingly. 'She's not likely to say anything for a while, sir. And we'll be very busy –'

'All the same,' Terry insisted. 'This is a major murder enquiry. We have to know.'

Cautiously, Harry climbed into the back of the ambulance and sat near Sharon's head. The paramedic fitted an oxygen mask over her mouth and nose and busied himself with a drip to her arm. Despite the pads he had strapped tightly across her stomach the blood was oozing into the blanket. Her face, what he could see of it, was as pale as the sheet and her hair was flecked with blood.

The paramedic handed him a bottle. 'Here, make yourself useful and hold this. Up in the air, make sure no bubbles get into the line. I'll try some adrenalin.'

The ambulance lurched into movement and Harry heard the crackle of the radio as the driver called in. '. . . serious stab wound to stomach . . . major haemorrhage . . . a full crash team . . . ETA seven minutes, with luck . . .'

The siren began to howl and the ambulance moved off. The paramedic was giving an injection into Sharon's leg. Nothing happened. He felt for a pulse, then lifted an eyelid, and bent his mouth close to her ear. 'Sharon? Come on, love, don't give up. Open your eyes, honey.'

Shocked, Harry watched as the eyelid flopped back; then, ten long seconds later, it began to flutter. Her eyes opened and gazed around her, confused.

'Sharon, are you with us? There's a good girl. You're in an ambulance, love, you'll be in hospital soon. Now what I want you to do, is take deep breaths from this mask on your face, all right? Fill your lungs, really good, slow, deep breaths.'

The eyes closed again. After a moment, he saw her chest rise and fall. Once, twice, three times. He heard her breathing inside the mask. Her eyes opened.

'That's great, Sharon, just great. You're doing fine. More deep breaths, now.'

She breathed deeply while they watched. The paramedic took her pulse again.

'That's brilliant, Sharon, brilliant. Now you just lie there and take deep breaths and we'll have you in hospital in no time. I'm going to give you another injection. You just look up at the ugly policeman who's come to protect you.'

As Sharon turned her head the oxygen mask slipped. 'Harry?'

'Don't worry, Sharon, you're going to be OK. We know who did it.'

'Sean?'

'Yeah. We'll get him, don't worry. Here, breathe this.'

Holding the bottle with his left hand, he replaced the oxygen mask with his right. She took a few more deep breaths, then pulled it away herself.

'Harry . . . my kid. Did he . . .?'

'No, she's fine, Sharon. Just fine. She's with a policewoman now. He never touched her.'

'Thank God. And . . . Wayne?'

'He's at school, isn't he? We'll send someone to pick him up.'

She nodded, put the mask back and took several long, shaky breaths. Harry swayed precariously on his seat as the ambulance, siren wailing, zigzagged through a set of red lights. She took off the mask again and tried a faint smile, her lips almost as pale as her teeth.

'You should try this, Harry. Good stuff.'

'Don't talk too much now, Sharon,' the paramedic warned. 'Save your strength.'

But the adrenalin injections seemed to have revived her. She breathed from the mask a couple more times, then said: 'He was the one who raped me before. Not Gary. He told me.'

'What, Sean? *He* was wearing the hood?'

She closed her eyes, then nodded faintly. 'That's not all . . . he did . . . other things . . .'

The effort seemed to be weakening her. She closed her eyes. The

340

paramedic replaced the mask firmly over her face. 'Come on now, Sharon. You can tell him all this later, when you're better. You just lie still and save your strength, OK?'

Harry glanced out of the window. They were crossing Lendal Bridge, weaving down the centre of the road through the traffic which was climbing the pavements to get out of their way. They should reach the hospital in three or four minutes. Sharon's eyes were closed. She seemed paler than before.

He glanced questioningly at the paramedic. The man shook his head and began to unwrap a third prepacked needle, larger than the others. He jabbed it into her chest, underneath the heart. She shuddered, then opened her eyes.

'That's a girl, Sharon. Come on now, love. Keep breathing. You're doing great.'

She took two shuddering breaths, her eyes wide and shocked. Then she turned to Harry and said something. 'Hhhhurklljasssshmintoooo.'

'What's that? Sharon, I can't hear.'

Harry reached to take off the mask but the paramedic held his arm. 'She can't talk now. You'll kill her.'

Sharon's eyes stared at his, wide and pleading. Harry shoved the man's arm aside.

'Just a couple of words. What is it, Sharon?'

'He killed . . . Jasmine . . . Hurst too.'

The words were like a whisper, scarcely louder than a breath. Her eyes closed abruptly. The paramedic clamped the mask over her face. 'Come on, Sharon, keep breathing. You can do it, Sharon, breathe deeply now. We're nearly there. You're doing great.'

The breaths came fainter and fainter and seemed to Harry to stop altogether. The ambulance drew up outside Accident and Emergency and in an instant the driver was round opening the back doors. They got the wheels of the stretcher down and hurried Sharon along the corridor into the emergency theatre, Harry running alongside still holding the bottle for the drip until a nurse took it from him.

He waited outside with the paramedics for a while, thinking of what he should tell Terry. Then a doctor came out. There was blood on his white coat. He shook his head sadly.

'Dead on arrival, I'm afraid. If she'd lasted a few minutes longer, perhaps . . .'

The paramedic glared at Harry. 'I told you,' he said.

'How long does it take?' Simon asked.

Sitting on the bench in the cell beside him, Lucy shrugged. 'How long is a piece of string? Half an hour, if they all agree at the start. Three hours, four – a day even, if they don't.'

'If they don't agree I'm free, aren't I?'

'Not necessarily.' Sarah paused from her pacing. 'If they can't agree after what the judge thinks is a reasonable time, he'll ask for a majority verdict. Eleven to one or ten to two. So if only three people think you're innocent . . .' She gave him a small, tight smile.

'You think we've lost, don't you?' Simon muttered, avoiding her eyes.

'The truth is I don't know, Simon. I really don't. Anyway what I think doesn't matter any more. There's nothing we can do about it now.'

'Christ!' Simon strode to the door, and banged his forehead against it, softly. 'This is the worst part of all, this waiting. They're deciding about my *life*, in there!'

'A lot of them were following your mother's speech closely, Simon,' Lucy said helpfully. 'Especially the younger ones . . .'

'And what about the old bat with the necklace? She hates me, you could see it in her eyes!' Simon swung round to face them. 'And those two old farts next to her. They'd have me shot, if they could!'

'You can't always tell from looks, Simon. Sometimes –'

There was a rattle of keys in the door. The three of them froze. A warder came in.

'Are they back?' Sarah asked.

'No, not yet, madam. It's the judge – he's called for you. Urgent, he says.'

'Oh? Right.' She glanced at the others apologetically. 'I'll be back.'

As Harry approached the Crown Court he wondered if Churchill would be there. He'd phoned Terry half an hour ago and learned that Sean and Gary had escaped. The patrol car had lost sight of them and they could be anywhere. Terry had put out an all car alert.

'How's Sharon?' Terry had asked.

'Dead on arrival, sir, I'm afraid. But she said something, in the ambulance.'

When Harry explained what he had heard, Terry insisted he go straight to the court to tell the judge. Harry was worried – this was direct interference in DCI Churchill's case. Shouldn't they consult him first?

'Just tell the judge, Harry,' Terry had insisted. 'That's an order. If it's wrong, it's my head on the block, not yours.'

Outside the court Harry saw Churchill in conversation with a tall, rustic-looking barrister in wig and gown and a fat, middle-aged solicitor, whom Harry took to be the prosecution team. Luckily, Churchill had his back to him. Harry strode swiftly past, located the court clerk, and a few minutes later was telling his story to the judge in chambers.

Judge Mookerjee sat back in his leather chair, drumming his fingers thoughtfully on his desk. 'You're quite sure of this, constable?'

'Perfectly, sir. It happened less than an hour ago. My superior officer ordered me to bring you the information immediately.'

'Quite so, quite so. Then I suppose I must disclose this to counsel. Though whether it can make a difference, at this stage . . . Wait there, will you?'

He picked up the phone and dialled.

'It seems to me that it makes all the difference in the world, my lord,' Sarah insisted. 'We all know there's been a series of unexplained rapes and murders in York, and now we have evidence that a man who has murdered again, this very day, has admitted to them all. Including the murder of which my son stands accused. You must stop this trial now. Any conviction in these new circumstances would be unsafe.'

'Hm. I see your point, of course. But there are difficulties.' Judge Mookerjee leaned forward. 'Mr Turner?'

Turner seemed reluctant to speak. He rubbed his ear thoughtfully. 'I'm sorry, but I can't see how this evidence can be admissible. It's hearsay. Hearsay at second hand, in fact, since DC Easby is telling us that he heard Sharon Gilbert tell him what she heard another person say. If, of course, he heard her words clearly at all. You were in an ambulance, constable, you say?'

'Yes, sir. Approaching York District Hospital.'

'Anyone else with you at the time?'

'Yes, sir. The paramedic. And the driver, of course.'

'Did the paramedic hear the words as well?'

'I don't know, sir. I haven't asked him. He was called away on another emergency shortly after we arrived.'

'Well, what do you think? Were the words clear enough for him to hear?'

Harry hesitated. This was not what he'd anticipated. As usual the lawyers were screwing things up. 'It was a whisper, sir. But he may have heard, I don't know. It was quite clear to me.'

'Was the siren sounding?'

'Yes, sir, of course.'

'Well, there we are then.' Turner turned back to the judge. 'Hearsay, at second hand, *whispered* in an emergency ambulance with the siren on. Another witness present who may well have heard nothing at all. It has to be inadmissible.'

'But there are clear exceptions to the hearsay rule,' Sarah intervened desperately. 'In homicide cases exactly like this. The law assumes that when a person is dying, as this woman was, what she says must be treated as truth. After all, what could she gain by lying?'

'If she said it at all,' Turner said, picking up a book from a row on the judge's desk.

'But she did. You heard her, didn't you, constable? There's no doubt in your mind?'

'No doubt at all,' Harry confirmed. '*He killed Jasmine Hurst too*. That's what she said.'

'Here it is. Article 39.' Turner began to read from the law book in his hands. '*The oral or written declaration of the deceased is admissible evidence of the cause of his death . . .*' he paused significantly, '*. . . at a trial for his murder or manslaughter, provided he was under a settled hopeless expectation of death when the statement was made, and provided he would have been a competent witness if called to give evidence at that time*. It seems to me that Ms Gilbert's statement fails on at least three grounds. Firstly, this is not a trial for her murder. Secondly, I doubt if she was under a "settled hopeless expectation of death" – do you think she knew she was dying, constable?'

'It's hard to say, sir,' Harry admitted hopelessly. 'It was all very sudden.'

'Exactly. And thirdly, would she have been a competent witness if called to give evidence in this trial? No, presumably, because it's still hearsay.'

'But this is a clear statement that my son is not guilty. Made by a woman who has just been murdered,' Sarah insisted. 'We know that this man – what's his name?'

'Sean Murphy,' Harry said. 'We think, anyway.'

'You *think*, exactly,' Turner interrupted. 'That's another element of doubt here.'

'But there's no element of doubt about the fact that he killed her, surely? So whatever his name is, we know he *is* a murderer. And he made this statement knowing that he was going to kill Sharon Gilbert, and therefore thinking that no one else would hear about it. So there was no reason why he shouldn't tell the truth. So surely, if this evidence was put before the jury, they would have to conclude that my son is innocent.'

Turner shook his head sadly. He seemed convinced by his argument, but embarrassed to meet her eyes. The judge peered at her reproachfully over his reading glasses, as though she were a student who'd handed in a sub-standard essay.

'Your argument is flawed on several grounds, Mrs Newby. Firstly, until this man is arrested, tried and convicted we cannot know for a fact any of these things – either that he is a murderer, or that he killed Sharon Gilbert, or that he made this statement knowing that he was about to kill her. Even if we accept that he did actually make the statement, it does not necessarily follow that he was telling the truth. In the absence of other evidence, it might be argued that he lied deliberately in order to frighten or torment his victim.'

'And the jury? I doubt if they would see it like that.'

'They might very well not. But it is my function, as trial judge, to decide what evidence does and does not go before this jury. And I regret to say that in view of its undoubted nature as hearsay at second hand, the evidence of DC Easby cannot be put before this jury.'

There was a silence, as the shorthand writer's fingers rattled out the decision on her keys. Sarah felt faint, as though a hand was squeezing her heart.

'And if other evidence comes to light? As it may very well do now that the police are investigating this man. What then?'

'Then, if your son is convicted, he will have grounds for an appeal.'

'After three or four years in prison.'

'That is the nature of the law, Mrs Newby. We cannot bend it to suit ourselves, as you well know.'

Sarah was struck dumb. She had lost another argument, the worst of all. She gazed at the judge helplessly, hoping for pity. He smiled faintly.

'After all, the jury are still out. They may well acquit him today.'

The traffic police spotted the van on the A64. When they stopped it two men got out and sprinted away across the fields, but one of the traffic policemen, a rugby back, brought down Gary with a fine tackle as he paused to cross a ditch. A second squad car arrived in time to rescue Sean from a farmer with a shotgun who had found him, covered in mud and cow pats, fiddling with wires under the dashboard of his Range Rover.

Terry watched as the pair of them were booked in by the custody sergeant. The knife, wrapped in a plastic bag, had already been checked in. In the back of the van the arresting officers had also found a rucksack, packed with clothes and other items.

'Is that yours, son?' Sergeant Chisholm asked Gary.

'No, it's his,' said Gary sullenly. 'All of it's his.'

'Yours, then,' said Sergeant Chisholm placidly, turning to Sean.

'Never seen it before in me life.'

Terry studied the man he had been hunting for so long. He was filthy after his attempted escape. Apart from that he was big, powerfully built like Gary, with the red-gold hair and boxer's nose they'd seen in the photofit. But it was the eyes that interested Terry mostly – the eyes that he was going to look into during the interrogation to come. As far as he could see they were flat, devoid of any obvious emotion – no fear, no panic, no resentment or anger at his predicament. Just emptiness, and a sense of sullen, reserved control. This was not over yet, clearly.

He turned his attention to the rucksack, which Sergeant Chisholm was unpacking methodically. Clothes mostly, and a few items of toiletry, as though for a journey. And then, at the bottom, a crumpled brown envelope. Sean shifted uneasily as the sergeant emptied it.

'A pair of female panties, white, stained – these yours, son?'

'None of it's mine.'

'No? And yet it's your rucksack, Gary says. And what's this – dog collar? And a scrapbook?' He opened it. 'Oh my God! Sir – I think you'd better have a look at this.'

Terry and Sergeant Chisholm leafed through the book together. News-paper cuttings, locks of hair, and photographs. Large, black and white pictures. The sort of quality any scenes of crime officer would die for. The sort of subject two women *had* died for.

Terry's phone trembled in his pocket. Hardly knowing what he was doing, he answered.

'Sir? It's Harry. I'm at the court now.'

'Oh yes, Harry. Good. Did you get the trial stopped?'

'No, sir. That's what I'm ringing about. The judge won't listen. Says Sharon's words are hearsay. Not real evidence.'

'What?' The graphic pictures in front of Terry's eyes were branding themselves on his brain. 'Why the hell not?'

'Usual lawyer crap, sir. Anyway the point is that the jury's still out but they may come back any time. I did my best, sir, but –'

'OK, Harry, just wait there. Tell them I'm on my way.'

Shoving his phone into his pocket, Terry slipped the scrapbook into an evidence bag. 'Book this out, sergeant. I need it for evidence.'

Sergeant Chisholm protested. 'Sir, you can't! I need to list each item separately.'

'Later. This is more important now. I'll take full responsibility.'

As he ran down the stairs, two at a time, the phone in his pocket said: 'DCI Churchill's here too, sir. He's not very happy . . .'

'This is it, then,' Lucy said. 'Chin up, Simon. Hope for the best.'

'Yeah, OK. Now or never, eh?'

Handcuffed to the security guards, Simon made his way up the grim concrete stairs. The court was full. Above him the public gallery creaked and hummed, fifty mouths muttering, a hundred eyes staring down. Lucy smiled encouragingly back at him as she took her seat.

In front of Lucy, he could see his mother's slim gown and the back of her horsehair wig. He wondered why she didn't turn and smile too when he came in, and if it might be a bad omen. Neither he nor Lucy had seen Sarah since she left them half an hour ago, and Lucy didn't know why she had gone.

The judge in his red robes entered, bowed and sat down. The clerk intoned the ancient formula: 'All those having to do with the case of the Crown versus S. Newby draw nigh and give your attendance. Her Majesty's Crown Court at York with His Lordship P.J. Mookerjee presiding is now in session.' The judge nodded to the usher to fetch the jury.

For a minute, perhaps longer, there was silence. Simon stared at his mother's neck, slender under the ribbons of the wig. Why doesn't she turn and smile, he wondered desperately? He crossed his fingers like a child. If only she turns and looks at me it'll be all right. Come on, Mum, turn. *Turn now!*

But she didn't.

Simon watched anxiously as the jurors filed back into court, willing them to meet his eyes. He had read somewhere that if they looked at you it was all right; if they avoided your eyes you were done for. Six of them glanced at him. Three of those looked away quickly when they met his eyes. None of them smiled.

When they had all taken their places the clerk of the court rose.

'Members of the jury, would your foreman please stand.'

Simon closed his eyes. When he opened them it was still true. The elderly woman at the back, the one with the grey hair and the string of pearls, was standing up. She wasn't looking at him. None of them were.

Terry drove with one hand on the wheel and the other holding the phone to his ear. Twice on the busy Fulford Road he had pulled out to overtake, once causing a car to hoot at him directly outside the police station. He was talking to Harry Easby.

'Look, Harry, I've got new evidence which proves it was him beyond a shadow of a doubt. You've got to get back in there and stop it, son, before it's too late.'

Harry was on the steps outside the court. 'I can't, sir, you don't understand. The lawyers have told DCI Churchill what I tried to do, and he's hopping mad, sir, I daren't go back in –'

'If you don't, Harry, there'll be a miscarriage of justice!'

'If I do there'll be murder, sir. You haven't seen him. Anyway I haven't got the evidence to show. You'll just have to bring it yourself before the jury come back.'

'That's what I'm trying to do, Harry – Christ!' Terry swerved to avoid a cyclist. 'I'm in Fishergate now, I'll be there in a couple of minutes. Just stall them till then, will you?'

Sarah couldn't face Simon. It was all she could do to sit here, facing the judge and the assembling jury. She was conscious of Phil Turner a few feet away, but couldn't meet his eyes. He had beaten her, persuaded the judge to disallow evidence that strongly suggested Simon's innocence. There was no justice in it but what did that matter? He had won the game of proof.

As the elderly woman identified herself as the jury foreman Sarah shuddered, as Simon had done. My worst enemy on the jury, the one who had fiddled in her handbag when I was making my strongest points.

'Madam foreman, have you reached a verdict?'

'We have, yes.' A thin clear voice, slightly more educated than Sarah had expected, but cold, too, without emotion.

'And is . . .'

A hand was tugging on Sarah's sleeve. Turning, she saw it was Harry Easby, the detective who'd brought the news of Sharon's death and Sean's confession. He was crouched, whispering something to her earnestly. 'Sorry, what?'

'DI Bateson's on his way. He's got more evidence. He says it proves Sean did it.'

'Yes, but it's too late now – look!'

The court clerk, irritated by their whispered conversation, frowned at them in reproof, before continuing, in a slightly louder voice. '. . . and is that the verdict of you all?'

'It is.'

'Very well. On count one, the murder of Jasmine Hurst, do you find the defendant, Simon Newby, guilty or . . .'

'He's got the proof,' Harry insisted. 'He'll be here in a minute. If you want to stop them now's the time . . .'

'. . . not guilty?'

'My lord.' Sarah rose to her feet, slowly, so slowly it seemed as if she was trying to run through water in a dream, a nightmare in which she had to act but couldn't because her muscles wouldn't obey her. She couldn't even seem to attract their attention; the clerk and the judge were both looking at the jury forewoman, not her, as though she wasn't there. Even her voice wasn't working. She tried again. 'My lord . . .'

'Not guilty.'

There was a gasp, a murmur of mingled outrage and relief from the public gallery behind her. At least they've heard me, Sarah thought, why hasn't the judge noticed yet? 'My lord . . .'

'Mrs Newby?' The judge studied her curiously, almost with compassion, rather than the anger she had expected. 'It's all right, Mrs Newby, there's no need any more.'

He looked past her and said, 'Simon Newby, you are free to go.'

And then it sank in. There was a roaring in Sarah's ears, and she sat down quite suddenly, like a puppet whose strings are cut. She heard talking around her and felt Lucy's soft hands on her shoulders but it was all a blur and her arms didn't seem to work. Judge Mookerjee, about to thank the jury and discharge them, noticed the commotion about Sarah and looked down, concerned. 'Mrs Newby, are you all right?'

Sarah looked up through a film of tears and straightened her spine as she had always done, all her life. 'Oh yes, my lord, thank you.' Then she turned to the jury, where the elderly woman was still on her feet, and said again, 'Thank you. Thank you all very much indeed.'

44

'So if you'd come in time, what were you going to show the judge?' Sarah asked Terry, as they strolled along the river bank the following day. Terry had meant to invite her to his office, but the atmosphere there was so poisonous after Churchill's humiliation that fresh air was a relief.

'Well, this first of all,' said Terry, passing her a photograph in a plastic cover. It was of Jasmine – a living, healthy Jasmine running along the track by the river, her hair blown back lightly from her face. 'You see the clothes are very different from the ones she was wearing on the day of her death.'

'Well, yes, exactly.' Sarah handed it back to him, surprised. 'It doesn't prove he killed her, Terry, the judge would never have stopped the trial for that.'

'He would have for this, though.' Terry passed her a second photograph, also of Jasmine. But this time a dead Jasmine, lying with her throat cut in the undergrowth. It was like the police photographs, except that this one had been taken at night, by flash.

Sarah studied it, transfixed. 'What did he want with a photo like this?'

'Gruesome, isn't it? But it's the context that explains it. Those photos were found with other things – newspaper clippings, several locks of hair, a pair of stained panties – and he was carrying a knife.'

'A complete sicko, then?' Sarah handed the photo back.

'Yes, and one like a magpie too. There weren't just things to do with Jasmine; there were trophies from all the other women he'd attacked as well.'

'You think he did them all, do you?' Sarah asked. 'Karen Whitaker, that girl Steersby, and Maria Clayton as well?'

'It looks like it. Karen Whitaker's boyfriend has already identified the camera as the one that was stolen from him when they were attacked. There were photos of Karen in this scrapbook too – probably the ones the boyfriend took. There were no photos of Maria but the rest of it fits. If we believe what he told Sharon, poor woman, before she died. Anyway we're testing the hair, and a little dog collar to see if belongs to Maria's dog, and the panties to see if they're Jasmine's. Hers were never found, were they?'

'No.' Sarah grimaced. 'And *he* raped Sharon too, you say. Not Gary after all?'

'So it seems. Though what I don't understand is, how Gary's hairs were in that hood, as well as Sean's.'

'No. Unless . . .' A sudden memory came to Sarah. 'When Gary attacked me in that shed, I pushed the hood into his face, to blind him, and he had to drag it off. Maybe then . . .'

'Maybe.' Terry frowned. 'I wish you'd told me before.'

'I never thought of it before.'

'No. Well, we're all human.' He picked up a stone and skimmed it across the water, where it bounced twice and sent a startled duck clattering into the air. 'It's not just Churchill who got things wrong. I had Gary down for them all – now it seems he's pure as the driven snow.'

'Week-old slush, more like,' said Sarah grimly. 'You're forgetting what he did to me. But what I don't understand is, how things worked out between those two. Why were they in that van together?'

'That's what I've been trying to understand too,' Terry said. 'Sean says nothing much, but Gary's positively voluble. He thinks he's been deceived. According to him, he thought Sean was just an ordinary decent thief, like himself. That's how they met, in prison, after all. He didn't think Sean was particularly interested in sex, and when I started trying to trace him Gary thought I was out to pin all these crimes on Sean in the same way as I'd tried to do with him. So he thought he'd help this innocent mate of his to get away – go back to Ireland, perhaps. Only he had the bright idea of asking Sean to visit Sharon on his behalf first, to make her admit that she'd got everything wrong. Fatal mistake – for Sharon, anyway.'

Briefly, Terry explained about the unsigned note they had found in Sharon's bedroom. 'Gary thought he could show it to the TV people. Like Sharon, he trusts TV more than he does the legal system.'

'Well, he has a point.' Sarah moved aside for a cyclist who passed between them. 'But why did Sean rape her, anyway?'

'Same reason he did everything. He hates women. No wonder, with a problem like his.'

'Problem? What's that?'

Briefly, Terry explained Sean's sexual disability. Sarah stopped dead, forcing two women pushing babies to move around her while she gawped in wonder. 'But . . . that's astonishing! Is it possible?'

'So the medicos tell me. Luckily, it only affects something like one man in a hundred thousand. Poor buggers.'

'But don't you understand what it means?' The two young mothers turned at the excitement in her voice, but Sarah didn't care. 'He could have raped Jasmine after all, and it wouldn't have left any semen. That would account for the bruising!'

The young mothers were rapt now, dawdling deliberately to hear what came next.

Terry smiled. 'So not only is your son not a murderer, he's not a rapist either.'

'No.' As Sarah shook her head, the emotion finally began to hit home.

She felt dizzy, and Terry grasped her shoulders to steady her. 'Just a great, lumbering, clumsy ignorant fool. Even last night when he was acquitted, I couldn't quite forgive him those bruises. Oh, Terry, you've made my day.'

'Glad to be of service.' He scowled at the rubber-necking mothers until they moved reluctantly away. 'Anyway, that's why Sean killed Maria and raped Sharon, as far as I can make out. They were both prostitutes and he'd hoped they might solve his problem, and when they didn't, he turned nasty and came back with revenge in mind instead. In Sharon's case, my guess is he probably *did* meet Gary that night. Gary told him how he'd quarrelled with Sharon over his watch, and Sean thought he'd get his mate's watch back and take his revenge at the same time.'

'But . . . why were the watch and hood found in Simon's shed?'

Terry shrugged. 'Well, I'm guessing, but we know both Gary and Sean used that shed for stolen goods. And it was just round the corner. Perhaps he changed his clothes there, so no one could trace them to him. And he left the watch because he knew Gary would come back there sometime and find it, and start to think . . . which isn't Gary's strong point, as you know. Perhaps the idea of Gary gawping at this watch in the shed amused him.'

'Until I turned up to distract him.' Sarah shuddered, remembering. 'In his alibi, Gary said Sean went off with a prostitute, didn't he?'

'Yes, I know. I should have taken that more seriously. But at the time . . .' Terry shook his head. 'Perhaps Sean did go with one, and things went wrong as they always did, which would have enraged him even more. So he decided to revenge himself on Sharon.'

'Poor woman.' Sarah sighed, remembering the sense of triumph she had felt after cross-examining Sharon in the witness box. And yet she had been right, after all – Sharon *hadn't* been able to identify her rapist, had she? Not that it seemed like much of a triumph, now. 'So what about Jasmine? How did Sean get involved with her?'

'Well, according to Gary, he'd been to Simon's house a few times – they both had, hiding stolen goods. So he must have met her there. Something about her must have attracted him.'

'Everything, probably, poor girl,' Sarah murmured sadly. 'After all, she looked like a film star, *and* she loved leading men on. But why didn't Simon notice? Or Gary, or anyone?'

'If you'd met him you'd see why,' said Terry, thinking of the cold, distant eyes that had faced him across the interview table. 'He gives nothing away, this lad. That's why he's survived so long. I doubt if he talks about women with anyone at all.'

'Just stalks them on his own, you mean?' Sarah shuddered, remembering the first photo of Jasmine Terry had shown her – the one taken days, weeks perhaps before her death, a young healthy girl running alone on the river path, unaware of the hidden maniac watching with his stolen camera. 'That would explain what she said to Mandy Kite.'

'Who?'

'A witness I wasn't allowed to use – one of the eco-warriors. Jasmine had told her she often felt she was being followed. The prosecution thought it was Simon and I suggested it was David Brodie, God forgive me! Bob was right . . . but what could I do?'

She stared away from him across the river, embarrassed by sudden tears. He hovered, wanting to put a comforting arm round her shoulders but uncertain how it would be received.

As always with Sarah, the tears were short-lived. She turned, brushing them away with her hand. 'And so he stalked her for a while, and then he followed her that night when she and Simon had their quarrel . . .'

'Probably.'

'. . . and then he jumped out at her somewhere and thought because she was two-timing both her boyfriends she wouldn't mind doing it with him as well. That's the way these perverts think, isn't it? Then when she refused, he pulled out his knife and – *Jesus, Terry!*'

She stopped, took hold of his arm. 'Let's not go any further, if you don't mind. You realize where we are, don't you?'

He looked, and saw what she meant. They were less than half a mile from where Jasmine's body had been found. They turned back towards the city.

'Of course, this is all speculation. The only confession he's made so far is to Sharon.'

'Which you'll have the devil of a job getting admitted in court. I couldn't.'

'There's lawyers for you,' Terry said, regretting it instantly. 'Sorry, I didn't mean . . .'

'Yes you did.' She walked on, looking down moodily. 'Everyone hates us, except when we're needed.'

He changed the subject. 'How's Simon taking it? Surely he must be grateful.'

'Oh yes.' She offered a wry smile. 'But to *you*, as much as to me. I'm surprised he hasn't been round to thank you. You're his hero, right now.'

'I'll look forward to it. And Bob? He must be pleased?'

'Yes, of course.' Sarah sighed. 'His problem is that not only did he shop Simon in the first place, he also believed in his guilt. Which makes things rather difficult in his relationship with Simon, you see. And in his relationship with me.'

Terry searched for an answer. 'You'll get over it. In time.'

'Will we, Terry?' She looked up at him. 'I wonder.'

They walked on for a while in silence. As they reached the car park, she turned and took both of his hands in hers. Over her shoulder he could see the Norman castle on its mound, and in front of it the elegant eighteenth-century law courts where so much was decided. For better or worse. She pressed his hand gently, and smiled.

'Anyway, we got something right in the end, between us, didn't we?'

She reached up, kissed him gently on the cheek, and was gone.

SMART
QUESTIONS

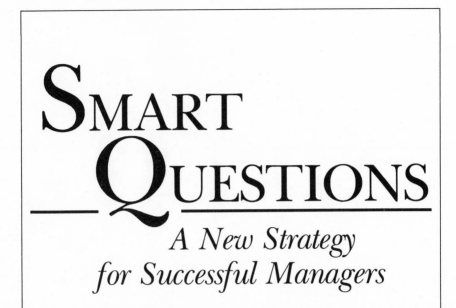

SMART QUESTIONS

A New Strategy for Successful Managers

DOROTHY LEEDS

McGraw-Hill Book Company

New York   St. Louis   San Francisco   Hamburg
Mexico   Toronto

3 4 5 6 7 8 9 D O C D O C 9 8

ISBN 0-07-036996-8

LIBRARY OF CONGRESS CATALOGING-IN-PUBLICATION DATA

Leeds, Dorothy.
    Smart questions.
    1. Management.   2. Personal management.
3. Questioning.   I. Title.
HD38.L3867   1986   658.4'52   86-27469
ISBN 0-07-036996-8

BOOK DESIGN BY PATRICE FODERO

For Nonny,
Laura,
and Ian,
with love

Contents

Part Three: Getting Ahead

Acknowledgments

In my seminars and speeches, I always say that there is nothing new under the sun—I am just the lucky catalyst to bring it out. In writing *Smart Questions*, I was the catalyst again. *Smart Questions* was definitely a team effort.

This book would not have been possible without the support, hard work, and involvement of so many people. Thank you to:

Tom Miller, my editor. This book would not be in its present state without his expert advice, persistence, and ability to conquer all obstacles.

Barbara Lowenstein, my agent. Without her original belief in *Smart Questions*, the concept would not have become a reality.

Gerry Miller, Bill Lee, Ed Weihenmayer, Allen Murray, Helen Galliand, Alan Barratt, Shel Caras, Harvey Schein, and Bill Granville, who have so graciously added their wisdom and time.

Anne Dalton for her encouragement and direction; when I struck out, she came to bat.

Judy Schwartz and Florence Levitt for their exceptional editing assistance.

Kathie Ness for her superior copy editing and knack of tying it all together.

Sanja Kabalin and Raquel Altreche, whose devoted administrative assistance have helped so much.

All the managers and supervisors at Mobil Oil, Duke Power, and Prudential-Bache who gave of their time to be interviewed and added so much through their participation in my questionnaires.

All the participants in my seminars and workshops, from whom I continue to learn the value of asking smart questions.

And to my other teams: my family and friends, who have been so lovingly involved and who have always tried to answer all my questions.
Onward and upward!

Introduction

One much-sought-after production chief in a high-tech industry told me, "Only 20 percent of my job is spent working with the computers; the other 80 percent is solving people problems."

As technology permeates every facet of the business world today, a manager's people skills often become his or her most valuable commodity. We are smack in the midst of what futurist John Naisbitt calls the "high-tech high-touch" society, when to get the most out of our machines we have to pay more attention than ever to people. At the same time, it's harder than ever to understand human feelings and motivations. Competition is keener, everything moves faster, machinery grows more complex.

Ultimately the day will come when the same technology that threatens to dull our humanity will actually enhance and even extend our own mental abilities. For now there is an uneasy alliance between the two. If human relationships break down, the machinery stops turning.

Now, I don't pretend to be the first management consultant to discover this basic truth. In fact, I add my voice to that of every expert writing in the field of business management today. The issue isn't recognizing the importance of human relationships in business, it's finding effective ways to improve these relationships.

Managers on all levels are searching out tools for building excellence

1

through people productivity, as well as through their own efforts. That's what *Smart Questions* does for you: it provides a tool for building excellence. And it does something else as well. Asking the right questions—of the right person and at the right time—gives the young manager a way to stand out.

Despite the trends of "new humanism" and "participative management," it's not easy to make yourself visible within a corporation. As good as a young executive may be, there are always others as good—or better. How can a newcomer stand out among so much talent? For a high-level executive in the upper reaches of management the problem might be somewhat different: how can he control the action and fast-moving events of modern business? The manager who knows how to ask smart questions can stand out in a crowd of giants and can also reduce much of the pressure that radiates from the centers of power.

Lee Iacocca, undoubtedly the most visible CEO in the nation, comments, "I've seen a lot of guys who are smarter than I am and a lot who know more about cars. And yet I've lost them in the smoke. Why? Because I'm tough? No. You don't succeed for very long by kicking people around. You've got to know how to talk to them, plain and simple."

Knowing how to "talk to them, plain and simple" involves knowing how to ask smart questions. Once you learn to ask the right questions, career success is the response you'll get.

Smart Questions offers a simple technique to help you reach your career goals. You don't have to adopt a special high-powered diet or get up at the crack of dawn to work out three times a week. Forget about dressing for success, meditating, or learning how to nab the right table at the best restaurants. No need to go back to school and collect professional degrees. And don't concern yourself with finding a lifetime mentor.

In fact, you don't need to do anything you haven't been doing all your life—you just have to do more of it, and in the right way. *Smart Questions* shows you how to turn an ordinary conversational skill—the art of asking questions—into a formidable business tool.

Does it sound as though I've discovered a secret code or a magic formula? Well, in a sense that's true. *Smart Questions* holds the secret to success the way a hieroglyph holds the key to a prehistoric civilization: once you understand the symbols, the story unfolds before you. Years of observing communication among executives has given me enough insight to break the code.

As a management consultant I have participated in hundreds of staff meetings, board meetings, coaching sessions, sales calls, job hirings—not to mention firings—and performance appraisals. As time went on, I noticed that the most successful leaders invariably asked the best questions. Effective questioners demonstrated both mastery over their jobs and consideration for other people, a highly desirable combination in modern business.

To test this observation, I devised a three-part questionnaire to measure the quantity and quality of questions asked by managers in various companies. Of more than five hundred managers from several large and small corporations, those considered by upper management to have the greatest potential for leadership all scored in the ninetieth percentile on each part of the questionnaire.

You may have a question about this theory. No, it's not enough to turn yourself loose and assault everyone you know with scores of questions. Shining up to your boss with "And how are you feeling today?" isn't going to do it. Dale Carnegie has always said that you win friends when you ask people about themselves. But good management is not a popularity contest. Good managers know how to use questions to get the most from other people, as well as to win allies.

They also know how to ask *themselves* smart questions. Routinely, the best managers ask themselves what they're doing and why, and what result they expect to achieve. Asking questions is an introspective process. The value of the system lies not only in what you ask other people but in how willing you are to question your own motivations and goals.

In a recent in-house newsletter Donald Petersen, chairman of Ford Motor Company, described his company's mission. One of the four guiding principles Petersen emphasized was this: "Asking more of the right questions and reducing the need to have all the answers. Having more discussions about how to make things happen instead of focusing on why they don't work."

In an interview for this book, Allen E. Murray, Chairman of Mobil Oil Corporation, told me, "In the final analysis, management is a skill of communication. Conveying ideas, work assignments, and priorities is based on communication. So is the ability to command loyalty and good performance." At Mobil one of the top priorities on each employee's annual performance appraisal is "communication skills."

As both Petersen and Murray so emphatically point out, communicating with people is essential for success. Executives who fill upper management positions are always reaching, and a crucial part of their jobs is reaching out to those they work with, trying to help them do their jobs better. At the same time, they're reaching upwards—trying to create footholds for climbing towards their own future in top management. Successful managers must also reach deep inside themselves to find positive and creative answers. Questions can help you reach out in all of these crucial directions.

Smart Questions is addressed to managers at every level, from trainees to vice presidents. All managers—even CEOs who must report to a board of directors—work in two directions. They strive to get maximum performance from their staff people. And they also strive to impress upper management with their own performance and to get ahead within the organization. Because of the bidirectional quality of their professional lives, we've divided *Smart Questions* into three sections.

Part One concentrates on the basic system of asking smart questions: why questions are powerful, how to pose good questions, and how to avoid questions that backfire. At the end of Part One we'll talk about targeting your questions to different personality types and using the special Smart Questions System in virtually any situation.

With the basics spelled out, you can begin to apply Smart Questions to the two primary aspects of every manager's life. In Part Two you will see how questions help you get the most from your staff. This section begins by describing questions that help you hire the best people. Once you have a high-quality staff, however, your job as a manager is just beginning. The following chapters show you how to use smart questions to keep your staff motivated: by delegating, by training and coaching to get your people through trouble spots, by counseling staff people who have special problems. Finally, we'll show how—by using questions—you can turn the ubiquitous performance appraisal into a prime motivating tool.

In Part Three we turn the Smart Questions System upwards, to show managers how to climb the corporate ladder by asking the right questions of the right people. Here we'll talk about using questions, particularly self questions, to solve business problems and make good decisions, and to become a sharper negotiator, especially when it comes to negotiating your own raise. We'll also talk about what to do if your career stalls out—how to use questions to find a new job with a big future—and about creating the special image that will let you pick out a career path in your organization. Finally, in an exclusive roundup of advice from top-level executives who were interviewed especially for this book, we're going to give you an overview of the star qualities that today's young managers must possess—or develop—to get ahead.

The best way to reach out to people, those who work for you and those who control your future, is with questions. People—clients, employees, bosses—will be moved not by how much you know but by how much you care, and how you show that you care. Smart questions demonstrate not only your intelligence but also the depth of your attention and concern. When you know how to ask the right questions you can make anything happen.

Part One
The System

"It is better to know some of the questions than to know all of the answers."

—James Thurber

1

The Quiz: Part One

Asking questions is a good thing, right? Right. It's productive, positive, creative, and helpful. Knowing how to ask a smart question can get you almost anything you want, anytime. So why don't we all do it? In fact, most of us think we do. We're certain that we ask plenty of questions, particularly in those situations known to require skillful probing.

I recall one of my clients, Barry, a senior vice president who was having a hard time building his staff; every new person he brought on board turned out to be a dud. He was convinced that his staffing problem stemmed from an inferior employee market.

Barry prided himself on his interviewing technique and told me that he always asked questions to uncover an applicant's potential. He readily agreed when I asked to sit in on one of his interview sessions. I was surprised to observe that, contrary to Barry's own impression, he talked throughout the entire interview, mostly from nervousness, and asked only the most rudimentary questions.

Looking for a convincing way to reveal to him his interviewing style, I suggested that we videotape his next interview. When he saw the videotape he was astounded: he couldn't believe that even though he *knew* he should be asking questions, he seldom did.

The truth is that most of us make statements most of the time. Even when we know better, impatience or nervousness or a need to get our point across pushes us into telling rather than asking, talking rather than listening. Ninety percent of us are talking 90 percent of the time.

The quizzes in *Smart Questions* are designed to help you change your basic communication approach, to put you in a questioning mode, so that by end of book you'll be thinking differently and responding differently. To get the greatest benefit from the questions in the quiz, do not ponder them; go with your first, automatic response. Before you can make smart questions a habit, you must look at your current style.

If you are honest, the quizzes will give you feedback in terms of how you use both self questions and direct questions. Learning to question yourself is as valuable as asking questions of others. Try to imagine each situation as if it were really happening to you, and then check the answer that comes closest to your immediate response. Remember, this quiz is for your own personal evaluation, and brutal honesty will give you the best information.

When you have answered all the questions, add up the points and read about the implications of your score.

Do You Use Questions Enough?

1. When a departmental report is criticized, you say:
   a. "I'm sorry, it's my fault."
   b. "What went wrong?"
   c. "Why does this always happen to me?"
   d. "My people never check their work."

2. When someone you call is "in a meeting," you:
   a. Say "I'll call back."
   b. Leave your name and hope he'll call back.
   c. Ask "When is the best time for me to call back?"
   d. Ask "Can you help me get through to your boss?"

3. You've been turned down for a raise. You:
   a. Quit, and start job hunting.
   b. Ask yourself "What's wrong with me?"
   c. Ask yourself "What can I do to get a yes?"

d. Stick with it, even though you feel demoralized and de-energized.

4. Toward the end of a busy day your boss asks, "What are you doing tonight?" You answer:

a. "I have an important appointment."

b. "Nothing."

c. "Why do you ask?"

d. "I was looking forward to having some time to myself."

5. In the space of one morning your boss gives you three top-priority projects, then brings in a fourth. You:

a. Plunge into all four assignments; you want to show that your boss can count on you, no matter what.

b. Accept the work load but feel furious inside because your boss has so little consideration.

c. Tell her straight out that there is no way all four jobs can be done at once.

d. Remind her of the four assignments and ask which she needs first.

6. When introduced to a new associate, in the first three minutes you:

a. Talk about yourself and try to make a good impression.

b. Ask questions to gain the advantage but resist revealing anything about yourself.

c. Draw the other person out by asking questions and talk about yourself when asked.

d. Don't say much and let the other person carry the ball.

7. The chairperson of a meeting of department heads says that your department should be more cooperative. You:

a. Ask the chairperson for specific suggestions after the meeting.

b. Say nothing, but later complain to your associates.

c. Immediately confront the meeting chairperson and ask how you can accomplish the change.

    d.   Nod your head in agreement.

8.   Your boss has criticized you severely for a simple error. You:

    a.   Worry for days because he doesn't like you.

    b.   Ask your boss to tell you more about what he expects from you.

    c.   Deny the criticism and loudly defend yourself.

    d.   At a calmer moment ask your boss how he would feel in the same situation.

9.   You are notified by mail that you have lost a major contract. You:

    a.   Accept the letter.

    b.   Plan to try again at the next bidding period.

    c.   Call up and ask why.

    d.   Register at the next sales seminar.

10.   You are asked by a high-level executive to volunteer for a project you do not want to do. You:

    a.   Agree reluctantly.

    b.   Say, "Can you tell me more about it?"

    c.   Refuse with a lengthy excuse.

    d.   Ask, "How important is this to you?"

11.   Without warning, you are asked to move to a smaller, less advantageous office. You:

    a.   Start packing.

    b.   Start looking for another job.

    c.   Tell the office manager "I'm on my way to a meeting; can we talk about this later?"

    d.   Ask your boss what's going on.

12.   You schedule a one-on-one meeting with a tough negotiator with whom you hope to do long-term business. To begin, you:

    a.   Ask a direct and leading question to gain control ("What's your bottom line?").

    b.   Ask a nonthreatening question to establish rapport ("What do you feel is the best way to start this?").

c. Let him start off.

d. Bring along a support person to set the stage.

13. When you have to make a work scheduling decision that will affect your staff, you usually:

a. Ask your boss's opinion.

b. Call a staff meeting and make a joint decision.

c. Weigh all the facts and decide for yourself.

d. Ask your staff to work it out among themselves.

14. When you are trying to show strength within a group, you usually:

a. Talk louder and longer.

b. Ask probing questions.

c. Listen.

d. Come well prepared with questions and statements.

15. Your CEO has just called and given you some instructions you don't understand. You:

a. Take notes and hope you'll eventually be able to figure them out.

b. Ask someone else to explain the instructions.

c. Say "I don't fully understand. Can you explain further?"

d. Ask "Can I call you back for further clarification after I digest this?"

16. A vice president from strategic planning gives you some advice regarding your projected move to another city. You:

a. Don't listen because you've already decided in favor of the move.

b. Ask why she's sharing this information with you.

c. Take in the information and mull it over later.

d. Listen, then later feel upset because you've made the wrong decision.

17. At an interview for a top position the interviewer opens with "Tell me about yourself." You answer:

a. "My first job was in the mail room at ABC; after I finished college I moved up to administrative assistant. Then I was office service manager for two years, and promoted to vice president of administrative services."

b. "That's a difficult question; I'm not sure where to begin."

c. "What specifically do you want to know?"

d. "I was born in Cleveland, but my folks moved to California when I was six."

18. At an important conference you make a poor presentation. You:

a. Vow never to make another public speech.

b. Go over and over all the things you did wrong.

c. Ask yourself "How can I improve the next time?"

d. Ask a more experienced, higher-level executive for constructive criticism.

19. As a job seeker, you are told after an interview, "We'll get back to you." You:

a. Ask "When can I expect to hear from you?"

b. Smile and say thank you.

c. Ask "When can I have an answer—I have other offers."

d. Ask, "When in the next ten days can I call you for an answer?"

20. At an important meeting the chairperson suddenly asks you, "Jim, what did you think of Elaine's point?" Your mind was wandering and you weren't listening to Elaine. You:

a. Try to change the subject.

b. Claim that you were still thinking about the preceding speaker's point.

c. Ask, "Could Elaine give an application of her point so I can answer more effectively?"

d. Admit with humor that you weren't listening.

21. When someone asks your advice about a problem, you:

a. Ask "Where do you hope to end up?"

    b.   Ask "What would you like to do?"

    c.   Ask "How can I specifically help?"

    d.   Ask "Whom else have you asked for advice?"

22.   In your opinion, the best way for a manager to use questions is to:

    a.   Gain information.

    b.   Gain commitment.

    c.   Control communications.

    d.   Gain the upper hand.

23.   During your three-week vacation you turn over your department to a highly power-oriented employee. You:

    a.   Ask the employee to clearly state the directives you've given.

    b.   Hope for the best.

    c.   Ask for a written statement of responsibilities and related authority.

    d.   Ask the employee to clearly define the limits of his or her authority.

24.   When dealing with a confrontational person, do you:

    a.   Feel uncomfortable?

    b.   Take the offensive?

    c.   Get angry, but acquiese?

    d.   Ask "Why do you say that?"

25.   An unresponsive person has been assigned to your team. You:

    a.   Ask "Why are you so quiet?"

    b.   Ask "What do I have to do to get you to respond?"

    c.   Leave him alone temporarily.

    d.   Ask "What projects are you working on now?"

Answers

1.   a = 2   b = 5   c = 1   d = 0

Automatically accepting the blame (*a*) when work is criticized is not a good answer, but at least it shows that you're not trying to pass the buck.

It's better than a woebegone "Why does this always happen to me?" (*c*) and certainly better than "My people never check their work" (*d*), which shows a lack of maturity on your part. Obviously, "What went wrong?" (*b*) is the best all-round answer.

2.   a = 2   b = 1   c = 4   d = 5

When someone you call is "in a meeting," the most normal—and least effective—response is to leave your name and hope the person will call back (*b*), unless you're Lee Iacocca or the President of the United States. "I'll call back" (*a*) gives you a little more control; "When is the best time for me to call back?" (*c*) is good, but leads to a lot of calls. "Can you help me get through to your boss?" (*d*) is the best possible answer because you get a commitment from someone else to help you.

3.   a = 0   b = 2   c = 5   d = 0

Only defensive, insecure people quit when they don't get what they want (*a*); and yet sticking it out (*d*) is also bad response, because you aren't any value to your company or yourself when you feel demoralized and de-energized. Blaming yourself (*b*) by asking "What's wrong with me?" is not very good either, but at least it means you are willing to take a look at yourself. Asking "What can I do to get a yes?" (*c*) is the most productive kind of self-questioning.

4.   a = 2   b = 0   c = 5   d = 3

When your boss asks "What are you doing tonight?" he or she has put you on the spot. If you're just trying to ward off another request to work overtime, "I have an important appointment" (*a*) is not a very good answer; you could miss out on something that might be more important. Answering "nothing" (*b*) leaves you open for a lot of work. "I was looking forward to having some time to myself" (*d*) is a pretty good answer, particularly if you sense that your boss is going to ask you to work overtime again. At least you're being honest and assertive. But the best possible answer is (*c*): "Why do you ask?" will give you all the information you need to make a choice.

5.   a = 1   b = 0   c = 3   d = 5

When your boss thoughtlessly piles on assignments, you can knock yourself out trying to do everything at once (*a*); at least it shows that you're eager and willing. It's better than accepting the workload while seething with anger (*b*). Telling your boss that you can't do all the jobs at once (*c*) is a pretty good answer; you're being assertive, but you're not offering any constructive solution. The best answer is (*d*): setting priorities helps your boss focus and helps you work efficiently.

6.   a = 1   b = 2   c = 5   d = 0

When introduced to a new associate, it's important to show sincere interest. Trying to make a good impression by talking about yourself (*a*) is not the worst thing you can do, but you're not learning much; (*b*) is a little better, although trying to gain the advantage is asking questions for the wrong reasons; letting the other person carry the ball (*d*) is the worst response because good managers should be actively involved in communication. The best response is (*c*): Ask questions and also talk about yourself; it's even better when you volunteer a little bit about yourself without being asked.

7.   a = 4   b = 0   c = 5   d = 1

When a meeting chairperson says your department should be cooperative, you have two good choices: asking for specific suggestions after the meeting (*a*) is a good response if it's a high-level meeting; but in most situations immediately confronting the chair (*c*) is the best response. Saying nothing (*b*) or nodding your head (*d*) doesn't help at all.

8.   a = 0   b = 5   c = 2   d = 4

Your boss has criticized you severely. Worrying for days (*a*) isn't going to help at all; nor will denying the criticism (*c*). A lot depends on what kind of relationship you have with your boss. If your boss criticizes you severely for a simple error, something else is probably bothering him. In this case (*b*) is the best response; asking your boss to tell you more about what he expects will help you get to the bottom of the problem. Waiting for your boss to cool down (*d*) and asking how he would feel in a similar situation is helpful, especially if this behavior is a pattern that you would like to avoid in the future.

9.   a = 0   b = 2   c = 5   d = 3

You've lost a major contract. Accepting it (*a*) after putting a lot of time and effort into it is not appropriate; people who want to get ahead have to be persistent. Planning to try again (*b*) isn't going to help too much either, but at least it shows some persistence. Registering at the next sales seminar (*d*) is not a bad idea, because learning is always helpful and it may give you some clues as to why you lost the contract. But the best answer is to call up and find out why (*c*). Then you know specifically what to do the next time.

10.   a = 2   b = 4   c = 0   d = 5

We're all asked to do things we don't want to do. Agreeing reluctantly (*a*) is not bad; "Can you tell me more about it?" (*b*) might help, because the assignment may be better than you think; refusing (*c*) isn't going to do you much good if you're upwardly mobile. "How important is this to you?" (*d*) is the best answer because the response may affect your decision: if it's not important, you may safely refuse; if it is very important, you may gain extra points for doing it.

11.   a = 0   b = 2   c = 5   d = 3

Unexpectedly being asked to move to a smaller office has happened to many people I know. It comes as a shock, and I've gotten more calls for advice about this situation than almost any other. My advice is, stall for time so you can think about the best way to deal with it. When you act immediately, you inevitably do the wrong thing. You don't want to start packing (*a*); there's no point in looking for another job yet (*b*). Stall for time (*c*), and ask them not to do anything until you can talk further. Asking your boss what's going on (*d*) couldn't hurt.

12.   a = 2   b = 5   c = 4   d = 0

The obvious answer when going one-on-one with a tough negotiator is (*a*)—try to gain control. But gaining control at the beginning is not always wise, even with a tough negotiator, especially when it concerns a long-term project. It's better to gain support. The best answer is (*b*)—establish rapport to gain trust over the long run. The next best answer is (*c*)—letting the other person start off builds trust. If you need a support person present with a tough negotiator (*d*), you'll lose Brownie points.

13.   a = 1   b = 5   c = 2   d = 3

Anytime you have to make a decision involving your staff, let them participate (*b*). If they can solve the issue without you, by all means let them do it and bring you the solution (*d*). It's all right to ask your boss's opinion, but not at the expense of involving your staff (*a*). There are some situations where you will want to make a solo decision (*c*), but for the most part, look for opportunities to involve your staff.

14.   a = 1   b = 4   c = 3   d = 5

It's hard to answer this question about yourself objectively. Ask someone to observe you in a group and to tell you honestly how you show strength. Talking louder and longer (*a*) doesn't help. Asking probing questions (*b*) is good; listening (*c*) is also good. But being well prepared with questions and statements (*d*) is obviously the best answer—especially if it's your style to talk a lot.

15.   a = 0   b = 1   c = 4   d = 5

Your CEO has just given you instructions you don't understand. Neither (*a*) nor (*b*) is a good response: faking your way through it or asking someone else for help is a dangerous way to go. Saying you don't understand and asking for further explanation (*c*) is not a bad response, but (*d*) is best: although you may not need to call back, always leave yourself an opening. Few people digest everything all at once, and it shows you're thinking ahead.

16.   a = 0   b = 5   c = 4   d = 1

You're about to move to a new location, and someone else sticks their nose in with advice. If you're too hotheaded to listen (*a*), you're not going to learn anything. To listen and mull it over later (*c*) is not bad, but you still don't know why the person is offering the advice. If you chose answer (*d*), at least you're willing to listen, although feeling upset isn't going to help. The best response is (*b*): "Why are you sharing this with me?" The person may have some valuable insight, but before you can judge the quality of the advice you need to know her motivation.

17.   a = 1   b = 3   c = 5   d = 0

"Tell me about yourself" is one of those awful questions that people ask all the time. The best possible answer is (*c*): "What specifically did you want to know?" Anything else and you're wandering off track.

18.   a = 0   b = 2   c = 4   d = 5

Never making another speech in public (*a*) is a sure way to put the brakes on your career. Going over all the things you did wrong (*b*) may help, if you also list all the things you did right. The best way to correct any mistake is to ask yourself "How can I improve the next time?" (*c*). But in this situation the very best thing to do is to ask a more experienced executive for constructive criticism (*d*): not only will you get the help you need, but you'll also develop that person's interest in you.

19.   a = 3   b = 0   c = 4   d = 5

When someone vaguely says "We'll get back to you," it's better, from your point of view, to nail down the specifics. As much as possible you want to be in control of the action. Therefore smiling and saying thank you (*b*) is a polite but useless response. "When can I expect to hear from you?" (*a*) is a good response. "When can I have an answer—I have other offers" (*c*) is better, if you feel confrontal on a given day; it lets the person know you're valued. But the best response is (*d*), "When in the next ten days can I call for an answer?" It is both specific and polite.

20.   a = 0   b = 1   c = 5   d = 3

When you're caught off guard, admitting with humor that you weren't listening (*d*) can sometimes pay off. If you do it right, it shows confidence. But since this is an important meeting, the best answer is "Could Elaine give an application of her point so I can answer more effectively" (*c*). It gives you the information you need in order to respond without revealing a lapse of attention on your part.

21.   a = 5   b = 4   c = 4   d = 2

We all like to be asked for advice, but to be useful to the other person— particularly if it's someone doing a job for you—the best answer is (*a*), "Where do you hope to end up?" because before you can help someone solve a problem you have to know their objective. "What would you like to do?" (*b*) is a good answer; it gets the person thinking for himself. "How can I specifically help?" (*c*) gets him to focus on what he really expects from you. "Whom else have you asked for advice?" (*d*) is a good question if you follow it with "What did they say?"

22.   a = 5   b = 5   c = 4   d = 1

For a manager the best use of questions is to gain information (*a*) and gain commitment (*b*). If you use questions to control communication in a positive sense, then (*c*) is also a good answer. I'd like to think that managers don't use questions to gain the upper hand (*d*), but questions are like any other skill—once you learn how to do it, you can use it any way you wish.

23.   a = 3   b = 1   c = 5   d = 3

When you have a power-oriented employee, you have to give clear guidelines as to what they can and can't do. If you sit back and hope for the best (*b*), that person is going to take over your job while you're away. You need a written statement of both responsibilities and extent of authority (*c*). Asking the employee to verbally state limits and directives (*a* and *d*) will help, but putting it in writing (*c*) encompasses everything.

24.   a = 1   b = 5   c = 1   d = 5

This is a question that you must answer in terms of your immediate reaction: what is your initial response when faced with a confrontal person? When dealing with confrontal people, taking the offensive in some way is the best strategy (*b* and *d*). "Why do you say that?" (*d*) is the best answer because it's a specific question.

25.   a = 1   b = 1   c = 3   d = 5

The worst thing you can ask an unresponsive person is "Why are you so quiet?" or "What do I have to do to get you to respond?" (*a* and *b*). You can leave the person alone temporarily and see what happens (*c*). But the best answer is to start asking about unthreatening subjects (*d*) to draw the person out.

Scoring

100–125 Points

You're self-confident and feel comfortable asking questions. You seek information and take action, no matter how difficult it may be. You are assertive, yet still able to establish long-term, supportive relationships with employees, colleagues, and clients. You take time to plan carefully and are persistent. Because you are secure you don't hesitate to ask others for help and advice. According to current business indicators, you possess the qualities of the manager of the 1980s.

90–100 Points

You are comfortable asking questions, but you don't seek the help and advice of others as often as you could. You feel that the best way to get more power is through your own achievement and recognition. You can take the lead and are visible within the company. You are ambitious, but to guarantee ultimate success you need to listen more and to tune in to new styles of people management.

75–90 Points

You are ambitious and want to get ahead, but you believe asking for help is a sign of weakness. When something goes wrong you tend to blame circumstances or other people. Asking questions will reduce some of your anxiety, help avoid costly mistakes, and let you develop a more people-oriented approach to your career.

Less than 75 Points

To make it to the top you will have to become more assertive. You tend to accept the blame for foul-ups, and you give up too easily. You are a hard worker and probably are overworked and under stress. You avoid confrontations at all costs. Asking questions in nonthreatening situations will bolster confidence and give you a way to assert yourself without anxiety.

You can see from the quiz that the art of asking smart questions is not always as easy as it sounds. There are few absolutely right or wrong answers. Nor is there a perfect response for every complex situation that crops up in day-to-day working and living. This book will help you develop a technique that allows you to deal with most situations in an intelligent and productive manner. To begin the journey into Smart Questions we're going to analyze the mysterious power that questions have over us all.

2

The Power of Questions

"If you could have three wishes at this moment, what would you wish?" Think about it. A question like that would make the most obstinate, closed-off, difficult person in the world open up. Like most smart questions, it's irresistible.

The main reason questions are so effective is that most people love to answer them. Questions stimulate the mind and offer people an opportunity to use their brains constructively. How else can you explain the continued popularity of question-and-answer quiz shows on radio and television? (What's a group of bears called? [A sleuth.] Where is it bad luck to say "Macbeth?" [The theater.])

One of the axioms of human communication is that most people prefer talking to listening. When you ask for someone's thoughts and opinions, you give him an opportunity to talk. For example, a manager who asks to hear an employee's ideas gains great measures of loyalty—and information—in return.

The impulse to answer a question—any question—is as automatic as the "fight or flight" response. Everyone, including that rare individual who refuses to answer, pays more attention to a question than to a statement. "This department is falling apart" is a statement that achieves nothing. Turned into a question—"If you were in my place, what would you do to turn things around?"—it invites innovation.

Hearing a question puts the listener on the alert. The phrasing and cadence instantly let him know he's expected to do more than listen: he's expected to respond. Even questions we really don't want to answer are compelling ("What are you doing tonight?" "How much rent do you pay?" "Why did you do that?" "What salary are you looking for?").

This answering reflex is fundamental to the Smart Questions system. And you can turn it to your advantage in a multiplicity of business situations.

When I was starting out in the advertising business, I worked with a staff of other junior account executives, photographers, copywriters, salespeople, and consultants. Our boss, the marketing director, was a harried, stressed person who would much rather deal with clients than with us. He was always lecturing us about how we should do a better job, develop better attitudes, work more closely with our customers. His comments, so generally phrased and so negative in tone, made me feel uncomfortable and inadequate. As a team we felt off balance because although our boss seemed so totally dissatisfied with our performance, we didn't know how to improve. Every day gloom permeated the atmosphere in the office.

I would often walk all the way home at night, mulling over the situation; I recognized that I would never be happy in the job unless I could find a way to relieve the constant frustration. Since it was clear that things were not going to change magically, I wondered what I could do to improve my circumstances. And one evening during one of my long walks I had an idea, but it involved taking a risk.

The next afternoon my boss came into the office and started giving us his standard lecture about client relations, ending with "You've just got to spend more time with your clients."

As we all shifted from one foot to the other, I looked him in the eye and said, "You approved my schedule and you know where I spend my time. Could you specifically say how I should change that?"

He looked at me, startled. Then he mumbled something like "Well, you'll just have to find a way," shuffled the papers he was holding, and walked out of the room.

That was a turning point in our relationship. He never lectured again, and he addressed me with new respect. We all began to talk over problems and work on ideas for improvement. I can't say he changed radically, but his behavior altered enough to make the work atmosphere more comfortable.

A Boon to Managers

Lee Iacocca, that wizard of the automobile industry, has said: "I've seen too many guys come along who are smart and talented . . . the go-getters who followed a plan, went to school, got a good job, worked hard—and then nothing came of it. Certainly luck plays a part. But a major reason capable people fail to advance is that they don't work well with their colleagues."

If the definition of management is getting things done through other people, then clearly working well with people is the best way to achieve success. And working well with people is 100 percent communication. Or, as Iacocca says, "talking to them plain and simple." Yet today's managers are expected to do even more than "get the job done." They are expected to help their employees make their own decisions and solve their own problems, thereby devising more imaginative solutions and achieving maximum excellence for both the company and themselves.

"Talking" now takes on even more import. A new communication style is needed to make this extra leap. Nothing can get people to take on and solve their own problems faster than a good question ("How would you do it?").

Managers today are also expected to function well in a wide range of circumstances and situations. When you know how to ask the right questions, you can talk to anyone about anything. You can be at ease in a conversation with a count or a cabdriver, an artist or an accountant. You can work smoothly with technical people and outside suppliers, with clients as well as upper management.

Asking questions doesn't require that you change yourself or try to be something you're not. You can work with anyone, or for anyone, whatever your basic nature.

When to Use Smart Questions

Knowing how to ask smart questions gives you the edge in virtually any situation. Did you know that questions help you:

- Persuade people
- Gain information
- Plant your own ideas

- Clear up fuzzy thinking
- Motivate employees
- Solve problems
- Take the sting out of criticism
- Open lines of communication among diverse peoples and departments
- Reduce mistakes
- Overcome objections
- Get cooperation
- Clarify instructions
- Reduce anxiety
- Defuse volatile situations
- Gain control in risky situations

Persuading People

No matter what your job, sooner or later you'll be in a situation where you want to sell someone something. It may be an idea, or a plan, or a pair of shoes. You may want to persuade someone to your point of view to gain their support. No matter what you're selling, questions will help you.

With a smart question you can find out what worries the other person and what would ease his doubts. A good question establishes rapport, gives the other person the sense that you care, and also gives you a more powerful forum for your pitch than you'd get by handing over gratuitous information.

No matter what you're selling, the same philosophy applies. Says Allen E. Murray, Chairman of the Mobil Oil Corporation, "Sometimes just a 'What do you think?' or 'How does it strike you?' or 'What's wrong with it?' can give me a sense of whether I'm succeeding."

When you want to persuade, you'll always get further by asking a question than by making a statement. In my business a good question will give me ammunition I can use in selling. I will often ask a client, "What are the benefits you'd like to see as a result of our working together?" Then I keep the answers in mind as I develop my proposal.

Getting Information

The most obvious use of questions is to gather information. Being well informed is essential to success in any field, and questions allow you to learn. Good managers need all the information they can absorb, and incomplete information or instructions can be costly.

I work with a client whose assistant vice president is a stickler for getting things right. After receiving any assignment, she invariably asks these questions: "Is there anything else I should know? Can I go over it with you one more time and clarify any miscommunication on my part? When can I call you if I have any questions?"

This manager is only 25 years old, and she is the fastest-rising vice president in her firm because she has a reputation for always turning in work that is virtually flawless.

No one can hope to know everything in this "information age." It's the ability to tap into the most accessible sources of information that's important. For example, the ability to listen to and cull the best ideas from staff people is the sign of a top manager. As humorist James Thurber said, "It is better to know some of the questions than to know all of the answers."

Planting Ideas

Often when you tell someone what you want, they fail to hear you: "Here's the plan—if you follow it everything will work out." Somehow they never quite follow the plan the way you described, because people naturally follow their own ideas better than they do someone else's. A clever use of questions is to plant your own idea in someone else's mind and then let them develop it as their own. William S. Lee, Chairman and CEO of Duke Power Company, describes how he uses the technique: "At a meeting, for example, ask, 'What do you think about incorporating Plan A and Plan B?' When the other person starts talking about it, once they've said it themselves, they own the idea—and I give them the credit for it."

Clearing up Thinking

For me, the most valuable use of questions is to clear up fuzzy or ambiguous thinking. Posing a question requires more concentration than making a statement. Asking questions means that you have to think things through more fully, and your thoughts become clearer as you shape each question. You must delve deeper into your own mind. For this reason alone asking questions immediately puts you a jump ahead of those managers who merely make statements.

For example, when I sit down with my staff to go over the week's priorities, we usually list what each of us hopes to accomplish during the week. Naturally I ask, "What has to be done?" But I also ask this question: "How specifically are you going to handle it?" That way, there are fewer misunderstandings and fewer unpleasant surprises.

A smart question organizes the problem—for yourself and for the person with whom you're speaking—and offers an opportunity to find a solution. When you ask a question you force the other person to think more clearly before answering. To answer you, he must organize his own thoughts and put them into words. Expressing thoughts aloud clarifies ideas, exposes any lapses in logic, and reinforces the strong points. So, as a two-way channel, questions create clearer, more direct communication.

We were involved in an especially busy time in our office when an unexpected direct-mail project turned up. Our marketing director felt swamped. I asked this simple question: "What do you think is the best way to work it out?" She stopped worrying, sat down, and developed a workable plan.

Often a person trying to express his ideas will say "I know what I mean and I just can't explain it." A well-turned question will help him clear things up: "What would you do first?" "How do you see the end result?"

Motivating Employees

One of the best ways to motivate employees is to encourage them to solve their own problems. For example, an employee tells you about an idea he has. After thinking it over a moment, you have your doubts. You might say:

"It will take too much time."

"It will be too costly."

"It's based on false assumptions."

What did you accomplish? You dealt with the idea swiftly, gave your staff person the benefit of your wisdom, and saved him from wasting his time on a chancy project. Or did you? What if instead you had said:

"How much time do you think it will take?"

"What do you estimate it will cost?"

"Does that equation seem profitable to you?"

What did you accomplish this time? By posing your thoughts as questions, you gave your employee your point of view in a more compelling way by allowing him to come to the same conclusion himself. Without creating ill will, you gave him the means to assess his idea, to see the flaws or strong points, and to make an independent judgment. And your receptiveness ensures that he will contribute his ideas again.

Problem Solving

Asking questions helps you get to the bottom of problems and make decisions that are fair to everyone concerned. Gerard A. Miller, Vice President Director of Finance, Merrill Lynch, Pierce, Fenner & Smith, Inc., says: "I use questions to locate pressure points and weak spots. It's important to get out and talk to your people; ask them what's going on. It's the only way you can discover problems before they mushroom."

I once observed two managers who solved problems in completely different ways. When one manager saw his people having difficulties he would say, "Oh, that's easy. I know you can take care of it." He believed that by taking a positive attitude he was building their confidence.

In similar situations, however, the second manager would ask, "What seems to be the problem?" He listened, then asked, "What solutions do you see?"

In the first instance, the staff had little respect for their manager; they felt he didn't care about their problems and that they had to struggle towards a solution alone. It always took them a lot of time to work things out.

In the second situation, the staff thought their manager was the best executive in the company. His simple questions showed interest and helped them think more clearly. As a result, they solved problems faster and more efficiently.

The most interesting aspect of these two examples is that both managers spent exactly the same amount of time and effort helping their staff. Yet one had a terrible time getting his people to solve problems and the other got them solved easily.

Taking the Sting out of Criticism

When you state an opinion, especially a critical one, the other person's hearing turns off and his guard goes up. Whether the person is your friend or your employee, your spouse or your child, direct criticism will put him or her on the defensive. Prefacing negative remarks with "Don't take this personally" doesn't help. Once aimed towards someone, criticism becomes personal. The only way to take the sting out of a negative appraisal is to get the person to see it—and say it—for himself.

A manager can use a question to take the sting out of criticism and at the same time secure a commitment for change. "You're always late" and "You are wrong" are statements that achieve nothing. Turned into questions—"How do you think lateness affects the department?" and "Why do you feel that way?"—they arouse thinking and encourage action. They involve the other person instead of alienating him.

Opening Communication between Diverse Groups

We've all heard about technical wizards who can solve the riddles of the universe but can't carry on a simple conversation with their next-door neighbor. As technological change speeds on, communication between technical and nontechnical people becomes more necessary, and more difficult, than ever.

In my consulting work I find that technicians suddenly promoted into managerial ranks often have trouble getting their ideas across to co-workers who don't speak their language. A nonverbal technical whiz will find he can talk to many different kinds of people, including his superiors, more easily once he learns to ask questions. A questioning approach makes him seem less aloof, more accessible and concerned. Asking questions lets the technical person talk less, listen more, and still establish rapport with co-workers.

Reducing Mistakes

One basic premise of communication is that your perception of a problem determines how you act on it. We go wrong not so much in what we do as in how we originally perceived the problem. Upon assigning a task, a manager will often ask an employee, "Do you understand?" The employee invariably nods affirmatively. To say he doesn't understand is tantamount to admitting that he's slow-witted.

Two weeks later the employee submits a report on the delegated task. The manager explodes. "This isn't what I wanted! I thought you said you understood!" The employee did indeed understand, but what he understood and what the manager understood were two completely different interpretations.

The manager asked the wrong question. Instead of "Do you understand?" he could have asked a smart feedback question: "To eliminate the guesswork, can you sum up what you're going to do as a result of this meeting?" He could then listen to the reply, correct any missteps, and clarify any vague instructions. Smart questions are a foolproof means of generating feedback and reducing mistakes.

When you establish an atmosphere of give-and-take, you can learn a great deal from such smart questions as "Is there anything more I can do to clarify the assignment before you begin?" or "Why don't you give it some thought and get back to me with any questions before you begin?"

Overcoming Objections

We all get into those binds where whatever we say is countered with a series of objections. "Yes, but . . ." is the most frequently heard. You can go on and on like this, offering one option after another, never getting anywhere. The solution? Stop . . . think . . . and ask.

"What are your major concerns about this [project, idea, product]?"

"What other choices do you see?"

"How can I help you?"

Getting Cooperation

Sometimes you get into a situation where you're trying to solve a business problem but can't seem to get attention or cooperation from anyone.

Charles, the head of a new publishing company, was trying to get permission to allow mail-order customers to charge their orders to a bank card. Charles spoke to eight different banks and from each received the same reply: no mail-order accounts because of previous bank losses. In desperation, he asked one bank officer in merchant sales, "Have you ever made an exception?" To Charles's surprise, the merchant saleswoman paused. "I'm not sure," she told him. "I think there was one instance . . . but I can't remember the details."

Charles became alert. "Would it be possible for you to find out for me? Maybe there's something else I can do."

The merchant saleswoman said she would try to find exceptions to the ruling. While waiting for a call back, Charles called five more bank officers in merchant sales and after being turned down, asked each the same question: "Have you ever made an exception?" In every case, the salesperson sought the exceptions, quoted the circumstances, and gave Charles something to go on.

By accumulating enough "exceptions," Charles was able to put together a passable application form and was eventually rewarded with permission to use a bank card. Many difficult legal cases are won in precisely this manner: accumulating the exceptions and building a case.

When faced with a blank wall, remember Charles: "Have you ever made an exception?" is one of the all-time great questions.

Clarifying Statements

The most immediate use of smart questions is to clarify statements of any kind. A new secretary once told me that she would reorganize my files so that I could more easily find things. I took for granted that this would be a positive maneuver. Lesson No. 1: Never assume. Naturally I came back to find that she had organized the files in a manner that was completely incomprehensible to me. The smart question I failed to ask: "How do you plan to do it?"

I remember another instance where an executive vice president of operations, in a state of frustration, addressed his staff with this statement: "What this organization needs is better communication."

He was totally shocked when he wound up with a new telephone system. No one asked him what he meant by "communication."

Stemming Anxiety

Most psychologists agree that anxiety arises from loss of control. Asking a smart question puts you in the driver's seat. Because the other person is compelled to answer, the power goes to the asker. Just watch the power shift when someone asks you, "Where are you going?" and you answer, "Why do you ask?"

With a question you choose the subject to be discussed, and you establish the tone of the exchange. The conversation continues along the lines of your questioning. The moment you feel the conversation turn in the wrong direction you can change the subject simply by shifting the focus of your questions.

It pays to be assertive. Terry's boss was a frantic workaholic, racing in and out of his office all morning with one assignment after another. Terry controlled the action and reduced his own tension with a smart question: "Which of these is most important to you, and what are the time limits?" Because smart questions put him in control, his anxiety abated.

Asking a question also forces you to think before you speak, and the better prepared you are, the more confident and in command you feel.

Defusing Volatile Encounters

Most of us shy away from direct confrontation with others because it threatens to set off an uncontrollable chain reaction of attack and counterattack. Asking questions gives you a way to confront people with minimal conflict. When you begin a confrontation with a question—"Can you tell me more about what you're feeling?"—you reduce the other person's defensiveness and open up the chance for communication.

Reducing Risks

To get to the top you often have to take risks. Melissa, an energetic and outgoing young project manager, was vying to handle an important new project for her company. Yet her boss couldn't seem to decide who would get the job. Melissa decided to take a calculated risk. She approached her boss:

"What are the key qualities I would need to do this job?" she asked.

"Tact, analytical thinking, follow-through, and good public-speaking abilities."

"Do you feel I have what it takes?"

"Yes and no."

"Can you clarify that?"

"You're good on your feet, you're an objective thinker, and you get the job done, but you also irritate a lot of people. You push too hard, and it puts people off."

"How important is that to you?"

"In this case, it's important. The client company has a complex inner structure, with lots of competitive departments and several people in authority who require subtle handling."

"Is that all that's holding me back from the job?"

"That's it."

"Let's say I got Vincent, the departmental diplomat, to handle the outside communication; would that satisfy you?"

"It's an interesting possibility. It might work. I'd be willing to give it a try."

In this case Melissa risked an outright rejection from her boss, which might have left a scar on their working relationship. It also could have confirmed his view of her as being too pushy and aggressive. If the situation had turned out that way, however, Melissa could have gained an important insight.

Her style might hold her back indefinitely in this particular company. It's possible, of course, that this situation might be an isolated case. To make certain, Melissa would need to probe further to see if the only people who get ahead in her company are indeed the diplomats. Were this the case she might get much further if she switched to a different job where her no-nonsense approach was considered an asset rather than a liability.

An Immediate Effect

These are some of the multitude of ways questions can work for you in business—both with your staff and with upper management. If you want to coach your employees, if you want to gain attention and respect from your boss, if you want to persuade, learn to ask questions. The best part about it is that you don't have to be a tactical genius to benefit from a questioning style. You learn how to do it simply by doing it. For one day, concentrate on asking questions. See for yourself how well you can make yourself understood by using questions instead of statements.

Many ordinary statements can be turned into questions. In your conversations, get into the habit of questioning—not just to get facts but to stimulate the other person's thinking, as well as your own. When you do make a statement, don't consider it complete unless you also ask for a reaction. If you try, you can quickly learn to restructure the way you communicate with people. You will become a better persuader almost immediately.

As you get into the habit of asking questions, you will find that your conversations are richer in information and more engaging to both the other person and yourself.

Now, obviously, going around asking questions willy-nilly of everyone you meet isn't going to turn you into an overnight success. The whole point of the Smart Questions technique is to ask the *right question,* at the *right time,* of the *right person.* And that's where skill, intuition, and good sense will make or break your success.

3

The Right Way to Ask

I remember two customer-service managers at a long-distance telephone company who used questions in different ways. The first manager answered customer complaints with this question: "Do you have a problem?" The response invariably was "You bet I have." The manager's ears burned with every telephone problem the customer had ever had. Customers ranted and raved, reliving every injustice ever perpetrated by telephone companies past and present. After all the grievances had been aired, the manager would eventually discover the immediate problem he was expected to solve.

The second manager avoided these long and exhausting encounters by using a different opening question. She would ask, "In what way may I help you?" Her question quickly got the customer off his gripes and got him thinking about a solution.

Even though smart questions have a broad application in almost every profession, they have to be used in the right way. Asking a smart question and asking it in the right way is an art. A thoughtlessly phrased question is like a loose cannon—it can set off wild repercussions. Likewise, too many questions, thoughtlessly phrased, make the questioner look and sound silly. But a thought-out, concise, and stimulating question shows that the questioner is intelligent and discerning. Fortunately it's fairly easy to arrive at this position.

The Two Types of Questions

There are many different types of questions, but most fall into two broad categories: the *closed question,* one that extracts a piece of information but precludes further discussion, and the *open question,* one that stimulates thought and encourages continued conversation. Smart questions invariably fall into the second category, but there are times when the closed question is useful.

Closed questions can be answered with a yes or no, or with a simple statement of fact. They are good for getting information in a hurry. Here are some examples:

"How many forms do you need?"

"Who is responsible for quality control?"

"What is our starting time?"

"Do you want to get ahead in this organization?"

"Is this the entire report?"

"Did the supplies come in on time?"

"Have we received all the payment invoices?"

"When is the meeting scheduled?"

"Did you phone for reservations?"

Closed questions usually get the sought-after information, and they can be useful for capturing someone's attention. William Granville, Manager of Technology Transfer at Mobil Oil Corporation, likes closed questions because "they save time and keep conversations properly directed." Interjecting a yes-or-no question into the stream of a conversation also can steer an undirected discussion back on course ("Didn't you tell me that the only really feasible course of action was to change the contract?").

You can also use a closed question to confirm an agreement: "Are we agreed then? Can we shake on it?"

But closed questions do not always serve a manager's needs, because they don't lead anywhere. The questions most valuable to managers—the questions that get results and encourage growth and development in virtually any situation—are like open roads, inviting exploration. At the same time they have purpose and intent.

The beauty of open questions is that they allow the other person to become involved, to participate in the exchange and come up with solutions of his or her own.

Open questions require a more in-depth response than a yes or no or a simple statement of fact. Some examples:

"How would *you* handle this situation?"

"What kind of people get ahead in this company?"

"What feedback are you getting from your people in the field?"

"How do you feel about this?"

"What is most important to you?"

"What is it you don't like about Brand X?"

"What are your priorities for this assignment?"

Open questions create a conversational tone. They eliminate the sense of interrogation typically associated with closed questions. In fact, the other person may not even be aware that questions are being asked. Open questions also encourage the other person to think about his answer. If he doesn't have the answer on the tip of his tongue, the natural pause that follows the question gives him a chance to think about it. If he does have an answer ready, you've given him an opportunity to express himself. By asking the question, you have invited the other person to offer his view.

An advertising man can earn points with a prospective client if he uses the open question technique:

"What would you like to see happen as a result of a new campaign?"

"Where do you think your previous agency fell short?"

"What's the message that you most want to get across to the public?"

"What do you think are the benefits of your product?"

"Why do you think someone should buy your product instead of the competing brand?"

With open questions you gain more than factual information, you get a good take on thoughts, attitudes, and emotions that influence the other person's actions. Open questions also help the other person clarify his thinking as he states his needs in his own words.

Open questions are prime motivating and coaching tools. We're going to talk more about this in Part Two. In a nutshell: The way to get employees past a problem is to get them involved in the solution. And the way to get them involved is to encourage them to verbalize the problem themselves. Instead of stating "I think your work would improve if you spent more time organizing yourself," ask "How do you think you could plan your time more efficiently?" or "In what way can you use your staff more productively?"

Knowing this, does it surprise you to learn that with all of these advantages, only one out of every twenty questions managers ask is phrased in an open style?

Open questions are vastly underused for two reasons. The first is sheer ignorance. Because questions are generally not part of the standard business communication repertoire, most people are unfamiliar with the technique and therefore don't know how to use it. The second reason is that it takes more effort to think up open questions and to pay the necessary close attention to the responses.

As a consultant working with a variety of corporations I have had plenty of opportunity to observe the difference between approaching my own clients with closed questions and with open questions. While it usually takes more time to think of an open question, ultimately I save much grinding, tedious effort. Here's an example of a management consultant using closed questions to elicit information from a potential client:

Consultant: Is your company involved in executive development?

Client: Yes.

Consultant: Who attends these sessions?

Client: First-line through middle managers.

Consultant: Do you use outside trainers?

Client: No.

Consultant: How often are these classes run?

Client: About once a month, or as needed.

Consultant: How long are they?

Client: One day each.

Consultant: What results do you see?

Client: Fair to good.

The consultant in this example garnered specific information with a series of six closed questions, but the conversation was rudimentary, and he is still a long way from landing the job. Suppose instead he had asked one smart open question:

Consultant: Can you tell me something about the kind of executive training you do?

Client: We have a limited menu of training and our managers are required to take five days of training each year. The courses usually last one day. They can select from the menu of courses, and their bosses okay the training. With cutbacks in budgets we'd like to do more, but we can't.

The word "limited" was a signal to the consultant that there was an opening. So was the information that the company confined itself to one-day courses. One day is not sufficient for many types of managerial training.

From the one question in this example the consultant acquired much valuable information. Also, the client was invited into the situation. Out of the client's own mouth came the answers that allowed the consultant to go on to make a strong case for his own employment.

Creating Smart Questions

A closed question is easily turned into an open question by adding one or two important words. "What," "how," and "could" are perfect examples.

Closed: Do you use word-processing equipment?

Open: To what extent do you use word-processing equipment?

Closed: Do you have any problems with that machine?

Open: What has been your experience with that machine?

Closed: Do you like to travel?

Open: How do you feel about traveling?

Closed: Can the department improve?

Open: How can the department improve?

Closed: Why did you do that?

Open: What could have been done differently?

Closed: Which idea is best?

Open: Could you describe several other options?

Closed: What do you use this for?

Open: Are there any other applications?

Ten Smart Open Questions

Tuck these ten smart and versatile open questions into your mind for future use in almost any situation.

1. "What can I do to help you?"
2. "What has to be done?"
3. "Can you explain the process?"
4. "How do you feel about it?"
5. "Can you explain that further?"
6. "From what standpoint are you asking?"
7. "What are some of the reasons this didn't work as well as we had hoped?"
8. "What can we change to make this work better?"
9. "What key results are we looking for?"
10. "From what standpoint do you ask?"

"Feeling" Questions

"Feeling" questions are wonderful for most people. (There is one important exception—a certain type of person of whom you should seldom ask a feeling question—which we will discuss in Chapter 5.)

For the most part, "How do you feel about that?" will generate a more in-depth response than "What do you think about that?" It's easy for someone to give you an offhand response to "What do you think?" They can hand you a quick opinion, or if they have no opinion, answer "I don't know." But whether or not you know anything about a topic, you can *feel* something about it. Exploring feelings also requires more personal commitment and, ultimately, deeper thinking.

This type of question, by the way, is the favorite of newscasters and reporters. The next time you watch the six o'clock news, listen to the reporters interviewing a subject.

Combine Questions with Third-Party Endorsements

Promoters, public-relations people, and marketers use a familiar persuasive device called "third-party endorsement." The premise here is that most people respond better to stories about other people than to abstract concepts. A promoter, for example, tells his listener a story about someone who struggled with a problem until the promoter's product provided the solution. By identifying with the third party, the listener is persuaded that the product can solve his problem too.

The same technique, combined with a question, works for managers. For example, you might help an employee grappling with a serious problem by saying "Joan once had a similar situation, which she solved this way." You proceed to describe the problem and how Joan coped with it. But that isn't enough. To make a third-party endorsement work as a managerial tool, you need to combine it with a smart question. When you finish Joan's story, ask an open question such as "How do you think that solution would work in this instance?"

A more subtle version of the third-person technique is used skillfully by interviewers when they discuss sensitive issues with celebrities. Let's say you want to get someone to level with you about his or her drinking problem, as Betty Rollin described in her book *Am I Getting Paid for This?*: "If you ask about it flat out," says Rollin, "they'll usually deny it. But if you say, 'A lot of people think it's easy to stop drinking, that all you need is a little willpower—what do you think?' Then you'll hear how it's not easy. And that's probably not all you'll hear. . . . Most people, even stars, seem to *want* to tell you about their true selves."

Questions Are Socially Appealing

You can learn a great deal about others by listening to the way they use—or don't use—questions. A very smart, attractive friend of mine says, "I wouldn't go out with a man who didn't ask me some questions about myself within the first five or ten minutes of our meeting. If he doesn't ask me anything about myself, I figure he's a self-centered sort of person. If he does ask me a few questions, it tells me that he's interested."

Questions are an enlivening conversational tool to help you breeze through any social situation. You needn't restrict your questions to the ordinary ("How do you feel?" "What have you been up to lately?"). Impersonal, imaginative questions can make for stimulating social conversation:

> "If you were stranded on an island, what ten books [tapes, video-cassettes] would you want? What man [woman] would you most want to be with?"
>
> "If you could live during any period in history, which would you choose?"
>
> "If you could marry any famous person in history, who would it be?"
>
> "If you were suddenly given a million dollars and told that you had to spend it just on yourself, what is the first thing you would buy?"

This is Barbara Walters's favorite conversation stimulator: "If you were hospitalized for three months but not really too sick, whom—and it can't be a relative—would you want in the next bed?"

Johnny Carson shot back: "The best damn doctor in town."

But Chet Huntley picked Charles de Gaulle. And Liberace chose Greta Garbo (so he could do all the talking). Whom would you choose?

Practice Makes It Happen

Creating smart questions is a skill that has to be developed. The next time you have a closed question or a statement on the tip of your tongue, stop and turn it into an open question. You will immediately notice the difference in personal response and communication. Like any other skill, however, your questioning technique will improve with practice. And don't limit your practice to the workplace. Get in the habit of asking questions in your personal interactions as well. In social situations make an effort to cast a few original questions towards other people. With friends, family, and colleagues, consciously try using open questions.

Like anything else, you're not going to get a hit every time. Questions are a wonderful tool, but you have to be careful about the way you use them. In the following chapters we're going to talk about staying out of questioning trouble and avoiding the real clinkers.

4

Questions That Backfire

My favorite dumb question was posed by Jimmy Durante in the movie *Jumbo*. As Durante tried to sneak his enormous circus elephant, Jumbo, out of the fairgrounds he was confronted by the sheriff and his deputies. "Where are you going with that elephant?" demanded the sheriff.

Standing in front of the elephant like a gnat trying to hide an airplane, Durante spread out his arms, looked inquiringly to either side, and innocently asked, "What elephant?"

Can questions ever lead you astray? They certainly can. Silly questions can make you look dumb. And smug questions, like smug statements, can make you wish you had a hole to fall through.

You've heard the story of the snappy young salesman who picked up his client at the airport and jauntily ushered him into a sparkling new Rolls Royce. "Is this your first time in one of these?" asked the salesman.

"My first time in the front seat," answered his amused client.

Everyone's entitled to make a fool of himself or herself occasionally. And questions that make you look foolish are not nearly as bad as questions that sound unfriendly, or even threatening. "May I be frank?," for example, is intimidating and almost always signals unpleasant criticism. Other questions can raise doubts or be aggravating.

I remember once asking a client, "What are some problems you're having with your staff?"

"Who said I was having any problems?" she shot back. She was so indignant that I was unable to steer the conversation back onto a neutral track. Although I had used this question dozens of times with other clients, it triggered a bad reaction in this particular person. For her, a less direct question would have worked better ("What are some of the things you're doing in that particular department?").

Certain questions generate a bad response in certain people, and it's not easy to know in advance how someone will respond. Permanently embedded in everyone's memory are parents and teachers:

"Where have you been?"

"How many times do I have to tell you . . . ?"

"When are you going to shape up?"

"How could you do such a thing?"

The wrong questions posed to the adult can trigger all these old feelings of guilt, inadequacy, and rejection.

Dangerous Questions

Of all the potentially dangerous questions you can ask, "Why?" may be the most harmful. Children use it to drive adults crazy. They eventually learn to stop asking "why" because it generates impatience in mothers, fathers, and teachers.

On an adult level, "Why?" frequently cuts off communication when it sounds judgmental or condescending ("Why are you doing it that way?" "Why do you feel that way?" "Why do you think that's a good idea?" "Why did you tell the client we'd send him an advance copy?").

"Why" is useful only when it is fully stripped of its negative connotations. It must be a sincere question, one that cannot be misread. A disapproving attitude can be expressed through your tone of voice, a gesture, even a raised eyebrow. If you accompany the question "Why?" with any of these signals, the other person automatically goes on the defensive.

Overall, "Why?" is one question that you can virtually eliminate from your stock of smart questions. Occasionally you'll be tempted to ask "why" to clarify an instruction, but even then you should take care. I recently overheard a man dining in a French restaurant make this request of the waiter:

"Would you bring me a new serving of butter? This one looks as if it's been used."

The waiter examined the pats of butter in the butter dish, which he had just brought out, and replied, "It's fresh, sir. It just looks ragged."

"Will you please bring me a new serving anyway?"

"Why?"

The customer lost his temper. "Because I asked you, that's why."

The waiter left in a huff and returned with a new plate of butter, which he promptly slammed on the table.

The customer grumbled to himself, and I could almost see him mentally cut the waiter's tip in half.

If you must ask "why" for information, remove the sting by rephrasing the question ("Could you tell me what the problem is?").

"Why?" can almost always be rephrased into "What," "how," and "could" questions. Consider these alternatives:

"Can you explain more fully?"

"What do you have in mind?"

"How do you feel about this?"

"Can you tell me more about why you want to do it this way?"

"How did you come to your decision?"

"If I knew what factors determined your decision, I could be more specific. Could you tell me?"

"Can you elaborate on that?"

"Can you give me some examples?"

"Why" works in some cases ("Why do you suppose that happened?"), but in general, think twice before you ask "why," and see if another question wouldn't get you a better result.

Manipulative Devices

Some people think they can use questions to gain the upper hand. Indirect questions fall into this category. My former boss used to ask,

"Wouldn't you like to get this for me?" or "Wouldn't you like to do this for me?" The whole point of such questions is to shift responsibility onto the other person, and that other person is bound to resent it. If you have to manipulate someone in order to be in control, you're already working from a tenuous position. People are much more willing to help if you ask straight out: "Please do this for me."

One of the most irritating indirect questions is this one: You're putting on your hat and coat and your boss (or colleague, or mother, or spouse) asks, "Are you going out?" What they really want to know is "Where are you going?" but they insist on taking the long way round.

Some people use questions to make it appear as if they are deeply interested in someone. They ask a string of questions to avoid revealing anything about themselves in the course of the conversation ("If I keep the chatter going, the other person will be happy and I won't have to volunteer a thing"). This assumes that people are so easily fooled that they're satisfied just running on and on about themselves ("How's your mom? Glad to hear it—how's your Dad? What about your little sister Amy? And your cousin who lives in Dubuque? What do you hear from Louie, that fellow you used to room with when you lived in Seattle?").

Some people ask questions because they're lazy or tired and don't have the energy to carry on a conversation. But communication means give-and-take. To make questions work, you have to be willing to talk about yourself.

At a medical convention Richard, a new advertising executive anxious to make contacts, meets a product manager of a pharmaceutical company. Richard has learned that a good conversationalist asks questions.

Richard: What sort of work do you do, Brad?

Brad: I'm in pharmaceutical marketing.

Richard: What company are you with?

Brad: Ross and Tompkins.

Richard: What kinds of products do you handle?

Brad: My division is devoted to over-the-counter drugs—we have the leading cold remedy. Some skin-care products, too.

Richard: Where is your office?

Brad: At Sixth Avenue and Fifty-first Street. It's not too far from Grand Central.

Richard: Do you commute?

Brad:	Every day. We moved up to New Rochelle a few years ago. It's not too bad, though. My wife and I both take the train.
Richard:	How long does the trip take?
Brad:	About an hour and ten minutes, door to door. It used to take me twenty minutes . . .
Richard:	How many children do you have?
Brad:	Two boys and a girl.
Richard:	How old are they?
Brad:	The boys are twelve and seven. Penney is five.

With each question Brad, gamely trying to develop the conversation, is feeling increasingly more irritated. All he can think about is how to get away from Richard and escape his verbal assault.

What does Richard think he's doing? He thinks he's being engaging. He has read that good social skills consist of drawing people out by asking them questions. But while Richard is patting himself on the back for being a diplomatic giant, Brad is getting ready to throttle him.

Hurling questions at people gives them the distinct impression that you're oblivious to their feelings. Lawyers are masters at this cross-examination technique, but what works in the courtroom may be a disaster in daily life.

How could this conversation have been different?

Richard:	What sort of work do you do, Brad?
Brad:	I'm in pharmaceutical marketing.
Richard:	That's interesting. Your job must be a tough one right now, with all the new regulations. Do you handle over-the-counter or prescription?
Brad:	OTC—and you're right. Nowadays, trying to sell any drug over the counter without saying anything out of line is a challenge. I'm temperamentally more suited to lying in the sun in Bermuda, but who can afford it?
Richard:	I sympathize—I'm one of the guys who try to help you guys come up with new ways to say the same old things.
Brad:	You must be in advertising. Creative or client side?

Richard: I'm an account executive. And from the looks of my bank balance I believe in my products. I guess I fall into the pattern of conspicuous consumption that everyone identifies with suburbanites. Are you one of us?

Brad: Oh yes, I'm on the run to New Rochelle. Whenever I have a nightmare there's always a commuter train in it. Actually, I like it pretty well. My wife and I both commute in the mornings and it gives us some time to talk without the kids around. I just complain because everyone else does.

In this version, even though Richard holds the initiative because he is the primary questioner, both men have talked about themselves, and both have enjoyed the conversation. Richard responded fully, rather than just collecting Brad's remarks like index cards and filing them away.

Richard has accomplished his purpose: he made a contact. He wasn't looking for a confirmed client or a best friend. He was looking to meet people and make a positive impression within his industry.

Showing Off with Questions

Some people use questions as a sneaky way to look smart. It's a good ploy, but it requires finesse. Recently I attended a seminar on diet and heart disease. The speaker was inexperienced and did not appear to be well informed. A knowledgeable show-off asked, "What about the study on how Type A behavior affects the development of atherosclerosis?" The asker was just showing off that he had as much knowledge as the speaker, and possibly more.

Too Curious

Prying questions are usually beyond the pale, but there are some exceptions. There are different kinds of prying—curious and nosy. You can often get away with being curious, but it's easy to go too far. (In New York you can ask "What rent do you pay?" In the South that might be out of line.) Curious questions fall somewhere into the gulf between needing to know and wanting to know. If you're asking a question because you want to satisfy your curiosity and really don't need the information, in certain situations it might be better to pass it up. You never want to make the other person feel uncomfortable.

Asking at the Wrong Time

In corporate life there's always a right time and a wrong time to ask questions. Stopping someone on his way out of the office is almost always the wrong time. Even if all times seem wrong—if, for example, your office is perpetually fighting a deadline—some moments are more wrong than others.

Before you ask anyone a question make sure you consider what the other person is doing. For instance, let's say you want to talk to your boss about a raise. You've spent a week working up your nerve, and you feel that it's now or never. You stride purposefully into his office:

"Have you got a minute?"

Your boss is obviously buried in paperwork, and both telephones are ringing. He looks up, harried and annoyed. "Sure. What do you need?"

Because you're so eager to make your pitch, you don't hear the warning bell go off. You don't hear the strain in his response. But you should have: clearly it's the wrong time.

Telephone callers, too, need to be aware of timing. "Is this a good time to call?" is a basic telephone question. As obvious as this is, most callers still plunge ahead, without consideration for the person on the other end of the line.

Recently a smart telephone solicitor called to ask me to contribute money to an alumni fund. She first asked, "Is this a good time to call? I only need one or two minutes of your time." Because of her courtesy, I took the time to listen, and she got the contribution.

Too Many Questions

One of the worst things you can do is to ask too many questions. If you go around your organization asking everyone questions all the time, you will get a backlash reaction. "Don't be in the business of asking questions like a child," advises Ed Weihenmayer, Vice President of Human Resources at Kidder, Peabody & Co. "Why, why, why—it's annoying and you might as well light it up on a marquee that you lack intelligence and initiative. To look smart, ask judicious questions, smart questions."

Answering a Question with Another Question

This can be effective when you're looking for clarification or when you don't have an answer to a difficult question. But to do it routinely ("Why are you asking?") makes people furious.

Say a customer asks, "How much will it cost me?" and you answer, "How much do you think it should cost you?" or, "What if I said it will cost you $500?" Well, kiss your good intentions good-bye. When a friend asks "Who wrote *The Managerial Practices of Nomadic Tribes?*" and you answer "You mean you don't know?" you have gone too far. Your questions have served merely to irritate, aggravate, and ridicule.

Dumb Question Rating Scale

Everyone is capable of asking stupid questions (but some of us are more incapable than others). And often it's self-serving or sophomoric motivations that prompt ill-advised queries. Think about your questioning style, and answer yes or no to the questions in both columns . . . honestly.

Column A:

You often use questions because you want to:

- Avoid talking to someone
- Put yourself in a power position
- Intimidate your subordinates
- Be clever by answering one question with another
- Get attention
- Show off
- Waste time
- Hide the fact that you can't think of anything else to say
- Disguise your emotions
- Aggravate or irritate someone

Column B:

You often ask questions because you want to:

- Hear and understand the answer
- Gather news, facts, or other information
- Form an opinion or reach a decision
- Learn someone else's opinion
- Obtain feedback
- Clarify a misunderstanding
- Encourage someone
- Discover hidden information
- Become an interested, helpful manager

Column A:

You often ask questions because you want to:

Get a reaction
Delay a solution or agreement
Add more stumbling blocks
Worm your way out of an uncomfortable spot
Be just plain ornery

Column B:

You often ask questions because you want to:

Solve the problem
Gain commitment
Encourage participation
Stay on track
Stay in control of a communication

If you answered yes to six or more questions in Column A, you're asking too many wrongheaded questions. Think about the circumstances that prompt such questions, and analyze your motives.

If you answered yes to eight or more questions in Column B, your questioning motivation is on the money.

More Stupid Questions

Some people are famous for using stupid questions to make you feel inadequate, unattractive, ignorant, and otherwise at your wit's end—usually to get you to do something you don't want to do. Mothers and fathers, bosses and best friends, spouses and your Aunt Millie can all get away with murderous manipulation. And if you complain, they say "I was only asking." Here are some classics:

"You're not leaving before you're done, are you?"

"You didn't have anything really important to do Sunday, did you?"

"How can you say that?"

"How come a pretty girl like you wants to be an engineer?"

"So, what do you think? You haven't said a thing all day."

"Have you considered the consequences?"

"You look so sad. Is something wrong?"

"Am I interrupting something?"

"Is this all?"

"Do you have a few minutes?"

"Give me a call, OK?"

"May I be frank?"

"Don't you think you should change [your clothes, shoes, hair, personality]?"

"You're not going to do that, are you?"

"Have you been putting on a little weight lately?"

"Are you going to eat all of that?"

"Don't you think you're playing that too loud?"

"Isn't your deadline today?"

Sometimes asking a dumb question is unavoidable. We're only human, after all, and talking is the most human of our attributes. It's bound to go wrong once in a while. One of the best ways to avoid asking dumb questions is to understand the special characteristics of the person with whom you're speaking. Different people respond well to different kinds of questions. Let's see who these different people are, and what kinds of questions appeal to them.

5

Making the Question Fit the Person

I once observed a convention planner at a national organization open a staff meeting with this mild, unthreatening question: "What did you think about the great feedback we got from our last convention?"

She expected an enthusiastic response. Instead, she got five completely different reactions. Joanne merely asked, "So what else is new?" She was already well into planning the next convention. Steve was eager to rehash the whole thing, and the manager had to cut him short. Harry jokingly asked, "Are we getting raises?" But she knew he meant it. And Sara was suspicious that the manager had an angle: "Why are you asking?" she said. And Jan didn't even respond. She was daydreaming about the new graphics for the next convention.

These are some of the frustrating differences in individual behavior that managers must deal with every day. Although there are obvious dangers in jumping to conclusions about people, there are advantages in gaining insight into the people you work with—what turns them on and what turns them off, what attracts some people and repels others, what some people find challenging and others find threatening.

It's clear that every question will not have the same effect on every person. Yet creating categories in which to slip something as prickly and awkward as the human psyche isn't easy. (But it's fun to try.)

Modern psychologists trace the systematic grouping of personality types to Hippocrates, who said that generally people fell into one of four categories: Choleric, people who take the lead; Sanguine, those who have a good time; Phlegmatic, the easygoing and group-oriented; and Melancholic, the analytical perfectionists. Later Carl Jung identified the Feeler, the Sensor, the Thinker, and the Intuitor.

Psychologists today often use tests, such as the Minnesota Multiphasic Personality Inventory (MMPI), and the Rorschach, or inkblot, to identify an individual's stress pattern. One of the things such personality surveys have suggested is that while we are all different, we aren't as different as we think we are. Most people fall into defined patterns of personality—with certain tendencies exaggerated or diminished.

A more practical survey for business—one that distinguishes how different personalities respond to questions—is a five-part system that I've developed, which I call "The Five C's."

The Five C's provide a modern version of Hippocrates' categories: The Choleric is called the Commander; the Sanguine, the Convincer; the Phlegmatic, the Carer-Nurturer; and the Melancholic, the Calculator. In addition, there is a fifth category which has always been an integral part of society in general, and today is more and more vital in business—that of the Creator.

I use the Five C's to help corporations discover the strengths of staff people, put together sales teams that can better relate to specific customers, and help build inter-company teams that promise maximum productivity and harmony. Managers can also discover why certain employees are in conflict with each other, and look for ways to resolve interpersonal problems. Above all, identifying personalities can help managers ask better questions.

Identifying Personalities

In terms of the five basic categories, we all tend to be a mixed bag. And yet knowing a person's personality tendencies gives you a valuable clue about how to communicate with him. Specifically, it tells you what approach and what kinds of questions that person will respond to most positively. Ask the right person the wrong question and you might as well wave a red flag at a bull. Ask the same person the right question and you win him to your side.

The tricky part of asking the right question is discovering the personality type. None of us walks around with a personality tag, nor can most of us even describe our own personality. But by observing a person's behavior it's possible to identify his or her personality type. Behavior can be observed, measured, dealt with objectively, and changed. This means that it is possible to identify a person's primary personality simply by observing his or her behavior.

And that's what we're going to do now. The Five C's are not infallible, but they do help. The following descriptions of the five categories contain behavior clues that should help you recognize the basic personality traits of the people you work with.

The Commanders

The Commander type personality is confident, direct, loves challenge and change, is willing to take charge and go for the action. These people don't wait for things to happen—they make them happen. Commander personalities are often aggressive, self-motivated, goal-oriented, and fast-moving. Surgeons, some entrepreneurs, stockbrokers, and project managers of any kind often have many Commander characteristics. Two renowned examples of the Commander personality were John Wayne and General George C. Patton. In television fiction, Beatrice Arthur's character, Maude, and Jackie Gleason's character, Ralph, are both Commanders.

People with a Commander personality often move up the ladder fast because they get results, but when they carry these qualities to the extreme they can be careless about securing their role within the company. Many consultants I know moved quickly up the corporate ladder because they had such a strong, result-oriented disposition. Eventually, however, they couldn't climb any farther because they had made too many enemies within the corporation. That's when they left and started their own consulting business.

How can you spot a Commander in his or her natural habitat? These merchants of action in the business arena tend to enjoy change in all areas of their lives. At work, Commanders are very conscious of using every minute productively; they like to work on several things at once, and their typical pattern is to arrive at the office early and stay late. Their offices are functional and demonstrate power; for example, visitors chairs are likely to face a window where the sun streams in. Off the job they look for ways to make leisure time or vacations "count." Time off, for its own sake, bores them.

In my seminars I ask Commanders, "How many of you like to solve problems?" They all raise their hands. My reply is "That's good, because you cause most of them."

And they all burst out laughing. Commanders, unlike most other personalities, will laugh at themselves. They also get the most ribbing from other people because they are stress carriers who can take a joke.

Commander personalities tend to be impatient. Their own questions are usually direct. (When they call you on the phone, they're likely to skip the hello. If my husband answers when my friend John calls, John says: "Nonny? John. Dorothy." Or if my secretary answers, he may not identify himself at all: "Is she there?" Some Commanders launch full tilt into the purpose of their call: "When can I get that report from you?") Their favorite question is "What's the bottom line?" Because they are blunt, it's tougher for them to learn how to use open questions to advantage.

Of the five groups, these are the men and women who are least approachable by questions. They don't want to talk, they want to move. One other thing you should know: Because control and power are important to them, Commanders need to have the upper hand. If they see your questions as a subtle attempt to get control, their defensiveness will know no bounds.

Commanders will keep right on pushing until someone stops them. When a Commander is running off the rails, don't hesitate to confront him. Miller, a bank president who hired a Commander to help him implement some new marketing plans, was appalled when the new man told the board of directors that the president didn't know anything about marketing. Later, when Miller went on vacation, the marketing man moved into his office. Miller, himself a Caring personality, was so shocked at this behavior that his only response was to fire the marketing man (although, being a nonconfrontal Caring type person, he gave him a year's severance pay). Direct confrontation would probably have turned the marketing man around: "What the hell are you doing in my office? Out."

Asking Questions of a Commander

When you want something from a Commander, pose a direct question. Keep it brief and to the point. Do not hedge or fool around. Remember that the Commander is interested in results, not details.

If you have a Commander on your staff, avoid boxing him in with specific instructions ("This is the only way to do it"). If you tell the Commander what to do, complain that he or she is falling behind, or throw down a win-lose challenge ("Do it my way or don't do it at all!"), you'll bring out his worst characteristics. If you try to drive or pressure a Commander, you risk a nasty blowup. No one can drive a Commander harder than he drives himself.

The kinds of questions that work best are direct: "What are your goals?"

"How much time will it take?"

"When can I expect to have it?"

"Do you need backup or help with details?"

If *you* work for a Commander, do your homework and act confident. Well-adjusted Commanders can be good to work for, because they are secure and will give you a chance to prove yourself. You can always go far with Commander bosses if you go beyond specifications, beat the competition, and make solid suggestions for improvement. But first make sure you deliver what they ask for. Once you've shown your mettle, they will leave you on your own.

Stay away from "feeling" questions. "How do you feel about this?" is not a smart question for a Commander. Ask questions that stick to the high points, not the little details, questions that get you the information you need to do your job. Smart questions that all Commanders like:

"Where do I need to end up with this assignment?"

"What is the overall purpose?"

"When do you want it?"

"What kind of help will I get?"

"When can we get moving?"

"What's the big picture?"

"How can we beat the other team?"

"What are you seeking to achieve?"

"How can we change that?"

"How can we do it better than everyone else?"

The Convincers

The Convincers are promoters, socializers, persuaders. They're emotional, enthusiastic, and tend to be disorganized. These folks would not be happy working in research, writing for long periods of time, or quietly living alone.

The Convincer's office looks neat when you show up for a meeting, but five minutes earlier he stacked up several piles of papers and put them in a closet. He'll spread them out again when the meeting is over. A sure giveaway: Convincers like to think they know where everything is, but they spend a lot of time looking for it, just the same.

The office will often have one big attention-getting item that is a guaranteed conversation starter (I know one Convincer who has a gravity machine in her office—she never uses it, just likes to explain it to visitors). They also tend to have unusual pets for the same reason.

Convincers are flexible and playful, and they go with the flow. They are open and outgoing, and enjoy working with people. They quickly move on to a first-name basis and are great huggers and touchers. They are seldom in their offices. They are the most stylish of the four types, usually dress well, and keep in shape.

You're likely to find Convincers in positions that require powers of persuasion, such as public speaking, sales, advertising, fund-raising, and public relations. Convincers can make first-rate trial attorneys and impressive evangelists, but they are an asset in any business because they are optimistic and help boost everyone's morale. Joan Rivers ("Can we talk?"), Lucille Ball, and Dom deLuise are classic Convincers.

Convincers are natural persuaders. They excel at motivating other people. When it comes to building better relations with clients or within the company, Convincers are without peers. They love to contact people—the telephone is an extension of their body. The worst torture you could devise for a Convincer would be to put him alone in a room without a telephone.

You can usually hear Convincers' enthusiasm in their voices. Thinking out loud and on their feet is second nature to them. They talk their ideas and then tend to forget them. Others are often disillusioned when the talking doesn't turn into doing, or when they follow through on the idea only to discover the Convincer has already forgotten about it.

In the extreme form, Convincers don't plan enough, and tend to jump to conclusions. They will stick to—and even argue—their opinion long after they are proved wrong. They're easily sidetracked. Too many

Convincers working together, for example, add up to a problem. Convincers tend to hire other Convincers so they'll have somebody to talk to, and as a result productivity may suffer.

A woman I know who headed an important government agency was herself a strong Commander and Convincer personality. Many people have a tendency to hire those with personalities similar to their own. She had a staff full of Commanders and Convincers. Everyone came up with innovations and got along well with people. But there was never anyone in the office doing the work.

Conversely, I once consulted with an old, established accounting firm which was facing some new competition. Everyone in the company was steady and detail oriented. They didn't like change. When they hired marketing consultants they hired people just like themselves. I suggested that they look for someone different—someone with Commander and Convincer characteristics who could shake things up a little.

Convincers often operate best from unconventional platforms. One Convincer executive I know in the beverage industry has a van outfitted with a kitchen and dining table. At noontime he collects whomever he has to do business with and drives them out to a lake for a picnic lunch with beer and wine. Colleagues love the break in routine, clients are enamored of his style, and he is in an environment where his creative juices flow most freely.

Convincers are usually popular, and fear rejection. They also have trouble saying no, because they want to please everyone. The worst thing you can tell a Convincer is that you don't like him. A Convincer will pick out the one person in a group who doesn't approve and will concentrate on getting that person to like him. I've fallen into that trap myself when addressing groups. If someone in the audience seems bored or unreceptive I tend to concentrate on winning that person over. I've trained myself not to react in this situation and to ignore the disapproving individual.

In general, you get the best results from Convincers if you make them feel special and if you are receptive to their ideas and creativity. Encourage their positive traits, and you'll get a positive result.

Asking Questions of Convincers

Convincers respond well to "How do you feel about this?" And "How would you like to do it?" Any question with "you" as the subject is a winner. After themselves, their favorite subject is other people. Don't ask Convincers "what," ask "who." "Whom will you need in this project?" "Who's the best person for this job?" "Who will hear about it?"

If you want to establish better communication with a Convincer, whether you work for him or he works for you, it's important to get him to slow down and organize his thoughts. Your goal is to help the Convincer channel some of his bountiful energy into specific action.

If you have Convincers on your staff, be very clear in your instructions. Get them to agree on what they're going to do and when. And always establish checkpoints for them to report back to you. Asking Convincers the right questions can help them become better focused and more productive. One key to getting their attention is to be persistent in your questions: "That's a very interesting point, John, but how, specifically, can we correct the problem?" The key is to not let them off the hook.

If your boss is a Convincer, you may find his or her personality frustrating. You may want to get to work when he or she wants to shoot the breeze. One executive described her Convincer boss: "He reminds me of my seventh-grade English teacher. We always knew we could deflect him from the subject at hand—grammar—by asking him to tell us about his summer trip to Europe. He would go on for the whole class period, and we'd never have to do any grammar. I loved that in the seventh grade. But now, at the office, I do all the work, and my boss sits around and chats with the client."

You may need a sense of humor to focus a Convincer. Try to pin him down when he's in a hurry: "We've only got five minutes. What are three key issues you want to discuss? I'm counting." Other good Convincer questions:

"What are your main problems?"

"Before we have the meeting can you give me an agenda and time-table?"

"What are the specifics?"

"What are the details?"

Jokingly say, "Can you restate our objectives in ten words or less?"
The next time your sociable boss is headed for a client lunch, write out a list of fact-gathering questions for him to ask.

The Carers

Caring personalities can get the job done and work harmoniously with a wide variety of people. They move slower and are more thoughtful than Convincers. They are good team players, and more and more companies are finding that those who succeed in business, especially in large companies, are Carers.

Carers never pick up and leave a job or a relationship easily. Because they are more loyal and more family oriented they're a great long-term investment for any company. However, if Carers have to choose between job and family, they suffer from the conflict.

How to identify this personality: The Carer works slowly and deliberately. He will be more inclined to leave the office on time, because he wants to be home with his family. They are good listeners and prefer one-on-one conversations. Their offices are comfortable, chairs facing each other. Photos of family and friends, framed letters, or drawings done by their children may decorate the desk and bookshelves.

They are wonderful at socializing and are always willing to come early and help out at parties. As long as they're with friends or family, they can relax and enjoy almost anything.

Carers work best in a relaxed atmosphere built upon sound relationships and harmony. Counseling, human resources, teaching young people, family practice medicine, and nursing are all careers that attract them. They thrive on cooperation and if possible will avoid competition. Group achievement is a Carer hallmark. A Carer would rather refine an existing practice to a high polish than to institute change.

Resistance to change can be a strength or a weakness, depending on the situation. In a balanced work group it is invaluable because the Carer thinks, analyzes, and assesses before committing to change.

Like the other personality categories, when the strengths of Carer personality are exaggerated they often become weaknesses. The Carer can be possessive and somewhat suspicious. Under stress, he or she will withdraw and miss deadlines. Carers tend to be grudge-carriers. They may appear passive, but underneath—because they dislike confrontation—they internalize and build up their resentments. A Carer can suddenly explode and surprise you with an ultimatum. I remember the dismay of one boss when after a routine assignment he found his Carer employee, whom he believed to be happy on the job, clearing out his desk and leaving without notice.

A Carer personality can sometimes be too concerned with the needs of others. More than most people, they have trouble firing someone—like Miller, the Carer bank president who fired his troublesome marketing man but gave him a year's severance pay. They also hesitate to delegate because they worry about overworking other people.

The worst thing you can do to a Carer is to overload or confuse him with sudden, risky changes. When you ask a Carer personality to implement something new, it's important that you explain everything, preferably in writing, so he or she can get a grip on each aspect. List all the advantages, and show how the plan fits into the bigger picture.

The Carer views the Convincer as too artificial, too eager to move without checking details; and he thinks the Commander is intimidating or overpowering. To get along better with a Carer personality, if you yourself are a Convincer or a Commander, be less direct. Show general concern and avoid confrontations. Emphasize cooperation and support.

If a Carer works for you, emphasize the relationship first. Coach and train in a nonthreatening tone, and motivate them by talking about how they can improve relationships.

Asking Questions of Carers

Carers respond best to "how to" or process questions and to "people" questions:

"How is the project being handled?"

"What systems need organizing?"

"Who needs help?"

"How can you make it work for the company and the team?"

"How can you build a better company/work-team environment?"

"How are we going to do it?"

The Calculators

Lily Tomlin once made this comment on her state of mind: "I'm as frustrated as a perfectionist who can't do anything right." That's a perfect description of the Calculator personality. Calculators are competent, conservative, correct, and conscientious. These are the people who follow the rules and regulations. They achieve their goals through planning, education, and persistence. These are the detail people, the perfectionists.

Engineers and accountants, mathematicians and researchers are usually Calculators. (I recently had a man come up to me in a seminar and tell me that now he understood why he had left accounting. He was a true Convincer, doing a Calculator's job.) In the corporate world, financial people are often Calculators. At their best, Calculators have precise minds and impressive analytical skills. In the days before computers, these people were the computers.

By nature, however, Calculators tend to be suspicious. They naturally question everything and worry a lot. If you have Calculators on your staff, don't make appointments with them in advance without explanation. For example, if you say on Monday, "Let's get together for a talk at the end of the week," they'll worry about it all week long.

If the Calculators in a company are too strong, the company might not be very innovative or competitive, but everything will be done perfectly. The Calculators will be holding things up, analyzing, measuring, counting. They may become overly focused on the quality of the task and fail to see the big picture.

Sometimes Calculators see their role as saving the company from the wild-eyed Commanders who will break the company into pieces with their schemes and changes. For success every company needs both sides of the equation, because the natural tension between the two groups creates its own system of checks and balances.

Calculators are sensitive and intuitive about events and people. Yet it is not in their nature to get personally involved. They leave this to Convincers and Carers.

How to identify Calculators: In his meticulous, formal office, a Calculator may have numerous graphs and charts lined up around the room or placed precisely on the walls. The favorite animal of Calculator person might be a Siamese cat or an owl. His car will be the most efficient and up-to-date, and he will know the precise value and use of every gadget in it. (His favorite publication is likely to be *Consumer Reports*.) Dick Cavett and the Mr. Spock character from *Star Trek* both appear to be Calculators.

I am more of a Convincer, and my husband has many Calculator characteristics. When it's my job to clean up after dinner I quickly and haphazardly load the dishwasher. If I go back into the kitchen later on, I'm likely to catch him carefully and systematically reloading my input.

Calculators are organized and precise. They talk in quality-control terms. Most Calculators (but not all) are silent types, but they will talk to you if they respect you. The better they know you, the more they'll open up.

Asking Questions of Calculators

The main thing to keep in mind about Calculators is that they can't stand criticism of their work. Asking personal questions is also a waste of time. The Calculator seldom volunteers information about herself. ("What did you think of it?" "I liked it." And a direct question will get you a blunt answer: "Is today your birthday?" "No.")

If a Calculator works for you, always give clear and accurate instructions. Give him a new piece of equipment to use, and he needs to know everything about it. He will ask many questions about how to do it, and then go over it with you to be sure. (Commanders and Convincers will take a quick look, say "Oh, I get it," only to go ahead and break it.)

If you work for a Calculator, you'll do well to recognize that they are task oriented. They respond best to specific, analytical questions that pertain to their professional concerns. They listen well to people who are clear and concise. Make a detailed outline of your work and what you plan to accomplish.

"How can we improve the quality of our product [our group, our system]?"

"How does it work?"

"How can it be done better?"

"What cross-checks are needed?"

"Who needs to be cross-trained?"

Calculators will lift their eyebrows if you give them an incomplete or inaccurate report. Prepare well for every encounter—whether it's in person, on the phone, or by letter, and always follow up. Calculators like to be presented with logical, planned options, and realistic trade-offs. I always hope my airplane pilots and the mechanics who work on the planes have a lot of Calculator characteristics. I always worry when the pilot is very talkative and effusive.

The Creators

The Creators are idea and concept oriented. In the business world you may find them working as designers, photographers, as new product developers, inventors, scientists, artists, or writers.

The world would be at a loss without the Creators. When I go through the functional areas of management in my seminars—planning, organization, controlling staff, leadership—one area I focus on is innovation. All managers and staff need to ask themselves, "How can I do it better?" People are valued in organizations not because they maintain the status quo, but because of the new ideas they come up with and the actions they take. Every time an individual discovers a better way to do things his creative part has been at work.

Creators are usually difficult bosses. They leave people alone and expect them to act and respond as they themselves would in every situation. Employees do not receive clear-cut standards to follow. Creators are not specific, nor are they sociable. They are blunt with others, but can be defensive and sensitive about receiving criticism themselves.

They often have a daydreamy quality. They tend not to make eye contact when talking to others, and often appear distracted.

Creators like to work alone. Rather than ask others for help, they prefer to figure things out and solve problems alone. They appear to work in spurts, although even when they seem to be doing nothing the creative process is often percolating inside their minds. When involved in a project they will work for days on end and never notice the time. Because they will keep at a task until it is flawless—which means that they are never completely finished with a job to their satisfaction—they need to be kept to deadlines. However, for them a rigid environment and following rules is high stress, and they do not function well in this kind of company. If you have Creators working or you, you'll get the best results if you leave them alone, but get them to agree to deadlines.

Creators will have an unusual work area that usually reveals their specialty. An architect's office will be laden with blueprints, a designer's with his favorite examples. They can be messy, not because they're disorganized (the driving principle behind the Creators' work is to bring order out of chaos and they are highly organized in their minds), but because outward messiness doesn't bother them. They are more concerned with thinking and creating. They might have papers on all the chairs and if you come to visit there's no place to sit.

Creators can be forgetful. (Their pets might be hungry because they forget to feed them.) There's the story about Albert Einstein who stopped to chat with some students as he was walking along a path at Princeton. After the discussion Einstein asked the students, "Which direction was I coming from?" The student pointed in the direction the famous scientist had been walking. "Good," said Einstein, "then I've already had lunch."

Creators are not strong in dealing with people, although they can be very caring if you can get their attention. Less creative people usually admire the talents of the Creators and their nonconforming style. But insecure people often feel uncomfortable or "inferior" around Creators.

Asking Questions of Creators

Creators do not usually make good listeners. This can be frustrating if your boss is a Creator because it's difficult to pin them down. They often agree with you just to get rid of you so they can go back to their project.

Creators can be unbearable and difficult during the creative process. To get the most from a Creator as a boss or employee you must understand their pattern and find times to deal with them when they are not preoccupied and can concentrate. The best time to talk to any Creator is between creative projects or shortly after the culmination of one, especially if its a success.

When talking to Creators, stay away from feeling-type questions. They don't mind them, but they are more thinkers than feelers. Creators respond best to creative questions, rather than people-oriented questions:

"What are you developing right now?"

"What do you think about it?"

"What are the aspects you are considering?"

"What ideas need developing?"

"What needs to be in place for your creative process?"

"What factors contribute to the whole?"

"What was your most satisfying creative effort?"

"Who can handle the nitty gritty so you can be free to think?"

Personality Combinations

There are some similarities and overlap among the five major behavioral styles. Commanders and Convincers both tend to be active and energetic; they like change and action. The Carers and Calculators are more slow moving and resistant to change; they are more oriented toward the status quo. Commanders, Calculators, and Creators are concerned with tasks, whereas Carers and Convincers are more concerned with people.

We all have all five dimensions in our personalities, but with varying degrees of intensity. One quick trick for learning something about a person's personality type is to ask them a simple question. For example, "Tell me what you enjoy most about your work. What do you like least?"

The Commander is likely to answer bluntly: "I enjoy outwitting the competition." "Bottom-line results." "Getting moving." "The adventure." "The chance for big gains." "That the job changes every day." "Having the whole project under my eyes." "What I like least is being bored."

The Convincer will probably go on at length, especially if you supplied the coffee: "I enjoy the flexibility." "The recognition." "Being where the action is." "Setting my own goals." "The challenge." "What I like least is writing reports."

The Carer might say, "Working with my team and feeling secure." "Developing the process." "Being part of an effective organization." "Helping people develop." "An environment where I can care about what I do and help others." "What I like least is sudden shift in policy."

The Calculator tends to reply: "Planning." "Analyzing situations and projects." "Getting the documentation right." "Having the time to do the job right." "What I like least is incomplete reporting or vague notions."

And the Creator might answer, "Conceptualizing. Freedom from restraints. Working alone. What I like least is being interrupted."

You don't need me to tell you that personality traits are not chiseled in stone. Because a person likes to place his pen precisely parallel to the top of his notepad doesn't automatically identify him as a Calculator. Nor does the fact that she sparkles at parties and can talk a blue streak mean that she's a Convincer in a business setting.

You must watch and listen. Even physical clues can be misleading. I recently planned a management development program with a client who had his office furniture arranged in an open style, with many photographs of his daughter around the room. I concluded that he was a Carer type. During the course of the meeting I asked him a question that I ask most clients: "What do you feel are the key points to include in the program?" I was surprised when he impatiently replied, "You're the expert. That's what I'm paying you for."

His response told me immediately that he was a Commander—someone who doesn't like questions. In this case, the superficial clues around his office were misleading. But when I heard his response to a single question I knew how to proceed. From then on I made all the decisions and just kept him informed of the results.

What Personality Type Are You?

It's important for managers to know their own personality traits and see how they are perceived by others. The following questions can give you a quick reading on your own personality:

Do you like to tell people what to do? (Commander)

Or do you prefer to persuade, cajole, or sell? (Convincer)

Are you a cooperative part of a working group? (Carer)

Are you interested in the task and the thoroughness and perfection in your work? (Calculator)

Do you like to think abstractly and daydream? (Creator)

If you identify yourself as a Commander-type manager, you can probably benefit by taking more time to ask your people questions and listen to their answers. Show that you care. Ask for feedback: "How do you feel about it?"

If you recognize yourself as a Convincer, you can think about how to talk less and listen more to details: "Can you explain to me specifically how we're to deal with this?"

If you're a Carer, you'll be interested in how you can use questions to focus a little more on results and actions: "How can we move things along a little more quickly?"

If you have many Calculator traits, instead of asking "How can it be more perfect?" you might want to ask more about the person you're dealing with: "How can you contribute?"

And if you're a Creator try to recognize that other people are not necessarily like you, and that you also need to depend on others. Spend time looking at and focusing on the people who work for you. They admire your creativity. They usually make exceptions for much of your unusual behavior because of your talents, but don't take advantage. Ask your staff, "How can I help you when I have time?" They will appreciate your concern and understand when you are preoccupied.

By observing a person's major personality traits you can ask questions that minimize hostility and anxiety and capitalize on that person's strengths. Behavioral assessments reveal what's important to different people, thereby suggesting a way of communicating well with them. While there are certain universal, fail-safe questions that work in almost any situation, for the most part when you ask questions—just as in any form of communication—you need to be supremely aware of the individual you're speaking with.

With that in mind, we're going to enter the heart of the Smart Questions System. The value of any system is that it has broad application in a variety of circumstances. When you understand how the Smart Questions System works you can use it across the board—whether you are trying to generate greater productivity from your staff, help people solve problems, or quicken your own pace as you move ahead in your organization.

6

The Smart Questions System

The Smart Questions System involves more than popping questions at random. It recognizes that asking smart questions is a thinking process. Once you learn the system you can gain the advantage in any situation— a job interview, asking for a raise, getting a promotion, handling an assignment, increasing productivity, coaching and leading your staff.

The question itself is only one element of the system. The Smart Questions System begins *before* you ask the question.

Step One: The Windup

Before you can ask a smart question, you need to *know your purpose*. Why are you asking? Ask yourself these smart questions:

1. "Exactly what do I want to gain with this question—cooperation, help, resources, information, commitment, better performance?"

2. "Whom am I asking? My boss? Someone else in upper management? A colleague? A member of the administrative staff? A subordinate?" (Not knowing whom you're talking to is like entering a room blindfolded.)

3. Put yourself in their shoes: "What are their goals?" "What do they want to happen?"

4. The final phase of the Windup is "How can I phrase this question to everyone's advantage?"

Christopher, the vice president of a real estate development firm, told me this story on himself. His firm was trying to get an important group of investors to commit to building a large shopping center. The investors had agreed to the terms of the proposal but were stalling about coming to a final signing. A face-to-face meeting had been postponed several times by the primary investor. Christopher, although certain that the agreement would eventaully go through, needed to get the contract off the ground. As time dragged by, his firm was losing both momentum and income. The company brass decided that the time had come to push harder and told Christopher to call the investor and insist on a meeting.

Christopher tried to develop an opening gambit for his phone call. He needed to convince the investor of the urgency of the situation without alienating him. He wrote out several paragraphs describing his company's objectives, the need to put the plans in action, why they should get started soon, when he would be available for a meeting, what they could hope to accomplish during the meeting, and so on.

When he finished Christopher had five handwritten pages. It occurred to him that he would have a terrible time having a one-on-one conversation with the investor if he had to read this epistle over the phone. Was there a way to get the investor to do some of the talking? He thought about the Smart Questions System and asked himself:

"Who is this investor?" (The head honcho, supposedly with the power to make decisions.)

"What is my purpose?" (To have a meeting during which he will sign the contract and give us a check.)

"What is the investor's problem?" (I don't know.)

Then Christopher threw out all of his notes and devised five smart questions to ask the investor during the phone conversation:

- "Is there something more you need from us to help you move the contract through?"

- "What can I do before we meet to make our time together maximally productive?"

- "Is there anyone else you would like us to talk to?"
- "When do you hope to see this project completed?"
- "When can we get together?"

Christopher then made the call. By asking only five questions, he stayed in control of the conversation, made clear his objectives, and helped the investor clarify his own thinking. As a result, Christopher got a firm appointment for a meeting, set the agenda in advance, and was able to come out of the meeting with a signed agreement and a start date.

Step Two: The Delivery

Once you've identified your purpose and have come up with the most appropriate question, the next step is to *ask the question*. You already know how to open up the question and invite the fullest response. When you ask, make sure you speak clearly, calmly, and directly, and don't rush the other person's thoughts. Maintain a positive attitude; don't let hidden feelings of disapproval or criticism creep into your voice. Because you have thought through the question, you should find it easy to speak without fumbling.

Don't toss the question off or bury it in a stream of other words. Let the person know you expect an answer. Look into his eyes, and let your warmth and intent show in your voice and manner. Let him or her know that you are interested in hearing the answer.

Step Three: The Response

A question is useless if you don't *listen carefully to the response*. At the opening of her seminars on negotiation, Tessa Albert Warschaw often asks participants to talk to as many people as they can within a period of ten minutes. In each encounter, the participants exchange answers to two questions. First, "What assets do you bring to a negotiation?" Second, "What liabilities?" The participants hear over and over again what's helping them and hurting them in their dealings with others.

But it's in their second meeting that the real test occurs. Once again, Warschaw asks the participants to speak to one another. "This time," she says, "tell the person you're talking to one thing you remember about him or her from what he or she told you last night."

Invariably this request is met with nervous laughter. To their intense embarrassment, the participants usually remember almost nothing from their conversations with one another. They realize that they've got to start "attending," as Warschaw calls it.

Much has been made of the virtues of listening. We talk about listening "between the lines," or listening to the "inner message," and a few authors suggest listening overtly—that is, paying attention to precisely what is said and not trying to decode hidden meanings.

Listening well is a skill that requires concentration and effort. For one thing, we think seven times faster than we speak. So while we're listening, our minds are racing ahead. Thus we often project our own ideas, associations, and judgments into what is being said to us. As a result we're not fully tuned in to what the other person is saying. It would be much more constructive to spend this surplus thinking time listening fully and constructing an interesting direction in which to take the interview, based on what you hear.

We also fail to listen when we feel an urgency to express ourselves. We're certain that if we can explain ourselves convincingly, the other person will see us as we wish to be seen. And the best resource we have for explaining ourselves is talking. Right? Wrong. One author lunching with his editor learned this lesson the hard way.

"I had a perfect opportunity," Jake said. "A chance to find out what trends my publisher saw in the book industry, what kinds of books she specifically was looking for, and how I fit into the scheme of this particular publisher's future. But I didn't find out anything."

Jake was so nervous that he spent the entire luncheon talking about himself. "I told her where I thought my career was going, how I wanted to develop as a writer. I learned absolutely nothing about her needs or the needs of the company. If she learned anything about me, it didn't result in any concrete suggestions for my future."

In other words, Jake presented himself as a person with a set of problems that needed to be solved and asked the editor to be his doctor. "*I* should have been the doctor," he said with sharp hindsight. "I should have found out her needs—symptoms—and looked to see what I could do to help her. I wasted an ideal opportunity."

Another typical reason for not paying attention is that we're not really interested in what the other person is talking about. But one way to make sure that you are interested is to ask questions.

When you're hopelessly bored while listening to someone else talk, consider this: Listening covers your weaknesses (you can never look or sound foolish, even if you're in way over your head). Listening gives you time to think and to consider all the information relevant to the particular situation. When you do speak your words have greater impact. Even though most of us feel compelled to talk, listening—when you learn to enjoy it—is actually less stressful than speaking.

But before you pat yourself on the back for being a good listener, remember that you can fall into your own trap. If you are listening in order to be thought captivating, don't let your eyes wander around the room as you nod your head agreeably. Rather than bask in your own charms, concentrate on what is being said. Some people are so enchanted with the impression they create as a good listener that they fail to hear what the other person is telling them.

Are You a Good Listener?

According to a recent report from Sperry Rand, 45 percent of a manager's time is spent listening. Listening absorbs your time in one-to-one conversations, in meetings, and on the telephone. There is no communication unless someone is listening.

You can judge your listening skills by asking yourself these questions:

Are you willing to learn about other people, places, and things?

Would you welcome your staff's opinion about your listening ability?

Do you listen for the main ideas being expressed?

Do you take care not to interrupt?

Do you curb the impulse to complete the other person's sentences?

Do you tune in to the speaker's feelings as well as his words?

Do you try to get beyond your own judgmental attitudes?

In other words, do you practice listening skills? If you have six or fewer yes answers, your listening could stand improvement. To quote Epictetus, one of the more observant Greek philosophers, "God has given us two ears and one mouth so we may hear twice as much as we speak."

Step Four: The Evaluation

As you listen, you need to *evaluate the answer.* This is the processing stage of the system. You may need to ask another question, or questions, before you get what you're looking for. You may want to ask a clarifying question to make sure you have the details straight. Or a probing question to get deeper into the heart of the issue or to discover where hidden resistance might be.

Good salespeople have learned that they can pin down a sale by asking questions that dig progressively deeper into the issues. The curtain rises on this conversation between a probing, calm, and concerned salesperson and the head of purchasing in a clothing manufacturing firm:

"Research has shown that our threads outlast our nearest competitor's by 17 percent, and other competitors' by much more than that. Yet our price is the same. Therefore our threads will save you money in the long run. How do you feel about saving money?"

"Well, who wouldn't like to save money? But convenience counts too. Our people are used to the present threads and salespeople. We're generally satisfied with what we've got now. With your product we'll have to change our threading process."

"When you say you're satisfied, does this mean that there are no problems?"

"We have a little trouble occasionally, but nothing we can't handle."

"I know nothing is perfect. What kind of trouble are you having?"

"Nothing serious, but I've noticed that we don't get as long a last from our present threads. We've been getting more garments returned because of split seams, and I've seen some reports about problems with the thread in the machines. It seems to break and put the machine out of commission for about ten or fifteen minutes until it's cleaned out.

"What percentage of returns are you getting?"

"I'd estimate about 8 percent."

"That's at least twice the number you should be getting. Our research shows that with our threads you should get returns down to 2 percent or even less. Can you judge how much total time you're losing?"

"Overall, we're averaging about fifteen to sixteen hours a week in lost time."

"You should only be losing about eight hours. With our easier threading and stronger thread, most of our customers lose only five or less. I'm comparing your company to companies with similar garments and number of employees. Wouldn't it be to your advantage to save problems with your machines and reduce the returned merchandise?"

"Yes, of course, but there's more to it than product viability. Threading is only a minor item in our production line. Replacing it with a new product could upset the procedure. Frankly, it isn't worth it. It means a new set of operating instructions and a period of confusion during the changeover, which usually means a lot of errors."

"I know what you mean—change is always upsetting. I can understand your wanting to avoid confusion and errors, but I wonder if this is likely to happen? How long have you been using your present product?"

"About three years."

"Then about three years ago you shifted from one thread to the brand you're now using. Is that right?"

"Yes, that's right. But what are you getting at?"

"I'm just looking to discover how difficult the transition period was. How much trouble do you recall having during that changeover?"

"Well, let's see. . . . Once or twice when things went wrong somebody blamed it on the new thread, but we straightened it out pretty easily."

"Then aren't you paying a lot more to avoid some trouble that isn't even likely to happen, from your own experience?"

"You know how people love to complain when you institute a change, and I don't always have the time or the energy to deal with it. On the other hand, I've been a little annoyed about the problems we've been having with the product. Maybe it wouldn't be that hard to switch, especially if the new stuff makes it easier to thread the machines. Suppose you send me a trial order of your thread and we'll see how it works out."

Through pointed questioning, this salesperson held the initiative all the way. The initial questions stirred the buyer's mind to activity rather than leaving him in a state of inertia. Subsequent questions moved his thinking until he himself reached out for a trial order.

Asking the first question, however, was only the first step. The critical factor was that the salesman _listened_ to each answer—and responded to the answer with another question.

I once called on a personnel director in a large advertising firm. When I asked what concerns she had, she answered, "I really don't have any concerns. We have several outside consultants and they all say we're doing a good job."

As I listened to her I recognized that her defenses were up, but I stuck with the questioning approach. "That must make you feel good. But there must have been one or two small things bothering you or you wouldn't have called me. Are there any areas in which you've never done training?"

As I probed around with nonthreatening questions, she agreed that there were a few minor things, and then went on to list many problem areas that were bothering her.

So stick with it. If you give up after asking one question, the conversation is probably over. Listen, evaluate the answer, and be ready to ask another question.

Step Five: The Payoff

You've asked a smart question, listened to the answer—and then what? To make smart questions pay off, a good manager must act on what he or she learns. You gain the respect of other people only if you capitalize on the information. If you ask for suggestions but fail to use them, people will stop volunteering.

The same thing is true of your colleagues and staff. When you ask for participation, when you ask people to delve into their minds and emotions to answer your questions and then ignore what they've told you, you've undermined all your good work. If you have a company suggestion box and never use it, people stop contributing. Likewise, if you ask for advice and disregard it, people stop providing it. What, after all, was the point?

Not every question and answer needs a direct action. Sometimes it's enough to listen and respond, letting the person know that you appreciate their thoughts and input.

Often action means simply following up. If an employee's work improves as a result of a questioning session, acknowledge it. Action can also mean mentally or physically filing away the information you gathered for future use. But, for example, if you discover in a questioning session that the reason deadlines have been missed in your department is because a supplier is consistently late, act on that information and solve the problem.

Taking action for the sake of doing something is not a good move. Just as smart questions, not just any questions, are the first step, smart actions are your goal. Knowing that your eventual aim is to take an appropriate action can help you to formulate your questions in the first place. The purpose of asking smart questions is to improve things, and that only happens when you act. Unless you go beyond what you have already mastered you'll never grow.

Five Steps for Best Results with the Smart Questions System

1. The Windup—know your purpose and your person
2. The Delivery—formulate your question
3. The Response—listen to the answer
4. The Evaluation—probe further if necessary
5. The Payoff—take action

Getting into the habit of asking smart questions takes some effort. It involves breaking an old habit (making statements) and creating a new one (asking questions). It's a matter of retraining your responses. However, when you try the Smart Questions System you see the benefits so quickly that it's easy to continue doing it. It's much easier to change when you see the rewards.

Asking smart questions is a technique that can become automatic, just like brushing your teeth, driving a car, or hitting a tennis ball. Studies show that it takes between seven and twenty-one conscious efforts to create a new habit. Pay attention to your communicating style for a week. Notice how you initiate conversations, how you talk to employees, how you respond when someone asks you a question. The next time you're ready to lecture someone or make a statement, stop yourself. Count to five and take a deep breath. And ask a question instead.

The Smart Questions System offers a wonderful and immediate reward. You will notice the difference the first time you use it, and those benefits will encourage you to keep experimenting. For the remainder of this book we're going to describe specific applications of the Smart Questions System. Part Two concentrates on your role as manager—how you can use smart questions to help everyone on your staff bring out his or her greatest potential.

PART TWO
Getting the Most from Your Staff

"Hard questions must have hard answers."

—Plutarch

7

The Quiz: Part Two

I once observed Sally, a customer-service manager, give instructions to her staff. "This is the way I want you to deal with complaints," she said, and she went on to describe the technique she wanted the representatives to use. Sally spoke quickly and to the point. At the end of her talk, she asked if there were any questions, but made it clear that she expected efficient action and not a lot of conversation. No one had any questions. Her staff, feeling not a little apprehensive, started to work. Over the next week, few of them were able to deal properly with customers. Sally was annoyed. She had been clear enough, hadn't she? Why hadn't anyone listened to her? A few weeks later she gave the lecture again, with the same poor results.

When it comes to getting the most from their staff, one common sin managers commit is telling people what to do but failing to discover if they've understood the instructions. Most managers like to lecture and feel uneasy with two-way conversations. A conversation means that you must ask questions and must establish an atmosphere that encourages people to ask questions of you as well. It takes more time, and it means that you leave yourself open to challenge. But a questioning approach is the way mistakes are corrected, comprehension is expanded, and co-operation becomes a byword of the department.

I ran into a similar problem with my own answering service. I recently called the service and gave the manager instructions on how I wanted my phones answered; I assumed that the information would be passed down to all the operators and it would work out. But they continued to make the same mistakes.

I called the manager again and asked, "How do you get the information to all the other operators?"

"We write it on your card," she said.

"How do you know that people read it?"

"We don't."

This was puzzling, but complaining didn't seem to solve the problem. So I asked a question: "What can you do to be sure that everyone who answers the phone gets this information and understands what has to be done?"

The manager thought about it, and came up with the idea of briefing all the operators at least once a day and asking for feedback to make sure everyone understood the new instructions. The same technique was used with the night shift. Only by verbal questions and answers would the information get through.

Part Two of *Smart Questions* deals with using questions to get the most from your staff and to establish better understanding so that people know what you need. The main reasons people fail at work are because they don't have the ability, they have a poor attitude, or they don't know what's expected of them. One way to be a superior boss is to clearly express your expectations. And smart questions will help you do that.

It will also help you develop your staff to their maximum potential. Many managers have talented people on tap, yet wind up doing much of the work themselves. Or they continue to use the same individuals for the same jobs, assuming that they know the abilities and goals of each person. But in fact we usually know very little about the people who work with us. By taking time to ask questions, managers can expand their knowledge of each individual on their staff and devise the most productive ways to make use of their talents and ambitions.

Again, it's important to answer these quiz questions with your first response. Before change can take place, it's necessary to become aware of the present reality. Only if you answer the questions honestly—not the way you think they should be answered—can you become a better questioner.

Are You Getting the Most from Your Staff?

1. When organizing a project team you usually:

   a. Select people you like.

   b. Ask "Who are the best people?"

   c. Ask yourself "What is the goal of the project and who are the best people for it?"

   d. Choose people you can control.

2. Recently your staff people have been making a lot of mistakes in written reports. You:

   a. Accept the situation as a normal part of doing business.

   b. Ask yourself how you might improve your instructions.

   c. Criticize them for not following directions.

   d. Ask them for solutions.

3. You can't decide between two qualified candidates for a position in your department. You:

   a. Ask a colleague to sit in on their interviews.

   b. Develop more probing questions to find out more about them.

   c. Look for a way to hire them both.

   d. Kick the decision upstairs and ask your boss to decide.

4. Your assistant tells you he can't meet an important deadline. Your immediate response is to:

   a. Ask "What am I going to tell the senior vice president?"

   b. Tell him he has no choice.

   c. Ask "What's the problem?"

   d. Tell him to get whatever help he needs to finish the job.

5. After giving an employee complex instructions for an assignment, you:

   a. Ask "Do you have any questions?"

    b.   Leave and give him time to work out the assignment for himself.

    c.   Ask him to repeat the instructions.

    d.   Ask him to describe in his own words how he interprets the assignment.

6.   You can't finish a project on time. You:

    a.   Think about which of your employees you can approach for help.

    b.   Stay up all night to finish because you assume your staff is overworked.

    c.   Ask your closest peer associate for help.

    d.   Ask yourself who else would most benefit from working on this project.

7.   Two of your best staff people are involved in a personal conflict. Your normal response is to:

    a.   Call them both into your office together for a problem-solving session.

    b.   Talk to each of them individually.

    c.   Tell them to work it out between them.

    d.   Transfer one person to another department to alleviate tension.

8.   When you plan a job interview for a prospective employee, you:

    a.   Write out a series of questions to ask.

    b.   Bring along the job description and use it as a guide.

    c.   Structure the interview around the applicant's resume.

    d.   Wing it, under the premise that spontaneity allows more freedom to explore the person's potential.

9.   One of your employees has a long-standing personal problem. You:

    a.   Get involved and try to solve it.

    b.   Send your employee to personnel.

    c.   Ignore it.

d.   Strongly advise getting professional help.

10.   You have a new supervisor reporting to you who doesn't delegate enough. In a coaching session, you:

a.   Laud the advantages of delegating.

b.   Tell her that she must delegate more.

c.   Ask her why delegating should be important to a manager.

d.   Send her for training in delegation.

11.   You schedule exit interviews with several employees who have resigned. You:

a.   Go through the formalities and wish them luck.

b.   Ask your remaining staff how they see the situation.

c.   Try to discover the real reasons for their leaving.

d.   Emphasize that they are making a big mistake by leaving.

12.   Morale is sagging in your department. To solve the problem, you begin by:

a.   Thinking it through objectively on your own.

b.   Calling a full staff meeting and ask for each person's contribution.

c.   Asking your key people to investigate.

d.   Asking the people who are most discontented how they perceive the difficulty.

13.   When you interview a new clerical employee, you say:

a.   "Tell me about yourself."

b.   "I guess personnel has told you all our policies."

c.   "What has personnel told you?"

d.   "What do you know about our company?"

14.   At a technical training session for your staff, you:

a.   Lecture and answer questions as they come up.

b.   Start off with a joke, then keep talking.

c.   Ask open-ended questions 75 percent of the time.

d.   Ask for frequent summaries throughout the session.

15. Your staff people have been late and ill a lot in recent months. You:

    a. Figure it must be the weather.

    b. Tell them to come in on time.

    c. Suggest they have physical checkups.

    d. Ask them, "What can we do to add more job satisfaction for you?"

16. You have a strong potential job candidate who was late for his first interview. You:

    a. Ignore it.

    b. Ask for his references and call them.

    c. Ask him why he was late.

    d. Ask him to come in for two or three interviews and see what happens.

17. You are always the last to know the bad news in your office. You:

    a. Ask yourself why you don't get this information earlier.

    b. Ask your group why they don't share with you.

    c. Complain that no one seems to care.

    d. Ask your boss for help.

18. You've hired two losers and are apprehensive about hiring the present job candidate. You:

    a. Ask "Can you describe in detail your previous job and the standards you were expected to fulfill?"

    b. Ask "What were your job duties?"

    c. Describe the job you have and ask, "Do you feel you can handle it?"

    d. Ask the personnel director for his or her opinion.

19. You feel uncomfortable in your new job because you are much younger than the people you've been hired to manage. You:

    a. Ask them "What do you feel makes a good manager?"

    b. Hope you'll prove your worth by actions.

    c. Try to cultivate your best personality so they'll get to like you.

    d.   Ask them for help in those areas where experience is important.

20.   You feel your staff does not operate as a team. You:

    a.   Give them a pep talk.

    b.   Talk to them individually.

    c.   Ask your corporate trainer about a team-building program.

    d.   Ask them, as a group, to bring to the next staff meeting suggestions for improvement.

21.   The third excellent employee you've hired has been lured away into another division of your firm. You:

    a.   Decide not to hire such good people.

    b.   Ask them why they go.

    c.   Register a complaint with your divisional vice president or the vice president of human resources.

    d.   Feel good that you have such a great network within the company and ask for a raise.

22.   Several of your staff people regularly come late to meetings. You:

    a.   Wait for the latecomers.

    b.   Ask your boss to come in for your next meeting.

    c.   Ask the staff to decide on a penalty for latecomers.

    d.   Start all meetings on time with important information for each person.

23.   During your summer vacation things fall apart in the office. You:

    a.   Wait for fall.

    b.   Plan a cross-training project.

    c.   Ask your employees for their suggestions.

    d.   Ask yourself if you've been delegating properly.

24.   Three of your top people have just returned from an expensive seminar. You:

    a.   Request a report from each.

    b.   Ask each one what he learned.

    c.   Ask each what he is going to do differently.

    d.   Watch to see the improvements.

25.   Managers succeed with their people because they:

    a.   Clearly express their expectations and ask their people to clarify their own expectations.

    b.   Have high goals.

    c.   Ask for frequent feedback.

    d.   Keep an open-door policy.

Answers

1.   a = 2   b = 3   c = 5   d = 1

We all prefer to have people we like on our project teams (*a*), but they aren't always the best choices. Nor are the all-round "best people" (*b*) always the right choice for a given project. The best answer is to match the people with the project (*c*), which should give you the best people for the particular job. You're in managerial trouble if you automatically choose people you can control (*d*).

2.   a = 0   b = 3   c = 0   d = 5

Your staff people recently have begun to make mistakes. The operative word in this question is "recently." If they had not been making mistakes before, something has gone wrong. The best answer is to ask them for solutions (*d*): your staff knows what is creating these problems. The answer would be totally different if you had a new staff and they were making a lot of mistakes. In that case, the best answer is to ask yourself how to improve your instructions (*b*).

3.   a = 1   b = 5   c = 2   d = 1

It's tough to decide between two qualified candidates. There's nothing wrong with asking a colleague for some help (*a*), but you must make your own decision. If you've got an unlimited budget, look for a way to hire them both (*c*), because you never can have enough good people.

And you might also ask your boss for advice; however, if you're looking to get ahead, don't ask your boss to decide for you (*d*). The best answer is to develop more probing questions to find out more about each candidate (*b*). It takes time and effort, but in the long run it's worth the trouble.

4.   a = 0   b = 1   c = 5   d = 3

Your assistant tells you he can't meet an important deadline. You lose if you condemn, immediately generate guilt, or worry about your own skin (*a* and *b*). Telling the person to get help (*d*) is not a bad answer because the realities of the workplace don't always allow time for individuals to complete their personal projects. But even when time is pressing, the best answer is (*c*): "What's the problem?" There may be a specific obstacle that can be worked out to allow your assistant to complete the project successfully.

5.   a = 2   b = 0   c = 4   d = 5

One reason people make so many mistakes is that managers don't ask for feedback. If you have a good working relationship with an employee, asking "Are there any questions?" is helpful (*a*). Letting the person work out the assignment for himself (*b*) is a waste of time unless the person is a mind reader. Both (*c*) and (*d*) are good answers, although just asking someone to repeat the instructions (*c*) can make the person feel like a child. Asking him to describe the assignment in his own words (*d*) is the most tactful and effective approach.

6.   a = 3   b = 0   c = 2   d = 5

Many new managers feel that when they're behind on a project it's up to them to stay up all night (*b*) or do whatever it takes to complete it alone. You may get the job done this way, but it's not a good solution. In an organization we all have to help each other. Asking your peers for help (*c*) does not take advantage of your managerial powers. Asking your employees for help (*a*) is a good idea, but you can maximize the situation by asking yourself "Who can benefit most from working on this project?" (*d*), thereby turning it into a growth experience for a staff person.

7.   a = 5   b = 1   c = 2   d = 1

When there are personal conflicts within your department, in most circumstances the best solution is to talk to the people together (*a*). Speaking to them individually (*b*) takes away their power to solve their problems jointly; and telling them to work it out between themselves (*c*) doesn't show enough concern on your part. Transferring one person (*d*) without getting to the bottom of the problem brands you as a manager who fails to deal with problems.

8.   a = 5   b = 4   c = 1   d = 0

The best way to interview prospective employees is to have a series of questions planned (*a*). The job description (*b*) is important, as long as you have read it before. Personally, I don't think resumes (*c*) are useful, from either the interviewer's or the candidate's point of view. Questions should be built around the job, not the resume. And while spontaneity sounds nice, a job interview isn't a party—far from it. If you wing it (*d*), you'll wind up with nothing.

9.   a = 0   b = 2   c = 0   d = 5

It's always difficult when employees have personal problems, but there's only one good answer here. As manager you can listen, but if an employee has a long-standing serious problem your goal is for the person to get professional help (*d*). Good managers often have a list of professionals or organizations to refer their people to. Sending someone to personnel (*b*) is passing the buck, although in some cases personnel might be able to help find the appropriate help.

10.   a = 2   b = 1   c = 5   d = 4

When a supervisor doesn't delegate enough, talking up the advantages of delegating (*a*) may help because at least it's positive; simply telling your employee to delegate more (*b*) is unlikely to have any effect. The two best answers are (*c*) and (*d*). Your goal is to get your employee to recognize for herself the benefits of delegating, which makes (*c*)—"Ask her why delegating should be important to a manager"—the best answer. It's also possible that an outside trainer (*d*) might help the person develop her delegating skills.

11.   a = 1   b = 3   c = 5   d = 0

Smart managers make exit interviews work for them. If you merely go through the formality of shaking hands (*a*) or pontificate that the person leaving is making a big mistake (*d*), you fail to maximize the opportunity. Since in this situation several people have resigned, asking your remaining staff how they see the situation (*b*) is a good choice. But the best solution is to ask questions of the people leaving, to discover the real reasons they are resigning (*c*). Such insight can help you correct situations in your department; you may also gain important feedback about your management style and how it affects your employees.

12.   a = 5   b = 3   c = 2   d = 4

Sagging morale rarely corrects itself. The best response is (*a*): before you take action, think through the problem objectively on your own; ask yourself some introspective smart questions about what's going on in your department. Then ask your problem people how they perceive the morale situation (*d*), since they are the ones having the problem. Asking your key people to investigate (*c*) is the least helpful of all the responses because your top people are not usually the ones having the problem. Calling a full staff meeting and asking for each person's contribution (*b*) can work, but it's taking the long way around. It's better to focus on those having the morale problem and try to correct it with them.

13.   a = 0   b = 1   c = 5   d = 1

"Tell me you about yourself" (*a*) is the worst question you can ask anyone during a job interview. It makes people feel defensive and confused, and seldom gets you any worthwhile or specific information. This question merely shows that you don't know what you're after. "I guess personnel has told you all our policies" (*b*) doesn't do you much good, either. Asking "What do you know about the company?" (*d*) has little value if you're hiring a clerical person but can be useful if you're interviewing someone for a management position. Overall, "What has personnel told you?" (*c*) is the best answer. It opens the conversation, it lets you find out what the person has already learned, it saves time, and it starts the interview off in a questioning mode.

14.   a = 5   b = 1   c = 1   d = 4

The key word in this question is "technical" training (as opposed to "human resources" training). To provide technical training for your staff you need to give input, but as with any training, you should also answer questions as they come up (*a*). Many technical trainers start off with a joke and then plunge into their talk (*b*), but this lecturing mode doesn't help people learn. Nor are open-ended questions (*c*) helpful when it comes to training someone in a specific skill (they're great for interpersonal or human resources training). In any training session, asking for frequent summaries (*d*) is good; summaries help reinforce the training and allow misinformation to surface and be corrected.

15.   a = 0   b = 2   c = 2   d = 5

When people come late or start calling in sick it's always a sign of deeper problems. Never ignore it (*a*). Telling them to come in on time (*b*) may work for a few days, but it won't solve the problem. They may have some physical problems (*c*), but don't count on it. Always investigate (*d*)—try to find out what's behind the lateness and sick days. If people are bored with their jobs you may not be able to do anything about it, but there's often the possibility of cross-training or other changes that might motivate your staff.

16.   a = 1   b = 4   c = 3   d = 5

What do you do when someone comes late for a first job interview: Do you assume they are always late? If punctuality is important in your office you don't want to ignore it (*a*), nor do you want to jump to conclusions. You can ask for an explanation (*c*), but that tends to get the interview off to a bad start (anyone can be late once). One good solution is to call the person's references and ask about past history (*b*); the best thing is to schedule two or three more interviews and see what happens (*d*).

17.   a = 5   b = 4   c = 1   d = 2

If you're the last to hear bad news in your office it means that people are afraid to tell you things. This happens to many managers, and it's dangerous. The best solution is to ask yourself why you don't get this information earlier (*a*), when you still have time to do something about it. Asking your group why they don't come to you when things go wrong (*b*) is not a bad approach, but if people are already afraid to talk to you they probably won't speak up. Complaining (*c*) and asking your boss for help (*d*) are not worth talking about.

18.   a = 5   b = 4   c = 2   d = 1

There's no foolproof way to select good job candidates, but your best chance comes if you can find out what the applicant did in his previous jobs and what standards he met (*a*). It's important to know what the person's job duties were (*b*), but without knowing the standards it isn't enough information. If you describe the job and ask the person "Can you handle it?" (*c*), you're doing the talking and the applicant naturally is likely to answer in the affirmative, which doesn't tell you much. And finally, asking personnel for an opinion (*d*) won't help you much because they can't know the job requirements as well as you do.

19.   a = 4   b = 3   c = 2   d = 5

When you're younger than the people you manage, it can help to ask them what they feel makes a good manager (*a*). They know as well as you that age has nothing to do with managing, and having to think about it will put them on the right track. But an even better strategy is to make the more mature people feel important (*d*). It's all right to prove your worth by actions (*b*), but it takes longer; try the other two strategies immediately. And putting on your most pleasing personality (*c*) may smooth the way temporarily, but you will still have to come to grips with the situation.

20.   a = 2   b = 3   c = 4   d = 5

If you want your people to operate as a team, giving them a pep talk (*a*) or talking to them individually (*b*) isn't going to do the job. Training (*c*) might help, but the best solution is to get them together as a group (*d*). A great way to start is to ask them to bring suggestions for improvement, and take it from there.

21.   a = 0   b = 4   c = 1   d = 5

Whenever you hire good people you run the risk that other departments will want them. Deciding not to hire such good people (*a*) is hurting yourself. Asking them why they accept the new offers (*b*) is a smart idea, because it may turn out that if all the top people are moving out of your division you might want to move out, too: you might work to change your management style if you discover that is the problem. Complaining to your boss (*c*) is silly. Overall, my philosophy is to enjoy the fact that you have such a good network in the company (*d*).

22.   a = 1   b = 3   c = 4   d = 5

The worst thing you can do with latecomers is wait for them (*a*), because then you're rewarding bad behavior. Asking your boss to attend the next meeting (*b*) is not a bad idea; and deciding on a penalty (*c*) has worked in many companies. But the more subtle, effective thing to do is to start the meetings on time, and start off with important information for each person, information that they cannot easily get elsewhere. It should cure the problem almost immediately.

23.   a = 1   b = 4   c = 3   d = 5

If things fall apart in your office when you're away, you must ask yourself if you're delegating properly (*d*). The next best thing is to plan a cross-training program (*b*) so that people can help each other when you're away. Asking employees for their suggestions (*c*) is not as specific, but it is helpful. The only thing that will happen if you wait until fall (*a*) is that the leaves will change color.

24.   a = 5   b = 3   c = 4   d = 2

When you've invested a lot of money sending people to a seminar you want to maximize its value. Asking for an extensive written report (*a*) helps reinforce the information and gives the seminar extra impact. It's also good to sit down and talk to each person who attended (*b*), but it's more important to find out what they're going to do differently in the future (*c*). (You might want to wait a while for the new information to sink in before asking this question.) If you passively watch to see the improvements (*d*), you are indicating that you don't really care if they learned anything and that sending them to a seminar was just going through the motions.

25.   a = 5   b = 3   c = 4   d = 1

The main cause of employee failure is unclear or unverbalized expectations. If you clearly express your expectations (*a*), you should be well on your way to being a successful manager. And the way to know if people understand your expectations is to ask for frequent feedback (*c*). High goals are important (*b*), but unless you express those goals clearly they remain your personal secret. I don't believe that managers should keep an open-door policy (*d*), because if they're available all the time people don't learn to make decisions on their own.

Scoring

100–125 Points

Your profile is the ideal for today's manager: you are concerned with both people and results. You ask questions throughout the workday, and you evaluate and act on the answers you receive. You are confident, calm, well organized, and able to delegate. Your people work hard for you and give you their best. You hire people at least as talented as yourself and don't feel threatened when they are promoted. Productivity in your department is high. You are respected by your staff as well as by upper management.

85–100 Points

Deep down, you really don't accept the fact that if your staff looks good, you look good. But you are ambitious. By asking more questions, listening more, and increasing your staff's involvement you could improve the overall performance of your department, as well as your own.

65–85 Points

Although you know that today's standards require you to be more of a people manager, you still hold on to an autocratic management style. Because you make all the decisions and insist that everything be done your way, your people do not produce as much as they could, and several of your employees feel frustrated. Because you take over so much, they don't feel fully involved in the job and consequently do not give it their maximum effort. You can improve if you give fewer orders, ask more questions, and listen more to your people.

Less than 65 Points

Managers who prefer to work alone are usually in this category. They are often detached and tend to avoid problems and confrontations.

Here also is the manager who can't say no. He is often overworked and disorganized, a person who relinquishes all control and decision making to other people, with little or no direction. This manager would like to put all his responsibility on others. As a result, staff people often feel he is both weak and unfair.

These two management styles are inadequate for today's business. Any manager who fits these profiles could improve his or her management skills and overall performance by developing a questioning approach.

The issues raised in Part Two of the Quiz are important because they show how your own management technique affects the morale and overall performance of your team. While managers can do much to enhance the enthusiasm and dedication of their people, success depends largely on choosing the right people to begin with. Selecting people with talent and ambition is your most demanding task. Your influence and success as a manager depend on your ability to make the right choice. The next chapter reveals how smart questions can help you find the best people for the job.

8

Quality Staffing: The Right Stuff

Volumes have been written about motivating employees and helping people bring out their best. But those managerial tasks are a thousand percent more profitable if the employee you're working with has "the right stuff" to begin with. Perhaps your most important function as manager is bringing on board the right personnel. And in this capacity smart questions serve as your shrewdest skill.

Set your standards high, and hire the best people to meet them. Sounds easy? It's not.

Jack was the production chief of a national magazine, and like production chiefs throughout the journalism industry he was overworked and understaffed. With a double issue going to press and a special year-end edition in preparation, Jack once again pleaded with upper management to add staff. The managing editor finally agreed and gave the necessary permission for Jack to look for someone new.

Jack was so anxious to relieve the pressure that he urged personnel to fill the job as soon as possible: "Get me a body, and get it fast."

And fast it was: he hired the first experienced person who passed the computer typesetting test. The result: four months later, his group of eighteen typesetters and proofreaders were squabbling among themselves, fighting over overtime, refusing to cooperate with each other—

in effect destroying the coordinated team effort essential to producing any regular publication on schedule. Why?

The new employee, it turned out, was fast on the computer but disaster on the team. Jack had completely missed the boat on the hiring decision. He thought he needed an extra pair of hands, but what he really needed was someone who would fit smoothly into the tightly knit group, remain cheerful under pressure, and be empathetic to a myriad of sensitive, volatile personalities—in other words, someone who could help the team function at peak performance. Competent hands were only a part of the task.

Jack hadn't taken time to ask himself the right questions: questions that, first, would help him *define the real job;* and second, that would help him know exactly *what kind of person* would best fill it.

Nowhere do you have more at stake than in hiring a new employee. Not only do you look bad if you choose the wrong person, but like Jack's, your company may be stuck paying thousands of dollars in unemployment compensation because of your mistake.

Many managers are like movie producers. Just as producers try to sign up big-name talent with proven box office draw, managers look to hire people with the right credentials, references, and experience. The reasoning in both cases is the same: self-protection in case something goes wrong. If the movie fails at the box office, the producer can look the investment banker in the eye and say, "I hired top names who had been successful in the past. It wasn't my fault if it didn't work." If an employee flops, the manager can say, "He went to Harvard and his references were impeccable. How could I know?"

This need for self-protection causes managers, like movie producers, to flop. Quality staffing is based on much more than credentials and references. Selecting the best person for the job requires that a manager be more than an executive—he or she must be something of a soothsayer.

Every day of the week, able people successfully step up into jobs they've never performed before. Sometimes it's brilliant strategy to take a chance on an individual of above-average ability, charisma, or ingenuity, especially when you're hiring for a growth job. An officer of a direct-mail marketing organization, interviewing senior account executives, discovered a candidate who had no experience in the field. But she did have all the vital attributes—ability to contact, establish a relationship, get information, sell creative concepts, close the deal. The firm took a risk, and the new employee helped multiply their business by 40 percent in the first six months.

What if you could accurately predict the future performance of any candidate who applied for a job? If you could pick winners and avoid personnel disasters? Obviously, if you hope to avoid the bad bets and spot the winners you've got to come up with the smartest possible questions to ask during the interview. And that means doing your homework. The reason that 90 percent of managers cannot pick a winner is that they're focused on the wrong aspect of the hiring process. They're willing to ask questions of the candidate, but they fail to ask questions about the job itself.

Before you can find the best person for the job you must, above all else, have a crystal clear understanding of the job itself. If you really know what the job is—not just the particular skill involved, but the kind of temperament needed to carry it out and the required level of performance—then finding the right person is relatively easy. You can never be 100 percent certain that the person you choose can do the job for you, but when you have a thorough understanding of the job's requirements, you can more easily take a chance and bet that he or she has what it takes.

Creating the Essential Job Profile

Reaching this thorough understanding is the key to hiring the right person. Most managers set out to hire "the best person for the job" without determining what is "best" for that particular position. It's the Rocky Graziano approach to hiring: "I pondered the situation—and it hit me!"

What you're after is a way to distinguish vital skills from irrelevant skills and to pinpoint the subtle qualities that will put the candidate over the top. By asking yourself some smart questions, you can put together the Essential Job Profile; from there you can go on to develop smart questions to ask during the actual interview.

The Essential Job Profile is a comprehensive outline which considers all aspects of the position—skills, personal traits, team fit, and special talents—the crucial as well as less important requirements.

To arrive at this profile you must answer four important questions:

- What type of person does your team need?
- What is the hidden job description?

- What are the success factors?
- How well do you want the job done?

Write each question on a separate sheet of paper. You can also ask people on your staff to help you with your homework by writing up their version of a particular Essential Job Profile. This can be an interesting project, and you and your group may learn a great deal from each other in the process.

What Type of Person Does Your Team Need?

Each time you hire a new person, the impact reverberates throughout your team. Everything shifts as the new employee finds his way to fit into the group and the group finds a way to adapt to him. This is true even if you run a two-person "group" and you are the only person the newcomer directly affects.

Understanding personality types is invaluable for smooth team transition. You also need to know something about your group's style. Take a good look at your team; think about how a new person might liven things up a little. If your people thrive on action and deadlines, then a slow-moving member might retard their momentum. On the other hand, such an addition might help moderate the team if it tends to foul up because of too high a speed.

Consider the descriptions in Chapter 4 of the 5 major categories of personality types. Commanders are the fast moving leaders, the merchants of change. Convincers will also come up with ideas, and will promote them. Carers will keep the peace, cooperate, and get the work done. Calculators will be sure it's done right. Creators will come up with new ideas and concepts. Most teams do best with all 5 types represented.

As a manager you also want your new employee to complement your own style. For example, if you're a Commander looking for a secretary or assistant, you should look for a Carer or Calculator to complement your weakness. *Hire your weakness*—someone who is strong in the areas where you are weak.

Ask yourself and your team these questions:

"How can I improve the group when I hire a new person?"

"What kind of person will fit into our team best?

"What talents or personality types would help to balance the team for maximum productivity?"

"Have I complemented my own weaknesses?"

"Can this person make up for my shortcomings?"

"Are we lacking a Carer or a Calculator type who would complement our group of Commanders and Convincers?"

"Do we need an idea person, or a peacemaker?"

"Do we need a person who loves detail, or someone who loves to talk to people?"

"Are there any parts of this job that someone else on the team would like to do?" (Hiring is a good time to reassess the team and see if other jobs should change.)

"Is there a way that this new circumstance will let me improve the present situation for my team?" (More space? Increased budget or more team training? This is a perfect question if you're hiring people to work with newly installed technology.)

Write down all your answers. They will form the basis of interview questions.

What Is the Hidden Job Description?

Many jobs already have a formal job description. A good one usually includes things like educational requirements, experience necessary, major responsibilities, lines of communication, and special considerations.

But every job also has a hidden job description—those things you wouldn't or couldn't or shouldn't write in the formal job description. A formal job description gives the facts: what the person is expected to do. The hidden job description covers the intangible requirements. You expect a salesperson to have confidence and to cope well with frequent rejection. And you want a copywriter to be sensitive to trends and change. And a personnel administrator who is a good listener.

Sometimes even the "best" skills are useless if the person isn't happy with the work. A simple question to ask yourself is "What should this person enjoy doing?" Or "What unusual circumstance should he or she be able to tolerate?"

David, who was hired as an administrative assistant in the training department, wanted to be a trainer although he had no experience. Even though he was a whiz on the word processor he resented it and peppered every passerby with comments like "Elaine is out there enjoying herself while I'm stuck at this miserable computer."

It's important to find people who really like their work. Hiring a manager who doesn't like people would be like hiring a chef who doesn't like food. Likewise, an administrator should love organized systems, and a secretary should enjoy being efficient. While these traits seem obvious, you can't take it for granted that because someone applies for a given job they automatically have the appropriate predilections.

Probing around these intangibles gives you the fodder to create a lot of smart interview questions. For example, if you note that frequent policy changes are a fact of life in your company, you should devise questions about the candidate's reaction to change. If several people have left recently for other companies, some interview questions may concern loyalty.

The hidden job description helps you focus on qualities, such as loyalty and energy, that can make a big difference when it comes to choosing the right person. To pin down these elusive factors, ask yourself—and your team—these ten smart questions:

"What personal qualities are necessary for this job?" (Enthusiasm, steadiness, flexibility, love of detail?)

"What type of behavior will suit this job?" (Energetic, placid, talkative, silent?)

"Who has failed in this job and why?"

"Who has succeeded in this job and why?"

"Who are the difficult people this individual will have to communicate with?"

"Are there any unusual circumstances in the organization that the person will have to cope with?" (Change? Moving? Working alone?)

"What are the toughest conditions of the job?"

"What kind of work should a person thrive on in order to be happy doing this particular job?"

"What kind of atmosphere should this person most enjoy?"

"If I had to describe the person who could best fill this job, what would I say?"

What Are the Success Factors?

There are almost always one or two outstanding characteristics that a person needs to excel in a job. I call these special talents or skills "success factors."

When you have defined the job and have determined the kind of personality that would best carry it out, you need to know something more: "What is the most important quality or ability the candidate must have to succeed in this particular job?" This could be both a quality or a skill or a combination.

Some people might say "An MBA," or "Writing reports." But those answers are wide of the mark. The success factor addresses itself to the essence of the job. For example, it's essential for the CEO of a controversial corporation (a power company, for example) to be a dynamic public speaker and a good media personality. And a telemarketing person must have a warm, confident telephone voice and the ability to close sales. A court stenographer must be able to record 150 words per minute. If the essence of a certain job involves complicated dealings with high-level authority, a candidate needs special talents for both politicking and negotiating. Desire and enthusiasm for the job are not enough. An opera singer, no matter how hard she works, cannot succeed without a great voice. These are the special abilities needed for these jobs—the keys that allow the person to excel.

If a job applicant is missing the success factor or factors, no other assets, no matter how exemplary, can make up for it. Too often we hire ducks for running and rabbits for swimming.

In my own office, for example, I hope that an administrative assistant will deal pleasantly on the telephone with clients, be an excellent typist, write good letters, and generally have good ideas for the company. But none of those assets is the success factor. The primary quality an administrative assistant must have is an unfailing ability to follow up and handle details.

Identifying the success factor can save a lot of time. If a Broadway producer or a real estate developer can raise funds, any other talents they have—or don't have—are irrelevant. Likewise, if a job requires 75 percent research, a highly gregarious Convincer, even if he or she is eager to tackle the research job, is the wrong choice.

You can sometimes arrive at the success factor if you think in terms of your company rather than an individual's capabilities. A prospective account executive may have a great track record landing new accounts, but perhaps his success has depended on a lavish expense account. Limited by the low budget your firm can afford, his hands will be tied. Another candidate may be able to land one king-size account in six months, but in fact you might need someone who can pull in several smaller accounts right away.

Janet Tweed, executive recruiter for Gilbert Tweed Associates, recently described one of their worst hiring decisions: "We wanted a president to oversee five companies, each with its own problems. The person chosen had unbelievable credentials with a Fortune 500 company. However, we learned he could manage different plants making the *same* product but lacked the flexibility to handle five *different* situations."

Some jobs have more than one success factor. There is the top success factor, and then others of lesser import. For example, many consultants whose business is conducted outside the office have trouble finding and keeping good secretaries because the person is alone so much. Although functioning well when alone is not the top success factor, it is vital and should be included. A good list of success factors should contain at least one—but not more than three—elements without which the job cannot be performed with excellence.

Five questions will help you determine the success factors for a particular job. Ask yourself, and write down your answers:

"What is the one talent and/or skill this person must have to do this job well?"

"Are there any other secondary qualities and/or skills necessary for good performance?"

"Are these factors crucial, or only important?"

"If a previous employee failed in this job, was there one quality lacking that made the difference?"

"How does that quality alter the list of success factors?"

Here's an example. Let's say that you have a position open for a technical researcher.

The first question is "What is the one talent and/or skill this person must have?" You answer: The person must be a persistent, dedicated researcher.

"Are there any other secondary qualities and/or skills necessary for good performance?" You answer:

1. Telephone interviewing.

2. Organizing a tight outline from many different sources.

3. Ability to write reports in clear, nontechnical prose.

4. Ability to type a clean, attractive presentation.

"Are these factors crucial, or only important?" You answer: Numbers 2 and 3 are crucial. Telephone interviewing and typing could be done by someone else.

"If a previous employee failed in this job, was there one quality lacking that made the difference?" You answer: The person who held the job before could amass information but had trouble picking out what was important.

"How does that quality alter the list of success factors?" You answer: I would change Number 2 to read: Ability to ferret out important information, *conceptualize,* and develop a tight outline from many different research sources.

After answering these self questions your list of success factors would read like this:

1. Dedicated, persistent researcher.

2. Able to select important information, conceptualize, and develop a tight outline from many different sources.

3. Able to translate outline into clear, nontechnical prose.

How Well Do You Want the Job Done?

The level of performance you would like to see in the work of an employee is the fourth vital element to add to your Essential Job Profile. During job interviews few things look more promising than an enthusiastic new employee; unfortunately, few things can be as misleading. Too often you find that your new employee's level of energy doesn't match his level of skills.

Managers often miss out on the right people because they fail to set standards of performance. Interviewers typically ask themselves "What is the job I have open?" A smarter question—the question that will get the best person—is "How well do I want the job done?"

A public-relations executive recently had to fire a newly hired account man; she realized that although he could write a press release in three days, she needed someone who could turn one out in half a day. Most of us have only a vague notion of the performance level we require in a job—someone who types "well," or someone who can handle a "variety" of projects.

When I ask in seminars "How fast do you want your secretary to type?" most executives answer "Around 50 words per minute." In my office I hire only people with 70 wpm or better. For most managers productivity will increase substantially if the secretary types 70 to 75 words per minute, and many people out there fill the bill.

Your interview questions aren't designed merely to learn what the applicant did in his last job; you want to find out how well he did it (and how well he would do it for you). Only when you establish the performance standard you require can you discover whether an applicant can perform at that level. If you want to excel, don't lower your standards— keep raising them.

Questions concerning standards will vary according to the job and the job requirements. Each major job requirement should have a matching performance standard. For example, if typing is one job requirement, you will have to set a minimum speed. You will have a separate performance standard for telemarketing, and so on. For each job requirement, ask yourself:

"What specific achievements do I expect from the new employee?"

"What do I want never to happen?" (No complaints from customers.)

"When do I expect the person to master the job?"

The questions should be aimed at the specific job at hand. For example, if a product manager will have to develop "several" new product lines over a twelve-month period, how many do you actually expect? How close to market-ready should suggested products be when presented to upper management? How successful do you expect them to be in their first year on the market?

Or if you're hiring a new account person: Do you expect him or her to eventually handle one or two product lines alone? Three or four? And how soon is "eventually"?

Or if you're hiring a new receptionist: Do you want the person simply to be pleasant and efficient? Or do you expect him or her to field tricky phone calls with tact and intelligence? Will you expect the receptionist to recognize all your clients after being with you a month? Two months?

Final Preparation of the Essential Job Profile

When you have answered these questions on your four sheets of paper, you have everything you need to arrive at the Essential Job Profile.

By developing the Essential Job Profile you are forced to think clearly about the forthcoming interview. Even if you do nothing further, you are already way out front in the hiring process.

However, it's best to take it one step further: to spell out a series of smart questions that will help you discover if the job applicant has the qualities revealed in the Essential Job Profile. Every hiring situation is different. As much as possible, each question you ask should be tailored to the particular situation and person involved. As you develop the Essential Job Profile for your job opening, put your notes in writing; outline important issues and start thinking of smart questions that relate to each issue.

A much-traveled-never-in-the-office colleague of mine asked me to help him hire an administrator to run his office. We used this system to create the Essential Job Profile. Here is what we wrote:

TEAM FIT:

Even-tempered; must complement me. Someone who enjoys being a self-starter and can work alone. Definitely need a Calculator personality.

HIDDEN JOB DESCRIPTION:

Someone to take over the administration and financial aspects of the business. Someone who will work overtime when necessary and not be a clock watcher. Want someone interested in doing the job right. Take-charge attitude, able to cope with high-pressure office. Clearly detail oriented.

SUCCESS FACTORS

1. Highly organized and detail oriented.

2. Must like to take over and operate without direction.

3. Must be able to hire good people.

PERFORMANCE STANDARDS

Record keeping: All books must be balanced each week with no errors.

Level of complaints: Complaints from clients are unacceptable.

Must be able to direct staff so that everyone is in office on time—without fail.

Here is the list of smart questions my colleague came up with to discover how job applicants matched his Essential Job Profile.

"What are your restrictions about overtime?"

"What in my ad attracted you?"

"In what specific ways do you consider yourself precise and detail oriented?"

"How would you define a self-starter?"

"Can you describe in detail the complexity of the projects in your last job?"

"How many projects did you have going on simultaneously?"

"What were your follow-up procedures? Your quality-control checks?"

"Describe how you interview a job candidate."

"May I talk with one of your former employers?"

The list of questions you devise will create a structure to carry you through the interview and keep you relaxed and on track, no more than that. Trying to follow a script is counterproductive. Overplanning and programmed questioning can be nervewracking to the interviewee and may lead to rigid and insipid answers.

Your goal is to have enough smart questions prepared so that in the interviews you will not be talking more than 30 percent of the time. (If you talk more than that, you're not finding out enough.)

Hiring Gives You a Competitive Edge

Hiring a new employee gives you the perfect opportunity to go beyond the ordinary and make a run for excellence. Aside from creating a first-class staff, nabbing the right person for a job is also a great way to make positive changes in your department and to shine up your image with upper management.

Each time you have such an opportunity, ask yourself these smart questions before you take any action:

"What goals do I want to achieve by hiring a new person?"

"Is there anyone else who should be involved in this hiring process?" (A peer whom the person may occasionally report to? A subordinate who will work closely with the person? Your own boss?)

"If so, what are their expectations?"

"What are the advantages (or disadvantages) of discussing the hiring decision with my boss?" (If you're perceived as weak in the decision-making department, you can prove otherwise by making an excellent choice by yourself. On the other hand, if you've been told you should be more of a team player, now is an ideal time to show that you do indeed value input from other people.)

"Where have I fouled up in the past in terms of hiring?" (Perhaps you weren't willing to spend money. Or you didn't really know what you were looking for. Or you chose someone because you liked him. Or you were afraid to hire someone who might outshine you.)

It is not uncommon for people to avoid hiring applicants who are "too good." One executive found a way to overcome her anxiety about hiring people who outperformed her: "I learned that coming up with good people made me look good. As a result one or two may have moved past me. But I'll tell you this: I've got the best network in the company." She has also earned herself a reputation for picking winners.

Managers who succeed understand that the best leaders follow this wisdom: Hire and promote people who are better than you are, because when they shine they make you look good. The eventual result is that when you reach a senior position, the entire organization is seeded with your talented charges.

The abiding philosophy of David Ogilvy, of the renowned Ogilvy & Mather advertising agency, is this: "If each of us hires people who are smaller than we are we shall become a company of dwarfs. But if each of us hires people who are bigger than we are, we shall become a company of giants."

People who get ahead in corporations see every hiring situation as an opportunity to thrust their careers forward. They ask themselves, consciously or unconsciously, this one smart question: "What can I do to maximize this experience—for myself, my team, and my organization?"

In the following chapter we're going to take quality staffing out of the theoretical and into the actual interview—one place where asking smart questions offers an immediate payoff.

9

The Smart Questions Way to Hire

You look across the desk. The job candidate smiles back at you. You notice that with his well-tailored blue suit and white shirt he's wearing gleaming black Italian loafers, an elegant tie, and a matching handkerchief peeking out from his breast pocket. "Why did you choose our company to apply to?" you ask.

Enthusiasm spills out of every pore: "I think what you're doing here is innovative. This organization is known to have its finger on what's happening around the country."

As you take in his appearance and his attitude, one question runs through your mind: "Is this person the right one? Is he the best possible addition to my team?"

There's only one way to find out. Resumes, credentials, and references can tell only part of the story. Impressions and "vibrations" add a little more. But your total picture of the applicant can be filled in only by asking right questions and evaluating each response.

When you interview a job candidate your immediate goal is to reduce tension and encourage forthright communication. Aim for a relaxed and unpressured pace.

The interview situation is likely to distort your sense of time, so don't rush things. Studies show that when interviewers estimate the length of a period of silence they typically magnify it by a factor of 10 to 100. As a result, whenever there is a pause in the conversation most interviewers rush to fill what they perceive as an awkward gap. Don't let anxiety make you answer your own questions because you can't bear the silence. Take your time and let the candidate fill the pauses with his own thoughts and answers.

Interviews should be one-on-one. If a colleague or your boss is also going to interview the candidate, their interviews should be in separate meetings. If the applicant must meet several people at once, for example a board of governors, let him know in advance and give him some advice on what to expect.

Always tell the applicant your purpose and objectives: "We're together to discuss the position that's open, and whether it's the right one for you. So this is a discovery process for us both." Suggest a give-and-take discussion.

One school of interview techniques is gaining popularity among managers desperately looking for easy answers to the hiring dilemma. This theory holds that the only purpose of the job interview is for you, the manager, to gather information. As the interviewer you give out as little information as possible and conduct the interview strictly as a question-and-answer session for yourself. I don't believe this method has value. High-quality candidates will not appreciate being treated like specimens to be examined at the discretion of the interviewer.

Many interviewers divide the interview into two parts—in the first part the interviewer asks questions, then during the second part the candidate can ask questions. This is better than the first technique, but it still creates unnecessary tension. In my opinion, conforming to such a rigid pattern is the sign of an insecure interviewer.

First-class interviewers encourage job candidates to ask questions throughout the interview. The idea is to establish a genuine rapport from the moment the session begins. Tell the person that you welcome questions, and then make it easy for him or her to ask: "I'll ask some questions, and feel free to ask any you might have as we go along."

Study the candidate's resume *before* the interview. You've got a real live person there, so don't relate to the paper when you can relate to the human being.

Some managers use the interview to sell applicants on the merits of the job—and later wonder why they hired the wrong person. Your success depends on your accurate assessment of *the candidate*, not vice versa.

Another fatal flaw: managers tend to hire people they like, or who are like them. Some managers are misled by the so-called halo effect. That is, they judge an individual in terms of the impression he or she makes. Managers often let the personal appeal of the candidate overshadow their judgment.

Interviewers must concentrate on past behavior as an indication of the person's potential. The fact that someone is charming, for example, doesn't guarantee that he or she can bargain with vendors for lowest prices. But the fact that the person had successfully run a dinner theater does strongly suggest that he can negotiate with a variety of suppliers for the best deal.

Begin with Open Questions

With the preliminaries over, just how does a manager go about asking the right questions? In a research project that concentrated on interviewing techniques, Samuel G. Trully, who teaches management courses for the School of Business Administration at the University of California, analyzed the recordings of one hundred job interviews. Trully discovered that successful interviewers always began with broad, open-ended questions and worked their way into sharper, more direct questions toward the end of the meeting.

If you ask closed questions right from the beginning, the interview becomes awkward: "Have you spoken to personnel?" "What are your salary requirements?" "What was your previous title?" "Did you get along with your last supervisor?" These questions are guaranteed to bring the conversation to a screeching halt.

In contrast, broad, open questions give the candidate plenty of room to reveal himself. He can talk about what he feels is important and can expand into areas that he thinks are vital. That means that you, the interviewer, have an opportunity to listen and learn.

Open questions stimulate discussion:

"What are some of the reasons you're interested in this position?"

"Why would you like to work for this company?" (Shows if the candidate has done some homework and found out anything about your company before the interview.)

"What has personnel told you?" (You find out what they know and don't know.)

If you succeed in establishing an easy flow with open questions, people will answer questions honestly. And because they encourage the person to talk freely, such open questions also let you learn about strengths, secrets, or problems that wouldn't be mentioned on a resume or in a more formal interview.

Later in the interview the conversational tone you've established will let you pose unusually intimate questions. For example, you might try the favorite interview questions of Robert Half, America's preeminent hiring pro:

"What did you do the day before yesterday—in detail?"

"Why do you think we should hire you?"

"Where does the power come from in your organization?"

Overall, however, you're searching to discover if the candidate has the strengths highlighted in the Essential Job Profile. Some interviewers probe for a person's weaknesses, but in fact, if the candidate fills the role described in the Essential Job Profile, his or her weaknesses are irrelevant. Everyone has weaknesses.

Matching the Essential Job Profile

The meat of the interview should involve questions that grow out of your Essential Job Profile. Here's where you find out whether the candidate's personality fits in with your team and matches the basics of the hidden job description; whether the applicant boasts the success factor or factors; whether in your judgment this person will perform up to your standards.

Looking for Team Fit

If the person you're looking for will have to deal with authority figures, you might ask:

"What kind of people did you have to deal with in your last job?"

"Can you describe the person or people with whom you got along best?"

"What were your least successful relationships? Why?"

"Tell me about two serious interpersonal relationship problems you've had on the job."

Even though I advocate a give-and-take exchange of information, it's important not to pose leading questions which have the answer built in: "You don't mind working alone, do you?" A better question is "What do you like best—working in a group or working solo?"

If they answer "both," press for a decision: "Give me examples." Or, "If you could choose between working on a team and doing research, which would you select?"

Probing for the Hidden Job Description

When considering the hidden job description, you should ask questions that reveal behavior tendencies and work style.

Past behavior is the best indicator of what someone can do for you. It's unrealistic to assume that a Convincer with loads of energy and a need for interaction is going to grow into a research job. If you know a person had a chronic problem meeting deadlines on their last job, it doesn't matter why. The only thing that matters is that the person isn't good at making deadlines.

The hidden job description often involves an individual's temperament and behavior patterns. Michael, the director of a pharmaceutical firm, hired a new vice president of direct marketing. Because the company was in the midst of growth and reorganizing, all of the new executive's time was devoted to budget and long-range planning instead of producing direct mail. He did such a good job that Michael offered him a promotion to do more of the same. But by this time the executive was ill from all the stress the job had caused him.

If you want to test temperament and behavior, try:

"Describe an interpersonal problem you had and how you resolved it."

"In what areas do you feel you would like to develop further?" (Look for concrete answers. A person might answer vaguely: "I'm looking for a job to sink my teeth into." Keep probing for specifics.)

"How do you plan to achieve these goals?"

"Can you tell me in more detail what you mean?"

"How do you see this job fitting in with your plans?"

This is also an appropriate time to find out whether the person is a Commander, Convincer, Carer, Calculator, or Creator. Ask questions that deal with working style, such as:

"Would you describe yourself as people oriented or task oriented?" Or, "Do you like to produce a product yourself, or do you like to delegate and supervise?"

"Can you explain why?"

"Do you solve problems by examining all the available data, or by creative trial and error?"

"What process do you follow in solving problems?"

"In groups do you often emerge as a dominant figure? What do you feel causes this?"

"Are you a competitor or a cooperator? Can you give an example?"

"When you have a problem with a co-worker, do you prefer direct confrontation or tact and delicacy?"

"What methods do you use to make decisions?"

An imaginative question can also reveal a person's behavioral tendencies: "Suppose you have to leave right away to sell a strange and totally unfamiliar product door to door. If you can ask only three things about the product before you go, what would they be?"

There is no right or wrong answer. If the candidate's unhesitating answer is "Price, product lifetime, primary use," you've got a quick thinker with an innate ability to pinpoint the bottom line—a Commander behavioral tendency.

On the other hand, an immediate response along the lines of "How will it make me feel or look better? What benefits does it have?" may indicate great marketing ability. This is more of a Convincer response.

Perhaps the candidate analyzes the question and comes up with "Who can fill me in on this product? How can I get the rest of the team involved in a sales campaign?" You probably have a Carer who presents a balanced view and likes to work with the full resources of a team behind him.

If the person asks "What are the facts about the product?" "Where is my sales manual?" you've got a Calculator. If he asks "What does this product do?" "How does it fit into the overall product line?" or "Why did you select me?—I'm not a good salesperson—I want to create a new product," you've got a Creator.

Don't stop after learning one dimension of the person. Probe further. For example, you might want to know how a candidate handles the issue of honoring company policy: "Were there ever times you had to get around, ignore, or change company policy in order to get a project done on schedule?"

If the applicant answers "Yes," don't jump to conclusions. Ask him or her to describe the details. Then follow it up with another question: "Was there ever a time that you followed company policy, even though you found it difficult?"

Since you've asked both questions, the applicant can't intuit the answer you're looking for. You're after a multi-dimensional picture of whether the person supports the organization he works for, and how he responds to rules and regulations.

When you're probing for the hidden job description, it's important to listen to *how* the person answers as well as what he says. Does the candidate have a pleasant voice or a grating one? Is he or she especially articulate, blunt, commanding, intimidating, tactful? Poised, outgoing and somewhat theatrical, full of irrepressible energy—or more like the Rock of Gibraltar and just as dignified? Careful observation can also give you keys to a candidate's personal strengths and perhaps to untapped potential.

Probing for Success Factors

Questions that probe for a given success factor will depend entirely on what kind of talent you're looking for. Seth, a clothing manufacturer, was looking for a designer who would develop four new lines each year and supervise a difficult, conflict-prone staff of twelve. The previous designer had ignored the people totally to meet the deadlines. When it came time to interview a new designer, Seth asked these smart questions:

"What were the pressures on your last job?"

"Most executives are jugglers. How do you handle the need to juggle many different elements?"

"In detail, what did you have to produce in your last job?"

"What kind of problems did your people have?"

"What results did you accomplish?"

"How did you develop your key people?"

"What do you consider your three greatest career achievements?"

"Why did these give you such satisfaction?"

"What are the most difficult aspects of your job? Not that you can't do them, but the ones that cost you the most time and effort?"

"If you had two people in serious conflict during a major deadline, what would you do?"

"If a key person wanted to quit during a deadline crisis, what would you do?"

"What do you consider the three essentials of success in developing four new lines and supervising a contentious staff?"

"If I were to interview a person on your staff, how might they describe you?"

"What is your interpretation of success?"

Smart Job Performance Questions

It's easy to ask a typist "How fast do you type?" It's more tricky to get subjective information about previous performance levels. Job applicants often know what success factor you're looking for and will give the expected answer. For example, I once made a poor hiring decision when I was looking for someone who was detail oriented. During the job interview I asked the applicant, "Are you good at details?" and she answered "Yes." I took her word for it, and went on to something else. I was impressed by her nice personality and by the ideas she had for running the office.

After the new person had been in the job for two weeks it became clear that while she had all the other necessary qualities, she was not interested in the follow-up work which was the heart of her job. When it came to the success factor, I should have probed beyond her immediate response and asked a series of questions designed to uncover this one important element. If I had been hiring an opera singer, I could have asked her to sing. But how do you audition an administrative assistant to discover if she's good at details? The only possibility is to ask smart questions:

"Are you good at details?"

"Describe how you handled the details of your last project."

"What have you done to ensure the quality of your employees' work?"

"Can you give me an example of how you would set up a cross-training program?"

Suppose you ask someone who was a project leader, "How well did your projects turn out?" You can bet they'll answer "Fine." Instead, try these smart questions:

"What kind of projects did you handle?"

"How did you select people for your projects?"

"To what extent did you delegate responsibility?"

"Tell me about a problem you had on a project."

"How did you handle it?"

Ask people for specifics:

"Describe a specific assignment and the specific results you achieved."

"What tools, resources, and people did you have to work with?"

"What were your accomplishments?"

"Over what period of time?"

"What was your budget?"

"If you had to do that project over again, what would you do differently?"

Listening and Evaluating

Since you've gone to so much trouble to devise smart questions, make sure you listen carefully to the answers. Throughout the interview, your questions should shift as you listen and evaluate the candidate's responses. Allen E. Murray, Chairman of the Mobil Corporation, says, "My first priority [when interviewing someone] is to make sure I hear and register all the answers, including the implications. After all, that's what prompts my next question."

What an Applicant's Questions Reveal

A good interviewer also listens carefully to the applicant's questions. If you've encouraged a mutual exchange throughout the interview, the candidate's questions will give you insight into the way his or her mind works. For example: "Where can I go in the company?" If an applicant asks this question in the first three or four minutes of the interview, you know this person is eager for a job with promotion potential.

Other questions asked early in the interview may suggest past problems or frustrations:

"Will I be responsible for coming up with ideas?"

"Will I have to present it in person?"

"How much red tape will I have to deal with?"

These questions require you to probe further. Ask "Is that a problem for you?" or "Why are you asking?" Make a genuine nonthreatening inquiry, so that you actually understand why the person is asking the question.

Before you answer any question, consider that you may learn more by first countering with a qualifying question:

Candidate:	Is there any overtime?
Interviewer:	Why do you ask? [It sounds as if she wants to make extra money, but that may not be the reason.]
Candidate:	Will I have to work late?
Interviewer:	Is that a problem for you?
Candidate:	Will there be much travel in this job?
Interviewer:	It's possible. How do you feel about traveling?
Candidate:	Some travel is all right, as long as it isn't too frequent.
Interviewer:	What do you mean by too frequent?
Candidate:	I don't want to be away all the time.
Interviewer:	Tell me what your specific travel concerns are.

If the job applicant doesn't ask any questions, you've learned something about her anyway. Supposing you're looking for a conscientious researcher, a newspaper reporter, or an aggressive salesperson? If the applicant doesn't probe they can't fit the bill.

Gaining the Winning Edge

You gain maximum advantage in the interview when you keep turning your question around until you get the most from the candidate's answer. When you ask a question, the first answer you get is often a programmed reply. Keep rolling the question over, keep probing, keep asking applicants to explain their answers: "Why did you say that?" "Under what circumstances did that happen?" "What would do if you were doing it again?" "Tell me more about that."

Ed Weihenmayer, Vice President of Human Resources at Kidder, Peabody & Co., says that during an interview he looks for a person's work ethic and their technical expertise. "I'll ask several questions to probe into these areas. The rule is, never let people off the hook. Be a detective. Move in on them. It makes for an incessantly tough but interesting and rewarding interview."

Ending the Interview

Significant bits of information are often revealed towards the end of the interview when participants have loosened up a bit. If you end too abruptly, you're likely to lose a valuable player. As you are getting to the last third of your questions, set up the ending: "Before we finish there are a few more things I'd like to go over with you." This gives the candidate a clue that the session is drawing to a close.

A brief summary also helps because it gives both participants something to think about afterwards. But get the *applicant* to summarize the interview. Here is the smartest interview question you can ask: "From our discussion so far, how do you see this job?"

When you bring the interview to a close, you don't want to commit yourself either way. But you do want to be cordial and to leave the person feeling good about himself: "Is there anything we haven't covered that you'd like to know?"

Part of the conclusion should consist of a plan of action, something to be done by either or both parties: "I'm interviewing several people for the job, but I will get back to you within two weeks. I thank you for coming in; I've enjoyed talking with you." Stand up and walk the person to the door and back to the reception area.

Post-Interview Analysis

During an interview, jot down notes of your impressions and the applicant's significant answers. These notes will help you reconstruct the interview at a later date. They also provide a framework for planning the next interview. Having something on paper lets you review the interview accurately. In the process, you may see flaws in your technique that may show you how to improve your approach. Without benefit of such hindsight, you tend to repeat your mistakes. Writing out overviews of the candidates can also help you compare applicants fairly so you can make the best choice.

Smart Questions for Reference Checking

Reference checking is often difficult these days because many people hesitate to give out any information about former employees. This means that it is even more important than ever to ask good questions when you check a job candidate's references.

I recently interviewed applicants for an office manager position. When I tried to call references I got the reply "Henry Rowan worked here" and that's all they would say. At first I accepted that, but by asking some nonthreatening questions I was able to get more information. For example, to one reference I said, "These new rules and regulations are really tough! What do *you* do when you need information about job applicants?" Soon we were talking and I got all the information I needed.

Here are some basic rules to remember when calling references:

1. Always let the candidate know beforehand that you will check their references.

2. When you call up for a reference, keep the conversation short, and concentrate on asking about those areas that most concern you, especially those that involve the success factors:

   "What kind of presentations did Elizabeth make?"

   "How much help and guidance did George need from you?"
   (This is a helpful question if the person must work on his own.)

3. Don't give away the answer you're looking for ("Was Elizabeth good about following company policy?" Better: "How did Elizabeth handle the issue of sticking to company policy?").

4. The smartest question: "If you could work with Elizabeth again, would you?" "Why?" "Why not?" If there is a significant pause, you can assume there were reservations. If possible, probe further. Usually if someone was a superior employee, questions are always welcome.

Great All-Purpose Interview Questions

Some interview questions apply in just about any situation. Put these on your list:

"How have your past job experiences prepared you directly or indirectly for this position?"

"Describe a normal day at your present job . . . a busy day . . . a great day."

"What did you like most about your last job? What did you like least?"

"How did the company's philosophy or attitudes affect you and your work?"

"How would you describe your previous boss's management style?"

"How did you work together?"

"In what ways were you alike—and different?"

"Who were your best employers and your worst?"

"What do you require from your boss?"

"Where did you fit on your last company's organizational chart?"

"What were your responsibilities?"

"What authority did you have?"

"What was your staff like?"

"What was your budget and how did you manage it?"

"What specifically were you accountable for?"

"What improvements did you make?"

"What or whom did you really go to bat for?"

"What were your three most impressive tangible contributions to your company?"

"What are your pet peeves—in a boss, in an organization?"

"Give some examples of situations in which you have been criticized."

"How did you react and why?"

Robert Half has said: "There is something that is much more scarce, something rarer than ability. It is the ability to recognize ability." When you ask smart questions, hiring becomes an art. Nothing can make a manager look better and perform more productively than a great team. Every time you are in a position to hire, you can enhance your opportunity for upward mobility. A good staff makes you less indispensable in your present position and more promotable.

I recently worked with a young woman who beat out three male engineers for an important promotion because she had gone into a failing department, hired some new people, and turned the department into a cohesive and productive work group. Because the department could then run on its own, upper management was convinced that she was the only person to handle the new and more challenging job.

Even when you have put together a superior team, however, your work as a people manager is just beginning. After you have them on board, you must look for ways to manage and motivate your staff on a day-to-day basis, to help them achieve their fullest potential. There are a number of vehicles with which to accomplish this, from encouraging them when things stall out, to offering direct advice on how to achieve their goals, to coaching and counseling. All of these techniques come under the umbrella of motivating your people to achieve maximum potential.

10

Ask the Most from Your People—And Get It

Millions of managers in thousands of different industries want the answer to the same question: "How can I motivate my people?"

Despite all the new management trends and alleged cure-alls, motivation remains a critical problem in today's business. Each of numerous theories has had its day in the sun, but no single idea can be applied universally. Theory X and Theory Y, job enlargement and job enrichment, increased responsibility, cross-training, job switching, situational leadership—all are good ideas that work in some instances and fail in others.

The fact is, managers cannot motivate other people. The best they can do is choose the right people for the right jobs, establish the right atmosphere, and ask for excellent performance.

Inspirational speaker and sales trainer Alan Cimberg often begins his seminars by asking a female member of the audience to come up and give him a kiss. Someone always fulfills his request.

"Why do I get the kiss?" he asks. "Because I ask for it. But when I ask the same woman, 'Will you take off all your clothes and give me another kiss?' she never does."

Cimberg's example graphically illustrates the difference between asking someone for something they can do or that they feel comfortable doing and asking for something they can't do or feel terrible doing. Understanding that difference is the essence of motivation.

As many experts on management emphasize, true motivation only comes from within. You cannot "start up" a human being the way you would switch on the ignition of a car. What a manager *can* do is help employees motivate themselves and get their own engines revved up to top speed.

The overriding question every manager should ask himself is "How can I encourage employees to perform with excellence because they want to?"

Smart Questions

You can motivate people only on their own terms. People respond for their own reasons, not yours. You may want someone to increase productivity to meet department quotas, or to enhance efficiency to reduce overtime. But the person actually carries out your program because he or she wants to go home on time, hopes to be paid well for satisfactory performance, or has some other personal motive. Sometimes the reason is that they want to please you. But motivation is most enduring when someone has his own inner goal, and when you recognize the nature of that goal. The reason most motivational techniques fail is that they do not focus on the individual.

The most universally successful way to motivate is based on discovering what the other person needs. And smart questions give you the tool for discovery. Smart questions are not limited to one company, or to a certain kind of person, or to a particular motivational technique. The right questions can help you discover the needs of individual staff members as they develop, and as jobs grow and change.

Self Questions to Get Started

To learn how to use questions as a motivating technique, begin by asking yourself:

"What do I want to happen as a result of my efforts to motivate?" (The answer is usually that you want people to *want* to do their best.)

"Why should this person want to do his best?" "What's in it for him if he does do his best?" (Promotion? Less strain? More challenging work in the future? More money? More freedom?)

"If I were this person, what would I need to get me moving?"

"What can I do to enhance his job so he will want to aim for peak performance?" (Make it more interesting? Give him more responsibility? Take away some of the pressure? Recognize his efforts?)

When you ask these questions, be specific, for this will bring you more in touch with the person's particular goals. For example, if you answered "Give him more responsibility," specify what kind of responsibility. More client contact? Seeing projects through?

Leadership Style

Even when we accept the idea that motivation must come from within, a manager still has to set the scene and develop the atmosphere that permits self-motivation to take over. You can't create the proper atmosphere simply by handing over the reins to your staff. The way to be democratic and at the same time maintain authority is by no means clear-cut. As one middle manager put it, "In my company, being a manager is still a choice between being a babysitter and being a son of a bitch."

Neither extreme will bring you much in the way of respect from your staff. Research shows that the most successful managers are flexible. They are able to adapt their styles to fit the situation and the people they're working with. True, a manager may need to be an autocrat in a crisis. But when things are running smoothly again, and you have talented people in your group, you should loosen your hold. Different situations call for different tactics. Brainstorming sessions, for example, require a free-wheeling, nonjudgmental atmosphere.

The successful leader is one who can respond appropriately in a variety of situations. If direction is in order, she is able to direct; if considerable participative freedom is called for, she's ready to grant such freedom. Thus in today's business world the successful manager is one who can accurately gauge the situation, determine the most suitable behavior, and act accordingly. Flexibility is the key.

Unfortunately, too many managers carry the same set of responses into every situation, especially if a certain method has served them well in the past. Jerry was hired by a large record company to pull the organization through a major crisis. He had built up a reputation of "saving" companies in tough times. This particular firm was faltering because it had failed to keep up with new technology in the industry. Just as he had in similar predicaments, Jerry clamored and pushed—and pulled the company through. Everyone rallied to his battle cry. But after the problems subsided, what did Jerry do?

He kept right on pushing. He treated every situation as though it were an emergency. He kept his people at such a stressful pace that everyone suffered from the daily strain. "It got so that ordering a taxi was a crisis," his secretary recalled. "Instead of walking to the elevator, he ran. Instead of making a request, he barked an order. It seemed we were forever throwing water on a fire that never got put out." The result was a big turnover in employees, as people grew tired of catering to his self-created tantrums.

Self Questions to Enhance Your Flexibility

We are all accustomed to reacting spontaneously in our usual way, whatever that "way" may be. It's difficult to let go of old habits and develop a more flexible managerial style. Leadership is tough. That's why corporate leadership is such a challenge.

Questions can help you become more flexible and establish an atmosphere where people can express the best in themselves. Here's one way to do it. When you encounter a problem, pose these quick questions to yourself:

"How is this situation unique?"

"What is my usual mode of dealing with people problems?"

"What works?"

"What doesn't?"

"What's the best way to handle this particular situation [or this particular person]?"

"When was the last time I handled something in a new way?"

"How might I change my approach to get the most out of each person on my team?"

"Where would applying pressure help?"

"Where would it hinder?"

"In terms of my bottom-line objective, how would I like this situation to turn out?"

"How can I get out of my own way and make that happen?"

Golden Rules of Motivation

Through hundreds of research reports one message rings out loud and clear: To increase motivation, create an atmosphere where people motivate themselves. When people feel personally involved in a plan, they work to make it happen. How do you do it? Show respect for the worker's opinion and experience; listen to ideas as well as problems; remove the obstacles that mar the employee's motivation.

There are seven questions that managers can ask themselves to help create a self-motivating atmosphere. Each one involves improving communication with your team.

1. Do Your People Know Your Plans?

Make it a point to share information vital to your business or organization—annual reports, quarterly updates, monthly operating results, comparative performance among divisions or units—with everyone on your team, including those at the entry level. Do all hands know, on a regular basis, how their group is performing according to the ten or fifteen most important criteria? How their group stacks up against other groups? Do they know how the standards were arrived at, and why?

It pays to be direct. Discard what Bob Collings, CEO of Data Terminal Systems in Massachusetts, calls the "Mushroom Theory of Management—the one that says keep your employees in the dark and throw a lot of manure on them." The best way to motivate people is to let them know the plan so they can participate in it. Tell them your goals and the goals of the organization. Let them see the picture as a whole and get a sense of their part in it.

Sharing builds motivation. As Collings says, "When people are highly motivated, it's easy to accomplish the impossible. And when they're not, it's impossible to accomplish the easy."

2. Do You Give Feedback?

People need feedback the way they need air. Even well-motivated employees "die" without it. They want to be encouraged if they're doing well, and if they're not doing well they want to know why. The more they know about how they're doing, the more effort they'll put into their work.

Give feedback immediately. When you see a good or a bad performance, tell the performer about it right then. Don't wait a year to correct a problem or to give recognition for a job well done. Pounce on it. Let the person know—now.

Feedback is a two-way process based on asking smart questions ("This looks good. Did you have any problems with it?"). When you give feedback you help keep communication channels open. If your people know you're willing to discuss performance with them, they'll be more likely to bring you their problems and questions and to keep you better informed. Feedback helps you avoid the NETMA (Nobody Ever Tells Me Anything) Syndrome. Create an atmosphere where people are not afraid to tell you when something is wrong, and you will have fewer surprises.

3. Do You Build on Strengths?

In their book, *Leaders,* Warren Bennis and Bert Nanus isolate several factors that mark superb leaders. At the top of the list: Instead of focusing on weaknesses, they build on strengths—their own as well as the strengths of their employees. When I train public speakers I ask people in the class to identify their strengths and their weaknesses. Invariably they say, "I don't know what my strengths are, but my weaknesses are. . . ." We've been so programmed to focus on weaknesses—as though any imperfection would negate or detract from any strength. But this is not so. All success comes from strengths. A person who is bright but shy succeeds because of his brightness and in spite of his shyness. If he merely dwelled on his shyness, he might not have allowed his intelligence to surface.

Once you get people operating from a position of strength, it is easier to motivate them. They will enjoy what they're doing and they will do it better. Positive—not negative—behavior should be looked at first.

For example, after a meeting, ask yourself: "What went right? How can I apply that in other situations?" Know the strengths of your people so you can help build on them. Know your own strengths so you also can continue to grow.

4. Do You Give Constructive Praise?

Successful managers sandwich criticism between layers of praise. Criticism and praise are both valuable parts of feedback, but some managers are reluctant to give either.

W. Timothy Gallwey, writing in *The Inner Game of Tennis,* observes that people wait for praise, and when they don't get it their performance falters. However, as Gallwey says, you cannot praise every move they make from start to finish. To help people learn, praise must be specific and precise. "You did a great job" is better than nothing, but if you want to help someone grow, try: "You did a great job. This is what made it great. . . ."

I have always admired the technique of a piano teacher who was known for launching superb pianists. After a student played a new passage during a lesson she would say, "That's very good. Try it with a little more action in the fingers." Or, "Try to draw out the legato in the fourth measure." Or any number of other improvements. She frequently made it seem as if she was correcting herself: "Let me see if I can give you a better fingering for this passage."

In other words, she *never* criticized, even when it was apparent that the student hadn't practiced or was giving a lackluster performance. As students followed her advice they saw and heard the improvement, and drove themselves until she would say, "Ah, that's much better. Keep doing that."

Her philosophy was that criticism kills pride, shatters self-esteem, and destroys desire. Constructive praise, on the other hand, builds new skills, stimulates self-confidence, and enriches performance.

For those times when criticism is necessary, engrave this message on your mind: *Give praise publicly; keep criticism private.* I will always remember one successful company president who made this offhand comment: "If you want to give a person credit, put it in writing and circulate it around the company. If you want to give him hell, do it on the phone."

Perhaps the most golden rule of people management is "Never be too tough on a person when he's down." When an individual is upset over failure, harping on the negative can hurt him and quench any incentive to improve. Even when giving criticism, you can create a positive framework: "I don't think this is up to your usual standard. What can we learn from it?"

5. Do You Give Rewards?

If people meet their agreed-upon objectives, they should be rewarded with more than kind words. Money and a promotion are among the tangible ways a company can proclaim a "Most Valuable Player." Adam Osborne, the one-time computer whiz who is now the head of Paperback Software International, Inc., in Berkeley, California, says, "Nothing is more important than developing a team that is willing to work with every bit of enthusiasm they have. The way you do that is by being fair—and a little bit more than fair—in the distribution of wealth that comes from your success."

But giving everyone the rewards isn't sound. When it comes to cost-of-living increases, for example, give the top performers the most, the satisfactory people a modest increase, and the poor performers nothing. Otherwise you are rewarding nonperformance.

The best-motivated organization that I've observed is a large graphics company where all raises and bonuses are based on merit and quality. If there are no errors or rejects, each month everyone gets a bonus. Individual merit is rewarded at the time of performance appraisal. The standards are clearly defined and everyone knows the rules. This company has very low absenteeism and is at the top of the industry in quality and creativity.

One of the best rewards you can give a high achiever is your time. Most managers spend the bulk of their time with the poor performers and let the best ones fend for themselves. When someone does a good job for you, recognize their efforts and set aside time to develop projects that will help them get ahead.

When you do give a person a raise, that's the time to increase his responsibilities. Reward him for what he's done and at the same time motivate him to do even more.

One good way *not* to motivate: If you always give someone else's work to a person who finishes a job quickly, then you're punishing, not rewarding. (You've rewarded the poor performer who was inefficient.) Or you might have someone on staff who helps out by doing a dirty job and doing it well. After a while, that person ends up with all the dirty jobs. A willing, effective worker should not be punished for being helpful; he or she should be given a raise, a promotion, or a new title or award. Or assign him a job he's eager to do.

6. Do You Listen and Learn?

It's reported that after finding himself at a dead end, out of money and out of prospects, Thomas Edison once asked his janitor this question: "I'd like to ask your advice, Pop. What do you think I should do in this situation?"

The janitor was stunned. "Nobody ever asked for my advice before," he replied.

"Well," said Edison, "then you should have a lot of good ideas stored up."

No matter what other techniques you employ in your quest to motivate your staff, you have to be prepared to ask questions and to listen at least as much as you talk. Managers who listen—to both ideas and problems—make the difference between a mediocre company and a great one.

It's essential that managers encourage all of their people to contribute and come up with ideas for improvements. Let's say you're in the manufacturing business. By asking questions and listening to your people in the field, you're able to develop products that are the direct result of demands from customers.

No one's ideas should be missed. Acknowledge all correspondence sent to you. You needn't seize on every suggestion, but if you don't at least get back to the person and say "That was a terrific idea" and thank him, he'll never give you another one. A thoughtful response lets people know they count with you. Always give proper recognition for every valid suggestion.

7. Do You Set an Example?

The best manager is a good role model. If you want your staff to perform in a stable, balanced manner, for instance, you cannot be an emotional yo-yo yourself.

A good manager accepts responsibility for the group, as opposed to expecting the group to be responsible for him. This means that he or she does not routinely delegate unpleasant matters. Anyone can muddle through ordinary events; it's the difficult tasks that show leadership. If you have to fire someone, for example, it's up to you to do it. If you don't handle unpleasant jobs personally, you forfeit clout and respect. Public relations expert Henry C. Rogers, author of the popular *Rogers' Rules for Success,* advises managers to "always take the blame, because doing so puts you in a leadership position and enhances your image." A good manager also knows how to say no, to be tough but fair.

Art Williams, founder and president of A. L. Williams, one of the fastest-growing life insurance and securities marketing organizations in the country, concurs: "I see so many of our leaders who talk about winning but who sit back and let others do the tough things. When one individual leads by example, he can become a very powerful force."

In other words, if you don't handle the responsibilities of your own leadership position, you can't expect your staff people to live up to their job responsibilities either.

Recognition of Performance

When you motivate effectively and your people consequently improve and succeed, what do you do next? You push them forward as fast as is practical. Such a policy is tonic to the ambitious, and it serves as a catalyst for the entire staff.

Business has come a long way in this regard over the past few years. Many big corporations used to have unwritten rules about cutoff points for certain employees (women, blacks, non–college grads)—points beyond which they could not move, regardless of their dedication or ability. Also, higher-ups often typecast individuals in their current roles and did not give them a chance to prove they could do more. For the promotion system to have a positive effect within a corporation, advancement must be based on merit. When an employee feels that movement is blocked regardless of performance, motivation falls off.

If the fact is that specific employees will not be promoted, for whatever reason, you, as a manager, have two choices. You can motivate them so they get the most enjoyment from what they're doing—switch job tasks, cross-train, look for ways to liven up the existing job. If they reach a point where they're no longer turned on and you cannot seem to spark any interest, you can move them somewhere else in the company. (Or, if there seems no alternative, suggest that they go elsewhere.)

Self Questions to Rate Your Motivational Skills

"Are my staff people in the right jobs?" (Every manager should strive to match the job with the person—and keep them matched. This is one important key to motivation.)

"Do my employees know specifically—not just vaguely—what I expect of them?" (Would each of them agree with your answer?)

"Can each person describe his job in terms of the Essential Job Profile?"

"Do I know what each person lacks to make him a good performer?"

"Do I show my concern about each person's performance in a helpful, nonthreatening way?"

"Are there any company policies or procedures which might be blocking them?"

"Do I consistently act in a supportive manner?"

"Do I frequently remark on their improvements?"

"Do I provide sufficient help and training for my staff?"

"When I delegate a task, do I also delegate authority?"

"Do I practice what I preach?"

"Am I careful not to punish good performance, and do I reward poor performance?"

"Do my employees have confidence in me?" (If you're the last one to know when there's a problem, your answer should be no. Remember the NETMA Syndrome.)

"Do I keep my people informed about company matters that are important to our department and to them?"

Any manager who can answer yes to twelve or more of these self questions can give himself a high rating in the motivational skills department.

Using Motivational Techniques

Managers generally think of motivating when employees aren't performing at peak levels. But in fact, successful managers are motivators all the time. They instinctively vary their approach to meet the needs of this person at this time, or that group at that time.

In his most vital role, a manager may motivate by *delegating, coaching, counseling,* or *confronting.* Each role is slightly different, but each has the same goal—to help people learn and grow, and to encourage creative ideas from all hands, all of which further your organization's overall purpose. When used skillfully, each method can stimulate motivation. When used inappropriately, however, the same methods can demotivate and crush morale. In the following chapters you will see how the Smart Questions System can make the most of each of these opportunities to motivate.

In all of these roles the manager is striving for maximum people potential—to get the best from the individuals who comprise his staff. And in all of these roles the Smart Questions System provides the key. The objective in every case is to ask questions that let the other person determine the means to growth, and to let that person take the responsibility for his or her own personal development.

11

Questions That Help You Delegate

Are you typical of many managers? Do you come in early and leave late while your employees are out having a good time and sleeping in? I once ran a three-day training program for the American Management Association during which one highly placed executive was always being called out to answer panicky telephone calls from his office; he missed one entire afternoon of the program because he had to attend to a staff emergency. By coincidence I was later called in to consult with his company. I learned that he was considered a poor manager because when he wasn't around everything fell apart.

Bear this in mind: If you've rendered your staff helpless without you, your boss won't be able to promote you—he'll know that chaos will result. You may have preserved your sense of control, but you've forfeited your chance for advancement. Further, refusing to delegate is the surest way to keep yourself bound to your desk twenty-four hours a day.

Delegating demands a sense of security. You have to trust others to come through without your constant coaching, and you have to be willing to give someone else a chance to succeed.

"The hard thing for me when I moved up to sales management," said a stockbroker promoted to branch manager, "was to admit that someone on my staff could sell as well as I used to, and in some cases even better. Even harder, though, was to learn to be patient with someone who wasn't as good as I was. To give them time to learn, instead of jumping in and doing it myself, was my managerial trial by fire."

Delegating is something you're expected to do for your own good. Yet even with all of the outstanding benefits—more time, less stress, greater productivity, more opportunities for growth—many managers still insist on being a one-person band. If you're inclined to do everything yourself because you think it's the only way it will get done right, then you are doing something wrong.

For you to get ahead, you have to learn how to delegate—to give other people important tasks and move aside so they can accomplish them. If your group doesn't stand out as a group, you will reach a managerial impasse.

Smart questions can help you delegate work imaginatively, in a way that gets the work done successfully and at the same time helps your people grow and develop.

Why Delegate?

Delegating is a superb tool for motivating your staff and getting the most from your team. The objective is the long-term development of each person, which in turn contributes to the performance of the team and ultimately the organization.

Frederick Herzberg, Professor and Chairman of the Psychology Department at Case Western Reserve University, has discovered that the only way to motivate an employee is to give him challenging work that is meaningful to him, for which he can assume responsibility. The message is that responsibility improves morale and encourages people to work harder and with more enthusiasm.

Finding the Right Approach

The most delicate part of using delegating as a motivational tool is making sure you don't demotivate the person in the process. A manager must tread the fine line between guiding the person and letting go so he can succeed on his own. If you give a person a task and then tell him not to come back until it's done, he may feel abandoned and in over his head. On the other hand, if you keep too tight a grip on the reins, you risk suffocating him. The latter error is more common—most managers tend toward too much control rather than too little. But both can cause you trouble.

It's essential that you learn to overcome that impulse to dominate the situation and yet never let the individual feel that you've lost interest in him. Good managing is personally guided autonomy, and you're the chief guide. You can turn things over to people gradually, with ever-widening intervals of reporting back to you, until they are ready to fly solo.

And if handling a task has given an employee a degree of expertise, let him follow through, especially in decision making. If you ask someone to research a new computer system for possible purchase, for example, let him or her be in on the final decision.

Delegating Authority

Nothing is more destructive—and self-defeating—than for a manager to delegate a job, then make it impossible for the employee to successfully carry it out. The easy part of leadership is telling people what to do; the hard part is giving them the authority to do it.

For example, Janice delegated a major time-study job which required a great deal of interaction with other departments. But instead of letting those involved speak directly to the person delegated to handle the job, all return calls had to go through Janice. Aside from being a waste of time, this was demoralizing to the staff person. Janice gave him responsibility, then essentially took it away.

In another instance, a manager in a word processing unit delegated the responsibility for hiring a team of skilled, quality-conscious workers. Although he told his subordinate to find the people, the manager made the hiring decisions. By reserving the final authority for himself he defeated the purpose of delegating.

Alex, a senior manager in a communications conglomerate (who should have known better), told Pat, a middle manager, to integrate three groups into one. Pat considered the assignment carefully, then offered her ideas for carrying out the process smoothly. Alex rejected the suggestions. "This is the way I see it," he said. "Do it my way."

Pat was forced to carry out a plan with which she did not agree and to defend the plan to the three diverse groups, who didn't want to be combined in the first place. There was no way for her to reach the goal on her own terms.

The result was unhappiness among the three groups, frustration for Pat, and a rough and disorganized transition period—all because Alex had insisted on doing it his way. It turned out that his middle manager knew the situation best because she had firsthand knowledge. Ultimately, because of employee dissatisfaction and union involvement, most of her original ideas were incorporated after all. But the overall result of the mishandled situation was distrust and disharmony between staff and management.

Thus, when you delegate a job, the two most important questions to ask yourself are:

(1) "Am I also delegating the appropriate amount of authority?"

(2) "Will this be a growth experience for the person, or merely more work?"

Good managing is making sure that others do their jobs smoothly, harmoniously, and productively. That means not only delegating tasks, but conceding the authority and status necessary to accomplish them.

Delegating Opportunities

When you delegate you should think of how you can polish and fine-tune the overall performance of your group. Look for opportunities for each person. If a new public-relations project comes in, you might give someone who normally implements and oversees projects a chance to become a promoter and improve his public speaking. When somebody leaves a team, see if another staff member might want to learn a new skill or take on some of the responsibilities the previous person held. Being given the chance to explore their potential is a tonic for boredom. When your people realize that you're looking to develop their potential and promote their careers, their interest level will continue to be high.

You can find opportunities to delegate in even the most static situations. At least part of what every manager considers routine would offer an interesting challenge for staff members. These routine tasks shouldn't be mere drudgery, however, but responsibilities that captured your own interest before you mastered them. In my office, making sales calls is routine for me but a great challenge to my assistant. Although it takes time and coaching to train her, it's worth it because of her great satisfaction when she makes a successful call.

There are other delegating possibilities: any project that has been sitting, stone cold, on the back burner. That one project you keep meaning to get around to someday—but somehow never do—is perfect for assigning to a staff member.

Another idea involves task swaps among staff members. There is bound to be interest and excitement for one person in what used to be a challenge for another. Your people may have their own notions of advantageous job swaps and promising projects. It's up to you to ask them.

The purpose of delegation is not to delegate chores you don't like. Nor should you keep all the boring or tough tasks for yourself. Self-sacrifice is not a virtue. Strive for a good mix for everyone on your staff. That doesn't mean you have to pass along a task you thoroughly enjoy. I know the managing editor of a publishing company that produces art books. She assigns a working editor to each book but always retains at least one book each season for which she does the hands-on editing because, as she explains, "I love it. I would be miserable in my job if I couldn't spend at least some time actually working on a book of my own."

When you delegate in this manner, what can you expect to happen? A number of staff members will respond wholeheartedly. Doing a tougher job will give them confidence; they will discover ambition. You won't get maximum results from everyone, but you can count on a heightened interest which will motivate staff members to build on their strengths.

Self Questions to Discover Opportunities

To be a good delegator you have to look for opportunities. Ask yourself these questions:

"Am I alert for situations where I can help people learn other jobs and take on new responsibilities?"

"Do I feel unthreatened by an individual's exceptional skill or ability?"

"Do I honestly want my people to succeed?"

"If not, why not?"

How Not to Delegate

Of course, there are some tasks that you should not delegate; never fall into the trap of thinking delegating is synonymous with passing the buck.

Employee conflicts, performance appraisals, any situation in which you risk losing face—these you've got to handle. Dumping on others all those things you hate to do is not the way to delegate.

Further, if you've agreed to personally take care of something for someone, you can't turn around and delegate it, regardless of how busy you are. One way to prevent this situation is to say, "My team will handle it for you. I trust that's all right?" or "We'll take care of it." Also, you shouldn't delegate anything you don't fully understand yourself. The idea, remember, is to assign tasks and improve the effectiveness of the team. You can't toss someone a problem and hope that somehow it will be resolved.

Cross-training can be valuable in many situations, but rotating people through various departments of a company with the idea that the movement will encourage them and keep them from getting bored presumes that all skills are interchangeable. They're not, and the people are more likely to get dizzy than inspired. It's as if a hospital administrator said about an obstetrician, "He's great on deliveries; next week let's have him do open-heart surgery." Having some experience in one area doesn't necessarily translate into skill in another.

If you force a switch on people, you risk losing their respect. Anna, the new owner of a large printing company, was looking for ways to reduce costly errors as well as eliminate some jobs. She observed that one group was responsible for setting type on the computers and another for proofreading galleys and checking for accuracy. Anna's idea was that she could increase efficiency and reduce errors if these two groups were combined. Also, with one person doing a job previously done by two, at least a few people could be dropped from the payroll. Anna quickly instituted a program to carry out cross-training: the typesetters would learn to proofread and copyedit, and the copyeditors would learn to set type.

This plan antagonized everyone involved. The typesetters felt that their job was impossible without excellent computer skills, good manual dexterity, and an ability to produce in a hectic, pressure-filled atmosphere. The copyeditors felt their job required thoughtfulness, a high degree of linguistic expertise, and a broad knowledge of many subjects. Both groups took pride in their own accomplishments. They all felt that the new owner had little understanding of what their jobs entailed and were furious when suddenly ordered to switch jobs and cross-train. Within the first two weeks, 80 percent of the staff left.

And yet Anna's idea could have worked. If she had understood their jobs, polled the people in both groups and asked who wanted to expand their skills, and matched up pairs in a positive manner, she might have pulled off a productive transition.

When to Delegate

The time to delegate is when you know your staff people are ready to take on more responsibility and make special contributions. Your staff then gets greater experience and a showcase for their talents.

Consider your team. If you have people who fit these descriptions you should be looking for opportunities to delegate:

Is there someone on the team whose performance is consistently high or exceptional?

Is there someone ready for promotion or increased responsibility?

Would it help to broaden someone's experience by exposing him or her to other areas of the department or the company?

Is there a promising performer who should be brought to the attention of colleagues or upper management?

What to Delegate

Many people don't delegate because they feel they must have one person to delegate an entire task to. But with analysis of the task and of the people on your staff, you can break a project into parts and have several people work on it. Take a good look at all the duties assigned to you personally, as well as to your group. Ask yourself these smart questions:

"What are my responsibilities?"

"What are the responsibilities of my department?"

"What can be delegated?"

"What would be gained?"

"Who is ready to do it?"

"Can it be broken into parts?"

"Who can carry out parts of the assignment?"

"Who could do it with training?"

Matching Assignments to People

Consider each individual in your group. Ask yourself:

"Who is a possible candidate for my job?"

"What particular skills does each of my people possess?"

"When does each person sparkle the most?"

"With whom does each one work the best?"

"What work does each one find most rewarding?"

"What are each person's long-range goals?"

You should have a delegating plan for each person on your team. Sit down with each individual and discuss what he or she wants to achieve. Before you assign a particular job to someone, ask yourself:

"What can he or she learn from this job?"

"What authority does he or she need to carry it out?"

Questions to Prepare the Person

Once you've decided what to delegate and to whom, smart questions can help the chosen employee get the most out of the opportunity. Before the work begins, ask the person:

"How do you see this project, overall?"

"Specifically, what is your objective?"

"What steps will you take to carry it out?"

"What kind of feedback do you plan to give me, to keep me abreast of your progress?"

"How often should I expect to hear from you?"

"In what form should I expect your final results?"

"When do you think you'll be finished?"

"How much authority do you need?"

"Do you need anything from me?"

Post-Delegation Questions

In terms of motivating your people, the most valuable questions are the ones you ask after the job is completed. The delegation process should always be a learning and growing experience for you and your employee. At the end of the project, ask the person:

"What's the most important thing you learned from this assignment?"

"How would you do it differently the next time?"

"What kinds of problems did you have?"

"How could you have anticipated problems sooner?"

"Should you have asked for more help?"

"Could you have done the job with less assistance?"

"Did you use all the resources available to you?"

"Did you enjoy and profit from your increased responsibilities?"

"How could I have been of more help?"

Overall, delegating is a superb motivational tool. It offers your people a way to develop their skills, show off their competency, and get ahead. It also offers you the chance to train your replacement, which means that you become more promotable.

Delegation is the essence of management. It works best when you have willing, problem-free employees. But managers also may need to use some special, often misunderstood, motivational techniques to help staff people develop. The most consistently valuable of these is training and coaching.

12

Questions That Train and Coach

When your Rolex watch goes on the blink, why don't you throw it out and get a new one? Because it's more practical and less expensive to have it repaired. The same philosophy applies to people management. When a person goes on the blink—when he or she loses motivation, or needs to develop new skills or sharpen old ones—it's much more productive to retrain than it is to hire someone else.

But a preconceived attitude works against many of us. We'd rather tell someone to go away than tell him how he's fouling up. We don't want the aggravation that comes with confronting a person with criticism. And yet managers who want to achieve a motivated, excited working group must tune in to the idea of helping people change. Asking smart questions offers a easy, rewarding way for managers to overcome their own resistance to training and coaching.

Training, coaching, and counseling are closely related motivational techniques, and many managers use the terms interchangeably. However, training is defined as a technique to teach new employees, or to train employees to use new equipment; coaching is used when an employee is failing in a specific task; and counseling is applied when an employee's overall performance is dropping. (Counseling often involves an employee's personal problems; for this reason, although the counseling technique is similar to coaching, it is treated as a separate subject in the following chapter.) All three techniques can be used spontaneously or in planned, formal sessions.

The hallmark of all three techniques is the Smart Questions system. The axiom is: People remember best those things they discover, learn, and experience themselves. If you want someone to digest and remember something, he has to think of it himself. The only way you help someone accept an idea as his own is to ask him a question and let him give the answer back to you.

I once observed the president of a sportswear chain put this principle into practice. Her vice president of marketing had to develop a sales promotion campaign for a new line of running shoes. The president had her own ideas about what would work, but rather than pushing them asked the vice president, who seemed stymied, this question: "If you were buying these shoes, what would get you excited?" That question got him started and he wound up with a great and successful campaign. I subsequently asked the president if their ideas had matched. She said she was pleased with the vice president's campaign, but never told me whether her ideas had been better.

The manager's role as a trainer or coach is to encourage and to educate. What you're looking for is better performance from your staff, but you also want to increase their self-confidence. To achieve both goals you must do three things: ask questions that encourage feedback, listen closely to the answers, and show appreciation for growth. Ask . . . listen . . . appreciate.

Feedback: The Principal Tool

Training and coaching the Smart Questions way is primarily a feedback technique that meets a genuine need from your staff. As a motivator you should continuously give feedback to let your people know how they're doing and to encourage them to strive to do even better. As a trainer and coach the second channel for feedback is open to you: you ask questions, and the person you're training or coaching feeds back information to you. This is the single most important element of successful coaching.

Feedback is the only way to confirm that your message has gotten across. Getting feedback on what may seem like simple instructions can save days, and even weeks, of work. More than that, by feeding back answers to your questions the individual discovers a way to solve the problem—whatever it is—for himself. Such independent discovery builds confidence and ensures that the information being learned is fully absorbed.

Showing Recognition

Questions are the main device for successful training and coaching. But there is one other valuable tool the manager must employ if he hopes to succeed: Always notice and reward progress in some way, even if it's just a thank you or an appreciative nod. And do it even when it's something you feel a person should have been doing all along, such as arriving at work on time. Many people disagree about this notion of reward when the person does what he's expected to do. But when you compliment a notoriously tardy person for arriving on time you're rewarding the change in behavior, not the person specifically. Change, even when it is relatively minor, is hard for everyone. Remember that if you want the change to become a permanent behavior, you must reinforce it with recognition.

By the same token, if you don't speak up when things go wrong, you're sending a signal that it doesn't matter. Even the most creative and spontaneous workers want guidelines.

Smart Questions That Train

Training is necessary when new systems or changes are instituted, or when an employee first joins the staff. The emphasis is on learning specific new material.

And yet in many companies new employees are simply brought in, shown to a desk, and within six weeks to three months evaluated on their performance. Often they aren't even told the difference between good performance and excellent performance.

Dr. Evans, physician-director of a surgical center in Kansas City, spent two hours telling four administrative assistants how to field phone inquiries. Evans's instructions included details about insurance forms and scheduling for surgery, as well as medical information about his specialty. At the end of the session, he asked, "Got that?" The four assistants nodded.

Dr. Evans went about his business. A few weeks later he tested the efficiency of his staff by asking a friend to call his office and pretend to be a prospective patient. The friend tape-recorded the disastrous results.

All four administrative assistants gave out wrong information about virtually everything. They did not know how to elicit information from a patient, nor were they able to answer the caller's questions. After hearing the tapes, Evans stormed into the office and fired everyone. He instructed the office manager to start hiring a new team, "and make sure you get people with brains this time."

This waste—of time, money, and human potential—could have been avoided had the doctor taken the time to ask a series of smart questions after his initial lecture. For example:

> "How would you describe in two or three brief sentences what services we offer?"
>
> "How would you advise a caller who has no medical insurance?"
>
> "What information must you always elicit from the caller?"
>
> "What will you say if the caller asks you a question you can't answer?"

Important Training Questions to Ask Yourself

Before you initiate any training program, ask yourself the Big Four Questions:

—"What do I want this person to know, or do, as a result of the training?"

—"What is the best way to impart this training?" (The more active and involved the method, the better. For example, questions and answers and hands-on training are better than lectures.)

—"Who is the best person to carry out this training?"

—"How can I reinforce this training?" (Ask for feedback and follow-up at scheduled intervals.)

Smart Questions That Coach

Coaching can take place all the time, under many different circumstances. It can be as informal as an enthusiastic cheer from the sidelines or as formal as a structured learning session. Whether it is informal or structured, coaching has a goal: to help a person improve performance in a specific area.

Coaching can be used to make simple, brief corrections, to improve poor performance in a specific task, and to provide encouragement before or after a "first" (first client presentation, first board meeting).

Many situations can be turned into informal coaching sessions. For example, a debriefing following a presentation illustrates the classic Smart Questions coaching formula. Immediately after the presentation (or meeting or production failure or submission of a written report), ask the person to think for a moment and then answer three questions:

1. *"What did you like about what you did?"*

Everyone has a gut feeling about what was right and what was wrong about their work. As time passes, however, they lose much of their objectivity. If they did a less than adequate job, for example, their memory clouds over as protective rationalization rushes to the defense. (An actress failing an audition may say, "I didn't get the job because the director wants his girlfriend in the part." An account man losing an account may say, "The client wasn't interested in doing something really different.")

On the other side, some people go too far the other way and berate themselves for the slightest flaws, losing sight of what they did well.

An evaluation is most accurate when it is done immediately after the event. Close to the reality, the individual usually comes out with a pretty fair assessment of what he or she did right.

2. *"If you could do it over again, what would you do differently? What would you change, and how?"*

Anyone performing a complex task should have the opportunity to look at what has been done, evaluate it, and consider what might have enhanced or enriched it, much like a writer revising a manuscript or an illustrator retouching a drawing.

Co-workers at an elite package-design firm make it a policy after each client presentation to evaluate the meeting. "We started doing it because our president does it on her own performance. After every presentation, she informally relives the meeting. She describes what was good about it, and then talks about how she might have made it better, how she could have answered a question better, or how she wished she had asked something or other. She doesn't berate herself, but she makes mental notes of how she would do it differently the next time. We all caught on to her style, and it's become a habit."

When you ask the first two questions most people readily uncover their major problems, especially when they are given support and feel they can express their thoughts without fear of negative criticism. During the evaluation the person may come upon a problem that he can't solve, which leads to the third and final smart question from you:

—3. *"What help do you need from me?"*

These three smart coaching questions let the person clearly evaluate what was right and what was wrong about the job at hand, and provide an avenue for change. You may have your own ideas about the person's performance and how you would do it differently. But the goal is for the person to discover for himself what he can do to improve. People can change only when they see the need for change.

When to Coach

Coaching can be used productively across the board to solve a variety of managerial problems. Athletic coaches, for example, do more than just train; they offer support, provide frequent advice, and keep people going. Ask yourself these smart questions:

"Does someone on my staff need specific information to enable them to contribute more fully?"

"Are people performing poorly?"

"Is someone showing signs of discontent—coming late, long lunches, many personal phone calls?"

"Are performance expectations unclear?"

"Does someone need to expand a specific skill?"

"Do I need stronger teamwork?"

"Are there some moderate performers in my group who need to push themselves?"

"Do I need an active way to show support for my group?"

"Do I need to show more enthusiasm?" (If you're feeling low and acting low, think about how tough it must be for your staff.)

If you answer yes to *any* of these questions, you have a situation that could benefit from coaching.

Whom to Coach

Before undertaking a formal coaching session with anyone on your team, you should ask yourself a series of questions. If you answer no to *any* of the following, coaching is in order.

"Could this person do the job if he or she wanted to?" (If the answer is yes, you might have an emotional issue on your hands. If the person isn't performing well because he or she is annoyed or demotivated, the situation may require counseling.)

"Does this person really know how to do the job?" (Always question the person directly about the training they received for the job. Then if your answer is "No, he doesn't really know how to do the job," coaching is appropriate.)

"Have the organization's goals been clearly communicated?"

"Did the person receive effective guidance?"

"Did I point out how to approach various people in the organization, and how to deal with them?"

"Have I spent enough time with the person?"

Rate Your Coaching Skills

To examine whether or not you as a manager are using coaching for maximum effectiveness, ask yourself:

"Do I show substantial support for my team?"

"Do I think team members would give me a high rating on understanding their problems?"

"When I apply pressure do I also offer support?"

"Do my people hear from me when they perform well?"

"Do I take time to encourage my team before an important event?"

"Do I repeat the encouragement afterwards?"

If you can answer yes to all of the above, you are using coaching skills consistently and productively.

The Coaching Session

The whole idea behind productive coaching is to help people to solve their own problems. You cannot and should not solve the problem, or tell them how to solve it. You can, however, contribute, and you can make suggestions.

The usual dialogue at a coaching session runs like this one between Linda, the manager of the electronic data processing department of a large toy manufacturing company, and Tom, one of her supervisors.

Linda: Tom, the monthly progress reports are late again.

Tom: I've been busy—half the people are out of the office with the flu.

Linda: I need to get the reports on time. It's making us look bad to the front office.

Tom: I'll do my best.

Linda: Thanks.

What's wrong with this approach? Everything. And the inevitable result is that the reports go out late again next month.

The interesting part about coaching is that given a chance to talk, most people have the solution to their own problems. However, people don't always come up with a neat answer the first time you ask; if it were that clear to them they'd be doing it right the first time. It's worth your while to do some imaginative probing and find out how to get the person headed in the right direction.

The first—and most difficult—step to productive coaching is getting the person to agree that a problem exists. Establishing an opening gambit is the toughest part of a coaching session, and this requires some creative questioning. Let's give Linda and her supervisor another chance, this time using the Smart Questions coaching system:

Linda: We need to talk about scheduling your reports. I'm not sure you see it in terms of its effect on the overall department. What do you think happens when reports are late? [Linda already knows the ramifications, but by asking the question she's transferring the thought to Tom's mind. She must wait and listen for Tom's answer.]

Tom: I guess the departmental report goes in late.

Linda: Anything else?

Tom: It makes you look inefficient.

Linda: What are some of the ways that might affect the position of our group with upper management?

Tom: We might not get the new computers we asked for. They might go back and use the outside consultants and cut down our staff.

Linda: Any other ideas?

Tom: We might not get much budget for raises or any bonuses at year end.

Linda: That's what I'm thinking, too. Do you agree that we have a problem? [Until Tom agrees that there's a problem, the manager can't move on to a solution. If Tom answers, "That's true, but. . . ." he hasn't agreed. "But" signals that he's unconvinced.]

Tom: Yes.

Linda: Let's talk about a solution. What are the main reasons for the delays?

Tom: We're short-staffed, and don't have the budget for overtime.

Linda: Any other reasons?

Tom: I don't like the details and checking the data. I tend to leave it for last.

Linda: What are your ideas for a solution?

Tom: I'll have to get to it earlier and spend more time on it. [Tom's response is not sufficient. He needs to tell the manager what specific actions he's going to take. If Tom continues to do the same thing, he'll continue to miss deadlines.]

Linda: How will you do that?

Tom: I could start collecting the information earlier in the month. I could also have a department meeting and set up a plan.

Linda: How would that work?

Tom: It would get everyone thinking about the problem and setting a schedule to meet the deadline.

Linda: You said you don't like checking the data. Any ideas about that?

Tom: I have one person in my group who's a stickler for accuracy. I could get him to check everything before I sign off on it. [The idea is for Tom to give his manager numerous solutions. Some of these might involve changes in the way other people do things—or even in the way the manager does things.]

Linda: Those sound like good possibilities. In terms of overall effectiveness, which solution do you think will work best?

Tom: Perhaps a combination, starting with a departmental meeting. We can set up a flowchart, and get people to check with me twice a week so I can gain better control.

Linda: Is there something I can do to help you put the plan into action?

Tom: What I would like is extra staff. Barring that, I think it would help if you came to the meeting yourself and reinforced the importance of the reports.

Linda: There's a company-wide hiring freeze on, so for the time being hiring outside people is not an option. If you still feel you need more staff after you implement the new plan, there may be an opportunity later to transfer someone in from another division. For now, I'll back you up in the meeting. So, what have we agreed on? What's the goal?

Tom: I'm going to implement a new plan for the monthly reports.

Linda: What's your first step?

Tom: I'll call a meeting for next week.

Linda: When can we expect to see some results?

Showing Support

Coaching means expressing approval or admiration, applauding, and commending small and large victories. But warm words are not enough. Coaching is the act of helping. While Tom's boss didn't solve the problem for him, she did ask what kind of help he needed. And she helped Tom solve the problem for himself. Like Tom, we all usually have the answer to a problem tucked away somewhere in our minds. A good manager looks for ways to build small successes into a solid track record. Support is shown by the personal commitment of the coach, proven through his or her consistent imaginative interest in helping each person progress.

The manager who has listened to an employee's problems and helped solve them is rewarded when he sees that person come into his own as a result. Training and coaching the Smart Questions way are fine motivational techniques that let managers accomplish this goal. But sometimes the root of the problem is emotional, and when this is the case the manager needs some very special motivational tools if he or she hopes to help. Emotional issues require sensitive, careful counseling from managers, and in extreme cases, a more dramatic confrontation. Both methods are difficult business techniques made simple by asking smart questions.

13

Problem Solving with Problem People

When the manager's job is to help an employee improve a specific performance problem, the best technique is coaching. But when a manager must deal with an employee who has personal or professional problems—problems that are damaging his overall effectiveness—a different technique is needed.

In some of my middle management training programs I use a problem called the Joe Bailey maze. Bailey is a fictional employee who is absent on too many Mondays. The problem is to decide how Joe's manager should deal with him. Seventy-five percent of the thousands of managers who have taken this program keep going around in the maze and never get out until they fire Joe or he quits, without ever getting to the root of the problem.

Smart questions offer managers a way through the maze. The manager's role as counselor is to ask a few opening questions, listen, and give support. The emphasis is on problem solving, with long-range change as the goal. The manager hopes to steer the individual towards renewed commitment, towards taking responsibility for his own problem. Throughout the counseling process the manager must be encouraging and positive.

The best way to begin is to ask one or two questions, and then be quiet and listen for a response. The worry is that a question the manager asks may be too intrusive. A thin line separates interest and concern from an invasion of privacy, and managers should guard against interfering in personal problems when their attention is unwelcome.

I once had a long-time employee who had always been reliable and whose work had always been excellent. Over a period of several weeks she had been arriving late and wasn't getting her work done on time. At staff meetings she was silent and contributed little. I knew I had to talk to her, but she seemed so withdrawn and defensive that I didn't know what to say. One day when she was in my office explaining why a report was late, I offered her a cup of tea and took the opportunity to bring up her unexplained drop in performance.

The company had come to rely on her excellent work, I started, "but lately you seem worried and distracted."

She didn't answer. I drank my tea and thought about what to say next. My first thought was, this counseling business isn't easy, but maybe I can get through it if I ask her a question.

"Is something wrong at home?" I asked. She nodded, but still didn't speak.

"Is there anything I could do to help?"

That one question unleashed the whole story. She was separated from her husband of twelve years and they were in the midst of divorce proceedings. She hadn't wanted to tell anyone about it and didn't want to offer her personal problems as an excuse for her diminished performance.

We talked for a long time, although not about her work performance. Afterwards, I inquired from time to time how things were going, but never asked her directly about her husband. Her work improved immensely. While I didn't solve her problem, it was enough that the two of us were able to talk about it.

It's up to the manager to decide the extent to which he or she should discuss an employee's personal life. But when personal problems become work problems, it may be more appropriate to step in than to pretend the problem doesn't exist.

Being a good counselor means going beyond the obvious, and this demands time and sensitivity. Some work problems can be smoothed over by correcting a misunderstanding or moving somebody into a different work station. But others will take patience and continued effort. Regardless of where the problem comes from—home or work—the counselor's role is to help the person understand the problem and then surmount it.

When to Counsel

Before you take on the counseling role in any situation, ask yourself one question: "Does the situation really call for it?"

A person should be given a reasonable chance to turn things around under his or her own power, with your wholehearted support but without your interference. Counseling is not another name for meddling—getting involved without the right or the invitation. Too soon can be as disastrous as too late. You should counsel only when asked, or when a performance problem seriously threatens an individual's job or the productivity of the team.

In most instances, you should counsel only if you have tried to coach first. There are one or two instances when counseling is applied immediately—for example, when someone suffers a sudden setback a little counseling can help him over the rough spots. But for the most part, counseling is preceded by coaching attempts.

A manager shouldn't try to be a psychologist. Some situations require help from professionals. If serious help is needed, be prepared to send the person on to someone else for professional assistance. It's a good idea to have some names that you can refer people to.

To discover if managerial counseling is appropriate, ask yourself these questions:

"Does the person who's not performing well have a solid track record?"

"Has training or coaching failed to make a difference?"

"Has the individual asked for my help during a personal crisis?"

"Does he or she seem to be at a loss, unsure of how to proceed?"

"Is someone having trouble coping because the organization is growing fast or is undergoing drastic changes?"

"Is an individual accustomed to success unable to bounce back after a failure or disappointment?" (This might occur unexpectedly when someone's role has been broadened by promotion.)

If you answered yes to any one of these questions, you have an individual and a situation in which counseling can help.

Pre-Counseling Self Questions

If you decide that counseling is warranted, it's time to extend a purposeful hand. Before setting up a counseling session, ask yourself these smart questions:

"What is my goal?" (Your overall goal is to make headway with the employee in order to get him or her back on track.)

"In what way do I expect the person to change his behavior?"

"What results can I expect?" (This is crucial; if you are vague or unclear in your own mind about what you want to accomplish, how can you hope to address someone else's confusion?)

"What is reasonable?" (If someone has been very depressed and looking terrible, you can't expect him to turn around and be Mr. Clean overnight.)

"What is my basic approach?" (Remember the 5 C's. Commanders will accept a direct approach. Carers will internalize all their grudges. Convincers will be easier to talk to. Calculators will be defensive, but will respond to a reasoning approach. Creators will be vague and withdrawn especially during the creative process.)

When you are prepared for the session, choose a time for the meeting. Counseling is a promise you must keep. Don't squeeze it in, and once you set the time, don't cancel. Pick a time when you both can give it your full attention, but do it during working hours. Sitting over a drink in the local cocktail lounge doesn't work.

Once you've chosen the time, ask the individual early in the day if he or she can meet with you at some later hour. Do not suggest an overnight—or even worse, a whole weekend—waiting period. If counseling is warranted people usually know something is wrong, and you instill needless anxiety by putting it off. Occasionally an opportunity will spontaneously present itself, but in most cases the best idea is to establish a time for the meeting and keep the appointment.

Counseling Questions

Here are some guidelines and questions that will help you through the Joe Bailey maze.

Open the session with a brief, straightforward statement of why you suggested the meeting: "I want you to be effective, and I know that you want to be effective. Let's see how we can work together to achieve that."

Let the person know that you are genuinely concerned about them. Try not to be intimidating or accusatory; that's the quickest way to seal the problem. Also, assure the person that whatever they say will be kept private. Once you open the discussion, lead the session with a few questions, and be prepared to listen.

"What do you think is at the root of the problem?"

"How do you think the problem could be solved?"

"Who or what has contributed to the problem?"

"How have I contributed to the situation?" (This is a tough question to ask, but be prepared to accept your own involvement as a possibility.)

Once you know where you're headed, establish the means to get there. Put together a plan of action.

"What needs to happen?"

"When?"

"What kind of assistance do you feel you will need?"

"What do you need from me?"

"Is there anyone else who should be told or involved?"

"Do you feel getting professional counseling would help?"

"What are you going to do to take action?"

"When would you like to talk again?"

Before the meeting ends, set up another one to check on how things are going and to see how you can help and support progress.

The key to a good session is understanding your role. You're not there as a psychologist—you're there as a manager. Your goal is always to get good people who have become problem people to solve their own problems. And by being supportive and asking the right questions you can create an environment that helps them do just that.

Elaine, an administrative assistant in a large law firm, was experiencing a problem with adapting to change. Not only did her boss install a new computer but he expected her to learn two software programs in two weeks. Elaine panicked, started arriving late or calling in sick, made careless mistakes in her work, and generally made her co-workers miserable. Her boss was furious.

Finally her boss calmed down and asked this question: "Since it's important for you to learn these systems within two weeks, what do you suggest?" He asked the question seriously, with the genuine intent of finding out how she would solve the problem.

Elaine came up with a perfect solution: the secretary could learn one while she learned the other. During the next month they would cross-train each other. For the same amount of money, the boss then had two people trained on the computer and was in good shape for future absences and vacations. This also reduced the stress that Elaine was feeling—the panic over sudden and extreme change—and allowed her to operate with much less daily tension.

Many problems are deeply personal. Dennis, ordinarily a fine team player, became withdrawn and uncooperative. When co-workers asked him what was wrong, Dennis answered, "Nothing." His manager was concerned and spent some time drawing him out:

Manager:	"I'm concerned about you and want to help. How do you see this problem affecting your work?"
Dennis:	"I can't help it. My wife's children have moved in with us and one of them is using drugs."
Manager:	"That's a tough one. How are you dealing with it?"
Dennis:	"I'm not, at least not very well. I don't know what to do."
Manager:	"I can suggest some help. A friend of mine had a similar problem, and got some help from one of the youth organizations. Would you like me to ask who he saw?"

If you run into resistance in an attempt to counsel, you can always ask:

"How long will it take to clear up the problem?"
"How can I help?"

And if the problem doesn't improve, you can try a follow-up counseling session. Although you have to set time limits, everyone goes through difficult periods sometimes. When I had cancer I was devastated by the experience. It took me several months to mentally recuperate. Fortunately, because I worked for myself I had a sympathetic employer, but I'm sure most employers would have been supportive if I had shared this problem with them.

Confrontation: When Counseling Isn't Enough

When performance problems persist despite repeated efforts to counsel—when an individual is undeniably failing in his or her current role—then it's time to bring things to a boil. It may be an employee who yesses you to death but never changes. Or a willing, amiable employee who for some reason cannot seem to do the job the way it needs to be done. Or it may be a conflict between two people or among a whole team. Occasionally, depending on the person you're dealing with, confrontation happens sooner rather than later. In a simple instance, when someone flatly refuses to come in on time, or fails to deal with customers pleasantly, you may cut directly to confrontation, bypassing coaching and counseling. The basic principles of confrontation are the same, whatever the situation.

Confrontation means that change is imperative. It means making a decision and setting a deadline to carry it out: job reassignment, restructuring of the current job, curtailing current job responsibilities, or dismissal.

Done by the best, confrontation is a forceful form of counseling in which the alternatives and consequences are clear and close at hand. Provided you previously did everything you could—coaching and counseling—to foster improvement, confronting can be a constructive, caring response to an individual's chronic low performance. Confrontation is always a face-to-face meeting where you bring a person's attention to the consequences of unacceptable performance. Confrontation is one of a manager's toughest responsibilities.

Even when viewed in its most positive light, confronting someone is an anxiety-producing situation. Frustrated managers often lose perspective and unload a personal attack or an ultimatum. There is a tendency to lecture and rehash previous discussions and harp on minor details. The greatest danger is that confrontation can flare into an all-out blaming session, in which you fire the person out of fury or the person quits in a huff.

The key to positive confrontation is to stay cool and to discuss sensitive issues without overdramatizing them. Both manager and employee have to be willing to get past the old obstacles and look ahead for solutions. A questioning approach allows you to confront different types of problem employees without letting things get out of hand. Asking smart questions gives you a way to get into the situation, minimize anxiety, and avoid becoming hostile: maximum results with minimum stress.

As a confronter, a manager must be positive, supportive, firm, and calm. The manager's job is to set limits, establish clear expectations, and stay centered on the subject.

Don't allow the employee to manipulate you ("You never told me that we had an inflexible deadline"). The normal reaction is to defend yourself ("I told you at least four times, and you're supposed to know it anyway"). The Smart Question reaction is never defensive ("I could have told you more *often*—but what do you think happens when you miss a deadline?").

Questions also get problem people to commit to change themselves. As in counseling, the key is to ask sensible questions and be willing to listen.

How to Confront

There are small confrontations and large ones. Letting a person know that he is abusing the lunch hour is a small confrontation. But a manager who deals with small problems immediately will have fewer large ones.

Confronting poor performance should never come as a surprise to the person. A true confrontation situation is always the last step, never the first. By the time you decide that the situation requires confrontation you both should be familiar with the issues.

All overtly nonconforming behavior is intended to get attention. You can help someone solve the problem if you build on their self-esteem. The better they feel about themselves, the more receptive they will be to your criticism.

One of my clients had a supervisor in the communications department who was always complaining, griping, and generally bad-mouthing everything and everyone. In addition, she was power-hungry and tried to pit people against each other. The director of the company, who valued this supervisor's creative contributions, repeatedly told her to improve her lousy attitude or she would never get ahead. But no change ever ensued.

After thinking over the director's problem, I suggested that he ask the supervisor a smart question: "How would you improve the low morale in the department?" Almost immediately she focused her attention on finding a creative solution. She got so much attention from her positive action program that she abandoned her gripes and complaints. It was a miraculous turnabout.

Decide that you will ask questions and provide assurance. Remember that people will resist what you tell them, even though deep down they might agree.

When Howard, a vice president of marketing, kept extending the lunch hour, his boss, Trevor, the executive vice president, was at his wit's end. Howard was great in the mornings but useless all afternoon. His unlimited expense account wasn't helping the situation. Previous suggestions to improve had not helped because Trevor, himself a likable and friendly Convincer, hated forcing the issue. Looking for a way to solve the problem without making an enemy of Howard, Trevor devised a strategic question. At their next meeting, he asked Howard, "What do you think will happen to your expense account if you continue like this?"

Now, Howard really loved the five-star restaurants and first-class travel arrangements. When he realized that Trevor was serious, he answered, "I'll probably lose it." That thought was so sobering that Howard made some serious changes in his work habits.

Think of ways you can use questions to get at the heart of the issue. Instead of offering a solution, ask for the solution: "What do you think would solve this problem?" The best way for a manager to improve poor performance is to get problem people to answer questions and arrive at their own decisions to change.

The biggest obstacle, as in counseling, is getting people to confess to having a problem. Sidney, the senior partner of a large law firm, was forced to confront a close friend and associate who had a long-term drinking problem. The lawyer in question for years had handled his alcoholism so that it didn't interfere with business. But in the last year his work began to slide markedly, and clients complained that the lawyer failed to file court documents on time, confused various legal papers, and was late with tax returns and other important financial matters.

Sidney confronted the lawyer and said, "Larry, you've got to straighten things out or we're in trouble." For a few months Larry improved. But then he rapidly deteriorated again, and soon became worse than before. A showdown was imminent. But Sidney couldn't get to first base:

Sidney: What's troubling you, Larry?

Larry: Nothing. Just been busier than usual.

Sidney: Are you drinking?

Larry: No, I've been on the wagon a long time. You know that.

Sidney: Because if you are, perhaps we could arrange a leave of absence for you at a sanitarium.

Larry: I said I wasn't drinking. I'm fine.

Sidney: Then what's happening to your work?

Larry: I don't know what you mean.

Sidney: The Vox Foundation taxes are long past due. Should I give that account to someone else until things ease up for you?

Larry: Certainly not. I've handled that account for eighteen years. I have a court extension, so there's nothing to worry about.

Sidney: But they don't want to be on extension.

Larry: I'll take care of it by next week.

If Sidney cannot get Larry to admit he has a problem in an agreeable way, he has only one recourse left: "If you can't solve this problem and improve performance, what might happen?" (There's only one answer· "I guess you might let me go.")

It's only when they actually believe that their behavior may have dire consequences that many problem people shape up. But if you keep barking threats at them without actually doing anything, no one is going to change. People will improve when they see that you stand behind the consequences.

It's too late for a "let's try this and see what happens" approach. By the end of the discussion you will have reached a definite plan of action. There is going to be a change in the structure of the present job, a shift to another job, or steps will be taken that lead to termination.

When to Confront

If you are considering confrontation, first ask yourself these smart questions:

"Have I given the person every reasonable opportunity to succeed?"

"Have I coached, trained, and removed any obstacles for achievement?"

"Am I sure this person understands what is expected of him?"

"Have I done enough counseling?"

"Have I really worked hard enough?"

If you answered yes to all of those questions, confrontation is in order. Now, ask yourself one more question: "Is this person worth the time and effort it will take to save him?"

If your answer is no, then try to find the gentlest and most expeditious way to fire the person.

If your answer is yes, then do not delay a confrontation. And be prepared to put in the effort and time necessary to deal with it.

Before the Confrontation

The people you have to confront are the people who've been giving you a hard time already. So you have to be extra strong and keep your objectives firmly in mind during the confrontation. Make sure you ask yourself this one question in advance: "What results can my team and my company live with?"

Smart Confrontation Questions

Before the session, think of the questions you're going to ask. When an employee displays apathy, for example, you might try:

"What are some of the things that you think make for a productive work atmosphere?"

"What do you think of the correlation between your behavior and productivity?"

"Six months ago you agreed there was a problem, but nothing has changed. What do you suggest we do about it?"

"What do you think is behind your lack of support and involvement?"

"Do you look forward to coming to work in the morning?" (If answer is yes, follow up with: "What can you do to show it more? I want to feel that you like to come to work." If the answer is no, then ask: "What do you want to do about it?")

"If you're not happy with the job, is there something specific we can do to change things?"

With a confident or more abrasive person, you can afford to be more blunt: "You're driving everyone around here nuts—what are you going to do about it?"

When the problem is poor performance, ask:

"How do you perceive this job?"

"What do you think I'm looking for in terms of results?"

"What do you think is getting in the way of your job performance?"

"How can it be solved?"

"What are you willing to do to solve it?"

"If you don't think it can be solved, what options do we have?"

"Do you see a way the job could be restructured that would help you?"

"Is there some other way that you feel you can contribute to the company?"

"If you don't think there are any solutions, then what is the alternative?"

Letting Someone Go

When you use smart questions during a confrontation the options become clear, and usually the individual will tell you what he thinks is the best solution. If he informs you that after examining all the possibilities he sees no way to improve his performance, then termination is the only option left.

Firing should never be a surprise. According to Robert Half, author of *Robert Half on Hiring,* "80 percent of us have been fired, and only 22 percent of the time was it a complete surprise."

When you decide to give up on someone you should act at once. Get him in your office, close the door, and tell him why, without mincing words. You owe it to him to let him know the full story. It's no favor to anyone to drag out a bad situation; the company is being shortchanged and so are the others in your group who must take up the slack. Certainly the person being fired is better off the quicker it's over with. For employees who simply cannot cope, it will be a distinct relief—the struggle is over and they can move on to something new. I'm sure that everybody who has ever lost a job because he or she was in the wrong business wishes in retrospect that somebody had recognized it earlier so they could have had a head start in some other career.

Act swiftly and with consideration. Do everything you can within company policy and Equal Employment Opportunity regulations to make it easy for the person. If possible, leave him the choice as to whether he would like to use the office for some period of notice or receive pay in lieu of notice. Find out what he would like others in the group to be told. In sum, treat him as well as you can. Or as you'd like to be treated in the same situation. Being thoughtful toward those who don't make the grade cannot fail to encourage those who do.

Exit Interviews

If done without bitterness, exit interviews can give you some good information for the future. Don't be afraid to ask the person who's leaving a few smart questions:

"How could I change?"

"How could the department change?"

"Why did you fail?"

You've motivated, trained, coached, and counseled, and even confronted. All of these techniques are important. But without the formal document described in the final chapter of this section you have no permanent record of what has transpired over the course of a year. The performance appraisal is a permanent record—not only of how the employee has progressed but also of how well you've been doing your job as manager/coach. Performance appraisal is a way to officially applaud progress and yet another opportunity to motivate employees to a higher standard of excellence.

14

Performance Appraisals That Work

Carrie, an engineer in a highly structured naval architecture firm, comes into her supervisor's office for her yearly appraisal. The boss smiles nervously and says, "Take a chair. Well, how are you?"

"Fine."

"I'm just going over the past year. You've done a fine job for us. But I can only give you a token raise because you don't get to work on time, and this really works against you here. We all have to punch the time clock. I've spoken to you about this before and you haven't done anything about it. If you make an effort to improve perhaps I can do something for you next time."

"OK."

"Is there anything you want to discuss?"

"Not really."

"Well, OK. Thanks for coming in."

The supervisor scratches a few notes on his rating sheet for this employee, including "excellent performance" and "lateness a problem." And yet he seems baffled when, three months later, Carrie informs him that she's leaving the company.

The performance appraisal is one of the manager's best tools for motivating people, yet it is seldom, if ever, exploited to its full potential. As typically handled, performance appraisals are virtually meaningless. When 200 managers in a large New York company were asked about their own last performance appraisal, only 10 of them said they had received a thorough give-and-take appraisal interview. Some had received no more than a token pat on the shoulder and a charge to keep up the good work. Others had been subjected to a harangue and a long list of gripes.

Yet almost all companies demand a review of each employee at least once a year. Such reviews may range from formal rating sheets where managers are asked to grade individuals on different skills to informal bull sessions.

Value of Performance Appraisals

What is the purpose of performance appraisals? Performance appraisal is usually a systemized, company-wide process by which a company rates people objectively, grants promotions and raises when due, and sets new objectives for the future. Such a review gives upper management a sense of what's happening with employees at all levels. The appraiser's task is to learn how a person has performed in his job during the year. Then the appraiser is supposed to match his perception of the individual's performance with the employee's own perception. Together, appraiser and employee are supposed to reach a consensus and plan for the coming year.

During a job appraisal a manager helps his people see how their objectives fit in with those of the department and the rest of the organization. The result is usually a written document that is passed on to personnel and upper management.

Everyone in the company is appraised, so the person doing the appraising will in turn be appraised by his or her boss. What we're going to discuss here is how you, as manager, can use performance appraisals of your staff as a tool for increased motivation.

Performance appraisal lets you develop each person on your team to full potential. The overall goal is to get each person to a higher level each year—or every six months—until ultimately they're working at their peak.

Regular appraisals, especially in a big company, keep good people from getting buried in the system. Equally important, nonproductive people don't have anywhere to hide.

Perhaps most important, a regular review system forces a dialogue between manager and staff. In an ideal world, no special structure would be necessary to ensure that kind of interaction. But even if a manager doesn't work closely with someone (he might, for example, have supervisory responsibility for someone in a different location), or if he doesn't get along well with a member of his staff, they still have to sit down and decide what they're going to accomplish together in the months ahead. Because there's no way to avoid this meeting, their working relationship is likely to improve as they gradually come to know each other better.

The performance appraisal gives managers an overview—as though on a panoramic screen—of how each person is coming along. Managers get to know their staff better and to establish themselves as thoughtful and interested leaders. Performance appraisals also let people sort out problems and prevent a buildup of aggravations and disappointments.

These are only a few of the benefits of a good performance appraisal. And yet these goals are seldom even touched upon in a typical appraisal.

Theoretically, appraisals should provide a nonthreatening structure for discussing sensitive topics with employees. The main reason they are shunned, however, is that the appraisal invariably involves giving criticism, and no one enjoys the anxiety inherent in such an emotionally laden situation.

It's difficult to be in a position where your judgment can affect a person's life. Further, managers hesitate to commit themselves to a statement that might cause trouble later. In companies that use a five-point appraisal scale, most managers sidestep the whole issue and rank everyone a three.

To be worthwhile, a performance appraisal takes both time and responsibility. Sure, it has the potential to be emotionally upsetting. And you can never predict how individuals will react. While a job appraisal can be couched in all-positive terms, no good appraisal will be 100 percent positive. A simple pat on the back or a smug "Keep up the good work" is by no means sufficient. Even if someone is doing a good job, you need to guide them as to where they can go from there.

Knowing how to ask smart questions helps you make any appraisal review fair and on target, and also softens the foreboding edge. Using questions as a guide gives both parties the opportunity to approach the situation objectively. Managers who ask smart questions get the most from performance appraisals and also eliminate tension by getting the person to be his own appraiser.

Timing of Appraisals

Most managers don't do appraisals frequently enough. Scheduling an appraisal only once a year turns it into an ominous day on the calendar. It also creates the temptation to let grievances and complaints pile up. "Hold it for the performance appraisal," you may think. Twelve months is too long between appraisals—and yet every week would be far too frequent. The optimal interval is every six months or every three, even if your company only officially requires they be done annually.

Whatever interval you establish, prepare yourself in advance for the appraisal interview. There's nothing worse than telling someone, "I don't think you're doing very well," and when they ask for examples your mind goes blank. Just as bad is giving a yearly rating based on the last thirty days.

It's better to evaluate as you go along: keep each person's file open and make regular notes on performance, including both achievements and trouble spots. Keep a daily or weekly list of pluses and problems. Write comments in terms of the person's observable behavior: "Fred's meeting with client went well today—he had done his homework and presented the ideas succinctly. When client asked questions Fred answered directly and to the point."

Or an entry might be something as simple as "Cy's department failed to meet production quality this month," "Cy hired a winner in Debbie," "Ben's performance appraisals for his group were incomplete." All notes should be specific and dated. A performance appraisal should never be general. During the appraisal you should always be able to refer to specific events and specific dates.

How Smart Questions Make Appraisals Productive

Smart questions turn performance appraisals into a prime motivational tool. Asking questions forces you to plan in advance. Questions help to clarify your thinking and also serve to clarify your employee's thinking. When people know they will be asked questions, they usually come to the meeting prepared to illustrate their past performance.

Consider these other benefits:

- By asking questions, you talk less and therefore obtain more information.

- You can lead the discussion without appearing to do so (because the other person will be doing most of the talking).

- Questions put responsibility on the other person. (If an employee protests "You give me too many things to do at once," you can say, "Can you give me specific examples?")

- Using questions keeps you both from becoming defensive. If the individual puts you on the spot with a question, you can always ask for clarification before jumping to conclusions. ("Before I can answer that, can you tell me more about why you're asking?" Or, "That's a good question. What's the reason behind it?")

- Questions encourage you both to be more objective, as opposed to getting caught up in personal value judgments. Instead of "You have a lousy attitude" or "You don't seem to care," ask, "How do you think your team feels when you leave early when we're in the middle of a crisis?"

   "You're so uncooperative" can be turned into: "Why didn't you help Steve when he needed it?" Or, "The last five times I've asked you to stay late you refused. Can you tell me why?"

   Accusations are a dead end: "You're doing the same thing all over again. You're all bogged down and nothing is getting done." Questions lead somewhere: "How do things get bogged down?" "What can we do to correct it?" "Let's look at your work flowchart and see where it's going." "Can we set a goal for improvement in that area?"

- Questions let you deal with a person's behavior—what they've done and what they're going to do—not with the person himself.

Let's go back to Carrie's performance appraisal and see what might have happened if her manager had asked a few smart questions:

Manager:	Good morning—come on in and have a chair. It's that time of year again. How's it going?
Carrie:	OK.
Manager:	Do you want to plunge right in, or is there something you want to talk about first?
Carrie:	Let's get to it.

Manager:	OK, why don't you tell me what you think went especially well this year?
Carrie:	I think we were running smoothly; the work got out quickly and efficiently. We were almost without mistakes. Adding Jim as a backup was a good idea because it freed me to concentrate on quality control. Overall, I think we were operating at top performance.
Manager:	I agree with you. Are you having any kinds of problems?
Carrie:	Well, the physical layout of the office is still a problem. I don't like being cooped up in that small inside office with Jim working at a table behind me. There's no privacy, and it's just too much togetherness, if you know what I mean.
Manager:	Well, nobody else even has a backup. I had to move heaven and earth just to add him to staff. How can I also request another office?
Carrie:	I don't know. You asked me, and I'm trying to tell you.
Manager:	OK. Let's put that on hold for a moment—we'll come back to it. Tell me, are you having any other problems?
Carrie:	Do you mean about being late in the mornings?
Manager:	Yes. There's got to be a reason—you're doing such a good job, and you know what a stickler the company is for punctuality. That time clock is a real pain for all of us. What's behind the coming in late in the mornings?
Carrie:	It's just hard getting up and getting downtown so early. I'm not a morning person.
Manager:	We all have to do it.
Carrie:	I'm not sure why. I'm often here until 7 or even 8 o'clock. No one needs me in the morning—I'm supposed to be here at 8:45 because that's what the company says, not because there's any particular reason for it.
Manager:	Well, just to take up your argument for a moment, how do you think everyone else in the group feels when they're at their desks at 8:45 and you come at 9:30 or 10 o'clock?
Carrie:	I see your point. It's just so restricting—the whole company is like being in the army.

Manager: Is that really what's bothering you? I mean, we all live with rules and regulations. It seems to me that something else is behind this. Can you get at it? Can you say what's really troubling you?

Carrie: I think I'm just bored, that there's nowhere for me to go. I think you'll have me sitting behind that same desk for the next twenty years. Nothing ever changes, and I can't help but feel that I'm smarter than a lot of other people upstairs.

You can see what's happening with Carrie's performance appraisal now. By continuing to ask questions, her manager has let Carrie fill out her own appraisal about her performance. He's also done a lot more. He has taken the opportunity of the performance appraisal and used it very much like a counseling session. Rather than merely scolding Carrie for not coming in on time, he's helped her uncover a fundamental dissatisfaction with her job.

Carrie has revealed herself to be a high achiever who's at the point where she needs a change. Lateness was not the real problem—the real problem was job dissatisfaction. If her manager doesn't find a way to move her up or add some interest to her job, he's going to lose her, in either body or spirit.

Many companies are satisfied with adequate performance and don't look for ways to challenge their people. For the last ten years I've met a scientist from a major computer company at an annual Christmas party. He's exceptionally bright, and his job bores him to death. He stays on board because of the financial security. Yet I know he can't possibly be giving his best to the company.

Job dissatisfaction shows itself in many ways. A sure sign of demotivation is when people become deeply involved in outside activities. When you have someone running for political office, or spending nights and weekends singing in a choral group or auditioning for plays, or accepting time-consuming positions in various outside organizations, you have people who are not deriving enough satisfaction from their work.

In Carrie's situation, chronic lateness was a clue that she was losing motivation, and it alerted her manager that he was in danger of losing a valuable member of his team. His next step is to see how he can help Carrie set goals that keep her productive and yet still tie in with the department's goals.

The Smart Questions Performance Appraisal

The biggest trap many appraisers fall into is the "lecture mode," where they monopolize the entire conversation. It's tempting to lecture, because you feel you have to defend any criticism as well as justify any praise. But if you ask four or five good questions you'll accomplish much more than if you lecture for a full hour. Before the session, keep this message in mind: "I'm not going to talk too much. I *am* going to ask questions."

When you handle job appraisals the Smart Questions way, your managerial role will begin to shift. Gradually you become less of an intimidating authority figure and more of a consultant.

The question to ask yourself throughout the whole process is "What are the strengths of this person, and how can I use them most effectively?" The only time to mention someone's shortcomings is when you bring them up in relation to their strengths. ("You're excellent on the telephone. I was surprised to see you had difficulties with that telemarketing project you assisted with last summer. What do you think happened?").

This is where you can build upon the golden rules of motivation. Concentrate on strengths, and ask people for feedback about their own performance: "Were you satisfied with the way the project turned out?" Usually, if you've established a trusting atmosphere, people are tougher on themselves than you would be.

If the person seems unresponsive or vague, be persistent. Keep asking. Rephrase the question and ask it again until the person gets the gist of what you're looking for and does give a response. Remember, you don't have to accept the first answer you receive. Keep turning the questions around and keep probing.

Don't be too predictable with your questions. Instead of setting up a tedious pattern, look upon the appraisal as a real opportunity to develop your questioning skills as well as to improve the person's attitude and productivity.

Openers

The normal procedure during an appraisal is to start with all the good things, then zap them with all the negative data you've been filing away.

Years of observing such interviews reveal that it's preferable to integrate the good with the bad throughout the interview.

Careful selection of opening questions is important because it establishes the tone of the meeting. Here are some smart openers:

"Is there any special place you would like to start this discussion?" (You're giving them the option to bring up something that's been weighing on their mind and get it out in the open.)

"How would you like this appraisal to work for you?"

"How would you like to feel at the end of our session?"

"What information would you like to have?"

"Of the objectives we agreed to last time, which is the one you'd like to start with?"

Exploring Questions

"How well is this current project being done?"

"How could it be better?"

"Tell me how you feel about what you've accomplished and what still needs to be done."

"One of your objectives was to improve communication with data processing—how did that go?"

As long as a person feels that he is not under fire and doesn't have to defend himself, he will undoubtedly be critical and objective and give you an accurate assessment of his performance.

You've eased the way by letting people evaluate themselves; that's why questions work so well. If they say they've done a good job, it's good for them to say so, and you can confirm it. If they criticize themselves, you can be supportive while they examine how they could have done better.

Expanding the Appraisal

The stage is now set to carry forward the performance appraisal so that it becomes a unique opportunity to build motivation. Consider these smart questions:

"What do you consider your main accomplishments this year?" (This is a smart question to discover whether the person's priorities coincide with your own.)

"What obstacles were most serious for you?"

"Which are permanent? Which are temporary?"

"What did you do to deal with them?"

"What could you do in the future to deal with them more effectively?"

"Where do you think you could improve?"

"How could I help you more?"

"If you could redo the year, given the same circumstances, what would you do differently?"

If your assessment of the job is radically different from the person's, ask: "Why do you think our ratings are so different?"

Setting Goals

The one final move that lets you exploit the performance appraisal to its fullest potential is asking the person what he hopes to accomplish during the next interval. First, this allows an individual to act as his own boss and to set his own goals. Second, it encourages self-motivation. Third, new ideas bubble up to the top because you're talking about more than one task or issue. Appraisals also force managers to consider what they expect their people to accomplish next and to learn how they intend to go about it.

This is the time to help the employee ask himself "What can I do this coming year that will make a noticeable difference—not only for my department but for the company?"

William Oncken, Jr., and Donald L. Wass, writing for the *Harvard Business Review,* have described the five degrees of initiative that managers can help their staff people pass through: (1) the lowest level is having the employee wait until instructed; (2) next, the employee should ask what to do; (3) then make recommendations and take actions; (4) act independently but feed results back to you immediately; and (5) at the highest level, act independently, then routinely report back at intervals.

Ideally, by setting higher goals with each appraisal you will be able to help each of your people to move through these levels of initiative until they can all function at the highest level in their key responsibilities.

When an employee states his goals, it's your responsibility to evaluate each one. For example, as someone describes what he hopes to do in the coming months, you can guide ("Is that a little ambitious?"), suggest ("It sounds good, but how will it affect your priorities?"), or approve ("That sounds good. Is there anything I can do to help you?").

People can set goals for themselves in various categories: personal development goals, key result goals, routine and procedural goals, and unusual contribution goals. Sometimes a member of your staff will set a goal for himself and fail to live up to it, because the goal was unrealistic, because of a mistake, or because the individual didn't follow through. Regular performance review gives you both enough time to salvage the situation. Because the employee set his own goal, he realizes that this is his problem.

When goals are not reviewed in this productive way, the person may hammer away at the wrong job for years, continually setting the wrong goals and continually failing to achieve them. Ultimately he falls into such a failure mode that he can't regain a positive footing.

Sometimes an employee reaches a level where no further promotion is possible. In these kinds of situations, however, the manager can be the most helpful if he's frank. In Carrie's case, for example, if there is clearly no promotional prospect for her—if there is simply nowhere to go or no more to learn within her department—her manager can be pretty sure that her enthusiasm for the job is going to deteriorate, as is already evidenced by her tardiness. Sometimes shifting job responsibilities or cross-training can help. If that isn't possible, the best thing the manager can do for Carrie is tell her the facts. Knowing where she stands and what her prospects are, Carrie is free to make her own decision.

As Harry Truman loved to say, "The buck stops here." When an individual's performance appraisal stops on your desk, that document should clearly reflect whether or not the employee has been doing his job and also whether you, as manager, have been living up to your obligations.

Regular performance appraisals bond people together in a constructive way, headed toward appropriate and agreed-upon objectives. They are, consequently, prime motivational tools. The Smart Questions performance appraisal can become a mutually satisfying experience—the mirror that shows how well you've been using your managerial skills to get the most from your staff.

In Part Two we've explored the primary tools at your disposal to help your people grow and develop, and have discussed how asking smart questions can maximize each of those techniques. In the final section of *Smart Questions* we're going to talk about you and your future—how asking smart questions can help you stand out in the crowd, gain visibility within your organization, and get ahead.

PART THREE
Getting Ahead

"Where do you want to go from here?"

—Cheshire Cat to Alice

15

The Quiz: Part Three

The final section of the quiz is designed to test your visibility quotient and your getting-ahead mentality.

Everyone wants to get ahead, but not everyone is willing to pay the price—which involves making yourself visible to upper management, striving for creativity, and working overtime to develop a smart-questioning approach. It's clear at this point that it's never enough to ask questions. You have to ask the *right* questions. That's what Part Three of the book is all about.

Those who get ahead regularly ask themselves one question: "What can I do to make myself stand out?" The top executives we interviewed for this section of *Smart Questions* pointed out certain essential areas: (1) figure out what needs to be done (fill the vacuum); (2) solve problems creatively; and (3) try to gain visibility in every area, from seeking job interviews to running meetings.

People who get ahead don't back into success. They know where they want to go, and they go after it. However, having ambition doesn't mean that you can rush into things. Introspection is the smart manager's most valuable asset. As a manager moves higher up, his or her actions become more visible, and each decision requires more time and thought. Smart managers stop, think, and ask the right questions of the right people.

With a questioning approach you stand a much better chance of gaining lasting success.

If you want to stand out, advance quickly, succeed where others fail, consider how you would cope with these situations.

Do You Use Questions to Get Ahead?

1. At a job interview you're told that the department you will head is functioning in very limited space. You:

    a. Accept the fact.

    b. Ask "What effect is the small space having on the staff?"

    c. Ask "Can I have a commitment for more space before I start the job?"

    d. Ask "Are there any other major problems?"

2. An opportunity to make a difficult, time-consuming presentation is given to you. Your response is:

    a. "When can I get started?"

    b. "Who will be there?"

    c. "What is the purpose of the presentation?"

    d. "How can I avoid this presentation, since I'd as soon jump off a bridge as make it?"

3. You are making a presentation when a key decision maker asks a question that you do not understand, and may not know the answer to. You:

    a. Ask the person to rephrase the question.

    b. Ask if they can see you after the presentation.

    c. Say "I don't know, but when do you need an answer?"

    d. Ask yourself, "How can I double-talk and blur the issue?"

4. You have an opportunity to work on a long project with a person whom you dislike intensely, but you know his expertise could save you at least a year of research. You:

    a. Ask yourself, "How can I set aside my emotions and make the best of this situation?"

b.   Ask your boss for advice.

c.   Ask "Why should I give myself all this stress?"

d.   Accept immediately.

5.   You are chairing a meeting and two of the three key people bow out. You:

    a.   Ask the two who canceled when they can commit to a definite time.

    b.   Ask your assistant to run the meeting.

    c.   Have a brief meeting with all three and ask if the third person can carry the ball.

    d.   Ask your boss to talk to the two key people.

6.   You've been asked to relocate in a company where moving is necessary for upward mobility. Your spouse has a great job and doesn't want to move. You:

    a.   Refuse the offer.

    b.   Accept, and deal with your spouse later.

    c.   Ask your boss and mentor for advice.

    d.   Go home and negotiate.

7.   Your boss has been overlooked for a promotion, and an outsider hired. You:

    a.   Ask yourself, "Should I look for another job?"

    b.   Ask "What can I do to lend support?"

    c.   Make friends with the new person.

    d.   Ask around to discover the reasons behind the decision.

8.   At a job interview the salary mentioned is lower than you expected. You:

    a.   Ask "Is there room for further negotiation?"

    b.   Say "I'm disappointed with such a low offer" and wait for a response.

    c.   Accept the offer and hope they'll give you a promotion when they see how good you are.

    d.   End the interview and walk out.

9. A few weeks into your new job you notice that everyone in the company seems to be working exceptionally hard and for long hours without necessarily being productive. You:

   a. Ask your boss, "Is this the company norm?"

   b. Start working longer and longer hours.

   c. Keep your normal schedule and refuse to work longer hours.

   d. Complain to your peers and staff.

10. You need help from two other department heads for a project that is running late. You:

    a. Do not impose on them because, after all, they are over-worked too.

    b. Ask "What can I do to help you, if you give me ten hours of help now?"

    c. Ask "Can I have your help for ten hours?"

    d. Decide to work around the clock for two days in order to finish.

11. You've been moved within your company into an area that is particularly volatile and political. You:

    a. Ask yourself, "Who can help me so I don't make too many wrong moves?"

    b. Decide to stay neutral, regardless.

    c. Figure your new boss, even though he's made enemies, should be your mentor.

    d. Ask the present political top banana, "How do you see the situation?"

12. You've been offered a better job for more money and plan to leave your present job. Then your boss matches the new offer in dollars. You:

    a. Stick with your decision; you don't want to appear weak.

    b. Go back to the "better job offer" and ask them to up the ante.

    c. Ask yourself if money is your only reason for leaving.

    d. Ask your boss what else he can offer.

13. When solving a difficult problem regarding increasing overtime costs, you:

   a. Ask your staff to cut back.

   b. Prepare a lengthy in-depth questionnaire and analysis of the situation.

   c. Call a department meeting and ask for input to get to the heart of the problem.

   d. Ask people individually about their problems.

14. When faced with a difficult decision, the first question you ask is:

   a. What are my options?

   b. What are the risks?

   c. What is my objective?

   d. What else do I need to know?

15. You are a new manager in a large computer-programming department. What do you do first:

   a. Nothing but ask a few questions, look, and listen.

   b. Call a staff meeting and ask for introductions.

   c. Ask for a meeting with your boss.

   d. Call a staff meeting to solve current problems.

16. You've been turned down twice by the finance committee for a budget increase request. You:

   a. Decide to wait for next year.

   b. Ask the chair of the committee for advice.

   c. Ask yourself what you've done wrong so far.

   d. Ask a negotiating expert for help.

17. You've been offered the presidency of an industry association, but you think it might conflict with your job and your boss. You:

   a. Accept and hope things will work out.

   b. Ask your boss for support.

   c. Ask your boss how this honor can help your department and the company.

d. Ask board members and former presidents of the asso-
    ciation how they worked things out with their employers.

18. Two senior vice presidents are talking together and not paying
     attention during your presentation. You:

a. Ask questions of other people, and subtly bring them into
    the discussion.

b. Call a break and privately ask for their support.

c. Ignore them, figuring that you can't expect their attention.

d. Question one of them directly.

19. Two of your peers are talking together and not paying attention
     during your presentation. You:

a. Stop and wait for their attention.

b. Ask one of them a specific question.

c. Walk over and stand behind them.

d. Ask "Is this a private meeting?"

20. Your creative juices for new ideas have run dry. You:

a. Ask your boss for funds to enroll in a creativity seminar.

b. Ask your staff for their input, rather than solving every-
    thing yourself.

c. Ask your boss for two weeks off to go to a retreat and rest.

d. Start reading and getting new input.

21. You are asked to contribute a weekly article for an important
     industry publication. You:

a. Ask your literary friends, "Do you know a good ghost-
    writer?"

b. Ask a staff member to write the column, and put your
    name on it.

c. Ask your entire staff for contributions, and share the credit.

d. Accept and ask personnel to enroll you in a good writing
    program.

22. Your boss has just locked horns with your mentor over a major
     policy issue. You:

a. Ask your mentor for advice.

    b.   Ask yourself, "What is right?"

    c.   Ask your boss for advice.

    d.   Ask yourself, "How soon could this situation wear itself out?"

23.   Your boss is afraid to let go of any authority. You:

    a.   Ask for a transfer.

    b.   Ask him, "What can I do to take over some of the work that you don't like?"

    c.   Ask "Have you ever felt frustrated by not having all the authority you need to do a good job?"

    d.   Ask "How could training your replacement make you look good?"

24.   You feel your highly regarded boss doesn't trust you. You:

    a.   Ask for a transfer.

    b.   Start looking for another job.

    c.   Ask your boss, "What can I do to gain your trust?"

    d.   Look for satisfaction in outside activities.

25.   In the washroom one day you overhear a rumor from reliable sources that your boss is going to get sacked. You:

    a.   Tell your boss immediately.

    b.   Ask the people the source of the rumor.

    c.   Ask your network if anyone else has heard anything.

    d.   Start packing your gear for your move into your boss's office.

Answers

1.   a = 0   b = 3   c = 4   d = 5

A smart manager should establish a power base when he or she is first interviewed for a job. This is an opportune time to make demands. In this case, the new manager is told there is a space problem. So asking "Can I have a commitment for more space before I start the job" (*c*) is an excellent tactic. But an even smarter question is "Are there any other major problems?" (*d*). Knowing what the problems are and getting a commitment from your new boss helps you achieve a strong position up front. If you answer (*b*)—"What effect is the small space having on the staff?"—you're asking a good question but not getting any action. And just accepting the fact (*a*) gets you nothing.

2.   a = 3   b = 5   c = 5   d = 0

No busy manager wants to get involved in a difficult, time-consuming presentation. While it's important to be enthusiastic (*a*), it's usually not smart to plunge in when you may get mired in a lengthy project with no payoff. If you want to get ahead, asking "What is the purpose of this presentation?" (*c*) and "Who will be there?" (*b*) will let you judge the potential impact of the project. Wriggling out of it (*d*) before you know the ramifications means that you might lose a great opportunity to make yourself visible.

3.   a = 5   b = 3   c = 4   d = 1

The answer to this question—what to do when a key person asks you a question that you do not understand—depends on who's doing the asking. Each of these answers has some merit, but unless you're a brilliant speaker, falling into double-talk to blur the issue (*d*) spells trouble. You may lose a few points if you admit that you don't know, but make up for it with "When do you need an answer?" (*c*), which shows that you'll find out and get back to the person. Asking the person to see you after the presentation (*b*) is not quite as effective, but can work if the person isn't challenging you head-on. It also suggests to the audience that you know the answer but don't want to take everyone else's time dealing with it. The smartest solution is to ask the person to rephrase the question (*a*). It gives you time to think; you can then come up with an answer or choose one of the other tactics.

4.   a = 5   b = 2   c = 0   d = 3

When you have an opportunity to save time by working with someone you dislike, do you jump to it? You do if you want to get ahead. The best question to ask yourself is "How can I set aside my emotions and make the best of this situation?" (*a*). The next-best response is to accept immediately (*d*). Your boss isn't going to help you solve your personal problems (b), although he or she may give you some advice in dealing with the person. Asking "Why should I give myself all this stress?" (c) is a useless question. If you're looking to get ahead, stress comes with the territory. You might as well get used to it.

5.   a = 3   b = 0   c = 5   d = 0

How many times do top people say they're going to come to a meeting and then get tied up elsewhere? It can turn a young manager's hair prematurely gray. Asking the two dropouts to commit to a new meeting is not a bad solution if you can get them to write the date in blood. But if you want to get ahead, you must do everything possible to avoid canceling meetings. So the best solution is to have a brief meeting with all three participants and ask if the third person can carry the ball (c). Neither (b) nor (d) is a suitable response. Turning the meeting over to your assistant just to make yourself look more important isn't worthwhile, and asking your boss to talk to the key people is passing the buck.

6.   a = 0   b = 4   c = 2   d = 5

If you want to get ahead, you certainly don't want to refuse the offer (a), even though it promises to cause problems with your spouse. The best plan is to go home and negotiate (d). People on big career paths need the support of their families, and ideally you can work out a win-win negotiation. The next-best solution, if you are looking to get ahead, is to accept the offer and deal with your spouse later (b). It's usually not wise to ask your boss or mentor to help with a personal matter (c).

7.   a = 2   b = 3   c = 3   d = 5

When someone is overlooked for a promotion, there's usually a reason. If that overlooked person is your boss, it's in your best interests to find out why. Therefore, asking around to discover the reasons behind the decision (d) is the best answer. You can usually lend support to your boss (b) and also make friends with the newly promoted person (c), and there's no reason not to do both. Immediately casting around for a new job (a) isn't intelligent, unless you discover that your company has adopted an "outside hire" philosophy. But don't act before you investigate the situation.

8.   a = 3   b = 5   c = 2   d = 0

If you've sold yourself at a job interview and the salary offer is too low, the best thing you can say is "I'm disappointed with such a low offer" (*b*)—and then *wait for a response*. The first person who talks is going to lose. The next-best response is to ask "Is there room for further negotiation?" (*a*), because it provides an opportunity to talk further. But this isn't nearly as good as (*b*). If you've sold yourself, it doesn't make sense to end the interview and walk out (*d*). And if you accept the offer with the idea that you'll get a raise when they see how good you are (*c*), it probably won't work out. If you're not assertive enough to ask for more money at the job interview, chances are you won't be assertive enough once you're on the job.

9.   a = 5   b = 3   c = 0   d = 1

For this question, the crucial thing to learn is whether long hours and excessive work is a corporate norm (*a*). Only when you know this can you make an intelligent decision. If it is a company norm and you want to get ahead, you will have to commit yourself to longer and longer hours (*b*). If you refuse to work long hours (*c*), you will not advance; it would be better for you to look for another job. (If it isn't a company norm, only a temporary circumstance, you will probably plunge in for the time being.) But you cannot act until you find out. Complaining to your peers and staff (*d*) is fruitless.

10.   a = 0   b = 5   c = 3   d = 2

If you want to get ahead, it's important to learn how to get help and work with other people. And yet powerful people don't want to be in someone's debt. Therefore to retain power when you need help, ask for it, but also negotiate for something you can do in return (*b*). This establishes a standard of give-and-take that will serve you throughout your career. Simply asking for specific help (*c*) isn't a bad solution, but without repaying in some way you're going to be in that person's debt. Being afraid to impose on someone (*a*) and killing yourself to achieve the task by yourself (*d*) are nonproductive solutions.

11.   a = 5   b = 2   c = 3   d = 3

When you're moved into a politically volatile area of the company, it pays to look around for the best advice so you can avoid making too many wrong moves (*a*). You cannot stay neutral too long (*b*); eventually you will have to position yourself. Although the most important person is always your boss, bosses are not necessarily the best mentors. So while (*c*) is not a terrible move, it isn't necessarily the best move. Asking the current top banana for help (*d*) could be the right move, but that person is likely to be biased. The smartest thing to do is stop, think, and ask a few smart questions before making any moves.

12.   a = 1   b = 3   c = 5   d = 3

When you accept a better job offer for more money and your boss makes a counteroffer, there's no reason why you can't change your mind. You're the one who loses if you stick to a decision just to appear strong (*a*). The best thing is to ask yourself an introspective question: "Is money my only reason for leaving?" (*c*). If money is the only reason you're changing jobs, you can negotiate with either the "better job offer" (*b*) or your boss (*d*). If money is not the main issue, if you're leaving because you're not happy in your job, then you have a different set of circumstances.

13.   a = 1   b = 1   c = 5   d = 2

When overtime costs are running your projects into the ground, asking your staff to cut back (*a*) isn't going to get to the root of the problem. And preparing a long in-depth questionnaire (*b*) will just drag the problem out. Asking people individually about their problems (*d*) could help, but it takes too much time. Your best shot is to call a department meeting (*c*) and ask for staff input. You will get to the bottom of the problem and also be able to institute immediate action.

14.   a = 3   b = 2   c = 5   d = 4

When faced with a difficult decision, all of these responses seem helpful. The important thing is to put them in sequence. The single most important question in the decision-making sequence is "What is my objective?" (*c*). Once you're clear about that, everything else falls into place. The next important question is "What else do I need to know?" (*d*). As you fill in these blanks, you automatically weigh options and risks (*a* and *b*).

15. a = 4   b = 4   c = 5   d = 1

The first thing to do when taking over any large department is to ask for a meeting with your boss (*c*). Almost as good is doing what Edward Finkelstein did when he took over Macy's: nothing but watch, listen, and learn (*a*). It's always good form to call a staff meeting and ask for introductions (*b*). But calling a meeting with the expectation of solving problems (*d*) won't work until you learn what the problems are.

16. a = 1   b = 5   c = 4   d = 3

When you are repeatedly turned down for budget increases, what can you do? If you wait for next year (*a*) to try again, you're leaving your future in other hands than your own. Asking yourself what you've been doing wrong so far (*c*) is a smart question if you can be objective about the answer. And by all means, if you have a negotiating expert around, ask for his or her advice (*d*). The most productive approach, however, is to ask the chair of the committee for advice (*b*). This is the only person who knows exactly why you're not getting the increases.

17. a = 1   b = 3   c = 5   d = 3

If you accept the presidency of an industry association for the prestige, the smartest thing you can do is ask your boss how this honor can help your department and the company (*c*). Asking your boss for support (*b*) and asking former presidents how they handled things with their employers (*d*) are good ideas because they give you internal support for the outside work that might take time away from your job. Simply hoping that things will work out (*a*) means that you will be unprepared if conflict does arise between your job and the honorary position.

18. a = 5   b = 3   c = 2   d = 0

What do you do when senior vice presidents start talking during your presentation? Calling a break and privately asking for their support (*b*) is a weak solution and may not even be possible in companies that have strict rules about how presentations are made. Ignoring them isn't going to help your credibility (*c*); and you're definitely not going to question them directly (*d*). The subtle approach will work best in this case; ask questions of other people at the meeting (*a*), which should generate discussion and gradually involve the vice presidents.

19.   a = 4   b = 5   c = 3   d = 2

The answers change if you're making a presentation to a meeting of your peers. Stopping and waiting for the attention of two talkative people may work (*a*), but if they are engrossed in conversation they may not even notice. Walking over and standing behind them (*c*) is a more subtle approach, but again, they may ignore you. Asking "Is this a private meeting?" is a rude and demeaning question (*d*) and unworthy of a smart manager. The best solution is to ask one of them a specific question (*b*). The question will get their attention, make them feel a twinge of guilt, let them know you want their input, and also get the meeting back on track.

20.   a = 3   b = 4   c = 2   d = 5

All of these solutions can help get the creative juices flowing again after a dry spell. The most helpful would be to start reading to stimulate your mind (*d*). Bringing in your staff can help (*b*), and going to a creativity seminar (*a*) certainly can't hurt. Even taking some time off (*c*), while the least direct method, may also do you some good.

21.   a = 3   b = 1   c = 5   d = 3

If you're asked to contribute a weekly article, you won't have time to do all the work yourself and it's unlikely that you have the money to hire a ghostwriter (*a*). And while it doesn't hurt anyone to become a good writer (*d*), that isn't what managing is all about. I believe that managers should take advantage of every opportunity to help staff people develop. But it's demoralizing to ask a staff member to write the column and then put your name on it (*b*). The best answer is to get the staff involved in the whole process—it will generate their interest and their enthusiasm. Use your name on it, along with theirs. Giving your staff credit makes you look good.

22.   a = 4   b = 5   c = 4   d = 4

When your boss and your mentor are at odds over a major policy issue, you have to look to yourself to discover what you think is right (*b*). This is a tough situation, but you must start with introspective questions about the situation, how you feel about it, and how you'd like things to end up. After you are clear about your own feelings, all of the remaining answers are helpful.

23.   a = 1   b = 5   c = 3   d = 4

People who are afraid to let go of authority usually feel insecure. Therefore a smart manager tries to wrestle authority and responsibility from his boss in an unthreatening manner. By taking on jobs he or she doesn't like (*b*) you help rid your boss of a burden, which is a big plus, and ease him into the habit of delegating. Asking about your boss's feelings (*c*) isn't bad, because you're trying to show some empathy, but it's a little too smug. And asking "How could training your replacement make you look good?" (*d*) would work only if your boss has some motivation to move up. Asking for a transfer (*a*) is avoiding the problem, and that's never a good managing solution.

24.   a = 4   b = 2   c = 5   d = 1

It is essential that your boss trust you. If he or she doesn't, you might think about asking for a transfer (*a*). But there might be another solution; before you give up, ask "What can I do to gain your trust?" (*c*). If there's something you can do, do it. If the answer is "Nothing," then ask for a transfer, or even start looking for another job (*b*). Looking for satisfaction in outside activities (*d*) doesn't work.

25.   a = 2   b = 4   c = 5   d = 1

When you hear a rumor that your boss is about to be fired, don't start dreaming of yourself sitting in his chair (*d*). Before running to your boss to tell him that he's about to get sacked (*a*), use your network to find out what else people have heard (*c*). There may be a lot more going on in the company. Next best is to learn the source of the rumor (*b*); it may be an unfounded bit of gossip. The two best answers both involve asking smart questions.

Scoring

100–125 Points

With a high score you are on target with your thinking as well as your questioning. You have the right balance between confrontation and tact and negotiation. You've done well in developing the Smart Questions approach to most situations, and that ability should be a big help in your career.

85–100 Points

You use questions well but need improvement if you want to move ahead faster. You need to practice the questioning approach until it becomes an integral part of your communication and thinking process. You also need practice in phrasing questions. Once you are emotionally committed, the phrasing should improve.

65–85 Points

You are either avoiding confrontation or making quick decisions and rushing off to the solution. You are not fully convinced that questions can help you. Although it is difficult to let go of an existing pattern, for example avoidance or fast decision making, the Smart Questions system can help you. In every planned situation—calls you make, meetings you initiate—start with questions. Write them out in advance and memorize them. Once you see the improvement for yourself, you'll change your style quickly.

Less than 65 Points

You need to change your style across the board: substitute more questions for statements both verbally and mentally. Try changing your approach. When faced with a new situation, instead of counting to ten and then reacting in your old way, stop and think about a suitable question to explore the situation.

There is no area more important for applying the Smart Questions technique than the advancement of your career. In the following chapters we're going to see the many ways—in getting a top job, seeking promotions and raises, coming up with creative ideas to solve problems—that asking smart questions can make the difference. In the final chapter a select group of leaders of America's major corporations ponder the issue of what distinguishes a rising star from the rest of the management pack. They offer their personal advice on how young managers can stand out in the corporate system, and what they have to say may surprise you.

16
Creative Ideas and Problem Solving

Sam and Rachel, both on the executive committee of a major association, were discussing whom to promote to the position of executive director. They quickly ruled out the present executive director's assistant, the most likely candidate, with "He never comes up with any original ideas." One way to hit a dead end in your career is to be labeled in this way.

Managers need to activate, not merely maintain the status quo, which means that they must come up with new ideas and better solutions to problems. If you are a manager looking to get ahead, generating good ideas and solving problems imaginatively are sure-fire ways to catapult yourself to success.

Most people believe that managers who think quickly and creatively are smarter than others, or have some kind of secret flair for solving problems. In fact, the secret they have is accessible to anyone. Creative thinking involves quiet "cerebration," as one well-known trial lawyer calls it, and the ability to ask smart questions.

Drs. Harold Bloomfield and Leonard Felder, authors of *The Achilles Syndrome*, advise managers to work less and think more. Creative thinking often begins with removing yourself mentally from the day-to-day routine of business. "A brilliant idea, a pivotal decision, a simple solution . . . in those five minutes you can accomplish more than shuffling papers for sixty hours."

Asking questions is a great way to stimulate creative thinking. Assigned to come up with a new product name for dill pickles, the product manager placed a big pickle on the table and asked a group of six people this question: "If you had never seen this object before, what would you call it?"

This one smart question sparked a wealth of imaginative names. Some of their answers: Crisper . . . Canoe . . . Pucker . . . Quencher . . . Greenith . . . Slimy Cuker . . . Cruncher . . .

Marketing strategists use smart questions in many kinds of brainstorming meetings, from inventing new products to naming existing ones, from long-range planning strategies to instant problem solving. The rules of these creative sessions are simple: panel members are encouraged to express any idea that comes into their minds, refrain from negative comments or criticism of any idea, and expand positively upon ideas expressed by other members.

For example, a packaged-goods manufacturer set up a brainstorming session to name a new fruit juice. The panel was comprised of seven people from various walks of life and a market researcher who served as moderator. The moderator asked the panel: "What does fruit juice make you think of?"

Everyone wrote down lists of the words that came to mind, such as:

health	mornings
outdoors	colors
trees	family

"Now," said the moderator, "forget about fruit juice, and let's build on just one word on the lists. What does 'mornings' make you think of?" Again, hundreds of different words popped up:

a.m.	coffee
sunlight	alarm clock
yawns	toothbrush
school	wake up
showers	fresh
cereal	start
eggs	beginning

"Let's try another word," the moderator said. "What do you associate the word 'health' with?"

After building on each word on the original list, the leader picked out a dozen of the most promising words and tested them among a sample of consumers. For example, "A.M." was tried out, and so was "Sunlight," "Wake Up," and "Fresh." In this case, "A.M." topped most people's lists and actually became the name of a product.

Sounds simple, doesn't it? Yet how often do most people, when presented with a new idea, immediately jump to criticize it? We seem to regard ideas as one would a ship—no matter how many good points it has, if there's a hole anywhere in the thinking, the whole thing is doomed to sink.

For some reason the ability to isolate the negatives of an idea—in other words, to criticize—is often more respected in our society than the ability to recognize potential. When faced with a new idea or solution to a problem, managers often struggle to come up with some critical comment that will make them look incisive and intelligent.

People who pounce on the flaws in an idea or seize the chance to play devil's advocate are often seen as quick and discerning. In terms of business, the ability to pick out flaws is undeniably valuable. But if "Can't be done" is your prompt response to anything new and different, you may be nipping your future in the bud. A stubborn resistance to change can only hold you back.

An irate banker once told an inventor to remove "that toy" from his office. That toy was the telephone. A young engineer, bored with laying out computer chips, asked his boss if he could work on designing a personal computer. The answer was no, so the engineer went home, built one on his own, and named it Apple. Many years ago, a young clerk working in a hardware store suggested to his boss that they set up a table in the middle of the store and sell off obsolete inventory items for a dime each. The sale was a success, and the clerk then suggested that they open a store that sold only nickel and dime items. His boss said he was crazy; they could never find enough items to sell at a nickel or a dime. Years later the boss lamented, "I figure every word I used in turning down Woolworth has cost me about a million dollars."

The ability to see the kernel of a great idea and build on it is much more profitable than the ability to criticize and discover the flaws in every idea. People who respond to the positive are rare, and refreshing to be around. Other people are eager to present their ideas to them because they'll be examined in the best light. People love to share their thoughts with those who see the good things.

That doesn't mean that everything you think of, or your staff thinks of, will pan out. On the contrary, only a few ideas are ultimately worthwhile. But to get one sensational idea, you have to welcome all ideas, no matter how bizarre. And to get one idea to the top, you have to be willing to push all ideas as far as they can go.

Most good ideas that succeed have been shaped and restructured to become workable; they don't just pop out of the air in perfect form. Inventors and innovators often seek out broad new concepts and original ways to meet unsatisfied needs, then work out the details of how to implement or execute them later. If you've got something worthwhile, you can usually iron out the problems and make it work.

Accent the Positive

The essence of modern creative thinking techniques is to build on the positive. As mentioned earlier, in brainstorming or think tanks, negative comments of any kind are usually forbidden because of their counterproductive effect. Negative comments inhibit people and often choke off valuable thoughts before they are explored. All ideas, however improbable, are assumed to be worthy of consideration. Participants are asked to build on ideas, not tear them down. What appears to be a wild and impractical approach often turns out to be the key to finding an imaginative and effective solution.

Use Your Team to Generate New Ideas

Creativity often derives from special knowledge. Ken Blanchard was in the field of management consulting for years before he wrote *The One Minute Manager* with Spencer Johnson. He knew the field thoroughly. Jonas Salk spent years in the research laboratory before discovering the vaccine for polio. New ideas may fester for years in the minds of the engineers who see the same products manufactured day in, day out. They are in a position to know what's practical and what's out of the question. Bookkeepers stuck with the same system for months on end may be dying to tell someone—anyone who would listen—about a better way.

If you are a manager looking for new ideas, doesn't it make sense to talk to the people involved, the people who know the most about your business, or about the idea or the problem?

Often creativity has been squelched for so long that the manager feels he needs a stick of dynamite to enliven things again. Smart managers find ways of encouraging their people to come up with creative innovations. If you are a manager looking towards the future, always let your people know that you are open, receptive, and positive. Tell them you're interested in their constructive input, since you know that no one knows the business—whatever business it is—better than the people who keep it running smoothly day after day.

Smart Questions Help Create Ideas

As we've seen, questions are a great device for coming up with new ideas. The next step is to evaluate that idea. Again, questions provide the best way to pinpoint the positives and systematically determine the value of the idea. When considering any new idea, ask yourself or your staff these smart questions:

"What specifically are the positive aspects of this idea?"

"What specifically are the negatives?"

"What is interesting about this idea?"

"What makes this idea unique or valuable?"

"In what ways can I build on the idea's advantages?"

"Are the possible advantages so great that it must be considered further?"

"Are the negatives so dominant that further thinking is a waste of time?"

"Can the basic concept be applied to different areas? Different products? Different departments?"

"Does this idea suggest any others that might work better?"

Smart Questions for Problem Solving

Creative thinking may also prove to be the key to solving some of your toughest on-the-job problems.

One newly hired executive in a growing pharmaceutical firm observed that various groups within the company were at loggerheads. Numerous major and minor mistakes were being made—on quantity and quality checks, in proofreading, and in other areas—costing the company possible lawsuits, poor publicity, and time and money. Department heads blamed each other and morale sagged across the board. Productivity declined.

The executive pondered this situation and came up with a series of solutions by asking herself some smart questions.

"What is the history of this problem?"

"When did it start?"

"What could be the source of the problem?"

"Who is involved?"

"What has been done about this in the past?"

As she tried to answer these questions, she realized that this was a relatively new problem that originated when the company began its expansion. Here was a large company with virtually no communication among its senior managers. In fact, no one had ever been out to the manufacturing plant. Once she recognized the problem for what it was, a solution was readily at hand.

As a result of her thinking, the executive came up with a program where everyone met as a group for one hour every month. At each meeting, members of one department gave a short presentation: how they fit into the big picture; what they needed from other departments—from manufacturing, advertising, marketing, and so on. Then they asked for feedback from the other groups. Every session concluded with questions from the floor. Speakers also gave out some written material so that anyone unable to attend the meeting could catch up on it. Tours were also developed, so every employee got to see how products were manufactured and packaged.

After a year, the program was reevaluated and it was discovered that many persistent, serious problems no longer existed. The executive who had come up with the plan received an important promotion.

When faced with a problem that seems to defy positive solution, smart questions can help you set a decisive course of action. Ask yourself:

"What is the source of the problem?"

"Who is involved?" (If the situation involves a problem with a specific individual, always examine the other person's point of view. Until you understand the problem as the other person sees it, you can't deal effectively with the problem itself.)

"What aspects of the problem are controllable?" (Managers often have more control over situations than they think. Don't assume anything until you know for certain.)

"What aspects about this situation require outside help?"

"What has been done in the past?"

"What worked? What didn't work?"

What Are Your Objectives?

When it comes to solving a problem, many people don't know what it is they're after. Sometimes the best way to discover what you want is to ask yourself what you don't want.

"What don't I want to happen?"

"What is the worst thing that could happen?"

"What is the best thing that could happen?"

Planning Strategy

"What are all the possible ways to approach this problem?" (Go for quantity at first, not quality.)

"What obstacles are we going to face?" (Be realistic, not negative. For example, if you will have to fight for approval, think of a creative way to do it.)

"What are the options?"

"What is the backup plan?" (Have at least one.)

"What are the trade-offs?"

"What's the bottom bottom line?" (Remember the story of the authoritative stranger who came into the office and asked, "Who's the Main Man around here?" The boss proudly stepped out and introduced himself. The man said, "I'm with the IRS." The boss quickly added, "Oh, you want the Main Main Man.")

"What help do I need to carry out the strategy?"

"From whom do I need support to put over the strategy?"

Personal Goals

"Did I choose this solution only because my associate or boss wants it?"

"Did I choose it because others expect it of me?"

"Did I choose it because it's the fashion?"

"Because it's easy?"

"Because it's hard?"

If you answer yes to any of the above, you should rethink your choice. Ask yourself one more smart question: "Is this the solution I really want?"

Using Your Team to Solve Problems

It is common today for companies to hire outside consultants to solve a variety of problems, from managerial to marketing to personnel-related difficulties. Frequently, one of the first things these consultants do is carefully interview the client firm's staff. Many companies, it seems, don't take the time or trouble to listen to their own people.

Many creative solutions do not involve a single decision or directive. More often, problem solving is a matter of discussion, cooperation, and an ongoing process of change. When you let your people actively participate in creative problem solving, you gain in two important ways: you are more likely to discover a solution that strikes directly at the heart of the problem, and you build the cooperation and loyalty of your staff.

People are often reluctant to come to a boss with problems, unless the boss has established an atmosphere where the bearer of bad news isn't shot on the spot. William S. Lee, Chairman and CEO of Duke Power Company, says that this is a sure sign of a poor manager: "Managers must build the right sort of climate where people can speak up and report unpleasant news upward."

You may find it valuable to hold regular team or staff meetings to discuss problems. Make it clear up front that these are not griping sessions or an excuse for mudslinging, but serious updates on serious business. At the same time, such meetings are worthless if people do not feel free to speak honestly without fear of disapproval. A good manager should be able to hear problems or suggestions without taking personal offense.

These sessions serve another purpose: potential problems may be cleared up before they become full-grown ones. The managers I know who have meaty problem-solving sessions never operate under crisis management.

How can a manager use staff people to solve problems imaginatively? Ask a few smart questions:

"How long have you been aware of this situation?"

"From your perspective, when and why did it start?"

"What factors do you think have contributed to the problem?"

"Is this particular problem part of a larger problem?"

"What ideas do you have to improve the situation on a day-to-day basis?"

"What steps might we take to solve the problem for the long term?"

"Can you point out any related problems?"

"What does this problem tell us about the larger picture and the way we are currently approaching our work?"

Of course, the ultimate responsibility for choosing any solution remains with the manager. And there will be problems that no outside input can help you solve.

The sign of an outstanding manager—a manager destined to move ahead and succeed within the organization—is the ability to make a decision and carry it out. The crucial part of any new brilliant idea or any imaginative solution is actually making the decision to go forward—and giving your brainchild every opportunity to succeed.

17

Dare to Decide

Nothing is valued more in organizations than a good decision. And nothing is criticized more—and remembered longer—than a poor one.

Lou, an executive vice president of a major insurance company, was promoted to run the West Coast office. As a result, he was asked to name his own replacement, a choice to be made from three of his best people. Each candidate had good qualities and all had been with the company for several years. Lou's final choice came down to which one could make the best decisions.

Before making his selection, Lou gave each candidate one important decision to make:

Candidate A was asked to choose the best marketing consultant for a new product line. "A" called up his cronies on the old boy network, found out whom they used, and went with their advice. Lou eliminated Candidate A because he did not interview and investigate on his own, and therefore had no assurance that he had gotten the best available consultant for the job. This wasn't the way Lou wanted his replacement to operate.

Candidate B was asked to select the best computer system for programming the new products. "B" methodically gathered the facts and made a thorough investigation. But as much as Lou pressed him, "B" put off making a decision. There were always more and more "essential bits of information that were still needed." Lou felt that no amount of prodding could help solve Candidate B's intense insecurity and fear of making a mistake. He eliminated Candidate B.

Candidate C had a reputation as an eager beaver. He was so energetic that he often rushed his decisions and failed to look at all sides of an issue. Lou asked "C" to develop the advertising plan and budget for the new line. Candidate C realized how much was at stake. Instead of following his usual pattern of jumping the gun, he went to Lou and asked for help. And this was the deciding factor for Lou. While none of the candidates was a first-class decision maker, Candidate C had the most potential because he was highly motivated and was willing to learn. Jim chose him as his replacement.

If I had to sum up the quality that's most essential for effective management, I'd say that it all comes down to decisiveness. You can use the most sophisticated computer in the world and you can gather all the charts and numbers available, but in the end you have to bring the information together, set up a timetable, and act.

Some people work their way up to the decision step, then are reluctant to act. Why? Because it's with the action—not the idea, not the analysis—that you win or lose. Every decision involves a risk. But each risk can be minimized.

Getting any idea off the ground involves two basic steps. First, you have to make a decision. Second, and equally important, you have to take action on what you've decided.

Step One: Making the Decision

It's important to understand the decision-making process to learn where you might go wrong. For example, do you tend to be overly conservative or to cave in under pressure?

Many managers let themselves get bogged down by the confusion of having to make rapid choices. And few businesses can afford the luxury of slow decision making. Obviously, you're responsible for gathering as many relevant facts and projections as you possibly can. But at some point you've got to make a decision based on your own instincts. Have confidence in your past successes. After all, decision making is a skill and if you did it right in the past, you're likely to do it right again.

Timing is everything. Even the right decision is wrong if it's made too late. A young designer I know took much longer than anticipated to bring out her important first line because she felt compelled to make it perfect. By the time the clothes were completed to her satisfaction, the fashion scene had found a new set of styles, and she had to start all over from scratch.

The fashion business, like so many businesses, is rooted in trends. Some trends move faster than others. Similarly, many products and services are seasonal, or dependent on shifting demographics or other factors. A manager must move heaven and earth to deliver the product to the marketplace before the marketplace shifts or even disappears. Whenever you make a decision—regardless of the nature of your business—you have to be aware of the clock ticking.

It's natural to want to see all the facts set out before you and to hold out for research that puts risk at a minimum or guarantees that a particular program will work. If you're going to invest money and resources, you want to be absolutely sure you're on the right track. But not every business problem can be solved by research. At some point, someone—some decisive manager—has to dare to decide.

How much information is enough? It's impossible to put a figure on it, but clearly when you move ahead with only 50 percent of the facts, the odds are stacked against you. At the same time, you'll never know 100 percent of what you need. When you must act with less than complete information—as all sharp managers must be able to do—there are things you can do to minimize the gamble.

First, make sure the information you do have is reliable. Know your people: your experience should tell you what sources are trustworthy and whose judgment is most sound and consistent. Encourage debate. This is just when you need feedback the most.

Make sure that whatever specific information you have makes sense. Don't take for granted that the list of figures you've been handed is accurate. As much as possible, check things out yourself.

It's important to recognize your own decision-making style. If you tend to be a Commander or Convincer decision maker, ask some caring team players or Calculating quality controllers in your group or organization for their opinion, to act as a balance and prevent a rash decision.

Listen to what others have to say, but listen more to your own instincts. Do you have any lurking doubts or feelings of uncertainty? Taking action often helps relieve nagging feelings of ambivalence and doubt, but don't act quickly merely to alleviate tension. A certain amount of uneasiness and uncertainty goes with the territory, and your subconscious may know something you don't know. Try to pin down what's bothering you.

Last, and most crucial, always monitor the success or failure of your decisions. One reason decisions are risky is that a manager never knows until afterwards—sometimes not until much later—whether it was a good decision. An example is hiring someone or deciding on a new product. And yet, short of making the decision to order a firing squad to shoot, most decisions are not irrevocable.

Research shows that once people make a decision, they do everything in their power to convince themselves it was the right one. Don't fall into this trap. Make it your business to get feedback. Make sure the decision is having the desired impact. If it's not, figure out why and help it along. Or if you realize that your first decision was a bad one, have the strength to change direction and cut your losses. This doesn't mean that you shouldn't stand by your decisions or that you should give up on a project the minute something goes wrong. It means that in certain situations, insisting that you're right when you've clearly made a mistake is much more costly in the long run. If you're digging a hole in the wrong place, digging it deeper or wider won't make it any better.

If you discover you've made an error, the most valuable thing you can do for yourself is to learn from the experience. All successful people use failure as a valuable teacher. It's a given that everyone makes mistakes, but only those who can analyze past failure to improve future performance emerge as winners.

So, making good decisions depends on knowing how to take calculated risks. When you don't have all the facts—which is most of the time—asking smart questions can give you a specific technique to speed decision making and help reduce the risk. When faced with choices, what kind of questions can you ask yourself in order to make the best decision? Realistically, most business decisions are not based on one clear-cut preference but on the lesser of several evils.

Exploring Your Options

Smart questions can help you explore the advantages of various options. List all your realistic alternatives and pose these questions about each one:

"What are the benefits of making this decision?"

"What are the risks?"

"What's the best possible result I can hope for?"

"What can I do to maximize the possibility of this happening?"

"Can I achieve this end in any other way?"

"What is the most probable result?" (Both positive and negative.)

"Does this satisfy my objectives? Will I be happy with this result?"

"What's the worst possible result?"

"Can I handle it?"

"If it's the wrong decision, how can I retrieve the situation and my self-esteem?"

"Should I alter my plans to avoid this possibility altogether?"

"Is there a way I can or should compromise?"

"If I'm a Commander, whom should I consult?"

Here's another issue to consider:

"Will my action go against the interest of some other part of the company?"

"Or of a colleague or team member?"

"Or against my own interests?"

"Is it worth this price?"

The Three Questions That Lead to a Winning Decision

Ultimately it takes only three very smart questions to reach a winning decision. Before you make *any* decision, be sure you know the answers:

1. "What will it cost—in money and resources?"
2. "What impact will this decision have?"
3. "What happens if we don't do it?"

Step Two: Taking Action

Taking the time to make a good decision and then failing to put the results into practice is like spending all your money on a beautiful house and failing to move in. Good decisions are worthless unless they're acted upon.

Once you have your decision, make the decision to *act*. Carrying out a plan or idea that has hitherto existed only abstractly can be a traumatic experience, but it's one that managers live with every day. It's like the author I know who finished a manuscript and locked it in his desk drawer. He couldn't face sending it out to publishers and risking the possibility of rejection. Or the would-be restaurateur who devised a fabulous thematic restaurant, spent months laboring over the plan, then dropped the whole idea when it came time to actually lease the property and open the doors. Or the speaker who developed scripts for a videocassette and couldn't decide which producer to go with.

The same thing happens frequently in all sorts of businesses. People spend time working up ideas, doing research, devising and planning innovations, and then let the whole thing slide away from them, just when they're ready to put it over the top. Why?

Perhaps because the closer you are to achievement the harder it all seems. There are also more subtle psychological reasons. When ideas and plans have taken a long time to evolve, people get attached to working on them. They hate to let the project go and send it on its way. For perfectionists, the work is never quite finished enough to turn loose. And if it's a particularly big plan, they might dread the actual implementation, which can be strenuous.

It's also hard to take the risk of testing your hard-won decisions, especially in a corporate world where putting yourself on the line is perceived as dangerous to your career. Many companies function on the principle of inertia, and in these organizations it's risky to rock the boat by promoting even a small change. But this means that the manager's career path will remain equally static.

Managers who succeed in making their ideas move have determination. Behind every enormous skyscraper that goes up there is a person determined to turn drawings into buildings. Donald Trump, the flamboyant real estate baron who has already made his mark on Manhattan's skyline, has said, "I never think of the negative. All obstacles can be overcome."

People who get ahead keep their eyes fixed on the end result—on what they want to achieve. And that end result is never the idea itself but the implementation of the idea. You can have the best ideas in the world, but upper management values and recognizes the person who turns ideas into actions.

Self Questions Create Successful Action

In some of my training programs I use an exercise called the Desert Survival Exercise. In this theoretical exercise, people are stranded in the desert with their gear. From the supplies on hand each person must arrange the items in order of their importance to his survival. Here's the important part of the exercise: If the person fails to set his objective first, he will make the wrong choices for survival. That is, he must first decide whether he will go forward or stay where he is. Every other decision is based on that objective.

Some managers are so eager to make a decision and get moving that they forget to set their objectives. So, every action you take should be preceded by this question: "What are my specific objectives? Short term? Long term?"

Then you can go on to the active part of the questioning:

"What specifically has to be done to carry them out?"

"How many people will this involve?"

"Who are the best people for the job(s)?"

"What information do they need?"

"How will they need my help?"

"Who else should be briefed to ensure success and cooperation?"

"How much time should I allot for each phase of the action?"

"What are the target due dates for each phase? What are the actual deadlines?"

"How will I get feedback on the ongoing progress?"

"How will I monitor long-term results?"

"Do I have any hidden resistance to seeing this project through?"

There is no such thing as a wishy-washy, insecure leader. Decisiveness is the essential element of success. The managers who get ahead make sound decisions and act on them. That doesn't mean they are perfect—every decision involves some risk, and you can't make the right choice every time. But asking the right questions in advance can reduce the risk and turn the odds in your favor.

Making your own decisions is one thing. Reaching a compromise with other people is another, equally important, sign of the manager with a future. How well and how smoothly you negotiate can affect your advancement.

18

Sharpen Your Negotiating Skills

Over lunch I asked one of the dynamic speaking agents I work with what she liked most about her job. She answered without hesitation and with a gleam in her eye: "Negotiating." Negotiating is a specialized form of problem solving. By definition, problem solving becomes negotiating when two people or groups start from opposing positions and attempt to reach a satisfactory middle ground, with each side hoping to give up as little as possible. It might more pointedly be described as the art of getting what you want with as little bloodshed as possible. Not all of us love it, but we all have to do it.

Negotiating and compromise are a fact of daily life and daily survival. Negotiating may involve money, power, and control. Or you can negotiate over who takes out the garbage, or who gets up to change the diapers on a crying baby. As a part of daily human interaction, negotiating is a tool that we all understand very well.

In the workplace negotiating may be relaxed and friendly, as it is when colleagues need to solve some relatively minor problem that's interfering with work. Or it may be complicated and emotional, as in situations involving unions and contracts. In business, the person who can negotiate in a variety of circumstances and conclude with everyone feeling satisfied about the outcome is worth his or her weight in gold to any organization. One of my clients is known as a masterful negotiator.

Her customers always say, "She can get me to say yes to anything and be happy about it."

The objective of negotiation is to reach some compromise acceptable to both parties; it should not be a game of win or lose. Compromise means the willingness to bargain, change, and keep an open mind. That's why the word "opponent" is not constructive. I prefer "counterpart." This makes it clear that you are in this together. You stand a better chance of negotiating successfully if your counterpart trusts you and respects you.

At the heart of all good negotiating is knowing how, and when, to ask questions. A good negotiator uses smart questions to gather information, and then to control the direction the negotiation takes.

I once watched a little girl playing with a small, flimsy sand pail on the beach. She saw a younger child playing with a larger, heftier pail. Instead of going over and grabbing the pail she wanted (which is a popular negotiating style, not only among children), she sized up the situation and went over to the younger kid and sweetly said, "That pail must be heavy for you. Wouldn't you like a pail that you could lift up easily?" The little girl happily walked away with the coveted pail, and the younger child was thrilled! That's a win-win negotiation.

Your Negotiating Style

As you can see, anyone can be a good negotiator. But to develop your skill it's important to recognize your own style and learn to accommodate it. You should know your own strengths and weaknesses. Your counterpart may know them well, and will not hesitate to take advantage of them. Are there certain issues or attitudes that tend to make you emotional and might cloud your judgment? In your heart, are you afraid you are a pushover? The time to bring these concerns to the surface is before you begin a negotiation, not during or after. The more in touch you are with yourself, the more confident you can be—and the better your results.

For example, Commanders are good hard-line negotiators—they are direct and self-contained, and are not apt to give out too much information. Because they thrive on confrontation, they are well suited for confrontational negotiations. They gather all the information they can, and they use it. On the down side, Commanders tend to be impatient and competitive. In any negotiation, patience is a virtue. To be more effective, Commander managers need to develop patience. They also need to damp down their competitive edge so they don't automatically approach others as combatants.

Convincers, because of their ability to express ideas well, can be adept at getting both sides to compromise in a negotiation. However, many Convincers are not organized enough to do all the preparation necessary to be a sharp negotiator. Convincers also may lose out on a deal because they care too much about social approval and don't want to be disliked even temporarily.

Carers are usually skillful at building the support and trust that serves as a base for the deal. But they are not confrontational and may give in under pressure. However, the fact that they are not direct communicators can be an advantage, especially when the counterparts in the negotiation are less direct.

C's, the Calculators, can really dig in their heels and be inflexible, but they'll have all the necessary facts and they'll stick at it. And this persistence may serve them well when it comes to pulling off a successful negotiation. They also may withdraw under pressure. Although Calculators are not direct communicators, their sensitivity and intuition can be a big help in negotiations. Creators are not strong negotiators and like to leave the negotiations to others. Material things don't matter too much to them, but when it's related to their "baby" they will fight for it like a tiger.

Confidence

A confident negotiating style goes a long way towards giving you the psychological advantage you need to win. Regardless of your style, all successful negotiators have one thing in common: they exude confidence. It can be a quiet confidence or a dominant presence. If you seem convinced that what you're asking for is the best choice, others will be too. If you waver, you send a signal that you're either unsure of what you want or unsure of how to get it.

I remember a lawsuit in which a public figure was suing a newspaper for libel. The newspaper corporation maintained its powerful image of integrity and honesty, even as it grew more and more doubtful that its case could be proved in court. The individual who was suing, despite the fact that things seemed to be going his way legally, appeared defensive and insecure. The power of the newspaper frightened him. As the pressure mounted, he backed down and withdrew the suit before a judgment could be reached.

A confident attitude should sink all the way into your bones. As Herb Cohen, negotiating expert and author of *You Can Negotiate Anything*, succinctly points out: "Power is based upon perception—if you think you've got it then you've got it. If you think you don't have it, even if you've got it, then you don't have it." Or as Sophia Loren likes to say, "Sex appeal is what the public thinks you've got."

Know Your Counterpart

To know your own negotiating style—your strengths and weaknesses— is one thing. It's equally, and sometimes more, important to recognize the negotiating style of your counterpart. Consider this axiom: "If I know more about you than you know about me, I can control the negotiation. And if I know more about you than *you* know about you, I can control you."

You must do as much research as possible on your counterpart. Remember the old saying "Know thine enemy"? Enemy or not, it pays to know the other side. You can't outmaneuver an unknown quantity.

If your counterpart is a Commander, give it to him fast and straight. If he is a Convincer, don't let yourself become sidetracked by extraneous issues. Nudge things along and keep bringing him back to the essential points.

If your counterpart is a Carer, constantly testing you, never show impatience. You can get him to agree because it's safe, secure, and good for his team. Never push a Stabilizer.

With Calculators you sometimes have to know when to push. I was once in a negotiation with a client for a series of seminars. He had agreed to twenty specific programs and then backed down to two. I sent him detailed background information on hundreds of previously successful programs and called frequently to see if he needed more. Finally, when we were face to face, I remembered his desire for perfection and his fear of criticism. I said, "You thought this was the right way to go two months ago and I know you make logical, sound decisions. Why change your mind now?" He made the decision on the spot to go with the whole program. So, if your counterpart is a stickler for details, wear him down with facts, logic, and information. And then make your move.

With Creators, let them feel you understand their ideas and concepts. Let them know that the deal under negotiation will free them from future worries over money, details, and people. Creators can often give in to get you off their backs, especially if they are in the midst of the creative process.

Reason vs. Emotion

Negotiation is above all an exercise in logic and clear thinking. Whenever emotion supercedes your reasoning power, for all intents and purposes you have lost. Negotiating requires a clear view of all the issues, all the shifting pros and cons, at all times. Getting angry or frustrated not only doesn't help; you are giving the advantage to your opponent.

A corollary to clear thinking is the ability to express yourself clearly. Negotiating is a specialized form of problem solving. If you fail to communicate your specific problems, needs, and bottom-line positions, you will probably not get what you want.

The Psychological Edge

You should always enter a negotiation armed with a list of concessions that you can make without any great sacrifice. But when you *do* give up something you consider minimal, create the impression that it's a significant compromise on your part. When a negotiator wins a major concession by giving up something insignificant, he gains a tremendous psychological boost. It's like trading a five-dollar bill for a ten.

Also, remember that the more time invested, the more the other party has at stake. When we were buying our computer we spent hours with each salesperson and at the end they kept giving us more and more concessions to get us to close the deal and make their time count.

If you are a Commander, remember that when it comes to negotiation, patience is indeed a virtue. I remember a line said by Oscar Homolka, playing a Russian general, in the film *War and Peace*. When news was brought to him that the French had won a victory in the field, Homolka smiled craftily and said, "That's all right. We can wait."

A negotiator who is anxious and impatient for a quick outcome cripples his chances of getting the best deal. Nobody wants a negotiation to go on for hours or days, but if you insist on pushing for an immediate resolution you're apt to give up much more than you have to. In fact, knowing that your counterpart is in a time bind may be a major advantage for your side. If you want something badly, holding back may turn out to be the best way to get it. Also, it's important to recognize the impact of the negotiation beyond the deal at hand. Could you actually be giving up something by winning? You might find yourself in the proverbial situation of winning the battle only to lose the war.

A manager I know recently spent several hours negotiating a simple misunderstanding with an outside consultant. "It was a trivial matter," she said, "and the problem would never have arisen if we had clearly understood the terms of our agreement before we started the job. As it was, we were at a standstill."

It seems that the consultant sent in a bill that reflected many more hours on the job than the manager had contracted for. "He said that with our various requests we had used up much more of his time than originally stated," the manager recalled. "Our position was that he didn't mention this extra time until he submitted his bill, which didn't leave us any options—that is, we were not given the opportunity to rethink our objectives and decide whether the extra hours were worth the price."

The manager and the consultant spent several hours on two different days working out a mutually satisfactory compromise. Why did the manager bother?

"Because I liked his work and hoped to continue working with him," she said. "Also, we wanted to avoid a more severe situation where we might wind up in a lawsuit. In the end, by taking time with the problem we both felt good about it. I appreciated all the extra effort he had put into the job, and we traded off some of that time for future jobs."

Smart Questions Negotiating

Good negotiating skills depend on your ability to ask smart questions and listen carefully to the answers. A negotiator's success depends on constantly "reading" his counterpart and responding with the proper strategy.

Big talkers, only interested in touting their point of view, are poor negotiators. Skillful negotiating means giving away as little as possible up front. Your first step in a negotiation is to gather information. Before you play your cards you should be getting a sense of your counterpart—his personality, his mind set, his attitudes, his weaknesses. The best way to accomplish this is to ask questions. Asking questions lets you listen more and reveal less.

Negotiating typically has three phases: preparation, opening bids, discussion and compromise.

Preparation

It is virtually impossible to be a good negotiator if you don't do your homework. If you're involved in a business negotiation with another company, for instance, it's vital to know the size and scope of the firm, their history, the resources at their disposal, their financial status, their corporate style and philosophy. All these elements will help you tune in to their point of view, their strengths and weaknesses, their bottom lines. As much as possible, have a grasp of whom you're dealing with before you start.

The more you know about the issues to be discussed, the better chance you will have of overcoming the objections and showing how you can both benefit. Try to find out as much as possible about the issues before going into negotiation. That may mean asking your counterpart for information, or you may want to go to others in the organization. Sometimes inside information can be the wild card you need.

ⓣ Part of your preparation is to set your goals. Before the negotiation, make sure you know the answers to these smart questions:

"What do I want to accomplish?"

"What are my real needs?"

"What is the most I could get?"

"What do I absolutely need?"

"Where specifically can I compromise?"

"What insignificant concessions can I make?"

"What concessions can I make that would hurt, but are still possible?"

"Do I have a clear understanding of what's at stake, what issues are involved, and all my bottom-line limitations?"

"What are my strengths?"

"What are my areas of vulnerability?"

"How can I deal with these?"

It is equally important for you to discover and fully understand what your counterpart is looking for. Do you know the answers to these two smart questions?

"What does my counterpart want?"

"Do I know why he wants it?"

You may think you know why someone wants something, and you may be completely off track. Warren, a vice president of a computer manufacturing firm, got into a head-to-head conflict with Jill, one of several fast-track managers on a planning committee to reorganize a production unit. Jill, an energetic, hardworking manager with her eye on advancement, did the research, developed the ideas with the team, and wrote the final version of the planning report. She insisted that she receive full credit for the task and that her name appear on the report cover. Warren, although appreciative of her work, wanted to submit the report under his name. It was company precedent for vice presidents to sign all reports emanating from their department.

"I did the work, I wrote the report," said Jill. "I deserve to have my name on it."

"To give credibility to the report and have influence with upper management, the report must be submitted under my umbrella and that of the planning committee," Warren argued.

Jill was dissatisfied and angry. Warren felt there was a danger that he might lose her, and she was the best of several managers who reported to him. Warren stewed over the problem and finally asked Jill to come in to see him, with the hope of smoothing over the problem.

"For some reason, when she walked in the office, a question popped into my mind," Warren recalled. "I asked her, 'Can you tell me a little more about why you want your name on the report?' "

"It's important to me to become more visible to upper management. I'm the first woman to produce such a report and it's important for me to set a precedent. I want them to know about my contribution."

Immediately, Warren had a different handle on the problem. "I'm not sure that putting your name on the cover is the best way to accomplish that," he said.

The solution they arrived at—the answer that satisfied them both— was to submit the report to top management with a cover letter describing Jill's contribution. In addition, when the report was presented orally, Jill would be the manager to deliver the presentation.

The point is this: Do not assume that you know the reason behind someone's demands. This amicable agreement was reached because one person took the trouble to discover the real reason—the "why"—behind the demands.

Questions for Opening Bids

It would be ideal if in all negotiations, you could both say simultaneously: "This is what I'd like, and this is what I'm willing to settle for." But in most cases the person who reveals this information first loses, unless he or she has the counterpart in a squeeze.

Formal and definite statements of position, especially at the start of a negotiation, sometimes polarize the negotiators. But if you ask your counterpart a few smart questions, informally, you can learn a lot of valuable information and at the same time open up the negotiation:

"What would you like to see happen here?"

"What are your goals?"

"What in your mind is really the crux of the matter?"

Questions That Lead to Discussion and Compromise

The golden rule of negotiating is "Make yourself ask for more than you want, and then be quiet and wait." But sooner or later you're going to have to say something. Smart questions allow you to find out all you need to know and guide the discussion in the way you want. Ask your counterpart:

"What do you see as areas of common ground or common interest?"

"Is there anything about my position that I haven't made clear?"

"Perhaps I can explain my position more fully. Are there specific areas where you feel I'm being inflexible or unreasonable?"

"Is there a more constructive way that we can approach this problem together?"

"Is there anything about your position that you'd like to clarify or expand on?"

"What sort of answers can we come up with that will be better for each of us?"

A good negotiator stays flexible. While patience is valuable, you may also need to be quick—quick to alter your strategy, quick to pick up on a new factor or pounce on an advantage, quick to change direction if necessary. On a moment's notice good negotiators can decide to forfeit certain prizes in order to get different ones.

The way to be alert to shifting opportunities is to constantly ask yourself certain key questions throughout the negotiation:

"What is my counterpart's stated reason for this particular demand?"

"What could be his underlying reason?"

"What is really going on?"

"What is my bottom line?"

"What is my bottom bottom line?"

"If my counterpart makes this particular concession, how can I help him save face?"

Throughout the negotiation, pay attention to eye contact and shifts in body stance. Ask yourself, "Is my counterpart sending any nonverbal signals? If so, what do they mean?"

Such a signal can tell you when to hold the line and when to push forward. I was once able to score a lucrative contract because I witnessed a change in my counterpart's stance. Throughout the negotiation he appeared nonchalant and casual. Then I noticed him checking his watch when he thought I wasn't looking. He started fidgeting. His body language gave away the fact that he was running out of time. I held to my bottom line and he gave in.

So, whether you're negotiating the price of a car, a deal with your landlord, or a labor contract for your company, watch for the unconscious signals the counterpart sends out.

Closing Negotiations

When you close a negotiation, make it firm. Sign, shake on it, whatever. But when it's done, it's done. End the negotiation with civility. Don't slip away as though you've taken your counterpart for a ride, because that's enough to make him feel that way. You and your counterpart should feel comfortable and confident with the results. One good, mutually beneficial deal paves the way for others.

Afterwards look for a way to follow up. Make an effort to speak to or write to your counterpart. Invite him or her out for a drink to celebrate. Or set a date for a future meeting. But don't just offer a token invitation. You must carry it out. You have everything to gain from establishing this kind of continuity. The next time you do business together you'll have a platform of mutual respect and understanding to begin from.

Negotiations are a fact of life. They take place in every business, in every circumstance. And managers who get ahead know how to make the most of each negotiating opportunity. But there's one special kind of negotiation that stands out in every successful manager's life. This particular negotiation has a tremendous personal impact on your present life and an even greater influence on your future: negotiating for a raise.

19

Negotiating a Raise

Do you feel you're paid as much as you're worth? Funny, I've never met anyone who answered "Yes" to that question. There's only one way to get more money: ask for it. It's not an unreasonable demand, and it's not asking for a favor. Raises are a normal part of business life. Everyone, including your boss, would like to take home a bigger slice of the pie.

In certain situations, it's actually more harmful *not* to ask. People in the corporate world are often judged by the size of their paycheck more than by their ability—even within the company. Also, if you don't request an increase after a certain amount of time, your boss may think you're crazy, or at least unambitious.

While annual or semiannual raises might be standard in the firm, your chances of securing a large sum are greater if you bring it up. During a debate with Sandra, a second-line supervisor for an airline, I reiterated that she would get ahead faster if she asked for a raise rather than waiting for review time. She countered, "It's never done in my company." But since she was ambitious, she decided to give it a try. Not only did she get the raise, and another at review time, but her boss (who had never thought her assertive enough to get ahead) began to groom her for future promotions. For the most part, bosses are proud of the go-getters in their departments.

* * *

Managers destined to get ahead always keep trying to increase their salary. If you allow yourself to be underpaid, you lose respect. Ironically, even your boss will probably value you more if he's paying you more. And you'll naturally be more motivated when you feel your talents are appreciated—especially when that appreciation is reflected in financial terms.

In other words, no raise or promotion is achieved in a vacuum. Both are functions of your value to your boss and to the company, and of your political position within the firm.

Timing Your Request

The most important element of asking for a raise is to time your request so that you (not your boss or your company) are in the strongest position possible. It may help if your boss is in a good mood and not particularly pressured or harried. But this will not get you your raise. What *will* get you a raise is if you've just brilliantly completed an important project, pulled off a major financial coup, or otherwise proved or underlined your special worth.

Recently I observed a young MBA graduate, hardworking and ambitious, get herself a $10,000 raise. Lesley works for a giant real estate development firm in Florida. She had done a phenomenal job in the year she had been with the company, and they wanted her to become their divisional manager in the Orlando area, with a salary increase of $2,500 a year. She knew she was needed and she also knew that she was much better at her job that other managers in the firm. Lesley surveyed the territory and accurately assessed that there were not enough good managers to match the company's rapid growth. She replied, "I feel the job is worth $10,000." That's all she said. She waited, and eventually received the full amount.

If you've got a very visible success story or some attention-getting ideas to show off, now is the time to pull them out of the hat. And stay alert for opportunities. If your boss has just lost two good people, that is an especially good time to ask. Or if several people in your department have just left, your experience and willingness to take on added responsibility could be priceless to your superiors at this time.

Self Questions to Evaluate Your Timing

Asking for a raise is usually a difficult and emotionally charged situation, but asking yourself some smart questions in advance can lessen anxiety and help you smoothly achieve your goal. Like any other negotiation, asking for a raise requires some homework. And the best way to do this is ask yourself some very smart questions.

Take a good look at corporate policy as well as the financial health of your company and even your industry. Periods of economic depression or widespread financial losses, for example, do not bode well for your chances, unless you are perceived as invaluable in solving the current problem.

To get an overall view of your company's status, ask yourself these smart questions:

"What had been the pattern of raises managers in my position have received in the past?"

"To what extent is compensation a fixed part of the budget process?"

"How much freedom does my boss have in deciding on raises?"

"What are the current conditions of business within the company? Within the industry?"

"What are the company's plans for the immediate future?"

"What is my role in those plans?"

The next step is to evaluate your position *vis à vis* your boss. How does your boss—and *her* boss—look upon raises in general, and how are they likely to feel about you when you make this particular request? To get an overall picture, ask yourself these questions:

"How does my boss treat me?"

"Does she seem to trust and value me?"

"Does she praise or criticize specific parts of my performance?"

"What is my boss's position in the firm? What are her ambitions for growth?"

"Does my boss take me for granted?"

"How well does she understand what I do?"

"How much does she know about my bottom-line value and contributions?"

"How does my boss talk about me to her peers and to upper management?"

The answers to these questions will point out the strengths and weaknesses of your position. For example, if your boss takes you for granted, it's up to you to change her attitude before asking for a raise. If she seems unaware of your contributions, you will have to make your bottom-line value obvious.

When considering your boss and your relationship with her, try to anticipate any criticisms that she might bring up so you can counter or negotiate around these points. Remember that no individual's performance is so flawless that it can't be legitimately criticized. You should never become offended or defensive in a negotiation, and the best way to keep your cool is to be prepared.

Ask yourself some tough questions in advance:

"Has my boss indicated dissatisfaction with any aspects of my performance in the past?"

"Have I followed up on her suggestions? Can I point to improvement?"

"Where else have I shown improved performance or increased productivity in the recent past?"

"In what areas might my boss say I could do better?"

"How can I respond in a positive way to these comments?"

"What special strengths or achievements can I bring up to counter weaker areas?"

Establishing Your Value

The best way to move ahead in any company is to establish your value to the organization and make your contributions visible. One way to establish your value is to keep adding to your Career and Confidence Inventory (discussed in the following chapter). Another is to interview for other jobs at least once a year. (Don't let anyone—including your boss—get too complacent.)

But the most important aspect of preparing for either a promotion or salary negotiations is pinning down your value to your firm. You're in the best position when you can prove your worth impressively in dollars, growth percentages, or other concrete terms.

Ed Weihenmayer, Vice President of Human Resources at Kidder, Peabody & Co., emphasizes this point: "No matter what task you're working on, always ask yourself, 'How does what I'm doing impact on the bottom line?' "

If you're in sales it's fairly simple to identify your bottom-line contribution to the company. But all employees should try to look for a bottom-line connection when getting ready to negotiate for a raise. If you're a copywriter in an advertising agency, for example, and you wrote a successful slogan that helped your agency keep an account that bills $2 million annually, that's a dollar value that's tough to refute.

You can also look for other ways to assess your corporate worth. What is your reputation within your department? Within your company? Within your industry?

And what is the value of someone in your position on the open market? You should always be aware of competitive salaries within your firm as well as outside it. If you can show that your firm is paying 10 percent less than its competition for the same level of job, you have a strong case. When other companies are willing to hire you for more money (or your company thinks they are), you will always appear more desirable. That's why I advise managers to go out and look once or twice a year. Occasional job interviewing keeps things in perspective. (You might also discover you're not worth as much as you think.) Going to professional conferences is another way to network within your industry and stay abreast of what's going on in terms of job openings and salaries.

Another smart question for you to ask yourself: "How easily can I be replaced?" If you have special talents or skills or experience, if it would be hard to replace you, you are in an excellent negotiating position.

But this strategy has been known to backfire. A company may be uncomfortable with someone who thinks he is "irreplaceable" and always has the firm over a barrel. Your assistant probably knows more about the job than you think —and when you come right down to it, no one is irreplaceable (only expensive). Know your worth, yes, but don't get carried away.

It's good strategy to demonstrate your value as often as you can. If you've saved hundred of hours by reorganizing department systems, be ready to say so. Or if you've been able to reduce overtime, shout it out.

Choose Your Strategy

Once you've defined your overall value, it's time to select a strategy. When you ask for either a raise or a promotion, you must have a specific approach planned out ahead of time. Given your particular circumstances, what is the best way to present your case to your boss?

The Straightforward Approach

If you have a long string of accomplishments, you may want to approach your boss in a fairly straightforward manner. You matter-of-factly point to your achievements and to documented evidence of increased profits, and ask for your well-deserved reward and recognition. You show confidence and control; there is no need to be demanding or emotional in any way.

The Ultimatum Strategy

The straightforward approach works well in many corporations. However, after examining your boss's attitudes and those of your company, you may decide that a stronger power play is necessary. Attempt this only when you have a lot of ammunition on your side—you feel you are indeed of great value and your firm is well aware of it—and you feel secure enough to take the risk. Ultimatums work best when you have an ace up your sleeve or some special knowledge that your boss needs. Your boss may not realize just how much he needs you until you force the issue. Perhaps you have a handle on the company's five major accounts and the client wants to deal only with you. Or an audit is coming up and you have the figures.

If you threaten to leave if your terms are not met, you must be fully prepared to pack up. If you wave another job offer in their faces, you should be quite willing to take it. This is not a good time to bluff; your job and your career could be at stake. When you play for high stakes, risk is part and parcel of the game.

Craig, a Commander, full of self-confidence and with an overinflated ego, was sure his company, a small public relations firm, couldn't do without him. Without preparation or a backup offer, he stormed into the president's office and demanded a large increase and a promotion to vice president of marketing, or else. The president, although valuing him, knew that Craig had serious flaws in his ability to deal with staff and decided that this was a good time to let him go. He refused the ultimatum and Craig had nowhere to go but out.

Even when you win with your ultimatum strategy, however, there could be other drawbacks. No one likes being painted into a corner, especially not your superiors. When you consider the ultimatum approach, take into account the ill will you may create. But also keep in mind that nice guys don't always make the most money, and that many people respect someone who drives a hard bargain. A subtle ultimatum, a veiled implication, can be very effective without spelling it out.

The Education Strategy

What if, after answering all the self questions about your performance and your boss's attitude, you reach the conclusion that you're not a superstar? What if you do good, steady work but have no startling figures to report? What if you have an adequate relationship with your boss, but he seems to take your work for granted? Are you still entitled to a raise? You bet you are. You simple need to employ a more subtle approach.

You must begin a campaign to educate your boss as to your true value long before the salary question is broached. Look for opportunities to clarify the skills and nuances necessary to performing well at your job. Let your boss know the strategies you've worked out that make his or her job easier and the operation run more smoothly. Your boss can't appreciate you fully when he doesn't know exactly what it is you do. While you're implementing this strategy, don't be overly self-congratulatory, and don't make it seem as if you're complaining about being overworked. Your attitude should remain positive and cooperative as you gradually make the powers-that-be aware of your difficulties and your successes.

The Promotion Strategy

The most obvious way to justify a raise is to first get a promotion, a new title, or increased job duties. To a certain extent, being promoted is the logical result of doing your job well and playing your political cards right. But sometimes you have to take things into your own hands.

Analyze the range of your job responsibilities. Then ask yourself two smart questions:

"Are there more visible, complicated, or sophisticated tasks that I can concentrate on?"

"Are there less important or more routine items that I can safely delegate?"

By answering fully these two questions, you can begin to carve out a promotional path for yourself. You may be able to subtly shift your job responsibilities to a higher level and gradually change the perimeters of the job itself. It's not uncommon for a hard worker hired as an office clerk to eventually run the office. Who hasn't heard of the secretary who became CEO? And once your job has changed, it's easy to prove your increased responsibilities and show that your salary should be adjusted accordingly.

The Attitude to Take

Whatever strategy you choose, a positive attitude is vital. Remember that you are entitled to a raise because of the good work and extra effort you put in. When you go in to make your claim, go with the assumption that you're going to win.

You should be confident and natural. Don't change your personality just because the issue is money!

Be pleasant. Accusing your boss of failing to appreciate you is not a good way to get him on your bandwagon. You might even begin by telling your boss that you value his support and fairness and that you know you can count on him in this instance too.

Reassure your boss that he's doing the right thing by raising your salary and that you will respond with renewed loyalty and enthusiasm.

And don't make it seem that money is your sole motivation for doing a good job. A fair salary should be just one way of compensating you for loyalty and hard work.

It is also a good idea to avoid the obvious statement "I want a raise," with its demanding and poutish feeling. Try something a little more sophisticated—"an adjustment in salary," "increased compensation," or "more monetary recognition."

A List of Don'ts

While you're rehearsing your positive attitude, it's helpful to examine this list of negatives:

Do not: plead (remember, you are not asking for a favor)
apologize
complain or whine
pester (unless your boss is a Commander or a Convincer)
get defensive
get angry or emotional

Don't

Setting Up the Meeting

In terms of actually setting a time for the initial meeting, some experts suggest that you schedule a formal appointment with your boss, specifically to deal with this topic. In my experience, however, this can lead to unnecessary tension and anxiety because of the negative implications surrounding the subject. If you refuse to explain in advance why you want to meet, this can also cause concern since it is automatically assumed that the topic must be serious and urgent.

In most cases, I feel it works better to tie your raise request in with some other private discussion you're having with your boss, whether it's a regular update meeting or a project review. This approach tends to be more successful since it reduces the need for a formal and perhaps awkward pronouncement and makes it clear (especially in your own mind) that your asking for a raise naturally evolves from your day-to-day work. But don't make the mistake of thinking that an informal approach means that you can be any less prepared.

Naming Your Figure

Whatever your strategy, you should always be the first to state the figure you had in mind. If your boss has the first word, he or she will undoubtedly name an amount that's too low, and you will be in the awkward position of having to say that's not enough.

Figure out what you think is a fair and realistic amount and then inflate it somewhat (if you'd settle for 15 percent, go for 20) so you will be in a position to negotiate down. Don't go wild and ask for the moon (unless you really and truly have a shot at it). Remember that you want to emerge from the negotiation in a winning position, so don't stack the odds against yourself. Aim for something you can realistically accomplish.

Smart Questions That Get Raises

How can you use questions to generate a positive response from your boss? Try these:

> "I've been doing two jobs for three months. Don't you think it's fair that I get paid for them?"
>
> "Do you believe that managers should be paid what they're worth?"
>
> "You don't want me to work without the reward, do you?"
>
> "I will be more productive and feel better about my position. Don't you think that would be best for both of us?"
>
> "Money is a symbol of what we think something is worth. Don't you agree?"
>
> "What would make you see me as more valuable?"
>
> "How can we both come out ahead here?"
>
> "What happens when a valued employee is paid less than he's worth?"
>
> "What about the $30,000 I saved the company last week?"
>
> "I increased my worth on the open market about $10,000 when I went from account executive to senior account executive. What compensation can you offer?"

Countering Your Boss's Strategies

There are several typical ways in which bosses try to evade the issue and thus avoid increasing your paycheck. I remember the first time I tried to get a raise. My boss was the champion guilt-producer in the company.

He cried "Poor ... No budget ... I'm harried by other problems ... Come back later." But I was well rehearsed and calmly kept coming back to the point: I had tripled my sales goals and wanted compensation. Although I did not get the raise, I was promoted to senior account executive; three months later, after two other "raise interviews," I got the compensation. Preparation, persistence, and patience are the keys to any negotiation.

So, if your boss tells you in confidence that the company or department is losing money, do not be angry, unbelieving, or unsympathetic—and do not feel guilty. Simply say that you fully understand, but you have your own financial needs to deal with. Fairness dictates that you be paid a proper amount for the work you do. Does the company charge less for its products or services when a consumer or client is in financial straits?

If the company is truly in trouble but you decide to stick it out, you might suggest stock options, profit sharing, or guaranteed bonuses when the financial outlook improves (get it in writing).

When an employer tells you that you deserve a raise but his hands are tied by company policy, there are several ways you can go. Ask these smart questions:

> "Have there been no exceptions?" (Make sure you've investigated in advance.)
>
> "Who can bend the rules?"

You may decide to go over your boss's head (with your boss's full knowledge), although this can create some bad blood. If you decide this is your best course of action, tell your boss that you completely understand his position and realize that he does not have the proper authority to fly in the face of company policy; then politely ask a smart question: "Who does?"

Smart Questions Can Get You Promoted

Even if your raise request is turned down flat, don't go away empty-handed. If there's a cap to what someone in your position can be paid, for example, it's a good time to negotiate for a promotion. Try these questions:

"If I can't get a raise right now, what else can you offer?" (Give your boss time to think it over; come back later for his answer.)

"As you know, I've been getting extra responsibility. How about a new title?"

"How can you increase my responsibilities?"

"Can I work more closely with you on the new departmental reorganization?"

"When can I receive more education?"

"Can I make the proposals to the management committee?"

"Can I work with upper management?"

"Will you send me to the industry's next top managerial conference?"

If you gain any of these concessions, you may get a direct promotion, or at least put yourself in line for a future promotion, greater opportunities, and ultimately more money. You've created the expectation, and your boss, if you do a good job, will want to help you.

When you negotiate for a raise, be strong, be confident. Never hesitate. Above all, do everything you can to perform your job with excellence. No boss wants to lose a winner. Think how you would feel if one of your key performers said he was leaving. You know how tough it is to recruit, select, and train a top achiever. You will do everything in your power, and more, to keep that person. If you're good—especially if you're great—at your job, your boss feels the same way about you. Believe in yourself and keep asking.

But what happens if your career path seems blocked in your company? What if the direction open to you is not the direction you choose? Can you change jobs, or even change careers, and win?

20

Finding a Job with a Future

Managers on the fast track look for ways to move up—and sometimes moving up means moving out. Can you hopscotch from company to company and come out on top? You certainly can, and if you're bogged down in your present organization you should calculate a career move.

Finding a job you love, and a job that will pull you ahead speedily, is a challenge. Don't dread it; look for ways to have fun with the experience. After all, if you work up until you are sixty-five you'll be working some 96,000 hours. You might as well make them count.

Two fundamental tasks take much of the guesswork out of getting ahead: deciding which job you want, and then marketing yourself to get it. The first part can actually be harder than the second. Choosing what you want to do involves a great deal of self-questioning. Once you choose the field, you need to select the companies that might be right for you and to figure out what specific jobs lie on your career path. From there, you must arrange an interview with the individual in each company who has the power to hire you. And sell yourself to that person.

Figuring Out the Path

While most companies do not have direct, rigid lines of ascent—that is, specific rules about promotions from one job to the next—it's usually pretty clear where the opportunities for advancement lie within a company. For example, in pharmaceutical companies top management is promoted from product managers, who frequently were promoted from the sales force. In automobile companies, plant managers usually come from production and related areas of plant operation, rather than from personnel or sales. In the steel industry, managers with ambition should not head for the advertising or marketing department. But in a company devoted to cosmetics or other consumer goods, advertising and marketing are in the front line, and these jobs tend to be positions with great potential for growth.

The key is to recognize that the exposure to top management depends upon the type of company you work for, and to select the most probable path of opportunity. The following method for finding a top job with a future has been developed over a long period of time and is based on my experience as a consultant to numerous corporations. I have sat through hundreds of job interviews and reviewed thousands of resumes. What you read here is a distillation of that experience—how to make it work for you. If you are thinking of changing jobs to jackrabbit your way to the top, or if you are looking to alter your career path in your present organization, here is the basic technique that will send you on your way. The process is so sound that it can work in either situation.

Five Steps to a Top Job

Finding the right job requires a targeted marketing approach. This is not an effort in mass marketing, but a highly selective undertaking. Your quest is comprised of five specific steps, each with a specific purpose. Although the overall goal is to secure a job, if you focus only on the end result you stand to miss out. Every step must receive your complete attention, and each must be fulfilled before going on to the next. In brief, the five steps are:

1. Develop a "Career and Confidence Inventory." A Career Inventory lists assignments you've had in the past, the actions you took for each one, and what you achieved with each. Ideally, when you finish your career inventory you will have a list of ten to twenty Assignments, Actions, and Achievements (AAA's). The object of this step is to define the offer you will ultimately make in Step 3.

2. Draw up a list of at least twenty targeted companies, each with the name of the person who might hire you. The objective is to compile or refine a workable mailing list. If you're looking within your present organization, make a list of the divisions and division heads whom you want to work for.

3. Send a carefully drafted letter targeted to the special interests of each person on your mailing list. The objective is to get their attention, and the letter will include your offer.

4. Establish a persistent phone call strategy to follow up the letters. The objective is to get an appointment for an interview.

5. Go to the interview. Your goals are to gather information about the company and to get a job offer.

Your Career and Confidence Inventory

Modesty, says renowned economist John Kenneth Galbraith, is a much overrated virtue. Looking for a job is no time to play shrinking violet. You have to sell yourself, and before you can do that you must believe in yourself. Creating your Career and Confidence Inventory is a way to build your self-esteem and also to define what you have to offer.

You deserve to have a good job and be well paid for it. Choosing the right sort of career involves delving into who you are, what you want, and where you are going with your life. And this is the hard part. Before you can sell yourself, you have to know what you're selling and why. To give yourself a start, answer these smart questions:

"What am I best at?"

"What do I like most?"

"Who's willing to pay me the most?"

"What exactly do I want to do?"

"Where do I want to do it?"

"Are there other departments or divisions in my own company where I would have these opportunities?"

"If not, which organizations interest me?"

"What are my long-term goals?"

"What price am I willing to pay for success?"

With your answers in mind, invest your time in developing your Career and Confidence Inventory. Employers are looking for people with skills in three basic areas: technical, human relations, or conceptual. Which category—or categories—do you want to fall into?

"What are my strongest technical talents?"

"What about my sales abilities and sales performance?"

"Do I seem to handle other people well?"

"Do I get along with most people?"

"How do I rate myself when it comes to thinking up new ideas?"

"How much money have I saved or made for my company?"

When you have selected one or two general categories that interest you, start to compile a list of ten to twenty Assignments, Actions, and Achievements (AAA's) that relate to those broad categories. To make the list you may need to work backwards. Begin by asking yourself some smart questions that will help you remember your accomplishments.

"Have I ever saved money or time?"

"What projects have I organized?"

"What excellent people have I hired?"

"How have I been innovative?"

"What difficult problems have I solved?"

"Have I made some tough decisions?"

These questions will help you remember all the impressive accomplishments that you may have forgotten. Once you've remembered the Accomplishment, go back and tie in the Assignment and the Action that led to the Accomplishment. Now, write out a complete list of your AAA's. Here's an example of one I used when I was looking for a job in sales and marketing:

Assignment: "My job was to open up the West Coast market for my company."

Action: "I achieved this by mobilizing a strategic marketing system."

Accomplishment: "At the end of the year the West Coast market accounted for 40 percent of my company's gross volume, which was 25 percent over our projections."

Your Mailing List

The approach I advocate is to make a list of twenty companies you want to work for and the job you might be interested in. If you're looking within your own organization, make a list of the division you want to work for and the job you want. Then send a specific letter to each person who is in a position to give it to you. Your best bets for finding this information are people you already know in the business or sources at the public library. The more specific your marketing approach, the better. Direct-mail marketers say the better the mailing list and the better the offer you make to the list, the more responses you get.

Forget about preparing a resume. Resumes are used primarily to screen people out. I've sat in on so many hiring sessions where we plowed through a pile of resumes, elimiating most of them. Why bother? Resumes are primarily for mass marketing or for lower-level jobs.

The Letter

The purpose of the letter is to get the attention of the prospective interviewer and make that person want to see you. Send your letter only to the people you have researched, who you know have the power to hire you. You don't need to know whether there is an actual job opening. People are always leaving, moving up or out or sideways, leaving vacant slots.

Your letter should be brief but packed with information, confidence, and benefits for your prospective employer. Start by telling about your experience—what you've done for others. Do this in one short, punchy opening line: "If you are looking for a dynamic results-oriented sales manager with a proven track record, look no further." Concentrate on what *you* can do for him and the company.

Include two AAA's, targeted to a specific job. The AAA's you describe must be something that could be applied to the company. For example, the Assignment and Accomplishment described earlier could be used for any marketing or sales job but would not be appropriate for a design job.

The Action step that you describe should be short and not too specific. You don't want to give them a blow-by-blow account of what you did; you want to tantalize the reader.

Above all, your letter must contain an irresistible offer. And that's what the AAA's give you. By concisely giving two AAA's you offer a track record—your past performance—which is the best indicator of what you can do for the reader. If your offer isn't tempting, everything else is irrelevant. Concentrate on how your AAA's might benefit this new company.

Don't tell the reader what he can do for you or what you are looking for. No one's looking for anyone to do favors for.

Conclude with "I will call you on _____ to make an appointment at your earliest convenience."

A resume can never do the job that this kind of letter can do. A resume is only an outline; the letter described here contains an irresistible offer. When you're going for a growth job, a letter, plus an interview, can be enough. In this kind of job search, you bypass personnel and appeal directly to the person you will work for. By definition, this will be a busy person who probably would ignore a resume but might read a short and enticing letter.

The Telephone Call

The follow-up telephone call has only one objective: to get the person to grant you an interview. Be persistent, but agreeably so. Keep asking for the appointment. Do not allow yourself to be screened out or interviewed over the telephone. The more you say on the phone, the less the person needs to see you. If you are asked a question, you might reply, "I can answer that much better in person. When can I come in to see you?" Once when I was trying to get an interview for an important job I rented a limousine and took the person to the airport. If you really want to see someone you will find a way.

Interview Goals

Once you've got the appointment, you have two objectives. The first goal is to find out as much as possible about the job, your potential boss, and the company. The second is to sell yourself. Whether or not to accept the job should always be *your* decision. Even if you don't want it, secure a job offer. You'll need all the selling practice you can get.

When you go for an offer, to get a "yes" you come into an interview with a different attitude. It's the difference between a dress rehearsal and an opening night. Show them that you want the job, not that you're desperate for it.

One reason to make sure that you interview well, no matter what, is that other possibilities may arise. A friend of mine applied for a position as production manager at an advertising agency. There was no opening, but because she seemed too good to lose they offered her a job as an account executive. She took it and is now a vice president.

Your main goal is to find out what the interviewer's problem is (the work he or she needs done), then to demonstrate how you can help solve it. Remember: you're doctor, he's the patient.

Beatrice Buckler, the former publisher and editor of *Working Woman*, told Jane Trahey how she felt about hiring staff for her magazine: "I want people who can convince me they are interested in my needs. I don't want to hear about their psyches. . . . I don't want to hear what her needs are. I want her to tell me how she will help me."

Even though you want a job that furthers your career, your attitude should be focused squarely on the present. Ask not so much where you can go as what you can do with the job available. And let that attitude show in the interview.

This is the usual scenario before a manager begins interviewing: "I'm desperate for a good person. My boss is furious that I've put off looking for so long, and my staff is overworked and dissatisfied. I've got so much pressure, so little time, and I've got five people to interview today." Never underestimate the anxiety of the person interviewing you—especially when that person is your future boss. (Personnel interviewers don't feel as anxious, since they are always interviewing.)

As unbelievable as it seems to a harried job-seeker, the interviewer has more at stake than you do. His or her job is on the line in a real way. Smart companies evaluate their managers by the people they hire, and too many poor hiring choices weaken the reputation of even the best managers. Knowing this fact when you are being interviewed gives you a distinct advantage. Remember that you are there to reassure them that you are the best person for the job. Anything you can do to reduce the interviewer's risks and anxieties will make it easier for him to say yes.

You have two important subtexts in the interview: "What's your problem? What can I do to help?" This is the attitude you make obvious to the interviewer. The second attitude is your secret agenda: "Is this the right job for me?"

Every question you ask should come out of these two contexts. An attitude of confidence and control should be evident from the first moments of the interview, especially if you are up for a responsible executive position. It takes an interviewer less than ten seconds to get a first impression of a candidate. Long before you have a chance to say anything intelligent, your attitude and your body language have conveyed volumes.

Positioning Yourself

The impression you make on the interviewer—your future boss—carries over into the job itself. If you position yourself as strong, capable, and ambitious in the interview, you begin to establish your position and reputation—your power base—for the future.

Most people do not realize it, but once someone has gambled on you and offered you a job you are in a powerful position. That person wants you to succeed. You must recognize this, and get all that you can up front in the way of equipment, money, staff, and resources to make a strong start.

You can shave years off your upward career path if you are wise to this idea. Leonard was offered a job as manager of an electronic data processing unit. Two things stood out at his job interview: the area he was to head had a long-standing complaint of being short-staffed and short on space. Before he took the job, Leonard got a commitment that he could hire necessary staff and get additional space. As a result, he started off in a strong position with his staff, since their previous two bosses had done nothing. At the same time, upper management respected him because of his astute bargaining. Down the line, Leonard was able to accomplish twice as much as other managers because of his fast start, and he continued to expand his power base.

To recapitulate: When you get the interview you're after, you have two goals. In the first part of the interview, get information. In the second part, actively sell yourself. In between, decide if you want the job. Smart questions can carry you through each of these phases with flying colors.

The Smart Questions Interview

You never know exactly how an interview will be conducted until you get there—which doesn't mean that you should wing it. On the contrary, you should be thoroughly prepared for anything. Do your homework.

You should already know a great deal about the company, and something about your potential boss. Sketch out a list of at least ten questions that you would like to have answered sometime during the course of the interview. Carry this list with you, and if your mind goes blank take it out of your briefcase and read it over. Or bring it out at the beginning and keep it in front of you. Remember that one of the ways smart interviewers evaluate you is by the quality of the questions you ask, so be prepared with good ones.

Nowadays there are some standard questions you can expect to be asked, and you should prepare in advance your answers concerning your own strengths and weaknesses. Some pointers: only reveal your strengths, even if you disguise some of them as weaknesses. For example, a positive weak point might be that you tend to be a bulldog—you never let go of a problem until it's solved. Another: you're too much of a perfectionist, but you're working on it. With these kinds of weaknesses, who needs strengths? But don't invent desirable qualities out of the blue; really examine yourself and select your most saleable strengths, and then make sure you communicate them. Don't just answer the questions you're asked—use them as an opportunity to tell the interviewer everything that you want him to know.

The interviewer should set the style and tone of the interview. If he's a skilled and experienced interviewer, which few people are, he's likely to suggest that you ask questions as the interview progresses. If he's insecure or inexperienced he may say, "I'll start off with some questions. If you have anything you want to ask, reserve your questions for the end. I'll allow plenty of time to answer." Or if the interviewer is a real game-player, he may say, "This is strictly a fact-gathering expedition. Our purpose right now is to find out something about you and if you will fit in with Continental Widgets. I hope you will answer freely. If you seem to be the right candidate, there will be time to discuss the job and any questions you have in a follow-up session."

Any of these scenarios is possible, and it's up to you to decide what you want to do about them. You may play by the rules the interviewer establishes, or you may object. But don't merely react blindly; tackle the situation with your eyes open.

The fact is, you cannot make a sound decision and sell yourself as the "doctor" until you get enough information. It's a given that the interviewer has more control over the situation than you do, and all of your preparation is based on trying to get some of that control for yourself.

The more questions you ask, the more control you have. Participate actively in the interview. Do not sit back and let the interviewer pick you over to see if you have the goods. What does he or she have to offer? What's this job all about? Whom would you report to? What are the department's greatest concerns?

Opening Gambits

Let's say that this is a normal interview situation, an exchange of questions and answers. Try to ask the first question—pleasantly. Take control smoothly and comfortably. Your objective is to find out as much as possible about the particular job, the people you'll be working with, and the potential for growth. You can begin by expressing interest in your interviewer. What is one serious mistake that many high-level job candidates make? They hesitate to ask questions that get their potential boss talking.

Every situation is different, but show in your questions that you have done some research about the company and are interested in learning how your interviewer fits in or contributes to the organization. If you can find out something about the person ahead of time, it gives you a distinct advantage: "I recently saw your name mentioned in the 'Business Today' section of the paper in relation to your upcoming union negotiations." Or "What are the things you feel have contributed to your success here?"

Suppose you've come through a recommendation. "John Smith has gotten us together because he thought there might be something mutually beneficial for us. What has he told you about me?" Or more casually, "How do you and John Smith know each other?"

Staying with the Interview

Questions can keep you in control and ensure that you reach your objectives:

"Your company is definitely on the move. What are the things you find most satisfying?"

"How did you come into your present position?" (You want to get a feeling for how career paths form in the company.)

"How many managers report to you?" (Seven is the magic number.

More than seven and the boss isn't going to have time for you.)

"How are managers cross-trained in your department?"

"Can you tell me what things you are most likely to delegate?"

"Are there certain things you don't like to delegate?"

"How often will you meet with me to discuss problems and issues?"

"What are your primary needs and concerns at the present time?"

Build questions as if *you* were hiring someone, but in reverse. Ask "How will I relate to the specific job, the team, the organization as a whole?"

As in other situations where control is vital, most of your time should be spent in asking smart questions and listening carefully to the answers—not in talking endlessly about yourself without a clue to what the other person actually needs to hear. Further, you will be judged by the quality of the questions you ask.

My own most challenging job interview was with a sharp sales manager at Bell and Howell. He saw that I had had a varied background and asked me: "Do you think this job could satisfy you because of your many interests?"

I realized that denying it wouldn't help, so I asked a smart question instead: "Does your job satisfy all of your talents?"

I was subsequently offered the job, and I believe that one question was the turning point.

Specific Job-Related Questions

During the course of the interview, make sure you learn the answers to these questions:

"What do you foresee as possible obstacles or problems I might have?"

"In terms of my major responsibilities, how much actual authority do I have?" ("How much money can I spend? How many people do I supervise? Do I have full power to hire and fire?")

"Do you have performance standards for my key job responsibilities?"

"If you hire me, what would your expectations be?"

The two smartest questions you can ask during any interview are these:

"If in the past someone has not fulfilled your expectations in this job, what were the main problems?"

"What do you think is the one major thing that would contribute to my excelling at this job?"

Team-Related Questions

"Is there some reason why you're not promoting someone within the company for this job?"

"How many people held this job within the last five years?"

"Are any of them still with the company? Would it be possible for me to talk with them?"

"With whom would I be working and may I talk with them?"

Company-Related Questions

"Since corporate fit is so important, how would you describe the ideal manager in your company?"

"How is job performance evaluated here?" ("How is it rewarded?")

"Since each corporation is unique, how would you describe the corporate climate here?"

"How are decisions made here?"

"What kind of decisions will I have to make?"

"How much time will I have to make them?"

"What kind of support will I get?"

"What happens if I make a mistake?"

"What happens if I win?"

If you are a woman or a member of a minority group, ask, "How many women [or minorities] are working in middle and upper management?"

Only when you have asked these or similar questions about the specific job, the team, and corporate fit should you ask questions about the potential for growth.

Questions for Your Future

Even though you're dealing with the present situation and the present job, the job interview is an appropriate time to consider your future with the company. Because you don't want to give the impression that your only interest is to get on the fast track, these questions are best asked towards the end of the interview.

Most companies today are concerned with succession and training people for the future. You should ask questions that probe for company policy in this area.

> "I see that your company is expanding in the Northeast—where do you see the company moving?"

> "What are you doing in terms of human resources planning to make that happen?"

> "What about career paths for new employees, as well as employees within the company?"

You must also interview your potential boss and find out whom he has promoted and what his career goals are. A dead-end boss can be a dead end for you, too. The most important question you can ask for your future is: "What can someone coming in at this level and performing in an outstanding way hope to achieve?"

Countering Questions During the Interview

The more information you get in the beginning of the interview, the better you can answer questions the interviewer puts to you.

Listen closely to questions you're asked. The less you're thinking about yourself and what you're going to say next, the better the interview will go. This is worth repeating: Nowhere is listening more important than in the job interview. Listen for the content and the intent all the time.

Only answer the question that's asked. Answer simply, directly, and briefly. Don't elaborate. If you're not 100 percent sure of what you're being asked, ask a clarifying question:

Interviewer: Tell me about yourself.

Candidate: What specifically do you want to know?

Interviewers typically ask questions that you should not or cannot answer properly without more information. Don't hesitate to ask for it.

Interviewer: What accomplishments make you most proud?

Candidate: I've done many things which please me. What areas are you interested in?

Tough Questions to Answer

Some interviewers enjoy trying to make you feel uncomfortable. Your best counter-move is to remain calm, never lose your cool, and use humor as much as possible. Don't be grim. It just *seems* like a matter of life and death.

You can be almost anything—aggressive, charming, funny—but never be defensive or angry.

Interviewer: What makes you think you're qualified to work for this company?

Defensive response: I've done . . . [You rattle off a list of reasons why you are qualified.]

Nondefensive answer: That's an interesting question. You're in a better position to answer than I am. What do you feel is the one thing that would make me qualified?

Or: That's an interesting question. I could answer that better if I knew more about the job, and more about the company.

If you think someone is deliberately trying to manipulate you, the best answer, said with humor, might be "What makes you think I'm not?"

Here's a tough one: "Tell me why you were fired from your last job." That's a damned if you do, damned if you don't kind of question. If you weren't fired, quickly say so. Otherwise, explain calmly that it was a mutually agreed-upon parting of the ways, and immediately ask another prepared question.

Interviewer: Do you like working with people or things?

This is a loaded question unless you know what the job is. As Dustin Hoffman said to the director in *Tootsie*, "Which answer will get me the job?"

Interviewer: What are several of your recurring problems?

Candidate: My definition of a professional is a person who recovers fast and seldom makes the same mistake twice. Do you agree?

By holding a nondefensive position you can consider the interview a challenging experience and enjoy it.

Talking Money

Never talk money until you know there's a job offer. This is a different tactic than negotiating for a raise. Wait until the interviewer is sold on you. No matter what. If you must, wait for the second or third interview. The more time they invest in you, the more they have at stake.

If the interviewer asks you early in the interview: "How much money are you looking for?" you counter, "Is this a job offer?"

Or if that seems too direct, ask another question: "I think it's more important that we talk about your needs first, and if I'm the right person we can talk about salary a little later." Then ask another question: "What would you say is the primary skill needed to succeed at this job?" Think of it as a game. Once you deflect a question or refuse to answer, you must throw the ball back in the other person's court by asking another question.

If the interviewer asks you about money at the right time, and you're ready to negotiate, your immediate task is to avoid naming the first figure. There are three levels of interviewers: people who can offer you any amount of money, people who can offer you a range, and people who can only offer you a fixed salary based on company policy. You need to know the authority of the person who's interviewing you.

Interviewer: How much money are you looking for?

Candidate: I know a manager can negotiate basically three types of salaries—unlimited, ranges, fixed salary. Which category does this job fit into, and what are you offering me?

Interviewer: What are you looking for?

Candidate: What I think I'm worth and what you think I'm worth may be very different. What are you offering? [Stick with it. If you mention salary first, you've lost the advantage.]

Finding the job of your choice takes belief in yourself. A specific marketing approach is the key. You can handle the most difficult job interviews if you have the techniques. Knowing how to ask smart questions can help you discover where and with whom you'll spend those 96,000 hours.

Getting started in the right job, however, is only one step in moving ahead. You may be in the slot, but you now have to maneuver your way through the corporate maze—all the way to the top.

21

Tuning In to the Corporate Culture

Jeffrey is a witty, stylish vice president of operations for a well-known brokerage firm. He is respected by his colleagues and knowledgeable in his field. He loves his job, but he also loves his own time. Jeffrey comes in to work at 9 A.M. and leaves between 5 and 6. Because Jeffrey is an excellent manager, and because he has fewer people in his area than the other vice presidents, his group functions perfectly within Jeffrey's time span. Twice Jeffrey's been passed over for senior vice president of operations. Why? Because the corporate norm is 7 to 10, not 9 to 5.

It's not enough to do your job well. You must find a way to tune in to the vibrations of the corporation, read the hidden messages, and pick up both obvious and faint signals that unerringly point the way to success.

If there are 500 managers in your corporation, 450 of them are anxious to move up. Unfortunately, a corporation seldom has clear rules about how to get ahead. Managers are not provided with a road map that they can use to pick out the fastest and most efficient way to get from here to there.

Frequently the corporation itself isn't even aware of its many paths to the top. It may have some vague mile markers but does not outline specific roads for its managers to reach them. Corporations are always moving—fluctuating, changing.

A jogging friend of mine recently left her hectic, demanding job as an account executive in advertising, where she was on call evenings and weekends. She had recently married and had taken up skiing and windsurfing. She wanted time on the weekends for her family and leisure activities. She was no longer willing to be part of a corporate culture which made such time-consuming demands. Fortunately she was able to go into her family's successful retail operation. Not everyone has such a viable alternative. But executives who want to move up must be aware of and compatible with the corporate culture, or find one that suits them.

One way *not* to get ahead is to ignore the corporate signals that do exist and set your own path. As William Granville, Manager of Technology Transfer at Mobil Oil Corporation, has pointed out: "Corporate fit is important. You must perceive the norms within the corporation. Either you must be flexible enough to adjust to them or you must find a corporation that matches your style perfectly. Corporations tend to promote people who fit the corporate structure, and then hire a team around those people."

Corporate Style

Even though many corporations today have some room for individual style, they still emphasize comformity. When you're looking to get ahead, it's important to know the culture of your organization. You needn't be a carbon copy of what you think the company wants, but your own personal style should be at least complementary to the company's ideals.

To quote human resources consultant Alan Barratt, "Managers tend to support people in their own image." Mavericks sometimes do succeed, but for the most part, if you behave differently from those who are respected and admired in your organization, you'll be slowing your own career momentum.

It's within your power to improve your image and your situation. Corporations are political institutions, with a lot of action and power shifts going on behind the scenes. So many people are in competition that getting close to the top isn't a matter of luck, it's largely a matter of honing your image so you can position yourself intelligently within your particular corporate culture.

When you examine behavior that is highly prized and rewarded in your organization, you may be surprised to find that much of it has little or nothing to do with getting the work done. Sometimes *how* you do something is more important than what actually gets accomplished.

Something as irrelevant as where people eat can turn out to be critical. In some companies, for example, executives are expected to lunch in the company dining room, and in others it's considered bad form. I know an account manager who recently went to work for an insurance firm with offices in the World Trade Center. During her first week on the job she was spotted lunching in the luxurious cafeteria in the lobby of the tower and was, fortunately, told the next day, "Our executives don't eat there."

Consider these seemingly innocuous factors: dress, manners, working hours, vacations, expense accounts, smoking, drinking, and the location, decor, and neatness of your office. Now, consider the executives in the upper reaches of management in your organization. How do they handle such things as dress and manners? Ask yourself:

"How well does my behavior fit?"

"Am I acting the way a successful person in my company is expected to act?"

"In what ways could my behavior be hurting my image and my career?"

Notice what leads to promotion and success in your organization. Corporations vary in terms of the styles of behavior that are rewarded. Take Ford and General Motors: from the beginning they represented two extremes of corporate styles. GM has always been clubby and genteel, with dozens of committees and multiple levels of management. Ford, by contrast, has a more competitive environment, with less staff review and more of an entrepreneurial spirit. The person who flourishes in the slow, well-ordered world of GM would undoubtedly founder in Ford waters—unless he tuned in to the difference and adapted his style.

At Mobil Oil, flexibility in relocating is deeply woven into the corporate culture. Only those executives willing to put time in at refineries in less glamorous parts of the world get a shot at the top.

Culture is often the result of a company's early needs and the personal style of its founders. Many brokerage and garment industry firms, for example, began as small family businesses and clung to this style long after they became large-scale corporations. They arrived late to the concepts of enlightened personnel development. Entrepreneurial in origin, they remain primarily interested in bottom-line objectives. According to these traditions, social skill, prudence, and loyalty to employees are qualities that come in second. Banks and utilities, on the other hand, possibly because they are traditionally concerned with an image of public service, pay more attention to the development of human resources.

To a certain extent culture is reflected across the spectrum of an industry, but within that image corporations often have varying styles. One of my clients manufactures a high-ticket item and the managers most valued within that corporation are polished, soft-spoken, and well dressed. Another manufacturing client, this one of novelties, couldn't care less how people dress as long as they can deal with the frenetic pace.

Corporate culture can be subtle. I knew a product manager who got fired because he used to walk into his boss's office without knocking. Although perceptive in other areas, his corporate antennae weren't hooked up. He failed to pick up the signal from his boss and other superiors that his behavior came across as too intimate. In that corporation the culture was formal, and executives were judged by the deference they inspired in their subordinates. The key to success in this case was to keep a polite distance.

Smart Self Questions for Getting Ahead

The concept that there is a corporate culture unique to every firm is not a new one. Nor is the notion that there are rebels who succeed in spite of the rules. But identifying the varied and individual factors that define a particular corporate culture can give you a definite advantage. The best way to isolate the corporate culture is to ask the right questions.

The answers will give you an overall view of all the little pieces that make up a company's corporate culture. Ask yourself these smart questions:

"How would I describe the type of person who is most successful in our corporation?"

"What is the company norm regarding working hours? Strictly 9 to 5?"

"Do important executives work late? On weekends?"

"Do they arrive at 7 A.M.?"

"Are they expected to wine and dine visiting clients?"

"What is the unstated dress code?"

"Are the company's leaders creative geniuses or buttoned-up administrative types?"

"Is the ambiance high-tech or high-touch?"

"Entrepreneurial or old-boy network?"

"Does the firm seek out academic degrees or street smarts?"

"Is getting the job done the thing that counts most—no matter what?"

"How fast do people move up the corporate ladder?"

"How many women and minorities are in middle to upper management? Line jobs or staff?"

"How often does the company promote from within?"

"Exactly who and what are being rewarded in the company? Who is really getting ahead?"

As you ask each question, apply the answer to your own temperament. Are you able to adapt yourself to suit this company? For example, if you're in a bottom-line-oriented company you could have a problem if your own priorities are people development and growth.

One of my clients is a computer support company performing all the programming and automated functions for several manufacturing firms. Executives who are valued are either highly creative programmers or calm, diplomatic individuals who can deal with the frustrations inherent in a support-type organization. An aggressive, pushing type of individual would not get far in this outfit.

Clothes, working hours, attitudes, can always be changed if you are willing to put in the effort. But a company culture that goes against the grain of your own personality and temperament is much tougher to come to terms with. Maybe the operation you're in will never make you happy and you should face that now. You may decide that rather than try to change yourself you should switch companies.

There are many different kinds of corporations. Many firms look for creative minds, while others seek out loyal, consistent individuals who will get along well with their colleagues and work hard. IBM, for example, is known for rewarding loyalty and service by taking care of its employees, offering excellent benefits and career security.

Hidden Messages

Sometimes it's hard to nail down the corporate culture. Firms frequently pay lip service to policies that have little to do with the realities of corporate life. Many companies send mixed messages. One overt message may be: "We want you to develop your people, bring them along, work with them, and focus on participative management." However, a penetrating look around will tell you that the people who get ahead are the steely-eyed, unyielding, bottom-line producers.

I work with a small manufacturing firm where the vice president of personnel earns over $100,000 a year, suggesting that the company is committed to developing its human resources. Yet the corporation does not spend any money at all throughout the year on professional seminars or training.

I'm also familiar with a large brokerage firm that proclaims it's out for quick profits. Yet top management is so conservative that it's hard to push anything through. In this corporate culture they do things very slowly, step by step. How they get the job done—safely and securely— is actually their biggest concern.

Perhaps your organization publicizes the fact that it's an equal-opportunity employer. When you take a good look, however, all top-level people are white male graduates of Ivy League schools. If you're a fast-track minority, you'll have to move mountains to change the culture. You may decide to switch to a company where there's greater opportunity.

Smart people recognize hidden messages. For example, suppose you receive a directive from your boss: "We assume that you'll take vacations and that your people will too."

You ask yourself, "Who gets ahead around here?" You observe that the CEO works around the clock and hasn't been on a vacation for the last five years. And that the managers who work for him are totally glued to their work and don't take vacations either. Those who actually take the time off that they're entitled to, on the other hand, rarely get promoted and don't stay around too long. Conclusion: If you want to get ahead, don't take vacations.

Some corporations tout reducing customer complaints and even give rewards for it. One customer-service manager in a large bank believed the overt corporate directive and concentrated on solving customer complaints. She was so successful at reaching this goal that she received an award at the end of the year. But her colleague, who ignored the directive, was promoted to vice president of customer relations. Why? This manager was responsible for bringing in a consultant who made the company $25 million with an innovative computerized direct-mail program.

Smart Questions for Tuning In

Developing a managerial style that fits with what's promotable in your company is important to your success. It's unlikely that you will ever find the ideal corporate culture to suit all your preferences. Nothing's perfect. Every new job and every new situation requires some adjustment on your part. You can't walk into a corporation and assume that the same norms you've been acting on in a previous organization will work in this one too. You may change the style of your dress, for example, if you switch from the fashion industry into banking.

Even as your job and level of responsibilities within your own company change, it's almost inevitable that you will need to make some changes in your style. Bosses and managers come and go; you join a new department or are promoted to. a different area. Many such situations call for sensitivity and minor adjustments.

Successful managers know how to ignore meaningless objectives and tune in to the real corporate culture. It is especially important to answer these practical questions during the first couple of weeks on a new job. Take a good look around and ask yourself:

"Which corporate objectives are really going to help me get ahead, and which are just there for show?"

"How are decisions made in this organization?" ("By consensus? By individuals?")

"Are quick-decision-makers considered valuable?"

"How do I get support for my projects?"

"How do I get to the top people?"

"How do I get on the best committees?"

"Whom do I need to know?"

"Who makes the decisions?"

One company executive told me he discovered something during his first weeks on the job that proved invaluable for his later success: "In my company if you do something wrong, you can't win if you dig your heels in and get defensive. But if you throw yourself on the mercy of the court, they tend to be forgiving."

So here are some more smart questions to ask yourself:

"What happens in this corporation when something goes wrong?"

"If I make a mistake, how do I get another chance?"

"What happens if a manager refuses an assignment?"

Adjusting Your Style

"Corporations will bring in an oddball if they feel it will save a particular situation, but that person might not fit afterwards," says J. Sheldon Caras, Senior Vice President of Marketing at The New England (formerly New England Life Insurance Co.).

The go-getter who charges in to solve a major problem and does so successfully may have to change drastically once his initial task is accomplished if he hopes to move up in the company.

Not everyone can do what Thomas Jefferson did after he finished all of his courses at William and Mary University in two years. The college insisted that if young Jefferson wanted to graduate he must stay for four years, no matter how many courses he had completed. Jefferson left and eventually started the University of Virginia, which from its founding was based on less rigid principles.

Can you change your style? Certainly. Tuning in to what's going on in your company is worthless unless you also analyze your own style and figure out what you need to do to adjust.

Ideally, adjusting your image to fit the corporate culture should be a matter of polishing up the fine points. If your company has a style and a culture that makes you uncomfortable, rather than torturing yourself you should look for another company. On the other hand, if your company has a style and a culture that appeals to you but you don't fit in, then look for ways to develop your image along company lines.

Louise, a talented and experienced operations manager in a large brokerage firm, was virtually unpromotable because she was overweight, spoke poorly, and lacked a college degree. Several times her vice president had suggested she "get her act together." Louise promised to improve but never did. Fortunately for her, the vice president was eager to maximize her potential and engaged in a little smart questioning: "Where would you like to go in the company?" he asked.

"To vice president of operations," Louise replied.

"How do you expect to get there?"

"As usual—working hard. Wheeling and dealing with the right people."

"Have you noticed who gets ahead in this company?"

"The well-dressed, smooth-talking MBAs."

"If that's so, what do you think you'll need to do?"

"After I shoot myself . . . I could lose some weight and go back to school."

"What's first?"

"I'd better start with school—it takes longest."

"Let's get the catalogs and sign you up for the next semester."

Louise was lucky. I also remember a lively junior account executive in a large advertising agency. John had the energy and the hustle to make a good account executive, but not the style. He dressed in polyester suits and wore clip-on ties. His shoes were run down at the heels. A senior account executive thought enough of him to tell him about the dress code that he had failed to observe for himself.

Now, you may not be lucky enough to have a boss who cares enough to help you out in this way. Most managers have to take themselves in hand. Like Louise and John, many people feel that hard work will gain them recognition. This simply is not always the case. Conveying an easily recognized, dynamic impression is often the key that unlocks the door to success. Whatever your career choice, a solid, believable image can help you reach your ultimate goal.

Tuning Up Your Image

Showing your awareness of the image expected by your corporation reflects professional savvy and dedication. Those who control your career development will recognize that you're paying attention to the details and to the overall picture of the corporation. In short, your image serves as a vehicle for communicating your competence. It is a reflection that bears long-lasting influence in your bid for success.

Another important point is that any image should be consistent. It doesn't work if you get yourself together on some days of the week, and then on others—say, when you don't have any important meetings—just let yourself go. If you're consistent in your style, your bosses feel secure; they know they can count on you to present a positive image at any given moment. If you're erratic they'll feel insecure, always a little worried, never quite sure that you'll be on target in front of a client or supplier.

A question I often hear is "Isn't it dishonest to present some sort of image, when that really isn't me?" The answer to that is, what shows *is* the reality. Your image is an expression of your best self. It is not something you put on like a dress or a suit. Your image should reinforce all of your best qualities. For example, if you continue to show confidence even when inside you feel unsure, you eventually will feel confident.

Personal styles can vary within an organization, but a strong image almost always reflects certain constants: self-confidence, reliability, the unmistakable aura of success.

Self Questions about Your Image

To get your image together, ask yourself these smart questions:

"How am I perceived now?"

"If I were my own boss (peer, employee), how would I describe me?"

"How do I feel about those perceptions?"

"How do those perceptions fit my corporation's culture?"

"What do I have to offer my company that is unique and special?"

"How can I make the most of my uniqueness and still fit in?"

"What are the most attractive points of my current image?"

"Which aspects detract?"

"What can I do to enhance my best qualities?"

The Courage to Change

How can you use smart questions directly to help you find the right corporate fit? Do a little undercover research; ask around. Your self-perception could conceivably be very different from how others see you.

One brave executive in a large department store used the Smart Questions system this way: Katherine, a sportswear buyer, passed out an anonymous questionnaire to all the divisional merchandising managers and to the firm's senior executives, asking what they thought of her. Here are the questions she asked:

"What are my chances for promotion?"

"Could I become CEO?"

"Why? Or why not?"

"How would you describe my corporate image?"

"What would you do to change it if you were me?"

Katherine was surprised to receive neatly typed, but unsigned, replies from almost every executive. She was more than surprised when she read them. There was a definite consensus among the respondents. Katherine discovered that she was perceived as abrasive (she thought she was people oriented). They didn't like her staff. Overall, the respondents did not think she was "part of the team." No one felt she could become CEO unless she radically changed her style.

Katherine was determined. At last count she had not made it to CEO, but through her nondefensive reaction to the feedback she has begun to alter her style. She was recently promoted to divisional merchandising manager and has her eye on the next rung. The questionnaire told her that the hidden corporate culture valued a team approach. Simply sending out the questionnaire indicated to top management that she wanted to be part of the team. Her story supports the idea that people—especially important people—like to be asked for their opinions.

If you do decide to do an image makeover, do it subtly and gradually. Like dyeing gray hair, if you do it a little at a time, you'll eventually end up with a major change but people won't suddenly be taken aback.

Remember that a good image cannot work unless you back it up with self-confidence. Henry C. Rogers, public relations expert and author of *Rogers' Rules for Success*, says, "Self-esteem and self-image are all important. The beginning of any success story comes when a person begins to feel good about himself."

One of the most important jobs you'll ever have is to tap into your strengths and express the most positive parts of your personality—for the sake of your happiness as well as for your corporate success. You may change your clothes to suit the corporate climate, but the intelligence and enthusiasm and personality—all integral parts of your image—are yours. Images can grow with you.

Tuning in to the corporate culture is step one on the path to success.

Your corporate fit is important, but only a piece of the giant corporate road map. You can't sit in your office all day looking good and expect to get to the top. You'll be glad to know that although image is important, it isn't everything. There's plenty of evidence that brains and hard work still count the most. To get ahead today, you must be very very good at your job.

22

Rising Stars and Powerful People

Who does get ahead in today's complex corporate jungle? It's both a tricky question and a fascinating one. I interviewed a number of CEOs of major corporations, as well as top executives from a wide variety of industries, and their answers may surprise you. The responses were highly individualistic and varied; yet I heard the same fundamental themes expressed again and again. In this chapter I will use their answers to define the basic principles of getting ahead and to suggest questions that will send you on your way.

From Harvey Schein, the Executive Vice President of News America Publishing, Inc.: "The very very able, and the very very smooth, inherit the world." I begin with this piece of wisdom because it clearly isolates the two main factors that go into making a corporate "star": ability and image. Let's start with ability, in itself a complicated concept.

Ability

What does ability really mean in business terms? For a corporation, ability is valuable only when it translates into high-quality performance. And high-quality performance includes many factors: hard work, dedication, loyalty, and results are the essential elements that make your ability abundantly clear. Personal talents and abilities that are not used to fulfill corporate goals are talents and abilities wasted. Your dedication and enthusiasm must help your company first, if they are to help you in the long run.

William S. Lee, Chairman and CEO of Duke Power Company, makes this comment: "To get ahead takes a combination of sensitivity and inner courage. You can't be defensive or afraid of change. You must be able to put your personal aspirations aside and do your best for the company."

William Granville, Manager of Technology Transfer for Mobil Oil, agrees that the company should come first: "To get ahead," says Granville, "you must support the principles of your organization. If your principles clash with your company's you're not going anywhere. Highest marks go to loyalty and competence."

Gerard A. Miller, Vice President, Director of Finance, Merrill Lynch and Co., Inc., adds that hard work is vital: "The person who gets ahead has the ability to get things done. He has a vision of where he's going and where the organization is going. A strong work ethic, coupled with commitment. You must be willing to pay the price—long work hours, and dedication."

And Alan Barratt, a human resources consultant and former Mobil executive, agrees: "You must have political and organizational sensitivity and a devotion to duty. You must be hardworking, self-starting, someone who's not going to put his foot in it."

Several corporate authorities say that they can spot a "comer" by his or her dedication and enthusiasm. "If the person always delivers on time," says J. Sheldon Caras, Senior Vice President of Marketing for The New England, formerly New England Life Insurance Co., "it tells you one thing. But if that person beats a timetable it tells you something else—that he's an eager beaver, and somebody to watch."

Supporting the company is also essential. The sure sign of a rising star, according to Helen Galland, President of Helen Galland Associates and former President and CEO of Bonwit Teller, is the person "who shows enthusiasm for projects—and endorses projects even if he or she isn't 100 percent in agreement."

It's clear that applying your capabilities to your firm by virtue of loyalty and hard work can turn your ability into star quality.

Always Say Yes?

Another aspect of having a lot of ability is deciding when to use it. Lois Wyse, president of the New York office of Wyse Advertising, was interviewed recently by *Success* magazine and advocated a policy of enthusiastic acceptance:

"I tell my daughter, 'Always say yes, because nothing ever happens to girls who say no.' It's true in business and it's true in life. 'Will you stay late and work?' If you say no, nothing good is going to happen to you. 'Can you take this extra assignment?' If you say no, *nothing* is going to happen to you. You have to learn to say yes."

Alan Barratt also advises that you take on a wide range of tasks in order to learn all you can: "Get a variety of jobs before age 35; if you're in a small company, move. If you're in a large organization, work in different divisions."

Film producer David Brown also credits his success with a "do-everything approach." "I was always willing to take on more than one job," he said in a recent magazine interview. "When magazine staffs were being cut back and organizations were being decimated by the Depression, I would do everything: I'd even be on the switchboard if necessary."

As a result, Brown learned everything about the publishing business. When a major reshuffling came about at his magazine, *Liberty*, Brown was the only person on the staff who had experience in all editorial departments and was the only person qualified to be editor-in-chief. It was this position that led him to a job with Darryl F. Zanuck, and eventually to the board of directors at Twentieth Century Fox.

The enthusiastic and adventurous attitude that these authorities suggest is clearly a plus for anyone looking to broaden his range of opportunities and gain attention as well as experience. But I would advise some caution. Saying yes to everything is fine in theory, but in the real world you have neither the time nor the energy to accomplish everything. Your time is valuable. In a corporate situation, when you're asked to volunteer, ask yourself if it's a project that you, your company, or your boss really values. If the project is a low priority with the company, or something that upper management really wouldn't pay attention to, it's foolish to devote weeks of energy to it. There are scores of other areas where your efforts would be appreciated.

It's great to get out there and handle the switchboard if your office runs into a crisis. But to let yourself get stuck doing double duty indefinitely because of some sense of idealism or martyrdom is a waste of

your talents and energy. Overall, do volunteer, do the job—any job—
but put your priorities and energy where they will count most.

"... And the Very Very Smooth"

As Harvey Schein pointed out, ability alone is not sufficient for success.
You must cultivate an image of power and success in order to distinguish
yourself from the group. Alan Barratt says: "You need to be a visionary,
to have a magical aura."

William Granville makes an attempt to address this elusive magic.
"The fact that you are worthy of respect travels along the grapevine; it
is never officially granted or acknowledged." Says Granville, "Present
yourself so people want to be associated with you. Dress the part, assume
control, forget about being part of the crowd. Stay out front. And when
you ask a question, ask a good one."

The smart question to ask yourself is: "How can I get positive attention without violating the prevailing corporate culture?"

J. Sheldon Caras told me, "In a dynamic organization, you need to
show more difference than sameness to rise to the top. You must be a
little bit of an iconoclast."

There's a fine line, yet a big difference, between the oddball and the
star performer. For example, in certain large brokerage firms a top
producer can be a little unconventional and still move up. You can wear
a striking color or carry a flashy briefcase and get away with it, especially
if it's not the dominant part of your image.

Herman Kahn, of think-tank fame, used to wear sneakers with his
business suits when he made client presentations. In the early days of
Doyle Dane Bernbach, when that original and creative agency was beginning to gain national recognition, one copywriter sent in his copy on
cocktail napkins.

I knew a manager in a large textile plant who had clocks that went
off and played a tune every hour. Because he was such a fine executive
and his plant was a top producer, the firm used to joke that perhaps
every manager should play the same tune. As Abraham Lincoln said
when told that General Grant was drinking too much whiskey, "Get me
the brand, and I'll send a barrel to my other generals."

On the other hand, the eccentricities of an average or poor performer
would be looked upon with considerably less humor. The corporate
culture will dictate the allowable degree of deviation.

Visibility

The main point, of course, is that you must be highly visible if you're going to rise to the top—but you have to be visible for the right reasons. There's a fine line to walk between being visible and being arrogant. Every company has its share of prima donnas; I'm sure you've run into someone who will do anything to draw attention to himself. If he's got the talent, he may be tolerated. He will certainly never become a trusted leader, however, and it's more likely that his showing off will get him shown to the door.

I know an extreme case where a top executive was hired by a cosmetics firm to help straighten out the marketing department. He went full steam ahead—and then ran right off the rails when he hired his own personal publicity agent. Theoretically the PR person was paid as a consultant to the company, but it soon became evident that his major concern was touting this one executive to the newspapers. This was a fatal error on the executive's part, and not surprisingly, he was fired.

On the other hand, a certain degree of self-promotion is natural and even necessary. If there's an opportunity to deal with the press or to comment publicly on something you've achieved, grab it. You don't want to hang back and stub your toe in the dirt. No one goes around checking to see if any wallflowers are in bloom. Ego, drive, and pride in self are all important for success.

But of course there's a world of difference between a strong ego—essential to any success—and an overblown one, which is destructive as well as offensive. The person with an overblown ego is always climbing over someone else to gain recognition and needs to be continually patted on the back. He thinks he's a cut above the others. And he typically talks down to the people who work for him, which immediately disqualifies him from being an effective manager or leader. The worst part about overblown egos, from a corporate viewpoint, is that they are easily manipulated. All anyone has to do to get the right response from them is to apply a little flattery.

The person with a strong ego, on the other hand, knows his own strengths. He's confident. He has a realistic idea of what he can accomplish, and he moves purposefully toward his goals.

How can you get visibility in your company without looking like an egomaniac? How can you be appreciated for your strengths and get the credit you deserve without spending all your time at it? You want to be visible—but you want to be visible in the right way.

The first thing you have to do is to develop a strategy for increasing your visibility. If your aim is the top, you have to start very early with a well-chiseled image that you will present to the world. Your image should be a common thread that runs through everything you do. It should be apparent in your letters, memos, clothes, relationships, every aspect of who you are.

Having this focus on yourself and your role will help you in all your responsibilities and job functions. It will help you do your job with more imagination, flair, and effectiveness. Start by asking yourself:

"How do I want to be perceived?"

"How do I want people to perceive my role in the company?"

"How do I want individuals (my boss, my peers, my staff) to perceive my relationship with them?"

"When I write a letter, a speech, a memo, or a presentation, what do I want the receiver to know (feel) about me?"

"How can my image help me to communicate and excel?"

Visibility and Power

Power, resources, and opportunity always flow to the visible high achiever. In fact, power and visibility go hand in hand. Whatever the fine points of your image, being a person of power has to be uppermost and consistent. As William Granville stated, you must "assume control."

You know when power is yours—and it always shows. You are listened to when you speak. People solicit your opinions. No phone calls go unreturned. You're invited to sit in on important meetings.

Power is sometimes acquired in the simplest ways. Inventory your verbal and nonverbal signals. Monitor your speech and manner. Stand and sit alertly. Walk briskly into a room as if you're in command of yourself.

Most important, ask the right questions and answer questions briefly and vigorously. Smart questions allow you to exhibit your competence and confidence. That sense of self-esteem will send out signals that others can't miss.

Allen E. Murray, Chairman of the Mobil Corporation, cautions that the misuse of questions can be devastating: "Questions that reveal that the other person hasn't been listening or hasn't studied a proposal are annoying and cast the questioner in an unfavorable light. I believe listening is a critical communication skill that should be mastered."

William Granville says this about questioning: "Questions give you power. Ask questions—but not a lot, and only the right ones."

When you do your homework and use your head, questions are by far your most valuable tool for gaining positive attention and respect at all times, whatever your strategy for visibility and success.

Increasing Your Visibility

Meetings are one perfect arena for you to show yourself. Every company has them—all the time. Surprisingly many executives overlook the opportunities meetings offer for increased visibility simply because there are so many of them that they take them for granted. It takes leadership abilities to run meetings or give talks, lectures, or seminars. But they are all good ways to build your visibility.

Speaking at a meeting is entirely different from private conversation. It requires thought and preparation. A speaker may be well informed, but if he hasn't thought out exactly what he wants to say today, and to this audience, he won't stand out.

It's imperative that you make the effort to learn how to speak effectively. Many fine speakers were shrinking violets when they started out. There are a lot of people out there with terrific ideas who have trouble explaining them to other people, but this needn't be the case. It's always a shame when a person with great talent can't tell the board or a committee what's in his head.

Self Questions to Enhance Your Performance

Examining how you perform at meetings, and then continually refining your technique, is a good way to boost your campaign for greater visibility and success. Try these self questions after every big meeting:

"How well planned was my presentation and contribution?"

"Did I have the right people there?"

"Whose support could add clout to my next meeting?"

"How did I perform in the leadership role?"

"Did I exhibit power and control in a charismatic way?"

"If the CEO of the company had been there, how would he have evaluated this meeting?"

"Did I enhance my image?"

"Did I ask smart questions?"

"Did I listen to the answers?"

And don't get discouraged if the responses you come up with are negative—just get better.

In addition to becoming a good public speaker and running results-oriented meetings, there are other ways to make yourself visible. For one thing, you can set out to become an expert in a particular area, and make yourself stand out in this way. Knowledge is power. Vera was an average manufacturing executive in a textile firm. She had studied the Asian markets in college and spoke some Chinese and Korean. Hence, when her company got involved in the Asian market, she became the expert and her career skyrocketed.

This can work in any field; the business world will always need its computer specialists, design kings, research whizzes. It takes talent and certain skills, yes, but like everything else, in most cases it's 99 percent determination and perspiration.

Publicity

Publicity is a terrific way to gain visibility. If you have an opportunity to be interviewed for a newspaper, magazine, or news program, say yes. But never, under any circumstances, allow yourself to be interviewed without first being prepared (unless it's on something you've talked about many times before). An interview can feel like a battle between you and the interviewer, and it's a battle you can win if you know what you want to get across. No matter what the interviewer says or asks, you answer with the points you want to emphasize. Observe politicians and others being interviewed on television and watch how they answer questions with their own answers, regardless of what the question was:

"Mr. So and So, is it true your company is planning to build an eighty-story building on the site of the old mill pond?"

"You know the wonderful thing about that, Bill? This new building will bring so much new vitality to this area. . . ." You get the idea.

Maintain the momentum of a locomotive. Whatever happens, you keep barreling along. Know your material inside and out. And before any interview, think of all the rotten questions an interviewer might throw at you, and figure out a maneuver to deflect each one.

Whatever you do, when you are interviewed, be brief. Thirty seconds should be enough for any answer.

Filling the Vacuum

Many executives I spoke to advocated this particular method of getting ahead, and it's among the most challenging and creative of all. "Organizations pay attention to vacuum-fillers," says Harvey Schein, "the people who can identify and grasp opportunities."

J. Sheldon Caras has this to add: "The person who gets ahead is able to think beyond the horizon—beyond the narrow furrow of his or her job."

And Ed Weihenmayer says, "Keep your eyes open for opportunities. There should be no boxes—no limits—on your imagination."

What are these high achievers suggesting? Simply that you do more than get your own job done and wait to be promoted through the regular channels. They are advocating that you take your career advancement into your own two hands and create a promotion track for yourself.

As an ambitious person today you can't simply wait for desirable jobs to open. Take the less conventional route: carve out your own position.

Identifying the Opportunities

Exactly how do you find these "vacuums" to fill? J. Sheldon Caras says that people who succeed know their organization's goals and expectations: "They stand back and ask themselves: 'What is the general direction of this organization? What has to be done to steer it that way? What is not being done now?' Then they come up with an answer and follow it through."

Harvey Schein adds that asking smart questions can help you spot any niche waiting to be filled:

"What problems does my company have?"

"What problems does my department have?"

"What are the issues involved?"

"Is upper management concerned about this problem?" (If the answer is no, forget the problem. If the answer if yes, then that's the one to try to solve.)

Harvey Schein's questions lead to others: "What does my company need? A new product line? A cost-cutting system? Another marketing approach?"

Take a good long look at the marketplace, as well as your industry and your competitors. Which way is the wind blowing? Ask yourself:

"Is the industry getting more high-tech? More high-touch?"

"Is the public demanding expanded services? More specialization?"

"Is the company keeping tabs on modern developments and trends?"

"Are there new ways to cut costs or overhead? Are we operating efficiently?"

Are you a manager who can anticipate the future and take advantage of it? When you have a vacuum-filling idea, do all the research you can. Figure out the potential ramifications for your company, yourself, and your job. Your final step is to write a thorough, practical, and well-documented proposal. Show it to your boss.

If he or she is uncooperative and unresponsive, try your boss's boss. In extreme situations, if your vision warrants such a drastic measure, go to the top.

Remember, nobody will be anxious to implement an idea for you simply to advance your career. Your suggestions must clearly benefit the company in a significant way.

A personnel director at a hospital developed a series of workshops that the hospital could offer to women in the evenings as part of a community service program. In her proposal, she showed the hospital administrator how they could exploit the wasted nighttime space that they paid rent and utilities for anyway, and gain public recognition in the process. Her program was a great success in the community, and as an additional benefit it ultimately brought new patients into the hospital.

An operations manager at a company that manufactured bed-spreads—a slowly declining industry—came up with a way the company could convert their looms to make draperies and wall hangings.

A vice president of sales promotion in a retail manufacturer thoroughly researched and developed a program to create a mail-order department for his company, expanding their business by 37 percent in a single year.

All of these projects took vision, insight, research, and hard work—and all of them were successful.

Help from Powerful People

An entirely different approach to getting ahead involves enlisting the aid of powerful people. In other words, finding a mentor.

Victor Kiam, CEO of Remington Products in Connecticut, said in a recent interview, "Never be associated with someone you can't be proud of, whether you work for him or he works for you."

But don't just latch onto someone because they wield power. William S. Lee suggests asking yourself this important question first: 'What do I need a mentor for?' If you need a mentor to learn from, then choose the person who can teach you the most in your field. Go with the best; whatever reason you need a mentor for, attach yourself to a fine example and learn from him or her. The value of a mentor is not getting ahead, but to develop and stretch yourself." And that, of course, is what ultimately leads you to success.

Make sure you consider what that particular mentor means to you. According to Ed Weihenmayer, "A mentor is usually not a kindly person being nice to you. It's someone who is interested enough to tell it to you straight. The mentor relationship relies on being candid. If you're the recipient, you must have the confidence and maturity to listen to what the mentor tells you."

In almost all of my interviews, everyone agreed that mentors are important. Everyone uses mentors in some way, shape, or form. But finding the right mentor might not be easy. Forget about the traditional form of mentoring, where a powerful person picks you out and guides you up the success path; it's great, but it's like winning the lottery—one chance in a million. If you're going to find the right mentor, you'll have to do it yourself.

Self Questions for Choosing a Mentor

Advice is a commodity seldom in short supply. Your challenge lies in identifying the person who can offer advice that's worthwhile. It's a good idea to begin your quest by asking yourself a few smart questions:

"What do I need mentoring in?"

"Who would be the best person to give it to me?"

"Do I respect the person enough to listen to him—and take his advice?"

When these questions are answered, you can go to the next step: "What is the best way to approach this person?"

Suppose you come up with the perfect mentor. You're going to ask him or her to do something for you, to give up time and energy and information. Working in your favor is his instinct to express his ideas. The desire to be helpful may also encourage him to share information. Make the process enjoyable for the person of your choice: ask him interesting questions, display your interest. Many people enjoy having a protégé and nurturing a career, turning their knowledge over to another. A mentor also may get satisfaction from exercising subtle power in order to help your career.

Look for ways you can meet the mentor's needs. Say a top-level executive has a strong personal interest in a charity. Offer your help and support. Freely give your time to help him do his thing—but you must make it your thing, too. You must sincerely and generously give of yourself, with no strings attached. This is not a business deal or a fair exchange. Give loyalty and respect if you want to get any in return.

A young performer I know has worked his way to the top of the nightclub circuit with the aid of a famous Broadway composer. The performer has a history of gaining the sponsorship of well-known show business personalities. How did he do it?

He's a genuinely giving and talented young man who offered his services to organize and catalog musical memorabilia and materials solely for the privilege of helping some of the older, currently less prominent names in the music business. He spent months in dusty basements going through boxes of disorganized and abandoned files, put them in order, and then typed out catalogs of everything he had found for the use of music scholars.

True, he was in the right place at the right time. But I'm convinced that he never used his connections in a calculated attempt to get a leg up in the world. When he met someone he respected, he looked for a way to offer help. If deep down he was conscious of every move he made, it certainly never showed.

A mentor is not something you go and fill out an application for.

When asked how to get a mentor, J. Sheldon Caras could only offer: "Natural affinity. Social friendship is unnecessary, but there must be mutual liking and respect. Work for a trusting relationship that works both ways." The mentor must trust you. If he feels you're looking out only for yourself, why should be help? And he added, "If you have one, and he or she is the right one, you're fortunate."

Having a Mentor

Gerard A. Miller says, "Mentors are vital for the creation of history in a corporation. They pass on to individuals the goals and aspirations of the organization. One important value of a mentor is to guide you in decision making. He can tell you what the norm is in your organization, tell you what top-level management takes into account when they make decisions."

And Helen Galland suggests that once you have a mentor there are certain things you should do, and certain things you should not do: "Never say 'no'—always try whatever your mentor suggests, or at least say you will. Even if the task seems difficult or impossible, always make an effort and show that you tried. But don't be a 'yes' man and jump at every request your mentor makes."

She continues, "Although many successful people don't have them, mentors do give you an advantage. There are many different kinds— passive mentors, someone just to talk to; active mentors, those who give you specific help by introducing you, making moves for you, generally paving the way."

William Granville agrees that having one powerful mentor may not always be the best way to get ahead and nurture a career. "You have to seek new sponsors at different levels and get different sponsors for different purposes, different components of your work. You may need a professional sponsor for one thing and a personal sponsor for another."

Alan Barratt explains how different mentors may be appropriate at different stages: "In the beginning of your career a mentor can help you identify who's got the power in the corporation structure. Later in your career a mentor can support you when you are trying to make moves in the organization. Still later, as you get toward the top, the best help a mentor can give you is to be your confidant."

Certainly mentors come in many different stripes, but three of the most basic are the mentor who offers technical training and information; the mentor who can help you politically, and the mentor who serves as a role model, someone you watch and emulate in terms of how they dress, think, or handle themselves. (In this case, your role models may not even know that they're your mentors.)

One last suggestion: When you ask for advice or mentoring, be sure you're looking in the right places. Power can be dispensed only by those who have it. Power is transitory; it shifts from hand to hand, from year to year. The question uppermost in your mind should be: "Does the person from whom I'm seeking power and help actually have it to give?"

To conclude this chapter on getting ahead I'd like to make a distinction between the specific goal of getting to the top and the broader concept of achieving success. Fran Tarkenton, former NFL quarterback and chairman of The Tarkenton Productivity Group, had this to say in a recent newspaper interview: "Success, in my view, is the willingness to strive for something you really want. The person not reaching the top is no less a success than the one who achieved it, if they both sweated blood and tears and overcame obstacles and fear. The failure to be perfect does not mean you are not a success.

"The people part of management is the hardest part," says Tarkenton, "but it's the most important part—making people feel like human beings, with a purpose in life."

If the future belongs to the very very good and the very very smooth, it also belongs to those perceptive and flexible human beings who can anticipate and recognize technological and social changes around them, and in the process still maintain a strong professional and personal image. This is the challenge managers face today. Those who can cope best with change, who can help their people adapt more quickly and comfortably, are the successful leaders of the future. One way to start is with smart questions.

The underlying advantages of developing a smart-questioning approach go far beyond the ability to handle specific job situations well. Once you have mastered a natural questioning response, you have disciplined your mind to think clearly and to respond creatively in almost any situation. And clear thinking has a positive effect not only on your job, but on your life.

People who think and ask smart questions before they act make fewer mistakes. All of us have made blunders that we wish we could take back. But when you're in the habit of asking good questions—getting all the angles and relevant information before taking action—you have a better chance of making a decision you can live with.

Smart questions let you make a major change in your life with relatively little effort. Getting in the habit of using your head to question yourself and then question others is not difficult. The most important step is to fully accept the power and value of asking smart questions and start putting them into practice whenever you can. It becomes easier as you gradually feel more and more in control of your situation and eventually your career.

Asking questions is obviously important in life, but it's essential in a successful manager. With all the responsibilities and stress a manager has to deal with, smart questions are the ideal way to break out of the running-in-place mode managers often find themselves in and to give your career a forward thrust. Only when you begin to ask the right questions do you begin to find the right answers.

Bibliography

Adams, James L. *Conceptual Blockbusting*: *A Guide to Better Ideas*. Second Edition. New York: W. W. Norton & Company, 1979.

Allio, Robert J., and Malcolm W. Pennington, eds. *Corporate Planning*: *Techniques and Applications*. New York: American Management Association, 1979.

Andersen, U. S. *Success Cybernetics*. North Hollywood, CA: Wilshire Book Company, 1975.

Bach, George R., and Dr. Herb Goldberg. *Creative Aggression*: *The Art of Assertive Living*. New York: Avon Books, 1974.

Batten, J. D. *Beyond Management by Objectives*. New York: American Management Association, 1966.

Belker, Loren B. *The Successful Secretary*: *You, Your Boss and the Top*. New York: American Management Association, 1981.

Bennett, Millard, and John D. Corrigan. *Successful Communications & Effective Speaking*. West Nyack, NY: Parker Publishing Co., 1979.

Bennis, Warren, and Nanus, Burt. *Leaders*: *The Strategies of Taking Charge*. New York: Harper & Row, 1985.

Birchall, David W., and Valerie J. Hammond. *Tomorrow's Office Today*: *Managing Technological Change*. New York: John Wiley & Sons, 1981.

Bittel, Lester R. *What Every Supervisor Should Know*. Third Edition. New York: McGraw-Hill, 1974.

Blanchard, Kenneth, and Spencer Johnson. *The One Minute Manager*. New York: William Morrow and Company, 1982.

Bloomfield, Harold H., and Leonard Felder. *Achilles Syndrome: Transforming Your Weaknesses into Strengths*. New York: Random House, 1985.

Boettinger, Henry M. *Moving Mountains or The Art of Letting Others See Things Your Way*. New York: Collier Books, 1969.

Bolles, Richard Nelson. *What Color Is Your Parachute? A Practical Manual for Job-Hunters & Career-Changers*. Revised Edition. Berkeley, CA: Ten Speed Press, 1975.

Bonoma, Thomas V., and Dennis P. Slevin. *Executive Survival Manual: A Program for Managerial Effectiveness*. Boston: CBI Publishing Company, Inc., 1978.

Bower, Sharon Anthony, and Gordon H. Bower. *Asserting Yourself: A Practical Guide for Positive Change*. Reading, MA: Addison-Wesley Publishing Company, 1976.

Brooks, William T., and Dan S. Kennedy. *It's About Time*. Phoenix: General Graphics and Printing, 1986.

Burger, Chester. *Creative Firing: Why Management Firings Happen . . . and How to Reduce Them*. New York: Litton Educational Publishing, 1972.

Bursk, Edward C., and John F. Chapman, eds. *New Decision-Making Tools for Managers*. New York: New American Library, 1963.

Campbell, David. *If I'm In Charge Here Why Is Everybody Laughing?* Allen, TX: Argus Communications, 1980.

———. *If You Don't Know Where You're Going, You'll Probably End Up Somewhere Else*. Allen, TX: Argus Communications, 1974.

———. *Take the Road to Creativity and Get Off Your Dead End*. Allen, TX: Argus Communications, 1977.

Caplow, Theodore. *How to Run Any Organization*. New York: Holt, Rinehart and Winston, 1976.

Carnegie, Dale. *How to Develop Self-Confidence & Influence People by Public Speaking*. New York: Pocket Books, 1956.

Carroll, Donald. *Why Didn't I Say That?—The Art of Verbal Self-Defense*. New York: Franklin Watts, 1980.

Christopher, William F. *Management for the 1980's*. New York: American Management Association, 1980.

Cohen, Herb. *You Can Negotiate Anything: How to Get What You Want*. Secaucus, NJ: Lyle Stuart, 1980.

Cooper, Joseph D. *The Art of Decision-Making*. Garden City, NY: Doubleday & Company, 1961.

Cooper, Ken. *Nonverbal Communication for Business Success*. New York: American Management Association, 1979.

Cribbin, James J. *Effective Managerial Leadership*. New York: American Management Association, 1972.

Crystal, John C., and Richard N. Bolles. *Where Do I Go From Here With My Life?* New York: Seabury Press, 1974.

De Bono, Edward. *Lateral Thinking: Creativity Step by Step*. New York: Harper & Row, Publishers, 1970.

Dible, Donald M., ed. *Business Startup Basics*. Fairfield, CA: The Entrepreneur Press, 1978.

Douglass, Merrill E. *The Time Management Workbook*. Grandville, MI: Time Management Center, 1978.

Doyle, Michael, and David Straus. *The New Interaction Method: How to Make Meetings Work*. Chicago: Playboy Press, 1976.

Drake, John D. *Interviewing for Managers: Sizing Up People*. New York: American Management Association, 1972.

Drucker, Peter F. *The Changing World of the Executive*. New York: Quadrangle/The New York Times Book Co., 1982.

———. *The Effective Executive*. New York: Harper & Row, Publishers, 1967.

———. *Management: Tasks, Responsibilities, Practices*. New York: Harper & Row, Publishers, 1974.

———. *The Practice of Management*. New York: Harper & Row, Publishers, 1954.

Dyer, William G. *Team Building: Issues and Alternatives*. Reading, MA: Addison-Wesley Publishing Company, 1977.

Elam, Houston G., and Norton Paley. *Marketing for the Non-Marketing Executive*. New York: American Management Association, 1978.

Elgin Haden, Suzette. *The Gentle Art of Verbal Self-Defense*. Englewood Cliffs, NJ: Prentice-Hall, 1980.

Famularo, Joseph J. *Organization Planning Manual*. Revised Edition. New York: American Management Association, 1971.

Farley, Jennie. *Affirmative Action and the Woman Worker: Guidelines for Personnel Management*. New York: American Management Association, 1979.

Fast, Julius. *Body Language*. New York: Pocket Books, 1970.

Fast, Julius, and Barbara Fast. *How We Mean More Than We Say*. New York: Viking Press, 1979.

Fielder, Fred E., and Martin M. Chemers. *Improving Leadership Effectiveness*: *The Leader Match Concept*. Revised Edition. New York: John Wiley & Sons, 1977.

Fine, Sidney A. *Functional Job Analysis Scales—A Desk Aid*. Kalamazoo, MI: The W. E. Upjohn Institute for Employment Research, 1973.

————. *Guidelines for the Design of New Careers*. Kalamazoo, MI: The W. E. Upjohn Institute for Employment Research, 1967.

Flesch, Rudolf. *The Art of Plain Talk*. New York: The Macmillan Co., 1951.

Fletcher, Winston. *Meetings, Meetings*: *How to Manipulate Them and Make Them More Fun*. London: Michael Joseph, 1983.

Follmann, Joseph F., Jr. *Helping the Troubled Employee*. New York: American Management Association, 1978.

French, Wendell L. *The Personnel Management Process*: *Human Resources Administration and Development*. Fourth Edition. Hopewell, NJ: Houghton Mifflin Company, 1978.

Friant, Ray J., Jr. *Preparing Effective Presentations*: *How to Make Presentations Pay Off!* New York: Pilot Industries, 1982.

Gallwey, W. Timothy. *Inner Game of Tennis*. New York: Bantam, 1979.

Gardner, James E. *Training the New Supervisor*. New York: American Management Association, 1980.

Gay, Ben, III, and Stephen Douglas Williford. *The Winner's Edge*. Volume One. Shingle Springs, CA: National Toll Free Marketing, 1985.

Gilbert, Michael A. *How to Win an Argument*. New York: McGraw-Hill Book Company, 1979.

Gold, Carol Sapin. *Solid Gold Customer Relations*. Englewood Cliffs, NJ: Prentice-Hall, 1983.

Goodworth, Clive T. *Interviewing Techniques*. Toronto: Coles Publishing Company, 1979.

Gordon, Thomas. *Leader Effective Training*. New York: Bantam Books, 1977.

Graham, Robert G., and Clifford F. Gray. *Business Games Hand Book*. New York: American Management Association, 1969.

Half, Robert. *Robert Half on Hiring*. New York: Crown, 1985.

Hanan, Mack. *Life-Styled Marketing*. Revised Edition. New York: American Management Association, 1972.

Harrison, Allen F., and Robert M. Bramson. *The Art of Thinking*: *Strategies for Asking Questions, Making Decisions, and Solving Problems*. New York: Berkley Books, 1982.

Hart, Lois B. *Learning from Conflict: A Handbook for Trainers and Group Leaders*. Reading, MA: Addison-Wesley Publishing Company, 1981.

Hegarty, Edward J. *How to Talk Your Way to the Top*. West Nyack, NY: Parker Publishing Company, 1973.

Henderson, Richard I. *Job Description: Critical Documents, Versatile Tools. A Guide to EEO Compliance*. New York: American Management Association, 1975.

Hennig, Margaret, and Anne Jardim. *The Managerial Woman*. Garden City, NY: Anchor Press/Doubleday, 1977.

Higginson, Margaret V., and Thomas L. Quick. *The Ambitious Woman's Guide to a Successful Career*. New York: American Management Association, 1975.

Humanic Designs, Division of Information Science Incorporated. *How to Eliminate Discriminatory Practices*. New York: American Management Association, 1975.

Humble, John W. *How to Manage by Objectives*. New York: American Management Association, 1973.

Huskey, Ken W. *Spokesperson*. Palm Springs, CA: K. W. Huskey Assoc., 1980.

Iacocca, Lee. *Iacocca: An Autobiography*. New York: Bantam Books, 1984.

Irish, Richard K. *Go Hire Yourself an Employer*. Garden City, NY: Anchor Press/Doubleday, 1973.

———. *If Things Don't Improve Soon I May Ask You to Fire Me. The Management Book for Everyone Who Works*. Garden City, NY: Anchor Press/Doubleday, 1976.

Jay, Antony. *The New Oratory*. New York: American Management Association, 1971.

Jongeward, Dorothy, and Muriel James. *Winning with People: Group Exercises in Transactional Analysis*. Reading, MA: Addison-Wesley Publishing Company, 1973.

Kanawaty, George, ed. *Managing and Developing New Forms of Work Organisation*. Management Development Series # 16. International Labour Office. Geneva: International Labour Organisation, 1980.

Kanter, Rosabeth Moss. *The Change Masters: Innovation and Entrepreneurship in the American Corporation*. New York: Simon & Schuster, 1983.

Kastens, Merritt L. *An Operating Manual: Long-Range Planning for Your Business*. New York, NY: American Management Association, 1976.

Kellogg, Marion S. *What to Do About Performance Appraisal*. Revised Edition. New York: American Management Association, 1975.

Korda, Michael. *Power! How to Get It, How to Use It*. New York: Ballantine Books, 1975.

Kotter, John P. *Power in Management: How to Understand, Acquire, and Use It*. New York: American Management Association, 1979.

Lakein, Alan. *How to Get Control of Your Time and Your Life*. New York: New American Library, 1973.

LeBoeuf, Michael. *The Greatest Management Principle in the World*. New York: G. P. Putnam's Sons, 1985.

Lesly, Philip, ed. *Lesly's Public Relations Handbook*. Englewood Cliffs, NJ: Prentice-Hall, 1971.

Lorayne, Harry. *Remembering People—The Key to Success*. New York: Stein & Day, 1975.

Lumsden, George J. *Impact Management: Personal Power Strategies for Success*. New York: American Management Association, 1979.

Lund, Philip R. *Compelling Spelling*. New York: American Management Association, 1978.

Lynch, Edith M. *The Woman's Guide to Management: How to Get to the Top and Stay There*. New York: Cornerstone Library, 1978.

McConkey, Dale D. *No-Nonsense Delegation*. New York: American Management Association, 1979.

McGill, Michael E. *Organization Development for Operating Managers*. New York: American Management Association, 1977.

MacKenzie, R. Alec. *The Time Trap: Managing Your Way Out*. New York: American Management Association, 1972.

Mager, N. H., S. K., and P. S., eds. and comps. *Power Writing, Power Speaking*. New York: William Morrow & Co., 1978.

Mager, Robert F. *Preparing Instructional Objectives*. Second Edition. Belmont, CA: Fearon Publishers, 1975.

Mager, Robert F., and Peter Pipe. *Analyzing Performance Problems, or, You Really Oughta Wanna*. Belmont, CA: Fearon Publishers, 1970.

Mandino, Og. *The Greatest Salesman in the World*. New York: Frederick Fell, 1968.

———. *The Greatest Secret in the World*. New York: Frederick Fell, 1972.

Marshall, Austin. *How to Get a Better Job*. New York: Hawthorn Books, 1964.

Marston, William Moulton. *Emotions of Normal People*. Minneapolis: Pierson Press, 1979.

Martin, Charles C. *Project Management: How to Make It Work*. New York: American Management Association, 1976.

Michalak, Donald F., and Edwin G. Yager. *Making the Training Process Work*. New York: Harper & Row, Publishers, 1979.

Midwest Center for Public Sector Labor Relations, Indiana University. *Questions and Answers on Contract Administration: A Practitioner's Guide*. Bloomington, IN: The Trustees of Indiana University, 1978.

Miller, Martin R. *Climbing the Corporate Pyramid*. New York: American Management Association, 1973.

Moffatt, Thomas L. *Selection Interviewing for Managers*. New York: Harper & Row, Publishers, 1979.

Montgomery, Robert L. *Listening Made Easy*. New York: American Management Association, 1981.

Morris, John O. *Make Yourself Clear!* New York: McGraw-Hill, 1972.

Morrisey, George L. *Effective Business & Technical Presentations*. Reading, MA: Addison-Wesley Publishing Co.–MOR Associates, 1982.

Mursell, James L. *Developmental Teaching*. New York: McGraw-Hill Book Company, 1949.

———. *Successful Teaching: Its Psychological Principles*. Second Edition. New York: McGraw-Hill Book Company, 1954.

Naisbitt, John. *Megatrends; Ten New Directions Transforming Our Lives*. New York: Warner Books, 1982.

Nash, Edward L. *Direct Marketing: Strategy, Planning, Execution*. New York: McGraw-Hill Book Company, 1982.

Neal, James E., Jr. *Effective Phrases for Performance Appraisals*. Perrysburg, OH: NEAL Publications, 1978.

Newman, Edwin. *A Civil Tongue*. New York: Warner Books, 1977.

———. *Strictly Speaking*. New York: Warner Books, 1975.

Neirenberg, Gerard I. *The Art of Negotiating: Psychological Strategies for Gaining Advantageous Bargains*. New York: Cornerstone Library Publications, 1968.

———. *How to Give and Receive Advice*. New York: Pocket Books, 1975.

Nierenberg, Gerard I., and Henry H. Calero. *How to Read A Person Like a Book*. New York: Pocket Books, 1971.

———. *Meta-Talk*. New York: Pocket Books, 1974.

Nirenberg, Jesse S. *Getting Through to People*. Englewood Cliffs, NJ: Prentice-Hall, 1963.

Noe, Robert M., ed. *Self-Assessment and Study Guide for Human Resource*

Management/Personnel. Alexandria, VA: The Personnel Accreditation Institute, 1985.

Ogden, Richard W. *How to Succeed in Business and Marriage*. New York: American Management Association, 1978.

Oncken, William, Jr., and Donald C. Wass. "Management Time: Who's Got the Monkey," *Harvard Business Review*, November–December 1974.

Organizational Dynamics: Managerial Decision Making. Revised Edition. Organization Behavior for Professional Managers. New York: American Management Association, 1973.

Organizational Dynamics. A Quarterly Review of Organizational Behavior for Professional Managers. New York, NY: American Management Association, Inc., Volume 7, Number 4, Spring 1979.

Osborn, Alex F. *Applied Imagination: Principles and Procedures of Creative Problem-Solving*. Third Revised Edition. New York: Charles Scribner's Sons, 1979.

Ouchi, William G. *Theory Z. How American Business Can Meet the Japanese Challenge*. Reading, MA: Addison-Wesley Publishing Company, 1981.

Owens, James. *Management Performance through Transactional Analysis and PA*. Washington, D. C.: Management Education, 1977.

———. *Time Management through Transactional Analysis and PA*. Washington, D.C.: Management Education, 1978.

Pascale, Richard Tanner, and Anthony G. Athos. *The Art of Japanese Management: Applications for American Executives*. New York: Simon & Schuster, 1981.

Payne, Richard A. *How to Get a Better Job Quicker*. New York: New American Library, 1972.

Payne, Stanley L. *The Art of Asking Questions*. Princeton, NJ: Princeton University Press, 1951.

Peters, Thomas J., and Robert H. Waterman, Jr. *In Search of Excellence: Lessons from America's Best-Run Companies*. New York: Harper & Row, Publishers, 1982.

Peters, Tom, and Nancy Austin. *A Passion for Excellence: The Leadership Difference*. New York: Random House, 1985.

Pleninger, Andrew. *How to Survive and Market Yourself in Management*. New York: American Management Association, 1977.

Pollock, Ted. *Managing Yourself Creatively*. New York: Hawthorn Books, 1971.

Potter, Beverly A. *Turning Around: The Behavioral Approach to Managing People*. New York: American Management Association, 1980.

Qubein, Nido R. *Communicate Like a Pro*. Englewood Cliffs, NJ: Prentice-Hall, 1983.

———. *Get the Best from Yourself: The Complete System of Personal and Professional Development*. Englewood Cliffs, NJ: Prentice-Hall, 1983.

———. *Nido Qubein's Professional Selling Techniques*. New York: Berkley Books, 1983.

Ringer, Robert J. *Looking Out for # 1*. New York: Fawcett Crest Books, 1977.

Roach, John M., and Mary Zippo, eds. *Behavior Modification: Selected Articles from AMACOM Publications*. New York: American Management Association, 1976.

Rogers, Carl R. *Carl Rogers on Personal Power*. New York: Dell Publishing Co., 1977.

Rogers, Henry C. *Rogers' Rules for Success: Tips That Will Take You to the Top by One of America's Foremost Public Relations Experts*. New York: St. Martin's, 1984.

Rohrer, Hibler & Replogle. *Managers for Tomorrow*. New York: New American Library of World Literature, 1965.

Rollin, Betty. *Am I Getting Paid for This?* New York: New American Library, 1984.

Rothschild, William E. *Motivational Theories and Applications for Managers*. New York: American Management Association, 1977.

———. *Putting It All Together: A Guide to Strategic Thinking*. New York: American Management Association, 1976.

Sales Manpower Foundation. *How to Land the Job You Want*. Revised Edition. New York: Sales Executives Club of New York, 1978.

Sanzotta, Donald. *The Manager's Guide to Interpersonal Relations*. New York: American Management Association, 1979.

Sarnoff, Dorothy. *Speech Can Change Your Life*. New York: Dell Publishing Co., 1972.

Scannell, Edward E., and John W. Newstrom. *Games Trainers Play: Experiential Learning Exercises*. New York: McGraw-Hill Book Company, 1980.

———. *More Games Trainers Play: Experiential Learning Exercises*. New York: McGraw-Hill Book Company, 1983.

Schoenberg, Robert J. *The Art of Being a Boss. Inside Intelligence from Top-Level Business Leaders and Young Executives on the Move*. New York: New American Library, 1978.

Simon, Sidney B. *Negative Criticism and What You Can Do About It*. Allen, TX: Argus Communications, 1978.

Simpson, James B., comp. *Comtemporary Quotations*. New York: Thomas Y. Crowell Company, 1964.

Sloma, Richard S. *No-Nonsense Management: A General Manager's Primer*. New York: Bantam Books, 1981.

Snell, Frank. *How to Hold a Better Meeting*. New York: Cornerstone Library, 1979.

———. *How to Stand Up & Speak Well in Business*. New York: Cornerstone Library, 1979.

Sperber, Philip. *The Science of Business Negotiation*. New York: Pilot Industries, 1979.

Stanton, Erwin S. *Successful Personnel Recruiting and Selection*. New York: American Management Association, 1977.

Steiner, Claude M. *The Other Side of Power: How to Become Powerful Without Being Power-Hungry*. New York: Grove Press, 1981.

Stewart, Nathaniel. *The Effective Woman Manager: Seven Vital Skills for Upward Mobility*. New York: John Wiley & Sons, 1978.

Stockard, James G. *Career Development and Job Training*. New York: American Management Association, 1977.

Szykitka, Walter, ed. *How to Be Your Own Boss: The Complete Handbook for Starting and Running a Small Business*. New York: New American Library, 1978.

Taffi, Donald J. *The Entrepreneur: A Corporate Strategy for the '80's*. New York: American Management Association, 1981.

Tarrant, John J. *How to Negotiate a Raise*. New York: Pocket Books, 1976.

The American Salesman. "Whipping Up Your Enthusiasm." Burlington, IA: National Research Bureau, January 1984.

Tracey, William R. *Designing Training and Development Systems*. New York: American Management Association, 1971.

———. *Managing Training and Development Systems*. New York: American Management Association, 1974.

Vandervelde, Maryanne. *The Changing Life of the Corporate Wife*. New York: Warner Books, 1979.

Van De Ven, Andrew H., and Diane L. Ferry. *Measuring and Assessing Organizations*. New York: John Wiley and Sons, 1980.

Varney, Glenn H. *Organization Development for Managers*. Reading, MA: Addison-Wesley Publishing Company, 1977.

Wachs, William. *Managerial Situations and How to Handle Them*. West Nyack, NY: Parker Publishing Company, 1976.

Walker, James W. *Human Resource Planning*. New York: McGraw-Hill, 1980.

Walters, Barbara. *How to Talk with Practically Anybody About Practically Anything*. New York: Dell Publishing Co., 1970.

Warschaw, Tessa Albert. *Winning by Negotiation*. New York: McGraw-Hill Book Company, 1980.

White, Richard M., Jr. *The Entrepreneur's Manual*. Radnor, PA: Chilton Book Company, 1977.

Woodcock, Mike. *Team Development Manual*. New York: John Wiley & Sons, 1979.

Wright, J. Patrick. *On a Clear Day You Can See General Motors: John Z. De Lorean's Look Inside the Automotive Giant*. Grosse Pointe, MI: Wright Enterprises, 1979.

Yaney, Joseph P., and Geary A. Rummler. *Labor Relations for the Supervisor*. Reading, MA: Addison-Wesley Publishing Company, 1968.

Index

A

Ability, 270–273
Achilles Syndrome, The (Bloomfield and Felder), 202
Am I Getting Paid for This? (Rollin), 42
Answering question with another question, 51
Anxiety, questions to reduce, 33
Appraisal (*see* Performance appraisal)
Authority, delegation of, 141–142
Awards, merit, 134–136

B

Barratt, Alan, 259, 271–273, 282
Bennis, Warren, 132
Blanchard, Ken, 205
Bloomfield, Harold, 202
Brainstorming, 203–204

Brown, David, 272
Buckler, Beatrice, 248

C

Calculator type personality, 63–65
    asking questions of, 65
    characteristics of, 63–65, 68
    managing, 65
    negotiating style of, 221, 222
    working for, 65
Caras, J. Sheldon, 265, 271, 273, 278, 282
Career and Confidence Inventory, 244–246
Career planning, 242–243
Carer type personality, 62–63
    asking questions of, 63
    characteristics of, 62–63, 68
    negotiating style of, 221, 222
Carnegie, Dale, 3

Postscript

Success is turning knowledge into positive action.

Dorothy Leeds' presentations, both live and on tape, will help you manage better, communicate more effectively, and improve your image and relationships. More importantly, they will help you to take your knowledge and use it.

If you want to know more about Dorothy Leeds' speeches, seminars, and audio-cassette programs, please call or write to:

Dorothy Leeds, President
Organizational Technologies, Inc., Suite 10A
800 West End Avenue
New York, NY 10025
(212) 864-2424

Her speeches and seminars include:

The Passionate Pursuit of Power
The Unique Strengths of Women
People Reading Strategies
The Smart Questions System
How to Market Yourself and Find the Job of Your Choice
How to Find and Hire the Right People
LifeChange Dynamics

Her audio-cassette programs are:

PowerSpeak: The Complete Guide to Persuasive Public Speaking and Presenting (6 Cassettes with Comprehensive Workbook) @$95.00 for set

How to Market Yourself and Get the Job of Your Choice (2 Cassettes with Comprehensive Workbook) @$39.95 for set

People Reading: Strategies for Engineering Better Relationships in Business (3 Cassettes with People Reading Guide) @$49.95 for set

The Motivational Manager: How to Get Top Performance from Your Staff (6 Cassettes with Assessments) @$95.00 for set

The Smart Questions System (4 Cassettes with Work Materials) @$59.95 for set

If you wish to receive her highly regarded, informative, complimentary newsletter, *The Leeds Letter*, please contact Organizational Technologies, Inc., at the above address.

When you order any three albums, you will receive Ms. Leeds' acclaimed cassette, *Success Is Turning Knowledge into Positive Action: A System for Change*, a retail value of $15.00, free of charge.

About the Author

Dorothy Leeds is the President of Organizational Technologies, Inc., management and sales development consultants. OTI specializes in maximizing people productivity by integrating present needs, projected growth, and future trends.

In addition to human resource consulting, Ms. Leeds develops and conducts management and sales seminars and workshops. Ms. Leeds works with a wide spectrum of organizations including Mobil Oil Corporation, Digital Equipment Corporation, Duke Power Company, Prudential-Bache, the City University of New York, and many others.

An international keynote speaker, Ms. Leeds has addressed many conferences and conventions, including those of Sales and Marketing Executives, the American Lung Association, and Meeting Planners International. She has appeared on *The Tonight Show*, *Straight Talk*, and television shows across the country.

Ms. Leeds came to the field of management consulting as a successful businesswoman. She has been a senior account executive for a leading retail advertising division of Grey Advertising and the owner of an international knitwear firm.

A graduate of Adelphi University, she holds an M.A. in Speech Education and Communication from Columbia University, and she is on the faculty of the American Management Association's Senior Management Course.